# Gloriana's Torch

# PATRICIA FINNEY

# Gloriana's Torch

ST. MARTIN'S PRESS ≈ NEW YORK

www.stmartins.com

Library of Congress Cataloging-in-Publication Data

Finney, Patricia, 1958–
Gloriana's torch / Patricia Finney.—1st U.S. ed.
p. cm.
ISBN 0-312-31285-7
1. Great Britain—History, Naval—Tudors, 1485–1603—Fiction.
2. Great Britain—History—Elizabeth, 1558–1603—Fiction.
3. Illegal arms transfer—Fiction. 4. Armada, 1588—Fiction.
I. Title.

PR6056.I519G58 2003
823'.914—dc22
2003058454

First published in Great Britian by Orion,
an imprint of the Orion Publishing Group Ltd

First U.S. Edition: November 2003

10 9 8 7 6 5 4 3 2 1

In memory of my best friend, lover and husband,
Chris Perry.

# Foreword

If I thank all the many people who have helped me with my long struggle to write this book, this foreword will stretch to Oscar-winning proportions.

The Author's Foundation generously made me an award of two thousand pounds so I could conduct gonzo historical research with the Sail Training Association aboard the Malcolm Miller sail-training ship, and also on the two-masted Phoenix of Charlestown, owned by Square Sail Shipyards, who also helped with my research. All descriptions of seasickness in this book are based on personal experience.

Ottakars bookshop in Truro offered me a sanctuary as an unofficial Writer in Residence, where I could sit and write the second draft without having thousands of domestic chores shouting at me. They treated me in the way I believe writers should always be treated – i.e. like royalty – and they also saved me from whaledom because my previous sanctuary in Café Three Zero in Truro sold far too many kinds of delicious food, not to mention puddings. Most of Ottakars' customers were charming and left me in peace to clatter away on my keyboard. There was one rather peppery elderly gentleman in statutory green fur-lined Barbour and tweed flat cap who was quietly making notes from guidebooks to Ireland at my (own folding antique) desk and very cross he was indeed at being asked nicely to move. Nor did he in fact buy a single one of the guidebooks he was consulting. But that was an isolated incident.

Many thanks to Andrew Forster, Louise Hale, Gwyneth Hemsley, Cyd Jupe, Andrew McKenzie and of course James Heneage, Ottakars' founder and MD who approved the idea. Many many thanks to Cyd Jupe who performed the heroic and essential task of reading my book in draft, making many sensible suggestions and saving me from some embarrassing mistakes. She also comforted my post-literary jitters and said she liked it, for which I was (and am) pathetically grateful.

vii

Another of the brave souls I call my non-professional readers is Kendall Britt, who e-mailed me about another book and has become a friend. She too read the book and made cogent suggestions, which I have adopted.

Keith Menadue gave valuable engineering and explosives advice on the best way to blow up London Bridge and also inspired me to do the research into the source of all that saltpetre the Elizabethans needed. Tristan Darkins kindly vetted the manuscript for nautical howlers.

I have always got on well with librarians, despite my diabolical lateness in returning most of the books I borrow. Living in Cornwall, I have found the local mobile library a vital resource and the librarian on my route, Angela Spurgin, has been the latest of that much underrated profession to seek diligently on my behalf for obscure tomes, lend them and then cope tactfully with my wild claims to have given them back. Where would we be without libraries and librarians?

Of course, despite all this help I have probably made silly mistakes – which are entirely my responsibility.

I would like to thank Clive Harrison, Tonia Cox and, especially, Danny Broderick for their personal support at a time of great difficulty for me. Heather Stanton has been a true friend and has taught me more than she may realise.

My thanks also go to Jane Wood and my publishers at Orion who were immensely patient as I struggled to get this onto paper, as deadlines came and passed unmet and as my private life went spectacularly supernova, they rescheduled again and never pressured me.

Patricia Finney
Truro, 2002

# Dramatis Personae

(* indicates a real person)

DAVID BECKET – sometime soldier and adventurer in the Netherlands. With Simon Ames (qui vide) he foiled a notable attempt against the Queen's life [*Firedrake's Eye*]. Later a swordmaster to Sir Philip Sidney, after the Poet's death he became involved in the suppression of a wicked libel against the Queen known as the Book of the Unicorn [*Unicorn's Blood*]. Unfortunately, during the course of it, he was mistaken for a Catholic priest and tortured in the Tower of London by means of the manacles, from which he is still not fully recovered.

SIMON AMES – now known as Simon Anriques, a Jew. Once a pursuivant and inquisitor for Walsingham, he was a partner with David Becket in preventing the Queen's assassination and also in the matter of the Book of the Unicorn. For reasons of State security, he changed his name when he retired from the Queen's service and married Rebecca Anriques (q.v.).

*DR HECTOR NUNEZ – Simon's uncle, physician to the Earl of Leicester, wealthy merchant and trader in tobacco, a notable independent contributor to Walsingham's intelligence network. Chief of the *marrano* Jewish refugees in London.

*SIR FRANCIS WALSINGHAM – Elizabeth's spymaster and energetic Puritan pursuer of Catholics.

*SIR FRANCIS DRAKE – known to the Spaniards as 'El Draco'. Elizabethan sailor, circumnavigator of the globe, pirate and Vice Admiral of the English fleet under Lord Charles Howard of Effingham.

*ELIZABETH TUDOR, QUEEN OF ENGLAND

MERULA – princess and upside-down woman of a slaving nation near the West Coast of Africa.

ANTHONY FANT – once a friend of Becket's, now his vehement enemy. A wealthy gentleman and trader, he lost his arm at the siege of Haarlem and his wife in the Tower.

\*ANTHONY MUNDAY – a pursuivant, inquisitor and future (mediocre) playwright.

REBECCA ANRIQUES – Simon Ames's wife, a Jewess from Bristol.

JOSEF PASQUALE – sometime Inquisitor at the Holy Office, then a clerk to the Spanish Ordnance office, of New Christian descent.

MICHAEL – a sailor

PHILIP BECKET – David Becket's older brother, a gentleman of reasonable means, living at Becket House, Middleton.

GOODWIFE (OR GOODY) BROWNLOW – the oldest woman in Middleton.

ELEANOR BECKET (NÉE FANT) – younger sister of Anthony Fant, married to Mr Philip Becket, gentlewoman.

ELIZABETH AND DAVID BECKET – their children.

\*BEN JONSON – a bricklayer's apprentice.

\*JOHN DONNE – a young gentleman.

PIERS LAMMETT – a Catholic Englishman in the service of Parma, the son of a friend of David Becket's father, and still a loyal subject to the Queen.

\*ROBERT CAREY – a courtier, rackety youngest son of Lord Hunsdon and a future Deputy Warden of the West March, among other things [see my books under the name of P.F. Chisholm].

\*THOMASINA DE PARIS – the Queen's Fool, a muliercula or midget and the Queen's most privy intelligencer.

EDWARD DORMER – would-be priest, assassin and soldier.

\*FR PERSONS – leader of the English Jesuits at Rheims.

\*ALEXANDER FARNESE, DUKE OF PARMA – Philip II's finest general in the Low Countries.

\*DON JUAN DE ACUNA VELA – in charge of the Spanish Royal Ordnance Office for the Armada.

SNAKE – Merula's lost son, Simon's friend and fellow slave.

\*ROBERT CECIL – second son of Lord Burleigh, already in the service of the Queen, a hunchback.

# BOOK I

# Prologue

Become a god with me, now. This is all about gods.

Come here, look at this. Remember these? Before computers and rainbow-flashing little discs? It's a book. Originally called a codex, a late Roman Christian invention, a scroll of paper, cut into sections, sewn together along one side, backed by something a little stronger than paper: wood, leather, cloth. A little heavy, but very portable, low-tech, convenient. The technology for creating it has changed, the thing, in its essence, hasn't.

Open it. You should recognise this one, despite multi-cultural education. It's a Bible. Big, heavy, the paper thick, strong, high on linen content, the print quite readable although peppered with those unfamiliar long 's's' to confuse the mental ear. Somebody has left an inky thumbprint on the page facing Genesis, Chapter I.

A century ago, two centuries ago, three centuries ago – if you owned any book at all, you owned this one. Perhaps you read a chapter aloud to your household every night, if you could read. Your children played with toys merchandised from it: Noah's arks, Christmas cribs. Now? Well, very few of us have actually read its strange mixture of Bronze Age Semitic myth and oral history, seventh century BC Jewish point-scoring, first century AD Aramaic oral history, Greek philosophising, letters, histories, accounts of (possibly prophetic) delirium. Politely edited highlights only, if at all. There is a friend-of-a-friend story about a girl selling jewellery in a shop who offered a customer a plain cross or one with a little man on it.

This particular Bible is in English. That was very radical in its day. Four hundred years ago men and women died over the question of whether they could read it in their own language, or have it interpreted for them by a priest from the inaccurate Vulgate Latin of St Jerome.

Four hundred years ago, men set sail in ships to fight and kill other men over interpretations of this book – which is at least partly about universal brotherhood and loving your enemies. Also partly

3

about betraying and destroying your enemies, beating them in battle and wiping them out down to their babies and their girl-children (see the book of Joshua for further details). The men who fought over it were, of course, in empirical genetic fact, far more closely related to each other than one chimp is to another chimp of the same tribe and yet . . . Blood flowed, people screamed and died, wood burned.

This way, fellow-god. Yes, be careful how you put it down. That particular book is older than the USA. It was printed before even the Jamestown colonies began, let alone the later date when the *Mayflower* sailed. I know, it is spooky to hold in your hands something older than a nation. It seems indecent really. How can a mere thing surf the centuries like a god, when real people cannot?

Now this book here was quite recently published, as you can tell from the excellent full-colour reproductions of paintings. It tells the story of the Spanish Armada, with potted boilings-down of the politics of the time, and a few notes on religion. Here's a picture of a man wearing a dunce's cap and a patterned cassock. Not looking too healthy, is he? Well, he's a New Christian, a Spanish Jew, a *marrano* (or pig) who has been tortured until he admitted to practising Judaism again. He's about to be burned at the stake for heresy. That's what he wore to parade through the town to the *auto de fe* for his burning.

Yes, the ships do look odd, don't they, with those little puffs of smoke from the cannon, like cotton wool, and their starched formal-dress sails. You have to be careful about relying on the paintings of the time: the painters were expected to transmit a great deal of information about the battle and were far more concerned to do it than give an accurate reproduction of reality. The painter of this one wasn't anywhere near the battle anyway and the picture was painted months, perhaps years, later. So the ships do look like toys – perhaps because he used models – and their perspective is one of status rather than mathematics. The English vessels are bigger than the Spanish, for instance, although the reverse was the case, just as the King in a medieval painting is always bigger than his council. The rigging doesn't actually make sense, although there are interesting clues to long-forgotten technicalities if you look close enough. But you could put your nose right next to the paper and still you can't climb in, hear the shouting, smell the salt.

So you have to become a god, like me. You have to come this way, into the dark. Put your foot here, the other one there, take my hand. We are not so very far from the past, you know. Look beyond the streetlight, stare at the stars: there, that one! The light from it started hurtling towards us four hundred years ago.

Look down – it's all right, you have no mass and therefore are invisible to gravity. You won't fall. London is in shades of brown and red, not grey. A complex crumpling of brick and wood and wattle and thatch, littering the Thames valley at the strategic place where the Romans built their bridge – where the river was still tidal enough to bring the ships in from the sea, but narrow enough to cross by round arches. It's a cramped and cluttered, semi-medieval city, with the insistent spires and towers of churches injecting the sky with their prayers. We'll follow the river, like the German bombers, that characteristic bend and arc – perhaps you subconsciously hear strains of a TV theme tune?

The Thames is not a blank, silver ribbon in this time but clotted and clustered with ships, entire forests transplanted to the water surface, crawling with humans. Yes, the shape is there as we skim over the cranes worked by the men inside the great wheels like hamsters, heading up river to the sprawling, mighty stone creature that is the Palace of Whitehall.

Barleysugar chimneys puff white woodsmoke into the air. The Queen will not have coal because she hates the smell and the smoke is dirty. We glimpse green as we go: surprising amounts. St James's park stretches to the north into farmland with the recently retired Lazar house in the middle. Nobody knows why leprosy is almost dying out in Europe now, while consumption replaces it as a scourge. Future bacteriologists will discover that the infective bacteria are related, for what that's worth.

Swoop down into the polite centre of Whitehall, into King Street where the Holbein Gate makes advertising statements about the power and justice of King Henry VIII (he of the six wives, two divorced, two executed, one dead in childbed, one widowed in the nick of time). There are folded queues of best-dressed people, waiting to reach a small entrance where a bored-looking bearded man in red velvet, holding his halberd – a thing like an old-fashioned tin-opener on a stick – takes the commoners' shillings and waves them on into the Queen's Court.

Follow the meek crowds, gawping around you at the painted walls, the high ceilings, the tiled floors. There's a flurry and a small group of young men in extraordinary puffed damask and velvet swing past, carrying silver and gold plates. Because we are gods we can tell, perhaps by their atomic composition, that the silk for the damask and velvet travelled clear across Eurasia from the fabled Far Eastern Empire to be unpicked and rewoven by marvellously skilled weavers in Flanders. We know that the gold came from mines in Bohemia but that the silver was dug up by sick and starving slaves at the great mine of Potosi and came to England as part of a spectacular haul of swag stolen by the foremost armed robber of the Kingdom, Sir Francis Drake.

Pay attention to this young man, Robert Carey. He's laughing politely, chestnut-haired under his much feathered cap, extremely elegant in forest green velvet and black damask, his sword at his side and a poniard dagger at his back. You've seen something like him on TV and at the theatre, no doubt, but this one is different. For a start, he smells rather strongly of man. Not dirty, not tramp-like (as his later descendants during the bacterial paradise of the seventeenth and eighteenth centuries would do). He just smells very much of himself, the (relatively unwashed) human male. He had a bath quite recently, two weeks ago, down at the Stews in Southwark, but deodorant hasn't been invented yet and his Queen abhors the smell of musk. Lavender, cloves and citron waft about his clothes but are hardly up to the job. He changes his extremely fine linen shirt at least every other day, more often if he is attending his fastidious Queen as a Gentleman of the Bedchamber, but . . .

There's a distinct niff in the air from all of them, in fact. Rosewater, some Seville orange, a lot of beer and wine. And the handsome young man who holds the chased silver chalice and its lid with such a graceful flourish has a wary, hard look. He isn't an actor, although he probably would be today. He's as athletic as a sportsman, he's very charming, something of a politician. In his own way, he is a celebrity. As a modern celebrity seeks to flatter and befriend and make his living out of his master, the seething democratic mass, so Robert Carey seeks to flatter and befriend and make his living out of his mistress, who is equally demanding. Except he is called a courtier and his mistress is a most well-educated, intelligent and temperamental Queen.

It's perfectly fine to ogle Robert Carey, if you like, although he has only a minor part to play in this particular story. He's a cousin of the Queen. He isn't going to notice you because, being massless, you do not reflect the light of his world. In any case, all around him are throngs of common people who stare at him as he passes them every day on his way to take part in the elaborate mummery of the

Queen's Dinner. He finds the ceremony boring but not ridiculous, although it has elements in it of a Catholic Mass. He and his elegant friends will be serving an empty chair under a magnificent cloth of estate with an extremely fine (if cold) meal involving stuffed partridges and venison pasties and spiced fish and manchet bread.

Her subjects and the many foreign visitors pay good money to come into her public rooms and gaze around at the bright colours and tut at the expensive silver-shot hangings. Each tapestry cost as much as a fully-fitted warship, but arguably does more for the cohesion of the kingdom – united in enjoyable shock at the expense. But the Queen is far too busy actually to sit and eat in front of them like a lioness at the menagerie by the Tower. At Easter and Christmas you might be privileged to see her (after paying triple for it), with perhaps Robert Carey kneeling at her side to hand her a drinking cup full of wine. The rest of the year, when it's his turn to do the business, Robert Carey kneels straight-backed and straight-faced to a velvet-covered wooden throne and its lion-infested canopy.

Four hundred years before the National Trust, the Queen permits hoi polloi to come chattering into her palace partly so they can see her queenly display of magnificence, but also because she cannot be so free with her physical presence as she was. A few years ago, the Dutch leader, William of Orange was assassinated by a young Belgian priest who walked up to him with a pistol and shot him. The Queen herself has been the object of a number of assassination plots, surviving one or two by the skin of her teeth. She wants her subjects to be intimate with her in a way that does not actually risk her life, hence the daft mummery of the Queen's Dinner. Her gentlemen eat the delicate meal afterwards and have quite forgotten the taste of hot food, which is a good thing since many of them have bad teeth from eating too much sugar. But this will be the last such occasion for a while, as there are more important things to do.

On this day, there are more than ever of the sightseers because everyone knows that the Armada is on its way.

However, nobody knows exactly when it will arrive, as radar and satellite surveillance are waiting another four hundred years for their invention. So there's tension in the air. The English are rather looking forward to meeting and beating the filthy Spaniards, since they are a bellicose people and have boundless (if often unwarranted) faith in their fighting men. They have even more faith in their navy, which is more reasonable, as it has been transformed by John Hawkins, the first completely honest and experienced seaman to be in charge of the Admiralty for generations. So honest is he that he put two Negroes in chains on his coat of arms as his proud boast that he made his fortune out of the slave trade and therefore had no need to take bribes.

London is buzzing with rumours, the trained bands are out training every morning at Smithfield, guns, swords, armour and gunpowder have all tripled in price and quite a few people are quietly buying gold to bury in their gardens.

Behind doors guarded by men who know every face that might have business there, the Queen is the apex of the Kingdom. She must seem accessible but not actually be so. No commoner is likely to get close to her without a very expensive appointment, except when she is on a summer progress.

So you must become a god again to pass through the walls. They are decorated and sumptuous in the places for common consumption, but whitewashed and raw in the warren of corridors behind the public parts, rather like backstage at a theatre. The corners are urine-stained as young men, who are allocated a daily ration of one gallon of beer, follow their natural inclinations. Ignore the hurrying servants carrying food, clothing, books, a hawk. Up one floor and here is a long panelled gallery that overlooks a garden.

Turn aside, pass through the door where another young man in buttercup yellow taffeta stands, hungover and bored. The Queen's audience chamber is lined with walls of stretched white satin, hung with caged and busily singing songbirds. Sitting on velvet cushions along one wall are half a dozen ladies and maids-in-waiting, mostly busy with embroidery or winding wool, chatting quietly. No servants these, they are the Queen's companions and usually related to the chief men of the kingdom, although their lives are tales of tedium, enlivened by gossip, competitive dressing and a little light, furtive dalliance with the crowds of young men who hanker after them. Three lapdogs, named Francis, Eric and Felipe, after discarded suitors of the Queen, snore in a hairy heap on a cushion. Two more young men in crimson silk doublets, holding halberds, stand behind the throne, also bored, hungover and rather tense. More men are standing around the walls pretending to have business there, including servants of the French, Scottish and Venetian embassies.

The Queen's throne has a canopy over it of red brocade

enlivened with lions, and is raised on a dais. At last, a fanfare blares. The Queen enters, white-damasked girls rearranging her train, mounts to the throne and sits on it. She has a Tudor's eye for appropriate ceremony and knows that important news is on its way. The beacons have been burning since the day before yesterday and the man sent post from Plymouth by Drake should be arriving at any time.

Therefore she is clad in carefully thought-out stark black and white, with turquoise ribbons and the jewel on her sleeve of the Serpent Wisdom. Normally there would also be a midget attending her, Thomasina de Paris, a muliercula in a startling elaborate gown of crimson and gold, trotting behind the pretty girls and waiting while they do their service to the Queen, before quietly coming to sit at the Queen's feet, like a very gaudy cat. However, at the moment, Thomasina's cushion on the dias is untenanted.

What does the Queen know, now, as the Armada of her enemies (with 129 ships remaining to them after the storms of Biscay) travel stately-fashion up the English Channel in their formal crescent formation, the winds for once in their favour? What is she thinking?

Since we are gods, not historians, we can prise apart the wings of her brows and look directly into the swirling, ten-dimensional maze of her mind.

Thomasina features in there, causing anxiety by her continued absence on a most dangerous mission, for the Queen loves her dearly. Two men who have done great service to the Queen in the past, David Becket and Simon Ames, also known as Simon Anriques, loom large in her thinking for she wonders where they are and how they are faring. Simon she thinks must be dead, but Becket . . . Who can tell?

Ames's faithful wife, Rebecca, is another main source of concern, although her tall black servant Merula is not. The Queen shares the mental blindness common to most Europeans of her time, and later, which cannot quite apply the definition human to someone with a skin coloured ebony.

What else preoccupies the Queen as she waits for news, as history sways undecided at a branching point? Is history, like a god, watching her?

Historians swim happily in the warm, dim waters of history, with documents filing past their noses, sergeant-majored by the card-file index or the database. History is a story they see from above. But when it is happening, history is only current events. And what

Elizabeth had been looking at month after month as she played her deadly game of correspondence chess with Philip II of Spain was the view from her bedchamber window, whether of Whitehall or Greenwich or Nonsuch or Hampton Court, looking out over whichever Privy Garden it happened to be. She could not see the vast activity of an empire diverting practically all its resources, its stored food and munitions, its money and able-bodied men, to fit out their original 150 ships of a motley variety against her. If anyone can be said to have seen it, that was the monkish King, Philip himself, battlemented by paper in his small study at San Lorenzo, now known to us as the Escorial.

What came to Elizabeth was hidden in signs and symptoms. She must diagnose her situation from letters written by men hoping for money, from the drone of one man making a report of what another man had told him he had seen in Antwerp, at the Hague, in Lisbon.

The idea of the Armada, of the attempt by Philip to take England by force when he had failed humiliatingly to take it by marriage, had hung over her like a Damoclean sword (as she herself remarked) for ten years and more. Was it true? Did it exist? Was there really such an attempt or was it all a bluff? Lord Treasurer Burghley certainly said it was just Philip doing what later generations would call sabre-rattling.

Important information was often blown in accidentally. A fishing vessel had seen ships in the mist . . . Merchants had had their ships confiscated at . . . Sir Francis Drake's famous attack on Cadiz in 1587 had been something of a reconnaissance in force as well as a barrel-burning expedition. What he had seen convinced most of the Privy Council but not Burghley, who evidently could not understand why the King of Spain would want to do such a silly thing. Letters came from Sir Horatio Palavicino, her banker, spin-merchant and Mr Fixit at the Hague where the money-markets were: Your Majesty's credit is halved because the money-men fear you will lose your kingdom. The Pope will give a million ducats to the King of Spain when Spanish troops land in England. The harvest is poor.

Some of her actions are still a mystery. Why, for instance, did she continue the peace talks at Dunkirk all the time the Armada was fitting out and indeed until well after it had sailed? It's true her old friend and 'Eyes', the Lord Treasurer Burghley was comfortably certain, as a cool and rational politician, that the whole Armada was a bogeyman, which would vanish into a puff of smoke if nicely spoken to and negotiated with. He had even sent his second son, Robert Cecil, to lead the delegation. Why did Elizabeth humour him with peace commissioners for so long? Did she believe it too?

More papers, more words trapped like butterflies in cobwebs of paper. And the Queen reads, listens, questions personally, hears testimony gathered by others, in a strange sense forced to be a historian of her own current events, trying to tease out late and inaccurately, what exactly was happening, had happened. Remember, the world was big then. It could take two days to get word from York. Think what can happen in two days.

She and her councillors had made the best preparations they could, mustered the country's trained bands, stockpiled shot and powder, poured money into the country's floating wooden walls. They were a small poor nation, compared to Spain, but . . . There are no guarantees in war. For a start, Elizabeth and her people – notoriously inefficient, drunken, unruly and inexperienced soldiers on land – were famously good at little raids, crazy plans and seacraft.

But it all had to wait until the Armada came. The news had arrived that the Armada had left Lisbon – it came to Dr Nunez first, perhaps by pigeon, and Dr Nunez rose from his dinner and went round the corner to Sir Francis Walsingham's house at Seething Lane to tell him. And then the news came that the Armada had been scattered by a storm and was in Corunna to refit. And then . . .

The tension slowly increased as the rumours solidified into fact, as the papers galloped into the sorting rooms of Seething Lane and Whitehall . . . Still, what Elizabeth saw was only the ceaseless swirl of Court faction and fashion, the gradual victory of spring over winter in her garden and then of early summer over spring. The weather was terrible, cold, stormy, rainy, but still the roses responded with buds.

At last! The Armada was sighted off Cornwall and the beacons lit, the land taking fire at its highest points from bearing to bearing, smoke rising in the day and fire prickling the land by night. At each place, a delay while watchers debated over what they had seen, saw confirmation from others in the network being lit, and took the slowmatch from their firepot to light their own high metal basket of brushwood and logs. Luckily, it wasn't raining that day. By evening, the news was in London and the capital was in an uproar, the Queen's court the very slow central processor from which orders radiated out across the kingdom.

And now a man gallops into the court gate on a lathered horse. He is met and escorted by Sir Walter Ralegh himself, resplendent in vibrant red silk brocade, straight through the Court, all the people seeing the young man's exhaustion, his mud-soaked boots and hose, his hair wet with sweat, turning, whispering, knowing why he is there. He has ridden post 200 miles, all the way from Plymouth to bring Her Majesty the true word on the Armada. This was an athletic feat like marathon-running, requiring extraordinary fitness, horsemanship and organisation. Riding post meant that every ten or fifteen miles you changed horses, so you could keep the pace at a canter or even a gallop for long distances. Apart from carrier pigeons, it was the fastest anyone could carry the quick-spoiling fish of military information.

Other young men are already behind him on the road, carrying further messages, small fast pinnaces likewise beating eastwards up the south coast, milking the land – and sea-breezes to carry their precious information to the place for which it was intended as fast as they possibly could. With luck, judgement, impeccable fitness and no accidents you could manage as much as a hundred miles a day.

Overwhelmed at being led by the Captain of the Queen's Guard the young man hurries drymouthed through the whispering passages, through the heavily guarded narrow corridor leading to the Queen's private chambers, up the stairs to the gallery. At the door to the Presence Chamber, Ralegh stops, reaches in his doublet sleeve pocket and holds out a chased silver flask.

'Drink,' he says with a nod and the young man accepts gratefully, gulps down excellent aqua vitae.

Ralegh leads him in, announces him and the young man drops to both his knees in front of the Queen before hurriedly fumbling out the sealed package from the Admiral of England, Lord Charles Howard of Effingham (not Drake, who was not aristocratic enough). The Queen snatches, tears, scans swiftly.

It tells a tale of disaster narrowly averted, since the English fleet had been resupplying in Plymouth when the Armada was sighted in Cornwall. With the wind against them, there had been a real risk of their being bottled up in the harbour. If Drake rather than the Duke of Medina Sidonia had been in charge of the Spanish, he would have snatched the all-important advantage of time and place and risked everything on a daring raid into Plymouth pool to attack the Queen's ships while they were helpless.

Fortunately, Medina Sidonia had orders not to try any such thing. The Spanish Armada hove-to just outside Plymouth for a Council of War and a Mass of thanksgiving.

The Queen questions her witness intently, while the messenger kneels desert-lipped before her. Yes, the young man has seen the Spanish ships himself, with his own eyes, most numerous, a dark alien forest laid on the sea, flying alien flags.

The Queen nods, her eyes darkening, and dismisses him with thanks, then leans back in her throne to reread the Lord Admiral's packet.

Being gods we can step backwards, rise above the complex wood and stone of Whitehall, high into orbit where we can reverse time and rifle back through the days, weeks, months, before diving low again and skimming down to the sun-soaked tree-plagued West Coast of Africa.

But we must be careful. Here they understand gods and have men and women who converse familiarly with the unseen. Here is one who might well see us and know what we are, who can speak to us directly.

# Merula

*The Slave Coast of Africa, Autumn 1587*

If I were as moon-white as you, you would call me a witch. You would torture me with water and weights and burn me with fire. But in my home where we are all dark and beautiful, we respect upside-down people.

I am not small and weak and slender like your pearl-faced women. I am tall and strong: my arms are like the black oak of your bogs; my legs are like the black fir trees of your forests; my body is as strong as any one of you strange pink men with your little pink manpiece. My breasts are towers of ebony, my face is a sculpture in onyx, my hair a wonder of black velvet.

Why did I come among the strange hairy ghosts of the cold north? There are no real people there, only you ghost-people with your foul milk skins and your hairy faces bristling red like a hog's, who wear great citadels of heavy and coloured and beautiful cloth. Do you know how badly you smell?

I am upside-down, so I do the opposite to everyone else. I came to the compound of my King, my brother, walking in on my hands so that his warriors were afraid to stop me.

I said, 'The Portingales and Arabs are bewitching us. They offer things such as cloth and guns for our strong fine men, who stumble in chains to the ports and never return. Surely such an evil is sorcery?'

My King blinked and shifted his golden collar. Behind him an adviser whispered behind the muzzle of his princely leopard skin. (I too have a leopard skin.)

'These men in chains are not my people,' said the King and flicked at a fly with his whisk. 'I have never sold any of my people. I only sell foreigners and criminals. Why should I not sell foreigners and criminals to the hairy ghosts?'

'Was my son – your nephew – a foreigner or a criminal?' I asked coldly and he flinched, began to sweat. He thought I did not know what had happened to the lad, or did not care. Wrong.

'Why do you think I sold him?' asked my King, cautiously. 'Why would I do that?'

Now here was a great hole in his speech where the words 'I did not do it' should have been. But he was afraid to lie to me as well. I walked up and down on my hands in front of him, the breasts that suckled my boy hanging down. Then I jumped and came right-side up, my head rushing with the change, smiled to show him my pointed teeth.

'The spirits told me.'

Strictly this was a lie because I had found it out from one of his own advisers whom I had made drunk and trusting with magic drinks.

The other adviser, the one the Arabs have bought, tapped his powder horn and tilted forward his gun. It was one of the few in the kingdom, a thing of great power and witchery. But without its magic powder to eat, it is dead. I had heard a great deal about this powder, I had even smelled and tasted some. It is sickening to taste, but nobody knows how to make it except the hairy ghosts.

So I bowed and touched the earth with my forehead, only I bowed not to my King but to his gun, his god.

My brother wanted more of the magic powder the guns eat. Any troublesome young man is a fair exchange for more magic powder. This is why there are no men for my sisters to marry, why they must go to old men and cripples for their children, why the fields are becoming smaller and the crops dwindle. And certainly any foolish young man who talks angrily against the King and has a claim to be King instead will be worth more in gunpowder. Most certainly. No doubt my brother the King felt merciful that he had not killed my boy.

'The hairy ghosts are my friends,' said my King. 'The English, the Portuguese, the Spanish. Even the Arabs. We have treaties, we have trade and trade is always good.' He paused, took a deep breath. 'I know nothing of your son.'

I smiled at him. It was, of course, true that he knew nothing of my son because nobody knows anything of those that are taken and bound by the Arabs and marched off towards the coast.

Once, long ago, I had a husband and so I had a son, praise be to the Queen Moon who gave him to me. But I was upside-down after the birth. When my husband beat me for it and I killed him, I gave my son to my sister whose baby had died. She came and took him and loved him. Then I went into the forest to hunt spirits and songs. Spirit time, song time is not the same as our time. When I came out of the forest again my son was grown and had passed his initiations, learned his secret songs, taken the scars of a young man, the snake that climbs up the right arm of men. My sister was the one who served him his beer afterwards. She was the mother who brought him to adulthood; I was only the mother who had spat him out of my womb. She wept for him when she came to me. But I did not weep. The King was foolish to sell him; more foolish to half-lie to me.

He looked away from my smile. 'Perhaps I could ask my friends the Arabs about your son?'

Oh certainly, he could do such a thing and tell them to see to it the boy was dead before sun up. Perhaps he would do that anyway, if he could. But why argue with stupidity? 'Let me go down to the port,' I said. 'I will sing and dance my son back to me.'

My King and his advisors looked at each other. I am likely to be a nuisance. Certainly a gun will shoot me dead, but then who knows where my soul will go or whose heart it might eat? Above their heads I could see their thoughts: the Arabs can have the curse for killing her after they capture her and find out how bad a slave she makes. My King's tubular, lead-spitting god sat on the sacred golden stool and smiled with his trigger under his long, tubular snout.

'You will not attack the Portuguese?' said the adviser. 'You will not frighten them away to trade with our enemies?'

'I am a woman,' I said. 'What do I know of fighting?'

'They won't take you as a gift, you fool,' sneered the other adviser, who had forgotten what he had told me. 'The Portuguese don't want to buy women, they say they have enough troubles of their own.'

'Nevertheless,' I told him, still smiling.

The King knocked his beautiful feathered and brass-bound spear on the ground, then reached out for the gun, which he put across his knees. A knife of light came through the leaves of his awning and softly cut the lock of the gun.

'You may go to the port,' said my King. 'You are the most upside-down woman we have ever seen, but there are others we can visit in the forest who are almost as upside-down, if we should need healing or to know the gods' sayings. You may go to hunt in the lands of the hairy ghosts.'

Of course, they were all glad to be rid of me, related to most of them as I am. Power comes down to me direct from the wise snake goddess who climbed a great many-boled tree in our land and mated with a golden bird; then she laid an egg in his nest and from the egg hatched the first of our line, alone, scaly, unbeaked, feathered by theft, male and female together, upside-down and right-side up. All of us, men and women, have such a snake climbing our arms, given in pain and blood when we became adult, very beautiful. So we are strange people and some of us see all the gods and spirits and become their friends.

I bowed again to the King and his advisers, and to their god, the gun, then I left them. In my poor King's enclosure where he must always stay except to go to battle, his great plump wives like hippopotami peeked between windowslats to see me go, whispering.

I laughed. I am a she-elephant – they are foolish cattle. I am a she-rhinoceros – they are frightened antelope. I am a she-snake – they are fat little birds.

To be upside-down is not always uncomfortable.

So with my best mantle of plush black and yellow fur, given me by a leopard most unwillingly, with my skirt of leather, with my stick and my pipe, my god-gifts hanging in a little frogskin bag at my neck and a leather net of dried meat over my shoulder, I went to the trail where the prisoners walk down, down to the sea, a river of them bowed in the sun.

Once, in the days of our great-grandparents, slaves would walk and walk northwards across the burning sands, across the rocky wastes of the north, walking in the night and the morning and resting in the brazen ugly day, when the Lion Sun stalks across the sky-desert and the world pants like a gazelle for breath. Half of them died on the way to the markets in the Arab lands by the Middle Sea.

Now there is no longer an ordeal by sand and thirst. The trail has widened and is used day after day and goes down to the sea. Now there is an ordeal by water and thirst. Then I knew nothing of it. All I knew is what I saw in that thin river of people: fine young men and a few crying women, some still weeping milk from their breasts for their dead babies, all walking walking walking down the trail. Many of the warriors were still wounded or dazed from being taken. They staggered with treetrunks necklacing each two together, and the tree bark wore great holes of meat in their shoulders and necks. It is

18

not good for slaves to be healthy, especially not strong young warriors, the most valuable ones when once they have been broken.

I stood on a treestump and took out my pipe and played to them. I played them sad songs and hopeful songs. They were indeed all foreigners, as my King had said, enemies. Their language was crooked and strange, hard for me to understand. They were descended from a different tree snake. Yet it seemed that they knew some of the songs I sang. One warrior answered my flute with whistling, a coming-of-age song. He had his manhood snake carved upon his cheek, not his arm.

One of their many guards was a cousin of mine, from my year-group, and he explained to his Arab master who I was. He should know, for I had brought his little brother safe from his mother's cave, when she had died of giving birth to him. He saw that I was hunting gods from my stick and my pipe, but he smiled and explained to the Arab that I was only a poor, mad healerwoman. The Arab nodded and I knew he was thinking that the hairy ghosts might give something for me because although I am certainly not pretty in the ghostly way of seeing things, I am as strong as a man.

*This is good*, said the Lady Leopard, walking in her other shape of a zebra by my side. Being ignorant hairy ghosts, you may not know that we are all trailed by the souls of anything we have killed. I myself am followed by a leopard, a zebra, many impala and smaller animals and a few men. But they are all my friendly ghosts, because I killed them fairly and honoured them afterwards. They help me.

My dreamsight flooded over me when I saw the Arab. There was his god: a golden word flaring bright above his head. He prayed to the writing, bowing down to it five times a day and I was entranced, fascinated, the first time I had ever seen such a god. The Arabs gave us their writing and some tell our king-tales for us to their paper rolls with pen and ink. To write is a very great magic and one day perhaps I will learn it.

When the first night fell, I slipped among the friendly trees to sleep and laid a little snare for the man the Arab would send to fetch me once my King's warriors were asleep, to beat me down and bring me in.

It didn't kill him, only broke his ankle. Poor man. I let him lie in pain to teach him better tracking, and his groaning was a bull bellowing in my sleep.

At dawn, the Arab sent my cousin to me to bow and ask politely what I wanted.

'I am seeking out my son who was sold by mistake,' I said. 'Have you seen him?'

My cousin knew the boy. He was shocked and yet it was interesting that he never asked how such a thing could have happened. The slave-traders and their guns make normal what was once terrible. 'No, of course not,' said my cousin. 'Do you think I could have seen him and not freed him? The King sent me away south last month.'

He was afraid of me, rightly, but I nodded to show I believed him. The next night I slept in a tree while heavyset men staggered about underneath looking for me. One of them was bitten by a snake. My black and yellow fur kept me warm.

On the third day, my cousin came to me as I slipped among the trees by the slavers' road.

'Tomorrow,' he said, sweating with fear, 'tomorrow . . . we will be near the fortress of the infidel and if you try to move through the trees and fields, their soldiers will take you or kill you, not knowing what you are. So after tomorrow it will be better for you to stay with us, whether you want to or not.'

Never have I been taken prisoner more politely.

'I will come back to you because you are intended to help me. But tonight I will sleep by myself,' I said to him firmly.

None of the Arab's men obeyed his orders to find me: they stamped about the forest, talking as loudly as they could and then went back to camp.

That night I made a fire with the sacred red wood that spits and wails as it burns; I broke my stick of power, weeping as I did it, and burnt it to ashes. I broke my flute and buried it. I ate the last of my meat, drank the last of my beer and burnt the bag and the calabash. I took them all full and pure into my heart where they could not be stolen.

*Now you must go into the lion's mouth*, said my Queen Moon and I saw that she was changed from a zebra to a leopard. I was afraid and sad.

I lay quietly by my fire and pretended to be asleep, pretended not to notice when the hairy ghosts sent by the Arab crept like elephants through the leaves in the dark and threw a net over me, rolled me in the leaflitter, bound my hands and arms like a buck.

'Why are you so afraid of me?' I asked, forgetting they would not speak my tongue, and the Queen Moon, my Lady Leopard pawed my lips to be silent and to listen and to watch. Truly, they were well worth watching for simple strangeness.

They smelled sour of milk and sweat and their pale skins glistened like a slug, except where they were boiled red from the sun or where their beards sprouted like monkeys'. I thought their bodies were not like ours for the strangeness of the shapes their clothing puts on them, though I learned better. They spoke hideously the language of the coast as they warned me not to try any tricks and to follow them.

Under the smiling plump face of the Queen Moon we went down to the port where the town rattled with traders, women, pens full of treetrunk bound men, sitting stunned with exhaustion and misery, some weeping in their sleep. Some swayed together and sang very low of how they had died and gone to live with the songs of their fathers, singing their own deathsongs, willing themselves to die. Perhaps they would. It does not always work.

The part of my heart that was not kidnapped and eaten by the gods was struck dumb and blind with fear at the stone squareness of the place. Around me, the Queen's light fell like water and the air was filled with flies that sting.

Soon we met the Arab and his train of captives, escorted by more of the hairy ghosts and no longer by my own cousin who had gone back to my King.

Now here was a great stone pen full of people guarded by Arabs with guns and hairy ghosts with guns and swords. So many people, men and women, but mostly men. The hairy ghosts prefer them for they can work harder, although they die quicker.

They had put iron bracelets on my wrists and a chain between, the same on my feet to hobble me, and a ring round my neck to lead me. It was heavy, awkward but not so bad. I am upside-down, a woman who brings back songs from the dreamtime to lift men's hearts, and so I sang to them, softly, under the heavy stars.

The day passed. Young men were bought in coffles of four. As I squatted in the dust, waiting, the Lion Sun patted my head with his golden paws and my mouth swelled with thirst. Nobody wanted to buy me, for I was not pretty to be bedded and they did not believe I was as strong as one of their men. The Arab scowled at me as though this was my fault and then clapped his hand to his head and sent a boy with a message.

At last, as the Lion Sun dropped down to be killed by the Night

Panther and his sister the Leopard Moon, here was a new hairy ghost. He was a scrawny creature, sweating in all his rich clothes, a cap on his balding head, his weak, pale brown eyes squinting behind glass windows.

He spoke quickly in a language of rich browns and golds, the tongue of the Portingales. The Arab beckoned me over and I shuffled to him.

'He wants to know if you can heal the flux?'

It depends on what kind and how bad it is and which demons are implicated.

'Yes,' I said.

More talk between them. 'He wants to know, can you look after a sick woman?'

'Yes.' I smiled. Why else do you think anyone tolerates upside-down people?

The Arab waved his arms with enthusiasm, words flooded from him. The little scrawny hairy ghost looked at me narrow-eyed and I looked back. The Arab thought I should show more respect and moved to strike me, but the little hairy ghost stopped him, rested his hand on my right shoulder briefly. More words passed, the Arab clearly thinking he was mad.

'He asks me to ask you, will you take service with him?' said the Arab, rolling his eyes at such absurdity.

I smiled and salaamed to the hairy ghost, while the leopard at my side swished her tail in pleasure. The hairy ghost gave a small purse to the Arab, who squatted down by his little enamel table to count it and then make patterns with his pen on a piece of paper.

The hairy ghost took the paper, put it inside his fortress of clothes, spoke again to the Arab.

'He says that you are to call him Mr Anriques. He desires to know your name.'

Names have great power. 'I have none for the Queen Moon ate it,' I said.

The Arab passed this on and Mr Anriques nodded as he spoke.

'He says that in that case he will call you Merula, which means blackbird, and you must come with him now.'

We came to a great stone lake built to pen the restless waters. Here was the sea and praise be to the Queen Moon who made it, for he is her husband. She turns to him and he rises to greet her, she turns away and he flees.

The sea was new to me, though I had heard tell of it many times. Here it sang like a forest in a storm, it glittered and spun like the wings of swarming beetles, and the Queen Moon laid down a road of her light upon it for me to travel the path.

And there in the stone lake floated the wonderful, great, wooden creatures that own the hairy ghosts.

What can I tell you about them? Now, I have lived in them, I have climbed amongst their trees and wings, I have made myself a part of them by pulling this or that thread of the rope spiderwebs they carry. I have been to them like a tick-pecking bird on a wildebeest.

At first my eyes were too unaccustomed to see them: I saw a forest moving in a breeze, heard the clicking and sucking of many small babies, thought the stone surrounding the lake to be the lake itself, heard the rattle from the trees and their folded wings as a small battle between tiny creatures I could not see.

Then my sight shifted and I knew them as sea creatures for I saw and recognised the water under them. I had seen boats on rivers; here they were, magnified.

There were three in the stone lake that night, their wings folded – these had two trees each to bear their wings, although I have known some of these great wooden sea creatures with as many as four trees each, especially among the wonderfully strange northern tribe of the English.

I was struck still with wonder. I stood and gasped, stared, planting my bare feet on the stone. The little hairy ghost who had bought me waited patiently, although he held a chain that led to the ring about my neck.

Lamps shone on them, I saw men walking on them. Thus I knew they were real and not only in my dreamsight. They were wonderful magics of the hairy ghosts, magics like wheels of the Arabs that raise water or the juice of a frog on an arrow which kills.

One of Mr Anriques' hairy followers rolled his eyes at me, in a face all covered with pimples. They wanted me to move on and when I had sung to my Lady the Queen Moon, I let them lead me, over the dust and cobbles, past piles of copper and bales of cloth and barrels of their firewater and magic powder to feed the guns, and a few stacked guns and coils of slowmatch. All of these were guarded by sweating hairy ghost soldiers.

Here is their cleverness. They sell us guns in exchange for a few young men. But the guns are not like spears or swords, once bought, for ever and completely bought. Nor are they like bows and arrows, for any bowman can make and fletch his own arrows. Nor are they like horses which must always eat, but which can eat grass and grain from anywhere. No, the guns from the north can be bought quite cheaply, considering what they are, but then magic powder must be bought and matches for the lock and bullets to fly out of the tube – and these things are used up, gone after even a small battle. Nor are they cheap. So each gun is like the first scout of an army, its food costs more and more men, for all the hairy ghosts want of us is ourselves. We are not as rich as we were either, for there has been much drought recently and we have all become poorer even without the wars.

Our kings and lords lust after guns and powder to feed their power: they use them to take more of each other's young men and more and more, so that between killing enemies with bullets and sending enemies away over the sea, the kings' enemies are destroyed. Better them than us, say the kings, and feel happy to be so rich and prosperous and safe.

But I am upside-down. I saw the guns as a forest fire, sucking trees towards itself and eating the air above it. And the metal fire of the north had sucked my child into it. Perhaps he was already dead, but even if he was, if I could find his spirit in the cold lands, I could bring him home with me. Any mother would wish to do it.

We came to the stone shore of the stone lake, where the hairy ghosts had me step down and sit in a wide canoe while two young men paddled for them. They tether their winged sea creatures away from the shore during the night.

Of course, I knew by then that they are only great boats, such as we have ourselves. But why not both? Large boats, winged sea creatures, why choose?

We clopped and splashed away from the stone and came under the wooden flank of one of the ships where there was a ladder. Mr Anriques gave the tether-chain to the younger of his servants and climbed briskly up, a little like an ape. Shouts between the hairy ghosts in the boat and those high above. An older hairy ghost, almost normal-coloured from the sun, unchained my arms. He pointed up the ladder and shouted at me, while the young pimpled one aimed a small handgun at me, the dull light of its match brightening and darkening as he waved it.

I shrugged, kilted my skirt, climbed the ladder. It was harder than I thought and I scraped my leg.

At the top was a wooden rail I must jump over and then a flat wooden floor like the roof of a temple, quite clean and decorated with rope. Jungle festoons of rope hung down or stretched like liana from the two great trees growing in the centre and far end of the floor. Here and there were large black calabashes, or iron pots, very long and narrow, which I did not then understand were the older brothers, the fathers and mothers of the guns that tempt our kings. The white wings of the ship were folded away upon the straight branches of their trees.

My dreamsight was dim but I could feel several gods over this strange sea creature.

One was the Suffering Jesus. Then there was his brother, a God of the Sea, Thundering Jehovah, worshipped by those mad, northerly hairy ghosts called the English. The great boat herself was a godling to some of her crew, of course. Below the gods, there was a battle. Souls that lived within the boat were battling a demon, an ugly flux demon that turns dung to water and flesh to fire until it withers and the soul departs. I could smell him clearly for the hairy ghosts are filthy, and like fools carry their dung in the belly of their boats. Smelled once, you shall always know him.

The old hairy ghost grabbed my hands and locked the iron bracelets on them again. They took me into a little wooden hut built under the floor of the boat. There was the man who thought himself my master, Mr Anriques, sitting by a cot, mopping the forehead of the one who lay in it. She was withered, her lips were drawn back from her teeth, her gums were black, she breathed hardly at all and her cream skin was dry.

He looked at me without hope when the old man pushed me down to the deck. I knelt. Why not? I am upside-down, it would have been more respectful to stand, but why should he know that?

Since then, I have found how very, very stupid are the hairy ghosts in the matter of demons. They know nothing. They do not know that flux demons and ague demons live in old water, they do not know that a flux demon must be fought with sweet water, they are like children in their ignorance.

From the way the scrawny ghost patted her head, I thought he might be her husband or her son – impossible to be sure since she was so withered.

Poor woman. Now the old ghost gave me a bucket with water in it and a cloth; the scrawny ghost gestured at his woman, said something. What did they want? Certainly she should drink – but was the water sweet? I tasted it with my finger. As I had heard of the sea, it was salty.

Not to drink then. To wash her? Ah, that was the answer. I took the cloth, squeezed it, made movements as if to wash the woman. Both of them nodded their heads.

I must tell them, though the poor woman would likely die. I looked on the little shelf by the cot. An empty cup. I took it, tipped it to her lips. Held it out. The old man brought a bottle, poured liquid. I smelled it – firewater. Poison to a woman so sick. So I poured it on the deck and the old man struck me.

So I put the bucket and the cup down and squatted. I am upside-down and I will be treated with respect. My face was a stone as the old man shouted and slapped at me, battered my back with his fists, and I waited for him to finish, staring at Mr Anriques.

Anriques approached. He took the cup, he dipped it in the bucket, held it, raised his brows. I turned my face, made a grimace at the salt. Now he shouted at the old man who marched away, muttering. We waited, Anriques and I, staring at each other. At last he came back, with sweet water in a leather jug and put it in the cup. I smelled it. Too sweet. I sprinkled a little salt water in it to clean it, then I gave it to the scrawny man and pointed at the woman's lips, made a mime of drinking.

They are so slow, these ghosts. At last his face cleared. He spoke sharply to the old man, he sat beside his woman and he began giving her the water.

I could not give it to the woman to drink myself – if she died, they would say I poisoned her.

So I took the bucket and the cloth and pulled back the cover, gagging at the reek of the flux demon. They had put rags against her legs to soak up what came from her, but not enough. You should know, by the way, that hairy ghosts are filthy creatures who never bathe because their lands are so cold and their rivers are cold and dirty. Also, they are terrified of the white ugliness of their skins and hide themselves beneath their clothes. Their garments are beautiful but underneath is stench and corruption.

I cleaned the poor woman like a baby and I sang to her to keep her strength up, to tell her soul to fight. She wore a shirt, stiff with sweat and dirt but very fine with an edging delicately plaited of thread and it was soiled. I wished to take it from her, to have her naked so her skin could breathe, to clean her properly for there were sore places on her. Gently I lifted her to strip her and Mr

26

Anriques turned away as I took the thing up and off her shoulders. She was a mother and had given suck, but where were her children? Then he was pushing another bundle of cloth at me, just as fine. At least it was a little cleaner. How could I tell him, she didn't need it? But it would have made no difference for the hairy ghosts believe they must always be hidden lest their whiteness offend the Moon and each other.

I shrugged and put the new shirt on her and then when she groaned and jack-knifed with more flux, I lifted her and put her on the close-stool in the corner, held her as she groaned, wiped her again and put her back in bed. I signalled for Anriques to give her more water. He seemed surprised but he did it, while I chanted her a chant of strengthening and victory over the flux demon.

So we worked together in silence and song. Anriques was a puzzle to me. He wore a little cap on his head to hide his baldness and perhaps his hair the colour of the drought-grass of the plains. His many clothes were of that cloth-fur they call velvet, rich browns and black, edged with black and gold and underneath I could see peeking out his white shirt. His fingers were long and thin. I saw no hard places on them and wondered what he was: a king, perhaps? Certainly, in a way, he was king of the boat, for the hairy ghosts that worked upon it came to speak to him often and I heard him giving orders.

He gave his woman water and gave her water and again and again, as I showed him. I lifted and cleaned and lifted and cleaned.

By morning the flux demon was weeping for mercy. I whistled to him, wishing for fire, wishing for my pipe that I had burnt, bidding him begone.

Sometimes the scrawny king, Mr Anriques spoke to me in many-coloured words. He used words that were rich crimson and indigo, he also used words that sounded pale blue and green, and I smiled and shook my head. He went out of the hut. It would be interesting to learn his languages. I hoped I would find someone to teach me.

There was a tramping and a moaning, many feet passing overhead, some of them singing their deathsongs. Even though I did not know their songs or their words, even though they were foreign prisoners taken in a war by a king I did not know, I crouched, shivering. My hair stood up and the world whirled about me and my dreamsight came crashing through the walls of my mind so all about me I saw the gods of the people, chattering, jostling, shapeshifting and fading.

The Queen Moon was a zebra beside me. *Be not afraid, I shine in all the lands you will visit,* she said.

Of course, I was still afraid, but her voice lifted me up and I stood. There was a croak beside me. The woman I had tended through the night had her eyes open: because the flux demon's heat in her flesh gave her dreamsight as it often does, she saw the Queen Moon and her eyes widened.

'Shhh,' I said to her, and stroked the striped muzzle of my Lady beside me. She still shrank back in fear. So as to be less frightening, I squatted by her cot again, and I sang her a baby's song, what I might sing to a girl-baby I had just helped from her mother's cave. The woman calmed and watched my Queen as she clattered her shining invisible hooves across the boards, spun around, reared up like a nightmare, to entertain her and show off her beauty.

Great weariness comes upon me when the dreamsight has taken me and I did not want to listen to the feet slapping on the boards and the clattering of the chains as the young men went down into the belly of the ship and were fastened there.

I rearranged the woman's covers. She saw my iron jewellery and frowned and I patted her hand, not to be concerned as I was not. My Lady Zebra nudged me. So I took off my leopard skin and laid it over her bed, the most powerful protection she could have. Then I lay down beside her cot on the straw mat, cool and comfortable with my head on my arm, and was rocked and rocked by the arms of the sea holding the womb of my captivity. So I slept.

I woke surrounded by movement and the floor tilting first one way, then the other, and then again, another way. I started up in fright, crouched, fell. The light was different, the whole hut swayed like a tree. Now came Anriques and spoke sharply, pointing to his woman. Behind him came the old man with his bucket, tutting.

I gestured him in return to make her drink and then when I had done with tending the woman, I went to peer out of the little door in the side of the hut. The ship was opening her wings, her sailors scuttled like beetles up the cobwebs on either side of her trees, and the other sailors heaved and sang and heaved and sang while the Leopard Moon rode pale and sleepy on one side of the sky and the Lion Sun stretched and shook out his mane on the other.

Now the sea creature who had slept in the stone-shored lake rose up and fell down like a northern camel, standing and sitting and standing and sitting again. Boats full of men, shouting to give each other the rhythm, pulled the sharp end round on ropes so that she was heading into the great sea desert. And below, the foreign prisoners wailed and moaned and screamed.

I stood staring, with joy rising between my breasts, latching on like a child, to see her wings outspread, to feel her move, to know her for the creature of wind and water that she was, a godling in her own place. I sang and ululated of my joy. The sailors frowned and made signs against bad luck. One of them shouted in some language and the old man behind, struck me on the back.

Why should I take offence? I heard the fear in their voices. I squatted again, making myself small, which is the way to make friends with the hairy half-men in the forest. As far as I could, I made the movements of a prayer of thanks to the Queen Moon, asking for a safe journey. They forgot about me in their busyness. Softly, quietly, I crept out of the door.

The land was falling away, the wind flapped my leather skirt and pulled chicken bumps in my skin. The sailors were working with the huge triangle of cloth at the sharp end, folding it and folding it, tying it up, turning its long branch on end to tilt it the other way and then unfolding again as if they were a woman showing fair cloth at a market. The ship tilted over suddenly and I fell again.

A fancy came on me to see the last of my land. I thought, perhaps I will never again see the zebras and hear the lion cough in the night. All about me are hairy ghosts, except for the foreign prisoners in the hold, and I could not talk to them except in song. Sorrow walked up from my heart and clutched my throat. The rivers of my brain overflowed. I shall climb that tree and say goodbye, I thought.

So quietly, I kilted my skirt, went to the side of the ship while they were all watching something else, hopped up to the railing where the sailors' feet had worn it smooth and began climbing the cobwebs made of rope that the sailors climbed. It was easier than a tree although the iron jewellery hampered me. Besides, Lady Leopard came and sat on my shoulder with her mischievous, whiskered face, lending me her grace and balance.

Up and up I went, up the middle tree, the one with square wings. The ship made the tree move up and down and sideways, but it seemed easy enough compared with some of the trees I had climbed to get at the frogs that hide high in their branches or for the mosses and lichens that grow on the bark. The ropes narrowed underneath a platform where you can stand to look out. I had watched to see how they did this thing: I climbed up and back on the ropes that led to its edge, hanging by my hands and feet like a monkey, then scrambled over the edge and past the great ropes and blocks for the next part, and stood on the platform. Some of the sailors turned to me, mouths open, eyes wide to see such a thing. Shouts came from below, but they were busy. They must move the sails to catch the wind, they would catch me later.

Another set of rope webladders stretching up, and up I went. So far to see, such a wide world. No other trees, only the pleated taffeta of the blue sea, a fringe of green where the faraway land met the sand.

I came to the second and highest branching where there was a place to sit of a barrel, nailed in place, and I stood on it, holding the topmost branch that had a pennant for its glory, which flapped against me in the wind. I held tight with my toes. The Queen Moon tutted at me lazily from her sleeping couch of clouds. I gave praise to her properly where no one could strike me. Perhaps I was loud. Below, I saw the ants running here and there, afraid.

Would I fall? Perhaps. But it was very fine to feel the dipping and swaying of the great tree in the wind and I laughed as the barrel flung me up and down and from side to side, like a wild zebra objecting to being ridden. No worse than that, and this tree would not bite.

Behind lay the green of my own land. When I die, my soul shall fly there, an arrow from the Moon's bow, away from the cold lands of the hairy ghosts where they bring themselves to bloody battle and their gods go out before them. They say they only worship one god, but they lie.

Below me I could see the faces, some red, some white, some brown, as the crew stared at me. They were little mushrooms eaten neatly by caterpillars, each white fungus eaten with three round holes. They looked so funny, I laughed. The Anriques ghost cupped his hands and shouted a few words I could not hear.

I had finished my praise. I climbed down into the barrel to look from and waved, then climbed carefully the rest of the way. As I jumped to the deck, the crew had a net ready and caught me up in it, as if I were a wild beast, and I laughed and laughed to smell their fear of me. A great argument began over me, but I was tired as I always am from a god-riding, and so I fell asleep.

Later I heard they had been within an inch of throwing me overboard for being mad and insane and unaccountable, fearful as they were of a sickness in my head. But the Queen Moon protected me, for Anriques needed a woman to tend his wife and had found only girls half-mad with raping in his hold. Now he had left our land and could buy no more.

They loaded me with iron tribute to slow me and keep me from climbing, and they tethered me to a ring on the wall of the woman's little hut. They knew I was a demon because of the blackness of my skin and the woolliness of my hair. That I was a woman only mattered because they were so distracted by my breasts. They were forbidden to take the foreign women out of the hold to use them and afraid to venture down where one of the young men might willingly give his life for the chance to crack a ghost's head open. But there I was, safely hobbled, they thought, fetching food and water in the service of the sick ghost woman. She had made me put on one of their shirts for modesty when she grew well enough to see me clear. I found it very strangling. My breasts languished for the touch of the air and it made no difference to the sailors who stared as greedily at me as before.

At last two of them plotted together and bribed their fellows for a clear bit of time at the beakhead when I was emptying buckets. They planned to catch me and hold me and make the man-woman dance with me, whether I would or not.

It was a sad and strange thing: I tried to warn them of Lady Leopard coming when they cornered me, but they did not understand me. Even when I tried the few words of English that the woman who believed herself my mistress had taught me, they still did not believe me. They thought they knew what I was.

Well, there was one man that had his jaw broken in so many places he never spoke clearly again. And the other was pitched into the sea screaming, leaving his manpiece behind.

These are the ways of the gods, they do not usually know mercy. I would have been kinder to the men, since they did not yet know me.

Anriques came to me where I lay bruised by the wooden wall in his wife's cabin, and asked me what had happened and I told him as best I could that I was not there at the time and they must have fallen.

Anriques spoke quietly to the fellows of the man who died and also to the man who lay wasting for lack of food below decks, because his jaw was jelly. The sailors muttered at me, watching me sidelong, and making gestures against the evil eye.

The sailors themselves had time to plot evil because we were becalmed in the heat of mid-ocean, where there is no land for miles and miles and all the windgods of all the nations play and dance together unceasingly. Except in the centre of their dance is a blank space where no one dances and seaweed floats past, and there we sat for day after day while our sweet water grew less and less, and more and more green.

A couple of days later, I knew that the men were planning something for they had been gathering in small knots and talking and then moving apart as if they were busy whenever one of the ship-chiefs came near. Some of them were proper men from the coast and they knew what sort of person I am, and told the others. The poor foreigners in the hold wailed and cried. Their water was down to half a pint per day. Even the hairy ghosts were only drinking a pint each. Corpses splashed into the sea every morning and some popped up from their ballasting and followed behind us, stinking.

'Is it true you are a witch?' said one sailor to me when I squatted washing shirts in salt water in a bucket. He was the ugly, barrel-chested man with a long pigtail dipped in tar, his face nearly burned human by the Lion Sun, the old man who served Anriques.

I shrugged.

'Can you call a wind like they say?' he demanded. 'We need a wind to get us out of the doldrums. Can you call one?'

'If I witch, you kill me,' I said, for I had heard them talking and even understood some of what the ship's priest had said during one of his brief sober moments, when he had darkly advised Anriques to throw me overboard before my devilish evil, as shown by my sin-stained skin, could poison his ship and himself. Mr Anriques had listened respectfully, pointed out that his wife was a great deal better of her flux, and poured the priest more spirits with his own hands.

The sailor shook his head. 'Eh? No, we won't kill you,' he said, lying.

'Burn me, eh?' I laughed.

'No.'

I looked at the sky, empty, sniffed the air, lifeless. Power was there, I could feel it.

Well, I did not like to drink only half a pint of green water in a day either. 'If master say, I go up.' I nodded up at the crow's nest, then lifted my hands and feet and stamped to make them jingle.

The man went to his chief and the chief to Anriques, who came and took the iron jewellery off.

'I personally do not believe you can do such a thing as call the wind,' he said to me, slowly so I could understand, in the crimson and indigo speech of the Portingales. 'There will be no punishment if you fail. But some of the crew from your country say you might be able to do it and we are in a bad enough case that it's worth the attempt. Take her up but keep watch on her, Michael,' he added, to the barrel-shaped crewman. 'And you do what he says, Merula.'

I bowed to him, then kilted my skirt, stepped up to the rail and climbed, with the ropewebs thrumming under my feet and hands, wrists and ankles itchy where the metal had bruised me, but wonderfully light and free now. The soft air did not so much as brush my cheek, the Lion Sun's mane covered the sky. Michael followed me, his face creased with determination and worry. Meanwhile, the priest my enemy lay unconscious, full of aqua vitae, nothing in his godspace save sleep.

I stood on the upper cross-trees and looked about and all the sea lay like a table, all the sky like an upturned cup, the Lion Sun was lord of all. To be thirsty is no bad thing for dreamsight. Where are the gods then, I wondered, where do they dance? I had had no dreamsight for days.

'Tie me here,' I said to Michael. 'I wait.'

'What?' Michael scowled.

Sometimes they punish crewmen by tying them to the crosstrees for a day until they are nearly thirsty and hot enough for the dreamsight to make them crazy. That had given me the idea.

'Just do the spell,' Michael added.

I sighed, shook my head. 'Tie me here,' I told him. I wished to ask him if he thought that gods are called for nothing, like a dog home to supper? I had taken no bitter herbs, I had eaten that day and drunk a little. Further, the beer they drink constantly and the firewater thay call aqua vitae in particular are death to the dreamsight. So I had seen very few gods, hardly any, only glimpses.

In the end, after I had got tired of saying it, he did as I asked and bound me against the mast as I stood on the lookout place, but with my arms free and my head bare. I stood with my arms out and waited, welcoming the paw-pats of the Lion Sun on my head, waiting patiently for it to come.

Soon the Lion Sun lay down to rest and the Leopard Moon came to smile at me and all the great glory of her children, shining in the night. I waited and waited, the Lion Sun woke and grew from cubhood and bullied his way over the desert of the sky and lay down to sleep in his bed of blood. Again the Leopard Moon came with her throngs of bright children. They sang and comforted me in the pain of my body, of my arms, of my mouth full of swollen salt longing for water, my head banging like a gong from the sun, my sickness spinning like a soul. When you seek out the gods, pain is the shortest way to go.

And at last it came, at last as the Lion Sun returned again and roared across the empty sky, I broke free of my body and went to walk in the dreamtime, searching for the gods who had deserted us . . .

Deep in the heart of a temple that is also a fortress and a palace, a hollow-eyed clerk bends over stacked piles of papers, a prisoner of his power and his god. His robe is dark velvet, his candles flicker the memory of bees into the air, and from beyond the wall comes the soothing iron chant of his priests praising his god. They sing beautifully, the black-robed shavenheaded men, singing of blood and mercy in a different tongue, the father of their own, a tongue of rust-red and purple.

Here and there on the papers leafed methodically before him, from one pile to another, the Kingly clerk writes in firm, rounded, tiny strokes an order, a request, a mordant comment. Every so often a respectful attendant comes carrying boxes of papers and goes away carrying more boxes. Out flow the papers, bubbles on the stream of power, and all over the cold northern lands of the hairy ghosts, armies march or hold, ships sail or dock, men live or die at the direction of the clerkish King's words. Or so he believes, devoutly. It is a desperate responsibility, one that exhausts him and has dried his face and body to a collection of luxuriously robed sticks.

Upon his wall hangs an idol of his god, a figure of a man tortured to death, most cunningly wrought, cross of silver, flesh of gold, agony delicately made with rubies for blood, a horrifying thing to worship. No wonder the hairy northern ghosts are so savage. The King looks at it without flinching, accustomed to such sights, reverencing the dreadful price paid for his rescue and the rescue of all his people from Hell. It is a rescue that must continue every day, he feels, never can he relax. In his mind echo the insistent demands that he believes come from his Suffering Jesus god: 'You must restore the heretic English to the rightful worship of My one and only True Church. (Thereby we shall also gain a populous kingdom

34

and heal the running sore in our empire caused by the revolting Netherlanders.) Your cause is holy, because it is Mine. The English have been lured into the worship of Satan by their Witch-Queen and her minions, and you are the only one who can save them by the destruction of this Queen and the conquest of their cloudy, wet land. It is a crusade against wickedness no less than when you broke the Turks at Lepanto, no less than when your grandparents Ferdinand and Isabella, destroyed the Moors and ejected the filthy Jews. Why do you delay in the face of My suffering? The English crucify me over and over again with their sin. When will you save the English from themselves?'

Of course, he has never visited the dreamtime, never found the rightful voice of his god: all he hears is the insistence of his own fear. Under the nagging words is a quietness, a breath of the heart, saying, *Be gentler, my son.*

Of course, he thinks it is the voice of a demon and ignores it.

All King Philip of Spain's dreams are of burning, of *autos da fe* where he himself burns, screaming eternally in the fires of his terrible sins of omission, of caution, of insufficient zeal. Poor creature, wherever did he get such a terrible god?

The rubies in the tortured man on his wall suddenly bulged and dripped as real blood down the gold. Then came my Queen Moon to find me, in a new guise, no leopard or zebra, but a woman in white and blue, standing on the serpent of wisdom, wearing the moon and stars on her brow to show who she is. She came in the scent of roses and took one of her pearl-white breasts and poured milk over the thing of horror and the white milk glistened and washed away the rust-red blood.

The Kingly clerk raised his head and blinked at his crucifix for a moment. He had seen something: blood and milk? He blinked again, shook his head, rubbed his eyes, returned to his marks on the paper. I sang a small song of pity for him and praise for this new shape of the Queen Moon.

She smiled at me and kissed me on the cheek and beckoned me to follow, and so I did, walking through the wall like mist, for the dreamtime has no spaces in it, to another mistier land where another clerk sat in another study, surrounded by papers, only this one wore black and white, most rich and clean, his black hair greying, his stern, intelligent face yellowed by his battle with the kidney stones that torture him. He scribbled and plotted, a great Queen's servant. This mirror clerk had no beautiful jewel of horror

35

on his wall, nor any images at all of his god; also his language is not the descendent of the rust-red and purple one, this is the pale blue and green that Mr Anriques had spoken to me also. It was colder in his room and rushes not tiles on the floor. Upon a small shelf by his elbow was his god, glowing in his sight: a stern, black book, marked with a simple cross, much thumbed.

And there in his godspace, bulged a great, a most mighty thundergod, an angry old man, ghost-white like his worshippers, his great white beard whipped and wracked by wind and storm, full of fury and caprice, all about his shoulders shone the bright orange light of storms, the blue-silver crackle of lightening. He rose like smoke out of the black-bound book and in his hand was the same book and from it came the great bolts of his lightning. Now here was a useful and interesting god, Thundering Jehovah, the god of the blue-green English.

I looked to see the Queen Moon and she was smiling, then she melted and became again my own darling Lady Leopard, who swished her tail and clicked her teeth at her scowling fellow god.

Yes, I thought, I have use for a god of storms. So I sang softly to the Thundering Jehovah and at last he took my scent, followed to see where I went. And as we loped back over the sea, the sea turned grey and the sky went to plush blue velvet, and the waves made slaps together to catch the white feathers of foam between them.

Since every inch of canvas was spread to catch the breeze, the sailors were running to take in sail. I was sick with so much dreamsight, with thirst and hunger and heat. I could not even lift my head and none came as high as I was. The sailors hung over the yards so I could see their pale backs between their shirts and their breeches. With frantic haste, they folded the sails and tied them tight, and turned the yards and lashed them hard to the mast, as the sea took the ship and flung it up and down and there was I left to be the storm's prey, high above the deck, every part of me shaking and juddering with the hard ending of god-hunting, my tongue swollen for lack of water and the lightening crackling around the mast tip.

Truly, it was glorious. Their fierce Thundering Jehovah was not angry, only playing and stamping about his sea like a boy in a pond. But the ship danced across the waves with the wind slapping my soaked shirt across my shoulders. I opened my mouth to catch raindrops and sucked the cloth, and cheered to see a god at play.

They are simple creatures, gods, in the main, simple and easily pleased, only dangerous because men make them so important.

Once when the wind howled and the lightning came too close, feeling for the sharp points of the mast, my own Queen Moon came galloping across the sky as a zebra to chase away the danger for me, and stayed to dance with the clouds.

The morning came again and the wind settled to a fresh easterly. At last, they remembered me as I slept quite peacefully, slumped against the ropes, and they came up to fetch me and bring me down in a bosun's chair, for I slept like the dead.

My mistress told me later the priest advised again that I be thrown overboard since I manifestly was a witch to call a storm like that. Anriques frowned at him and spoke sharply. He rated the man for superstition, to think that any creature, woman, witch or even Satan, could control the weather, which was, after all, the kingdom of the Almighty. A storm had come while I was tied to the mast and had blown us all out of the doldrums. It was mere chance, the throw of the dice, that was all.

I had never meant to frighten them so. Poor hairy ghosts, they are so afraid of real people.

With reason, of course.

# David Becket

Spring away from the fragile wooden ship bobbing on the swell, step forwards in time now, for we shall visit an old friend.

David Becket goes doggedly about his duties as Deputy Clerk of the Ordnance for Sir Francis Walsingham. It's a come-down for him. He has been Sir Philip Sidney's swordmaster, but owing to a most unfortunate mistake he was tortured by the manacles in the Tower and believes he can no longer be a swordmaster. The blow to his head that robbed him then temporarily of his memory, has left him with what we would call mild temporal lobe epilepsy and what he calls the falling sickness, or fits of prophecy.

And who is to say that such subtle damage to the marvellously complex jelly that is a human brain could not cause its possessor to think past the barriers of time and space and see into a possible future? Or perhaps it is no more than a phantasy from too much phlegmatic humour.

Swoop through the clouds to the sodden eastern fringes of London where everything that stinks industrially must be sited, where the tanneries and soap-boilers war to pollute the air and water. At the edge of a still worse place is a post-inn where they keep horses ready for use by the Queen's servants, with a dormitory below and small stale rooms above, each overwhelmed by old beds with lumpy mattresses. In one of them lies Becket in his shirt, the blanket thrown off and fingers of moonlight slitting the shutters to touch his face as he whines in his sleep like a dog.

A dream is whipping through his skull like a hurricane, making him shake. In his dream it is already the autumn of 1588 and he has become, by some unknown means, Sir David Becket, Captain-General of the hard-bitten West Country army, looking for the Duke of Parma and his Spanish tercios to bring him to battle and stop him reaching Bristol . . .

*They were a little to the south of Dorchester as they came in the late afternoon upon the unmistakeable signs of Parma's army, slowly eating its* way across the land like a vast bloodthirsty slug. Trodden fields, shattered hedges, chewed-up lanes and the small fat unfortified English villages, pillaged and burned.

It was like the worst parts of the Netherlands in his youth. Worse, because this was country he knew. Had ridden across many times.

Sir David sent out scouts to be sure they did not find any of Parma's tercios by walking into them and also because he was wondering . . . He couldn't help it. He had not been home since that night his father broke his nose, threw him out and disinherited him for reasons that had seemed wholly ridiculous when Becket was a lad of twenty, but now seemed cogent and sensible to the thirty-five-year-old man of authority.

One of the scouts clattered back at the gallop in the late afternoon, whey-faced, stammered something reluctant. Sir David Becket looked at him, shook his head. He had to go and see.

He thought there was no likelihood of meeting Parma anywhere near, from the reports of the other scouts. Perhaps the Spaniards had withdrawn back to London for the winter. Becket was praying for a good hard one and so far the autumn had looked promising, setting in wet and with bitter nights. He had some ideas about uses to which you could put a frozen Thames.

But first he had to see for himself what had happened to his family.

Hand easing the small of his back, which was aching, he told his second-in-command where he was going, listened to the remonstrations and then repeated where he was going. His second-in-command was not happy and said so; Becket swore at him and then allowed the man to order up a bodyguard of forty riders, which he felt he had no need of at all. The rest of the column would make camp where they were. In the morning they would turn north, to be sure Parma was not feinting north for Bristol and incidentally, perhaps, draw some of Medina Sidonia's besiegers south-westwards from Oxford. This might then make it easier for Sir Robert Carey to relieve the Queen there, supposing he got through in time with his father's motley Borderers.

Becket had been in the saddle since two hours before dawn and had eaten on the move. His stomach was rumbling, as it usually was, but at least he had not got the piles or the squits like many of his men. Permanent tiredness was a normal condition of war, after all.

The forty lads of his guard sorted themselves out eventually, jostling to be nearest the Queen's Captain-General, trying to impress him with their smartness and hardness. He sighed. He was now surrounded by a pack of twitchy young gentlemen with no sense, on nervy young horses with no *brains. By God, he knew he stood a better chance on his own with one outrider.*

*Becket's shoulders and wrists were aching, his hands buzzing as they often did when he was tired and also in wet weather. The ugly white scarring on his wrists seemed to make his hands colder. He rubbed them, trying to get the blood flowing and his sleeping body did likewise, a habitual gesture, awake or not.*

*Then, in the world of his mind, he turned his horse's head south, took the road he remembered, despite its churned-up state, and pricked the animal to a canter on the bits that were passable.*

*It took them two hours to reach Middleton, passing two other burned villages on the way. Somebody witty had dressed a sheep in a stolen hat and cloak and then amused themselves shooting at it while it tried to run away. This Becket took as a good sign, in terms of Parma's grip on his chronically unpaid troops, and a bad sign for himself and his house.*

*The village had been burned, of course, the lychgate broken, the cottages ransacked. Here and there lay corpses; Goody Brownlow had made a fight of it, seemingly, since she was pinned to her cottage door with a pike through her and a woodaxe still in her fist. Over a fire made of pews from the church, now without its lead roof, hung the charred remains of a pig.*

*The forty lads of his guard looked at each other and sideways at him. They knew where they were, why they had come.*

*'Half of you keep watch,' he said wearily. 'Half see if you can find anything worth keeping.'*

*Becket turned his horse, who snorted in protest, and carried on up the trampled lane towards his father's house, built from the ruins of the local priory. His expert eye fell on some small and inadequate ditches dug in the ruined orchard and herb garden, ludicrous attempts made at fences and traps. Oh Lord God, had his brother tried to make a siege of it?*

*Becket House had been burned and still smelled of smoke, still occasionally crackled as another beam dropped. Becket walked in slowly through the door his father had booted him out of fifteen years ago. It was now drunkenly off its hinges and shattered by axes. He went through the lobby and into the small hall, once proudly hammer-beamed, now open to the sky.*

*He could hear somebody singing, a woman or a boy. Taking his dag from his belt, he stood in a corner to shot and wind it, then went forward into the parlour behind the hall, which still seemed to have most of its roof.*

*It was a place where somebody had made a little cave from the remains of a bed, and a small fire from the broken panelling and roofbeams.*

*He advanced carefully, for the singing had now stopped, trying to see what was there in the dusk and flickering light. Inside the little cave lay two children and a baby, he thought, carefully tucked up under a blanket. Were they his nephews, nieces? He didn't know. He took his morion helmet off, for he knew it made him seem monstrous with its plume and fancy chasing.*

*'Don't be afraid,' he said softly to the children. 'I'm no Spaniard. Where has your father gone?'*

*None of the little forms moved. He bent closer, shifted the blanket and froze. What he had taken to be a girl, by her fair hair, had no face but a broken shattered wound. The boy had the broken end of a pike still in him. And the babe ... It had been cloven in two and the pieces put back together. Carefully.*

*He replaced the blanket and turned away to vomit. Then he heard the hissing of a match.*

*The woman was coming towards him, limping and barefoot, something dark and sticky making her feet and the tatters of her kirtle filthy. Her beaten face was twisted with effort for the caliver was heavy for her to hold and her hands were shaking. The bright match in the lock wavered. Perhaps she had thought to load it, perhaps not. More than likely she would miss. But she might not.*

*Becket stayed still, put up the hand not holding his helmet.*

*'Mistress,' he said hoarsely, 'Mistress, where is Mr Philip Becket?'*

*'My husband is engaged and cannot receive visitors. Please let my children sleep, sir, I have only just this minute got them to settle.'*

*Becket drew in a shaky breath. 'Will you call him, Mistress Becket? I have some important news for him.'*

*The woman smiled quite sweetly, tilted her face up and called, 'Philip! Husband! There's an English Spaniard come to visit.'*

*Becket knew what he would see when he looked up, for he had seen it often before, not only in England but also in the Netherlands.*

*His brother hung swinging from a roofbeam, his face a purple joke with its swollen tongue.*

*The Queen's Captain-General blinked and swallowed, found the tears trickling into his beard. 'Mistress,' he whispered, his throat too tight to speak, 'if you will put down your firearm, perhaps I could conduct you somewhere ... better.'*

*'No,' she said, still smiling, 'you see, I cannot possibly leave the children until ... until things are arranged.'*

*'But mistress, your children are—'*

*Her face curdled, she lifted the caliver and Becket threw himself sideways as it went off, perhaps cracked, perhaps double-charged, and exploded in her arms. She looked down serenely at the rags of her hands and her ribcage, then crumpled to the earth.*

*Becket rolled to his feet, looked himself over, found a couple of cuts where bits of caliver had hit him, but his buff-coat and cuirass had protected him. He picked up his helmet, put it on and went to look at his sister-in-law, whose guts were spilling as she jack-knifed in agony.*

*The sound of hooves in the lane. Good. He had a job for them. Becket took out his dag, put it carefully to his sister-in-law's head, and fired.*

*Weeping, he went out to where his lads were galloping up in rescue, to tell them to dig five graves for his family. They would put the death date of 5 September 1588.*

Becket woke, still weeping, his heart pounding like a prisoner beating the walls of his chest. He sat for a while, arms wrapped round his knees, trying to stop gasping, to remember what had been in his dream to frighten him so. It was not the same as the usual nightmares, where he was back in the Tower not knowing who he was. This had been different. He had been leading men as he had in his twenties, there had been a smell of burning, a woman . . .

It was gone. Below in the inn courtyard, the lads were already shouting and leading out the post horses for their exercise, the daylight sliding over the eastern horizon. And he was not in the West Country, he was in Essex where the Thames trickled fat and sour into the sea. And now he should rise and make ready to visit the greatest midden in England.

Groaning and scratching, Becket swung his legs over the side of the bed, felt for the chamberpot. Thank God as a Deputy Clerk of the Ordnance, he could now afford a room by himself and no longer had to share beds with snoring, stinking, farting strangers. He took a drink from the flask under his pillow to ease his headache and went in search of his hose.

It seems I am fated always to be wading through the shite, thought Becket a few hours later, coughing and trying not to breathe through his nose. Before him stretched a foul plain down to the Thames mudflats, studded with little hills. The nearest steamed gently before him: a dunghill of magnificent, epic size. Stench of piss and shit many weeks old was making the air blue above them and the number of different mephitic and disease-laden odours hardly bore thinking about.

Becket put his nose deep in the little bunch of herbs he had been given and breathed in. It didn't help at all:

'This pile is not ripe, of course,' said the fastidiously dressed little man standing beside him, unmoved by Becket's nausea. He wore a silver pomander around his neck against disease but seemed nasally immune.

A cart squelched past them and over to the nearest most pungent hill, pulled by a scabby donkey. A troll-like creature hunched on the bench pulled a string, the board slurped and lifted, and the latest haul of London's nightsoil slithered out.

A shout went up from huts by the river. Three scrawny children wrapped in rags came running out and started scrabbling among the leavings. The littlest found something valuable, a piece of bright blue cloth, hardly marked, and put it triumphantly on his head, only to have it snatched away by the biggest.

'When ... er ... when will it ripen, Mr Jarvis?' Becket asked, trying to ignore the shrill screams and sounds of fist-fighting.

'Not for a few years. It is the next, over there, that is looking fair for harvest. Would you care ...' Mr Jarvis coughed, hesitated, dry-washed his hands. Never had Becket seen a more painfully clean person: his small ruff was like snow, his nails had been pared until they bled. Only his boots were crusted. 'Would you care to ... er ... water the pile?'

'What?' Becket was trying to settle his stomach with a gulp of aqua vitae from his worn flask. That did nothing for the stink either. He wiped a few drops off his beard and sighed.

Mr Jarvis trembled. Mr Becket smelled of drink, his grey eyes were dull and bloodshot, his belly strained the pewter buttons of his worn velvet doublet. Only the hat sitting on his greasy black ringlets was new and tolerably fine. He looked like a broken-down soldier who had been bought the position of Deputy Clerk to the Ordnance by a wealthy patron, which indeed was what he was. However, his patron was Sir Francis Walsingham and his purpose seemed to be to ferret out all Jarvis's comfortable little doings, instead of sitting back and drawing his stipend like a reasonable man.

'Your ... er ... predecessor liked to er ... water the heap.' Poor old Staveling, dead of some mysterious jaundice. Now there was a peaceable fellow with no mad questions to disturb anyone's quiet.

'What?' Becket had swung his bulk round to glare at Jarvis. He stood like a Smithfield bully boy, he had a worn-hilted, very

43

businesslike sword on his belt, he was two yards high and at least a yard broad, and there was something about him that had the sullen unpredictability of a thundercloud.

'To ... er ... piss on the heap, sir.' Jarvis was sweating and wishing he had kept his mouth shut. 'It ... er ... it helps the saltpetre to grow, sir. Urine, or indeed blood from the Shambles, sprinkled on the surface, followed by a dusting of earth, sir.' Occasionally the blood did not come from the Shambles and was brought still in its body at dead of night by men working for Pickering, the King of the London thieves, while Jarvis made sure he was somewhere else. 'It's a very nice mixture indeed, to encourage our treasure to grow.'

Becket grunted and put his flask away, pointedly without offering it. 'Sounds like a truffle.'

'In a way, sir, in a way. Certainly a strange alchemy takes place in these heaps of ... er ... London's waste. Cover up the ... er ... turds of London, sprinkle with piss or blood, bury, leave for a few years, return and dig and there you have it, sir, alchemical magic, the treasure in the dunghill, the very aquila albus itself. How it comes there is a philosophical mystery, but come there it does.'

Becket belched and then laughed. Never had Mr Jarvis heard a laugh less humorous. 'Ay, well, anything to get it to grow faster.' He unlaced and watered at large like a boy. 'Asperges me Dominum cum hyssopo and so forth. Enough?'

'Indeed, sir,' said Jarvis, smiling tightly as he sidled to avoid the puddles oozing in his direction. 'Are you satisfied with your inspection?'

'No, by God, I'm not. Who digs it up? Where does it go from there?'

They left the track and squelched along a path to where gloomy men were hard at work with shovels to excavate trenches through another mound, a little flatter than the first. The pale brown lumps they found were slung into handcarts, which were trundled by older boys than the urchins into a long low building with many chimneys.

Unhappily, and only after Becket had insisted thrice, Jarvis conducted him into the place, infernally hot and stinking to take your head off. There miserable women tended a long row of large pelicans, bellied alchemists' pots with a beaklike tube at the top leading to a smaller pot, sitting on a blazing fire. The stink came from the neat squares of dried turd they were economically using to feed the fire.

44

'Here we may see the alchemical wonder of the aquila albus, the white eagle, saltpetre. When it is heated, it does not melt but flies directly to a white smoke which being directed to another pot and cooled is thereby instantly cleaned of gravel or any other dirt and may be gathered and packed in barrels.'

Becket blinked at the brown-clad women trudging about and wondered blearily if the late Sir Philip Sidney, onetime Queen's Secretary of the Armoury had ever come here. Probably not, for if he had there would most certainly have been an elegant rhyme in Latin or English to celebrate the fact. The man had been incorrigible.

'And here we pack the pure crystals of saltpetre in barrels, as you see, branded with the Tower portcullis, and then it is sent to Her Majesty's mill at Wilmington.'

Explaining the familiar routines had begun to make Jarvis relax, so his heart nearly stopped when Becket swung round to scowl at him.

'Oh is it, by God?'

Jarvis dabbed at his mouth with a handkerchief and swallowed. 'Sir?'

None of the women were worth looking at, yellow-skinned and haggard the lot of them, though they were looking at him. Becket hooked his thumbs in his belt and leaned back to address the blacked beams above, his eyes hooding themselves behind heavily lashed lids.

'Mr Jarvis,' he intoned like a schoolmaster, 'I have it on excellent authority that more gunpowder is arriving at the Hague and, by implication, Lisbon than ever we see at the Tower. I have it from Wilmington that they are constantly hampered by the shortage of saltpetre. As you may know, gunpowder is a receipt compounded of one part charcoal, two parts sulphur and seven parts saltpetre.' This was a studied insult, to tell Jarvis the composition of gunpowder, as if he were a child. 'Neither serpentine nor milled powder can be made without saltpetre, therefore. As well make a sword without iron. Now at the Tower, what we receive is serpentine powder, with about the strength of a mouse's fart, on account of its age and separated condition, and no prettier a smell. They tell me that serpentine needs less saltpetre to make, which I know to be a black lie as well as you do.'

Jarvis, who had been about to agree that it certainly was, swallowed again. 'Sir?'

'Now this would have been of no particular moment as short a time ago as last autumn, but, Mr Jarvis, you may perhaps have heard tell even here in the wilds of Essex, that His Most Catholic Majesty the King of Spain is preparing a great fleet for to land his tercios in England, sack London, shoot the Queen and have his Jesuits rape every boy south of the Humber.'

Since the balladmongers had been singing of little else for six months, Jarvis did indeed know and he resented Becket's sarcasm. He felt it was really nothing to do with him. He could hardly be expected to change the ancient practices, established by his father who had bought the office and by the Lord Treasurer who had sold it to him.

'Now, Mr Jarvis,' Becket continued heavily while the women listened as they worked, glad of the entertainment and to see Mr Jarvis discomfited, 'I have seen tercios in action and you, I suspect, have not. It is only thanks to the love of God and Drake's raid on Cadiz this summer that the Spaniards are not marching through Kent as we speak. I would prefer Drake and his ships to blow them all to hell before ever the tercios set foot in England.'

'Amen,' said Jarvis piously, wondering where this was going and how much longer it would take.

Becket stepped closer and leaned over Jarvis. Some of the women stopped their toiling over the fires to watch. Jarvis was somehow cornered, in his own kingdom, and he started to sweat.

'Amen, you say.' Becket's rumble was thoughtful. 'Amen? And yet what is Drake to blow them to hell with, eh? Answer me that? For every eighteen-pound ball his demi-culverins fire, it takes nine pounds of milled or eighteen pounds of serpentine to loft the shot. He has told me he cannot get the powder he needs, neither milled nor serpentine, no matter how he begs. And I come and ask here and there, and ask and ask, and I am assured on all sides that the powder is in the making, but where it might be hiding, Mr Jarvis, truly, nobody knows.'

Becket's breath stank of aqua vitae as well as his sweat, thought Jarvis, feeling sick, and he was much too close and too large. It was unfair. Jarvis had never done anything worse than anybody else.

A broad finger and thumb reached out to pinch Jarvis's carefully slashed and trimmed tawny velvet doublet.

'I like your duds, Jarvis,' Becket said heavily. 'What did you pay for them? And with what, eh? While we're about it? At fifty pound per annum, your stipend would not buy you a sleeve of it, let alone the suit.'

'M . . . my wife has money.'

Becket stared at him unblinking. Jarvis pulled away from him and stalked out of the shed, nose high.

Becket was about to go after him, when he found his way blocked by two of the broadest women, brawny arms folded over their aprons. He had been right; they did stink, pungently.

'Sir,' said one, 'if we was to lay information against Mr Jarvis, would he lose his place?'

'He might,' allowed Becket. 'But I can pay you now, if you like.'

The two women exchanged looks. 'How much?'

'What's the information?'

'Where your saltpetre goes to.'

For answer Becket reached under his doublet and brought out his purse, pulled some shillings out and gave the women two each. They smiled at him gap-toothed as the shillings disappeared beneath their stays, and took him to the door, pointed down at the sulky sea lapping an inlet.

'Small boats. They take it out to the Dutch fly-boats – they can come right in close, you know, sir, they don't mind if the tide's up or no. And they pay for it, but we never get nothing.'

Becket nodded. Probably most of the missing saltpetre went to the Dutch for use against Spain, or perhaps they sold it on to the Spanish. He had heard the sorry, mercenary, brainless tale over and over again in the last couple of months. Englishmen who thought only of money had sold guns, ammunition and powder to men who thought only of power. Worse, to Papists, to Spaniards. He had never been one to think the best of any man but the sheer blind stupidity of them all made him long to kill someone. If he could find out whose corruption, whose permission licensed the quiet pillage of the Queen's Ordnance, then perhaps he could watch the man hanged, drawn and quartered. He would enjoy that, he thought savagely, for all his new-grown squeamishness.

'When do they come?'

'When they choose, sir. Mr Jarvis takes all the money, never gives us none. Do you think it's right dealing, sir?'

Their indignation made them red and self-righteous. Becket felt suddenly exhausted. Would they care if the Spaniards landed? Would they know until the tercios came and burned their hovels and spitted their revolting spawn on long lances? Of course not.

'Thank you, goodwives,' he said and shouldered past them into relatively fresher air. Jarvis was waiting by the horses.

Becket untethered his horse, climbed into the saddle and found his stirrups. 'Mr Jarvis,' he said, 'Englishmen will die for your pretty duds and so will you. Do you think the Spaniards will care how you helped them when they come to hang you?'

Jarvis opened his mouth with some excuse and Becket stopped him with a raised hand.

'Mr Jarvis, by my estimate, you are capable of producing twice as much saltpetre from here as you do, according to your accounts. This is what I expect to see coming up to Wilmington. If it does not, I will be back with a warrant for your arrest on a misprision of treason and Mr Norton will be given you to examine to be sure you are not some bastard Papist in disguise. Understand?'

Jarvis gobbled at him helplessly, 'But ... but ... we cannot possibly do it, the saltpetre grows slowly and—'

'And you have four untouched mounds ripe and ready. What are you saving them for, you fool? Dig them up and send us the saltpetre!'

Shaking his head, Becket touched his heels to the horse's flanks and the nag trotted up the path, dropping his own contribution to the Ordnance as he went.

After a night at Walsingham's household in Seething Lane where he had lodgings, Becket was on the road again, heading west for Bristol, Gloucester and the Forest of Dean to inspect the gunmaking there. With the ease of long practice, he dozed as he rode, because his sleep was mantrapped with ugly dreams that woke him shouting and fighting the blankets. Even Walsingham had noticed the black rings under his eyes and asked after his health when he finished making his report. Lady Walsingham had insisted on giving him a little bottle of tincture of St John's Wort, sovereign against melancholy and sleeplessness and after tasting it once, he had tipped it out in the road and refilled it with aqua vitae, which was a much surer medicine.

Although it had not prevented another dream, which had again woken him that morning. That had been doubly confusing, for in his dream he had been woken by a courtier, white-faced and shaking ...

'Sir, sir, Mr Becket, sir. The Queen wants you!'

The dreaming Becket had sat up, rubbed his eyes full of hangover, blinked uncomprehending at the young man. 'What? Why?'

'The Spaniards have landed. They took Gravesend last night.'

And in the dream his belly had swooped and clenched and he had changed his shirt, combed his hair, put on his buff-coat over his doublet, strapped on his sword and run ahead of the courtier to Walsingham's stables, which boiled with frightened men and terrified horses. He had to punch a groom to get his hands on a horse and he galloped for Westminster through streets that were already full of people asking each other what had happened, what should they do?

He knew something was odd, even in his dreaming self, for St James's Park was leafy and plump with greenery, not pale with spring buds. Late summer of 1588, the year that would end an Empire, according to the prophecy.

Two of Ralegh's guards waited for him at the Court Gate. He was hurried past knots of grim-faced, shouting men, weeping women, taken straight into the Queen's Presence chamber and found her flanked by Ralegh and his tall red-clad men. She was ivory-faced but most splendidly dressed in black velvet sprinkled with pearls and her crown on her head.

Becket dropped to both knees and bowed his head, feeling his heart thump, somehow more painfully aware of the print of rush matting into his kneecaps than he was of the girls sobbing behind him. The Queen swept down from the dais and stood before him, and he saw that with her knack for the dramatic, she was wearing a poniard dagger on her belt, very splendidly jewelled with rubies.

'Mr Becket,' she said, 'we thank you for coming in our hour of need. Will you do us a great service?'

'I am Your Majesty's liegeman,' said Becket, wondering what suicidal madness she was going to ask him to undertake now.

'Mr David Becket,' she had said, her voice ringing through the room, 'we hereby appoint you Captain of the Rearguard, with complete powers over our sovereign city of London in its defence.'

Becket blinked for a moment. Ah, that suicidal madness. Something inside him wondered cynically what had happened to the Lord Mayor and his aldermen. Rumour had whispered the week before that they had been locked up in the Tower on account of selling ordnance to the Spanish.

'In my name, you are to delay, frustrate, annoy and murder the Spanish for as long as you possibly can, using every advantage and ally that London affords. You will deny to the Spaniards any benefit that you can. You may not surrender the city under any circumstances.'

Looked at one way, it was very unlikely that Parma would ask him to,

49

*seeing that London had no walls and could not stand siege. Looked at another, it was a backhanded compliment to him that the possibility might even be considered, a compliment typical of the Queen's corkscrew mind.*

*'Further, Mr Becket, I desire that you shall not permit yourself to be killed or taken and when the time comes that you shall rejoin us in Oxford.'*

*It was a thought to make his booze-battered brain reel, that she was giving him any command at all, no matter what the situation. Gravesend. They had taken Gravesend in the night. Obvious, when you thought of it, for Tilbury was too well-defended and Gravesend, on the opposite bank of the Thames, controlled the river as well. His mouth was full of dust.*

*'Mr Becket?'*

*Something in her voice made him look up. She was smiling at him.*

*'If we are still alive in a month, make no doubt we shall reward you with great honour,' and the dry humour in her voice said she perfectly well knew what men said of her promises, and didn't care. Then she put a heavy gold chain over his head.*

The jasmine and rosewater scents of her had woken him, clutching his chest where the chain had seemed to burn him.

And now, in the Forest of Dean, he looked around him, puzzled to see early spring not late summer. A few green shoots were already scouting out the hedges although the landscape around him was blasted as if some Welsh dragon in league with the Spaniards had passed by and casually scorched it. Fences divided the woods into a patchwork where they were newly coppiced and needed protecting from deer and rabbits. In the parts that were ready to be coppiced again, the saplings grew thick. Charcoal burners moved among them, cutting them judiciously, piling the staves into mounds and skilfully burying the mounds with turves before lighting them and watching through the night as the wood part-burned into charcoal. Smoke rose lazily from turf mounds in all directions.

It had taken him two days clear to get the stench of Essex out of his nostrils and now he was coming into another place that stank volcanically, only of fire and metal, not ordure.

He had a great many things to do and he wanted to get back to London as soon as he could. As he took his horse up to a canter on a slightly less rutted piece of road, he came round a corner and had to haul the poor animal back on its haunches to stop himself riding into a line of charcoal burners' carts trailing slowly up a hill that looked like a manor in hell.

All the trees were bare and had been turned into frames for holding weights. At the top of the hill a great brick furnace bellowed fire and sparks into the air, the water wheel behind it making a strange, stately *whoomf-suck* noise as it moved a giant bellows to pump up and down. With each blast of air, the fire in the furnace blazed hotter.

Becket tried to pick his way past the plodding donkeys and their carts, none of which would move aside for him, their drivers stolidly pretending he didn't exist.

Muttering with impatience, he spotted what seemed a clear path and turned his horse into it. He found himself riding beside what looked like a long, straight, empty streambed made of burned earth. It was designed like a tree of Jesse, heading down the hill, so each branch ended in a sink hole of clay, surrounded by gravel. At each branching stood a flagstone on end, to dam the main channel. And in each pot hole, as if in a strange obscenity, a giant's fancy, hung a long pole dependent on a tree-frame so it did not touch the sides nor the bottom.

'Damn it,' said Becket, suddenly understanding where he was and what he was riding in. Very carefully, he turned his horse again, urged it up between the scorched trees where men were already waving at him to warn him. At the top where the heat and smell of smoke was choking, he slid down from the saddle gratefully, staggered for a minute, then led the reluctant nag on to the place at the base of the huge chimney where the foundry-master stood, staring at him as if he was mad.

'Ay,' said the foundry-master gravely, looking at Becket's warrant upside-down before handing it back. 'You have come at a good time, sir. Only I'd be much obliged if you wouldn't stand your horse in the casting channel again, on account of it might spoil the guns to have horseflesh in the metal.'

'My mistake, Mr Arlott,' said Becket ruefully. 'I hope I've not caused damage.'

'A man's checking it. Now then, no doubt you are here for the casting.'

'Of course,' said Becket, although this was the first he had heard of it.

'Second casting this year already and the biggest we ever tried. Two cannon, two demi-cannon, four culverins, two sakers, two falcons, a falconet and a cast murderer. Breech-loading murderer. We'll saw out the chamber and see if we can make magazines to fit. Bit of an experiment, to tell you the truth, sir. They say that Holzhammer managed it last autumn, but I ain't seen the gun proved . . .'

The foundry master was not in fact talking to Becket at all but into his chest, watching the flames and metal crucible in the furnace intently. Behind it all the wheel creaked round and the bellows pumped. Arlott ran out of words, seemed to forget all about Becket, and began putting on wetted leather armour and a helmet that covered his face, also of leather. As the sparks mounted in the mouth of hell and the colour paled, a lad tugged Becket's elbow to move him back.

Arlott waited, watching the fire intently, poised on his toes. Suddenly he darted forwards, carrying a long pole. He flung aside a door across the mouth of hell. Becket found his horse whinnying frantically and hauling backwards away from the terror of it, so he hitched the animal to a tree, turned back to watch.

Black against the golden, Arlott leaned in with his pole and deftly tipped the crucible. Out poured white hot metal and flooded down the channel built for it.

'First stoppers!' roared Arlott. Two men in leather jumped forward and stood by the first stone dams. The metal whirled its way into the gun moulds. As the white metal brimmed and overflowed, so they lifted the flagstones on the end of chains and the metal raced onward, crusting a little as it stopped at the next branching. 'Second stoppers!'

So two demi-cannon were born in smoke and flame and brimming metal and another set of flagstones went up amongst the bare scorched branches. Mould after mould filled from the pouring crucible, a vast river of earth's blood from a man-made volcano, until the last trickles sulked their way into the small murderer moulds lying ready for them at the bottom of the channel. The whole side of the hill was smoking and burning and smelling pungently of iron, the channels between clearing slowly as metal congealed. Amongst the pools of molten metal leaped Arlott, dainty as a deer among puddles that would fry his foot in its heavy boot if he slipped. He visited each sullenly smoking mould, tapping with his hammer, watching, tapping again. Once he shook his head as a big bubble came up from the hole, made a cross in the earth by a demi-cannon mould.

One of Arlott's assistants tilted the empty crucible upright again, pushed it back into the furnace on its cradle and shut the furnace door. Other men disconnected the wheel from the bellows and stood panting for breath as the bricks dulled to red.

Arlott came prancing back and looked surprised to see Becket still there.

'By God, Mr Arlott,' rumbled Becket, taking a gulp of aqua vitae. 'That was a sight to behold. I never knew cannon-founding was like the wrath of Jehovah.'

Arlott looked as if he had never thought of this. 'Not far off as dangerous, sir, and your beard is smouldering.'

Becket slapped out the burning and thought he should have got his beard trimmed. All the men tending the furnace and Arlott himself were clean-shaven and noticeably piebald with burn-scars.

'What else can you show me of your craft, Master Arlott, before you go to your well-earned rest.'

'Shan't rest tonight, sir. The last tapping is near enough ready for proving.'

The foundry-master was stripping off his leathers again, handing them to the lad who had moved Becket out of danger. Under the helmet, Arlott's face was wrinkled with sweat. He jerked his head at Becket and they began trudging down a little incline and up another hill.

Becket heard the screeling and screeching long before they came to it. There were vast high frames built of the tallest trees, well enough away from the furnace that no sparks would set light to them. Suspended mouth down from the top of the nearest frame was a demi-cannon, the long pole of the boring iron going deep into it. Below the boring iron, turning the blades so it spun, was a patient, blindfolded horse, pacing round and round in the shafts of his converted milling wheel, while a little tent above protected them from the filings and sand as the boring iron ground and groaned in its cavity, boring it out, smoothing it down, so the demi-cannon could eventually be fired.

Arlott stepped up to the horse, muttering to it, patted its neck as it stoically continued round, following the carrots it could smell but had never learned it would only catch at sunset. He climbed up on the wheel, pulled a corner of the tent aside and squinted up at the cavity, then jumped down.

'Not so bad,' he grunted. 'The new sand is answering.'

Becket had no more time to waste in sightseeing. 'Master Arlott,' he said, 'how many guns might you approve from each tapping after casting, boring, polishing and the rest?'

'Can't say, sir. About six or eight. It depends on the weather, the charcoal, the blooms.'

'How often do you make a full casting?'

'We cup about once every two weeks, working flat out to remake the moulds. Takes a week or so after to saw off the filling heads.'

'After which it takes another . . . ten days to bore out the guns?'

'Depends on the gun, sir. A little falconet might only take two days if it cast well.'

'So shall we say, roughly, you could expect to make ten to fifteen new guns every month, here?'

'With luck. If it didn't rain.'

'Fewer in winter, no doubt.'

'None at all, sir. We make the blooms in winter, stockpile the clay, design the models. Winter's no good for gunfounding. We're casting so early this year because of the demand.'

'You make for six months of the year, then?'

'Something like that, ay.'

They were walking away from the blasted part of the forest and in the distance Becket could hear the roaring of other furnaces, the pumping of other bellows, the screeching of other borers.

'And this is only one of many foundries in the Forest of Dean.'

'The best, sir,' said Arlott flintily. 'We work the best, make the best guns and the most.'

'So I was informed, Master Arlott, which was why I came here.'

Arlott grunted, slightly mollified. They paced on, at least beginning to find undergrowth, astonishingly even a few sick and scrawny bluebells.

'Allowing for accidents, shall we say as a modest guess that you can expect to make forty guns in a year, of various sizes.'

Arlott sucked his teeth, scratched his ear, consulted the sky. 'Ay, sir. Though Sir Francis Drake is forever at us to make culverins and no sakers or falcons, which is slower in the casting. But that'd be a good rate.'

'No other problems? No Dutchmen coming to take them in tribute?'

'Eh?'

Becket sighed. 'I came to ask who is stealing them, Mr Arlott?'

Obstinate blank ignorance suffused Mr Arlott's scarred, dried-out face.

'Shall we have a drink, Mr Arlott?'

'I'm a busy man. Got to inspect the polisher and then—'

'So am I, Mr Arlott, but it can all wait. Is that an alehouse over there? You must be thirsty after all your efforts, to be sure, sir.'

Raw suspicion replaced the ignorance and the man was obviously about to balk. Becket put his thumbs in his swordbelt and leaned slightly, staring him down. Arlott might jump around puddles of white hot metal like a doe in the springtime watermeadows, but it seemed Becket could still impress when he wanted.

They continued to the very small reed-thatched alehouse that served the thirsty men of the foundry.

Inside, an ugly old woman glared at Becket, served him sour beer with insolence and gave Arlott her best brew from a different barrel. Becket sighed and paid the outrageous reckoning, not having energy to spare to make anything of it.

'I have a mystery here, Mr Arlott, and I very much hope that you can cast some light on it.' Becket sat down foursquare on the bench, feeling it creak and give beneath him. He fumbled out a grubby notebook, opened it, pointed with a square finger, its nail bitten down to the quick. Arlott blinked wisely at the incomprehensible script.

'Forty guns a year from this foundry alone. From Currer's foundry, another thirty. Holzhammer, ten to thirty, depending if he's sober or not. And there are about forty foundries here in the Forest of Dean alone. By my reckoning I should be seeing eight hundred guns a year from the Forest of Dean. I only took up my position last summer, Mr Arlott, but in that time I have seen a grand total of two hundred guns, all types, delivered to Her Majesty's Armoury.'

'Don't rightly know what you're talking about.'

'My fault, I'm sure, Mr Arlott. I never pretended to any abilities as a clerk, but I have in my time quarter-mastered a troop of soldiers and I can add and subtract. Let's put it another way. Let's say I was a baker and from my oven I expected to get . . . oh . . . say eight hundred penny loaves . . . Let's say six hundred, to be fair, to allow for the ones that burn and the ones that are dropped and the ones that don't rise. Six hundred, to be fair. And in my shop I find I only have two hundred penny loaves. What would you say, Mr Arlott?'

'I'd say there was a mistake in your adding.'

Becket rubbed the singed patch on his chin, smiled sweetly.

'Could be, could well be. Show me where I'm wrong, make two hundred guns sum up to six hundred.'

Arlott coughed. 'Well, there's Bristol and the ships there. We send off about fifty a year to them. And Southampton and Plymouth.'

'I've included those.'

'I don't rightly know what you're asking, Mr Becket.'

'Every year, something around three to four hundred pieces of top-quality English ordnance goes missing. It disappears. Some of it leaves Bristol, supposedly being shipped to Plymouth but it never arrives. Some of it leaves Southampton, on its way, apparently to Bristol. Never gets there. Plymouth to Southampton. The same. All the paperwork is in order, you can't fault the clerks. The papers say, the guns went here, arrived here, were shipped there ... It's wonderful what they say. I've spent months tracking them down. And at the end of the trail, Mr Arlott, what do I find?'

Arlott drank his beer and kept his mouth shut.

Becket's fist came down on the table top. 'Nothing,' he said, very softly. 'No guns, not brass, not iron. Nothing.'

Arlott took another pull of beer.

'What do you think of all your hard work ending at the bottom of the sea or in Elfland? Because that must surely be what's going on. Surely to God no man would be stupid enough to sell to Spain guns that will be used against England?'

Arlott coughed, stared at the floor. 'Well,' he said, 'I don't rightly know. There's a special order. They're more decorated, very pretty, specially modelled dolphins and all, but we don't put our mark on them, only the date. Go off special to Plymouth, usually the Flemish ships take them. We get a big fancy piece of paper for them and that gets sent up to London with the rest of the guns.'

'What is written on the paper?'

'Don't rightly know, sir. I can reckon out my name and numbers of course, but I can't make out all that fancy clerk-writing. Or sometimes Portuguese carracks take them and the certificates say Bristol on them, I can make that out.'

Becket sighed and rubbed his face.

'Mind I never said any of this. You put me on a witness stand, Mr Becket, and I'll be struck dumb with terror.'

'Nothing could be further from my intention, Mr Arlott. Only you could, of course, be selling off the guns yourself for gold.'

Arlott finished his beer, took breath to speak, and stopped. He nodded. 'Fair enough. Come and look.'

In the corner of the vast store yard full of iron blooms, charcoal, pine trees, and clay, stood a neat wooden shed. At the back, under coils of rope and slabs of wax was a locked trunk and inside it lay the ornately and beautifully written bankers' drafts. Mostly they drew on funds in the Medici bank, some on the Fuggers. Some were signed by Don Juan de Acuna Vela, Captain-General of the Spanish Ordnance. All of them were made out to Elizabeth's faithful friend, the Lord Treasurer Burghley.

Becket squatted by the trunk and stared into space, gazing at last at the cold hard evidence of more extraordinary complacency than even he had expected. Then he caught sight of the date.

'Good God, he's *still* selling them?'

'Ay, sir. I spoke to Sir Robert Cecil, his son, who says his reverend father is certain sure we shall have peace. Reckons Parma's only trying to frighten the Queen into concessions for the peace commissioners at Dunkirk.'

Becket blinked slowly at Arlott and couldn't think what to say, so Arlott filled the silence.

'Sir Robert's a decent man, sir, for all his body's so twisted, treats you right if you follow. He said to me that if there's any guns I'm not perfectly sure of, any I've a bad feeling about on account of damp or bubbles or so on, I'm to put those in the special order.'

Becket nodded. 'What do you put in the books about these guns?'

'Some went to Bristol, some to Southampton . . .'

'All right.' Becket gathered up the bankers' drafts. 'I'll deliver these to my Lord Treasurer personally, I think.'

'I can't stop you, I suppose, sir, not with the Queen's Warrant.' Arlott's voice was distant, he was staring at a cat sleeping on a pile of wax blocks. He could stop Becket, of course he could, he had his men in earshot. 'Wouldn't be legal, would it?'

'No, Mr Arlott, it wouldn't. You can say you tried to stop me if you like.'

Becket folded the wad of papers and put them in the inside pocket of his doublet. 'When is the next special shipment?'

'We've a big special order for demi-cannon and culverins, should be ready by the end of the month, if the weather holds.'

'I think the weather might be bad, Mr Arlott. I think the shipment might be delayed.'

'Never can tell with weather, sir.'

'Quite. Shocking damp it's been, hasn't it?'

'Ay, sir.'

Sighing and shaking his head, Becket rode east from the mouth of hell where the great guns cooled slowly in their pits, waiting to have the filling heads sawn off and the bores smoothed and their sides polished and their touch holes drilled, ready to be shipped to Spain.

The nightmare woke him weeping from his sleep, the smell of burning, of blood and death, the terrible desolation of death. He had been at Middleton again, the village where he was born ... Something was terribly wrong there. He had had the dream so often now that he could remember many details, though his mind still shrank from recalling what was in the ruined parlour. He abandoned all hope of more sleep, tired though he was, got up, drank aqua vitae, dressed and clattered down the stairs to the common room where a lad was trotting around with wooden trenchers laden with hot new bread and cheese and big jacks of mild ale.

He rode on, stunned with weariness and depression until he came to the market town where he was to change horses and reined in suddenly, struck to the heart by its familiarity.

He asked the name of the place of the ostler who brought his remount and was quite dumb with shock to find he was, in very truth, only ten miles from where he was born, for the first time in years.

He had mounted, ridden down the street to the market cross where he stopped and tried to think, at war with himself. His horse quietly sidled towards a yew tree it thought might be tasty. That woke him from his reverie; he pulled the horse away from the poisonous leaves, tethered it by an alehouse, so he could go in and consider.

He had been beaten up, thrown out and disinherited by his father in 1572 or 1573, now he couldn't truthfully tell you which. A long time ago, fifteen, sixteen years. As the younger son he hadn't stood to inherit much anyway, some property from his mother's family, he thought. But it rankled that his father had denied him to be his son. The years had passed and he had sent no letter, nor received none, partly because of the sheer press of living and partly because of pride.

To visit Becket House would not take him much out of his way, nor delay him by much. He had the bankers' orders proving Burghley's treason crackling in his doublet front and perhaps he should not hurry to take them to London. It might be better to consider how to bring them to the Queen. Becket was not a courtier, had not even met Elizabeth Tudor, the woman whose service had brought him so close to death, had taken so much from him.

On the other hand . . . What did he want with old man Becket? What if his father refused to see him, turned him out again? What if . . . ?

As often happened, Becket's hands began to tingle and buzz and he rubbed them carefully as Dr Nunez advised, circling motions, not forgetting the knotted scar tissue around his wrists.

What to do? He sat there for an hour, nursing his quart of ale, until the alewife glowered at him every time she passed. At last he took out a new penny, held it up and flipped it. Let Lady Luck decide for him. Heads I go home, tails I carry on, he said solemnly to himself and watched himself from far away as he snapped the penny out of the air and slapped it on his wrist. Heads.

Like a sleepwalker he mounted and turned the nag's head south and west instead of eastwards, while twin voices argued for and against over and over in his head. That was about eleven o'clock. He rode slowly, slower and slower, as if wading through a swamp of reluctance. The horse felt his ill-humour and clopped sullenly along the lanes.

A little past one in the afternoon, he trotted down the muddy lane and into the village green where somebody had built a new shed next to the church and taken out the ancient saint-carved Papist lychgate to replace it with a respectable plain one. As if memory was an animal and could bite, he recalled his hysterical giggling when he and Anthony Fant had found the carving of a woman's quim in one corner of the gate. His big brother Philip had been so shocked when brought to see it, he had gone red as a raspberry.

He smiled at the memory, then frowned. To think of Anthony Fant was like prodding an old scar, it still hurt him that the man was now one of his bitterest enemies. And how often had they sworn to be blood brothers over the hilts of their boys' blunt practice swords? He looked around himself, blinking.

It seemed he was a ghost. Nobody knew him. Of course, they wondered what a gentleman in London clothes was doing in their village and while he watered the horse at the duckpond, he looked around himself, lonelier than he had been in his life. There were people he didn't know at all in a village he had skirmished through thousands of times, playing war with Fant and his brother and the Strangways brothers, battling their enemies, led by Henry Smith, the blacksmith's boy.

Some grubby children were hiding behind the oak to get a sight of him and he tipped his hat gravely to them. Well, in a minute he would remount and ride away and that would be the end of it . . .

'Good afternoon, sir. May I be of assistance?'

It was Philip Becket, his brother, heir to the lord of the manor, run for by one of the children and no doubt sent by his father, after a sprint to fetch his swordbelt and a stately walk down from the house to catch his breath. He must have been out inspecting drainage ditches by the mud on his lamentable old boots.

Becket turned, bowed, opened his mouth to speak and found his voice stopped in his throat. What in the name of God could he say?

'Sir?' said Philip, nervous as ever, not understanding his silence, of course, hand dropping awkwardly to the sword he had probably never used in anger, slightly short-sighted eyes crinkling in puzzlement. 'I think I should know you, sir, but I fear I—'

'Brother.' It came out hoarsely, unexpected.

We are often better known by our voices than our bodies. Philip's jaw dropped, he stared, blinked, stared again.

'Christ Almighty God, is it *David*?'

Becket nodded and then found himself suddenly wrapped in his brother's arms.

'David! Is it? Is it truly? By God, by God . . .' Philip pulled back from him, held him by the shoulders, stared hard at his eyes, up and down his body and the tears were brimming in his eyes, so that more answered in Becket's eyes and he had to cough. His brother embraced him again, swearing quite shockingly for him, banged his back over and over again.

It seemed that the village, which had looked empty, suddenly erupted with people. He was shaken and pummelled and his head uncovered and stared at by the blacksmith who had let them play with bent nails behind his forge and the carpenter and the orchardman and Goody Brownlow who said she supposed he must be David for the way he looked like his old dad in his youth, may he rest in peace . . .

And that was how he learned that the man who had broken his

nose was dead. It was too much. He didn't know what to do after that, having had some half-thought-out hope of a prodigal son's welcome, maybe not as extravagant as a fatted calf but perhaps a pig . . .

And they had all faded far away, the shouting friendly crowd, like the waves of the sea, far, far away, while he thought how he could have come back at any time. He could have hired a horse while he was swordmastering Sir Philip Sidney and comparatively respectable, or even the first time he came back from the Netherlands with plunder in his pocket, he could have come back at any time and been welcomed . . .

He was wiping his face and stammering and wondering where the rain was coming from when Philip suddenly took his arm and led him away from the shouting throng and through the lychgate into the churchyard. It wasn't until they were there that the rain began again, so he knew to mop his eyes and blow his nose.

The grave was old enough to have a headstone, though of course the marble was newly cut and still looked like the inside of a sugarloaf, shining with rain. Nearby the headstone of his mother's grave was more weathered.

'When did he die?' He heard his voice from a distance, as deep and rough as one of the bears on the South Bank.

'A little after the Christmas before last.' Philip had calmed down as well and was leaning against a yew tree with his thumbs in his belt, smiling foolishly at Becket. 'We sent to London for you but no one could tell us where you were.'

Becket ducked his head, shut his eyes. Under his dank, greasy cloak, his hands tried to turn themselves into fists, but still lacked their old strength. He spoke only when he was sure his voice could be steady.

'I was . . . um . . .' He had to lie. He could hardly explain to his brother that he had been in the Tower, slowly recovering from torture and half-mad, now could he? Philip was no longer the thin, nervous, elderly, young man he had once been. Now he was a thin, nervous, elderly, middle-aged man. Philip had never given their father five minutes of worry and their father had despised him roundly for it. Philip might well faint on the spot at the news that his disgraced and disinherited younger brother had ever been prisoner in the Tower, no matter how mistakenly. 'I was in

Flanders.' The lie came smoothly, since he had used it before. 'Recovering from wounds I got at . . . er . . . Zutphen.'

His brother flushed and nodded. 'I had heard tell that you were with Sir Philip Sidney himself.'

'Yes.' Becket sighed. 'I was his swordmaster. I was with him when he was wounded and I saw him just before his death.'

'A glorious death,' said Philip fervently, his pale eyes brightening, bony hand clutching the hilt of a gentleman's sword that was certainly too ornate and probably too heavy for him. Well, his father's sword would be, of course. It was more David Becket's weight. Before torture had ruined his grip, of course.

'Not really,' Becket said, not expecting to be heard. The balladmongers had done their work too well. 'His wound sickened and rotted because he would not have his leg cut off after an arquebus ball broke the bone.'

'I meant, the fight at Zutphen.'

Becket shook his head. Tell him that, owing to the Earl of Leicester being of the opinion that scouts were a waste of time and effort, the fight had been the nearest thing to a bloody defeat that could be painted up as a victory. Fight the combined force of balladmongers and pulpit? Hardly.

'Yes,' said Becket. 'I suppose it was.'

'And you were there?' Philip fairly glowed with pride, as the rain spattered on his thinning hair. 'I told Father you would do well in the end.'

What to say? He should never have come back. A stupid impulse. 'Thank you.'

'He forgave you before he died.'

Probably a lie, but a kindly one. Becket lifted his head and contemplated this, the rain dipping its cold beak amongst his curls, for he still held his hat to his chest in respect.

'Truly he did,' Philip repeated earnestly, leaning towards him. 'I think he repented of driving you out a few weeks after he did it, only he would never say so, of course.'

'Of course.' What had they quarrelled over, all those years ago? Oh yes. Becket's debts mostly. Gambling, swordschools and women had been surprisingly expensive. His twenty-year-old self had known his debts to be eminently reasonable and quite small, whereas his older wiser self was no longer so sure.

As the years had ground off his sharp edges, he had found himself siding with his father's opinion in the matter more and more. But at the time his father's accusations had hurt him, mainly for being true. He had become angry, sullen and insolent. His father had lost his temper and cuffed his ear like a boy. Undoubtedly he had sinned grievously in trying to punch his father. And even more undoubtedly, his father had been the better man then and certainly the better fighter.

Unconsciously, Becket put his hand to his slightly bent nose: was it before or after the old man kicked me in the cods that he broke my nose for me and threw me bodily out of the house? His memory of landing in the ditch, the world fading and then coming back in pain and blood down his face, bit him sharply with misery. He had never really believed that would be the last time he would see the old buzzard.

Becket looked down at the grave again and wished for a pipe.

'I promised him I would speak to you if I saw you,' said Philip. 'I'll tell you what he said and did, David. But shall we go in and get warm?'

'Ay, might as well,' said Becket, more willing than he sounded, shaking rain out of his hair and putting his hat back on, longing for a drink.

They squelched through the village – the churchyard was only at the other end. Twice Philip stopped: once to frown at some tattered thatch and once to gently urge out of their path a large sow who was obviously in pig, calling her by name, which was Buttercup. She belonged to Goodwife Brownlow, who had a bad hip, so surreptitiously, lest one of his tenants be offended by seeing the lord herding swine, Philip shooed Buttercup into her little sty and checked to see she had water, before knocking on the cottage's horn window and calling through that if the Goodwife let her pig roam free in the evening again, she must not be surprised if some ill-affected Papist had her bacon to his supper.

'Is that young David with you?' demanded Goody Brownlow, wrenching back the horn pane and peering out. 'I was going to say, he's looking very fine in his London suit and all. Brought any plunder back from Antwerp, eh? You still owe me for them chickens you stole.'

'It wasn't me, Goody,' Becket said, although it had been.

'Hah! Spent all your plunder on cards and loose women, no doubt. Such a wicked boy, you know, Mr Becket, sir, not a moment out of trouble since the day he was weaned . . .'

Philip smiled. 'Keep Buttercup in at night, Goody.'

They walked on. 'The pig seems to know you well enough.'

'She should,' said Philip ruefully. 'I put her to bed nearly every night.'

Becket hid a grin.

Becket House shone with expansive welcome, for Philip's wife had brought out the precious wax candles in honour of their guest and no doubt hidden away all the tallow dips and their holders. And she had gone to the length of killing a couple of chickens and a duck to honour the prodigal brother because the scent of the fowls roasting in front of the kitchen fire filled the house.

Becket made his bow to Eleanor Fant that was now Eleanor Becket. Astonishing to find that Philip had caught himself such a wife as none other than Anthony Fant's youngest sister, who had come to the Becket household from her brother with a dowry of three villages and two London properties and a jointure worth two hundred pounds. Or so Philip had boasted on the trudge back through the village.

Mistress Becket was a short, plump, busy person with a round face and a round belly on her where another niece or nephew for David lay hiding in ambush. There were two more of them upstairs with their nurse, no doubt having their hair combed and their faces scrubbed sore and clean collars put on by main force. Becket crushed the strange chill he felt at seeing her, as if she were a ghost he recognised, a shadow from his nightmare. He shook himself like a horse.

The children came trooping downstairs to do their courtesy to their uncle, a fair little girl named Elizabeth as most girls tended to be and a stout, serious, black-haired boy, just into breeches, who bent his knee and told Becket that his name was David as well.

Knowing his place, Becket tipped them each a shilling and promised sword lessons to the boy when he was old enough.

Two lads and a hot-looking village girl laid a table in the parlour and as they sat down, Becket found himself being cross-examined by Eleanor Becket as to whether he had married and if he meant to and when he might do it. He complimented her on her brood and she told him the first of her babies was born too soon and was buried in the grave of Becket's mother who would surely look after it until Judgement came.

'I'm sorry for that . . .' Becket said awkwardly as a break came in his sister-in-law's flow of words because she wanted to chew and swallow, and the duck was slightly tough.

'Oh stuff,' said Eleanor briskly. 'It was my own fault for I rode to hounds the day before the pains started. And God gave us Lizzy and then David and now whatever this one is.'

Once again Becket found his eyeballs prickling treacherously. No doubt it was something in the country air, though it was astonishing to him that they had named their eldest son after him and it touched him more than he would ever have thought possible.

'To be sure, I say it is the only thing I dislike about being with child, not being able to ride.'

'You should see her,' said Philip. 'Terrifies and completely outrides me, will take any fence and seems to think her neck is made of steel.'

'Phooey.' Eleanor grinned at her lord. 'You should try a sidesaddle some time, it is almost impossible to fall out of. Stuff, brother,' she added, when Becket tried to stumble out something about the honour of their naming their son after him, 'we were hoping he would find himself an uncle grown rich at the wars and snaffle a pretty legacy.' And she grinned at him and wrinkled her nose so cynically, Becket started envying his elder brother even more than he had before.

He said this and found that it pleased her so she laughed and told him it was lucky he had wanted to visit his reverend father's grave, for she had been in her wet larder, looking like a female scarecrow in her oldest and most unbecoming English gown when the boy came running up from the village to tell her who he was, and it was very uncivil of him not to send a man ahead to warn them of his arrival so she would not be in the middle of the very messiest and smelliest meat-pickle when he came. Since she was wearing a perfectly respectable cramoisie velvet gown and a french hood over her cap, with not the faintest taint of vinegar, he assumed there had been something of a flurry, which was quite flattering. Looking at her roundness and happiness, he found it marvellous, like a buttercup growing in a snowfield.

'David!'

'Eh?' Philip had asked him something and he hadn't heard. 'I cry you pardon, Philip, I was lost in admiration of your wife.' At least it was true, though perhaps overgallant.

Philip only smiled while Eleanor blushed satisfactorily. 'I am very sure there are thousands of women in London far prettier than me,' she said complacently.

'True,' said Becket, to be rewarded by a frown. 'But only from a distance. Once you get close enough to scrape off the paint . . .' He shook his head and sighed. 'Such a lot of disappointments.' Eleanor giggled like a girl.

Philip pushed away the last of his candied carrots and went to the sideboard for his locked tobacco box, bought in Bristol and proudly displayed along with some good plate. Becket filled his pipe gratefully and Eleanor bustled away to supervise the servingmen at clearing and the kitchen boys at washing and then to go and say goodnight to her favourite gelding in the stables.

Wreathed in clouds of very vile tobacco smoke, Philip asked his question again. 'What do you think to the Spanish, David? Having fought them?'

'The Spanish,' Becket said, not knowing where to begin.

'When I go to muster, when the Spanish come, what should I bring?'

Becket puffed on his pipe and coughed. There sat his brother, never fired a gun in anger, never so much as fought since he was a boy, and he was smiling in pleased anticipation of more excitement than a simple hunt for deer or hares or foxes. He was launching into a long account of who was coming and who would stay and what their weapons would be and the difficulty of getting calivers, not that most of the men round about would have the least idea how to use them or even which end to point with, but what of longbows – after all, David knew John Denton had always been a fine shot and so was Henry Smith and . . .

Becket listened and wondered what to say. He tried to imagine his brother and his tenants facing the tight-lipped discipline of a tercio, but he simply could not because it made his blood run cold.

'David?' Philip's voice was uncertain. 'What is it?'

Becket took a long shaky breath and prepared himself to lie heroically. 'The tercios of Spain are very great fighters,' he said, 'but they can be shot and killed like any men . . . Only it's better to do it from behind a ditch when they are not expecting you. And better still not to let them land.'

Philip laughed. 'What will you be doing if they land?'

*Sudden dream-memory of the Queen putting a gold chain round his neck.* 'Brother, I shall be a great Captain with my own company as I was in Flanders for a while, and I'll come and fortify Becket House and make it the biggest grave of Spaniards since the harbour at Cadiz.'

I'll be dead, he thought to himself, dead trying to defend London with the decayed and separated serpentine powder at the Tower and old guns too rotten to be fired. God knows, if I ever come sword to sword with a Spaniard, he'll cut me down like a butter man at a banquet.

Eleanor came bustling back, smelling slightly of horses, waving a leather bottle and spoon. She dosed them both firmly with a vile green liquid that was certain sure to protect them from scurvy and keep their teeth in their heads. Philip said this was woman's foolishness, since he had never suffered from scurvy. Eleanor retorted that that was clearly thanks to her physic and there was no sense taking chances. It sounded like an argument they had every year, as comfortable as an old shirt. Then she sat down by the fire with her embroidery hoop.

Philip immediately launched proudly into some nonsensical proposals for fortifying Becket House without damaging the orchard on which he had clearly spent a great deal of time and thought. Becket watched him and wished he knew as little about war as his brother.

'Oh yes, brother, a fine plan,' he agreed and Eleanor looked at him sternly while her needle flashed. He looked away, unwilling to be found out.

'And what was it brought you here at last?' she asked him. Relieved, he told her of his work for Mr Secretary Walsingham and the mystery of the missing ordnance. Something in her face changed, somehow, went from enlightenment to caution and then back to a proper womanly admiration. It was so swift, he decided he had imagined the change.

'. . . but surely we make the finest guns in all Europe,' Philip said. 'The Reverend Poyning said so in his last sermon.'

'No, the Germans make those,' said Becket pedantically, shocking his brother again. 'We make more of them. Not the finest in Europe, but the most. Many times more than France or Spain. So there should be no shortage of guns and yet . . .'

'Yet?'

'Yet where are they? The Queen's ships still want more, the merchantmen want more, there aren't enough to defend London, let alone powder and shot enough for them. Where have they all gone?'

67

'Do you know?'

'I suspect the Spaniards have a good number of our guns and the arms merchants at the Hague have the rest.'

'Surely not,' said Philip confidently. 'Who could possibly be stupid enough to sell weapons of war to the Spaniards?'

It was on the tip of Becket's tongue to say 'My Lord Treasurer Burghley', to watch him stare and protest and gasp, to pierce the quotidian armour of confidence in his betters that his brother wore. Instead, he made jokes, passed on court gossip, told carefully edited tales of his exploits in the Netherlands, some of which had happened to other men.

At last Eleanor took a candle and said she would see to it that David's bed had been properly warmed and left him alone with his brother.

'Father spoke of you before he died.' Philip sucked thoughtfully on the long pipestem and then blew smoke rings, a skill he was clearly very proud of.

Becket inhaled deep into his lungs and coughed. 'If he cursed me with his dying breath, I had rather not know,' he said, only half a grim joke.

Philip shook his head, smiling in puzzlement. 'Did you know him so little?' he asked. 'Who are his very spit and image? Father and you both have . . . had . . . terrible tempers, always at odds, but for God's sake, he always loved you best.'

Becket muttered something childish.

'How could he show it than by trying to keep you away from boozing kens and save you from poxing yourself? Besides, I'll not quarrel with you, brother. I'm not the same as you. I'm a man for business and our lands and tenants have prospered since I have had the running of them. I like things to be tidy and in their right places, you know. And I have been trying to find you ever since he died. I even sent to the Privy Council to see if they had word of you, for Father left you property in his will and we must transfer the deeds.'

'*Father* left me property?' If Philip had revealed that his true sire was Edward VI, Becket could not have been more staggered.

'Of course he did. If he had not, I would have told him to do it. But there was no need.'

'Well . . . but what did he leave me?'

'Some houses that once belonged to an old monastery in London – snapped them up in forty-seven I think, what was the place?

Blackfriars? No, Whitefriars. Facing a courtyard. Hanging Sword Court, I think, not far off Salisbury Place.'

Becket couldn't help it, he had to laugh at the ludicrous coincidence.

Philip almost feared for his brother's sanity to see him put his head in his hands and laugh and laugh. He had thought to please David with his revelation and he thought he had, but there was something about David that chilled him. Less than half of what his brother had said at the dinner table had been the truth, he thought, and what in the name of Christ had caused the wicked scarring peeping out under his shirt cuffs on both his wrists? Had he been a galley-slave at some time? Philip longed to ask, but dared not.

Later, when they had done the business and transferred the deeds, after Becket had gulped down the last of her very own best double-distilled aqua vitae from their own cider, and embraced his brother goodnight, Eleanor led him personally to the guest room above the hall, newly built since he was gone.

'Will you stay a few days with us, brother?' she asked.

Becket's fingers seemed oddly clumsy as he began to undo the buttons of his doublet. Eleanor ignored the hint.

'Will I have Philip's man come to help you undress?'

'No, thank you.' Becket gave up on the buttons for the moment and went in search of booze, which he found in the jack of spiced ale by the side of the big guest bed. 'I cry you pardon, sister, but I cannot stay. I fear I must hurry back to London. I must . . .' He stopped, looked gloomy. 'I must report my findings to Mr Secretary Walsingham.'

'Mm.' Eleanor made her decision. There was no help for it, if he wouldn't stay, she'd do it now. Though she would instinctively have preferred to let him get a night's sleep before presenting him with a mystery. He looked exhausted and careworn, poor man, not at all the dashing swordsman Philip had described to her.

She came in, tapped her candle down on the lid of the chest, poked at the fire and sat herself down beside it. Becket squinted at her unhappily, recognising permanency when he saw it.

'Eleanor?' he asked warily. 'How is your brother Anthony?'

She smiled at him, liking his taking of the bull by the horns. So like the old Mr Becket. Philip, bless him, would have pottered around the subject for another hour. 'Well enough. He finally married again last year, you know.' Becket nodded. 'A rich widower with five children, I'm astonished he escaped this long,' she added. 'Though God knows, he's grouchy enough. Wouldn't even buy a lovely colt off me last year for his eldest boy. His new wife's a friend of mine and—'

'What does he say about me, which you have carefully not told Philip and which you want me to tell you the truth of?' Becket was clearly doing his best not to sound belligerent, which only made him more like his father.

She smiled again. 'Why, that you have been at your old coat-changing practices. That you were in the Tower on a charge of treason the Christmas before last but that somehow you got away and convinced Walsingham you are a loyal Englishman when Anthony knows you for a Spaniard and a Papist in your black and ugly heart. That's what he said in his letter.'

Becket sighed. 'I'm sorry for your brother's other enemies.'

'It's as if all the charity and kindness in his body was left behind in Haarlem with his arm,' said Eleanor thoughtfully. 'I'm to tell him at once if you turn up, by the way. Is any of it true?'

'It's true I was in the Tower.' Becket spoke slowly and quite without emotion, which told Eleanor how hard this was for him. 'It was a misunderstanding. I was working for Sidney in a matter of intelligence and got scooped up by Walsingham's pursuivants in a raid on a Mass, knocked on the head. They mistook me for a priest and since the blow had scrambled my brains somewhat, it took a while to . . . to convince them otherwise. Why did you not pass on Fant's letter to Philip?'

Eleanor smiled fondly. 'It would distress him terribly. He worried over you when you were children, I know, and still does it. And he hates to think of hatred or evil.'

'Then God help him if the Spaniards land.'

'Amen,' said Eleanor, deciding to take the bull – or perhaps the bear – by the horns herself. 'Do you think as little of Philip's careful plans for defence as I do?'

The expression on David's face was so desperate as to be frightening by itself. He said nothing.

'My own opinion is,' she said to help him, 'that if we try to make a defence of it with Becket House quite without walls and the village as it is, then the house will be burnt and all of us infallibly shall be killed. But of course, I am only a weak foolish woman and—'

'Entirely correct.' Becket's voice was harsh, but amused. 'It seems to me, sister, if I may speak plain, that England is like a virgin with a bosom full of gold blinking at an alley lined with footpads.'

'So what should we do, brother? If they land? What do they do to fight the Spaniards in the Low Countries? Not romantic nonsense, but the truth?'

He drank a cup of ale and she waited for his answer.

'It depends where they land,' he said at last. 'If they land in the West Country or the Isle of Wight, then the minute you get a true word of it, gather the children, everyone in the village that cannot fight, take food, blankets and horses and all your cattle and herds and go north. Take the lead off the church roof, burn your house and your fields and orchards and granaries behind you and see to it that everyone does likewise. Get into the Welsh mountains and stay there until all the Spaniards are dead or King Philip is proclaimed the rightful sovereign from the pulpit.'

She swallowed. 'Burn the house?'

He hadn't wanted to frighten her, that was clear, he hadn't wanted to burst the bubble of faith and safety he thought she lived in, but now he had begun with the truth he could not stop. But she had nursed her brother Anthony through two fevers when he came back from the Low Countries and had learned more of war from him in his delirium than he had thought she did.

'Burn everything you cannot carry and that cannot run. Give the bastards nothing to feed themselves with and get out of their path. Armies move slowly, you know. At the best, they cover ten miles in a day, with the scouts ranging out ten miles ahead of that. If you move promptly when you first have proper word from someone you trust, then you need never clap eyes on a tercio. Which would be best, believe me, sister.'

*Sudden gut-freezing picture of her, skirts foul with blood, aiming a caliver at him . . .*

'And there was I thinking to form mine own Amazon cavalry regiment and charge Parma down with sword and pistol.'

'If anything could frighten the man, I believe that would.' Becket managed some gallantry. 'If they land at the Thames mouth – do as I told you, but head west. If I am able at all, I shall send you word myself, but do not wait for it, go when you have the news.'

'Are Anthony's tales of what the Spaniards do in the Low Countries true?'

'Yes,' said Becket, without needing to know what the tales were. 'Both sides do evil. I myself have played games when I bet how

71

many burning arrows it would take to fire a butter-eater's barn, with the man hanging upside-down from a tree beside me, stripped and crying it was his livelihood. I thought it was funny at the time. It is in the nature of war that men do evil in it. And the answer is either to kill them first or not to be there when they do it.'

He poured himself more ale and drank and she thought that he had sad grey eyes and that he had not told her the half of the evil he had seen or done.

She nodded. 'David,' she said hesitantly, 'I must tell you . . . this summer, a strange man came visiting the house, a thin man in a soldier's buff coat like yours. He said he was a Mr Piers Lammett, the son of an old friend of your father's, who was a Papist and removed to the Continent with your father's help when the Queen came to the throne. He was much afraid of pursuivants and Philip was not at all happy to be giving him house-room only I made him. He stayed the night and then was away again in the morning before sun-up. When Philip would not speak to him, he talked to me instead. He had come for to find you, crossed the sea secretly and ridden at risk of his life from Southampton to the place his father had told him was your home. He said he had met you in Arnheim under the name of Smith where he gave you word of a libel against the Queen called the Book of the Unicorn.'

Now that had an effect. Becket was white as a sheet, gripping his hands together so she would not see how they shook.

'He said he had intelligence that he wanted to give you, but when he found we knew not where you were, he left a packet here with me privily, and went back to his ship. As far as I know he got away again.'

She took a packet out of the pocket of her petticoat and gave it to him.

'Ah,' Becket was blinking at the thing in his hand as if it contained a viper.

She was very much hoping he would open it while she was there so she could find out what was in it and scratch the itch of curiosity which had been worse than a bed-bug's bite since the summer. Alas, he put it on the table for later.

She sighed. 'Are you one of Walsingham's pursuivants?' she asked.

'At least you don't ask me if I am a traitor, as Fant paints me.'

She sniffed. 'Lord above, what a foolish thing to ask. Whatever you truly are, you will surely answer no. Are you a pursuivant?'

David bowed with mock ceremony. 'In a manner of speaking, very reluctantly, yes.'

'Why? Philip said you were a swordmaster, a soldier of fortune.'

'No longer, I think. I'm getting old for that game.'

Not true, despite the silver in his hair. He was only in his thirties. There was something else.

'No doubt I'll resign from Walsingham's service once the Spaniard is whipped back to his kennel. Now I have the rents on the Whitefriars properties, I shall be a rich man. Whatever shall I do with myself?'

'Marry at last?' She grinned naughtily at him. 'Instead of burning.'

'Have mercy, sister.' Becket said, 'Don't match-make for me yet.'

'Me? Match-make? Never!'

He half-smiled at her, blinking at the mysterious packet again. It was time to let him look at it. She stood, he stood, staring at her as if his heart was too heavy to speak. He bowed, she curtsied, left pen and ink upon the chest next to the candle and rustled from the room.

Becket was better trained in dealing with mysterious letters than he had been. After several more cups of ale to fortify himself, he smelled it, examined the waxed silk it was sewn into, looked closely at the borders of the wax seal, which had an impression on it he vaguely recalled, checked the seams for evenness of stitching. Then he put on his riding gloves and used the tip of his poniard to slit it open.

A single blank sheet of paper fell out, accompanied by the faint scent of Seville oranges. His mouth was dry. His hands shook when he took the paper and held it near the heat of the candle flame, watched as the writing came clear and brown. He was poised to note it down in case it was enciphered, but it was in clear and he copied the letters.

The handwriting was firm, a little flowery, and to the point.

Greetings

Parma has a three-part plan against England. First, there is the Armada. Second, his army in Flanders, which is to be carried over when the Armada have taken control of the Narrow Seas. So much is known to all. But the third part makes or mars all. It is the lynchpin of the whole enterprise. I

73

could not find it out, for a fear that Parma suspects me. I only
know that they name it their Miracle of Beauty.

Your old friend from Arnheim.

Smith

Not his friend. By no means his friend. He vaguely remembered
Henry Lammett, his Protestant father's Catholic friend, from the
time when he was a little boy, still in skirts, still under the care of
his nurse. Henry Lammett had protected them in the frightening
days of Bloody Queen Mary and then gone overseas with his
father's quiet help in 1560. There had been a son, a boy somewhat
older than him. It made sense, although he hadn't recognised the
man at all when he met him at Arnheim in 1586.

Becket sighed and sat back, weariness and despair washing over
him like a flood tide.

No more. He could do no more in the Queen's service. He was
utterly exhausted, as much by warfare within as by the world
without. He had no idea how he would bring to the Queen those
bankers' drafts that proved Burghley's stupid treason. What would
Walsingham do with the information? Would he pass it on to Her
Majesty? Becket suspected not. Walsingham believed as an article
of faith that the less women were told, the less trouble they caused.
The fact that this had been proven wrong, certainly with regard to
the Queen, over and over, troubled the man not at all. And further,
he would not wish to waste such a prime weapon of blackmail
against his old enemy in the Council. On no account could Becket
go to Walsingham.

And now this. He had no stomach for any of it, none at all. He
could not so much as glimpse a man dressed plainly in black and
white without flinching; every pleasant memory of Christmas was
scarred across, slashed to ribbons by unbidden recall of his sojourn
in the Tower.

The Christmas of 1587 he had spent in bed, struck down by a
melancholy so deep that Lady Walsingham had called Dr Nunez in
to physic him and a surgeon to bleed him. If only he could be bled
dry of memory. Sometimes memory, which had been so frail and
elusive in the Tower, became like Hercules and rose up and gripped
his throat and hands so he stared and could not breathe and folk
would look at him strangely. He was constantly terrified of the
falling sickness, and yet he also longed for it to take him while he
was on horseback so he could fall, crack his head open and make a
guiltless end of it all. He was not so old, in what some called the

74

prime of life, but he felt as worn as an old man. It was taking him all his time to bring himself to rise from his bed in the mornings and saddle his horse and ride wherever he happened to be sent by peremptory notes from Walsingham or Phelippes, his clerk, or Phelippes' son. Often the only thing that got him through the day was the promise of booze and oblivion at the end of it.

He scrubbed his tired eyes with the palm of his hand, felt for his flask and drank a couple of gulps. Not much effect, so he finished it. As he slowly, painfully, unbuttoned to go to bed, he thought that perhaps he could give Dr Nunez in London this unwanted information from Piers Lammett, his unwanted contact at Parma's court. Nunez could decide what to do about it, refer it to Simon Ames – or Anriques as he now was – who should be back from his slaving voyage. Ames would know what to do with such a dangerous sliver of information and how important it might be. Nunez understood these things as well, was experienced and wise in the ways of espionage, as was his nephew Simon Ames/Anriques. Not him. The Queen had had the best of him. He was a broken down ex-swordmaster with weak hands, no more. Christ have mercy. No more.

# Merula

*South America, Autumn 1587 (Portugal, Spring 1588)*

Now I will dance across the days as a storyteller must do. We sailed over sea that changed from grey to green to blue, day after day, while they repaired the damage from the storm. My mistress spoke to me in the red-purple words of the Portuguese, in the blue-green words of the English, speaking to me as if I were a child so I could learn it easily. She was called Rebecca Anriques, she was wife to my master and she spoke sadly of their children, whom she had left in the far north with their nurse and her father's family. She stood between me and death many times, for she argued with the priest who was my enemy – no doubt because I had called the god and he had not been able to – and she spoke vehemently to her husband when Anriques said that for the sake of peace with the priest and the crew, he would sell me ashore in New Spain.

We came to a harbour in a place that was hot and steamy, full of trees, with a raw little fort and slave pens newly built. Everyone spoke the crimson-indigo tongue. There the poor slaves were unlocked from the hold and marched down the gangplank, staggering, scrawny, even the noble young men gone down to skin and bone and greyness. My master watched them and frowned. He said to the ship's captain, 'Why are so few left?' And the captain grunted and told him that on every voyage they lost at least a third of the blacks, sometimes half and this was not so very bad.

They call us blacks, Negroes, as if we were nothing but our skin.

Mr Anriques nodded, still frowning, said nothing more.

A little later, he had Michael put the iron jewellery on my arms and legs again. Michael scowled and did it as slowly as possible. Mr Anriques was hidden inside a cold, haughty disdain. Michael gave my hand a squeeze, as if he was saying he was sorry.

Then Mr Anriques bade me follow him down the rope ladder into the ship's boat, and we were rowed in silence to the quayside. It was true that his wife was recovered of her flux and now I only helped her to put on her tight breast-cage in the morning, which the savage hairy ghosts have their women wear to imprison them and make them short of breath. She was asleep. I think he had given her poppy juice so she could not argue with him.

There was heaviness deep in my bowels. I must stay with them, I must be with the hairy ghosts, not doing whatever their captives do in New Spain. This was the wrong path for me and for Anriques and for my son – he was not in New Spain, I was sure of it. I had felt his spirit when I went god-hunting on the masthead and it was in a different direction, northerly, for all there are no such things as directions in the dreamtime.

Help me, Lady, help me, I muttered and hummed a song for guidance. There are places where the world splits and this was one of them: Lady, Lady of the shining face, of the shining hooves, black and white zebra woman, spotted golden leopard lady, help me find my right path . . .

Anriques walked ahead, towing me on a chain to my wrists. He walked quietly, no swagger. If you did not know him, you might not see him. His clothes were too rich and heavy for the heat; he sweated profusely into his shirt, which already smelled bad. I knew it did, for I had been washing the Anriques shirts and salt water rots the cloth.

In the sunlight he spoke to a few merchants, asking questions. He spoke Portuguese quickly and easily, but I understood more than he thought. He was asking where I would get a good price. Yes, he was going to sell me. Some men laughed and directed him to a bawdy-house. Now this I could not allow.

'Mr Ames,' I said, using his rightful name, which he hardly ever did, 'do not sell me there.'

He squinted at me, not seeing. 'The sailors are frightened of you, the priest says you are a witch. I'm faced with mutiny if I go to Lisbon with you. Why did you call me Ames?'

'It is the name your Witch-Queen knows you by.'

A shudder passed over his face, he was afraid of me. Now he too believed I was a witch, although of course I could have learnt his former name from his wife while she was feverish. But once you get the name of a witch, everything you do is more evidence for it, especially to superstitious northern savages.

'What will my mistress your wife say to you when you come back without me?' I asked him and he frowned.

'She is my woman, she must do as I tell her.' Like many men of my own country, he believed that this is what she usually did. 'And she should not have told you my right name. It's dangerous.'

He was angry as well. Queen Moon, Lady Leopard, come to me, help me, show me my right path.

She came to me, Lady Leopard, sharp teeth, whiskers, soft, soft fur. Her fur is delicious to stroke; her mouth bites and tears. *Do not think you understand a god.*

Did she want me to strike Anriques, beat him down with my iron jewellery? No, it seemed not. She sat, waiting beside me, whiskers bright, eyes wide, ears perked, tail swishing. Oh she was in a good humour, which meant there might be blood. And she was strong here: they worshipped her here under another name, in another tongue, but in a very similar shape. I felt my heart moving, knew my stomach was folding away, all my arms and legs were full of golden fireflies.

Anriques led me down a narrow, bright alley, where the sunlight fell and the awnings held it back, where the shadows were black dark, white bright, like a zebra's hide. At its end was a place full of shadows, where women waited to serve men in the game of the two-backed beast. And halfway down the alley waited two hungry men who thought Anriques might be worth a scuffle for his purse.

Only a fool steps from bright light into dark shadow and keeps walking. If Anriques had had any sense, he would have stopped for a moment to let his eyes change. But he did not because he was fretful and impatient, going against his inner wisdom in favour of what seemed to be the safe thing to do. This is one of the things the gods do to entertain themselves: they show us a safe-looking path and one that looks frightening. When we choose the safe one, they step back to reveal the crocodiles and lions hidden beside it and watch us bleed.

So my master walked straight into the ambush. One man threw a cloak over his head, caught him round the neck, the other robber patted him down for hidden purses after cutting the small leather bag on his belt.

No wonder Lady Leopard was happy: I smiled at her, she leaped into me. I crossed my wrists, stepped behind the man with the purse-cutting knife and dropped the looped chain over his head, then pulled sharply and his neck broke. I put my wrists together and brought the chain down on the other one's head and he dropped Anriques in a slippery pile of dung, turned with a blade in his fist. My feet were chained, so I jumped up and over Anriques and kicked both legs sideways as in a dance and so caught the man in the ribs. He tumbled over, I crashed down on top of him, he scrambled away from me while I was still stunned and tangled, dropped his cloak and ran.

I could have run, also. I could have skipped into the shadows while Anriques fought with the cloak that was suffocating him. I wanted to at first, I, the person I once was before I became upside-down, yes, I did want to run. But Lady Leopard still rode me and she said, *Stay with him.*

So I did. I untangled Anriques from the cloak, helped him up from the mud, found his hat for him.

I smiled, laughed, jingled the chains. 'You not sell me, Simon Ames, Mr Anriques. You not break my path. I come find my son, take him home or sing his spirit quiet. Now you . . . You too break . . . here!'

The knife of the man I killed lay in the dust. I caught it, saw Anriques' indrawn gasp of alarm, before I slammed it into the dirt.

'Choose. Kill me or keep me with you.' His nostrils flared, his lips were pinched. 'One day, you is glad.'

He did not want to do as I said, a woman as well as a slave, but he was also a just man for all he dealt in human flesh. And I had not run and I had helped him when he was attacked.

Finally he nodded, picked the knife up out of the dirt and put it in his belt, led the way back to the quayside. Out of my heart leaped my Lady Leopard, swishing her tail, a robber's soul in her teeth.

We sailed from New Spain two months later, after the great hairy ghost festival of the birth of the Suffering Jesus. This is a very good festival, full of good food and singing and sweet-smelling incense, the telling of the god-tale with fine mysterious ceremonies in the candled dark, though no sacrifices. It is touching that the wild northerners worship a baby-god, surely the least mad of the hairy ghost superstitions.

When we set sail, it is dangerous, for the ocean was still swarming with storms. I spoke to them kindly and they left us alone. Mr Anriques was in a hurry to complete his business. As we sailed north and east, Rebecca my mistress began praying to her own god. A strange god for a woman, behind letters like the Arab but also with much of the English Thundering Jehovah in him. She did not want to go to Portugal, to Lisbon, I knew that, but her husband was obstinate. There was something vital he must do there and he would do it, no matter what she said.

Herein the gods were restless again, each contending with each.

Rebecca had ghost-skin but she had dark straight hair and very dark eyes. She wore many clothes, which she was teaching me to put on for her, so many, such a complication of them, nobody could run or bend or work in them. She only wore what she called English gowns at sea, but now she must find and wear her farthingale for Spain – this meant rousting out the supplies in the hold to find the canvas bag with a great wheel of bone and cane-threaded canvas to make it like a bell. Quite wonderful.

Over the ribs and pillars of her undergarments, she put crimson velvet and black satin, most costly and beautiful to look at. Her husband likewise clothed himself in velvet and satin. As the last touch, as we came with the tide into the vast outer harbour of Lisbon, she took out of her casket a small plain gold cross for him and a jewelled one for her, glinting even in the small light of the cabin. Anriques stopped her when she would have passed the chain over his head.

'No.'

'Why not?' she asked.

He did not answer. She put her own cross on the table next to his.

'You wear yours, Rebecca.'

'My husband, either we both wear a cross or neither of us.'

'It doesn't matter for you, it does for me.'

'As my husband does, so shall I,' said Rebecca with the defiant submission I have occasionally seen in Kings' wives. Anriques sighed and put the cross over his head.

'Take Merula with you.'

'What? Why?'

She smiled. 'You have always needed a bodyguard, and she will make a good attendant for you.'

He sighed. 'Well, she can't go dressed like that.'

They could not find women's clothes for me. Certainly Rebecca's could no more fit me than a child's. And so they found a suit of men's clothes, of doublet and hose and two shirts, which had belonged to the man whose jaw my Lady Leopard broke and who died a little after, months ago now. He was my height and my breadth, but they were terribly uncomfortable, with the cloth between my legs chafing my woman's place and the shoulders too wide and the chest too narrow. Rebecca did some work with needle and thread and a pair of shears, and in the end they pronounced me decent, or nearly, seeing as it was a great sin for a woman to wear men's clothes. I agreed with them – why should I make myself ugly like a man, when I am made in the holy shape of the Queen Moon? But then, what else could I do, for the hairy ghosts are terrified of skin and so mine must be covered up like theirs.

Ames spoke to me slowly and clearly, as if I was a fool, first in Portuguese and then in English, which I found quite comfortable to my tongue by then. He was explaining the situation.

While his cargo of sugar was being unloaded, he must go into the town of Lisbon and meet diverse men for reasons of business. My work was to stand by him, do his bidding and if any attacked him, to do as I did in New Spain. I must be quiet as well because some of what he did must be secret.

Here I should tell you that in this land of the Kingly clerk Philip II of Spain and Portugal, the Suffering Jesus god is very strong and his priests are as powerful as princes. He has certain priests called the Inquisitors of the Holy Office who search out any that do not believe in and serve the Suffering Jesus. These are arrested, tortured, then burnt to death. Yes, this is true. It is not even for a burnt sacrifice, which would make some sense, for they do not believe that the Suffering Jesus eats the souls of the burned ones, or any souls at all. Never mind what other gods the victims may serve; all must serve the Suffering Jesus or die, even the Arabs or the English who serve Thundering Jehovah or those like Anriques and his wife who worship the secret-named god. To the Kingly clerk, there can be no one in all the land who worships any other god, or . . . These priests say the Suffering Jesus will be angry and disaster will befall all of them.

In their ignorance, these ghosts have made of their kindly god a most terrible monster.

'Must I worship him?' I asked Rebecca, when she explained all this to me while Anriques had gone on deck to shout at the dawdling men in their cranes and the hold-master. I wondered what the Queen Moon would make of that. No doubt she would find it funny. 'What does this god like for his gifts? Are there songs I should learn?'

Rebecca coughed, shook her head. 'I'm afraid you are not allowed simply to add him to all the other gods. You must give up your other gods and serve only him.'

'But why? Surely my other gods will be angry?'

She shook her head again. 'In fact, I don't think it matters for you, Merula. You are black and they know blacks are heathens. So long as you are respectful, I think they will not care enough about you to worry about your soul. Many of them say you have no soul at all, being black.'

Well, how convenient. I grinned at her. 'We say the same of you,' I told her, but I am glad to say I spoke in my own tongue.

'But what does the Suffering Jesus think of all this burning?' I asked. 'Does he approve what his priests do?'

'It seems so,' said Rebecca thinly.

'But has anyone asked? Has anyone gone to the dreamtime to talk to him?'

Rebecca blinked at me. 'What? Of course not. You can't talk to the Almighty, not that way, and certainly not to a man who was no doubt a great Prophet but died fifteen hundred years ago.'

Ah. Again, how convenient. So it was I found the root of this constant tribal fighting between the savages of the north: none of them have rightly trained, upside-down people who can go spirit walking. They cannot send someone to visit the dreamtime and find out what their gods really want. We fight each other for sensible, civilised things like gold and land and captives and food and watercourses; they fight for these things but also for their gods, which become ever stronger and greedier as a result of all the blood poured out for them.

'You have a different god from the Suffering Jesus,' I told her.

'No.' She paused, thought and said, 'Well, yes. But they do not understand it. Say nothing, don't discuss anything to do with God while we are here.'

I bowed to her. Wearing men's clothes was making me feel very much like a man, especially as I was so much taller than most of them. I thought of the warriors in their leopard skins who guarded my King and went out before him in war and it made me smile. Here was a way I could be.

When I joined Anriques on deck, he mentioned nothing of his problem with the gods, for he saw no reason to. Why should he explain things to me? I was his slave. All he did say, out of the side of his mouth, was that if ever he swore by the name of Jesus Christ, I must escape immediately, not even try to fight for him, but go back to the ship immediately and guard Rebecca.

Now this I found funny and I laughed. Anriques did not like it, he felt I was disrespectful to him. I could smell the fear on him.

So I went to one knee, touched his foot as a warrior would show respect. 'If the priests are so dangerous, why not stay here on the ship, my lord?'

'I must do my business.'

'Send somebody. You are king of this ship, you could send your clerk. Or the priest.'

'Nobody else can do what I must.' Anriques straightened, pulled back his shoulders, put on a sword, then changed his mind and took it off again. He wrapped around a most marvellous dark green brocade gown, made of wormsilk that the Arabs love also and get from the east. He put on a velvet cap. Now Spain is not as hot as my own country, but still hot enough. He began to sweat immediately, stinking of fear, and I thought gloomily of washing his shirt.

We climbed down the ladder to the quay, and he set off, pale as milk, glistening with fright, firm of step. Behind him I walked, softly humming a song of warriors setting out to raid, in his honour.

All morning we walked in the bright sun from small white house to large white house. The buildings of the northern hairy ghosts are wonderful works, smooth stone raised up so high, looming out of the huts and pigpens and little courtyards with lemon trees and marble carved like lace.

Once we went into a temple where the idol of the Suffering Jesus hung at one end, bleeding silently into the pleasant cool. Anriques took his hat off as he went in, bobbed his knees to the altar where a lamp was burning. I copied him, hoping the god was in a good mood today. I pushed away my dreamsight as far as I could, lest he overwhelm me. Anriques sat on one of the side benches by the wall and waited. Another man came, in a black gown, trimming candles. Anriques followed him and I paced behind Anriques to a small inner room behind the altar, decked with many beautiful silver and gold cups and fine linen and priest-robes hanging, covered in the beautiful embroidery of the north, to show sacrifices and animals and magic signs. They have a wonderful craft to make pictures of things as if they truly were there, and not made of paint and shadow. Being simpler minded than real people, the hairy ghosts do not understand that you can show a thing by its meaning, they think in their ignorance that it must look like what it is.

I stood by the door of the room, while Anriques and the man in black spoke in a guttural language I had never heard before. Neither looked at me. Sniffing, I could smell incense, wine, a little oil. A strange temple, although so beautiful. There was no old blood.

Certainly, blood was painted everywhere, as spattered as a battle-field, but there was no actual blood, neither human nor animal anywhere. Not even on the altar where the small golden cupboard stood with its light next to it.

To one side of the altar was one of their northern pictures, very fine, as if you were looking through a window, of the Queen Moon, shown in their primitive way, with ghost-skin: pale and young, she stood as she always does, on the full moon, her servant the serpent of wisdom wrapped about her feet, with stars in her hair and the crescent moon crowning her. A marvellous picture. Lady Leopard paced up and down in front of the picture, lashing her tail, agreeing it was good.

Out came Anriques, looking frustrated. He bobbed his knees and so did I, then he walked out of the temple and across the square paved space to sit under an awning at a wineshop, sipping wine. I stood by him, as the warriors of the King do, my arms gravely folded. In a little while, a man in red and yellow wool came past, and Anriques followed him to another wineshop.

I was unhappy. There was something I was not seeing and Lady Leopard was impatient with me for not noticing. She paced by my side, yawning sometimes, lashing her tail back and forth, patting her paw on flickers of light on the cobbles. I turned about, turned about, snuffed the air.

'Sir,' I said to him as he sat drinking again and I stood by, 'something is not right.'

'What?'

I shook my head.

'Don't be afraid, Merula,' he said patronisingly, 'I have nearly finished my business. You will like the next meeting.'

On we went to a man's house where his little girls played in a swing hanging on an ancient olive tree. They wore little gowns of rose silk and were in wonder over my skin, while Anriques talked with their father. I heard him asking about galleases. What had the man heard of these four, strange, new, hybrid galley-galleons being built for Admiral Santa Cruz in Naples? Surely there was something important about them, they must have some special purpose when the Invincible Armada sailed to take England? No, said the man, he only knew they were designed to carry heavy guns.

I sat down in the dust between the two little girls and they asked their hundreds of questions. They had seen Africans before in the market – was it true we came from the place where lions lived? Yes,

I said, I myself have sung the lion-friend song to stop them from hunting me on the plains. Did our mothers dip us in paint when we were born? No, I said, this is how we grow. Did the colour come off? No, I said, holding up my arm, see – rub it or wash it, there it stays. 'What happened to your skin?' I asked the little girl, laughing. 'Poor child, why are you so pale and pink?'

'How did it happen that we are so different?' asked the littler one.

'Perhaps God made all people like me at first,' I said to her, 'but when your tribe went into the far northern lands, the cold froze your skins to ice.'

The older girl shook her head bossily. She told a fine god-tale of the first people, whom the hairy ghosts call Adam and Eve, and how they had two sons first, and one called Cain, killed the other called Abel. And God banished Cain and marked him and all his children for the crime with a black skin.

I laughed to hear it. Only hairy ghosts could believe such foolishness: are they not the only ones who look as they do? Well, then. Who has been marked?

Anriques left that place looking worried. We went to the shops in the richest marketplace, full of people talking and laughing and swatting away the beggars. He bought a book in one place and left it in another.

At last he relaxed. As he sat at yet another wineshop, he bought me a lemon sherbert when he had one himself, as I was thirsty by then. It was full of bright sourness of lemons and sugar and water, very delicious.

'Nearly finished, Merula,' he said. 'All I must do now is visit the harbour master to complete the sailing paperwork and then we can weigh anchor and go with the next tide.'

His face was still tense, the moisture beading his forehead, but he seemed less afraid. Still frustrated, he had not found what he came for, but he could see the path back. I thought he was wrong and my feet stamped themselves up and down in a small war dance, Lady Leopard flowing round me, her whiskers twitching with excitement. I looked at the marketplace, at the beggars and knew what I had not liked.

'Sir,' I said to him, 'look at them. What are they?'

He followed where I pointed and frowned, told me the name.

'Why have no beggars begged from us?' I asked. 'They have left us alone as if we had a plague. Look!'

He shrugged, unwilling to be frightened again. 'Didn't like the looks of you, perhaps, Merula.'

'No, no,' I said impatiently, 'they know we are dangerous to approach.' I glared around, trying to see who was following us, but there were so many people, all so brightly dressed and talking, and hairy ghosts all look alike anyway.

'It doesn't matter, we'll soon be gone,' he said, obstinately blind and I spat with impatience.

'Sir,' I hissed at him fiercely, 'go back to the ship and sail away.'

He only shook his head. 'I must visit the harbour master for my papers, and one more meeting. Come on.'

So we walked, untroubled by any beggars or street-hawkers at all, to another place by the water, made in white stone. The harbour master in his office smelled of fear and he looked at me sideways.

'What is that?' he demanded of Anriques.

'My slave,' said Anriques. 'She is my attendant.'

'Leave it outside.'

I made a two-fisted bow to him, as a warrior might to his enemy, and stepped outside. As I did, just in the tail of my eye, I saw the last of a file of men, shining with their curving peaked helmets and smooth metal breastplates, carrying the long axe-spears of the north, as they went quietly down an alleyway at the side of the big white harbour master's building to a sidedoor.

Lady Leopard looked at me, swished her tail, climbed quite catlike on my shoulder. She weighed nothing.

I followed the way the file of men had gone, to see the door shutting behind the last of them. I saw a window, open but covered by a carved and beautiful grill made of metal peacocks to keep out the sun, and I climbed up some baskets to the window ledge and looked through it.

And there was Anriques facing the harbour master. Behind Anriques in the corner stood a clerk behind a high desk, impassively dipping his pen, a white gull's feather in his back velvet cap. Something about the clerk's face was familiar.

From the way Anriques stood, I knew he was afraid, and what he was afraid of was another man who sat at the table, his back to my window, wearing a black suit of clothes, very fine silk brocade, but black, black, black, dull as squid ink, with a great strange white wheel about his neck made of linen and a black hat on his head. Anriques bowed to him and as he straightened, he caught sight of me, my shape against the sunlight through the metal peacock I was clinging to.

Nothing in his face changed, but he spoke up loudly. 'I swear by the Lord Jesus Christ that I am only a merchant, dealing in sugar,' he said very clearly and slowly. 'Your informer is lying, Christ have mercy on him, no doubt so you at the Holy Office will let him die, Señor Inquisitor Pasquale.'

The man in black was elegant, with a pale, slender, gentle face. He looked sadly at Anriques. 'No, Mr Anriques, I think not. I think you were here to meet a traitor named Francis Ames and receive vital intelligence about His Majesty's Armada.'

Anriques stood still. The world hung. How interesting, I thought. Now he was like a warrior when he had not been one in the alley-ambush in New Spain on the other side of the sea. Now he was poised and calm. Yes, his face was concerned, afraid, as it should be, of course. But his body, calm.

'Who is this Francis Ames who speaks ill of me?' he asked.

The harbour master's clerk was watching intently, his pen poised to record.

'Your friend,' said the Inquisitor. 'He said so when we arrested him. You bought him with stolen English gold.'

The clerk smiled briefly, bent to write again. Mr Anriques/Ames too relaxed a little. The soldiers I had seen filed in from the anteroom where they had been waiting.

'Please make no fuss, Mr Anriques,' said the Inquisitor. 'We prefer to do these things quietly.'

'By the Lord Jesus Christ, sir, I am innocent.'

I climbed higher, stepped from one grill to the next, peeked around the corner. Then men at arms surrounded Anriques' slight body, and marched him off, with Señor Pasquale in the lead. I looked back at the clerk, still writing away, staring fixedly at the page. He felt my stare, glanced at me – then he looked down again.

Anriques had sworn by the Suffering Jesus who was not his god, therefore what he said was a lie and he was giving me the signal to go back to the ship. And I felt sure that there was more to the harbour master's clerk than met the eye.

I leaped down from the window ledge, and looked about me at all the crowded hurrying people. Would the harbour master tell the men-at-arms that Mr Anriques had had an attendant? Would he think of it? Would he assume I had simply made my escape?

Ha! He might. I bent down, picked up a broken basket full of bones, and put it on my head, then I walked out into the square. What shall I do, Queen Moon? I asked. Shall I go now to the ship?

*Oh yes, first the ship,* came the soft tickling voice of Lady Leopard at my ear, *there is a thing you must do there.*

So I sang her songs as I carried my basket of scraps and when I came to the ship, tied tight to the quayside, I scattered the scraps out across the stones and the seagulls swooped down, quarrelling to pick them up. The men with ropes to the yards were swaying up the last great bags of sugar loaves and swinging them out onto the quay. Every bag of sugar was one slave's life – cutting the cane in the hot sun, boiling and straining it – and in my dreamsight, blood dripped. But I had no time for dreamsight.

I walked over the gangplank onto the ship, saw Michael high on the yards, and went straight to where Rebecca waited in the cabin, staring at papers. When she saw me alone she gulped like a frog.

'Where is he?'

*Not to frighten her,* said Lady Leopard. *Be gentle but quick.*

I had wanted to sing my mistress a woman-warrior's song, but this was not customary to her people and the strange music might confuse her. So I went to one knee at her feet, where her soft crimson gown flowed onto the wood like blood, like blood.

'My mistress,' I whispered, although being upside-down, now I was the one in command as her world tipped itself up around her, 'come with me now, take gold and a cloak and come.'

On the harbour side I heard the squawking and alarm calls as something frightened off the seagulls eating the scraps. I went to the bed, took my leopard skin and scooped the jewels from her casket into it, making it like a bag. There was the sound of marching feet, the sound of shouting.

Rebecca went whiter, and her eyes became like gazelles' eyes. She sat still, not breathing, truly a gazelle in the gaze of a lion.

*Go, go,* whispered Lady Leopard.

I looked and there was a window that opened to the air, at the flat end of the ship, aftwards, looking over the rudder. They had had the best cabin on the ship, being the owners.

I took Rebecca's hand and led her to the window while she stared and paled and paled and stared. Through the little window, I could see the sea, only a little way below, dirty, to be sure, but water is quite soft if not too far away.

More shouts. She was little and I was big, and I had lifted her like a child while she was sick. So I picked her up and pushed her through the window, head first, skirts and all, shoving her through past her bumroll, she squawking a little in shock. She pitched into the water with a muffled cry, her skirts billowing around her, and then with my Lady Leopard blinking down on me with distaste from the rudder, I squeezed through still knotting my leopard skin, dropped it and followed her laughing, with a great splash.

Well, she was drowning now in a sodden tangle of silk and canvas, and I was surprised at the foul saltiness of the water, but I found her head, and got it above water, and when she grabbed at me, I caught her by her hair and towed her to the side of the next ship along, where we clung, gasping and watched the men in their bright helmets and breastplates, carrying their dark guns, marching on board the Anriques' ship and claiming it and its cargo impounded for the Holy Office.

High above was Michael, still leaning over the yard, staring down on the soldiers tramping over the deck. Had he seen us? Some of them shouted up at him, one pointed a caliver and he sidled along the yard, riding it like a horse now, to the very tip where it hung over the water. A shot rang out, a hole in the sail . . . He stood on the yard and dived.

Water is very hard if it is a long way away. I hoped the fall wouldn't kill him.

Rebecca was gripping the anchor chain next to me, her small hands slipping and gleaming while she wept, gasping harshly through her square mouth, as if she were in childbirth. Poor lady. I patted her shoulder and pulled her along with me to the next ship, where she suddenly began to moan and tear at her breast-wrappings of canvas. Suddenly I understood that the canvas was shrinking and killing her. I found her little knife in her belt and cut through the lacings of her bodice and then her stays where I had bound her up in all her cloth that morning, like a baby, and she breathed better. Then I found the fastenings for her great kirtle of silk and the farthingale and cut that free, and dragged her on to the next moored ship, riding and rocking.

There was no sign of Michael. No doubt he had drowned.

We felt our way on round the ship, and we found a little place where the steps went up from the sea, and we crawled out there, and hid, at the bottom of the steps, dripping with foul, cold water, my man's suit as heavy as lead around me. I could not swim or stay on the surface any longer. Rebecca sat on the steps and gripped her hair in her fists and wept as silently as she could, ah ah, she prayed to her strange word-god, and wept and moaned, silently, while the men in breastplates began searching the ship. But then she looked at me.

'How was he taken?' she whispered.

'At the harbour master's place,' I said. 'They waited for him.'

'Had he . . . had he met Francis Ames, his brother?'

'The man who took him said that Francis Ames was his friend, bought for money.'

'No, no, his elder brother. They must have the name but nothing else. Did they meet?'

I shook my head. 'He met many people this morning.'

'In his hat . . . a gull's feather?'

Then I laughed and thought of the familiar-faced harbour master's clerk. What cold nerve to stand and watch your brother taken. I liked him already and I told Rebecca of it.

'And it was certainly the Holy Office?'

'When he swore by Jesus to give me the signal, he named them that.'

She gulped hard. 'Oh, may he die quickly.'

I smiled at her. 'Your man faced them as a warrior.'

She stared at me as if she was not sure whether I was making fun of her, but being upside-down I do not do that. Then she put her hands across her body to hold her arms as if she was holding herself in one piece by force and shuddered.

'Thank you, Merula,' she said sadly. 'I suppose you had better go now.'

'Go?'

'Run away. Escape. You can be free now.'

Now here was a great singing in my head, and a laughing from my gods, for this was fine. To have my freedom was a fine thing, if I had ever lost it, which I had not. But I had come to find my son and I still had no idea where to start.

'I am not your captive,' I told her. 'All that has happened has been at the will of God. I am here to find my son or his spirit and take him home.'

She blinked at me in astonishment, as if I could not have a purpose other than freedom, as if I had no quests of my own to seek.

I took off all my clothes and squeezed them out, stood and stretched. It was good to feel the sun on my breasts again, not to be imprisoned in cloth. Well, I did not like the oily look of the water but I had to find my leopard skin. The sun was going down, perhaps they would not see me.

There was a hippopotamus splashing and gasping, and round the edge of the quay came Michael, pushing a bolt of floating wood. He saw me and paddled over and I helped him up the steps.

The tide was going out as the sun set, and while my mistress was helping Michael and talking to him, I slid back into the water and paddled from one ship to the other until I came to the Anriques' ship, which was now flying the flag of the Holy Office.

At the back of it I ducked under, looking in the murk and mud and dropped spars and cut anchors, for my leopard skin. My Lady Leopard would have nothing to do with this, but at last my fingers brushed soft sodden fur and I brought it up, still tied, and paddled back to the steps under the overhang where I had left my mistress and found her still there, still sodden and bedraggled, though if she had had the sense to take her clothes off, they might almost have dried. Though her petticoat was dyed with the colour of her skirts, her bodice hung from her where I had cut it and there were cuts in her skin where I had been in a hurry. She still shook and twisted her hands together and tried to push back the tears coming out of her eyes with her fists. I touched her arm, shook myself and showed her the jewels I had rescued.

Then she smiled and so did Michael. Michael took a necklace of pearls with him and went out to the shops and drinking dens that serve the docks.

While the darkness deepened swiftly, I climbed to the quayside and paced along it, quietly on my bare feet, waiting. There were guards on our ship and soldiers of the Holy Office at the gates. Once there was a clatter and shouting as one came through that they knew.

I went back to where Rebecca was hiding, and as I went, I knew that someone else was quietly walking that way. I paused and then followed, stalking him. He was walking along the quayside, looking at the water. He asked questions at the other ships' anchor-watches.

He turned his face and I saw it, knew him for the clerk who had had a gull's feather in his cap. So I paced up behind him and whispered to him, 'Are you looking for Rebecca?'

He moved fast for a hairy ghost. He had his arm at my throat and a knife prickling my neck under my ear before I could dodge him – he was a warrior where his brother was none. I smiled at the neatness of it, let my muscles relax. Lady Leopard was watching from a mooring post.

'Shh,' I said. 'Mr Ames, if you wear a gull's feather for a sign, give it to me and I will fetch her.'

Slowly he let go.

'You saw me today when my master your brother was taken,' I told him, speaking the blue-green tongue of the English. 'Now give me your sign.'

He gave it to me, and I went to where Rebecca still sat, waiting. Now I knew what she had been waiting for, apart from not knowing where to go and having no clothes to hide the ugliness of her skin.

She told me to bring him and so I did and he hurried down the steps to clasp her in his arms, and she wept into his shoulder.

'I am so afraid of burning,' she said, 'Simon is so brave, he said he must come, but I am so afraid . . .'

To burn to death is very bad, I thought, as I stood at the top of the steps to keep watch, with my arms folded as a warrior. The Suffering Jesus must be greedy.

'I'm sorry, Rebecca, I could do nothing. Not without getting arrested myself . . .'

'I know that. It would have been pointless. What information did you have to tell him.'

'This.' He whispered in Rebecca's ear.

She frowned and stared at him. 'Is that all?'

'It cost the life of my finest spy to get it. Take it to the Queen, it may help her.'

'*The galleases are for the Miracle of Beauty*. That's all?'

'That's all. It is the greatest secret of the Spanish enterprise. Admiral Santa Cruz told no one after he set it in motion. I had it from one of his counting-house clerks. The Duke of Parma knows, but that's all.'

'But isn't there—'

'Rebecca, in the matter of intelligence, often all you can know is a small part of the whole, but sometimes the small part you hold is the key. Make sure this gets to the Queen.'

She shook her head. 'I'll take it to Walsingham.'

'No. The Queen. He does not tell her everything and Burghley is taking money from Spain. You can tell her that too. But give it to the Queen only. I saw Michael buying boys' clothes for you. When he comes back, you must go to the two-master, the *San Antonio*.

The captain is one of ours.' He kissed her again. 'I am sorry,' he said. 'I hoped Simon would not bring you.'

'I made him. Is it true that if you breathe in the flames deliberately, your lungs shrivel up and you die quicker?'

He patted her arm. After all, no death is easy.

And then he was gone, slipping away into the shadows again, then walking directly from the ship with the Holy Office flag over it, yawning and rubbing his eyes, a resentful harbour master's clerk kept up to deliver a message, and he spent ten minutes complaining of it to the soldiers at the gate until they let him pass for sheer boredom.

# David Becket

*West Country, Spring 1588*

In the comfortable bed in the best guest-chamber at Becket House, with its crewel-worked curtains hanging down to keep out the bad airs, David Becket dreamed he was only a boy, a boy full of mixed fear and delight at the drama and excitement that had overtaken his life . . .

*His pony clattered past men sweating to unload cartloads of paint and painter's spirit that had been taken from the dockyards on the South Bank of the Thames. He trotted on under the hedgehog's winter armour of traitors' heads perched above London Bridge Gate, and imagined Fr Campion's skull praising the skies with empty eye sockets for the landing of the Papists. The pony's small hooves clopped on under the high brick arch.*

*All the bridge houses were empty except for a couple of cats glaring from the roof of a privy hanging out like a swallow's nest over the Thames.*

*The pony slowed to a walk and sidled, for all the boy's drumming heels, not liking the emptiness and darkness. Also, to be fair to him, Smudge was tired from the long gallop up the road from Greenwich.*

*They came into a long, narrow street entirely surrounded by tall, shuttered houses, with light dropping into it only from the oblong of sky above. The boy kicked unmercifully, hearing more voices, and the pony ungraciously clopped on. Through another arch and onto a wide place where you could look west and east at the river, eerily scoured of traffic. Eastwards gouts of smoke blackened the sky. Westwards was more smoke, coming he thought from the kilns in Scotland Yard, next to Whitehall Palace. Why were they firing the kilns?*

*It seemed that anyone with a boat had gone upriver away from Parma on the incoming tide. Many of the ships that had been in the Pool of London had cut their anchors and fled on the ebb, hoping to get past Tilbury without Parma noticing. Another arch, lower this time. Where was the Queen's Captain of the Rearguard?*

*Another wide place with a rail each side where there was theoretically a drawbridge that had never been raised in all his memory. He could hear a sound of chopping with axes right underneath, and something complicated* involving ropes and barrels seemed to be happening over the side. A cart was blocking the street, men were heaving barrels that smelled of bad eggs, shouts of 'Steady! To you, heave!'

It was there, under the arch, that he finally found the man he had been sent to. The Queen's Captain of the Rearguard. A big bear of a man, very impressive, standing foursquare on the cart shouting orders, his morion helmet gleaming dully over black curls, a scuffed buff coat covered by a fine, blued steel breastplace and over the chest hung the gold chain of esses only worn by a high officer of state.

'Sir!' called the lad, sweating and praying his voice wouldn't break. 'Sir, Captain Becket, sir!'

The man turned, took in the boy's sweat-marked pony and frightened face. 'Donne,' he said to a young man in front of him, 'go back along the bridge and make sure every window is shut, every shutter bolted, but each house must have its door open. Understand?'

'Aye, sir. Windows shut, shutters bolted, door open.'

Becket jumped surprisingly lightly from the cart as Donne flourished his hat and jog-trotted back down across the bridge. He came over, took the pony's bridle, led them both aside.

'Where are they?'

'Greenwich, sir. And they've took some ships that was trying to get out on the ebb.'

'The palace?'

'Yes, sir. Parma's standard is over it.'

'How many tercios?'

'Don't rightly know, sir. Lots. More men than you could count.'

'I mean, how many banners?'

'At least twenty. More. I heard tell they've been bringing them over, fast as they can since they took Gravesend. I heard tell Drake's dead, sir, of a fever. I heard tell he's had Mass said in the Queen's own chapel. Parma, that is. Not Drake 'cos he's dead, see. Mass in the Queen's palace!'

Captain Becket didn't seem shocked, but only grunted. 'Horse?'

'Oh, plenty of horses, sir, he sent some men off on horses to see what's ahead. Poor old Smudge had to run as fast as he could to get ahead of them.'

'What's his ordnance? Did you see any guns?'

'Didn't see none, sir. What are you going to do, sir? Is it right the Queen's gone north, sir?'

'I'm going to amuse the Spaniard. Now what's your name?'

'Ben Jonson, sir.'

'Well, Ben. You can walk on northwards if you like, because I am

95

commandeering your pony in the name of the Queen. The Great North Road will be blocked solid with carts and folk but you're small, you might get through. Or you can stay here and carry messages for me in case we can give your pony back, but if you stay here you might be killed.'

'Want to get back to Greenwich, sir, see after me mam.'

'Well, if you try that, you most certainly will be killed.'

'I'll stay here, sir.'

'Good man.'

Smudge was already protesting and nipping at being loaded up with sacks full of sawdust when he clearly deserved a rest and a full nosebag. Two men manhandled more barrels into the building next to them. Captain Becket turned to speak to someone else.

Nosily, not wanting to miss anything, Ben followed the men with the barrels and found them being piled up in the middle of a fine showroom, still lined with bolts of cloth, and nymphs and cupids painted on the walls. Ben helped pour out the sawdust from a sack round the barrels onto fine black and white tiles.

'Why sawdust?' he asked, coughing. The man shrugged. 'Captain says. Paint too.'

'What about the merchant what owns this ken?'

The man grinned. 'Captain Becket came with the Queen's Warrant and some of the Life Guard this morning and turfed the lot of them out at gunpoint. You never heard such a fuss. If Parma don't come, Captain Becket will be in the Hall of Westminster answering twenty lawsuits by next week.'

Ben grinned back. 'That must have been a sight to see.'

'Almost worth it. Almost.' The man sighed. 'Seems a pity to blow it up.'

For two hours they worked to fill London Bridge with powder while to the north, London boiled with terror. To the south, the poorer whores and the bearmasters and tumblers at Paris Garden were philosophically preparing for a new influx of customers. The richer ones had already left, paying a great deal of gold for a boat-crossing that normally cost tuppence.

Ben found a little brooch of coral and pearls dropped on the floor and pocketed it quietly. He ended up carrying the smaller bags of sawdust, seeing as he was quite strong for his age. He stayed in sight of the Captain, though. Every so often someone would come sprinting up to Becket with a new rumour and some titbits of information about Parma. Rumour swirled around the soldiers on the bridge like counterfeit coin. The Queen was dead, shot in the breast. The Queen was already in Oxford, she'd gone upriver in her barge. The Queen was standing at Tyburn taking a tax in gold off every cart that passed up the Edgeware Road. The Queen was still *at Whitehall where fires burned away at the enormous heaps of paper stored there.*

*Under the drawbridge at slack water, Thames watermen sweated to draw up an entire wherry snug under the aged oak beams, filled full of powder and chain-shot.*

*'When will you set light to it, sir?' Ben asked cheekily, when Captain Becket came past again.*

*'When I choose.'*

*In the houses south of the bridge that lined the Southwark Road, Becket placed men with calivers and arquebuses, grenadoes and bows. Many of them were watermen, with their wherries drawn up behind the houses that had watersteps. Ben wanted to stay with them since it seemed they would get to fight the Spaniard first. They told him no. He whined and protested and was summarily carried back to the middle of the bridge by a lowering giant of a man who promised him the belting of his life if he set foot on the South Bank again. Ben couldn't understand it at all. Why shouldn't he get some glory too?*

*The afternoon was waning. Was Parma coming up the road? Another young man arrived on a sweating horse, spoke urgently to the Captain and suddenly they were all being ordered northwards off the bridge to wait in Cheapside, which was shuttered and bare after the flight of all the goldsmiths. Ben decided to stick close to Captain Becket, in case he could get poor Smudge back again. Also he wanted to go back to his mam once the battle was finished and the Spaniards were beaten.*

*Becket had a horse now, a big solid hunter, and sat on it, looking grim. Smudge was standing with the other horses, head hanging down. Becket had slowmatch slung in coils round his body and curled expertly in his hand. He was absent-mindedly loading a dag from the pistol case before him.*

*A short, round man in a very well-cut wool suit came up to his stirrup and spoke quietly, 'It's all set, Captain.'*

*Becket looked down at him. 'Thank you, Mr Pickering.'*

*The man nodded, walked away to an alleyway where a ragged beggar covered in pustules waited for him. Becket beckoned Ben towards him.*

*'Now, Ben, I have a very important message for you. You can have your pony again, here's money for your journey and a warrant that makes you a Queen's Messenger. I hereby order you, in the name of the Queen, to ride to the village of Middleton, ten miles south of Dorchester, and go to Becket House. If it's still standing when you reach it, tell the lady of the house, Mistress Eleanor Becket, that the time has come to do as they do in the Low Countries. Here is a ring for her, which you must guard like your life, for*

*it tells her who you come from. Then you do as she says, for she'll look after you until you can go back to your mam. Can you do it?'*

*Ben's heart swelled with pride. He grabbed off his hat, ducked a bow and took the ring, which went on his forefinger quite snugly. It was a pretty ring, more for a woman than a man, set with diamond sparks and turquoise and pearls like a flower.*

*'Ay, sir, I'll do it, my word on it. I'll tell her.'*

*He cocked his head. Men were singing in Latin, far away. He listened a moment, wondering what they were saying. He knew Latin, had gone to school for a bit, before he had to be apprenticed as a bricklayer, and he'd been good at it. He was sorry to leave.*

*'Good.' Captain Becket was listening too. He smiled at Ben. 'I rely on you, Mr Jonson. Go now. Take the Great West Road.'*

*Ben jumped astride Smudge, who punished him with a small crow-hop. He clattered his heels on the pony's ribs until the animal went very unhappily up to a choppy canter, heading west.*

*As happens in dreams sometimes, the dreamer's eye changed its focus, dived into the self it had been watching . . .*

*Becket left his horse tethered to a rail, walked quickly down through the deserted bridge to stand looking out like a shopkeeper at his door, under the skulls of dead Papists. He heard them clearer now, the drumbeats and the singing. The tercios marched to a Latin hymn, a deep-voiced growl.*

*'Te Deum laudamus, te Dominum confitemur, te aeternum Patrem omnis terra veneratur . . .'*

*He had sung it himself while pretending to be a priest at the English Seminary in Rheims. We praise you, God, we confess you lord, you the eternal father that all the world worships . . . Something like that.*

*Becket knew it was Parma's habit to have his men sing that hymn when they took possession of a conquered city. A little premature, aren't we, Your Grace? He waited until his ears were full as the drumbeats came louder and the sound of thousands of horses' hooves and men's feet and the grinding of wagons behind . . . Any minute now they would come in sight.*

*He ducked inside the bridge gatehouse with his slowmatch burning, took it and lit the first and longest fuse. He had set the fuses himself, using all the slowmatch he could find in the bowels of the Tower, never mind its age and rottenness.*

*He had to lean right over the balustrade, almost upend himself to light the fuses under the carefully weakened drawbridge. It reminded him of his old friend Simon, and his throat ached for the man, awkward bastard though he was, and almost certainly lost in the dungeons of the Inquisition of Spain.*

98

He ran on, watched by the nearest watermen and soldiers, a heavyset, clumsy-looking man, yet very light on his feet, as he set his burning match to one fuse after another as if preparing fireworks for an Accession Day display. Which it was, in its kind. Who needed the excitable Signor Giambelli's fireships loaded with gunpowder and called hellburners, to break a bridge? He would do it with gunpowder alone, as he had years ago in the Netherlands.

A roar erupted from many thousand Spanish throats. Had they seen him? No – they had seen the heads of the traitors over the gatehouse.

Orders shouted, the column halted. Please God, let Parma be at their head to ride into London, let no one delay them, let them not feel the need to send scouts ahead.

He had argued until he was hoarse for this extravagant trap, with only Ralegh's support. The Queen had listened and, at last, given her assent. Let it work, please God . . . They would send scouts ahead who would understand what the hissing and the smell meant and warn off the others. It would all be for nothing . . .

No. They were marching again, they would not wait, they surged ahead, flags flying, drums beating . . . Ah, they had moved their sacred, Papally blessed banner to the vanguard now, carried by four young men in black. The officers had their helmets off in respect for the martyrs over the gate. How touching.

The Spaniards broke step on the bridge and it rumbled with tramping feet as Becket quietly ran lighting fuses ahead of them. Come on, come to Papa, get your standards over the drawbridge.

He was still lighting at the City end, when the first barrel of gunpowder blew with a great bellowing WHOOMF! and the walls of the house it was in blew outwards. The top three storeys paused in the air as the walls crumbled under them, another deep voiced boom as the next barrel blew.

He had fused them to blow in sequence from each end; one misfired but the next went so it must have been bad powder, not the fuses.

Suddenly, unmistakeably, a baby's cry rang out from the top, fourth storey of one of the houses, crying and bawling. Some fool nurse must have left him behind. Nothing anyone could do about it, there wasn't time to climb to one storey, let alone four . . . In the seconds before the next explosion, and after it, the babe screamed rage at the brutal world that had woken him.

In the street down the middle of the bridge, Becket could see in his mind's eye the terror and chaos of the vanguard, as the explosions stepped inwards to the drawbridge from each end. They would be running to and fro to escape the masonry and fire, crowding together, horses going mad, *yes, there were a couple of men on the parapet looking down at the water as it purled through the narrow arches. One jumped, then another, veterans who knew perfectly well what had happened and what was coming next and were willing to exchange certain death for death merely probable in the roaring waters below. A few more jumped and then . . .*

*BOOM! BOOM! Like a child's mud bridge kicked by an invisible foot, house after house thundered, broke and fell inwards, the brick crumbling to dust, the wood turning into a spiked straw heap before the sawdust and paint and booze finally did their job and the flames took hold. No more crying from that poor baby.*

*The middle of the bridge burst out in a bellow of light and smoke and bits of wood and limbs and chainshot thrown high in the air.*

*Wishing to God he had more men, Becket heard the calivers and muskets of the watermen shooting the column of Spaniards from the Southwark house-windows. He longed for proper troops he could have held in reserve until now. In a year's time, Becket knew he would have such troops. But not yet.*

*The head of Parma's triumphant column had been snapped off, along with their fancy banner. The middle of the column now writhed under fire from the houses around. But these were the finest troops in Europe, the unbeaten tercios of Spain. They staggered, backed, retreated from the bridge in good order, relined under fire, brought muskets and small murderer guns on the carts to bear and began methodically clearing one Southwark house after the other. The watermen ran for it when they had to and could, and rowed their boats for the other side of the Thames, most of them shot down before they got very far, their boats tumbling on downriver.*

*Screams still echoed from the bridge, no more babies, thank God, mainly horses, as the buildings burned on into the dusk. Becket did not think he had managed to kill Parma himself, but it was still a good blow against him. The Duke would be more careful next time he crossed a bridge and that in itself would slow him down.*

*Becket mounted his horse, who stamped and whinnied at the horrible sounds from the bridge. There was Lawrence Pickering, King of the London thieves, now sitting on a sweating pony. His hands were clenched.*

*'Never thought I'd see the day,' he muttered, tears in his eyes as he stared at the burning broken wonder of London town. 'Never thought it. We'll make them sons of whores regret every brick.'*

*Becket had almost no gunpowder left and a city in riot ahead of him. He turned his head north and west, full of satisfaction . . .*

And woke, staring at the embroidered tester, hearing the songbirds and the crows squabbling and astonished that there was no horse between his legs, no prickling stench of gunpowder in the air. The dream fled from him as he reached for it, more vivid than a play, more frightening than an ambush.

He was exhausted, wrung out, as if he had in truth been blowing up London Bridge, rather than snoring away the spring night in the guestroom of Becket House. That much he recalled. Parma marching in to the city and him blowing the bridge. Well, so he would, if he had to. It had seemed a sound enough plan, perfectly workable, given the powder and the authority.

The authority. Given that . . . Was that why he had been spared, why so many things that should have killed him had not done so? Did God intend him to be the Queen's Captain-General against the Spaniard when he landed?

Shaking his head he slid from between the covers and murdered the last dregs of his dream with a long swallow of aqua vitae from his flask.

Philip would not hear of his brother travelling up to London on his own, a journey he took far more seriously than Becket did, who was so accustomed to days in the saddle and the tedium of bad roads that he occasionally wondered if his arse would one day be as tough as his buff coat. He said as much, vigorously supported by Eleanor, but Philip set his bottom lip and looked mulish and said he was planning to go and look at David's property in London in any case and if David wouldn't ride with him, why he would ride by himself.

Ungraciously, Becket gave in. There was a flurry as Philip's man packed a bag for him and Eleanor unlocked their casket to get travel money for him. She paused and then picked something out of it, gave it to Becket who blinked down at the ring, ice running suddenly down his back at sight of it.

'If you send me word as we discussed,' she said quietly to him, 'prove it with this ring.'

Becket nodded wordlessly, transfixed by the pretty flower made of diamond sparks and turquoise and pearls. He slipped it onto his left little finger.

Determined to discourage his brother into going home again as soon as possible, Becket said hardly a word to him for the two days it took them, travelling by the Queen's post for which Becket had a warrant, changing horses every morning and afternoon and sleeping at the warranty inn overnight – a process that impressed Philip.

They could have got to the city in the evening had they hurried, but Becket took a room at an inn in the village of Kensington so he could write letters and copy out Piers Lammett's message. Philip was pressing to come to Seething Lane with him, perhaps to be introduced to the great Mr Secretary Walsingham himself . . .

'Why? Do you want to be a pursuivant?' Becket asked rudely, pouring more aqua vitae and regretting the extra stop. They were finishing their supper at one end of the common room, near the fire.

'No, of course not, though it must be wonderfully interesting to serve the Queen by hunting down Spanish spies and priests.'

Interesting. Christ. *Interesting!* Becket's mouth twisted. 'I tell you what, brother. I'll change places with you, take your house, your wife, your children and live quiet in the country and you can be the pursuivant. Hmm? Say the word, and I'll do it.'

Philip blinked at him, shocked more by his voice than by what he said.

'It's no bad thing to have a tidy mind for business, the money can be good enough if you're successful at picking up estates from arrested Papists. Anthony Munday has himself quite a little bundle of them by now, may he pox himself and die.'

Philip had leaned back and was looking seriously at him across the scarred inn table, not bothering to drink his own silver cup of spirits. Becket tossed off his and poured some more.

'Why so bitter, David?' Philip asked softly. 'What happened to you?'

Becket shook his head. Jesu, where to start? It was simpler to keep silent.

No, Philip would not be put off. He leaned across the table, caught his brother's left hand and pushed back the grimy lace cuff. Then he whistled air in through his teeth at the ugliness of the knotted scars braceleting Becket's thick wrist. Becket fought down the urge to punch him.

'Were you a galley-slave, David?'

Becket shook his head.

'What was it then?'

Always, across his mind and heart, slashed the memories: exhausting cold cramped misery of the tiny dank cell called Little Ease, the cluttered basement of the White Tower, Mr Secretary

Davison questioning him in his fog of forgetfulness. He had wept, he remembered weeping because of the pain in his arms and shoulders and back, although God was a little merciful and did not allow anyone to remember the pain itself. Only his hands tingled with the ghosts of agony.

Philip was still looking, seeing the cording as Becket's hand turned, not very well, to a fist. 'Who did this to you, brother?' he asked huskily. 'Is there any vengeance we could take?'

Becket slammed his other fist on the table, pulled his wrist out of Philip's grip and covered it again with his shirtcuff, drank his aqua vitae. Damn it, the cup rattled on his teeth with his shaking.

'Take Walsingham to court, why don't you?' he snarled. 'Take Anthony Munday, pursuivant, and Mr Secretary Davison the length of Westminster Hall on my account, for assault, battery . . .'

Philip frowned. 'Not Spaniards? Not the Inquisition?'

Oh God, he was naïve. 'The first time, it was Spaniards, yes. At Haarlem. But the Christmas before last, true Englishmen, Anthony Munday and his bumboy James Ramme, under the authority of Mr Secretary Davison and William Norton, Englishmen of good Protestant religion, hung me up from a pillar under the White Tower by my wrists, twice, and flogged me for good measure.'

'*Flogged* you?'

Poor Philip was so shocked at such a thing happening to his own brother, a gentleman.

'Jesu, Philip, that wasn't what did the harm, it was hanging up all day from my wrists. You get better from a flogging, it doesn't even make your back stiff if you remember to touch your toes every hour while it heals. It was my own weight on my wrists in the manacles . . .'

Philip's face was white. Becket wished to stop, wanted to protect his brother's cosy world where only Spaniards did evil, but once he had begun, his misery rose like a tide and he could not stop.

'They thought I was a priest. They took me in a raid on a Mass where I was spying on them in disguise as a Papist, and the pursuivants cracked my head so well in taking of me, when I woke I knew nothing of myself. And until I cursed them for Papists they thought I was a Jesuit and treated me as they generally do treat Jesuits, God have mercy on them.'

Philip put his hand to his mouth, took a shaky breath to talk, thought better of it and poured himself some aqua vitae. Becket gulped his own down and was able to speak better for it.

'Do not upset yourself over it,' he growled, hoping Philip would listen. 'It was an honest mistake and they righted it when once they understood what I was. Walsingham even made me an ex-gratia payment afterwards. But you see ... My wrists ... something happened to them. My hands no longer answer my will, they prickle and burn sometimes, they are clumsy and weak. See, I could not even make a proper fist to hit you with. If we arm-wrestled, you would win for the first time. So I am no longer a swordmaster and must make my way as a pursuivant, for I cannot wield even a veney-stick.'

Christ Almighty, those were tears again. He was bawling like a babe for his lost swordplay, what in the name of God was he turning into? Becket put his cold hands over his face and fought for control.

He felt the give on the bench as Philip sat himself down next to him, felt the weight of his brother's arm across his back, found himself turning into his embrace so he could hide his face on his brother's shoulder. Philip said nothing, only sat there next to him on the bench until he could cough and blow his nose and in general behave like a grown man again. At last Philip handed him another cup of aqua vitae. But Becket felt sick now, and only sipped. It did help. God knew, it was often the only thing that did.

When he eventually looked at Philip's face, he found no contempt as he feared, nor pity as he dreaded. Only a sort of kindly wonder.

'Lord, brother, Eleanor was right when she likened you to a wounded bear.'

Becket coughed. 'Will you do the deal then, Philip?' he said, less huskily. 'You have my "interesting" life and I'll have ... why, I'll let you keep the house and the brood and I'll settle for your wife by herself, in her smock.'

'Steady,' said Philip dryly. 'I think I can make shift to fight you for her.'

'And beat me now, I'm sure,' said Becket sadly. 'But you see why I am not so eager to introduce you to Walsingham. He'll have you writing to him with intelligence before you know it.'

'More than ever I am glad that father remembered you in his will. At least you will not be scraping for money any more.'

It was a comfortable thought. And he did feel better, it was true, to find that Philip was still on his side. Although the poor man looked older still.

He patted Philip's knee to reassure him, called the potboy over and asked for the reckoning and a receipt, since it was occasionally possible to get your money back from Walsingham's clerk, Phelippes – if you docketed everything in writing.

'I'll see what I can do,' he said. 'Only keep well out of any matter of Walsingham's, for what will I say to Eleanor if you turn pursuivant?'

They took a boat downriver in the morning, so that Philip could enjoy the sight of the river frontage with the Palace of Westminster and the rich men's gardens and then the fine ships in the Pool. They landed at Temple steps so that Philip could go up the lane and see his lawyer and man of business, Peregrine Howard, while Becket walked up Ludgate Hill and into the City. He had thought long and hard what to do about his discovery that Burghley was still selling ordnance overseas, eclipsed though it had been in his eyes by Piers Lammett's information about the Miracle of Beauty.

In the end, he left a package containing all his information for Thomasina de Paris at Dr Nunez' house in Poor Jewry, marked for the Queen's eyes only. And then he took the same report to Walsingham, similarly marked, without mentioning his other conduit to the Queen. He thought it was an experiment the Queen might enjoy, whatever the result.

He was just leaving to join his brother for dinner, when he was grabbed by Phelippes the younger in great relief and asked to go and meet some Dutchman called Van Groenig at the Belle Sauvage in Ludgate, on account of his speaking Dutch.

'Send Munday,' growled Becket.

'Speaks no Dutch,' said Phelippes. 'Or I would, believe me, Mr Becket.'

'What's so urgent about it?'

Phelippes squinted at a piece of paper. 'Claims to be Parma's mapmaker. Says he has vital information about a plot against the Queen and the realm. The usual.'

Becket sighed and rolled his eyes. 'Not again?'

Phelippes smiled in his prosiac, lips-tucked fashion. 'I am afraid so.'

'How many this month?'

'Twenty-two.'

'His letter?'

Phelippes handed it over and Becket assessed it with an expertise he was unaware of. The handwriting was good, the Dutch literate, no great whirligigs of hyperbole about how very dangerous and important and unique the information was. It had not been penned in blood and no angels had dictated it, which was a relief.

'All must at least be seen,' said Phelippes unnecessarily. 'And my father particularly asked that it be you. Van Groenig takes his dinner at the Belle Sauvage every midday . . .'

'Sensible of him. I like their bag puddings.'

'Their hard sauce of sack and butter also is excellent,' murmured Phelippes. 'I recommend it with the almond pudding. And I shall, of course, see to your expenses myself.'

Becket sighed.

The first Philip knew of the enterprise was his brother banging through the door of the Cheshire Cheese and beckoning him over.

'If you want to be a pursuivant, you can see what I spend my days doing,' Becket said, heading up the alley towards Fleet Street. 'Wasting my days, if you like. Every madman in Europe with angels sitting whispering on his shoulder, every single one comes to London with divine knowledge of Parma's plans. And Walsingham says we have to talk to each one, just in case there might be something in it.'

'Well, mightn't there be?'

'You have evidently not spoken to as many Protestant madmen as I have,' said his brother heavily.

Philip felt his brother was very ill-suited to be a pursuivant. As far as he could make out, Becket mishandled the interview with Van Groenig at the Belle Sauvage. For a start, he marched straight up to the squat man in an unmistakeably German doublet who sat with his back in a corner, by a window onto the great courtyard where the carrier's wagons made ready for their journeys up the Great North Road every morning.

Becket loomed over him deliberately and spoke in a bored tone of voice. 'Mijnheer Van Groenig?'

'Have you got the money?' asked the man in a heavy Low Dutch accent, munching away on a piece of pie.

Becket said something in Dutch. Groenig gave him an ugly look, snarled something in the same language and then continued to speak English. 'I told you. First the money, then the story. Parma is look for me. To hide, I must money have. I want your Valseenam protect me.'

Becket put his hand on the table and leaned in. 'I don't buy no pigs in pokes, nothing I haven't seen. I've been caught that way before.'

Van Groenig shrugged, stolidly continued to eat his steak and kidney pie.

'Shall I speak to Mr Munday about you?' hissed Becket. 'I'm surprised you haven't been arrested and taken to meet Mr Rackmaster Norton.'

'I also,' Van Groenig sneered. 'So why not? I also would do that.' He looked theatrically round the room. 'Oh, you have no men. So sit down, Mijnheer Priest Hunter.'

Becket sat down, while Philip stood over in the corner, trying to hear what was going on without staring or seeming to eavesdrop. He thought he would at least have tried to be pleasant first.

'You listen,' said Van Groenig, making a face as he drank the beer, 'not threaten. What I sell is worth the kingdom, understand? The kingdom.'

'Parma's secret plans for invasion?' asked Becket, his eyes half shut, his voice heavy with disbelief.

Van Groenig flushed angrily. 'It happens, *ja*.'

Becket sighed. 'And you want for this . . . ?'

'Fifty pounds. Gold.'

'Oh. Is that all?'

'Is a bargain for a kingdom, even yours. It is, how you say, good cheap?'

'Who told you the plan?'

'Nobody. I find it by my work.'

Becket rolled his eyes.

'You not believe me?'

'Mijnheer, put yourself in my place. Why should I believe you? Ever since last summer, I have had one madman after another try to sell me Parma's secret plans for invading his realm. My master would certainly pay fifty pounds for such information, but not for some lunatic's phantastical spew.'

Van Groenig's lips shut tight. 'I not a lunatic.'

'Having once been very good friends with a lunatic, I can assure you that they never admit what they are. Nor even know it, maybe. So please, Mr Van Groenig, convince me. Help me. What, for instance, is your trade?'

'I am a scholar, a geographer and a cartographer.'

'A mapmaker? So what?'

'I make maps. I go to a place, a city, I walk around, I count my steps, I sit on a hill and sketch. Later, I make a map. I am very good mapmaker.'

'Who for?'

Van Groenig smiled. 'For who pays good money. For Cunning Prince Wilhelm before the priest shot him. For the Duc d'Anjou. For Parma.'

'Who's paying you now?'

'No one. I am look for a patron.'

'Why are you talking to me?'

'Mijnheer Priest Hunter, to work for Spain is hungry business. He promise much, but he not pay. Give me gold and I am your Queen's mapmaker.'

'We don't need a map of London. We know our way around.'

Van Groenig smiled again. 'I have for Parma a map made, a very secret map. So secret, instead of pay me, he try for arrest me.'

'A map of what?'

'A city, *natürlich*. But of where? A-ha. Money first.'

Becket sighed. 'I have no authority to pay you, Mr Van Groenig. Nor do I have a pound of gold on me, leave alone fifty of them.'

Van Groenig slapped his hand on the table in disgust. 'Why should I with the boy speak when I have information for the master. You go tell your master,' a broad, ink-stained finger prodded Becket's doublet, 'you go tell your Valseenum, if he does not to me listen, Parma eats his liver next summer.'

And Van Groenig turned away and ostentatiously filled his mouth with kidney and piecrust.

Becket stumped away from the table and sat next to Philip, calling for ale. Philip had philosophically ordered some pie for both of them, which Becket began to demolish at speed.

Philip thought they should go to Seething Lane again to report, but Becket thought not. Instead they finished their food, then left the room, but waited by the great gate of the inn until the Dutchman left.

He stamped out of the common room door shortly after and they followed him discreetly. It wasn't difficult. Van Groenig seemed too angry to pay much attention to what was behind him, although he had scanned the street before he started. That worried Philip. Disappointment made sense, if the man was a fraud, but not anger. Becket only grunted when he pointed this out.

Van Groenig had lodgings in the small rents to the north of the Strand. They waited outside as the Dutchman bought himself an apple and raisin pasty on credit from a stallholder, went upstairs. They heard the bang of his door.

Becket rubbed his face wearily, scratched the margins of his beard, which needed trimming. He could have changed his shirt that morning as well. Eleanor had given him three that had once been his father's and were wide enough. Philip changed his shirt every second day.

'Perhaps he should be picked up,' Becket said meditatively. 'I don't like him running around loose if Parma is after him, and Anthony Munday may be better at prising him open than I am.'

'Is Munday a friend of yours?'

'No, I told you, he's an inquisitor.' Becket's chin dropped to his regrettable falling-band, and his voice rumbled. 'Not my friend.'

Philip remembered then when he had heard the name before and could have kicked himself. Do you have any friends, David? he wanted to ask, but didn't.

Becket rubbed his face again. Sighed. 'God curse it, the butter-eater has me half-convinced. Do you know where Seething Lane is, Philip?'

Philip looked around wildly at the choked, winding streets. 'If you could tell me . . .'

Becket scowled. 'I'll run to Walsingham and tell them to pick him up. You stay here.'

'What shall I do if he leaves?'

'I doubt he will but if he does, don't try to follow him, you'll only lose him and yourself. Mark which direction he goes in, but then stay here to tell me when I come back.'

Philip nodded uncertainly and Becket jogged off through the crowds, hand tilting his sword to keep it out of his way and his sheer size cutting him a passage. Philip watched him go, worried that he wouldn't know what to do if something happened.

He sat down, called for ale, tried to pretend he was not watching the house across the street. There was no sign of the Dutchman but someone else came out of the door, a young man with brown hair and an open, handsome face in a well-cut grey suit of fine wool, trimmed with black braid. There was something that obscurely worried Philip about him, what was it? Not that he was whistling something, not the jaunty way he walked, nor the pallor of his face, nor the way he paused briefly to look at some elderly fish displayed on a street stall and then hurried on. He looked over his shoulder and their eyes met, briefly. What was it about him? His hands moved obscurely under his cloak, putting something away.

Unnamed instinct got Philip off the bench, over to the small street door. The stairs were narrow and turned as they went up.

'Good day?' he called. 'Um . . . anyone there?'

No answer. And what was that dark drop on the muddy board in front of him?

Philip climbed the stairs two at a time, went through the open door, into the small room with its bare paint-plaster walls, its overstuffed bed with the dusty curtains, the table, the chest which was open and the contents scattered, the stout body of a man sprawled on the rushes . . .

Van Groenig had his mouth open, he was snorting like a pig. Philip bent over him, wondering what was wrong. There was no obvious wound, no blood . . .

One eye rolled to focus on Philip, the other . . . Oh Jesus, the other eye was full of blood and something grey and creamy . . . Oh God . . .

Philip put his hand over his mouth, swallowing sourness. The other eye rolled, the one that wasn't a deep pond of blood and brain, fixed on him, struggled to see.

'*Ka . . . Het is kaaa . . .*' said Van Groenig desperately, caught at Philip, gripping hard. '*Ka.*'

His head went back, the undestroyed eye blackened, became jelly, his spine contracted, jolted, his legs worked as if he was trying to run away from death.

Philip stepped back unsteadily. That was what he had glimpsed. The young man had been carefully wiping a knife under his short cloak . . .

He stumbled down the stairs, his head almost bursting, his guts working. It was like a dream. What could he do? He squinted desperately down the street, saw no sign of the young man in any direction, no sign that anyone had even noticed. He stumbled one way, then another. Nothing. But he had to do something to settle his stomach, and Becket had told him to wait. So he went back to the alehouse opposite, ordered aqua vitae, swallowed the greasy fluid in one gulp and nearly puked again because it was so bad.

He sat there, staring and sweating, the picture of Van Groenig sweeping across his mind unbidden every second moment, wondering what the hell to do, until his brother jogged up, breathing hard and gripped his shoulder.

'Munday will be here with pursuivants in a quarter hour, we can
... Philip? What is it?'

Philip looked up at his brother mutely. I'm sorry, David, he
wanted to say except his mouth was too dry, I'm not used to seeing
things like that.

Becket spun on his heel, crossed the street like a bear going after
a dog in the bearpit, was up the stairs and into the room with Philip
behind him, wanting obscurely to prevent his younger brother
seeing anything so nasty ... Stupid of him.

He cannoned into his brother's broad back as Becket stood just
inside the door.

'God rot it,' said Becket, taking it all in wearily. 'God rot it to hell
and damnation.'

In five minutes he had searched the cooling body and the room,
under the mattress on the bed, opening the seams of the mattress
and the pillows, checked the chest for a false bottom, kicked
through Van Groenig's shirts and netherhose lying scattered on the
thin old rushes. He sat down on the bed, making it creak, spotted
something that had rolled against the wall. He bent and picked it
up, held it to the light. 'French coin,' he said, 'a pistole, I think.'

'He must have been—'

'Ay,' rumbled Becket, shutting his eyes. 'Perhaps he was telling
the truth. Somebody thought so. Did you see who did it?'

'A young man came out of the place, dressed in dark grey wool
... um ... Hat. Brown hair. Ruff. Er ... short cloak. Long pale
face.'

'Would you know him again? Draw a picture of him? You're
good at limning.'

Philip frowned. 'Perhaps. Yes, I could.'

'Watch out for him. Did he see you?'

'I think so, though I didn't know then ... I just wondered who he
was.'

'Did Van Groenig say anything to you before he died?'

'No,' said Philip, wanting to forget everything about what he had
seen, the one eye staring at him, the other eye destroyed. 'He tried,
but it was Dutch ... It sounded like 'cat' or 'can' but he couldn't say
it. I'm sorry, David.'

'And you didn't see the young man go in?'

'No.'

'Must have been waiting for him. Yes. Mapmaker. Perhaps

recently in France if the pistole didn't come from someone else, like the assassin. Damn it.'

'Walsingham should have paid the fifty pounds.'

'Oh, he would have, Philip. I was going to recommend it. Come on. There's no maps here.'

He pushed past Philip, clattered halfway down the stairs.

'Should we not wait for your . . . for Mr Munday? For the Watch and the magistrates and the inquest and—'

'Hell with the lot of them,' said Becket, shocking him with his lack of responsibility. 'Mr Recorder Fleetwood can sort it out with Munday. Besides, they might arrest you for the crime. You were here at the time, after all.'

Philip gasped though he couldn't fault the logic. He followed Becket back down the narrow stairs.

It was not as shocking as all that, for after a while of hurrying through London at a jog-trot behind his brother, Philip realised that Becket was calling out his affinity, in much the same way he himself would have done at Middleton if there had been a band of sturdy beggars in the area or a mysterious murder done. Except his brother's affinity seemed to consist mainly of the kind of people Philip would call out his own affinity *against*. First Becket stopped at Temple Bar and grabbed one of the sore-covered beggars waving a bowl at a hurrying lawyer. He spoke quite softly in the man's ear and then left him. They went up Ludgate Hill to Paul's Churchyard and caught a boy in a ragged wool suit who was trying to convince some farmers that Duke Humphrey's tomb was filled up with gold and jewels and if they paid him a penny each, he would use his influence to get them in to see it. Becket muttered in his ear and gave him a penny. The boy nodded nervously.

They took a boat from Temple steps and visited what Philip was sure was a stews on the South Bank where Becket seemed on worryingly friendly terms with the Madam and then called in on the famous bear-baiting ring where Philip was introduced to both Harry Hunks and Tom of Lincoln, both of whom seemed polite enough gentlemen, if extremely hairy and smelly. Harry Hunks roared when he saw Becket and Becket took the orangeado full of sugar he had bought from a pie woman on the corner and lobbed it into Harry Hunks's cage. The bear picked up the orangeado and sat with it in his paws, snuffling and licking away. Philip smiled to see it.

'I always bring him something,' Becket explained half-shame-faced. 'He's an old friend of mine. Saved my life a couple of years back, though he's grown old and long in the tooth now, if he had any, that is.' He talked intently to the bearwarden and the ticket seller.

They walked back over the bridge, with Philip trying not to gawp like the farmer he really was at all the wonderful fabrics displayed in the clear glass windows, the devore and stamped velvets, the silks, the brocades from the Far East that Eleanor would sigh over and he could never hope to buy her. They stopped for beer at a small boozing ken with the usual red lattices and nothing whatever interesting or unusual about it except that the beer was magnificent and there was a flight of polished stairs leading to a carved and locked door. Everywhere previously Becket had described the man he was looking for and everywhere he got fearful looks and promises of obedience. Except in this last place, called the Seven Stars, where a short round man with a round happy face and an extremely rich brocade doublet greeted Becket like an old friend and embraced him.

'Now Mr Pickering, may I present my brother, Mr Philip Becket of Becket House, Middleton. Brother, this is Mr Lawrence Pickering . . . whom some call the King of London.'

'Not in my hearing, Mr Becket,' said Pickering with an admonishing smile. 'Mr Secretary Walsingham don't like it.'

'My apologies, Mr Pickering. I was only relaying the common opinion.'

Despite the way his sharp London voice was at odds with his silk doublet, Philip made a small bow, which Pickering matched.

'More trouble wiv priests, Mr Becket?' Mr Pickering was also wearing some remarkably large jewelled rings on his fingers.

'Not priests, but certainly some manner of Papist.' Pickering tutted. Becket told the story of the killing again and Pickering was entirely unshocked though somewhat annoyed that it had happened, as he put it, 'on his manor'. They discussed the method of dispatch in the manner of carpenters disputing the merits of an adze.

'It's a good way, but it takes confidence,' Pickering said consideringly. 'Me, I prefer a kidney jab with a poniard because they can't see you coming and the pain stops 'em squealing.'

Philip stared from him to his brother who was nodding wisely. 'Must have been waiting behind the door for him, caught his hair and . . .' He made a stabbing motion with his fist. 'You could do it with a short, thin knife though, one you could put on your wrist, for example. Only takes a couple of inches in the eye. Which of Van Groenig's eyes was stabbed, brother, can you remember?'

'Um . . . his right,' said Philip, trying to hide the sourness in the back of his throat at the thought of it.

'No help there then. Right-handed,' said Pickering, rubbing his lower lip with his thumb. 'Well, Mr Becket, I'll put the word out for the sake of His Honour the Secretary and yourself, of course. Do you think it might be serious?'

'Perhaps, Mr Pickering, perhaps. At the very least, I'd like to know where a man who kills like that came from, how he got here, where he's been staying. He might pay for passage with pistoles, by the way.'

Pickering nodded. 'And the usual arrangement for your brother?'

'I would take that very kindly, Mr Pickering, very kindly indeed.'

'Consider it done, Mr Becket. Can I tempt you with a very fine apricot water?'

'No, thank you, I must go back to Seething Lane again. Another time.'

And with great mutual courtesy, they left, while Philip wondered which parts of the conversation had eluded him.

'Arrangement?' he asked tentatively.

Becket was deep in thought. 'Hmm? Oh, it means none of his filches or drabs will bother you or tip you any lays while you are in London. Or if they do, you'll have your money back the next morning and the taker of it in the Thames.'

'Who is he?'

'I told you. That was the King of London, the leader of the London thieves.'

'Ah. Um . . . how do you . . . er . . . ?'

'Used to work for him. Now I work for much worse men. Pickering at least is an honest thief and whoremaster and becoming very rich. His brother-in-law's the London hangman. If all goes well, his grandson could be a lord.'

Philip nodded, not at all sure what to think.

They ate in the small crowded hall at Seething Lane, paying for their meal with inordinately long prayers before and after, as Becket complained. A plump, complacent-looking man in a well-cut black suit came bustling up to Becket and began berating him for leaving him to deal with Van Groenig's corpse like that. Becket just stared

114

down at the man as if at a worm, waited pointedly until he had finished complaining, and then introduced him to Philip as Anthony Munday.

Coldness slid down Philip's back as he thought to himself, This man tortured my brother, and yet I cannot, for respectability, kill him or even hit him.

'Please be so good as not to arrest my brother by mistake, Mr Munday,' Becket said sourly and Munday flushed.

Philip as usual had his lodgings in Gray's Inn and so they went back there. He watched his brother as they drank malmsey by the fire. Becket was silent and morose, and drank his way steadily through what seemed to Philip to be at least a quart of malmsey without showing much effect. All attempts at conversation fell flat and Philip found himself regretting how much of a battered stranger David now was, wondering how much was left of the proud, open-hearted, quick-tempered, fighting-obsessed young man he had been.

He thought longingly of Eleanor all evening, for she would have known how to talk to David, could have drawn him out of his blank stare at the fire. What would she have said? he wondered. How would she have gentled the wounded bear that his brother had truly become? In the end, he was so lonely for her, he extravagantly spent a penny on a piece of paper and a pen and ink and wrote her a letter, telling her all about the mapmaker and how he had tried to say something and about the young man who had killed him and Becket's silence and thirst for booze. In the margin he drew pictures: of St Paul's, of a beggar, of the young man, if only to fix the killer's face in his own mind. He ended with his love to her and the children and added a postscript of how he thanked God for his good fortune in such a wife as he could write to in such terms.

He left it with the innkeeper to send to the carrier for Bristol to be dropped off at Middleton. Philip went to his bedroom soon after, weary with country habits, leaving Becket still sitting, still drinking, still staring at the fire. They were in separate rooms despite the expense, since Philip had discovered on the way to London that his brother snored even more loudly than his wife did.

Becket moaned, asleep in his chair.

*He was the Queen. Somewhere under the weirdness of the dream, he knew that he was no such thing, but in the way of dreams, he believed it. He was* the Queen of England, facing death and ruin in the thirtieth summer of her reign.

Before dawn the white-faced mud-spattered man had clattered under the Court Gate, shouting incoherently, and her women had come weeping to her, bringing him into her very chamber as she sat wrapped in the Tzar of Muscovy's sable dressing gown.

The rider smelled so strongly of male sweat, of fear and horses and mud and blood and gunpowder, she had nearly retched, but this was no time to demand sweet-scentedness of a man. He dropped with a thud to his knees in front of her and gasped for breath and she gripped the arms of her chair and waited for him to compose himself.

'Your Majesty,' he had said, with tears in his eyes, 'Your Majesty, the Spanish have taken Gravesend.'

'Gravesend,' she repeated.

The Earl of Essex had sent him. While the Lord Admiral Charles Howard of Effingham and Sir Francis Drake and their ragged, empty, stinking ships had finally been forced to refit and resupply in Portsmouth and Southampton, the mouth of the Thames had fallen to the Duke of Medina Sidonia. His galleases had rowed against the wind, their heavy guns had pounded the defences at Gravesend and one had cut the expensive chain of boats with its sharp, bronze beak. The Spanish soldiers had gone ashore in rowing boats and the town had fallen within two hours. On the other side of the Thames mouth, Tilbury Fort, full of soldiers and ordnance, had watched impotently as the fight rampaged and the town burned, for their bridge of boats was gone and they could not row across against the weight of ordnance in the four galleases.

It was well done. Drake, even sick as he was, would have been proud of the raid.

She had called her Privy Council to meet before breakfast, requiring the advice of men in the man's world of battle.

But in the way of men, her Council had crumpled. Some, like Burghley, had advised more negotiations with Spain, a truce. Surely, this was a feint. She had asked him to his face how much Philip of Spain was paying him and had he not earned enough from selling all her guns and powder? He had made noises in his throat, unable to answer.

Walsingham had predictably counselled the immediate murder of every Papist that could be found. The Earl of Leicester . . . He had been red in the face with rage and importance, he had begged, no, demanded to be sent out with the London trained bands and every man they could scrape up to fight Parma before he got to London.

Sir Walter Ralegh had held his silence until every other man had said *his say at least thrice. She had appointed him to the Privy Council pro tempora when the disaster began, against the alarm of Burghley. He, at least, did not disappoint her. When at last she called for his opinion, he had waited with dignity until the secondary arguments and spitting fits had died away amongst the learned and noble counsellors.*

'Your Majesty,' he said, softly and evenly, the only man among them not shouting, 'I advise your instant departure. Be very sure that Parma is bringing his best troops over as we speak, with every ship that will float. They will be on the road to London the day after tomorrow at the latest. London is unwalled and unmunitioned. It is not defensible. The trained bands are youths and striplings and not as well-armed as the least of Parma's cooks. No matter how brilliantly led,' with a bow to Leicester that could have been a compliment or the least tilting of an insult, 'they cannot stand against a properly led tercio. They will be trampled underfoot, or more likely they will break and run—'

'How dare you, sir!' roared Leicester. 'How dare you call the men of London cowards?'

'My advice to you, Most Gracious Majesty,' Ralegh continued unruffled, 'is to leave London now, waste no lives nor treasure defending it.'

She held up her hand for silence, knowing that he was right and yet his advice could not be followed. For reasons of politics, of expedience, the young men of London must spend their lives. While her heart clenched against her breastbone at the terrible waste of it, her stomach which she had said only weeks before was that of a King, knew and understood the necessity.

'My lord Earl of Leicester,' she said gently to her old friend, 'my lord, will you face Parma for me?'

Spontaneity was rare in the formal world of the Court. Leicester stood and planted his fists on the table. Underneath the silt of fat and pomposity, the young man she had loved stood proud. He smiled directly at her. She thought he might make some sort of speech about how he had longed all his life to serve her on the field of battle.

'Of course,' he said, and came round the table and knelt before her. 'Whatever can be done, I will do. And gladly.' For the first time in years, he spoke without bombast.

He knew as well, then. He understood.

'Give me your sword.'

He drew it and Burghley sucked in his breath disapprovingly: a naked blade in the presence of the sovereign was utterly forbidden, on pain of a traitor's death. Babbington had died for much less. But she had ordered Leicester to draw. She was making, as it were, a point.

She took the ornate weapon from him and held it, feeling the weight.

*Alas, she was too old now to learn the Art of Defence, even if David Becket had been available to teach her. Then, careful of her fingers on the oiled blade, she held it up cruciform in front of them all, brought it down and kissed the blade before giving it back to Leicester. He kissed the hand she held out to him, stood and strode from the room, holding his sword still unsheathed.*

*All her court understood the arts dramatical.*

*I killed my cousin, Mary Queen of Scots and now I am sending my best friend to his death, she thought, desolate.*

*She waved her hand to dismiss the councillors and they filed out, all except for Walsingham. He came up to her, full of fire and brimstone. 'Your Majesty,' he said urgently, 'The Papists must be rounded up and—'*

*'The Papists will spend the first week in shocked prayers after which they will rush to fight the filthy foreigners.'*

*'Those that are not fighting for them.'*

*Her patience snapped. She stood. 'Mr Secretary,' she shouted, weary to the core of his suspicious mind, 'I took your advice last year to execute my cousin the Queen of Scots, the which foolishness has now led to this invasion and may yet lead to our destruction. This is not armageddon, wherein Christ shall come to our reinforcement, leading the charge against Parma with mailed angels in serried rank behind him.' Walsingham flinched at her sarcasm. Yes, he had in fact genuinely thought that. 'This, Mr Secretary, is war between Princes, this is the English against the world and if you think above a hundred of my Catholic subjects shall deign to fight on Parma's behalf, you know your own people very little. Now, go send out your intelligencers to find me information of Parma and his strength and his movements, and later we may discuss at leisure wherefore we had no knowledge of this plot? What happened to Mr Anriques and his wife? Why did Howard have no powder and shot after the second day? And find me Mr David Becket if he is anywhere in London. Go!'*

*Finally, blinking with shock, Walsingham had the sense to bow and depart. She was left alone as she so rarely was, staring at the golden carved oak walls. At last she could allow the tears to spring into her eyes. She let them fall for the first and last time, unheeded. She would never allow such a womanish luxury again until the last Spaniard on her ground was dead.*

*Or, of course, until she was dead.*

Christ have mercy, he had tears in his eyes and the smell of rosewater in his nostrils. Becket had been sleeping slouched in front of the fire in the common room, and the curfew was over the coals, his neck was cricked and his back ached. What the devil was wrong with him? He had had no more attacks of the falling sickness but why were these dreams plaguing him? They had more sense in them than most dreams, they hung shining in his memory, parts of them made his heart beat like a drum. The Queen. He had dreamt that he was the Queen. Wasn't such a dream halfway to treason? Or madness?

He stood up, stretched and cracked his shoulder muscles, used the chamberpot, found his flask and finished what was in it, wished there was more because it was by no means enough to make him sleep. If he had not been in so respectable place as an Inn of Court, he might perhaps have found a drab to help him catch some sleep in her softness.

As it was, he stumbled heavily up the stairs to the bedroom Philip had taken for him, shucked his clothes and climbed in amongst the curtains and sheets while the bed-strapping creaked in protest. The dream was waiting, lying behind his eyelids, ready to pounce the minute he let go . . .

*Again he was the Queen, sitting sidesaddle on her horse as they came to the brow of Hampstead Hill. Sidesaddle! Never, by God, had he sat sidesaddle, he was no feeble woman and . . . Briefly he struggled with the dream, but it was too powerful.*

*The Queen reined in and paused, snuffed the air like a dog. Then she turned and spurred past the pond to the look-out point where the brazier on its pillar still smouldered, to gaze down unblinking into her City of London.*

*Not hers. Now it belonged to the Duke of Parma and to Spain.*

*A kind of growl came from it, very faint, borne on the winds that had carried Parma and his army across from Flanders. In the west smudged pillows of black smoke, in the east likewise. The wind carried the smell with it.*

*She took a deep breath and held it, let it out shakily. Beside her moved the Captain of her Guard, immaculate in red velvet and a buff coat, sitting his horse like a centaur, his lean face intent. By God, he was a good-looking man, was Ralegh.*

*The chief city of her realm groaned like a struck animal. She couldn't see it, wondered if she imagined that she could hear the fighting in its streets. Tears threatened again. She lifted her chin and ordered them back, watery troops she had no use for. There was a flash in the middle of the tumble of houses and then, after a strange suspended heartbeat, a low cracking boom that made her horse sidle and snort.*

'What was that?'

Ralegh smiled. 'Mr Becket blowing London Bridge, I believe. Let us pray that Parma was on it at the time.'

'Amen.'

Another flash, a sequence of booms like a giant playing drums. Smoke rose from the middle of the houses.

'Quite a firework display.'

'Something of the sort. I hope Mr Becket has used up all the powder in the Tower.'

'Why?'

'To frighten the Spaniards, to make them cautious, to deny them its use. Mr Becket had some excellent plans. I think Parma will take longer to possess himself of London than he expects.'

'Such destruction. Such waste of life.' Before she had finished saying them, she regretted the words, heavy though they lay on her heart.

Ralegh turned to her, his eyes blazing. 'Madam,' he said, 'may I speak my mind?'

And they could have been on a summer hunting expedition so fair was the weather: the trees whispered in the little coppice, although the Heath itself was bare from overgrazing.

She tilted her head in permission.

'Your Majesty has been a most wise, tender and merciful Prince in our happy realm of peace. But now we have crossed over the border into the land of war, as they have in Ireland, where the laws are different. Wisdom is still needed, but not tenderness and not mercy.'

'What happened to you in Ireland when you were young, Water?'

'I learnt the laws of the land of war.'

'And?'

'Why, at the age of sixteen I killed my first man, in a little skirmish somewhere in the Wicklow hills and puked my guts up for half an hour after. By the time I came home, I had lost count of the number of men I had killed, though I could remember every one of their faces, especially the six hundred Spanish prisoners I helped to massacre.'

She winced. His deep Devon burr was quite passionless as he spoke. 'Why did you kill them if they had surrendered?'

He showed his teeth. 'Because we could neither feed them nor guard them safely. I would do it again tomorrow.'

She waited.

'Your Majesty, there are no half-measures in war. If we fight the Spaniard, we must fight him until we win, no matter how much it costs or what is destroyed. If Whitehall burns, we can rebuild it. When men die, there will be others willing to fight. But only if we fight to win.'

'Water, answer me truthfully. Can we win, against Parma and his tercios, now?'

'Yes, Your Majesty, we can. He's a man like any other. But only if you will lead us, only if you will do as you said at Tilbury and again yesterday at St Paul's and be our Warrior Queen. If you have not the stomach for it, Madam, then let us save time and much blood and surrender. I myself will ride down to Parma with your terms, if you order it. I am your liegeman and I will do it.'

He was staring at her, not boldly, more than that. As if she were a man and he had just challenged her to a duel. Mind, it had pleased her to be called a Warrior Queen. Which, she knew, was why he had used the phrase. He understood her and she understood him.

Yesterday, or the day before, she thought it was, she had spoken just as Ralegh had. She had gone on horseback, wearing the white velvet and the silver gorget of Tilbury, her father's ruby-studded poniard on her belt, surrounded by her young men in red. The criers had announced her, the people of London had flocked to the place, terrified by rumour, by the panic at the Royal Exchange. For the King of Spain had now released the gift of a million gold ducats promised by the Pope, to be paid when Spanish troops set foot in England. Elizabeth's credit was gone to nothing. The rich merchants of London had been fleeing down to their ships with as much wealth as they could carry.

She had stood in the pulpit at the St Paul's preaching place, where no woman had stood before, and she had spoken to her people ex tempore, her voice lent wings by pure rage. She had told them the bald truth: Parma had landed, the trained bands under her beloved Earl would set out to stop them and with God's will, would do it. But if he lost the battle, then London would fall.

Never would she forget the sucked-in breath, the visceral groan. Only the fact that they knew her and knew she loved them had kept them quiet, still standing there.

She could not rightly remember what she had said: she had called for anything they could give her, their plate, their jewels, their money. Keep your weapons, she said, you shall need them. I have given Mr David Becket the Captainship of the Rearguard and as you love me, you shall do as he says. Those who would leave and have a place to go, gather up every horse, every cart, every bale of hay, every peck of flour, every herd from the fields, take everything north and west. She had paused for a beat, taken breath, words came to her from somewhere.

'Be sure that God is watching us and will be with us. Be sure that we will fight the Spaniard, I, Elizabeth, shall be your Captain and I myself shall fight him. We shall fight him wherever he goes. We shall fight him in the noonday and at midnight. When he lies down to sleep, we shall fight him and when he wakes to march, we shall fight him. Never ever will we give in.'

They had growled and the growl had turned into a cheer. She waited since there was more to say, and they fell silent. She had said, 'I know I have the body of a weak and feeble woman, but I have the heart and stomach of a King and a King of England too . . .' They had interrupted her with another cheer at that and she had held up her hand so she could continue, fury lifting the words into her mouth. 'Proud Parma shall most bitterly rue the day he entered upon this my realm of England. This shall be his grave and all his soldiers with him. For I am Queen under God of a mighty and valiant people and we shall prevail!'

By God, how they had roared and cheered for her, she had shaken with the power of their love and anger for her, so she had almost been lifted up by it. The ordinary people brought her cartloads of plate, barrels full of jewels, their sons to fight. And die.

But that was the day before yesterday and now she looked down the hill onto ruin and disaster. Parma was raping her land.

The red-clad men of her guard were close around her, so few, and starting to look nervous. After all, she knew she might have left it too late, that for all Mr Becket's soldierly skill, Parma would have sent the fastest riders he could find up the road to capture her. In the past three days she had sent her women by boat to Oxford with her older courtiers, all the treasure that was left and, God help her, Lord Treasurer Burghley to command them in her absence, in the certain knowledge that he would do absolutely nothing. He seemed a broken man, blinking and staring, quite abstracted. As well he might be, the treacherous bastard.

Ralegh was still staring at her. 'What of it, Your Majesty?' he asked softly. 'Shall we surrender?'

'I never thought to hear you say that.'

Ralegh did an extraordinary thing. He moved his horse close enough to put his hand on her arm. She felt the weight of it, heavy, more intimate than she was used to, bringing back memories of her youth.

'I wish to God I had been born twenty years earlier,' whispered Ralegh, 'for then . . . then I might have been your King and Parma would never have landed.'

She smiled at this outrageous insolence. 'Are you so sure you would have been my King?'

'Oh yes. Very sure.' Ralegh had bowled over her maids of honour like so many overdressed ninepins, perhaps he had a right to be sure. He smiled, more like a wolf than a lover. 'As for Leicester, I would have called him out over you, if need be, and killed him too. But you, Elizabeth, you I would have taken to my bed.'

He went too far, much, much too far, as he often did. Once she would have had him in the Tower for less.

But both of the other two men who had ever called her Elizabeth were dead: one by execution when she was fifteen; the other, Leicester, now lay on a field near Dartford, perhaps the crows had had his eyes already. Unless Parma had put his head on a pole to frighten her with. They said he had died well, after a disastrously stupid piece of generalship had trapped his men between the Spaniards and the River Dart. She had heard that when the trained bands of London ran in horror from the musketry and ordnance of the tercios of Lombardy, he had roared and thrashed about him with his sword, trying to get them to stand, until a better aimed ball knocked him off his horse and completed the rout.

Leicester, unlike Ralegh, had been a stupid man.

Elizabeth smiled at the Captain of her Guard. I am fifty-five and will never have a child. 'Water,' she said, still softly, 'why do you think I sent my lord of Leicester out to fight Parma?'

'I had believed it was because you did not like my advice.'

'Your military advice was the best. But I know more than that. I sent Leicester to fight and die to get him safely martyred and to wake the English up. And he did gain us an extra day. Do you think I wanted him as my General in Chief? Good God, man, I had rather have Will Kemp. Now, will you be my General?'

His eyes darkened and his hand on her arm gripped tight enough to hurt. 'Yes, Elizabeth.'

'I too understand the laws of the land of war,' she said as she disengaged him and turned her horse away from the lost world of London. Then she checked and turned again, to look one more time.

God knows, I will have Parma's guts. He shall be defeated by a mere heretic woman and every last Spaniard in this my blessed land shall die.

Ralegh watched, concerned. The men of her guard also looked, their eyes whitened by a fear that none of them could admit. Ah, they were worried because her lips had drawn back from her teeth in a visceral and unbecoming snarl.

Elizabeth stripped off her left glove and held it up so they could see it, then flung it down the hill towards London. The defiance made them blink.

In the morning, Becket sat by the window holding his head and staring out at the flood of people walking up Gray's Inn Lane to the farms and fields and market gardens where they worked. It was certain sure he was mad. To be having such dreams, to believe in his sleep that he was the Queen – well, he supposed some might find it funny but he did not. He wished he could talk to his friend Simon about it, who might have some ingenious explanation for him, composed of Cabbala and Euclid, no doubt, with a sprinkling of Lucretius.

Thank God, some of it was fading now. He could return to his more familiar worries about the repercussions from the various reports he had made and delivered: Burghley's idiocy and perfidy in still selling ordnance abroad; Piers Lammett's information; the death of Van Groenig the mapmaker. Dread sat in the pit of his belly like a squat ugly toad, refusing to leave. Everything he did required double effort, not just against weariness and aqua vitae, but against the feeling that it was all completely hopeless. To become a prophet, to see the world as it would be in fire and blood when Parma had landed . . . Why? Why should he have such dreams and not the Queen herself, for Christ's sake, why couldn't she have the bloody things and not him? He had enough to contend with in just living. The last thing he wanted was to live another nocturnal life as the Queen of England, nor yet her bloody Captain. Although he did think he would make a good fist at such an office, but still . . .

He rubbed his eyes, groaned and gulped his first drink of the day. Half an hour later he sat at table with his brother, munching tasteless manchet bread and cheese for breakfast. A boy came with a letter for him. Philip was trying to make light conversation about the prospects for planting apricots along the south-facing wall of the house and how Eleanor was set upon it if he could but get the plants and he had heard that my lord Burghley . . .

Dr Nunez had invited them to dinner. Like most things, the invitation filled him with forboding, but Philip was interested and honoured at being bidden to the table of the Earl of Leicester's own physician. They spent the morning viewing Becket's property in Hanging Sword Court and Philip's lawyer, Peregrine Howard, murmured that he had heard that one of the Queen's greatest courtiers might be interested in making a purchase if the right price could be agreed . . . Then they strolled sightseeing along Cheapside, past the goldsmiths' windows, while Becket fought his ghostly impressions of Spanish troops marching in triumph down the centre of it. Philip was delighted with all of it, as ever.

They both knew there had been some kind of catastrophe as soon as they entered the Nunez house in Poor Jewry. Leonora Nunez had clearly been crying, the servants were scurrying about looking grim and when Dr Nunez came to welcome them, his face was drawn as if he had not had a good night's sleep for a week.

Becket took his hand. 'What's happened, Doctor?' he asked, low and urgent.

'It's Simon,' said Nunez simply. 'We have had news of him at last.'

'Not shipwrecked?'

Nunez shook his head. 'Worse than shipwrecked,' he said.

What was worse than that? Becket was about to ask when Nunez noticed Philip and collected himself, was introduced, they made their bows and Philip continued looking about himself with wonder at the richness of the house and its indefinable air of foreignness. It was not only from the complex Turkey rugs on the walls and the plate on display and the finely tiled floors with not a trace of rushes, but even the smell was somehow foreign. He tried to hide his wonder as best he could, almost as impressed at the way Becket seemed to know the reverend doctor.

Nunez showed them into a parlour where a woman sat all in black, her face hidden by a black veil, and next to her stood the most extraordinary large Negress, looming as tall as Becket himself, wearing a man's tawny suit with the doublet straining open under the pressure from her magnificent breasts, a man's hat with a feather on her woolly head and a very businesslike shortsword on her belt. Her arms were folded and she gave back stare for stare as if she were very amused by them. Philip felt his mouth drop open and was a little comforted that Becket was staring too.

'Gentlemen, may I present Mrs Rebecca Anriques, my nephew's wife.'

Becket set his jaw and sat down heavily at the parlour table, rested his forearms on the finely worked pink and grey silk rug laid on it, clasped his hands. Simon's wife was clearly in mourning. Nunez sighed and sat opposite, Philipp drew up one of the stools.

'Mr Becket ... I shall begin at the beginning,' said Dr Nunez sadly. 'Late last summer my nephew Simon went to the Slave Coast with iron, cloth and some guns and there bought slaves.'

No movement from the Negress at all, though presumably this

was where she had come from. Philip was having terrible trouble keeping his eyes from a woman wearing breeches like a man, but Becket was intent on the doctor.

'From there he went to Cartagena in New Spain and loaded sugar. Thence, after Christmas, he travelled to Lisbon. And at Lisbon—'

'He was taken by the Inquisition?' interrupted Becket hollowly. The doctor nodded.

There was a short, flat silence while Philip looked from one to another, trying to be as serious as they were and all the time thinking how strange to be only a few days from Middleton and speaking of the Inquisition, of New Spain, looking at a Negress in breeches . . .

'Is there anything we can do?' Becket asked. 'Can he be bought out?'

'In normal times, yes,' said Nunez, 'with the Queen's help, which she would give, of course.'

'Of course.'

'It's possible that if they have finished interrogating him, they might relax him to the secular arm and in these times of war, he might then be sentenced to hard labour and then we might be able . . .'

Becket sat back, utterly appalled. Unconsciously he was rubbing the scars on his wrists. Simon, with his arms like reeds and his legs like willow twigs, put to the question, sentenced to hard labour? Impossible. It would kill him for certain. Probably already had.

'Oh Doctor. Mrs Ames . . . um . . . Anriques.' He didn't know what to say, how to tell them of the sorrow filling his heart. Poor Simon. He was brave, a great deal tougher then he looked, Jesus, it would be so hard for him. He turned to the veiled woman. 'Mistress, if there is anything I can . . . if I may serve . . .' He paused, swallowed hard, spoke more firmly. 'If it were not for your husband, Mrs Anriques, I would have died last year. I am sure Dr Nunez is far more able than I am in anything of this kind, but if there is any service I may do you, please only say so.'

Mrs Anriques tilted her head graciously. 'Thank you, Mr Becket,'' she said and her voice was quite calm. 'My husband spoke often of you and his respect for your courage and abilities and his pleasure in your friendship. I am sure that you will be able to help me.'

'How?'

'Perhaps we should wait,' said Nunez with a warning sound in his voice.

'What do you have in mind, Doctor?'

'Not I, it is none of my devising, indeed, I think very little of the scheme, but . . . no. I will wait to hear your decision. Mistress de Paris will be here to conduct you to a . . . meeting.'

'Thomasina?' Becket smiled. 'And how is she?'

'Much as usual. She seems not to age at all. I would give a great deal to know if she has ever had her menses, but . . .'

It was a determined change of subject and Becket went with it. Philip could hardly believe his ears at such talk. The whole thing was too strange to imagine. He would spend two pennies on paper and write a very long letter to Eleanor tonight. Good Lord, he had never even seen a Negro before and now here was one standing near enough to touch, and a woman wearing men's clothes as well. Were the blacks reversed? Perhaps their men were the weak and gentle ones and their women the ones who fought? Certainly, looking her over, Philip felt he would prefer not to fight the Negress. Did she speak English? Could she talk? Did she have a tail? What was she thinking as she stood there impassively by her mistress with her arms folded?

He stared as frankly as a boy without the least idea of what he was doing, until the Negress caught his eye and winked at him.

He blushed beetroot colour and looked away. Mistress Nunez came to join them, followed by servants carrying silver dishes full of delicious-smelling food, lamb in saffron, salt beef with mustard sauce, potherbs and little pasties full of new cheese. The wine was excellent too. Philip concentrated on drinking and eating as much as he could while the conversation passed to the likely composition of the Spanish Enterprise against England and the ladies spoke quietly in a foreign language Philip supposed to be Portuguese.

Nunez had a new book that he invited Becket to look at and when Philip looked as well, he realised it was in foreign. Becket could read it and said that it was published by the King of Spain for to frighten the English. It was an account of the composition of the Invincible Armada; lists of ships and their tonnage along with armaments and men.

Becket turned the pages quickly, grunting to himself. 'One hundred and fifty ships including the galleys, which will sink. They must have scraped up every hulk in Spain and Portugal. They are short of ordnance like us, it seems,' he said. 'And look at all the soldiers they're boasting of. They'll have trouble watering that lot.'

'We had word recently that the Duke of Parma has taken the mouth of the Rhine and it's true that Admiral Santa Cruz died last month.'

'It's true?' Becket boomed a grim laugh. 'Why, that's wonderful. Best news I've heard for a long time. Who will command instead?'

'I would imagine that the Duke of Medina Sidonia is the only grandee senior enough with the right experience, if he can be got to take the office. He is said to be very timid.'

'Medina Sidonia.' Becket's face had fallen. 'Damn.'

'Why? What have you heard of him?'

Becket shook his head. 'He may not be as timid as all that. And Parma has Sluys.'

'He has built canals for the barges. Meanwhile, my lord Burghley tells me he is certain sure that all of this is simply to bring the Queen to terms by frightening her.'

Becket hooted with ugly laughter. 'Oh ay, no doubt. He's hoping not to face the choice of hearing Mass or burning.'

'So you are quite satisfied they are in earnest?'

'What? That the King of Spain intends to invade? Oh yes. With the cost of it, the men, the prestige . . . Parma will have lost a year's campaigning against the Netherlanders for this. Believe me. They mean to take us.'

'So I had thought, but my lord Burghley is very persuasive.'

'Don't listen to the old nanny goat, listen to Ralegh. There's a man who knows war.'

Philip was shocked at such disrespectful gossiping about the Queen's counsellors.

Nunez fingered his curly beard and nodded. 'Ralegh is on fire to go to sea.'

'She'll never let him.'

Philip noticed that a richly dressed child had come into the room, but that instead of waiting to be noticed or curtseying to the adults, she marched straight up to where Nunez sat and tapped him on the shoulder.

And Nunez made an obeisance to her, which she returned with aplomb, before smiling at Becket who kissed her hand as if she were a lady.

Philip rubbed his eyes, tried not to stare again. Becket grinned and introduced her. 'Mistress Thomasina de Paris, the Queen's Fool.'

Was she ...? Good God, was she a muliercula, a miniature woman? Philip had heard of such things but never seen one. Yes, there were faint crow's feet on either side of her eyes, frown lines between her eyebrows. She was polite, but refused to sit with them and instead whisked Becket, Mrs Ames and her Negress away with her, leaving Philip very much alone among these strange foreigners who were his brother's friends, who were kind enough to him and tried to talk to him, but were so utterly alien he could think of nothing to say.

At last he made his excuses and since Becket had not returned, they sent a boy with him to guide him back to the Inns of Court. And when he got there, he found a message for a Mr Becket, very urgent. Naturally he opened it, only to find that Mr Pickering sent his compliments and the man Mr Becket sought was about to leave the Pool of London on the ebb tide that night, sailing on the *Fortune of Lubeck*.

The Queen's Mews was a building in its own right, fitly made of stone, at the back of the enormous busy stables at Charing Cross that served the Court and mounted all the Queen's messengers. Thomasina had brought them in by a back route that skirted the smoking kilns at Scotland Yard, sharing a litter with Mrs Anriques and leaning out of it to shout directions at the sweating bearers. The Negress paced easily and silently behind the litter.

At a back gate opened by a silent man in green, Thomasina vaulted down and Mrs Ames was helped out by her woman. Then they crossed courtyards, climbed stairs and waited in a room that smelled like a chicken coop, being blindly observed by rows of hooded and unhooded hunting birds sitting on their perches, the jingle of their jesses like a very small dance.

There was the sound of footsteps, of talk and laughter, and Becket suddenly found the black and ugly toad in his belly urging him to go, go now, this was his last chance.

'Who are we meeting, Thomasina?' he demanded again.

'Hush,' she said, impish with mischief. 'Who do you think?'

A horrible suspicion dawned fully. 'What? Why the devil didn't you tell me? At least I could have changed my shirt.'

'Oh stuff,' said Thomasina with a grin. 'Why do you think I suggested the mews, Becket? I know you.'

Becket gave her a look that was all the dirtier for her being completely right.

He had never met the woman who came sauntering through the door at her ease, wearing a forest green hunting dress with a doublet-bodice and scenes of stag-hunting on the false front of her petticoat, a small cage of pearls, emeralds and diamonds lighting up her curly red wig and causing the nearest unhooded falcons to eye it with thoughtful greed. She rested on the arm of a chestnut-haired young man also in forest green, whose face bore a distinct family resemblance to hers, and the Royal Falconer led them, pompously discoursing about new hoods in the French style.

Becket went to his knees, heart thundering, trying not to think of all the things he knew about this woman, which she would certainly have him beheaded rather than so much as breathe.

Christ! I've still got my hat on, he thought suddenly and clutched it off his head, wishing devoutly that he had been to a barber recently, wondered if he should stand, go forward, stay where he was . . . He never wanted to meet the Queen, damn it! What was Thomasina thinking of? He was no scented, prinked-up courtier like whatsisname over there, holding out his arm for the Queen so prettily. Come to think of it, hadn't he taught the boy some swordplay? Yes, he had. In fact, he wasn't bad: short temper, tendency to attack without thinking, but quick on his feet and able to plan while he fought. Robert something . . . Robert Carey. One of Lord Chamberlain Hunsdon's many sons. Memory stirred uncomfortably. Carey's name had been in his dreams.

And had he just put his right knee on a bird's turd?

The Queen smiled at Carey. 'Now, Robin,' she said, 'do as I told you.'

One elegant eyebrow up, the courtier escorted the Royal Falconer back to the door and out before the man had a chance to protest. Then he bowed, backed and shut the door after himself. One of the birds bated, blinking fiercely at the shiny stuff on the Queen's head. They were alone with the Queen of England.

Thomasina curtseyed. 'Your Majesty,' she said, 'may I present Mr David Becket, of Mr Secretary Walsingham's service. Mrs Anriques you already know, of course.'

The Queen rustled forwards and Becket found he was looking at the pointed end of her stomacher, which had a fan hanging from it and an enamelled jewel of a white hart. Where was the jewelled poniard, then? Oh no, that was in his dream. He swallowed hard in a completely dry throat, not at all helped by the suffocating smell of bird. A long, white hand heavy with rings appeared in his vision and he remembered just enough of his manners to take it and kiss it.

'For God's sake, man, get off your knees. No one can think down there. Come on, up.'

He climbed to his feet, longing to dust off the one that would have a smear of white on it.

'Give me your hands.' Hesitation, a long time, that phrase still had the power to clench his belly, chill his neck. At last he did so, put them in her long white fingers as if swearing allegiance to her in the old way. She held his paws lightly, only the tips of her long cold fingers, turned them over like a mother examining for dirty nails (which his were, where not bitten down to the quick), pushed back his grimy lace cuffs. She paused, hissed in her breath at the sight of the scars on his wrists. It came to him that she probably had never before seen the results of her servants' work. By God, he'd better not take his shirt off then, she might faint dead away. At least one young whore had, which the older ones had found immensely funny.

'Are you recovered of your stay in the Tower, Mr Becket?'

'Ah . . . yes, Your Majesty.'

'Really?'

'Don't lie to her,' hissed Thomasina at his elbow as she stood on his toe.

'Um . . . no, Your Majesty.'

She simply waited in silence for him to go on, still holding his hands in hers. He struggled against yet another ludicrous great lump in his throat.

'My back is stiff, Your Majesty, and my shoulders catch now and then, and my left shoulder was put out when I fell off my horse last month . . .' It had hurt so badly he was sure it was broken, until he managed to ride to the next town and find a horse-doctor who used a couple of straps and a knee to get his joint back in again, a crescendo of pain and then sudden relief so blessed it almost made him faint.

She was still listening, her head cocked slightly to the side and the hanging diamonds on her hair-decoration trembling. He swallowed.

'. . . but it's my grip that's been worst hurt. The other is only natural. But I cannot firmly hold a sword any longer although at least I can make a fist . . .'

She looked down suddenly and he found he had done it without intending to.

'Mr Becket,' the Queen said softly, 'this was done to you in our name and in the name of our policy, to our continued regret and sorrow. To *my* regret and sorrow. We have as you know, chastised that man Davison who so ill-used you, and we have seen to it that no such mistake shall be made with you again.'

Becket ducked his head, blinking, thinking that apologies, even royal apologies, were all very well. They hardly mended broken grips.

'Know that we are much in your debt, Mr Becket, which is not a thing lightly said by princes.'

For the first time, Becket lifted his shaggy head and stared straight into her eyes. Yes, by God, Madam, he thought, you *are* in my debt. So what dramatic piece of heroism have you in mind to kill me off safely, hmm?

'After all,' said the Queen, speaking more lightly, 'we have not yet thanked you personally for your efforts in our behalf last year.'

'Your Majesty . . .' Becket tried to think what to say and had just settled on something suitably modest when the Queen swept on.

'We are also delighted at your discretion in all matters of state.'

Yes there had been the faintest hint of an accent on the word 'all' so Becket decided he would stay silent now until she asked him a direct question.

'Mr Becket, we are not so overpressed with able servants that we can afford to ignore your abilities. We have therefore approved a gift from the Privy Purse, in earnest of our thankfulness, of lands to the value of one hundred pounds per annum.'

Now he had to say something. 'Your Majesty is very kind and generous,' he stammered, stunned at how fortunes could turn. With that and the rents on the Whitefriars property, he would be rich if he could just stay away from Pickering's card games. And the booze and women of course.

'Thomasina shall see to it. Now this is a gift and for services already rendered in our service. Not to mention what you have done personally for me.' She paused significantly. 'I know you have been sorely hurt in my service and so I will not order this. But if you feel you are able, we have another request to make of you, Mr Becket.'

Here it comes, said the black toad in Becket's belly, here is the thing that will kill you. And you could have been a lord.

She let go his hands, stepped back a little. He loomed over her since she was only medium-sized for a woman. She smiled up at him, a most charming smile, despite the fact that she was certainly over fifty and her teeth were brown.

Becket found himself smiling back at her, caught by the wicked gleam in her fine eyes. The thought came to him unbidden that every man in the kingdom must have been a catamite to let her go unbedded and unwed in her youth. Well, unwed at any rate.

'Come,' she said, and he found that she had taken his arm and was moving them past the rows of falcons to the other end of the room, the other two women following silently. Thomasina trotted with them, her old-young face impassive.

At the end of the room, the falcons could not decide whom to watch, the woman with the shiny interesting stuff on her, or the little one with shiny stuff or the big man. The other two women were not interesting. None of them had food, so most of the birds settled on watching the door carefully for their friend and feeder, the Falconer.

In the corner, by a rack full of delicately worked little leather hoods, each hanging on a hook labelled with a bird's name, the Queen turned to face Becket. 'I understand you are a clerk of the Ordnance at the moment.'

'Yes, Your Majesty.'

'I received your information about my lord Burghley from one source, but not the other, which I find interesting although not surprising.'

Becket nodded cynically. 'Ay,' he said, 'I thought that might amuse you . . . Majesty.'

'Well, so it did. And I like your thinking behind it. The other information . . . I have no idea what kind of credence to place in it. This man called "Smith" – is he a friend of yours?'

'In a manner of speaking, Your Majesty. I met him once when I was serving Sir Philip Sidney. I believe his real name is Lammett, the son of an old friend of my father's. To be sure he is a Catholic, but he is an Englishman first. It was he first warned me of a . . . of the wicked libel against yourself.'

'Ah.' There was a world of chilly reminiscence and warning in that vowel.

Becket shifted his feet, wondering how she could make him sweat just by looking at him. And it wasn't just her regal power, it was in her eyes. He looked down.

'So perhaps we should listen to him?' she said.

'I think so, except for the vagueness. A third part to Parma's plan, a Miracle of Beauty? Not much there.'

'Might it have anything to do with the four galleases Mr Ames was investigating for me?'

'Of course it might. Anything might.'

'What would you use a galleas for?'

'I don't know, Majesty, I have never seen one. And Ames in any case is . . . is lost.'

Her lips tightened. 'I had heard. Now, Mr Becket, the thing I am about to ask of you is no easier or safer service than Ames's, I fear, although it may give you a chance to find out what happened to him.'

By falling into the clutches of the Inquisition myself, no doubt, Madam, Becket thought but didn't say.

'We are proposing to become even more indebted to you, in a matter of great urgency, touching the safety of the kingdom. It may be that if all goes well we shall eventually owe you not only our life, not merely our reputation but our very throne.' She turned her formal words with relish, as pleased with them as a poet, then leaned forward. 'To be bald with you, Mr Becket, you may be killed or taken, I fear.'

So do I, Madam, you have no notion how I fear. The black toad was self-satisfied, justified, its dire predictions vindicated.

She glanced at Rebecca, still standing, head bowed, hands clasped, her black woman looming at her shoulder. 'Will I explain your plan to Mr Becket, Mrs Anriques?'

Simon's widow curtseyed. 'If you please, Your Majesty. I am not good at explanations.'

Becket listened, not quite believing his own ears, as the Queen laid out to him the crazy, half-witted plan she had invented.

Rebecca had suggested that in order to make search of her husband, she should take a ship with a cargo of supplies to Lisbon, to give her countenance, perhaps cheeses or hides or rope. Once in the Spanish harbour, it would no doubt be impounded but she would at least be in Spain, in the place where she had last had sight of her husband, and with the names and money she would bring, might be able to find him.

But the Queen had taken this little plan, which needed her permission, and from it she had made a veritable Trojan horse.

'Guns?' said Becket heavily, breaking etiquette by interrupting the Queen, but needing to be sure he had heard right. 'You want me to take *guns* to the Spaniards and instruct them in gunnery?'

'Yes, Mr Becket,' said the Queen.

'But . . . will they be faulty?'

'Some may, most will not. They are already bought and paid for by the Spanish, as you know, so they will be expecting them.'

'But—'

'Mr Becket, hear me out!' rapped the Queen and Becket fell silent again, glaring at the floor. 'You shall take Mrs Anriques' ship, loaded with the guns of the latest shipment, but no powder of course, for of that we have very little. Guns are not our worst problem, Mr Becket, for all Drake's fretting, we make more than all the Spaniards, Frogs and Butter-eaters do put together. It is powder and shot we lack, principally powder. In any case, you shall be taking the smaller weaponry with less throwing power. When you have brought the guns to the Duke of Medina Sidonia, you, Mr Becket shall use every art in your power to find out the truth of this third part of the Armada plan, this so-called Miracle of Beauty.'

Becket's jaw dropped. He tried to take a breath. 'You want *me* to join the Armada?'

'Yes, Mr Becket. For two excellent reasons. Firstly, so that you may harm and confuse their gunnery and ordnance, and secondly so that you can enquire as to the Miracle of Beauty and when you have found it out, you must find a way to tell my lord Admiral Howard of Effingham.'

Becket stood there, utterly at a loss.

'I have spoken privily with my Lord Treasurer Burghley and with . . . others who will be necessary for the matter. To be short, even if you cannot find out about the plan, I desire you to be my eyes and ears in the Armada. The guns are already sold by my Lord Treasurer, so they will be expected, and you will sail first to Flanders and then to Lisbon to join the Spanish fleet. You shall claim you are from Flanders and there will be papers to prove it. They will welcome you with open arms, for they greatly desire more guns. Further, they are even shorter of gunners than of guns and so if you present yourself as a gunner, they will certainly take you with them.'

Find it out . . . find a way . . . What did she think he was? Jesus bloody Christ, to walk on water and deliver a letter to the *Ark Royal*?

'To which end, Mrs Anriques and her woman shall go with you, since it is Mrs Anriques' ship.'

'*What?*'

'Mrs Anriques is giving me a ship for this matter and she has said that since she desires to go to Lisbon to find out what she can about her husband, she intends to go with you.'

'Impossible. Insane even to think of it, the Armada is no place—'

'I have no intention of joining the Armada, Mr Becket,' said the voice of Rebecca behind her veil. 'My intention is to find my husband. Besides, the Queen desires him rescued from the Inquisition as much as I do . . .'

Becket was rocking with shock and dismay. A *woman*? In a matter like this? Never!

'. . . and if you have any success at all in discovering this mysterious Miracle of Beauty, well, then I may also be the means of bringing it home.'

Becket had the sense of walking across a bridge that had no beginning or end but was suspended on a silken spider's web of feminine devices. The Queen looked at him quite as coldly as the falcons, as did Thomasina, Rebecca and the Negress.

'Have I any choice?' he asked bitterly.

'Of course you do, Mr Becket,' said the Queen with asperity. 'I told you that if you do not feel able for this matter, then Mrs Anriques and Thomasina shall conduct it themselves.'

'Thomasina as well?'

'Certainly.'

'But . . . but I . . . but it's dangerous. The Inquisition . . .'

The Queen smiled at him kindly. 'Mr Becket, the Inquisition make no distinction of man or woman in these things and so nor do I. Moreover, while I do not believe that women should have any place in high policy, which are reserved only to Princes, this is a most pious and proper thing for any wife to do, to search out and find whether her husband be dead or no.'

'Mrs Anriques, I'm sorry, but surely . . . surely Simon is dead.'

The veiled head tilted slightly. 'He may be,' said Rebecca coldly, 'but I intend to be certain. And if he is not dead, then I intend to free him by whatever means there are.'

'It will do him no good if his wife is hanged up and tortured next to him.'

There was an intake of breath as if he had slapped her, as in a way he had. And intended it. He had never heard such madness.

'Enough, Mr Becket,' said the Queen. 'I know you mean nothing but chivalry yet there is in fact only one thing for you to decide – whether you shall be party to this enterprise or no. In a way, this is a fishing expedition. I am setting a sprat to catch a mackerel, or perhaps a shark to catch Leviathan. And there may be no answer to the riddle of the miracle, or you may fail in finding it or—'

'Or I may be caught and put to the question.'

'Certainly you may, Mr Becket,' said the Queen in a more gentle voice, 'which is why we do not order this of you. I ask it, only ask.'

I kept silence when they hanged me up in the Tower, my memory hid itself, *she thinks me torture-proof.* Oh Christ.

'Why me?' It was like a child's complaint, he was embarrassed by it.

'Who else is there? And why not you, Mr Becket? You are a man of courage and integrity, of determination and quick thought.'

I am not torture-proof, he thought, but didn't say. No one is. Believe me.

'I have many who wish to serve me, Mr Becket, but very few as seasoned and as apt to this task as you. None, I think. Will you do it?'

She had said nothing of reward, which question hung in the air along with the chicken-coop choke nonetheless. But certainly, no man will put his head in the lion's mouth for mere pay. There must be something else.

He looked slowly at the small erect figure of Simon's valiant little widow. 'Must she come?'

'It is her ship.'

He sighed. 'It will be hard enough to do without that I must protect my friend's wife as well.'

Mrs Anriques made an impatient 'tchah!' noise for no reason Becket could see.

The Queen smiled and pounced. 'But you will do it?'

They waited for him, all watching him, while his thoughts scattered in all directions and he found himself wondering in a dishevelled fashion which Greek king it was got himself ripped apart by Maenads and if these women had looked like them.

He shut his mouth, coughed bird-smell. His hands clasped themselves together and pressed until his fingers were white and he watched their antics as if they didn't belong to him. He wanted to ask if they couldn't find anyone else, and of course he knew they couldn't. Could Munday do such a thing? Never. None other of

Walsingham's followers knew as much as he did or understood half of what he did.

Simon would do as much for him, he knew that. And how could he let his friend's wife go foolishly into such danger without a man to guide her? And insane though the plan was, it was the sort of insanity that did in fact sometimes work. He bowed to the Queen and the implacable Furies around her.

'Yes, Your Majesty,' he said with as much flourish as he could muster. 'I will be part of this enterprise.'

He got back to the inn late, his head still whirling and found no Philip waiting for him, only a couple of messages. One was from Pickering, which had been opened, no doubt by Philip who was also called Mr Becket. The other was from Philip himself.

Brother
    I have sent a note to Mr Secretary Walsingham at Seething Lane and another to Dr Nunez, but as I have waited an hour and the tide is about to turn, I have gone down to the Pool to find the man.
    Your loving brother
    Philip

Becket hired a horse and galloped like a madman to Seething Lane to demand what the devil had happened, to discover they had only just received the message sent by Philip because the innkeeper's boy carrying it had got involved in a football match. He went down to the Pool of London with the Watch, Munday and a troop of men, to find that the *Fortune of Lubeck* had weighed anchor and warped out of the Pool on the ebb tide about an hour before he had ever seen the message.

Philip was nowhere to be seen.

Becket marched up and down the dock, questioning the anchor watch on the two ships either side of the *Fortune*. Yes, there had been a scuffle, but nobody had been very interested, this being the Pool of London. Oh it was over there, sir, the fight, behind the bales. Over quickly, yes. No, nobody dragged away.

Sick with fear, Becket went to the bales, poked behind them, circled them, backed and nearly tripped on something hard and soft together.

Munday came at the run when he heard Becket's roar of anguish, to find him bent over the still shape of a man who had been stabbed in the eye.

# Edward Dormer

Pull back, up and up, out of the London docks, into the smoky sky, and step sideways and a little back across the map of time, so that we may examine another part of it, another thread in our tapestry.

Here he is, young, rawboned, kneeling with his fellows in the little Chapel of the Jesuit English Seminary at Rheims in northern France, hearing Mass as he does every day. Nowadays we would call him a traitor, plain and simple. To himself, however, he is only a servant of a higher and nobler cause than a mere country or Queen. He is a true son of the one true Church and the greatest service he could give his country would be to help convert all the people back to Catholicism and so save them from Hell. He does believe that without the Catholic church, all of the English are doomed to Hell. There are no colours in his moral universe, only simple black and white.

Edward Dormer is an ungrown seed, a young Englishman struggling with all his heart to be a priest but in fact, on this cold wintry morning with no signs yet of spring, he is sinfully far away from the Sacrament. He is dreaming of battle and blood and victory.

*Pushed skimming over the waves by the oars, the longboats drove in towards the sandy English beach. Sunlight caught the frothing tips of the waves and made small rainbows in the spray. Behind them the cannon roared over the water at the cheeky little English ships, battering their hulls and murdering their men. Starved of ordnance by their penny-pinching Witch-Queen, the English had neither shot nor powder left to fight.*

*The men in the longboats kept their heads low, some clutching rosaries and muttering Salve Marias and Pater Nosters over and over to themselves. Others drank from hipflasks. One or two were voiding their guts over the side. Musket fire sputtered from the beach and even some ridiculously old-fashioned arrows, which buried themselves in the wood of the boats.*

*Edward Dormer carefully lit the fuse of a grenado with the slowmatch of his pistol, waited while the saltpetre sputtered into life, then stood and threw it overarm. It burst perfectly in the air, scattering nails and flints among the waiting English soldiers on the beach, scything ragged gaps in their ranks. In that second their boat grounded on sand.*

*Dormer leaped over the side into the freezing water, staggered as the weight of his cuirass and morion helmet almost pulled him down, then gasping and lurching, ran through the red waves up onto the beach. Behind him his men followed with shouts of Jesu and Santa Maria, the holy patroness of the invasion. Dormer's boots crunched in sand and shale. He dropped to one knee, fired his pistol and saw the red flower in the chest of a noble English lord. Bullets and arrows flung themselves harmlessly past him, maybe one or two of his men were down – but only the sinners, only the scoffers and drinkers, the men who were there for money and power. God spared the good soldiers, those who truly believed in the crusade, like him.*

*And then Dormer led the charge onto his native soil, sword flashing in the sun, cutting down the miserable common bowmen, slicing open the heretics who were staring in horror at the realisation that yet again, England was being conquered.*

*More troops came ashore as the longboats flung themselves in towards the sand. The tercio soldiers, the best troops in Europe, formed themselves into lines behind him and began setting up a terrible withering fire at the heretics, still shooting at them cowardly-fashion from the dunes. One fell, another fell, and the heretics ran again. They were withdrawing from the field, leaving Edward Dormer at the crest of the dunes, breathless, his morion shining the sun, blood on his sword. The beach-head had been taken for the King of Spain, for Holy Mother Church.*

*Dropping devoutly to his knees where he was, Edward Dormer raised his voice clear and strong in a Te Deum, followed by the ringing bronze response of his men, who knelt likewise among the blood and bodies of their fallen . . .*

'Vere dignum et . . . Snnnfff . . . justum est aequum et salutare . . . Snnnfff . . . nos tibi semper et ubique gratias agere . . . Snnnfffle harumph!'

Edward Dormer was jerked back to the present by his belly rumbling and cramping under his breastbone. He realised with black depression that he had just daydreamed his way through the Canon of the Mass and had yet another sin to report to his confessor.

He struggled to bring his mind back to God, to speak the Pater Noster properly, the words that the Saviour, and Captain of their Society, had given, in the very same words he had said, reverberating down through fifteen centuries freighted with holiness and power . . .

The words jumbled and turned themselves to mockery. His boredom was extreme, a physical pain. The celebrant had a head cold and snorted constantly, the patten, ciborium and chalice glittered but the little church was icy, the black soutane Edward was wearing was third-hand and very threadbare, and the ominous smell of cabbage soup was already insinuating oily, quotidian fingers between the drifts of incense.

Then a voice in his head, so loud Edward looked around to see who had spoken. *You are not priestly material, my son.*

Nobody had said anything, the voice was inside Edward's skull. Was he going mad? Had God spoken? Surely not, surely God would confirm the thing he had worked so hard for all his life. After all, he ought to be used to threadbare magnificence and cabbage soup by now, both had been staples of his family life before the Seminary. And he was the priest, the one destined to go abroad and be ordained, leaving their impoverished lands near Worcester in the capable hands of his practical older brother. He was the one whose life work it would be to pray for his elder brothers and sisters, forced by the evil Witch-Queen's laws to pretend to her heretical mummery of a religion. It was what he had prepared for all his young life . . .

*You are bored*, protested the voice. *You hate it all. You want a woman. You want to fight someone. You hate using the discipline. You hate hairshirts. You would die for Me if you must, but not as a priest. Have mercy on yourself, my son. Go home.*

Edward bowed his head, squeezed his eyes shut, shaking. He was going mad. What would people think? He pulled out his rosary, smooth ebony, a cross cut in the capital beads so he could tell them in his pocket. He pressed his steepled fingers against his lips to be sure he wasn't speaking sotto voce.

*You will never make a priest and I do not want you to be one*, said the voice in his head again. *I want priests who rejoice in their priesthood, not miserable, dutiful slaves.*

Usually the feel of the beads slipping through his fingers, the monotony of the words Ave Maria, gratia plenum, Dominus tecum

. . . repeated over and over calmed him, focused his rebellious mind, steadied his nerves.

His heart thundered on oblivious. He couldn't breathe. The air was too thick, laden with cabbage and frankincense, and the voice in his head would not let him be.

*Tell them you do not want to be a Jesuit priest. You have no vocation. If there is an opposite to vocation, this is it. I am calling you not to be a priest. Go home, my son. Your mother is sick and misses you more than she will admit, go home to her.*

Even though it was quite friendly, a firm, humorous, affectionate voice, as he sometimes imagined the voice of Jesus during Gospel readings, he was terrified. He gulped over and over again, sweating, his head spinning. He loosened his tight collar, tried to compose his mind.

Louder and louder boomed the cannon fire of his heart, round and round went the contents of his skull, up and down went his chest until the Edward inside stepped away from the Edward in such bodily distress. He looked down on his own body with grave sympathy until the cramps started in his limbs and chest and blackness rolled up.

His head was bleeding where he had cracked it on the ground. Around him knelt his fellow students, iron in their discipline, while the infirmerar was just hurrying from the back of the chapel, waving a couple of the sturdier men to help carry him out. A couple watched covertly from under eyelids, wondering if he was being favoured with a vision as some occasionally were, especially in the hungry season between Christmas and Easter when everyone's joints ached and their gums bled.

But as they carried him gently out, Edward knew he was a fake. He had no vision, only madness from his fear, only a panic-stricken collapse – because he was bored?

Settled at last, sustained with rough aqua vitae, his head roughly bandaged, Edward doddered his way to the little chamber belonging to the head of the English Seminary at Rheims.

Fr Persons smiled kindly at him, offered him a dish of sallet herbs to dip in oil. They tasted peppery and made his mouth flood so he could hardly speak.

'What happened, my son?'

Edward gulped down the sallet leaves. He could not keep his mind on things. Even now in front of the saintly leader of the English Jesuits he kept seeing the letters he wrote at the beginning of every exercise, every letter. AMDG, Ad Maiorem Dei Gloria – to the greater glory of God.

'I felt ill ... afraid. I was ... I'm sorry, Father, my mind was not on the Blessed Sacrament.'

'What was it on?'

'Sinful self-indulgence,' said Edward sadly, then saw the stern hardening of Fr Persons' face. 'Nothing like ... nothing ... er ... fleshly.'

'Good. You have been troubled by succubi in the past?'

'Not recently, Father.'

'Good.'

'This was ... different. I was thinking of ... of leading the assault on England, being first ashore to reconquer England for the True Faith.'

'Hmm.' Persons' face crumpled with sad understanding. 'I think many of us have such dreams. Nor do I think they are sinful, save they should not be indulged in during Mass.'

'Yes, Father. But then there was this voice ... like a voice. In my head – not outside, nobody spoke in the chapel. But the voice said I am not priestly material.'

'What did you do?'

'I tried to pray my rosary, but the voice went on about how ... how I hate all this, how I ... all I want is to fight ... Like that, Father. So of course, I tried to pray harder and somehow the air became thick and I could not breathe and then I fell down.' It sounded even more childish, put like that. 'That was all, sir.'

'Hmm. Do you think it was a holy vision?'

'No, sir, of course not. St Jerome teaches us to enquire of how we feel after such a visitation, since a true vision, from God or an angel, will make us feel better and a false vision from the devil will make us feel worse.'

'Perhaps. Although our noble founder has more to say on the discernment of spirits, which is that if we are turned away from God's true path for us, we shall find the touch of God painful. Did you feel it was unholy?'

'Well, Father ... Certainly I feel worse.' Edward's constantly rumbling stomach twisted, appalled. Oh no, more fasting, more praying, perhaps greater use of the discipline prescribed to help oust the demon. Oh God, no, please. I don't think I am possessed by an evil spirit. Of course, an evil spirit would make him think that. Perhaps he should be exorcised.

'If the choice were yours, Mr Dormer,' said Fr Persons, 'if your mother had not intended you for the Society of Jesus and you, as a dutiful son, obeyed, what would you do?'

'I would go to the Duke of Parma and offer him my sword, my wits, my body, everything I have, so he can return England to the True Faith and I can go home.'

The words had burst out of him, shaking with passion frustrated. Edward bent his head with embarrassment.

'I cry you pardon, Father, I will try harder.'

Fr Persons reached across the little desk where lay a piece of stale bread he had somehow forgotten long enough for it to have a trace of blue mould on it, and found a most stately piece of paper, deciphered in the spaces between the lines. He looked up at Dormer, who had to drag his hungry eyes away from the bread.

'All your masters concur. They approve your dedication and determination to become a priest and your devotion to Our Lord and the sacraments, but they say they have only once found a man less suited to the calling of priest and he turned out to be a heretic English spy. Your swordsmanship is excellent, your understanding of gunnery excellent, your analysis of Joshua's campaign of conquest in the Holy Land masterly. But in theology you struggle, you have mastered none of Loyola's precepts and you are constantly bored and miserable.' Edward bent his head at this devastating indictment of his faults, which he knew to be true, feeling the flush climbing his face and making his spots tingle. Fr Persons smiled at him. 'Mr Dormer, we would have had this interview in any case, but it seems that Jesus Christ, our Saviour and Captain, is also in agreement.'

'It was His voice? But why me?'

'Now why should you be the only one of His creatures that Our Lord does not take an interest in? What arrogance.' Parsons was still smiling kindly. 'Why not His voice? In times of misery and labour, He will try to speak to us. All we must do is listen.'

Dormer clasped his hands, trying to control his despair. They would tell him to leave. He had failed catastrophically at the thing to which he had dedicated his whole life. This was the end.

*Fear not*, said the soft voice at the back of his skull, *now you can go home*.

Well, that was obviously impossible, his mother would never forgive him, and there would be no room for him in the large draughty house with its empty larders.

'I am not to be a member of the Society of Jesus,' he said dully.

'No, Mr Dormer. It would be cruelty to admit you.'

Quite objectively, he noted that his knuckles had gone white and so were the quicks of his bitten nails. He was young enough that it was still a surprise to him how large and bony his hands had become.

'Mr Dormer.'

'Yes, Father?'

'I have need of an active young man to carry some dispatches for me to His Grace the Duke of Parma. I have written a letter of introduction for you to His Grace and I am sure he will find work that is worthy of you in the Great Enterprise of England.'

Edward blinked. 'I am sure he has many servants far more able than I—'

'On the contrary,' said Fr Persons, smiling his dry smile, 'God, as I have often noted, works strangely. You will find it in Isaiah, chapter fifty-five, his thoughts are not our thoughts, his ways not our ways. The worst heresy in the world tells God what He should do. As indeed the Protestants tell Him. Now here I have a letter from His Grace the Duke of Parma, which arrived this morning from Antwerp. He asks for a young Englishman for a most important mission into England in connection with the King of Spain's great Enterprise of England. He would prefer one that has taken no Holy Orders since there may well be fighting and certainly some unpriestlike behaviour involved. It could end in your death, Edward, in fact it quite likely will. It could end as it did for young Father Campion, with the public hangman gutting and castrating you in the sight of the London mob, before cutting you in four. Are you ready for that, if need be?'

'Of course, Father.' Edward answered in what he hoped was a firm voice. Was this right? Was Fr Persons making fun of him? *Go home!* shouted the voice of the little demon inside him.

'Hmm,' said Fr Persons. 'Well, let us hope and pray that the heretic bastard's murder of the saintly Queen of Scots is the last such martyrdom in England.'

'It will be if I can make it so,' said Edward, having to crush the urge to laugh. 'I can go to Parma?'

'Yes, my son. Go and change back into your old clothes – which may be a little loose for you – take your sword, hire a horse with the money I shall give you and go to Flanders. Parma awaits your arrival with eager anticipation – or he would if he knew you.'

'I'm not to be a priest?' Edward knew he was repeating himself, but he had to be sure.

'No, my son. Not now. Not ever, perhaps. God requires of you a more active kind of service.'

The joy bubbling up inside Dormer was almost too much to bear. He knelt to kiss Fr Persons' ring, blessed by Loyola himself, and then let himself into the little white-washed passage, crudely painted with the Sacrifice of Isaac. There he silently jumped and punched the air at the glory of his release.

He couldn't go home just yet, which was a pity. But he could go home in glory, with the plunder of London, to rescue his family from poverty and want and outrageous recusant fines.

He took horse later that day with just enough money to get him to Flanders if he was not robbed, a doublet that creased and wrinkled on him like a sack and a belt in which he had to cut another notch. His sword felt so heavy when he put it on he nearly dropped it and the bony nag between his flabby thighs stumbled and sighed at every step through the meanly cobbled streets of Rheims, since she could perfectly tell that he had not the power in him to make her behave.

One day perhaps, thought Edward, when I ride into London with the liberating tercios, perhaps on that day I will be happier. He hummed Laudate Deum omnes gentes to himself as the poor nag groaned and stumbled her way into the countryside.

Antwerp was a maze of streets, some of them still singed or shot-holed in places from the great Fury of Antwerp when the Spanish troops had mutinied after Queen Elizabeth stole their wages from the Genoan treasure ships.

Edward was tired and had run out of money by the time he reached the place, and he got lost. He only trailed into Parma's headquarters late in the evening. He handed in his package and letter of introduction from Fr Persons without much hope that it would help him find lodging for the night.

To his astonishment, after a short time waiting by the fire in the porter's chamber, he was led by a brisk functionary in black damask and an icy ruff, through a series of anterooms filled with a vast variety of men, soldiers, servants, clerks, priests, a series of doors guarded by impassive soldiers in high polished morions, and at last brought to a halt at a curtain that had candlelight trickling under it.

146

'Who are you bringing me to?' Edward asked in French and then again in Latin.

The functionary blinked and answered, also in Latin, 'To His Grace, of course.'

That Edward had simply never expected. He felt a little sick. 'But sir, should I not wash, prepare myself . . . ?'

Eat? asked his stomach and made a mighty rumble.

'His Grace is a very busy man and he can only fit you in now,' said the functionary blankly.

Please God, stop my stomach rumbling. The functionary jerked his head for Edward to follow, and they went into the high-ceilinged office where a man in black and cramoisie figured velvet bent his head over a desk under a blaze of wax candles.

'Your Grace, may I present Mr Edward Dormer, late of the English Seminary at Rheims.'

Alexander Farnese, Duke of Parma turned and nodded. Edward stepped forward, heart thundering, traitor-guts gurgling and managed to make it down to one knee without too much disgrace. The Duke held out a ring for Edward to kiss, which he did.

'Mr Dormer,' said Parma, 'I believe I know your aunt. Did she once attend Her Majesty the Queen of Spain?'

'Yes, Your Grace.' Edward could feel his spots tingling.

'Hmm.' The dark, intelligent face looked thoughtful. 'I have a vital and urgent mission for you, Mr Dormer.'

Edward's stomach gurgled again. He tightened his stomach muscles and gulped. 'Yes, Your Grace?'

It was a simple mission in essence, but very difficult, Parma explained, slowly and carefully in his accented Latin, while Edward knelt before him, praying frantically that he would not fart.

It seemed Parma had no need of more clerks or secretaries and nor did he lack for young lieutenants. What he did need was someone who spoke fluent English, who was not known to the English priest hunters. What he most especially needed was someone who could travel to England in disguise and swiftly track down a traitor, who was probably on the point of selling some very important information to Walsingham, the Queen's spymaster.

'And then, Your Grace?' Edward asked nervously.

The dark, chiselled chin creaked on the ruff as Parma looked at the candles. 'Kill him, of course.'

Edward gulped. He had not in fact killed anyone in his life, which he hoped Parma did not know.

'Your Grace . . .' He was about to say that he felt utterly inadequate for such an important mission. His guts were ahead of him. The most appalling gurgle and growling resounded through the office. Parma's aristocratic face did not so much as twitch, although Edward blushed crimson.

'You need not take this mission, if your heart forbids it,' said Parma, looking at him shrewdly. 'There can be no room for doubt here.'

*Go home!*

'I have no doubts,' said Edward firmly. 'Of course I'll find this traitor and . . . and kill him, Your Grace.'

Parma handed him two pieces of paper. 'That is all the information we have on the man, Van Groenig. He is a mapmaker, incidentally. If you have the chance, you must search him and his dwelling and retrieve any stolen maps he may have. The other is a plenary indulgence from the Holy Father, so that whatever mortal sins you commit in this mission are already forgiven you since they are in the cause of God's Holy Church. This means that if you are captured, you can go to your death unshriven, joyful in the knowledge that all your sins are forgiven. Naturally you must be careful not to abuse such a trust.'

Edward found the paper slippery to his fingers, which were sweating. He gulped again. 'Of course, Your Grace.'

'When you have committed the information to memory, please burn the paper. The indulgence you may keep with your or leave here as you please.'

'Your Grace, how should I . . . er . . . how should I kill him?'

'In any way that seems proper to you, Mr Dormer, I do not interfere in matters of judgement. You will be given instruction by our Mr Lammett while we make you ready for your journey, but I beseech you not to speak of your mission to anyone, since it seems remarkable to me how much Walsingham knows of my decisions.'

'Yes, Your Grace.'

'It's the way of the world, alas, that so many can be bought by the heretics. If you should come upon an Englishman called David Becket and happen to have a good opportunity, you would do a great work for our blessed Mother Church if you could kill him too. However, he is not an easy man to kill and is one of Walsingham's most dangerous servants, so your first task must be Van Groenig.'

'Your Grace, you honour me greatly with such—' Arughluglglug, said Edward's stomach demon, determined to destroy him.

148

Parma looked briefly sad, as if there was a great deal he had no intention of telling Edward. 'Please don't thank me, Mr Dormer. I shall thank you personally if you should return. Now go and tell my man to feed you.'

Edward got himself up on his feet again without too much disaster, bowed very clumsily because his head felt light, and whisked out under the curtain. He had got as far as the corridor where the functionary was waiting for him before he had to let go. Loudly. He felt resentful: the most important interview of his life and his infuriating Brother Ass of a body had to make a farce of it.

But he forgot all about his resentment when they gave him a plate of bread and sausage and pease-pottage that would have served for three meals in the seminary. He wolfed it down with the excellent Flemish beer. Then they took him to a small room where two other men snorted on a bed, and gave him a straw pallet on the floor, sheets and blankets to cover himself. Edward undressed, almost blind with weariness, then stretched out feeling quite guilty at all the luxury: no bare boards, no hairshirt, no breviary to stumble through with eyes dropping shut by themselves with tiredness. And he was warm. He tried to say a couple of prayers of thanksgiving but only got through the first half of the Lord's Prayer.

In the morning, he slept late, until a serving boy came to fetch him at eight o'clock. There was fresh bread and soft cheese, and more good Flemish beer for breakfast and then he was led to another part of the palace where he was measured for a new suit of clothes to be made for him by an English tailor. After that he was introduced to an Englishman called Piers Lammett, who had a weary, shut face like a turtle's, and a lean body in a worn buff coat.

'Mr Dormer,' he said in English, 'I understand you will be journeying to England on a vital mission.'

'I am going to England, yes,' said Edward carefully.

'And what will you be doing?'

'Carrying dispatches, I expect.'

Lammett smiled and nodded. He picked up a blunt practice sword and threw another one to Edward who caught it. 'Attack me, Mr Dormer, any way you like.'

Edward was invigorated by food, good sleep and the excitement of the trust place in him. He attacked with such vim that he somehow got through Lammett's guard and caught him in the ribs with a sideways cut.

Lammett made a surprised 'Ooof!' sound, and staggered back for a moment, cradling his ribs. Edward waited politely for him, and Lammett fleched straight into Edward's solar plexus with the blunted point of the sword. Edward sat down crowing for air. Lammett bent over him, caught his hair and brought the blade of the sword round gently against his neck.

'Less of the gentleman, Mr Dormer,' he said dryly. 'If you come through someone's guard like that, don't waste your chance.'

'Uhhh ... huhhh ... I haven't practised with a ... sword for uhhh ... years.'

'Is that so? Well, Mr Dormer, you must have a natural gift for it, for I never saw such a pretty attack. Come on, up with you.'

Lammett spent the morning taking Edward through all the various varieties of Defence: sword and buckler, rapier, sword and dagger, dagger alone. Edward's legs and arms were trembling and his shirt soaked with sweat when he sat down to eat and again found twice as much on his plate as he was used to. He gulped it all down, took a siesta and went back to Lammett.

It seemed there were numerous ways to kill someone and Lammett knew most of them. The lean Englishman favoured the crossbow for long-distance work and the garrotte for close work or a very sharp stiletto into the eye. None of these methods caused noise or a great deal of mess, as he put it, so there was at least the possibility of escape.

'Possibility?' Edward asked.

'I put it no higher.' Lammett met his eye coldly. 'Be sure you have made your confession before you leave.'

'What about this famous henchman of Walsingham's, David Becket? Do you know him?'

Lammett blinked at him for a moment. 'By reputation, yes. Although I've heard he's less handy with a blade than he was.'

Well, that was good to hear. Edward nodded, wondering if he should ask about how best to kill Van Groenig.

'I taught the use of a crossbow to a young man that had a plan to assassinate the Witch-Queen of England,' said Lammett thoughtfully, 'and it was Becket who foiled the plot. Sir Philip Sidney sent Becket to pretend to be a priest at Rheims a couple of years later to find out the truth of a rumoured libel against the Witch-Queen. He went with poor Fr Tom Hart to England and, of course, that all ended badly as well.'

'Becket was at Rheims?'

'Briefly. Walsingham is often successful at getting men into the

Seminary, mainly because Fr Persons is a good and holy man who generally believes what he's told. I had heard that Becket was injured and not able to fight any more, but even so, he's a dangerous man.'

Lammett came at him again with the wooden dagger and Edward used a trick his poor father had taught him, took it off him and gently dipped the blade towards Lammett's eye.

'Very good, Mr Dormer. Very good indeed.'

Edward nodded, trying to look serious and modest and thought how splendid it would be to defeat this evil servant of Walsingham's in a fair fight and kill him.

A week later, wearing a new and more fashionable grey wool suit trimmed with black brocade, carrying a sword and stiletto and a pouch full of French livres tournois, Edward travelled as a French merchant dealing in pearls across the storm-tossed, evil, grey Channel to Dover where the Tunnage and Poundage men were as easy to bribe as Lammett had predicted.

He rested to recover from his seasickness for a few days, then hired a livery horse at Hobson's Stables and travelled up the boggy road to London, feeling very strange to be back so soon, and very much a foreigner. It was hard to see how a mapmaker could be so important as to need killing. Perhaps he was going to sell a map of Antwerp to Walsingham, or a map of the troop-carrying canals that Parma was having built in the Scheldt estuary to carry the barges full of soldiers across the Narrow Sea when the Armada had taken control of it. It was impossible that Parma would order such a thing as an assassination without very good reason.

England was not so cold as Rheims, or perhaps it was just that he was eating so much more: big solid steak and kidney puddings, spit-roasts of pork with apples and bread sippets, high, proud pies full of gamebirds and rabbit. At night the dank air beyond the bed curtains caught his lungs sometimes and made him cough.

The paper Parma had given him had carried a full description of Van Groenig. It was burned now, but impressed on his memory. He thought often, especially in bed at night, about how he would do the killing. Sometimes he thought of his home on the marches of Wales and wished he could go and see his mother and his sisters, but not yet. First he would complete his mission. He was very frightened about the killing. Certainly he had learned a great deal from Lammett, but would he be able to do it properly, in cold blood, as the heroic young Belgian priest who had shot the heretic William the Silent had done?

He never thought about being captured. For all Lammett's gloom, he did not expect it. God had called him to do this work, he was certain. God had spoken personally to him, telling him not to be a priest and to serve Parma. Therefore all would be well. Theoretically, God might want him for a martyr, but he didn't expect such an honour. He knew for sure that he was being led into the greater and better service of God and His Holy Church, and that was good enough for him.

He stayed at the house of a good Catholic woman in London, who often hid priests. She called him by the name he gave her, fed him good plain food and asked not a single question. He was impressed. He knew very little of women, apart from his mother and sisters, but he knew that the Church Fathers taught truthfully that they were weak, foolish chatterboxes.

The following day he went in search of the Dutch mapmaker. First he changed some of his French money into shillings and pennies at Gresham's Exchange. Then he began with the great carrier's inns and had gone to all of them when it occurred to him that Van Groenig would want to be near Walsingham but not inside the city so he could move about more easily at night. There were some addresses he had been given of people who rented out rooms to foreign businessmen. Painstakingly he visited each one in turn, claiming to be one of Walsingham's pursuivants. One of them had turned down a Dutchman wanting a room with too weak a story of what he was doing here. He had sent the Dutchman off to the Strand rents where there were always rooms free because most people disliked sharing them with rats and cockroaches . . .

Hurrying there, Edward went from one to another asking for a Dutchman called Van Blauw and found himself looking at the face of the man he had come to kill the fourth time he knocked.

'I'm sorry to trouble you, sir,' he said, 'I have a message for a Netherlander.'

'*Ja?*' said the man suspiciously, with a jowelly face and heavy pockmarks under his beard. 'I am Netherlander.'

'Mr Van Blauw?'

'Nein, my name is Van Groenig.'

Edward felt himself flush, hoped the man would see that as irritation or embarrassment. He muttered apologies and hurried away, remembering just in time to carry on asking at other doors.

Then he settled down at the alehouse opposite with a quart of mild and some bread and cheese, listened to some desperate lute-playing by a scrawny young man, and watched until Van Groenig went out, presumably for his dinner.

Then he went back into the rents and up the stairs, took out the lockpicks Lammett had given him. It took a horribly long time to open the simple lock and latch. He had never sweated so much in his life, he was trembling by the time he got the door open and went in and then he had to lock the door again, which took another hour, so it seemed, and he only finished a moment before he heard heavy angry steps on the stairs.

He stepped behind the door where the Dutchman had hung his cloak. His knees were trembling. This is madness. I'm supposed to be a priest. Why am I here? Why am I doing this? What if I fail?

He took a deep breath, drew his stiletto from the scabbard at his back, prayed incoherently for strength. *Why are you doing this, my son?* asked the little voice of the devil deep inside him and he answered it proudly: Ad Maiorem Dei Gloria – to the greater glory of God.

The door slammed open. Van Groenig stamped in, muttering to himself. Edward reached out to grab his greasy yellow hair, pull him back, left hand over his mouth, as Lammett had shown him, plunge the blade in, felt the thin bone at the back of the eyesocket resist and then crack to his blade like an eggshell . . .

It was over. All finished. Van Groenig gulped, snorted, his back arched and Edward let him down gently so as not to make a clatter. He shut the door, then went methodically to the furthest corner of the room and began searching. He found money, he found some heretical books and then . . . he found two maps. Rolling them up, he slipped them in his doublet, looked around and decided he could make use of the cloak better than Van Groenig. He took it down, swept it round his shoulders. His stiletto still poked out of Van Groenig's eye, which made him feel sick, so he pulled it out, saw that Van Groenig still breathed. It was sad that he had to die, one of God's creatures after all, even though he was a heretic. Sadder still that his immortal soul would go to hell.

Crossing himself, Edward knelt beside the man he had killed and prayed for the repose of his soul, then wiped his stiletto on Van Groenig's doublet. An impulse slowed him down. Could he? Dare he? Perhaps Parma would require proof he had succeeded in killing the mapmaker? Half embarrassed to be doing it, he used the stiletto's blade to saw off some of the dirty blond hair, made it neatly into a knot, just as he had the lock of his mother's hair she gave him when he left home, put it in his pouch. Then he hurried down the stairs. Preoccupied with getting the smear of blood off his hands and the stiletto's hilt, he was halfway down the street before he looked up and met the eyes of a tall, thin man with sandy hair and grey eyes, watching him from the same alehouse he himself had been sitting in.

Edward hurried on, still feeling sick, but starting to believe that perhaps he had done it, he had actually managed to kill his first man, he had stopped the Dutch mapmaker from betraying the Duke of Parma. Triumph filled him like wine. He'd done it. If now he could only get aboard ship and away from the shore with the next tide, he would be able to take the purloined maps back to Parma.

He had succeeded. God be praised.

He spent the afternoon moving from alehouse to alehouse, drinking only mild ale. In one place, he found a dark corner in a booth and opened up the maps. They both showed a walled city with a citadel, built around a harbour. It looked teasingly familiar but there was no label, no key. One of the maps showed shading in the waters of the harbour, which he thought might be sandbanks or currents. Something about the way it was laid out tickled his memory and he squinted at it, trying to remember.

There were two men at the serving hatch, asking the man there about another. Edward glanced at them, saw that one was a big, burly, ugly bear of a man, the other the thinner one with sandy hair that had watched him leave Van Groenig's. They were asking for someone of his description. Edward froze where he sat, then made himself lean back in the booth, pull his hat down over his nose and look as if he was dozing off. Under the hat's brim, he watched the two pursuivants leave the boozing ken and it took him all the discipline against his natural inclinations that he had learned at Rheims to stay exactly where he was and not bolt. In fact, he decided to stay there until the next day, since he knew it was one place the pursuivants would not search again. And as they would be searching the docks, he decided to stay the night.

The following evening, he took a boat downriver to the dock where the *Fortune of Lubeck* was moored, went aboard and showed the Master his letter from Parma.

The Master sighed and held out his hand for gold, which Edward gave him.

Starting to relax, he sat in the Master and Commander's cabin and drank aqua vitae to fortify himself against the seasickness to come.

While he waited, a lone pursuivant came and asked the sailors if a man answering his description had come aboard, which the sailors, paid in gold, all denied. The pursuivant, the sandy-haired thin man who had been watching Van Groenig's lodging, said that his name was Becket and at that point, Edward made his decision.

Parma had said he could do a great work for the cause of goodness and Holy Mother Church if he could manage to kill David Becket, and here was the very man, walking down the gangplank and onto the shadowy quay, full of silent cranes and piles of boxes and coiled rope.

Before he could have time to feel frightened again, Edward put down his cup, walked swiftly out of the cabin, down the plank, caught up with the man just as he passed by a pile of pulleys and ropes, grabbed him from behind and stabbed him in the eye. It was less neatly done, this time. The man cried out, tried to fight, draw his sword, but then was quiet. Edward stood over him, panting, delighted with himself. Surely God was with him, to be able to kill the formidable David Becket so easily. For his own satisfaction, he cut a lock of Becket's hair, just as he had of Van Groenig's, knotted it and put it in his belt-pouch. Then he crossed himself, said a Pater Noster for the repose of Becket's soul, strode back aboard the ship and advised the Master to leave at once. The sailors looked at him with great respect as he cleaned his stiletto again with a cloth and sharpened and oiled it. He ignored them, feeling light and clean and released from responsibility, comfortable in the proven certainty of God's favour.

They warped away from the quay, and then the Master had the longboats out because the tide was not quite turned, so the *Fortune of Lubeck* was pulled down the Thames towards the sea by the creak and swing of the sailors at the oars of the longboats.

By the evening, Edward was being miserably seasick into a bucket again.

# Merula

## England, Spring 1588

Look out across the great highway of God, find again the wandering black thread of Merula, step down into time again and there she stops and looks at us, speaks to us. Argues with us?

With respect, gods, you are quite wrong. Time is not a road, as you hairy ghost gods would have it. Time is not a river either, nor a carpet. Time is a reflection: there when you look, not when you don't. Times passes only because we are here to see it go.

Rebecca and Michael found the two-masted *San Antonio*, as Francis Ames had told them to, and talked to the captain. So *San Antonio* cut her anchor and sailed out on the ebb tide early in the morning. In the Bay of Biscay where Thundering Jehovah and Suffering Jesus dance and play and wrestle together like the brothers they are, we weathered a storm that carried us north faster than we could ever have hoped and we landed in England at Southampton.

Then came a long weary time to travel up to London, for Rebecca would not ride – hating horses, she must have a litter – and we walked up the busy road from Southampton to London, ten or fifteen miles a day and so I saw for the first time the strange land of the blue-green English.

To begin with, it is dark and cold for all the summer days are so long. The reason for your hairy ghost addiction to citadels of cloth became clear to me even before we came to harbour. I shivered and shook in the wind and the rain and the nights froze me. Rebecca was concerned. She gave me a waistcoat to wear under my doublet and two shirts and a thick oily cloak to go over the top and still I was never warm. When the Lion Sun shines in England, he is nothing but a little newborn cub, he hardly roars light across the sky since the clouds blot him out most of the time. Instead of having a Rainy Season for the rain to fall in, like a civilised country, in England the rain falls constantly, summer or winter, weeps from the sky for days and days and everything becomes dank and mournful and colder than ever. When the Cub Sun goes down, there is a long time when it is neither day nor night and the light fades slowly, as if it is too tired to leave the world to follow the Sun into the dreamtime. And the same in the morning, the light creeps up as if it were ashamed, which it should be since it is so feeble.

And so everything in the land of England is ruled by the feebleness of the sun and the constant rain. To be poor in England is not only to be hungry, as it is everywhere, it is also to be constantly cold. My mistress was not poor, indeed her family was rich, but as I walked behind her slow litter, I looked about and saw poor folk travelling the roads, scrawny and wrapped in rags. Several times men came by, galloping on horses, shouting to us to make way in the name of the Queen, carrying the Queen's messages.

I was looking forward to seeing this Queen and her compound and her husbands. Rebecca had spoken of her, how great her palace was and the magnificence of her robes and the sharpness of her tongue. I wondered if she would ask me to go to the dreamtime for her and call in her god to help her, but when I asked, Rebecca only told me to hush.

Now another thing that is strange about England is that the animals are different. The cows are fat and the sheep very woolly and the pigs are fat and the horses too. They have no lions, nor antelope, nor giraffes nor zebras nor leopards. They have deer and they have wolves but the animals are mostly only for the service of men and this makes them very conceited as to their own importance to the Lady Moon. They believe that all of the world was made to serve them.

They have forests, true, but not very rich and with strange plants growing there. Nor do they have any of the half-men living in the forest to teach the use of plants.

Their houses are like ours, only square and often made in baked mud-bricks, and their temples are magnificently built in stone with long pointed towers. The English mainly have their temples plain on the inside, though they have an art to make coloured glass pictures, very fine, and their singing is magnificent, if strangely flat and unrhythmic. Their music weaves around itself like a nest of snakes.

When they travel, they do not make a fire and camp, the land is too wet and cold. They have great caravanserais all along the road, every twenty miles or so, with a courtyard where the wagons are hitched and a common room where hairy ghost men would stare and stare at me as I ordered my mistress's food, and fair rooms above with beds that are in themselves tents made of cloth, for to keep out the damp and cold. I slept in Rebecca's room, on a little bed that was pulled out from under the great tented bed, until she grew tired of listening to my teeth chatter in the night, and called me to come into her bed with her so we could both be warm. It was better so, with my two shirts and waistcoat and the cap she gave me, but ah Lady Leopard, the ugliness of waking in the dawn to light the brazier in the cold morning. So cold a place, no wonder they wish to come to our lands.

As we came near to the Queen's city, the gardens stretched out all about us, the fields full of their fat cattle, the roads were crowded with wagons bringing food to feed so many people. Southampton was like the place with the harbour that we had left so long ago, but as we came to London, I was astonished at the people and the houses of stone and brick filling the swamps by the river. And then we came to the bridge over the river and I fell silent for what I had thought was London was only its fringes, and before us lay a great jungle made of wood and stone, a jungle full of hairy ghosts and a bridge made of houses to cross the river tumbling below it.

Above the gate of the bridge, just as we would do at home, the Queen had put the captured heads of her enemies so that their souls could help to guard her city. At least that made sense, so I was a little comforted by the stinking skulls with their attendance of crows in the midst of the greatness and strangeness of the place.

By that time my nose was stunned to the stench of the hairy ghosts and I had grown used to the small beer and aqua vitae that we drank, but it meant my godsight was feeble and I could only sometimes see the swirling dreams of the people when I myself dreamed. It frightened me that I should become right-side up again, for what if the Queen should ask me to travel into the dreamtime for her? And so I drank plain water on the evening when we came to London and to the great house of Rebecca's uncle, Dr Nunez, which immediately gave me a flux to help my sight. Lady Leopard is always quick and clean in the way she brings about what she wants. My head rocked with fever and I must run out to the jakes in the back yard half dozen times a day, but I refused to go to bed or be dosed as Rebecca wanted since I did not want to waste the helpful heat. In so cold a land, I had no Lion Sun to help me climb into the place where the gods live.

Word went to the Queen, taken by Dr Nunez, word came back from the Queen by means of a letter, sealed with her seal and written with her name. Rebecca showed me it: most fit for a Queen, curling and winding in and about itself, a magnificent pattern.

We went by boat to the great Palace of Whitehall, vast, stone built, raging with men, hung with woven cloths and all most confusing to the eye since they take such pride in making flat cloth or wood painted with paint seem like reality. I leaped out to help up Rebecca from the boat and found the red-coated Queen's guard there also, who looked at me once as they might look at another man, and then again, sideways, staring, when they realised I was a woman, and they muttered between each other that this was outrageous and shocking and the Queen would dislike it extremely.

By this time, I could have had woman's clothes to wear, and indeed Nunez had bought me some, which I found such agony and made me so ugly, that I had rather have my thighs rubbed by padding and swagger about like their menfolk, than learn to breathe with only half my chest the way their women must do.

Still, they had been told to bring us to the Queen and so they did. We walked through many beautiful rooms, one which had the Queen's chair and her canopy just as my King had, and at last out into a little garden all filled with well-disciplined plants I did not know, and some smelled sweet and some savoury so that it was a garden for the nose as well as the eye.

I was still sick for all this time, the flux demon raged about my guts and my heart made fire to fight it with. I was thirsty, which made the flux demon strong, so my head spun and swelled and narrowed like the lungs of a dying antelope.

We stood in the centre of a winding path made of little carved brushes, Rebecca and I and a young man that had guided us, and I swayed in the winds of the dreamtime, waiting with interest to see the Queen and perhaps even her husbands.

She came at last, briskly along the path. Women walked behind her with three yapping little dogs on leads. The dogs saw me and smelled me and set up a wild barking with their hackles up, until the oldest of the serving women gestured at the two youngest maids to take them within. The girls were finely dressed in white and black and rose and crimson and greens and golds and stared freely at me since they had never seen a true human being before and they went very slowly away, craning their necks for another look.

Rebecca and I both knelt to the Queen. In my light-headed state, she shocked me too. In my heart, I had expected a strong, proper-coloured woman like myself to rule over the hairy ghosts, but of course she was a hairy ghost as well. Her skin was white and pearly and painted to be more white and pink. Her hair was copper red. I have heard of women-kings and here was one. I have heard of witch-queens and here was one. She walked to us, ghost face under fiery hair, black velvet and white damask to make the walls of the soft house she carried on her back for clothing, like a snail. Her high red leather boots marked the pebbles of the path as she stamped around and about the maze, her face thunderous.

It was no wonder she was angry, imprisoned in her robes as she was, as much as my own king's wives are imprisoned by their fat. It is still astonishing to me what the hairy ghosts will put on their bodies. True, they have no gold and copper rings to wear on their necks and arms to show their wealth. So velvet piled on damask piled on taffety and to top it all a high-wired white veil behind her head as if she wore a mist for her crown.

She spoke to Rebecca and my head clanged like a gong with words I did not rightly follow. Mainly, I think Rebecca was telling the Queen again what had happened to her husband Simon. The news distressed the Queen greatly. She clasped her hands together and milked her fingers, her thin lips tightening to disappearance.

'Did you mean what you added to the petition Dr Nunez brought me?' asked the Queen. Rebecca looked up at her and I felt her vibrate through the air, heard her swallow stickily. It came to me that Rebecca was truly afraid of this Queen, which was good and as it should be.

'Your Majesty—'

'Come, my dear,' said the Queen in a voice she no doubt used to her husbands, 'you added a very interesting postscriptum to your petition. Did you mean it?'

'Yes.'

'Is the ship yours to loan or your father's?'

'Mine,' said Rebecca.

The Queen tilted Rebecca's chin to look up at her. 'You are well-dowered and rich. Is there no other man you could marry? Could you not wait until word comes that your husband is dead, or wait seven years, and then you would officially be a widow and free to wed as you wished?'

In the reeling of my head and the pounding of the flux demon in my blood I could feel the rage lighting Rebecca's soul. She stared straight up at the Queen, fury in her dark eyes.

'Your Majesty,' she whispered, 'there is no other man I wish to marry. I have loved my husband since I first saw him, when I refused to marry him because he was still in thrall to you. I would not share him then or now. I love him now even when he may not be alive. Until I see his body or his grave, I shall still love him.'

'Commendable,' said the Queen, still coldly, not at all concerned by Rebecca's anger, which she must have heard. 'Appropriate. But why put yourself in such danger to find him? Certainly, if you are willing to loan your ship for this venture, we are grateful to you. But as for you yourself going with the ship into the teeth of danger, right back into the arms of the Inquisition—'

'Your Majesty,' Rebecca interrupted, then paused and smiled at her. 'I deal with sea-captains and their crews all the time. As do you. This is a matter of great moment to me and I wish to be sure that my orders are obeyed and that they do as I require.'

'You wish to supervise them?'

'I wish to remind them of what we are about.'

The Queen smiled, no, she grinned at Rebecca. 'By God, how I have longed to do the same. Sea-captains are the flightiest creatures on earth, worse than a pack of maids-in-waiting. Always gallivanting off to the Azores in hopes of a treasure ship. Of course, I will send a man much experienced in these matters to command. If he agrees.'

'Who?'

'Your husband's friend, David Becket.'

Rebecca frowned then. I knew that although she had not met the man, she did not like him for the reason that it was to rescue him from the Tower that Simon had left her side eighteen months before and become embroiled in a piece of madness that ended with him being wounded by a halberd and chased by dogs across south London.

But she could find no cogent objection to him so contented herself with a submissive 'Yes, Your Majesty.'

The Queen looked straight at her, very serious. 'There may be no chance for you to find Simon on this mission.'

Rebecca shrugged. 'It's in the hands of the Almighty in any case, Your Majesty. If He wills it, I will find Simon.'

The Queen nodded. 'This love you say you feel for your husband. What is it like?' She was prying, what business was it of hers?

To my surprise Rebecca answered slowly. 'It's like fear, only it feels happy,' she said, placing her words exactly. 'My husband is not a strong man, and certainly he has faults, many of them. But when a room full of people has no Simon in it, then it is empty. And when an empty room has Simon in it, then it is full.'

I looked sideways at her, surprised at the passion in her light, high voice. And envious, for I had never felt any such thing. When I looked at the Queen, I was surprised again for not only was she smiling at Rebecca, there were tears standing in her eyes. In my fever-sight, the tears branched out like crystals, across the gap between her and Rebecca, a bridge of diamond. A-ha, I thought, she has looked at a man that way, and loved him for all his faults. Rebecca understood it too and smiled back.

'Your Majesty, I am a lucky woman, I know,' she said. 'Many women must marry men who bore them, who make them unhappy, who empty their lives instead of filling them. But I have been happy as Simon's wife and in his bed, and now he needs me, I will quarter the world to find him.'

Rebecca reached out, took the Queen's white hand and kissed it, made bold by the diamond bridge between them. 'As my most merciful and kindly Prince, I know you will allow me to do it.'

'You have children. What if you die, what if the Inquisition catches you and burns you?'

'What if I catch plague here in London and die of it? They have my father and mother and nurses to love them in Bristol. All is in the hands of the Almighty.'

I waited, feeling the dampness in the pebbles striking up through my hose into my knees while my fever mounted and my head whirled and at last in came my godsight, crashing through the walls of beer and aqua vitae, taking me so I could hardly speak what I saw.

I saw the Queen naked in the dreamtime as she walked about her garden, thinking. I saw her near-naked in a ragged shirt with a poor battered shield and a small though sharp sword in her hand. Ranged against her in her mind was the Kingly clerk, her enemy Philip of Spain, grown monstrous tall and big, wielding a hammer as tall as she was to beat her down.

And in her godspace was no god at all. Never have I seen a creature more alone. About her crowded her ghosts – there was a wide, fierce, laughing giant with red hair and clothes bulging with jewels; a dark, shadowy woman with a sword wound in her neck; a tall cousin Queen clad in red; a laughing, rash young man, many young men indeed, since she was a Queen and must often order men to their deaths.

Also I saw her multiplicities of husbands, ranged about her, wildly dressed, peacocking, fighting to show her their power and strength and beauty, and she enjoyed all of them, but took none to her bed for fear they would then try to rule her. She believed God had given her the burden to carry and carry it she would with all her heart and despite her loneliness. But now she was afraid that through her fault her people would be conquered. Very afraid. She called to God when she worshipped in her palace temple and got no answer, she questioned all the time as she read her papers and consulted her advisors, and she got no answers except what she came to herself. She waited for her options to narrow down to only two, and then she chose and all the time, the doubt that she was right gnawed away at her and could never be revealed.

Now the intricacies of her garden maze lay before her, a labyrinth of time and action with many paths to follow. Yet so many led to blood and fire and the victory of her enemy Philip of Spain. Only a few led to her survival and to peace in the end and nor could she see clearly from where she was which ones those might be. Her thin, dark-faced servant Walsingham sought impatiently for battle between England and Spain, the ugly game between his god Thundering Jehovah and his devil, the Suffering Jesus. His Queen saw the maze about her grow, become an ever-changing flux, with chessmen roaming its paths and doing battle when they met while Thundering Jehovah and Suffering Jesus faced each other, growling across the narrow seas.

We were standing where a path split in a dreamtime, which I could see.

I should stay silent, but I must speak. I must ask her about my son. I am upside-down, I do the opposite.

'Your Majesty,' I said to her softly from where I knelt, not to frighten her, 'Great Queen, may I speak with you?'

She blinked at me. I had interrupted my mistress just as she finished expounding her plan. The Queen, like Rebecca, took my words as something like rebellion. Nor, frankly, did she expect a face so black to be able to speak English to her at all.

'Yes?' she said, her voice very chilly.

'Here I am, Your Majesty, I am a woman of power, and upside-down. If you ask me to, I can visit the dreamtime for you and ask the will of your god.'

'A prophetess?' she asked.

I did not know the word. Rebecca told me and I shook my head. 'No, Majesty, I do not know the future, there are so many. One in particular where you are victorious and alone, one where you are defeated and happy. Nor do I know how to get to a particular one from here. But I can ask the will of your thunder-god and find out what gifts he might like to destroy your enemies for you.'

'A witch?' she asked and I heard doubtful fear and interest fighting each other in her voice.

It is hard to explain what I do to the ignorant and superstitious hairy ghosts.

'No, Great Majesty, I am no maker of spells. I am the greatest upside-down person there has ever been but now I am hunting my son through the swamps of the world. He was sold last summer on the Slave Coast. If you will help me find my son, I will speak to Your Majesty's gods for you.'

It was a fair and generous offer, but the answer was cold.

'There is only one God,' she said flatly and turned away. Rebecca murmured to her what I had told her of my son.

'One, truly, but our eyes are small, so where there is one, we see many parts,' I said, not thinking to be heard. 'Perhaps you would prefer to call them angels.'

Cloth rustled on cloth as the Queen turned back to me. 'Mrs Anriques says you called a storm for the ship when you were becalmed in the doldrums.'

I smiled. 'To be truthful, Majesty, I sought out your own storm god, a mighty angel, and I brought him to us because I myself was tired of drinking a very little green water.'

'Perhaps you should talk to Dr Dee when he comes back from Bohemia. He claims to be talking with angels too.' Her voice still doubted but did not jeer.

'I am not so eager to seek out gods, for the road is very hard,' I told her. 'It is only that I desire to do Your Majesty a service so that you will help me find my son or his corpse and this is the only service I know how to do.'

'I have nothing to do with African slaves,' said the Queen. She took taxes off those who made their fortunes with the bodies of men, but it had nothing to do with her. Oh no. 'How would your son be known if we found him?'

I undid lacings and pulled up the sleeve of my doublet to show her my woman-snake winding round my left arm. 'He has a snake also, but on his right arm. And his year-group has zig-zags for its patterning.'

'I will ask Mr Secretary Hawkins to make a search of his own merchandise for you and ask his fellow merchants, in thanks for the service you have already rendered me by saving my servant Mrs Anriques. And if you should come across this storm angel again, perhaps you would ask him from me to protect this my land.'

I salaamed to her. Gods, angels, wild spirits, there is no difference. Call them what you like, they can be vain and greedy creatures and they enjoy worship. I could certainly ask for her. But I thought I had failed here.

'Your dreams are wise,' I told her, at last, a free gift to her. 'Listen to them, Great Majesty.'

She whitened under the paint and her eyes were angry. She spoke a few more words to Rebecca and dismissed us.

As we were led away, Rebecca rounded on me furiously. 'How could you risk what I was trying to do? How *dare* you speak to the Queen like that?'

'How dare I?' I smiled. 'I am upside-down and the sister of a King. I will help you find your man, Rebecca Anriques, but only if you help me find mine.'

'It's impossible,' she snapped.

I shrugged and locked my mouth against her. She did not understand what I had done. She thought I had been insolent, she had corrected me and now I was at last silent. She had no idea how dangerous my silence can be. Lady Leopard walked swishing her tail behind her as we threaded our way again through the white-washed passageways and by a looping direction, back to the water steps.

'At least the Queen likes my idea,' said Rebecca to me. 'We will have another meeting with Becket just as soon as he arrives in London and then we will begin.'

I smiled and said nothing.

Here you see, the time is patchy, for I was sick of the flux and took a while to recover and Rebecca did not notice that I had locked my mouth against her.

Then came David Becket, of whom I had heard so much in that household. He came to dinner at the Nunez house and arrived bringing his brother with him, who was slender and tall and had little lines of anxiety across his brow. Becket himself was taller than I am and a great deal broader and stood at all times like a warrior, although he had some injury to his wrists and his face was blurred by drink and furrowed by sorrow. Not the hungriest hairy ghost maiden could call the man good-looking, he smelled worse than many, and his cloud-coloured eyes and long lashes gave a mismatched look to his face. And he had a fair few spirits of his own killing to follow him. He saw me only as Rebecca's servant and after a good stare at my breasts behind my buttoned doublet, and another at my legs in their canions and hose and boots, he left off so much as thinking of me. His brother could hardly keep his eyes away from me, which made me want to tease him and so I did. He nearly fainted when I winked at him.

Little Thomasina de Paris, the Queen's Fool, came personally to bring us to the Queen and Becket trailed along complaining that he hated mysteries and why should he go to see falcons and hawks and what was the point of taking a boat and why did the women have to come – these were Rebecca and Thomasina in the litter and myself in attendance behind. If I concentrated, I could see his godspace, which had a very angry god indeed lowering in it, and dark clouds of unhappiness all about the man. And also he had had an injury to his head that had made him at least a little upside-down, for I could see swirling about him the dancing possibilities of a prophet. I wondered if he knew what he was and whether he minded.

When we met the Queen in the mews, she began by rewarding him for some service and then, most skilfully, to ask of him the thing that she and Rebecca had agreed upon by letters borne by Thomasina all the days while I was sick. He was appalled and horrified, and he bowed over as if he would weep at the thought. And then he agreed.

Now here came some days of preparation. Thomasina went to an armourer she knew and had made two strange little implements, which she said all the whores in London used. It was a knife that took apart at the hilt and the blade could be hidden inside the hilt, which was hollow and had a cord at one end. This she said made it easy to hide for a woman and even a man could hide it if he must. I looked at the shape and laughed, and took the one she had for me and went to the jakes and hid it in my woman's place. Rebecca also took her little knife and blushed fiercely as she promised to do the same.

More importantly, there was a letter from Hawkins, which Rebecca read to me. It said that there had been no English slaving voyages at all, official or unofficial, in the time when my son was sold, which helped me greatly for it told me that there would be no finding him in the blue-green lands of my mistress. And so I must journey to the crimson-and-purple lands, to the brown-and-gold lands where the Inquisition burn their unsacrifices. If he was not in New Spain and not in England, then he was there, for no others of the tribes of the north deal in black people, apart from the Dutch, a little. It was hard for me to wait while letters went back and forth. I carried messages, or guarded my mistress when she went to speak to the masters of ships. I carried several letters to houses around London. At one large fair stone house by the name of Fant Place, I saw a creature carved in a stone above the door that made me think of my home, for it could only have been an elephant carved by someone who had never seen such a one but had had it described to him. By the front door were the tusks of the beast, magnificently carved and I wondered what was the tale of the elephant and how it came to the cold northern lands. Eventually my mistress had acquired a new ship called the *Salamander of London*, after a mysterious and complex deal with a Bristol merchant who also needed a ship to trade with Ireland and had one to lend.

Becket was raging at the death of his brother. He rode home with the corpse to his own lands and came back, white and weary and tight-lipped, and found me in the Nunez kitchen drinking by myself. For it is a fact, alas for it, that although it angered my Lady Leopard, I was growing to like the aqua vitae they drank so much and while the forests of my own lands are never lonely for they are filled with gods and animals and spirits, the human jungle of London was empty of any folk I could really speak to.

I remember it now, how it came about. Becket creaked into the kitchen with mud caking his boots and his legs, smelling of horses and weariness, and tried to pour himself a tankard of beer from the barrel in the corner by the wet larder. The cook had gone to market and taken both the scullions with him, which was why I was there, for quietness. But the injury that had happened to his hands made them weak and the tap was stiff and he could not turn it. He cursed and banged the thing with his fist, and for the sake of quietness, I stood and took the tankard from him and poured him ale.

'Thank you,' he said, which was more than any others of the household did when I served them.

I smiled at him and he refilled my tankard, handed it to me. 'Never drink alone,' he rumbled. 'It's bad for the spirit.'

Now this was certainly true and if I had had a proper human being to drink with, I would not have been so lonely and nor would I have drunk so much.

The broad hairy ghost sat across the scrubbed table from me and lifted his tankard to me. 'Your health,' he said. 'You're a fine-looking nigger-woman. I wonder if it's true what Mrs Anriques says about you, that you called a storm.'

'In a way,' I told him, my tongue unready from being locked against Rebecca.

He looked shocked, as if he had been talking to a horse and had never expected an answer. 'You speak English then?'

I smiled and nodded and drank. My Lady Leopard seemed to be asleep, curled up by the fire. Or perhaps that was the blurred tabby cat I liked so well. With the booze winding its tendrils around the gates of my mind, they were becoming hard to open.

'What was it happened to Simon Ames, then? How did the Inquisition take him alive?'

I paused and then I told him the tale, as I have told you, and made it as well as I could and he listened, only cursing at the end.

'Rebecca says you are a soothsayer,' he said. 'So can you tell me, how could I have known in my dreams that the Inquisition had him in their dungeons before your ship so much as landed.'

'In our dreams we can walk in the dreamtime,' I told him. 'And sometimes from the dreamtime we can look into the past and sometimes into the future. And sometimes we can see the gods, or angels as you call them here.'

'Does that mean my dreams will come true?'

'It might.'

He blinked at me. 'What if all my dreams showed a terrible future that was good for me, wherein I was a man of rank and command?'

I felt a prickle on my neck, where the Lady Leopard's whiskers caught me. *Be careful*, she said.

'There may be another path,' I told him, 'but it may mean your death. Or it may all be a phantasy made by the hurt to your head you got last year.'

'How can I find out which?'

I leaned towards him and put my hand on his wrist, where the scarring was. He flinched slightly, but I held him – to be sure, he was only afraid because I looked so different from any of his ghost-women.

'Mr Becket,' I said to him, 'you cannot. All you can do is what seems good to you.'

He grunted, ducked his head, drank some more.

'You are a swordmaster,' I said to him.

He shrugged and his mouth twisted sadly. 'I was.'

'Well, sir, will you teach me the right use of this?' I showed him the short sword I had been given. 'And also to fire guns? And where the powder comes from?'

'Women can't learn swordplay. They're too weak.'

'Some women are, I am not. I am stronger than you now, Mr Becket, I think.'

He spat, laughed grimly. 'No.'

'I am. And I need to learn to fight with your weapons. I know the use of a spear already, and a club, but a sword or a gun . . . not yet. So teach me.'

He put up his right arm with the bent elbow on the table and smiled lazily, his eyes half-shut. 'Prove your strength. Hold me to a draw. I'll bet you a sword lesson that you can't.'

I did not know the game of arm-wrestling but he explained it and I bent my arm and leaned my hand against his.

Of course, I won. First I held him to a draw and then as I felt where the weakness in his grip was, I twisted and so beat him.

And he sighed and refilled his tankard. 'Are all the other African women as mighty as you?'

'Some,' I told him. 'Some are much weaker, some are fat as the hippopotamus and giggle all day. Now pay your bet.'

By the time the cook came back we were both in our shirtsleeves and he had me holding a bolt of wood from the pile by the fire and making the shapes in the air that they set store by. The cook was angry for we had broken some dishes and the scullions stood to stare at such a sight. Becket had been reluctant enough to start with but now he was paying attention and instructing me properly and I had liked the lesson, although the tabby cat had gone away from the fire in a great hissing.

As we were driven from the kitchen with the fury of the cook behind us, Becket clapped me on the back and threw me my doublet. 'By God, Merula, if the black women are like you, what are the men like?'

'Mighty warriors,' I said. 'Taller than me and stronger, but not so clever, alas. And also not immune to gunfire.'

'Well, thank Christ for it, or you would be foraying to England to make slaves of us.'

I smiled, but did not say what I thought, which was, Why would we want hairy ghosts for slaves when they are so savage and primitive that they must be told of the dreamtime?

I know that this was the beginning of my destruction. It began in beer and aqua vitae and the closing of the doors in my mind, the turning of myself right-side up, as if I were a man of their kind. I had come in search of my son and also in search of the secret of gunpowder to take them both home. Here was where my path began to twist. I can see it now, of course, but I half-saw it then too for I could see the Lady Leopard when I lay down by Rebecca to sleep and she had her back to me, her tail lashing. But I saw no harm in learning swordplay from a man wise in the way of teaching it. And I saw no harm in making a friend of Becket, who was so unhappy except when he was teaching me to fight. Nor did I mind how he watched me when I slashed with the bolt of wood, for I had been manless for a long time and was also lonely. Why was the Lady Leopard in a temper with me, I wondered a little, but I had no wish to go into the dreamtime to ask her, which was so hard and painful. One night in sorrow I tried to sing to the Queen Moon as she lay in her couch of clouds, but Rebecca told me to hush and the night was silent. So I drank some more of the aqua vitae in the cup by Rebecca's bed and fell asleep to dream no dreams.

Walk across the days like a flamingo with me, dipping your beak upside-down into the hours for details. Here is a memory of myself and Becket learning swordskills in the Nunez courtyard: we had progressed to using heavy blunt metal swords and I laughed as I wielded mine, for I could feel there was a god whose business I was learning, a new god was taking an interest in me. Lady Leopard was angry. Her back and lashing tail were all I could see. So here I came, making my blows count and here came Becket, fighting back, his sword tied to his hand so he would not drop it. He was slow and careful not to hurt me when he struck me, wonderfully light on his feet for so big a man. And he turned and suddenly caught my arm under his, holding tightly and so I dropped my sword and was caught.

'Now what?' he said breathlessly, showing his teeth.

I stood, wondering, for without my Lady Leopard to give me savagery, I truly did not know. Also, I didn't want to use savagery on Becket, I liked him for all his scowling and bad temper. And when you fight a man, you know him, you learn his body as you might if you danced with him, and so he becomes known to you. This is so even with men you must kill; much more so with a man who is teaching you to fight.

'Well? By now I have broken your arm and stabbed you. What will you do?'

I brought my knee up, caught only his thigh for he was quick to dodge, and he had his own blunted blade in the pit of my stomach.

'You're dead, Merula.'

'What should I do?' He was very close, only the sword was between us, and his grey eyes danced with mischief. I still have my man's part as well as my woman's cave, the part where delight lives, that the Arabs, in their fear, like to cut away.

'Think about it. How many hands have I? Only one. I'm no better off than you are, for although I've trapped your sword arm, I'm close enough for you to strike . . .'

I brought my fist up, hit his jaw gently.

'Ay, so, and if you have a buckler in your left hand, all the better. Again.'

And we practised it, he trapping my arm, and myself striking him gently, left-handed and each time he was closer until the last time he changed his stance and bore me back againt the wall of the jakes with the blunt blade of his sword pinning me there. If it had been anyone else, one of the sailors who tried to dance the man and woman dance with me, I would have known what to do and Lady Leopard herself would have come to help me, but here and now, with the hairy ghost man pinning me there less with his strength than his cloud-coloured eyes . . . I was confused. I felt helpless, as if I was only the girl I was when I was first married to my husband, and knew nothing of being upside-down, only carrying water, growing crops and raising children.

'Now,' he was breathing hard, 'now you may fight like a man, Merula, but anyone can lose a fight and if you do . . . it will go harder with you for it, do you understand?'

I did understand what he was saying. He wanted to take me himself, but he hid this from himself in his warning. I knew the ways of men – do you think all of the nearby tribes were frightened enough of the gods and ghosts in the forests? There had been men who had come to find me and break into my cave in the early days, after all.

Suddenly, I thought, well, what of it if I let him into my cave? I am not sworn to virginity, after all. I have borne a manchild, and if I have been manless for a long time, it was more for the reason that they were afraid of my upside-down state. And also of the heads and manpieces of those who had come to find me in the forest, which I displayed on the trees near their villages.

So I reached and took his wrist, where the scarring was and moved the blade aside so there was no longer anything between us. 'Do you think I am a girl?' I asked him, not knowing the word for virgin. 'Do you think I have never known a man? I have a son, and no god lay with me to make him. What do you want?'

To hairy ghosts, to be black is to be devilish, not human. To me, he was a hairy ghost, not human. But we were close and I am a woman and he is a man.

He dropped his sword, lifted his wrist where I had hold of it and kissed the back of my hand, very courtly, as men commonly do to women among the hairy ghosts. I let go and stroked the furriness of his beard, as I wished to know if it was rough or smooth. Rough.

He shook his head, smiled downwards as if at a secret joke. 'Ah Merula,' he said. Then he let me go, and I bent to pick up the swords we had dropped. 'Why do you wear men's clothes?' he asked me suddenly.

'In this land it is too cold to go bare with only a leather skirt. Men's clothes are uncomfortable,' I said. 'But I have never worn women's stays all my life and they make my breath come short and how can I be my mistress's guard if my legs are wrapped around with petticoats.'

'It looks . . . strange,' he said. 'One minute one thing, the next something else.'

'Make no mistake,' I told him. 'I am a woman and no man.'

'Fights like a man, dresses like a man, drinks like a man, is as strong as a man . . .' He was smiling, teasing me. But there was an edge.

I felt tired of his teasing and his doubts, so I swung on him and caught him under his codpiece, where he lived, and he yelped as they always do. Then I took his hand and put it under my own crotch.

'What do you feel there?'

'Nothing?'

I had him and he was still, his face going red as the hairy ghosts do, most revealing of their feelings.

'More than nothing,' I told him. 'Less than something.' I moved his hand up to put it on my breast, under my doublet. 'Now?'

'Yes,' he growled, starting to breathe fast again. 'Yes, very much something.'

And he grinned suddenly, for all I had his balls in my hand and could have twisted, he grinned and cupped his own hand to squeeze my breast quite gently.

I was answered, so I smiled and let him go and stepped back. He blew breath out of his lips like a horse and rearranged himself and we went back into the house while he looked at me sideways when he thought I would not see, looked and looked away, as if he was considering something new.

I was a little happier. The battlements of their clothes make the hairy ghosts very easy to confuse, and I wished him to know what I was. Being savage, the hairy ghosts like to keep things very simple: they want a woman to do only what all women do and a man to do only what men do. But we are not so simple, and when they have no spaces in their he- and she-boxes for such as me, then they make their lives confusing. I will be seen for what I am and I wished Becket to see it.

And he did. I think he did.

At least one part of my quest was successful. I learned from him the secret of gunpowder. It is a simple thing, something that was first made as a medicine, no doubt for constipation by which the hairy ghosts are plagued. Then somebody cooked it and nearly died of the explosion. Of saltpetre seven parts, of sulphur two parts and of charcoal one part. Mix it together fine ground and you have the sand-like serpentine powder. Wet the powder, make it into cakes, dry it and (very carefully) grind it small and you have the better milled powder. For *this* our Kings have been selling our young men. Becket told it to me, and showed me the few barrels that were loaded on the *Salamander of London*, the ship that was Rebecca's passport into the Armada. He showed me the use and loading of handguns: an arquebus, a caliver and a dag. He took me to Newington Butts, south of the river where they have targets for archers to shoot at and an earthbanked place for shooting. It took a great deal of argument by Becket and a bribe to the man who owned the shooting range, but I learned the business of cleaning and loading and priming, became less afraid of the glowing match next to my eye and the kick-back of the gun as it fired no longer made me cry out and drop the weapon, though my shoulder was aching and bruised.

I could have gone then. I could have taken my knowledge, stolen money and found a ship, come back to my own country and gone to my King. I could have said to him: give me the brown lumps that grow in dungheaps, give me sulphur from the south, give me charcoal and some men to work and I will give you the magic powder to feed your guns so you will not need to feed young men to the Arabs or the hairy ghosts. I could have done that, yes. Many things would have changed. Perhaps that is why my Lady Leopard turned her back on me. But I was not so interested in gunpowder as I was in my son. Or as I was in aqua vitae. Or as I was in Becket.

Becket spent the day before we sailed closeted close with Dr Nunez and came out with his eyes sadder than ever and his face full of doubt. I had served behind Rebecca at table while she spoke in Portuguese to her aunt and then in English to her ship's Captain that they would sail first to the Netherlands to construct a false past for themselves that the Spaniards would believe.

Afterwards Becket came to me and laid his hand on my shoulder, as if I were a man. 'Let's go and get drunk before we sail, Merula,' he rumbled.

I was cold and afraid and weary of locking my mouth against Rebecca, who still seemed not to notice. She disapproved of it when I went to learn swordplay with Becket, as if I were a maiden she must guard. So when I had helped her to take off her gown and kirtle and her wrapping stays and all the underpinnings that made her womanly in the hairy ghosts eyes, I asked if I could have some hours by myself. Grudgingly she said yes.

We went to a small boozing ken, just outside the City walls, Becket and I, on a road called High Holborn, where the tall, shelved houses of the Sergeants' Inn topple over the street. There we played at cards with other men known to Becket, and I made some money from the shilling Becket lent me, for even with the dreamtime closed to me, I could still make out the godspaces and fears of the other players.

When I had taken their money and they had gone off angrily, threatening to tell Mr Recorder Fleetwood of the heathen witch Becket had had them lose to, Becket looked seriously at me. 'You could buy your freedom with that money, if you wish, Merula.'

Now I knew why he had done it and I was touched to my heart. As always, his hands were clasped on the table in front of him and now they began their uneasy wrestling.

'In this venture, the likelihood is that we will be taken by the

Inquisition,' he said heavily. 'I trust I'll be able to do them some damage first, but that's the truth. In the end, they'll know us and take us. I make no hopes of finding out the Queen's riddle of the Miracle of Beauty.'

I nodded, hearing his distress. He had told me something of what had happened to him the winter before last and although his body had mainly recovered, his spirit clearly had not. In another time or life I would have gone to the dreamtime for him to find out where his spirit was hiding and perhaps even fetch it back to him again. But such witchery would have frightened him to his primitive soul. So I could do nothing for him except listen when he talked. Now he swallowed firewater, swallowed again, licked his lips and continued.

'When they take us, if there is better or worse in the hands of the Inquisition, they will treat you worst, Merula. Rebecca is small and weak and they will be afraid of killing her with their ill-treatment, although . . . well, there is plenty they can try even so. But you . . . you are strong and brave and they will use you against her.'

'What about you, Becket?' I said to him. 'What will they do to you?'

His right hand gripped his left and the two contended like men who hated each other. 'No doubt what they have done before and with luck it will kill me this time. I have plenty of information to give them which will do them no good, so I might not fare so badly . . . but you and Rebecca . . .' He drank again, finished and beckoned the boy over for another refill.

'I think you are too gloomy.' I said to him, touching his thumb with my forefinger. 'I see no reason why they should catch us, why they should put us to the question. Among so many ships and so many people, sailing over the sea, why should they notice us?'

'Because of Rebecca,' said Becket sadly. 'She will be asking of her husband and of the riddle and being a woman they will want to know why. She will be the undoing of us.'

'So?'

'Take the money you won. Go to your mistress. Say that you will not go upon this voyage with her and here is the money that Simon paid to buy you, and will she manumit you so that you are not forced upon the journey, which might kill you. She is a just woman, for all her obstinate foolishness.'

I nodded at him. 'And you? Why will you go?'

'The Queen asked me to.'

'Only that?'

'She'll reward me if I return.'

'What good will that do you if you are dead?'

'I feel I must, then, Merula. I don't want to, but I must.'

'Why?' I pressed him. He growled at me, his eyebrows nearly meeting. 'Tell me, when you dream of the evil future, where are you in your dreams?'

'I am a great Captain, leading men to victory as the Spaniards march across England.'

I smiled at him, hearing the awkwardness. 'And?'

'I also ... dream foolishness.'

'It's possible to dream we are quite different from what we are,' I told him to make it easier. 'I myself have dreamed I am a leopard and also a man.'

He coughed, looked sidelong at me because he never liked it when I read his mind. 'Well, then, I dream that I am the Queen, fighting the Spaniard also and that ... well, I am happy.'

And so the decision was made. I need not have gone with them on their voyage, and I need not have done what I did that night. The strangeness of Becket's cloud-coloured eyes was some of it, the way he looked at me when we practised, as if one minute he could see my breasts and another minute all he could see was the darkness of my skin. And the Queen Moon was there as well, of course, as she always is, although I could not see her or hear her and thought she had left me.

I laid my hand full on his, drank aqua vitae, left my hand there. The hairy ghosts are always cocooned by cloth, as I have said, and so they are sensitive to touch. With my other hand, I unbuttoned the top of my doublet and untied the strings of my shirt with its falling-band. They rarely see women's breasts, save at the stews where the whores sit about with their breasts perched high on the top of their stays, and so he was not used to seeing any breasts pressing against a shirt as mine were.

'Merula ...' he said hoarsely, 'don't do that.'

'Why not?'

'Because ... I ... because ...'

'Do you think I am a virgin?' I asked him, having found out the word I needed.

'Married?'

I felt my lip curling in a smile at him. 'My husband is dead. If I were only another woman, you would already have tried to kiss me.'

He stopped in what he was going to say, stared, blinked, stared again and his skin started to ruddy and darken, as theirs do when they are thinking what they believe to be evil thoughts.

'Do you think I would be offended by your kiss?' I asked. 'Or would you perhaps be offended by my kiss?'

He swallowed. 'I haven't thought of you as . . .' He stopped himself, knowing that I most certainly would be offended if he told he thought of me as a man, even though I knew perfectly well that he did. 'And you are black and it's strange . . .'

'Is it too strange for you?' I asked, not surprised, for it had taken me a long time to see past his paleness.

He looked down again, then moved, sat next to me on the bench, not opposite. There was hardly room for us both, for as I have said, he is broad and I am neither small nor slender.

'There's strangeness, sure,' he said, running his fingers along my hand to my wrist, and then up to the side of my mouth and down the cord of my neck. 'You are very strange, Merula.'

The word 'but' hung like a bird from the perch of my name and I laughed and tipped my head so his eyes could follow his fingers down into the darkness where my breasts lay. I let him kiss me first, beautiful though his bulk felt against me, I held back until he had put his lips to mine, so he would know he had seduced me and not the other way about. And he had, of course. To be manless is possible, but never pleasant, after all. And to be womanless except for those you can buy, no man likes it either.

He took my hand, went to the innkeeper, spoke quickly, and then caught the key that was thrown to him and so we went up the creaking stairs to a room overwhelmed with a broken-backed bed and a sagging mattress and curtains in tatters all about and a bowl in the corner. It stank of the fish-swimming of other two-backed beasts, but I didn't care. Becket locked the door behind us, then stood facing me, took my hands and swung them out and kissed my lips properly, so I could taste him and the booze he drank and he could taste me and the booze I drank. Then I unbuttoned the rest of my doublet and opened my shirt so he could taste my breasts as well.

'Do you know, I have no idea how to undress you,' he said laughing and muffled, as his hands fought the ties of my anions.

I bent my lips to his ear. 'You work at your clothes and I'll work at mine.'

'You see how wrong you are to wear hose? If you wore skirts, this would be simple,' he grumbled and turned away while I did the same. Well, we left our shirts, for the pleasure of lifting them off each other and there we were at last, himself in shades of pink and white and quite remarkably hairy and myself . . . I have said that I am beautiful and so he said as well, enjoying my pointed breasts and flat flanks and belly with his hands, burying his face between my breasts and mounting and riding me while I lay back and went happily to the place where pleasure sings.

Afterwards we lay cupped together in the hollow of the broken-backed bed, which had lost a couple more straps thanks to us, and while he dozed I sat up and looked to see what had been hidden all this time by his clothes. I have no desire for boys who are unmarked by the world, but it made my heart lurch to see just how much the world had marked him. Scars on hairy ghosts are rather ugly and pink when new, and silvery white like a slug's trail when old. His back was a snail's carnival of stripes and there were healed cuts on his shoulders, his leg, a raised place on his ribcage where he had been hit by something hard and broken a rib or two. Quite apart from the scar bracelets he wore on each wrist.

His eyes fluttered open again and he shook his head at me, rolled on his back, reached out to bring my face closer and stopped when he saw my left arm.

'Good God, what's that?' He was staring at the world-snake coiling up my arm, which was made when my woman's cave first gave blood, to show that I knew how to bear pain. It is made by cutting the skin and putting clean stones in the cuts to raise up welts and it hurts a great deal. Some die of it because the scars do not heal and become full of flies and sickness and heat: we say the world-snake has eaten them early. Becket reached out to touch it gently.

'It is my own world-snake who laid the egg that the world hatched out of and sits in the tree of knowledge as the Queen Moon to teach us all she knows.'

'Oh.' He frowned. 'To us, a snake is evil.'

'Perhaps your northern snakes are evil, but our snakes are very wise. All my people carry her on their arms, the women on the left arm to make it strong to carry babies and the men on the right arm to make it strong to fight our enemies.'

His fingers followed the spiral to where the head is on the shoulder. 'It looks like a carving.'

'It was carved.' With emphasis, I looked over his naked pink hairy chest and his belly and passed my hand down to his lower nest of hair. 'Look, you have a snake too.'

He laughed and lo, his snake rose up to tell me how happy it was. Well, I was happy to see it too, and had a warm cave ready for it to explore.

We had to roll off the bed before the last few straps broke, which made me laugh, and when we had both got our breath back, he told me he had never had a woman ride him like that before. I asked him what kind of fools hairy ghost women are, not to know how to be a frog for the pleasure of their man. He said for a woman to ride a man was sinful and I laughed again.

The gods of the hairy ghosts are quite extraordinary, for not only do they tell their people whom they may mate with and when, which is normal for gods who are busybodies that way, they tell them in what way they may mate and what positions. Which is surely none of any god's business, but Becket was worried his angry storm-god would be offended.

So I told him some of the god-stories of my people, where the feathered serpent tricks the hippopotamus and the Lady Moon's egg-laying at the beginning of the world and he told me their own god-tale of a garden where a god made people and told them not to eat fruit from a certain tree and a serpent came and told the woman to eat and she did and gave it to her man and so they were driven from the garden and had to work and suffer.

It was a very strange tale indeed, especially as the hairy ghosts say that it shows women are weak and foolish because it was a woman who ate the fruit first. I say, she was clearly the first upside-down person, to see through the god's tricks and listen to the wise serpent, so that she could capture the knowledge of good and evil for herself. I say, she was brave and bold to risk it. And kindly too, since she shared with her ignorant and ungrateful man. But Becket told me to hush since I did not know what I said and was in any case speaking blasphemy.

The hairy ghost gods are very easily offended – touchy, oversensitive and short-tempered. No doubt it is from never being visited in the dreamtime.

We lay down to sleep together, skin to skin, most delightful especially for me as I had been sleeping wrapped in shirts next to Rebecca, whose snores were high-pitched, and I much preferred the salty bulk of David Becket.

And so it came about that I went dream-riding with him . . .

*He was riding his horse half-asleep and the horse itself near ready to drop for weariness. He had had no sleep for three days, except the occasional doze for ten minutes while they waited for the stragglers to catch up, and nothing to eat for a day. They were heading up the Oxford Road and near enough to Oxford to see the hills around it, the fields empty though still unburned. Behind them, perhaps a day or two behind, perhaps less, came the Spanish army, Parma's finest tercios, driving north-west up the road to catch and destroy them.*

*It went against the grain to be running away, but he knew he had to do it. He had held Parma for ten days, used all the labrynthine complexity of London to stop him, given the Queen precious time to ride for the second city of her Kingdom, given the barges and boats full of supplies time to go up the Thames, bought some time for Lord Hunsdon to raise troops in the Border country. He had lost most of his men and London was a smoking wreck behind him, but he had stolen the one thing Parma had very little of – time.*

*And now that Parma had broken out to the Edgeware Road, he was riding like hell for Oxford with what remained to him, a couple of hundred horse and a number of the remnants of the London trained bands running grim-faced at their stirrups. Most of them were ahead of him on the road of course, with scouts out ahead of that. He was with the Rearguard arquebusiers, to form an ambush if Parma should manage to come to contact with them.*

*His head was spinning with his hunger for sleep as dusk came down. There was some blockage – oh yes, one of the last two wagons with guns and weapons and a couple of barrels of powder, it had naturally broken an axle within a few miles of their goal. The men who had been with it were feverishly trying to unload it.*

*'Leave it,' he ordered, 'Prime the barrel and leave the fastest rider to blow it up when Parma comes.'*

*They were young, hollow-eyed and weary, and very frightened. They looked at each other, not knowing how to choose which one to risk almost certain death.*

*'Draw straws for it, gentlemen,' said Becket quietly as he and his four outriders went past.*

*Something was happening ahead, some stir among the exhausted men plodding along the rutted muddy road, a sound of hoofbeats, easily distinguishable from their own horses because they were bright, firm, not stumbling.*

*For one second, Becket's empty belly griped as he wondered if Parma could possibly have stolen a march on him . . . No. It was impossible. Unless he had fitted wings to his horses.*

*And here they came, the Queen's General-in-Chief of England, newly-made the Earl of Sherborne, Walter Ralegh himself riding towards him with his breastplate bright and shiny under his double chain of esses and his buff-coat clean and a woman's glove pinned to his shoulder as if he were a knight at a tourney.*

*Too tired to think what else to do, Becket simply turned his horse to meet Ralegh's, wishing with all his heart he could have had a rest and changed his clothes and washed before meeting the Queen's Favourite. Ralegh would no doubt look down his long courtier's nose at Becket's face still blackened with the smuts of London's smoke and a throbbing slash on his cheek from a few frantic moments when it had seemed as if Parma's men had caught him after all.*

*Ralegh was mounted on a magnificent chestnut animal . . . That was another thing they had him to thank for, the few days they had needed to move the Queen's entire stables north and west. The horse stopped and Ralegh waited for his own outriders to catch up.*

*Ralegh knew he was being watched, you could see it in the tilt of his head. Becket waited dully for arrogance and then . . .*

*Ralegh swept his hat off and bowed in the saddle to him. Becket found his mouth was opening, shut it, clutched at his helmet to take it off, then gave up and simply bowed back. What?*

*'Captain Becket,' said Ralegh clearly and loudly, 'Her Majesty the Queen bids me tell you that she is most mightily delighted with your valour and wisdom in that you have held back Parma for twice as long as she ever could have hoped and so given her time to reach and fortify Oxford. To which end, Captain, she has given me at my own request, her gracious permission that I may dub you knight, here and now as we stand in the field.'*

*Becket sat blinking while his soggy brains caught up with the honour. Around him his men muttered and a scattered clapping began, then a few cheers and then more. Young John Donne was at his elbow, grinning and delighted.*

*'Now, my lord?' Becket asked, a little bewildered.*

*'Now sir, if it pleases you,' said Ralegh, quite gently. He dismounted, gave his horse's reins to one of his riders, then came striding over and held Becket's stirrup for him.*

*Becket slid from his horse, not quite able to feel his feet and wondering if he would be able to stand up at all. Luckily, instinct and a skilled shove from Ralegh's shoulder kept him upright. It was true what they said, Ralegh was unreasonably tall. Becket was not at all accustomed to looking up at anyone.*

'A few minutes here to make you a knight,' said Ralegh, his Devonshire burr only a breath in Becket's ear. 'Then we'll be up the road in an hour and you in your bed.'

'But I—'

'It will please your men, at least. And the Queen will have it.'

John Donne was at his elbow again, whispering something ... Oh he was being told to kneel here, away from the deeper mud. What did it matter? His legs were caked already.

Shaking his head like a bear, Becket knelt, fumbled the straps of his morion, took the helmet off at last, shook his curls free and tried to settle his mind. Ralegh was before him, clean buff leather, polished blued steel ... Well, he had some mud splashes on his boots too.

There was a hiss and scrape as he drew the long Damascene rapier and Becket felt the flat of it on his shoulder, right, left and right again. There was a rumble of approval and amazingly loud cheering and clapping again.

Ralegh looked around at the men. 'Rise Sir David Becket, most valiant and glorious knight of the Queen.'

Becket heaved himself up, sincerely terrified he was going to faint, to find Ralegh gripping his hand.

'Did you know you won me forty pounds, Sir David?' said Ralegh conversationally.

Becket blinked and then half-grinned. 'You made a book on how long we'd last?'

'Of course. None of the others would dare venture past five days, but I struck out for ten. So I am personally indebted to you besides the Queen.'

'How is she?'

Ralegh shook his head and smiled. 'Extraordinary. Better than I have seen her in months. And very angry.'

'Good. You know Parma's on my tail.'

'Ah yes.' Once again Ralegh held Becket's stirrup and he climbed into the saddle while every muscle in him protested virulently at the outrage. 'Tell me on the road.'

By the time they came past the huge earthworks still being feverishly dug by shirt-sleeved young students, old men and women, while the children carried baskets of earth up to the tops of the banks, Ralegh had skilfully filleted out the whole tale of Becket's doings from his exhausted ramblings. And somewhere at the back of his mind, Becket thought he had come on a new thing. He had seen the Prince of Orange many years ago while he was fighting in the Netherlands, and he had served under Sir John Neville, under many captains in fact. But with Ralegh's lean face *tilted towards him attentively, it suddenly came to him that just as she had found herself the perfect bureaucrat in Cecil, Lord Burghley to be her Lord Treasurer during the peacetime, the perfect spymaster in Walsingham during the strained arm's-length non-war over the past ten years or so, now the Queen had found herself the perfect warrior to be her General-in-Chief. It was typical of her. For the first time since early spring, most unlikely, most irrationally, his misery and horror began to lift, it began to seem possible that Parma could be fought and destroyed.*

I woke and Becket himself dreamed on, less powerfully, floating women, sea-snakes, coupling with strange creatures.

It had been a dream of prophecy; there was no mistaking the brightness of it, the strength, the sense it made. No wonder he was haunted and weary. Nothing tires the spirit more than prophecy.

A little later, when I had dressed myself again, I woke him and when he had roused himself most unwillingly and drunk ale and dressed, we went primly down the stairs and out into High Holborn and Becket seemed not able to look straight at me any more. I wondered if he was afraid I would want more of him, so I smiled and chinked my purse. He said nothing of his new dream, and nor did I speak of it, not wishing to frighten him.

Rebecca was cold to me. She did not like it that I went and disappeared with her husband's best friend, nor did she like it that I returned bright-eyed and loose-limbed when I had said I would. I offered her the money for my manumission and she sat and stared for a long while.

'Whose idea is it?'

'Becket's,' I told her. 'But it seems that my son is not here in this cold place, so I must go to Portugal again.'

Her lips tightened and she looked in the purse. 'Keep it,' she told me and bade me fetch pen and paper, which I did, and she wrote out a manumission that her aunt and Dr Nunez signed. But when I had the paper in my breast, I felt no different.

'What will you do now?' she asked.

'Seek service again,' I answered, knowing what she was thinking. 'I might go and stand by the servingman's pillar in St Paul's.'

'I still have need of an attendant.'

I smiled and bowed to her.

The *Salamander of London*, two masts, was moved to the lower Pool of London, to have the sails rerigged. But at dead of night on the ebb tibe, with Rebecca and myself and Becket and little Thomasina de Paris on the bridge, she slipped her anchor and drifted out, silent as a ghost with a friendly wind to push at her lateen sail, down the Thames, past Tilbury Fort and Gravesend and so in to the Narrow Seas.

We sailed as quick as we could, afraid of the flyte-boats that would take us as a pretty prize, and came into the Hague two days later, another city like London except that their streets were made of water, and the people sounding and looking much the same to me only more guttural. We had crossed so quickly that Rebecca and Becket were still puking when we came to the quay.

Rebecca stayed with her father's Factor there, an elderly close-faced man with a richly furnished house who treated her with great respect and the rest of us with none.

Particularly me. He had me sleep in one of the outhouses, empty at that time, but there were ring-bolts in the stone walls and a door that locked on the outside. I lay on the straw pallet Rebecca had insisted I be given, and sniffed the air full of sorrow, and tried not to be enraged. Once perhaps I might have invited my Leopard Lady to ride me and take a terrible revenge, but by then I was well-mired in the hairy ghost stupidity of good sense. After all, Rebecca would be asking for news of my son, as she had promised.

The next day I went shopping with Rebecca to buy Dutch clothes for all of us. She had a moneybelt and she passed up and down the great second-hand clothes market, muttering her list to herself.

We met Becket at a boozing ken where she and he spoke only Dutch and so I was left marooned by words again, not understanding what was said.

Everything about Becket smelled of weariness and fear.

At last the thing he had feared came about, for he brought it. I was attending my mistress to her chamber for the night, following her up the stairs. Thomasina she had sent on some errand. Becket came after me suddenly.

'Merula, a word,' he said and drew me onto a landing. 'I'm sorry . . .' he began and while I waited to hear what he was sorry for and my Lady Leopard turned her back on me, he brought his fist up and hit me on the chin.

I went down like a poled ox, for he caught me right on the point and I felt only the thud of his fist connecting and then the floor hitting me and a black hole and then his boot in my gut to be sure I stayed there. The air became my enemy as I fought it for breath.

Rebecca spun on the stairs, stared.

'Mrs Anriques, you will do as I say.'

And then I heard her little footsteps running on up, her skirts lifted, the slam of a door as she rushed through it, and then she was back out again, a wheel-lock dag held in both her hands.

Fireflies fluttered round the two of them as they faced each other, for blackness was coming over me again. I had got to my hands and knees and waited gasping, but Becket saw and kicked me again. I thought the planks of the landing a better way to rest, and collapsed.

'I have been commissioned to see to it that you do not risk yourself in the dungeons of Inquisition. When I have done the Queen's mission, I will make full search for Simon . . .'

'Mr Becket,' said Rebecca, cold and furious. 'Whatever my uncle may have paid you to keep me out of harm's way, you may not do it.'

Becket went up one stair. 'Put the gun down,' he said coaxingly. 'Please, Mrs Anriques, for your husband's sake I had rather not lay hands on his wife, but if you try to shoot me you will find it jumps in your hand and breaks your wrist and further you will probably not hit me even at this distance . . . So give over this foolishness and let me lock you safely in your room until I have gone to the ship.'

'He said you would do this, he told me you would play me false.'

Becket went up one more step, but Rebecca stood firm. I rather thought she might shoot him in fact, or at least try to because he was telling the truth, it's hard to hit anything with a handgun.

'Who did?'

And that was when the road through time we were walking upon suddenly split, for out of the shadows below the stairs stepped a tall, grey-haired man I did not know, backed by other men of his own affinity, and another handgun held in his right hand. He had long lost his left arm: his sleeve was pinned to his shoulder and he was grim with satisfaction.

And now Becket was afraid, truly afraid. 'By God,' he said, 'you knew.'

'Of course, I knew,' snapped Rebecca. 'Do you think I'm blind or deaf or do not know my uncle? He gave in far too easily. Go down the stairs ahead of me and take your black bitch with you.'

Becket hooked his fingers in my collar and dragged me until I wobbled myself up to my feet, still panting for breath, still bent, my head banging like a gong and the hinges of my jaw hurting.

'Mr Fant, we shall do as we planned.'

'It would be better to kill him,' said the one-armed man. 'He's a coat-changing traitor and he'll betray us.'

'No,' said Rebecca. 'No noise and no corpses. In there, Mr Becket. And you, Merula.'

I had known nothing of it, but it seemed she thought I did and had not told her. Becket's nearly breaking my jaw had no effect on her.

Indeed I should have seen it coming, the Lady Leopard should have warned me, but the booze had dulled me until I was no more than the hairy ghosts. I may be able to speak to the gods, but I have no gifts of prophecy.

Becket blinked at the man who hated him, whose last remaining hand was steady to hold a dag and was backed by henchmen who looked quite able to deal with both of us. 'You don't understand, Fant,' he said, 'You have completely mistaken—'

'I saw Haarlem fall because you betrayed us, I saw all the garrison butchered, I saw . . . You cloak your treason and most people are fooled by you, but not me and now not Mrs Anriques.'

Becket looked at him considering, then spoke directly to Rebecca. 'Who will be the gunner for you, to give you countenance among the Spanish?'

'I will,' said Fant. 'Do you think I learned nothing about gunnery during the siege? I know Dutch as well as you do, if not better. And at least I will not sell her to the Inquisition the minute we're safely in Lisbon.'

'And the other, the Queen's mission?'

'I shall find it out better without you to hamper me,' said Rebecca. 'The innkeeper has orders to let you and your black whore out tomorrow morning when we will be safely gone. Then you can shift for yourself. I have already written to my uncle.'

Becket nodded. That was all. Once he might have thought of something to try; now he made no more protest, for his heart was filled with a great black weariness. As for me, among the fireflies from being struck and the sick breathlessness, I could just make out the shadow of my Lady Leopard, twitching her tail in the shadows of the room full of barrels and hanging hams that we were led to, and locked inside in the dim light and the pungent smell of pickles and salt beef and salt cod.

Becket sat down on a barrel and put his face in his hands. I squatted down in the pungent dimness, rested my back against the swell of another barrel and looked up at the little barred window. At least in that place, if they forgot us, we would not starve although we might die of thirst since everything was so salty. My mind was spinning strangely, most dizzy, most split from one thought to another. It took a long while for me to be able to think more than two thoughts in a row. And my face hurt.

Rebecca had called me Becket's black whore. It is their word for a woman who lies with men for money. To them any woman who does so unwed is a whore, they are as bad as the Arabs for it. When I had lain with Becket, I had done so for the pleasure of it – even when I first became upside-down, there were men who came to me in the forest that I did not geld or kill, although they were few because the warriors feared me and there were plenty of other less dangerous, more willing and younger girls after all. To be sacred to a god, it is not necessary for us to be chaste, only to listen. It was not lying with Becket that had made me deaf to the Lady Leopard.

But I had never thought it would make Rebecca jealous enough of me to hate me. How strange that she should think I must be faithful to her in that way as well.

Becket was silent for an hour before he lifted his head and blinked at me. I smiled at him, ate some of the ham I had cut from the nearest hock and offered him a slice off my knife. He offered me some of his little flask of aqua vitae, which warmed my throat.

'Who is the old enemy of yours?' I asked him.

His grey eyes chilled as he stared straight ahead. 'Anthony Fant. We were friends once, when we first went to the Low Countries to fight the Spanish.'

'Is it true you betrayed a city?'

'Yes.' He spoke in a voice that was lead-coloured. 'In a way. At the siege of Haarlem, I was carrying a message about the relief force and the Spaniards captured me, put me . . . questioned me. I . . . was fooled by one of them I thought was a friend. I was tired and stupid and . . . weakened and I believed him when he said he would help me get the message to the city. So yes, when Haarlem fell and the Spaniards massacred the garrison, it was my fault.'

I wrinkled my eyes, trying to see what was happening in his godspace. Did he have a city-full of ghosts following him? It seemed not, though I could not be sure with the doors of my mind closed. So I drank more aqua vitae, gave him the flask back.

'And that man was in the city?'

'It's where he lost his arm. He's more angry with me than ever now. He even believes I betrayed my own brother to his death. His sister Eleanor was my own sister-in-law and he knows how she sorrows for poor Philip. Whatever happens, you know, Merula, whatever I do, no matter how I try, it seems I must destroy the people around me.' His voice was soft and flat.

I leaned over and patted his arm. 'Not me,' I told him. 'I am very hard to destroy. You are more likely to be destroyed by me, truly.'

He looked at me properly at last and tried to smile. 'Well, at least it would make a change.'

We slept on the uncomfortable stone flags of the wet-larder, curled into each other like fish packed in a barrel, his head on my flank and my head on his.

Once more I went dream-riding with him . . .

*This time he was the Queen. I saw him twist and turn within the dream-carapace, not to be such a thing, and yet the dream carried him on, the sharp knife of its prophecy breaking through his mind, wielded by the Queen Moon in her hairy ghost guise, pale and dressed in blue, crowned with stars, dancing with the serpent between her feet. She smiled when she saw me there, as if at last I had done something that pleased her well.*

*I was the hairy ghost queen along with Becket.*

*And the Queen sat in the tower of one of the Oxford colleges, blinking like a ginger cat through the window, waiting for Ralegh to return.*

*He had scraped up every fighting man he could, woken Becket from his exhausted sleep to command the Vanguard. Among the arquebusiers there were some of the stronger women of the town, they were so desperate for men who were able to lift one. The Queen had tried to forbid it, considering it an abomination that women should try to wield a weapon in the dirt and reek of fighting. It was the business of men to protect women, she had said. The goodwives told her with flinty respect that they had heard the townswomen in the Netherlands had done as much and more, which Becket confirmed. They added that they had rather die honestly in battle than be raped by Spanish soldiers. Elizabeth had said this showed how little they knew of the matter. Then Ralegh himself had pointed out that most of the men knew no more of fighting than they did and so long as the women could hold their nerve at least as well as the men, and fire off their arquebuses at least once, that would be all he asked.*

*Reluctantly she had given her permission and watched the broad-armed wide townswomen shoulder muskets and march off with the men, their skirts hooked up out of the mud and their petticoats swinging.*

*They were still pitifully few. Perhaps three thousand untried foot and a thousand horse against Parma's tercios, fresh from the sack of London.*

*Thanks to Becket they had some ordnance and even some powder, newly made in Wales. But still . . .*

*That was the day before. She had sat in Magdalene tower all the afternoon, just as she was now, and when Philadelphia Carey came to coax her down for some food and rest, she had sworn at her and thrown a slipper.*

*This morning there had been sounds from down the London Road. Banging from the guns, clattering from the arquebuses, a low roar, all of it thinned and made inconsequential by distance.*

*She stared and stared, as if she could punch holes through the miles by the simple intensity of her eyes. Trees waved in the wind. It was quite quiet now, though she thought she had heard cheering. Whose? The Spaniards?*

*She waited, fear trickling through all her body, like a silver thread of ice, knitting up every humour into a knot that sat in her belly as if she had swallowed a stone. A crow came in because the tower was so quiet, and was hopping across the floor when she moved and it flurried off, cawing angrily at the outrage of a glittery statue being alive. Still she sat, no sounds, no movement on the road. No sign of an army victorious, whether English or Spanish. Nothing. As the afternoon wore on, perhaps her eyes glazed. She knew she had felt like this before and remembered after some effort. When she had been in the Tower, in her sister's reign. Then she had felt like this.*

*A puff of movement, somebody on horseback galloping up the road. A result.*

*She rose, very stately, a little stiff, smoothed down the black damask of her kirtle and started down the stairs of the tower, to go out and stand on the bridge, ready for whatever Fate should send. She had agreed with Ralegh that if it all went wrong, she would break Magdalene bridge and leave artillery at the top of the tower, then withdraw behind the ramparts and make terms with Parma if she heard nothing from Robert Carey and Lord Hunsdon in a week.*

*She knew she could do that, but Oh please God, let Ralegh not be killed, let him survive . . .*

*She waited on the London side of the bridge.*

*It was a boy, not a man, mud-caked from head to foot. The autumn rains of 1588 had begun early, melting into the foul storms of late summer that had done such damage to the English fleet beating up and down outside Calais. No matter now, Ralegh said the rain was excellent for it would hamper the Spanish ordnance and give the Papists flux and foot rot.*

*The lad tumbled from the saddle like an avalanche before running over to her and kneeling very clumsily.*

*'Oh Queen,' he panted, 'he won, he won it, Ralegh won it.'*

*All the silver lump of ice inside her suddenly burst like a seedpod and filled her head with sunshine. She laughed. 'Thank you for riding to tell me of God's bountiful mercy, but you really should make attempt to call me Your Majesty.'*

*He went pink, scrabbled off his cap, and said, 'I forgot, see. I'm sorry. Your Majesty. Only it was such a great victory . . . We waited for them, see, in ambush I suppose, and when they come up to us, Ralegh . . . I mean, my lord Earl of Sherborne, he says, very quiet, "Hold boys, wait." And then cavalry come galloping straight down the road and hit them – CRASH! like that, missus, and there was a great big fight and we shot at them from the hills. He rolled 'em up, horse, foot and guns, he pounded them, and hit them with the horses, he shot them to bits and they was all bloody and broken and then when they ran, we all got to chase them and kill them. Look, missus! Look what I got!'*

*It was unmistakeably an ear, already starting to dry.*

*Elizabeth stopped smiling and swallowed. 'Many congratulations,' she said. 'And is my lord Earl of Sherbourne well?'*

*'Oh yes, Majesty, he sent you this letter and he says not to tell you of his leg, it'll be well soon, he's sure of it.'*

*'His leg?'*

*'He took a musket ball in it, but the barber's seen to it and searched it and it'll be right as rain soon . . .'*

*Her heart had turned back to grey ice. That sounded too much like Sidney.*

*She opened the letter, which had been dictated. It told the tale of the victory, more eloquently but less vividly, and it said that Parma was alive but utterly routed, and the great tercio of Lombardy utterly shattered. The Spaniards had run and Sir David Becket had taken their entire siege train, many horses and any quantity you like of food and weaponry. Ralegh signed it with his old nickname of Water and added a drawing of a bucket, just to make a point. She smiled again. There was no mention of his wound. But at the bottom, in a very unclerkly scrawl, was a note that read: 'Your Majesty, in God's name order my lord of Sherborne for to have his leg cut off or he will end like Sidney, which I saw. Your loyal and obedient subject, Sir David Becket.'*

*And so the Queen put on her cloak and called for the whitest horse from her stables, which she mounted astride because most of the sidesaddles had been left in Whitehall. It was very uncomfortable and insecure but she put up with it.*

*Then she gathered all the wagons she could, commandeered oxen out of the fields and some of the students to guard them and they set out down the road to meet the victorious troops.*

*They met in an hour. At the head of the raggedly happy army rode the Earl of Oxford, white from the jail fever still, and transparently thin. There were few of them and utterly weary, and they were bringing in the heavy guns before the road was made worse by the return of the rest of the army of Oxford.*

*Elizabeth gave them the yokes of oxen she had brought and continued on to the camp Ralegh had made. She told the alarmed young men that they were to gather up all those who had fought and she would speak to them directly.*

*In the centre was a makeshift lean-to walled with canvas and inside it, as she swept aside the men of her lifeguard who knelt to her and muddied their velvet even further, lay Ralegh. He was sleeping, propped up in bed, clammy and white with pain. She sniffed carefully, found a smell of the hunting field but no scent of the midden nor the mousehole that predicted gangrene. So she sat down beside him on the camp stool and waited patiently. There was a heavy squelching and Sir David blocked the light as he came in, then knelt to her.*

*'Up,' she said. 'How is he?'*

*'He says Your Majesty will never countenance a one-legged man as her general.'*

*'What stuff. For all his victory, he is still a vain, arrogant man. Does he think I value the prettiness of his legs above his life?'*

*Becket smiled. 'He certainly does, I think.'*

*'Go and fetch the barber-surgeon.'*

*Becket bowed and walked out. The Queen took up the long fingers, flaccid now, and gripped them.*

*Ralegh's eyes were open, bright with fever, resting on her. 'Your Majesty, Parma is broken for the time being.'*

*She smiled and gripped his hand, which answered her feebly. 'I have it on good authority that Drake is now recovered of his fever and gathering up all the ships he can in Southampton. He will retake Gravesend for us with Justin of Nassau. Your victory has given us the autumn and the winter to rest and recharge ourselves.'*

*Ralegh lifted her hand and kissed it. 'Elizabeth,' he whispered, 'marry me.'*

*'What?'*

*'If you marry me, I'll have the surgeon take my leg. It's all I ask. You need not make me your King unless you desire it, only make me your husband.'*

'This is no time for courtierly, romantical nonsense, Water. I am far too old for you and you should find yourself some sweet-faced girl to give you babies.'

'Your Majesty has had men mutilated for saying such things.'

'That was then. Now it is I, Elizabeth, who speak. For me to marry you, Water, would be ridiculous. I am an old woman and barren; you are a young man who has never hesitated to bed any girl that took your fancy and was foolish enough to listen to your charming words. The thing will never do.'

'Then let's take it for policy. If I am your husband, my authority over all your soldiers is assured. Walsingham will be unable to challenge it, nor will young Essex try anything. As your husband, if anything should happen to you, I will be able to finish the fight.'

'You might betray me to Spain or you might decide to take the kingship yourself,' snapped Elizabeth.

'But Elizabeth, I could do that in any case. And as your husband, not your king, but your husband, I supplant Philip's claim to the throne.'

'And if I die?'

'I shall be Regent until I can find and marry Arabella Stuart. Our issue shall rule.'

'You may die of the amputation.'

'Yes. And I had rather die your wedded man than your liegeman, Elizabeth. It's true I have bedded many foolish maidens, but not a one of them failed to bore me to distraction as soon as we were done, for a vainer pack of empty-headed jilts I have never found than among your own waiting women.'

Elizabeth snorted with amusement.

'But you . . . you Elizabeth . . . Yes, I professed undying love for you like everyone else for flattery and advancement, of course I did. Except then it became true.'

Elizabeth sighed and stared into space. 'You spoke once of the different laws of the land of war.'

'I did. One of them being, carpe diem.'

'If you have your leg cut off . . .'

He lifted his head, moving uneasily under the blankets, gripping her hand so her fingertips went white. 'No, Elizabeth, I know your ways. Your promises are as empty as your women's heads. You marry me first. Then I have my leg cut off.'

At court, this honesty would have been met by thrown slippers and roars of profanity. Now Elizabeth lowered her gaze and coloured.

David Becket was waiting at the door of the lean-to with the surgeon.

*When they were called in it was to send for a churchman and witness the most extraordinary proceedings as Elizabeth Tudor, spinster of the parish of Whitehall, was wedded to Walter Ralegh, bachelor of the same.*

*And then the surgeon rolled up his sleeves and produced his straps and saw, and Elizabeth sat by her new husband while the surgeon sawed and the blood flowed.*

Again I woke before Becket, to find sunlight shining into the storeroom and my hip aching from sleeping on the flagstones.

About me hung the silent hams and sides of beef, rose the towers of pickle barrels. It all smelled very pungent but not unpleasant.

Rebecca would have sailed by now with her new helper, Anthony Fant, sailed and gone. And I was left here in Flanders, a land where I did not speak the language, with Becket whom I had ridden but whose prophecies were utterly strange to me. Nor, if I am truthful, did I much care which hairy ghost tribe ruled the cold muddy island that was his home. Let their gods contend against each other, for in that cold morning, all I could think of was that my son was still a slave and I could do nothing for him.

I had hardly seen him while I was upside-down. The gods and spirits of the forest had been my family, and my sister had loved him and brought him to manhood, given him beer when his newly carved snake still throbbed and bled on his right arm and his hand shook so he could hardly drink. She was the mother of his heart, true, but I had given him suck and he had been a fat little boy of three, running in mischief from puddle to tree to wall to find more ways of terrifying me when the Queen Moon had swooped down into my head and caused me to kill my husband when he beat me again for straying in his dreams. Upside-down, I could think of my son in the terrible hands of the hairy ghosts and not tremble, for the spirit world was realer to me than this one. Now I had turned right-side up again, without warning, turned by beer and aqua vitae. All I could think was that the chains would hurt his chubby little neck terribly. He was a grown man and I had seen him as a man, but still he was the child of my heart and my heart wept blood for him.

To help with that, I drank up half of Becket's aqua vitae and went to cut him some ham. As dawn came, the innkeeper came with his brother, carrying clubs, to open the door to the storeroom and let us out. Our bill had at least been paid, although the innkeeper wanted us to recompense him for the ham we had taken for breakfast until Becket threatened to see the magistrates to lay charges of false imprisonment and robbery.

We stumbled wearily out into the street and Becket insisted on going straight to the quay where the *Salamander of London* had been moored. She was gone of course. Slipped out on the morning tide.

We looked at the money we had – a few shillings and a couple of crowns. Not enough to last more than a couple of days.

Becket sat nursing a jug of ale in a boozing ken, blinking into space, while I hummed to myself a song of accusation against the Lady Leopard, whose shadow sat with its back to me in a corner, lashing her tail. I still had a headache and my face was swollen up from Becket's ill-treatment of me, nor could I chew the hard bread they brought to go with the ale since my jaw-hinges were sore as well. I sucked down ale instead and it made me dizzy.

Finally Becket slapped his hand flat on the table and said, 'We'll go to Dunkirk.'

I nodded owlishly at him.

'It's where the peace commissioners are based and we can ask Robert Cecil to send a message to the Queen that her plan went awry before it was properly started. Perhaps we could find work as their guards or messengers or some such. Are you with me, Merula?'

Again I could have told him no. I could have told him to take himself to Dunkirk by all means and then gone and hired on as a hand on one of the ships sailing to Africa for to buy slaves. I could have done it, for there would have been at least one sailing from that port in a month's time. But I was unwilling and afraid, unhappy to be alone in a land where most would think me an escaped slave, and in any case I did not speak the language. To be with Becket at least gave me countenance and some protection against those who would sell me to a whorehouse. How had I become so cowardly? In the cold world that you find when the god dismounts and abandons you, to be cowardly is only sensible.

Besides I wanted to be with Becket. My heart took light from his touch, even when all we did was sleep, his dreams of prophecy carried me where I had once travelled by myself, carried only by my own intention. The Queen Moon must have laughed at what a sad, sensible creature I had become, how I had fallen from being upside-down just when I needed it most.

So I said to Becket, 'Certainly I am with you. Do you think they will hire me?'

'Why not?' he said, grinning. 'If only to humour me.'

We played cards that night, just the two of us together, for thousands of ducats and Becket wound up owing me ten thousand ducats for which I accepted a part-payment in kind. In the morning we hired horses and headed south and west along the line of the coast, which Becket said would bring us to Dunkirk.

# BOOK II

# Señor Josef Pasquale

The Church of the Blessed Virgin was cool and dim; only a few candles were lit and none of the side chapels showing the Virgin's life could be seen, because the shadows were so black. In summer, through the high windows, you could see the day blazing from the iridescent lapis lazuli of the sky, but the sun could not shine directly into the church, except through the rainbow filter of the great window behind the altar. The Virgin in her elaborate chapel beside the High Altar was dressed in her usual clothes, the green silks of Ordinary Time, not the heavy gold or red brocades of festivals. His own mother had embroidered that green gown with the Glorious Mysteries of the rosary. Herself, with her own hands, in thanks for his birth. The candlelight glinted occasionally on the Virgin's plump pink cheeks, and on her baby Son's upraised fingers.

Señor Josef Pasqale knelt to say his customary rosary, asking for strength and determination, to steel himself against pity, to understand that the Holy Office had a vital though humble part to play in the greatness of the Catholic Church. For it was in the nature of purity that it was easily damaged; and as long as that great cesspool of corrupt doctrine festered in the north, so there was always the risk that the Spanish peninsular might be infected and likewise become gangrenous with heresy.

He thought he knew what kind of evil he was dealing with in Simon Anriques, so-called. He suspected. He only had to apply the right pressure, and he would find it out. Everything.

Holy Mother, he whispered in the darkness, keep my heart pure, let me not be seduced into pleasure at what I do, vouchsafe only that by my diligence I may preserve your purity and the purity of my Holy Mother Church. Help me to find out the heretics, wherever they may be, and destroy them. Help me to resist their sinful miasmas.

There was no answer, as usual. He rose, genuflected, crossed himself, ready to go. Was that a crystal tear under the blue glass eyes, just glimpsed as he turned away? No, only a trick of the light.

He was far too sinful to be given a vision. And besides, why should the Virgin weep when he was doing her work?

He crossed himself again with Holy Water. He felt better, for he always dreaded interrogations. The pleading, the screams . . . It was a hard vocation. But coming to church first gave him strength, and guarded him from the sickness and greed of some others in the Holy Office, who were interested only in what rich estates they might confiscate. He treated rich and poor exactly alike.

They brought Anriques, the suspected English heretic, up from the cells, where he had had a couple of days to consider his position. He was very angry, loud and pugnacious, standing square on the tiled floor of Pasquale's office, dishevelled, unshaven.

'Sir, I protest!' he said. 'I am, as you know, a merchant in sugar and I demand to know the nature of any accusation against me—'

'We do not find it appropriate to answer your questions,' said Pasquale. 'Please answer ours. Your name?'

'Simon Anriques.'

'Your place of birth?'

He claimed to have been born in the New World, in Cartagena, which certainly was the last place his ship had docked. His ship was registered in Antwerp, where the priest who had reported him was taken on. There were people called Anriques living there and also in Cartagena. It was possible. Of course, it depended what you meant by people.

They went through the whole rigmarole, how he was Portuguese by descent, indeed, more Portuguese than the King. How he was the son of a merchant now dead, how his uncle had helped finance his voyage, how he had traded guns and gunpowder down to the Slave Coast, loaded slaves . . . Yes, he had a *permesso* – it was on his ship. If he could go there and fetch it . . .

The searchers had found no such thing, but Señor Pasquale did not say so.

Señor Pasquale took careful notes, cross-questioned. The tale was solid, it was possible he told some of the truth. If there had been no other information than what Anriques said, if there had been no scrawled and booze-spattered affidavit from the ship's chaplain, perhaps he would have got away with no more than the confiscation of his ship and deportation.

They went through it twice, Anriques getting more and more agitated, swearing over and over by Christ and every saint there was that he did not know what the Inquisition wanted with him . . .

Another little clue. Interesting. Was it possible? His Portuguese was very good, as was his Spanish.

The man had meandered to a halt. Pasquale looked through his notes for a long moment and then nodded at his three assistants. Two of them held Anriques carefully, while his manacles were taken off and they removed his clothes except for his shirt. He squawked at them, as men always did, denying, expostulating . . . Pasquale thought it overdone.

Still struggling, Anriques was strapped to the long table with the gutters and the little block to go under the small of the back, to keep the chest arched upwards. He was scrawny, not at all well-built, and gave the assistants no real trouble. Even if he had not had his own preferred method, Pasquale would not have used a rack or the strappado on Anriques for fear of killing him accidentally.

At Pasquale's nod, they inserted the smallest metal gag to keep Anriques' mouth open and fed in the funnel of cloth. For some reason, the block of wood pressing against the spine prevented vomiting. Anriques' eyes rolled, his chest heaved, his neck corded. One of the assistants bound his head more firmly down to the table.

'Two jugs,' said Pasquale, and turned to sit down with his back to the prisoner.

The trickling of water was spoiled by the sound of choking, coughing, more choking. Enough water would go down Anriques' gullet to distend his stomach and make it press down on the block against his spine, and all the time he would be drowning slowly as the water trickled down the funnel in his throat.

Generally speaking, Pasquale rarely found it took more than four jugs to get at the truth.

When the two jugs had gone, Pasquale sent the assistants to draw more water – and it was always the best water, pure from the well, no filth in it as some liked to do – and went to stand by Anriques' head while he coughed and gasped and strained. His tongue was bloody from the gag holding his teeth apart, bloody spittle dripping down his cheeks.

'Please. I would prefer not to trouble you any more,' Pasquale said, as he always did. 'I take no pleasure from this, believe me. But I simply must have the truth.'

Of course, Anriques couldn't answer with his mouth open and the metal gag pressing against his tongue, but he could move his head just enough to nod. His eyes bugged as he nodded. Good.

'Now, I desire to know where you were born. And I desire to

know when and where you were christened. And I desire to know your business here.'

Very carefully, in case of being bitten, which had happened once or twice before, Pasquale removed the gag.

'I told you . . . I was born in Cartagena in the New World . . .'

Pasquale sighed. He held the man's nose and slipped the gag back in again, before the prisoner could imperil his immortal soul any more. His assistants came back with the jugs, reinserted the cloth funnel and began pouring again, very slowly. You had to be careful because if you split a man's belly, of course he would die, and then he couldn't confess and be shriven of his sins. Also it took great skill to keep someone on the edge of drowning, so that they went in and out of consciousness without actually killing them. Pasquale usually timed it by saying an Ave Maria. Any more than three Aves and the man would start to die. Once they had brought a prisoner round with great difficulty, only to find he had turned into an idiot.

There was also the problem of the way water affected people: it was possible for someone to die simply of drinking too much water, extraordinary as that might seem. You had to let them up to be sick occasionally. Which was the reason for the basins let into the table. Pasquale had designed it himself since he had no wish to trouble his cleaners with stains on his tiles, of any kind.

It seemed that this Anriques was quite weak, because he passed out completely for longer periods each time. On the fourth time they took the gag out, he began babbling in some Germanic tongue, Flemish or English as he started coming round. This was interesting and encouraging, so Pasquale nodded, and the assistants unbound all but his right hand so he could turn over and vomit his pregnant belly empty. He did immediately, helplessly, on all fours, gasping and gagging. His nose started bleeding, which was a bad sign. Unfortunately, he had lost control of himself when he passed out the last time, so with care, while he continued to spew, they cut his shirt off and sluiced him with more water. Anriques finally finished emptying his guts again, and collapsed half-conscious on his side. And that was when Pasquale finally recognised the sign, realised what they really had here. This wasn't just an English heretic spy.

It was a Jew.

Pasquale couldn't help himself. He stared. There had officially been no Jews in the holy and pure land of Spain since the reign of the Catholic Princes, King Ferdinand and Queen Isabella. A little less than a hundred years before, all Christ-killers had been ordered to convert to the true Religion or be expelled. The Holy Office had in fact been instituted in order to enforce the law that said once he had been converted to Christianity, no matter how forcibly, any Jew returning to his old ways was a heretic and could therefore be burned by the Secular Arm. It was a nicety of law that few appreciated: the Jews were never persecuted for being Jews, only expelled as filth no Christian nation could tolerate. If they wanted to stay in the country of their birth, they had only to convert to Catholicism. But then, if they started following Jewish ways again, *then* they could be burned. And were, sometimes in their hundreds. Apart from a few Turkish galley-slaves, there were no circumcised men in Spain.

And this . . . this man had been circumcised.

Pasquale drew his dagger, stepped up to the table and used the point delicately to lift the abomination. No mistake. No accident. He was entire . . . except for his foreskin. And he was no Moor because his skin was too pale.

Pasquale shuddered, put his dagger away.

'Jesus Christ also was circumcised, as I am.' Anriques was lying in the remnants of his spasms, still bleeding from the nose and mouth. His voice was down to a croak – one of the disadvantages of the use of the jugs, since subjects could often only whisper afterwards.

'I beg your pardon?'

The half-shut eyes stretched in a bruised smile. 'Jesus was circumcised. Says so. In the Bible. Because he was a Jew.'

Pasquale lost control of himself. Pure rage caused him to lift his fist, punch the filthy creature in the face. It was inexcusable, even in the circumstances.

He put his dagger away, wiped his hand with a napkin hanging on a rail under the table, stepped away.

When he was sure his voice would not shake, he said, 'You spoke English while you were unconscious. I know that you are an English heretic, trading illegally.'

The Jew's mouth was bleeding badly, breath caught raggedly in a swollen throat. 'So?'

'And you are . . . a Jew.' Pasquale was still upset, he was dabbing his napkin on his split knuckles. He should have known better. The devil's spawn had sharp teeth.

The devil's spawn lifted itself up on its elbow, looked down at itself, spat out one of its teeth. 'Yes, I am. Since you ask,' it whispered. 'I have always been a Jew. I was circumcised, like Christ, at eight days old. At fourteen, like Christ, I had my Bar Mitzvah. You asked . . .' He paused to cough again, spat some more blood, '. . . when and where I was christened. I was not christened. I have never been christened. I was born in London just before Passover in 1553, and in all my life I have never been a Christian. I have observed, to the best of my poor abilities, the Jewish faith.'

This new horror had not occurred to Pasquale. Surely even heretics took the trouble to ensure some orthodoxy? Certainly they did against the True Religion. Surely they did not tolerate the filth of Judaism in England?

'Are you surprised, Señor?' asked the Jew. 'The Queen of England has granted dispensation. To all of us.'

This interview had gone wrong. Somehow Pasquale had lost the initiative, worse, he had lost his natural and normal ascendancy over a Killer of Christ. His assistants, one of whom was trained in law, stared at him in alarm. The abominable whispering went on.

'Señor, you cannot accuse me of Judaising or apostasy. I have never been a Christian so I cannot have returned to the religion I never . . . ptah . . . left. I am simply a merchant. If you had not arrested me, I would have been gone from this country, in accordance with the old sentence of exile.' The pale brown eyes watered with more violent coughing. 'I have committed no crime against the law here and you have no legal hold on me. I demand that you release me and return my ship to me.'

Pasquale rammed the gag back in the creature's mouth and retired to his desk to think, while the devil's spawn sat naked on the table, cross-legged, comfortable despite the right wrist still bound to a corner. It coughed in paroxysms through the O of the gag, trying to clear the water from its lungs. Pasquale went to the prie-dieu in the corner and prayed briefly for guidance.

At last, he regained enough control to speak calmly to his assistants. 'Clean it. Give it something to cover itself. Take it back to the cells.'

He had to wash his hands over and over until the jug was empty, to get the feeling of pollution off. Then he went to the nearby church of St Simeon, where he lit a candle and prayed fervently for guidance. For what the Christ-Killer had said was true. He had absolutely no legal hold on it.

Afterwards, Pasquale tried to write his report while his assistants cleaned and scrubbed the table. Pasquale was always careful in his reports. He used the shorthand account his clerk took of the dialogue and he made sure he separated his opinions from the facts of what the accused might have said.

There was, however, no way of covering up the lamentable fact that the Jew had legality on his side. The letter of the law was on the Jew's side, but of course the spirit of it clearly could not be. Pasquale went into some detail as he explained exactly why he felt that the only correct action was immediate relaxation of the Jew to the secular arm, followed by burning at the next *auto de fe*.

But he could not concentrate. It took him a long time to write, was not as polished as he would have wished. In the end he left his draft to be fair-copied for tomorrow by his clerk, who might be able to clear up some of the trailing ends of thoughts that had intruded as he worked. He scanned the draft to be sure there were no traces of sin. For sin seemed to surround him like a miasma again, strong and pungent from his rage at the Jew.

Pasquale left to have his dinner. He often went home to keep his mother company while she sucked and dribbled on the carefully mashed foods her woman prepared for her, but Pasquale felt he was not up to the strain of making one-sided conversation for appearance's sake. He went to a tavern instead, asked for the ordinary of the day and then when it came, a novelty dish of pork in a sauce of New Spanish fruit, sat there looking at it, his stomach churning and his head full of fragmented pictures.

He was often unsettled in this way after an interrogation, even if it had gone well. He was similar to a physician in many ways, a doctor of the State. Just as a physician who was brave enough to treat plague or smallpox ran the risk of catching the disease himself, so Pasquale's proximity to sin often infected him with it. For a long time he had been able to keep succubi and sinful thoughts at bay by praying and fasting. But there had been the suspected Jewess last year, the woman who would not eat pork. He had interrogated her and after she broke and admitted everything, he had been so full of heat and the devilish exudations from her, that he had . . .

The memory broke out again, what he had done. He had only been trying to avoid sin . . . No, if he was honest, he had not. He had sought out sin because he had come to such a pitch that he felt the mortal sin of fornication would be less bad than the constant nagging of images in his head that made him abstracted and unable to concentrate, unable to sleep.

Was that what he needed this time? Did he need to visit the little house in the old Moorish quarter? With the metal grills and the veiled women who took charge of him? It would mean a great penance when he confessed, of course, but it would be worth it if he could think straight and function afterwards.

Suddenly decisive, he left money for his uneaten meal, and swept off, walking swiftly through the blazing sun, through almost empty streets, black robe flapping behind him as he took a deliberately twisty, doubling-back route through the little white streets, down the steps, across the tiny courtyard almost filled by the orange tree.

The heavy door was locked, as always. He knocked, waited, knocked again. They would be looking at him from one of the forbidden upstairs rooms, from behind a screen.

He had heard of the address from one of his assistants, overheard it really since the man had been laughing at a cousin of his who made regular visits. The address had burned in his head for a month. At last he had stumbled to the place, drunk one night after a man had died while he was being interrogated. They had wanted a recommendation, a password: it was like visiting a nunnery, arguing back and forth through the grill in the door. He had passed two gold pieces through the wires and at last the door had opened. They had insisted on blindfolding him, that first time, which had somehow served only to increase his heat. To trust such people, probably poor New Christians who could earn their bread no other way, to consign himself helpless into their care . . . It had made his heart thunder and his loins swell, he had been hotter and more aching with the miserable pressure of sin than ever before. And the women there had soothed him, gently commanded him, eased his dreadful stress, reassured him of his rightness. They had sung to him, done what he desired and not laughed when he wept helplessly under his blindfold.

In time they had come to trust him and allowed him to enter the long, low, ornately screened room without a blindfold. He didn't really see why it had been necessary because he never saw any of their faces. Even when they were dancing oiled and naked for him, they kept a Moorish veil across the lower part of their faces and no matter how he begged, not one of them would reveal herself. Sometimes he was alone, but more often there were others there, tactfully hidden by curtains and screens, revealed only by moans and occasional sharp noises beyond the clouds of Moroccan incense. It was like the Paradise of the Moors, a place of ecstasy and guilt.

He went as often as he could afford it for months, happily fasting as his confessor ordered so that he could save the money. Then once his first frenzy was calmed, he went when he needed to and they welcomed him.

It was strange how badly he needed women, and yet he had no desire to marry. Of course at the moment, it would hardly be very suitable. But he had never fallen in love with any of the girls who had sat demure and formal in the garden of his mother's house.

The black door opened and the woman who opened it had only her eyes showing under her veil, in the Moorish way. He knew her by her eyes alone, which were large and almond shaped. She was the one with broad, lush hips and heavy breasts, soft as butter and about the same colour. When he smiled at her humbly, she gripped his hand and led him into the long, dim room, screened by marble, filled with cushions and curtains and little hookahs of tobacco and incense mixed. There were the familiar heavy scents in the air, jasmine and musk and women, that strangely rounded, tip-tilted smell of woman. He gave the doorwoman his money and when she had put it in the bound carved box, the two other women, also veiled, came to him and laughing at him, humming at him, took his robe and doublet off for him. They led him, trembling already, to one of the curtained alcoves and then bound his hands with silk scarves to the screen, gagged him with another scarf so he could not shame himself by pleading or crying out. He was utterly in their hands, at their mercy, helpless ... And then, as he felt his body melting and boiling, softening and hardening, they delicately forced him into the wickedness of fornication that he so desperately needed and desired.

Every time he always felt he might die from the pleasure of it, from that heart-pounding dagger of joy. The first time he had been terrified that the wetness he felt was his blood. Now he knew better. But every time it was as sharp, as unendurable as before. If he had not been restrained, he would not have been able to allow it, so wild did it make him.

Afterwards, when they had taken the scarf from between his teeth, he lay and panted and they fanned him and cleaned him, untied his hands and massaged them, wiped his face with orange flower water. As his heart slowed from a gallop to a canter to a trot, he always promised that this would be the last time he sought out sin. Always he promised it, always meaning it.

He dozed away the siesta hour until the women tapped him and told him in their soft voices that he must go. He languorously put on his clothes again, while one of the women knelt to do his laces at the back. And then she firmly led him to the door and out again. As always, hearing the door shut and lock on Paradise behind him, he felt like a sleeper awakening.

Then as always, he went straight to confession, walking as fast as he could, terrified that he might suddenly be struck down by some footpad or an attack of plague and go to hell because he had not had time to be shriven.

He alternated between four different churches for his confession, so as not to shock the priest, and found that each had his favourite penance for fornication: a couple of rosaries in one, a donation to church funds in another, a hairshirt to be worn for a week or nightly use of the discipline at another and the fourth would normally recommend a month of abstaining from meat, except once in Lent when he had ordered a week-long fast. That had been very difficult, but Pasquale had performed it diligently, welcoming the night sweats and the dizzy weakness during the day because at least he felt no need to sin while he was thinking of food all the time. He tried conscientiously not to sin again before he had paid off the penance for the last time.

It was the fourth church's turn today. He slipped into the dark booth, saw the shadow of the priest's face behind the grill, and began as soon as the priest had closed his book. He gabbled his prayers, anxious to be absolved and waited expectantly.

'My son,' said the priest with a sigh, 'I have heard this tale from you before. Last month, in fact. And the month before.'

Pasquale flushed although the priest couldn't see him through the grill. 'Father?'

'This sin of fornication is regular, is it, my son?'

Pasquale coughed, stuttered. The priest sighed again.

'Are you in holy orders?'

'Minor orders, only, Father.'

'Well then, my son, have you considered the holy state of matrimony?'

'I—'

'Consider it. As St Paul says, it is better to marry than to burn. In the meantime I would like you to refrain from meat for the rest of this month and if you cannot marry, may I suggest an adventure.'

'A . . . what?'

'An adventure. If you have no pressing familial ties, go on a voyage, enter the service of His Majesty the King, become a soldier. Something that will take you away from the occasion of your sin.'

Pasquale was shocked to the point of gobbling as he tried to think of reasons why it was impossible. Except that it wasn't, of course, apart from his mother.

So he refrained from meat, knowing that it would make him easily tired but also that his humours would be less hot as a result which would be a good thing. And the suggestion of the priest at the church he no longer visited stayed in his mind like a stone in his shoe.

In due course, the Jew came to trial. Pasquale worked at his case in the week leading up to the trial, was up all that night with a flux born of pure nerves. He prayed before he went in front of the judge, did his very best – and found that the judge was clearly insane.

After the judgement, Señor Pasquale was outraged, unable to believe his ears. He went back to the judge to make his representations, wondering if he should approach the Cortes for a retrial. The judge received him in his chamber and listened courteously to three hours of Pasquale's arguments that all Christ-Killers should die and in particular one as insolent as Anriques.

'Certainly he is insolent, certainly,' agreed the judge, 'and if this were a normal time, I would be in agreement with you, Señor. However ...' He passed over a piece of official paper, properly watermarked and signed by the King himself.

Pasquale read the King's appeal to all judges that in any cases where there was the slightest shadow of doubt, they should sentence to the galleys instead of to death. There was a desperate call for men of all sizes to row the oars of the four new galleases being delivered from Naples for the Enterprise of England.

'I understand from my contacts that they have eighteen oars on each side and that because of the high freeboard, the sweeps are very long and require seven men each,' explained the judge. Señor Pasquale's lips moved as he tried to calculate how many fresh galley slaves this required. 'Of course, there must be at least two hundred and fifty-two slaves in each galleas, one thousand and eight all told, plus fifty or so in the hold to replace wastage. In fact we have been told to find two thousand of them, to allow for losses.'

'Excellency, what is a galleas?'

209

'I believe it is a new invention of His Grace, Lord Admiral Santa Cruz, a cross between a galleon and a galley. It has three masts and it carries a great weight of ordnance. This is all I know. It is intended for a special purpose, which is a secret, in the Holy Enterprise of England. Now tell me, Señor, which is more important? To burn one Jew or to help save the souls of all the poor heretics lost in the toils of the Witch-Queen of England?'

Señor Pasquale bowed and withdrew all his objections.

Along with the priest's suggestion of a few weeks before, the King's appeal stirred his blood. He prayed about it as he returned to his mother's house that evening, partly to avoid looking at the noble ladies who took the air.

When he entered his mother's chamber to say goodnight, he found the old lady well tucked up, her lace-trimmed nightcap tied a little too tight about her chin. She had been terribly afflicted by a syncope the year before and could only move one arm a little and speak hardly at all. Sometimes she wept with rage as she told the amethyst beads of her rosary, but sometimes she was calm, as she was today. She had withered in the past year, her skin become flaccid and baggy and pale. Only her eyes still made her beautiful, wide, almond-shaped, liquid and brown, her black brows still winged above them, and the frown lines between making the body of the bird. The whites had become a little yellow but the pupils were so large and velvet, it hardly mattered. Many, many times as a child, Josef had heard his reverend father praise his mother's eyes. Once he had teased her, saying that only among the Moors and the *marranos* were there women with such beautiful eyes and his mother had flashed lightning under her brows and sworn angrily at her husband, saying that she came of an excellent Old Christian family and never forget it. They had made up the quarrel in bed, while Josef hid his head under a pillow and tried not to listen. When his father died at Lepanto, his mother had taken to wearing mourning always, and become thinner and less curved – but still her eyes were where her soul lived. Now they were the only part of her that could speak clearly and they rested on Josef, full of love? Perhaps. He prayed to the Virgin every day that he could be a good son to her in her need.

He leaned over and retied the ribbons under her chin so they would be more comfortable. Then he knelt by his mother's bed.

'Mother, I have a very important matter to discuss with you. How are you feeling?'

She looked at him and firmed her lip, which was inclined to slacken. He wiped a little spit from it with a clean cloth. 'Yesh,' she said.

'Mother, you have heard Father Juarez preach of the Holy Enterprise of England?'

'Yesh,' she said, frowning at the sound of her voice.

'Mother, the Holy Office will be set up in London once Parma has taken the city. It will be a great and holy work to bring the heretics back to the arms of Holy Mother Church. All the best men will be needed.'

She said nothing, waited, staring at him like a little bird.

'Mother,' he faltered, knowing how hard was the thing that he was asking of her, 'if I can find you a pleasant and kindly convent to enter, if I am found worthy of going with the Enterprise . . . m . . . may I . . . may I go?'

He was afraid she would rage at him, forbid him, as she had when he had wanted to go to Flanders five years before. He was her son and he knew he must obey her if she asked him to stay because she needed him.

The good hand, the one that always held the rosary, clutched convulsively and he held it.

'Yesh,' she said, quite clearly, hauling the waxy folds of her face into half of a smile. 'God . . . with . . . you . . . Josef.'

His heart soared and he kissed her poor hand. She held tight.

'Write . . . to . . .' She frowned, struggled, breathing harshly, with the effort of remembering, 'to . . . my cousin . . . Juan de Acuna Vela.'

Of course! Her aunt's son, now the King's Secretary for Ships' Ordnance. Wonderful. Pasquale would write tomorrow; one of his assistants had already suggested a pleasant, respectable convent where the nuns would care for his mother well until he returned. He thought he was senior enough in the Holy Office that if he expressed a desire to go with the Enterprise, his cousin would find a way of allowing him. Certainly, if it was God's will that he go, then there would be no lasting obstacle. The priest who gave fasting penances had been right.

He would be like those famous men of the Society of Jesus who had gone among the benighted heathen savages of the New World, and brought them, in their thousands, to be baptised. He could see himself, standing in the sun at St Paul's, watching the Host in the reconsecration procession as it passed the cheering, genuflecting crowds of the newly freed English.

It was the mission he had been born to fulfil.

# Suleiman

Suleiman always looked forward to seeing the new men unwrapped, not only because he enjoyed the sight, but also because you could start to see what they were. Since they had all usually been in prison for a while before, it was less important how big their muscles were than how they stood, how they looked around, how they walked.

He was a voluntary, of course he was. As soon as he had heard that the fascinating galleases were recruiting, he had gone to volunteer, even though his true loves were the slim and deadly galleys, with their sharp beaks, their centre-line cannon, everything about them stripped to the essentials, graceful and beautiful as a cat. He liked cats. To row in a galley was not a sentence, not a servitude, but an honour, as he always told his bench. This was why he had made the galleys his life.

But it had been obvious after the English El Draco beat Santa Cruz's very own galleys at Cadiz that they might have been Queens of the Mediterranean, but they could not cope with the Atlantic seas or the Atlantic ships. For this reason, Santa Cruz had ordered the building of the strange hybrids that were galleases. And as soon as he heard the first whisper about them in a wineshop, Suleiman had been on fire to see one, row in one.

He had come aboard the day before, newly shaved at the most expensive barber's in town, blowing the last of his money on it, carrying only his dagger, his water bottle and his whip. The Señors had greeted him with open arms, delighted to have such an experienced man, who had rowed at Lepanto. They had given him charge of two sweeps, thirteen men, since they were so short of voluntaries for this Enterprise.

Suleiman wasn't at all sure where this England was and didn't particularly care why one brand of Christian wanted to conquer another. Once he had prayed to Mecca five times daily, now he felt proud of himself if he remembered once a day. Nobody troubled him to be baptised now; he thought he had been a couple of times, but couldn't remember. Only on voyages was he truly alive. The times between tended to fade into the wine and aqua vitae he drank.

Yesterday he had persuaded one of the riggers to show him round his new ship, the *San Lorenzo*, flagship of the four galleases. It wasn't much like a galley, in fact, being high in the water, with three decks and three masts. This was going to be very heavy to row. They were also carrying a complement of sailors for the sails and gunners for the guns – there were gunports all along the top deck – but not all the gunports had a gun. There was still a shortage of ordnance, although the galleases were getting the pick of them.

The rigger took him down to the oardeck. It was not open to the sky as a galley's was, but closed in under the top deck, although pierced at intervals with gratings. Suleiman brushed his moustache with the back of his hand and frowned. Eighteen sweeps either side, grouped in two fives and two fours, with gunports between the groups. The sweeps must be immense because of the great angle needed to reach the water from so high above it, but they had not yet been rigged, so the oar holes with their leather padding and hanging iron rings were open. The lowest bench was a few feet from the oar hole, the second at an angle and so on built up to the central walkway. That steep angle would be a problem with a ship so heavy. Suleiman frowned again. Six men plus the Padron to each double bench, how would they do it? And water would be a problem too, once the oars were in, for the guns took up the space they usually used for water barrels. Santa Cruz may have been a great admiral but he had never rowed a galley.

'How many are they giving us?' he asked the rigger, kicking the ringbolts on the nearest bench to see if they were firm.

'About two hundred and seventy,' said the man, staring around him curiously. 'Don't the oars chafe in the holes?'

Suleiman put his hand on the nearest pivot chain with its great ring to take the oar. 'Train the men right and the oars never need to touch the sides,' he said and pulled on the ring to be sure it was firm. Well, at least that had been done properly. But two hundred and seventy men were not going to be enough because unless they could solve the water problem they would lose a lot to heat and thirst the first time they took them out. They would be sailing some time soon, after the slaves were in, when the winds were fair.

He climbed up from the bench pits to the wide walkway, walked along it. They hadn't rigged the guardnets yet because the slaves hadn't been installed. And it all smelled of new wood and sawing.

The floor was unnaturally clean, the gutters and drains clear, the benches sharp-edged and unworn.

He was sure there would be problems in heavy seas because of the way the sweeps were angled and they would certainly need the sails to get them started. This was very different from a galley, not nearly so beautiful or so cleverly designed. A galley was such an ancient thing, although individually most of them were no more than twenty or thirty years old because of ship-worms. There was nothing in a galley that had not been tested over hundreds of years and kept only because it was efficient. Here the thing was new, there were many compromises and he had not yet even seen the sweeps. He would bet that the handrails on them would be angled wrong and probably not firm enough.

They needed three hundred men per ship to allow for injuries. He had told the Señor of the Benches so and the man had laughed at him.

Now, today, looking at the slaves as they cluttered up the quay in their chains, some scowling, some blank-faced, some clearly terrified, Suleiman's heart sank. Gaston was cutting their clothes off and some showed marks of torture, some were deformed, some diseased. Allah, that one had leprosy!

Outraged, Suleiman went to argue with the Señor of the Benches, who took one look and blanched. At least the leper was taken out of the chains, sent back to prison to rot.

He passed along through the crowds of chained, frightened men, assessing, judging. He chose two gangs that seemed marginally less useless than the others, at least there were a couple of blacks in one gang and one in another. One in each gang was clearly the runt, there was always one: you needed a short man to go down next to the oarport, though it helped if he was strong to steady it, a miner or a blacksmith. Neither of these were. One was some kind of scrawny clerk with the unmistakeable red rash of a hairshirt all over him and ... oh ... Was he Musselman? Well, no matter, he'd probably die the first time they rowed for more than an hour. The other was an attractive boy, with curly hair and a peach of an arse.

Suleiman slipped the guard his very last coin for the two gangs, then led them all a little aside.

'I am your Padron,' he said to them, brushing his moustache with the end of his whip, enjoying the eyes on him, the licked lips. 'My name is Suleiman. You are right to fear me because I am the hardest Padron there has ever been. But you will be the best oarsmen in the

215

world, whether you want it or not, and thus we will help the ship to live. For you are the ship. If the ship dies, you die. You are her soul, her speed. To row in a galley is not slavery, but an honour.'

He paused impressively in case anyone wanted to laugh or argue and give him a chance to demonstrate the use of his whip. Nobody did.

'Now this is all I require of you and then you will be fed and not beaten. You obey me. You do as I say no matter how foolish it may seem. If I say stand, then stand. If sit, sit. And you do not speak. Now sit.'

He said it quietly, to see who was listening. About half of them squatted, the experienced ones, the other half looked round puzzled or started for the ground or stared at him.

'Once more. All stand.'

Now some were squatting, having caught up with his first order, some standing. He was patient until they were all up.

'Sit,' he told them gently.

About half of them squatted, including the scrawny clerk who had been staring like a halfwit. But of the men still standing, some were narrowing their eyes at this. They weren't aboard yet, you could feel them thinking, why did they have to obey him now?

He went up to the biggest one, an ugly, scarred ex-soldier with heavy muscles. He had to look up at the man.

'Do you have a problem with sitting?' he asked softly. 'Are you sick, have you the piles?'

'I am not a dog,' rumbled the man stupidly.

Suleiman reached down and grabbed the man's privates, wrenched and twisted. The ex-soldier hooted, bent double, his eyes crossed.

'You are less than a dog,' said Suleiman, squeezing and pulling down. 'Sit, doggy.' The soldier squatted, making high, whining noises between his teeth. Suleiman let go with a final twist, stood and kicked the man in the face, knocking him backwards and breaking his nose with a satisfying crack.

He brushed his moustache, stared at the men. 'Does anyone else have difficulty sitting?'

Nobody spoke. Excellent. The beautiful boy was crying as quietly as he could. Well, perhaps he would learn that Suleiman could be kind as well as harsh.

He moved them up to the gangplank when he calculated that the sweeps he wanted would be boarding. A couple of sailors threw buckets of water, handfuls of slaked lime to kill the vermin, making them choke and cough. They jingled aboard, the ex-soldier still nursing his nose and bleeding in drips onto the clean wood.

Installing new slaves on their benches was always a difficult business. Suleiman was pleased to see that their ankle chains were individually and separately passed through the ringbolts in the bench. It was the only way to do it: if you tried simply passing one chain through the rings and manacling the men to the chain, you might think you had saved time in fitting out, but then the first time a slave died and you had to release him, you had a mutiny on your hands and would end up having to flog an entire bench to death, which was both wasteful and tedious.

The noise of hammering and talking was loud in the space under the top deck. This was going to be a noisy ship and Suleiman hoped devoutly that nobody was a loud snorer. His two gangs waited, then shuffled carefully down the companion way to the oardeck, the little clerk tripping and nearly pitching on his head. There were guards on the oardeck of course, ready to kill anyone who thought he might have a chance of escape in the confusion of fitting out. Sometimes it worked; more usually, the enterprising ones died. Of course, it was the last possible chance of escape before you were chained in the place where you would eat, shit and work for the rest of your life, however short that turned out to be. You couldn't blame them.

Suleiman tapped his whip on his legs and stood in the lefthand oarpit while his two gangs shuffled themselves alongside the new benches.

'Sit. On the bench.'

All of them sat with alacrity. Good. They sat, staring at him, looking around them. The clerk peered out of the oarhole, and then up at the high roof above them; it was twice as high as a normal tween-decks space because the oardeck took the upper half of the hold as well. There was a reason for that, which the clerk would find out in good time.

Suleiman sat on the walkway, dangling his legs, watching them, waiting for the first man to talk. One of them did, he made a joke of some sort. Suleiman flicked his whip out lazily, caught the top of the joker's ear.

'Don't talk,' he said. 'Now stand.'

All of them stood. Good.

The blacksmith arrived with his tools and began the process of taking the chains between the men's feet off, leaving only the leg irons. Suleiman moved among them. The clerk was in the right place, down by the oarport. Next to him Suleiman placed one of the two blacks in that gang, then a well-built peasant, then the soldier, then the other black, then the tallest of them. He nodded at the blacksmith to continue. One at a time the blacksmith riveted a steel chain to the left ankle-ring, passed it through the ringbolt on the deck, attached it to the right ankle and riveted it on. He had a small anvil and a narrow ballpeen hammer and he was skilful enough, didn't bruise too many of them. Most of the new slaves stared into space, pretending they didn't care and perhaps some of them didn't. The clerk watched the process intently, as if he wanted to learn something important. When he was finished with the leg-chains, the blacksmith took off each man's manacles. Most of the men rubbed their wrists gratefully, some stretched their arms out. The clerk was staring out of the oarport thoughtfully. He looked down at the gutter between his feet.

'Does anyone want to take a shit?' Suleiman asked genially.

They all looked at him as if he was mad, annd then as the more intelligent of them began to think, they worked out what was the purpose of the gutter between the benches at right angles to the side of the ship, why they were naked, why galleys were notorious for their stench.

'No one? Good. If you take my advice, you'll shit in the morning or the evening, but not during the day because it makes the deck slippery.'

Some of them were open-mouthed with horror. Suleiman knew half his men would be constipated by the end of the week and he had even laid in a special store of figs to help them. His benches were always the healthiest because he cared for them as if they were his sons. He rarely lost a man, he never had a mutiny. They were the best because he was the best.

'Stand,' he said. Some stayed sitting, still staring at their legs, the boy was crying again. The soldier stood, the clerk stood. 'Sit.' He sighed. 'These are not words. They are commands. There are not many but you must learn to obey them. Or you will die. There is "Take Hold!" When we have the sweeps rigged, we will practise that. There is "Down!" which means lie down under the bench and stay there. There is "Up!" – you must sit in your place on your bench. And then there are "Stand!" and "Sit!" We will practise them now.'

They did. He had them standing and sitting and sitting and standing for an hour until he was satisfied they all knew what he was talking about, even the blacks who spoke no Christian languages. By that ttime, the noise of hammering had stopped because all the slaves were finally aboard and the oardeck was beginning to heat up with all the bodies in it. Suleiman had heard that the north was cold even in summer and he hoped it was true because otherwise they were going to lose an awful lot to overheating, what with being closed in and the water barrel problem.

He left them under the eye of the soldiers assigned to that bench and went to look for barrels of water and wine, and also for wrist-guards and handstraps. He was delighted to find some goatskins that nobody else had the imagination to want and grabbed six of them. He thought he would be able to hang them under the walkway where there was a space. But there were no handstraps available and only a few tattered wrist-guards. He had his own smart, carved, leather wrist-guards of course. He was one of the first to come looking for food and managed to talk a large piece of dried sausage out of the cook's stores.

Back with his men he came between the benches, cutting off some sausage for each man.

'Hold your hands out, cupped,' he told the first one. 'This is how I will give you your food. If I do not, it is because there is not enough or becaause I think you have not worked hard enough. Or perhaps because I feel like starving you a little. I will give you the best and the most food that I can. You will eat whatever I give you no matter what it looks like or how bad it smells.'

As he came to each one he asked what the man was before, did he have illnesses or injuries, had he ever been in battle. The soldier claimed to have fought in a tercio, claimed to have an old war wound, claimed to have been in battle. His eyes were blackening, and he could hardly speak because his nose was so swollen. Suleiman reached out, caught the nose and twisted the septum back into place before the man could do more than squawk.

'It'll heal straight now,' he said.

Last of all was the clerk. His face was blank, stony, and his pale brown eyes squinted past Suleiman without any expression.

'What were you before?'

'A merchant's clerk, sir.' His Portuguese was precise, cultured.

'Morisco?' asked Suleiman, pointed at the man's privates.

'No sir. *Marrano*.'

Suleiman's eyebrows rose. 'Ah? So that's why you are here?'

'Yes, sir.'

'You call me Padron.'

'Yes, Padron.'

'Injuries?'

'My lungs are weak, Padron.'

'Rowing in a galley will either cure your lungs or kill you. Have you fought in battle?'

The pale brown eyes contemplated this question, contemplated Suleiman. 'Not in battle, no,' he said eventually. 'Padron.' there was the white mark of a spear wound in his shoulder but Suleiman left it.

'Fussy eater?'

'I prefer not to eat pork, Padron.'

'Too bad,' said Suleiman. 'Eat it anyway.'

He watched while the clerk took the sausage, looked at it and then ate it. Good. No trouble there.

Suleiman was reasonably happy with his two benches. Tomorrow they would rig the oars and practise Taking Hold and the next day, no doubt, they would put to sea for sea-trials and all hell would let loose.

Well, no doubt the clerk would get his hand caught and crushed or his head stove in or would simply keel over as so many did. Suleiman was quite sure he wouldn't last. They had about twenty more men, mostly escapers, caged down in the hold to take the places of the losses, but that was all and he knew it wasn't enough. He'd have to shake out his no-hopers quickly, so he could get his pick of the replacements.

The slaves spent a quiet night, which wasn't to say they slept. After the nets had been rigged, Suleiman brought in his bedroll and slept on the walkway above them. None of the slaves had blankets or pallets, of course, and they hadn't learned yet to huddle up in rows like sardines in a barrel to get a bit of warmth from the man next door, they were still shy. They would soon lose that. Of all people, galley slaves had the least use for shyness or modesty. Once the oars were in they would find they had even less space.

Suleiman slept very well. It was like a lullaby to him, the sound of an oardeck with two hundred and fifty-two men in it, sleeping, snoring, muttering, farting.

In the morning, they brought the oars and it was just as much of a nightmare as Suleiman had expected. The ship swarmed with riggers, cursing, shouting, hauling. The riggers had to put each sweep through the oarport by crane from the outside, hammer the cross-piece into the hole drilled for it, attach the pulley rope to the ring at the end, and then each bench had to haul in their own oar until it was pulled up at an angle in its sling at precisely the right position, the paddle-end just by the port and the business-end, with the handrails, triced up tight to the ceiling formed by the upper deck above them. Suleiman recognised the system; it was the one used for the lower deck of an old-fashioned trireme. One after another went in until one side of the oardeck was as full of oars as a herring full of bones and then they had to warp the ship around and put the other row in. You couldn't do it from the sea, the sweeps were too big and heavy – each sweep was made from two individual pinetrees lashed together and shaped with adzes to the form of an enormous oar.

The oardeck filled with the smells of new pinewood and lard, with sweat and tar. He had his men stowed under their bench, out of the way. Thirty-six trees criss-crossing the oardeck, one above, one below, gave a very snug fit indeed when you added two hundred and fifty-two men. The whole process took a day and a half.

Of course, they couldn't possibly practise rowing until they were at sea. They couldn't even run the oars out, on account of the quay being in the way. Suleiman went up on deck to report and found the sailors in the new rigging, ready to make sail as they caught the tide. He watched them monkeying around the ropes for a while, fascinated. He never ever wanted to do it himself because he was terrified of heights.

The Captain of the Oardeck and the Señor of the Benches were arguing with a pretty boy aristocrat in the service of Hugo de Moncada, the Admiral of the Galleases. The Captain of the Oardeck beckoned Suleiman over. He made an obeisance to the pretty boy, who didn't bother to return it.

'This is Suleiman, one of our most experienced and successful Padrons,' said the Captain of the Oardeck. 'He'll tell you.'

The pretty boy glinted in the sun, what with his tawny satin doublet and a great quantity of gold brocade. Suleiman looked at him and indulged himself in the fantasy of seeing the boy stripped and chained to one of his benches.

'With such men as you directing the work, there would be no problem rowing out of port, would there, Suleiman?' said the pretty boy with a brilliant, confiding smile.

Suleiman brushed his moustache and sucked his teeth. 'How many replacements have we got in the hold?'

'Twenty,' said the Captain, who knew he knew this.

'Find me another sixty, Señor, and I'll do it.'

Pretty boy laughed. 'Oh surely,' he neighed, 'you wouldn't expect to lose that many?'

'They're all new, Señor, none of them know their arses from their elbows. Could be more. And of course we'll need to come back to port for refitting to replace the oars we'll break. And we'd need plenty of space around us . . .'

'But I myself have seen galleys come up to the quayside at full speed, back water and rest up against the quay as sweet as a kiss,' said the boy, who obviously had some romantic notion about showing off his new suit on the deck of a ship under oars, no doubt to someone equally pretty on the quay.

'Give me a month to work the men and we will do that, Señor,' said Suleiman, 'but not today. With respect.'

The pretty boy looked sulky but left the point.

'Is he the officer in charge of this ship?' Suleiman asked. It was possible. He had seen stupider choices of Commander.

'No,' answered the Señor of the Benches. 'Thank the Blessed Virgin, we are the flagship. His Excellency Hugo de Moncada will be the Captain of this ship as well as Admiral of the Galleas squadron.'

At least that one had some idea of what he was doing. Suleiman nodded. 'Señor,' he said, 'I have one question to ask of you.'

'Yes, Suleiman?'

'Water barrels. Where are they?'

The Señor of the Benches stared at his boots and the Captain of the Oardeck looked miserable.

'They're on their way, Padron.'

Suleiman gazed unwaveringly at him until the Captain of the Oardeck looked away.

'Señor,' said Suleiman, 'this is a serious matter. Without water, the men cannot row. There must be water available.'

The Captain had evidently heard this from the other Padrons. He nodded and then shrugged.

Suleiman went down to the oardeck again, unconsciously chewing the underside of his moustache. Galley slaves could row without food for a remarkably long time, far longer than anyone ever thought possible. But without water they would be unable to row in a day and dead in another two.

The Englishman El Draco was to blame of course. When he had burned the seasoned barrel staves the year before, he had set back the supply of the Armada by three years, not one. But the King didn't understand about barrels and water, and had ordered them on without regard to the problem. Suleiman went to talk to the other Padrons about it.

The ship heeled slightly as they cast off for their practice run and the warping ropes took hold. Once they were away from the quay, the sails part filled with wind and the hull began to rock in the mild waves of the harbour.

They only sailed a little way because they needed the space. They hove-to in the outer pool.

Suleiman went to stand on the walkway, stripped to the waist, his moustache magnificently waxed. From where he stood, he could take hold of the cross-bar at the end of the oar when it was run out for he was the seventh man on it. He had a junior Padron for his second bench who was experienced enough to do as he was told.

The first time you put the ours out; like taking a boy's virginity. A ticklish and delicate process and one that needed a certain boldness. The Captain of the Oardeck stood at the aftmost point holding his speaking trumpet, with the drummer beside him.

'Stand!' said Suleiman to his benches. Most of them stood at once, hunched by the mass of the oar above them. 'Clerk, do you know how to cast off a line and put a stopper on?'

The clerk nodded, then shouted, 'Yes, Padron!' The beautiful boy at the other oarport didn't know of course, and had to be shown by Suleiman's junior.

The oardeck was full of noise as normal. The Captain of the Oardeck roared for silence, then gave the order and two hundred and fifty-two men tried to let thirty-six enormous oars slip gently through their oarports and stop them at the right point. Most of them failed. The oars were run up and they tried again. And failed again. One oar went all the way because one bench let go. It stuck fast by its cross-piece, with the Padron of that bench cursing and beating. Suleiman watched impassively. At least his men were trying. He didn't believe in too much beating; slaves would lose their fear of the whip. He tried to make sure all of them tasted it in the first few days so they knew it hurt, and then he kept it as a threat. Of course, if he ever did have occasions to beat someone properly they might well not survive so he did it rarely.

They had sorted out the stuck oar, they ran them up and tried again. And again. Hugo de Moncada was watching from the hatchway, not over-concerned at the chaos.

The oardeck was heating up already as the men worked on the ropes, up and down, up and down, some of them panting and slipping. The soldier was thoroughly cowed, doing his best. The two blacks worked without seeming to understand or care what they were doing. The tall one on the end was already crowing for breath, though they hadn't done anything yet. So far, to Suleiman's surprise, the clerk had managed to keep his hands clear of the oar as it thundered through the port and he had managed to cast the rope on and off and pull on it without getting knocked out.

They went through it twenty times before the Captain of the Oardeck let them keep the oars out. Many Padrons never went into their oarpit once the nets were rigged, but Suleiman slipped round the net and dropped to the deck, walked between two rows of chained men to the oarport.

'Clerk,' he said to the man, 'you have an important job. You must clip on the ring.' Suleiman pulled down the huge iron ring on its thick chain, opened it, passed it round the oar at the reinforced place and bolted it. The clerk watched short-sightedly. He undid it again. 'Now you try.' The clerk jumped to reach it, put it on, clamped it too loosely. Suleiman showed him again, and he tried again. Not so bad. He left the ring as it was, went to show the beautiful boy with the good arse the same thing. That took longer.

At last Suleiman picked his way back to the walkway and jumped up, knowing he was being stared at by the other Padrons who didn't know him. So what if many Padrons didn't care to go among their benches for fear of being killed by a slave who didn't care how he died so long as the Padron did too. Suleiman felt that if a slave wanted to try it on with him, he was welcome to have a go. It was only fair. If Suleiman wasn't the best fighter, he shouldn't be the Padron.

The command came: 'Rings on!' Plenty of fumbling, swearing from Padrons shouting orders. Suleiman brushed his moustache. His benches were the only ones with their oars secured. The Señor of the Benches came along the walkway, making sure the rings were on properly, reported to the Captain of the Oardeck. Then came the order that still thrilled Suleiman after fifteen years of it.

'Take Hold!'

Once more, he jumped down, showed his men how to put their hands round the rail bolted to the oar. The oar itself was far too thick for a man to hold. When you took hold, you did it for the duration, there could be no slipping or letting go or the oar might go wild with the waves and break the others. Discipline was essential. Here in the pool it might not be too serious and if they broke an oar or two they could refit, but later there would be no such leeway.

He told them about it. 'Once you take hold, you hold until you hear the order Let Go,' he said. 'Any man who lets go without the order, I shall beat him. If he does it again, I shall personally bind his hands to the rail. Once you take hold, you never let go. Never.'

They all gulped in unison, looked at their hands on the rail, mostly pale and soft as uncooked sausages. Only the peasant seemed unworried.

Suleiman said, 'Let go.' Half of them didn't. And he sighed. 'Likewise,' he told them, 'if you fail to let go on the order, it may be that your hand will be ripped off. So let go.' And they did.

He ordered them to take hold again, took hold himself at the top end where you needed the greatest skill and strength to control it, unhitched the rope from the ring at the end of the oar and put it on the hook on the beam beside him, and that was it, they had control of the enormous sweep.

'Do you remember when I taught you to stand and sit?' he asked them. Probably they had forgotten. 'Now, when I give the command, you must stand and sit, and all the time you keep hold of your oar. Understand?'

Some of them nodded, others stared.

'When I ask you if you understand, you say, "Yes, Padron!" Firmly, like that. So I know you are still alive and worth feeding.'

'Yes, Padron,' they chorused dolefully.

Suleiman could hear orders being shouted above, Hugo de Moncada was looking down the hatchway again. We are going for a small rowing voyage now, he thought, and this is when we lose the first ones. Very good. Let's shake them out.

The Captain of the Oardeck gave the order: 'Ready! Stroke!'

'Stand!' roared Suleiman. 'Sit!'

As the oarsmen stood up the sweep dipped into the water. As they sat, it moved back through the air.

Chaos was instant as the forward oars heard the order later than the aftward oars and some stood and some sat. On the larboard side of the ship there was a crack as two oars slammed together and the sound of shrieking as somebody's arm was broken. But you couldn't stop, or rest.

'Stand. Sit. Stand. Sit!' roared Suleiman as he walked forward when they stood and backward as they sat. He had the least effort, but the most movement. The clerk down by the oarhole had the least movement and the most effort.

The soldier let go to look at a blister. Suleiman never paused in his movement and his roaring of orders, but he laid the lash across the broad shoulders so the blood came. The soldier took hold again.

In the calm waters of the Lisbon outer pool, with very little wind, the effort to move the high, clumsy galleas through the water was brutal. The men launched themselves off from the bench, pushing their weight against the oar, and then collapsed backwards onto the bench again. And again. And again.

Hugo de Moncada was looking through the hatchway again, measuring their speed through the water. The galleases had been sailed to Lisbon from Naples but they had had sea-trials with professional oarsmen, which had allowed adjustments to be made and the best way of stowing and controlling the oars discovered. Then they had been thoroughly cleaned and fitted out and galleries attached to extend the oardeck and allow space for two extra men per oar, hence the new wood in the gutters, which was already staining yellow with urine.

And again. And again. Each time Suleiman roared, 'Stand!' they all stood. Soon he knew the whole oardeck would take his stroke simply because he had the best ear for it. Each galley had its own natural rhythm, subtly different from the next because no two were alike, any more than men were alike. The galleas would be the same, but he hadn't found the right rhythm yet. Eventually the slaves would be able to take their cue from the drummer, but that day was far off.

They stood and they sat for an hour before the order came to raise oars while the sails were trimmed. Suleiman took a waterskin out from under the walkway and went down between the benches, pouring water soured with wine into the men's gasping mouths. They were all heaving and crowing for breath, most of their legs were trembling, many had bruises and grazes on their arses and the backs of their legs, several had his lash marks on their shoulders and backs for letting go. The clerk's breath rattled in his throat and he could hardly gulp the water down, and there was blood coming between his fingers where he gripped the rail.

Then they rowed for another hour with the temperature in the oardeck rising to a steambath heat. Eventually four slaves on other benches, whose Padrons did not bother to water them, had fallen between the benches, one juddering in the convulsions that usually marked a man killed by heatstroke. Two more oars broke as a result. At last they were given the order to raise oars again.

'Make fast.' Suleiman attached the hauling line to the ring on the end of the oar. 'Rowers, let go!'

As he had expected, most of them couldn't do it. Suleiman went back down into the oarpit with his wineskin over his shoulder again, poured water onto the back of hands, rubbed forearms, helped them to unpeel their fingers and then rinsed the hand rail of blood and bits of skin. He picked up the hauling line and gave it to them. One look at the clerk and the boy, who were both half-conscious, told him there was no point expecting them to unclamp the ring, so he did it himself and then ran lightly along the bench under the oar and vaulted up onto the walkway. They hauled the oars up to their rest position, some of them coughing and puking as they did it, and then Suleiman was about to vault down again to make the line fast when he found that the clerk had roused himself to wind the rope round the knightshead and coiled it as well. His junior, Gaston, did the job for the nice-looking boy who was crying again.

'Down,' he said to them gently, and they all, even the peasant, collapsed, under the bench and lay there limply. Once more he walked between them with his waterskin. He felt mildly sorry for them, because he remembered very well how bad the first few days were. It had been no different for him when he was a young man captured by Christian pirates from Malta and put to one of their oars. The first day you thought you would die; the second day you wondered why you hadn't; the third day you were no longer sure whether you were alive or not, and by the fourth day, either things stopped getting worse or you did indeed die.

And one more thing to do, a special trick he had learned from an old Christian galley-slave on his second voyage. He had his own special barrel of cheap aqua vitae that he used for it, and a metal helmet with the padding taken out to use for a bowl. He filled the bowl with aqua vitae and hopped down into the oarpit again, not caring that some of the other Padrons who didn't know him were staring at him again. He was the best, they could learn from him.

The tall young man lay on his back still gasping like a fish. Suleiman told him to sit up, open his hands. Obviously he had done some manual work, despite his weakness, his hands weren't too bad but Suleiman had him put them in the aqua vitae for a few heartbeats. The black was not too bad, the soldier was bleeding a little on his palms, the peasant had no problems at all, the other black was bleeding too and the poor clerk . . . Well, he wasn't going to last so it probably didn't matter, but both his hands were blistered and bleeding, particularly across the palms.

'Put your hands in the spirit, clerk,' Suleiman said. The clerk hesitated, not looking up, his face slack with exhaustion. 'Yes, it will be like fire, but it will help in the long run.' He wasn't sure why he was being so gentle with the clerk, perhaps because the clerk had made the rope fast even when he could hardly stand, perhaps because he was probably going to die soon. The clerk did what he was told and shuddered and sweated with the pain of it. But he didn't say anything, which impressed Suleiman against his will, and he waited until Suleiman said he could take them out.

They rested the slaves while the galleas went back to her anchorage in Lisbon harbour by the power of wind, lurching and rolling in the water. She wasn't really a very happy kind of animal, thought Suleiman: she was very hard to row and also, it seemed, to sail. The galleas *San Lorenzo* was neither a horse nor a donkey, but a mule, poor creature, and just as difficult and bad-tempered.

The new movement of the ship caused more chaos because about half the slaves were trying to be sick on their empty stomachs, spitting and hawking and groaning. The gutters were full and the smell was making others puke so the Señor of the Benches asked the Captain of the Oardeck to send up to the main deck asking for pumps to be rigged. After a certain amount of fumbling, the pumps were ready and water started flowing in through the hatchways and grills. Some of the slaves moaned as the cold seawater hit them, others tried to move nearer the water to cool off and gradually the foul gutters cleared down to the gallery.

Suleiman hopped onto the bench and went down to the end where the clerk was now sitting under the oar, his back against one of the bench supports, eyes shut.

'Wake up,' said Suleiman, nudging with his foot. When the clerk climbed wearily to his feet, Suleiman got the sweeper from its hook, made the movements he wanted, gave it to him.

Blankly, the clerk swept the sewage overboard through the

scuppers let into the gallery, his nostrils flaring as he worked. Interestingly he was the only one on the bench who had not been sick and nor was he now, so his stomach was clearly stronger than he was. When he finished, Suleiman showed him where to stow the sweeper. The clerk looked up the stepped bench at the other men who were grinning with relief that they weren't the ones who had to do that job, shrugged and slipped down to sit with his back against the bench. His hands had started bleeding again.

Next, after the rations were given out, Suleiman brought them food – quite a feast: black bread, olives, sausage, Manchegan cheese that was only a few years old, vineleaves full of rice. Most of them ate ravenously, except the clerk who looked at what was in his hands and then shut his eyes again.

Did he have a fever? Suleiman went back and reached over to feel his head. The clerk flinched. Suleiman stood on his bare toes.

'Are you sick, clerk?'

The clerk had a breathy, whispery voice of a kind Suleiman had heard before; this one must have been in the hands of the Holy Office for a while.

'No, Padron.'

'Why not eat?'

'I'm not hungry.'

'You must be. You worked today.'

The clerk shook his head, shut his eyes. The black beside him was watching with interest. Suleiman leaned over the clerk, thinking he was probably wasting his time but that he must do what he did because he was the best.

'Listen, clerk, I am your Padron, you are like my own son. You say you are not hungry. I say you must eat. There is nothing wrong with the food, it is not rotten, there is plenty of it. So eat it.'

'I'll have it, Padron,' said one of the others, the peasant who had already finished his.

'Anyone who steals food from another man will get my fist in his teeth,' snarled Suleiman, shutting the fool up. Later on in the voyage they would certainly fight over food, you couldn't stop them, but there was no need while there was plenty around.

'Will you beat me if I don't eat?' asked the clerk, not sounding fearful but as if he was merely trying to find out the facts of the matter.

'Of course I will,' said Suleiman genially. 'But first I'll tie your hands to the bench and stuff the food down your neck. So why not eat?'

'Yes, Padron,' said the clerk stonily and started fumbling the food into his mouth, spitting olive pits. Suleiman brought the waterskin along again, and they passed the horn cup docilely between them. Most of them lay down again afterwards and shut their eyes.

He let them sleep rather than getting them up again to grease the blade of the oar, because they could do it in the morning. After all, they would have the next day and the day after to practise rowing again. He decided to open a book on which was going to die first, the tall young man or the clerk.

Over the next few days they settled the men in, shook out the weaklings. The other Padrons who had bet on the tall young man to die first had taken their money and tobacco. Suleiman too made money on it. Unfortunately he had needed to kill one of the men on his other bench for trying to seduce the one next to him, who happened to be the beautiful boy Suleiman himself had his eye on, only the boy had squealed in the night. This would make Suleiman's plans for the pretty boy more difficult to achieve because Don Hugo de Moncada had sent down to know what had caused the trouble and the Captain of the Oardeck had later made a little speech about impurity and its consequences. Full of savage rage, Suleiman had called up the blacksmith to release the man from his bench, hung him upside-down from the hatchway and beaten him to death.

They brought in a replacement out of the hold, a lash-scarred old hand in the galleys, who had been sentenced to ten years for heresy and never released. So that was an improvement.

Swirling patterns of clouds decorate the planet with paradigms of complexity. Out on the Atlantic, a vast storm-system is forming, unwatched by any satellites save the Moon. If we ride a seagull, we can swoop down into Lisbon harbour from a still blue sky to see a vast procession of people, sweating in the warm day, playing solemn, aggressive music of pipes and drums, paced with a stern Latin chant of monks. The crowds cheer and weep and cross themselves as the magnificent embroidered banner passes them. It was blessed by the Pope for his Crusade against heresy, it is sacred. The banner slowly flaps its way above the sweating young priests carrying it, down to the quayside where the flagship of the Invincible, the Blessed Armada is moored. Horses clatter, flags flutter, women and children cheer their noble menfolk in their crustacean helmets and breastplates, marching down to embark for the great Crusade against the evil English.

Most of the thousands of soldiers are already aboard the ships scattered at anchor all over the inner pool, scoffing precious supplies at a terrifying rate. This Armada is an Enterprise that creaks right from the start, the uttermost effort of a newly-wealthy nation to crush and absorb a smaller one. A very heavily leveraged hostile takeover bid, you might say.

Incense billows, more prayers fly up into the sky, bothering the scrap-hunting seagulls not at all. The ceremonies are glittering, beautiful, endless. Here comes the Admiral on a white horse, the Duke of Medina Sidonia, appointed only a few months ago to sort out the unholy administrative mess left by the late great Admiral Santa Cruz. Now he must turn by God's grace from a capable and conscientious administrator into a dashing leader of men. Small, sallow, with a constant anxious frown, he still has the invincible dignity of a true Spanish grandee as he dismounts from his horse and kneels reverently to kiss the crusading flag.

A few words, audible only by those nearest to him, he walks up the gangplank with his attendants, lurches a little at the tiny heel of the ship, and stands to wave at the cheering crowds while the gangplank is winched up and stowed, the mooring ropes unhooked. Four longboats, rowed by professionals, take the strain and the great galleon *San Martin* – 1,000 tons burthen, 48 guns, carrying 300 soldiers and 177 sailors, flagship of the entire Armada – moves away from the shore. Guns fire from the fort, the people cheer, flags flutter, the rest of the fleet follow her slowly.

From the roof of the harbour master's building, a clerk releases four pigeons into the blue.

Suleiman had expected the clerk to die on the fourth day. They had rowed most of the afternoon, their first day fully at sea, beyond any harbour's protection, heading north up the coast of Portugal. Several times Suleiman had had to touch him up with the whip for letting go. When the order came to draw up the oars at last, the clerk had not seemed to hear, and when the Padron came down the bench to find out what was happening, he had been standing there with the rope in his hands, looking as if he had killed someone. Blood covered his hands to the wrists. Since all the slaves had wide raw patches on their palms by then, no matter what their trade had been, it wasn't surprising.

Suleiman took the rope from him, hauled up, made fast. The clerk nearly lost his head as the oar came thundering in and didn't seem particularly concerned by it. On the order 'Down,' he collapsed bonelessly, as if he was a puppet whose strings had been cut. Nor did he stir when Suleiman kicked him. Suleiman was about to order up the blacksmith to take the leg irons off so they could slip the clerk out through the oar hole and get someone stronger in his place, when the man muttered something in a language Suleiman did not know.

'What was that?' he demanded, squatting down with one hand braced on the bench. The black sitting next to the clerk sidled away from him, looking frightened. The clerk was curled underneath the bench, hardly breathing. 'What did you say?'

'I said, I am not dead yet, Padron.'

'You said something different.'

'I spoke in English.'

'Ah?' Suleiman was interested. He had had a couple of English galley slaves in his time, and they were as crazy as everyone said they were. One had even tried to kill him. Nearly succeeded too. 'Why do you speak English?'

'I was born in England, Padron.'

'Do they have galleys there?'

It was a very strange conversation, the clerk was lying where he had collapsed but whispering quite coherently.

There was a pause, the clerk blinked his pale brown eyes. 'One or two, I think. But the seas around England are too heavy for galleys, the weather is too bad.' His breathy voice was almost inaudible. 'They have many sailing ships.'

England was where they were sailing to, somewhere vaguely in the north. Suleiman still wasn't that interested.

'Are you going to die tonight, clerk?'

The man shrugged a bruised shoulder.

'If you can, eh?'

With enormous effort, the clerk lifted himself up on his elbow, reached down to scratch the chafed place under his ankle ring. 'So you can win all your bets, Padron?' he said. 'No.'

Suleiman laughed. The clerk lay down again on the stinking planks, one arm under his head, his hands still oozing. Suleiman sloshed aqua vitae on them on general principle and left him to rest.

That night as they sailed northwards, the storm hit them like a beast leaping out of the sky, putting the ship almost on her side with the onset.

Suleiman was on his feet before he was properly awake, roaring at everyone to wake, get their bums moving, lashing the sleepy ones with his whip. The oarports had not been properly battened down and the sea was coming in; the oars weren't lashed up tight enough and they swayed enormously above their heads. The Captain of the Oardeck slept up in one of the poop cabins, away from the stink, the Señor of the Oardeck had found a place somewhere else, Don Hugo de Moncada was probably even now being woken and in the meantime, unless somebody took action, the galleas would sink. Which would be bad for the officers and sailors and certain death for the slaves.

The other Padrons were looking at him to tell them what to do, because of course, he was the best. Suleiman jumped up to the walkway, found the drum by touch and beat a tattoo on it.

'Listen!' he roared. 'End men, shut the oarport hatches, batten them shut. NOW!'

The waves washed in again, the ship was turning sideways, then up again, then sideways deeper, scooping up more water with each roll so that the oarpits were knee deep already. Some of the slaves were groaning and crying and flailing about in the water to pull uselessly on their chains. Stupid fools.

'SHUT THE OARPORTS!' he roared again, and then once more in Turkish for good measure. They hadn't practised it. Suleiman was trying to light the lantern of the watchlight swinging over the drum and as the flame took, he heard one slam. When there was light, he saw two hundred and fifty-one bald men staring at him, and one of them was next to his closed oarport and in the middle of fitting the batten across. It was the clerk.

'Do as the clerk did!' he shouted. 'End men, shut the ports.' Most of them were looking up at the swinging creaking oars, some were still pulling at their chains. Two of the Padrons made a break for the companionway, obviously forgetting that the hatch was locked shut at night. Suleiman flicked both of them with his whip.

'I'm not running,' he said to them. 'Why are you?'

To the rowers he added, 'Nobody leaves. Never mind the oars, if more water gets in, we all die anyway. Shut the ports.'

At last they were doing it, there were more slams. The ship scooped again, this time, less water came in. Suleiman ran down his bench, and starting with the aftmost ports, he ran along the gallery by the oarports, checking they were battened shut properly, helping the ones who were still too bewildered to act. Pretty-arse nearly trapped his fingers, but after another few minutes, there was no more water coming in by the ports. Just as well, because it was up to thigh-height by then, with puke from those who had lost their suppers and worse floating in it. But it was starting to run out of the scuppers as *San Lorenzo* heaved herself up and tilted again under the vicious lashing of the wind.

The sailors had to get her head down, run before the wind, there was simply no other option. Suleiman looked again at the oars, thought the slings and ropes would probably hold for the moment and roared again, 'Down! Everyone under the benches until the ship is better-trimmed.' Most of the slaves frowned at him with puzzlement. 'Until I say.'

Enough water had drained out again that they could squat with their chins out of the water under the benches, which would give them a little protection from the wildly swinging herringbone of oars. They did as he said and then watched as Suleiman roared at the other Padrons to help him with the sweeps.

He hated being so high up, hated climbing among the ropes and swinging timber, but if he didn't do it, nobody else would dare. He sucked in his stomach, growled and forced himself to climb up the ropes. Two of the younger ones climbed up after him and helped to steady them as the stronger Padrons hauled the slings up tight under the roof, pulled the lines up hard until the whole mass creaked to and fro but did not rock so wildly.

By that time the ship was aft on to the wind, flying before it and rolling with the choppy waves of Biscay. They had just got the oars sorted out and most of the water had drained away when one of the oardeck guns broke loose from its lashing and crashed slowly across the deck into one of the benches. Two men were crushed screaming under its weight and as the ship heeled again, the gun rumbled inexorably across to the other bench and the men who were going to be crushed could only pull madly on their ankle rings to try and get away. There was another crash, a shrieking, blood spurting.

The ship rolled again and the gun went with it, past Suleiman's own bench on its deadly zigzag course – except all the rowers of Suleiman's bench were standing on the bench by then, and the gun rolled harmlessly past.

'Onto the benches,' bellowed Suleiman, cutting one of the nets free. He waited for the moment when the gun was still against the wood of the gallery, then ran forward with the net and threw it over the gun. He thrust the ropes into the men's hands, ordered some to pull, others to hold steady.

He and two of the other Padrons got the gun tied down where it had landed and made safe against the gallery. Then Suleiman went from gun to gun adding ropes, tricing up tight, making fast. There were a ridiculous number of guns, very big ones, stern chasers mostly, forty- or fifty-pounders. Two between each bank of four or five oars. Whatever for? he wondered briefly, then put it down to the congenital madness of the Señors.

He told the men to sweep out the water, quick as they could, and they obeyed, occasionally falling when they tried to steady themselves against the heel of the ship and got caught by an ankle chain.

When all was as safe as it could be, bearing in mind that they were in a cockleshell of wood out on the vast range of the sea at the mercy of Allah's breath, Suleiman went to look at the men who had been crushed. All three of them were beyond help, one had already died, one was bubbling blood from his mouth, the other grey-skinned and silent and still, but conscious.

'You must put them out of their agony,' Suleiman said quietly to their Padron, who had been one of the ones hiding under the aftmost bench while he and the better men were making the oars and the gun safe. The Padron stared at him, shook his head. Suleiman sighed.

'Are you in pain?' he asked the one who was silent and still, whose hips and legs were a bloody, jelly-like mass. For answer the man shut his eyes. 'They will both be dead in the morning,' Suleiman said to their Padron. 'Why make them suffer? Give them mercy.'

The Padron put his hands behind him and backed away. Suleiman knelt down beside the one who bubbled blood with every breath.

'My son, do you agree that I must kill you?' he said softly, and the man shut his eyes, nodded convulsively. Suleiman drew his knife again, put his hand over the man's eyes and stabbed him under his ear. The other one was waiting for the question and sighed, 'Yes.' There were tears in his eyes. Again the yield of jugular to his knife, again the gush of blood, the writhing of the body unwilling to release its soul, the smell of sewage.

Suleiman imagined their souls flying free to meet Allah in Paradise. He went to the clerk, who was squatting under his bench again. The black lay beside him, wheezing for breath and even in the flickering light of the lantern, he looked greyish, which was the shade blacks went when they were sick.

Suleiman stopped what he was going to say and reached out to feel the black's forehead. It was burning. 'What's wrong with him?'

'He took sick yesterday,' said the clerk tonelessly. 'The food disagreed with him.'

This was an ill-omened voyage, Suleiman decided. Never had he lost a man so quickly – well, he'd killed the one on his other bench, but that had been for a good reason. Suleiman sighed. 'Do what you can for him, clerk.'

'What can I do, Padron? He needs medicine and good nursing, a warm dry place to sleep, rest. Can I give him those?'

'No,' said Suleiman. 'Was it you thought of getting up on the bench when the gun went past?'

A fraction of hesitation. The peasant answered for him. 'It was, Padron. He thought of it, gave us the order when we didn't know what to do.'

The clerk was studying the deck where water and blood still swirled. 'Well done,' said Suleiman quietly. 'You must have the heart of a Padron.'

The merest flick of the man's pale eyes told Suleiman that the clerk did not take this as a compliment.

'Or the heart of a lord,' he added, smiling, not offended, 'You were also the first to shut an oarport. Well done, again.'

The clerk nodded but said nothing, still studying the deck. 'Will you not put him out his pain?' he asked as Suleiman turned to go, pointing at the black who was so sick.

'No.' Suleiman was grave to answer this; if the clerk was going to be a Padron he needed to understand. 'He might get better, and if he does or not is for Allah to decide. The men that were crushed were not going to get better, but it would have taken them until the morning to die, perhaps longer. Why should they suffer more and hurt our ears with their moaning?'

The clerk looked as if he had more to say but thought better of it. Suleiman went back to his bedroll, found it was wet, hung it up in the hope it might dry one day, and went to curl up against his junior Padron by the drums where it was driest.

Morning came and they were still running before the howling wind, as the rain battered down and the ship rolled from wave to wave. The Captain of the Oardeck and the Señor of the Benches appeared at last with the blacksmith, to inspect the casualties of the night. One after another the bodies were released from the ankle rings and slipped through one open oarport into the water. Nobody said any prayers because they were only dead slaves, except the peasant who crossed himself. The Captain of the Oardeck left that one oarport open for air and a little light, said nothing to Suleiman about the hatches, complimentary or not. No doubt he was terrified of Hugo de Moncada finding out that his lack of care had nearly sunk the ship.

Although it had nearly killed Suleiman, he thought on the whole he didn't blame the Captain for his negligence. This was supposedly summer, why should anyone expect such a vicious storm with so little warning? But then they were out on the grey and hostile Atlantic. Even in the fair blue Mediterranean you sometimes got ferocious summer storms. Except there, of course, in a proper galley, you would be safe in port at night anyway.

It was dark in the oardeck, all that day, with the little lamp burning and nothing to do except rock with the heel and roll and twiddle of the heavily pooped galleas being driven across the miles of grey. At least the deck had been cleaned by the sea, which had now gone out through the scuppers, so the men lay down and most tried to sleep, those who weren't still puking. With no rowing, it was cold. Some of then huddled together for warmth, others just lay and shivered. Suleiman found the clerk hunched up next to the black, who was stiff and still.

The clerk shook his head and Suleiman went wearily to the hatchway to tell the officers that another slave was dead.

After the black had splashed out of the oarport, there was the sound of orders and the Captain of the Oardeck came down the companionway, followed by the blacksmith and four more slaves under guard. Two of them were black, all of them showed the traces of half-healed flogging, so they were men who had tried to escape. Already? thought Suleiman, we're already down to the escapers and madmen? Allah preserve us.

Never mind, he would do honour to the clerk, who showed signs of promise. He led the chained men over to the clerk's end of the bench.

'Clerk,' he said, and the man climbed to his feet, stood with his legs braced against the bench. He was drawn and weary.

'Yes, Padron.'

'Which one do you want for your oarmate?'

It was a privilege to be allowed to choose. The clerk understood this, being clearly an intelligent man. He blinked and looked closely at the blacks. One immediately interested him. He reached out, touched an upper right arm. A magnificent snake had somehow been carved into the black skin and scarred so that when the muscles rippled, it looked as if it breathed.

'Him,' said the clerk.

No doubt he thought the snake would be a talisman against the fever that had killed his first oarmate. Suleiman nodded to the blacksmith to do his job and when the hammering was over and the new rower safely locked in place, he said to the clerk, 'You may not wish it, clerk, but you cannot help being what you are, with the heart of a Padron or a lord. When the oarports are open again, I want you to look through them and tell me anything you happen to see. If you do it well, I will give you a loincloth.'

The clerk looked down at himself and then smiled sourly. 'I cannot do that, Padron,' he answered. 'My sight is too bad. If I had spectacles perhaps . . . but I can barely see my toes from here.'

Suleiman sighed, patted the clerk on the back and left him to it. As he went, he heard the man say to the black next to him, 'Do you understand me?'

'A little.'

The clerk pointed at the snake-scar, said something about a world-snake.

Suleiman looked back over his shoulder. The black was staring at the clerk. He spoke softly, the clerk answered, and then suddenly the black was embracing the clerk like a brother. For a moment Suleiman wanted to go over and demand to know why, but then he stopped himself. He could find out later, at the moment he had to supervise the installation of three more slaves in their right places.

Later, when he had given the slaves permission to talk but told them that they would not be fed that day because they were not working, he found himself shivering as well. That did it. This was stupid. So he went up the companionway, asked permission to come on deck and went up to the Captain of the Oardeck and bowed to him.

'Señor,' he said, 'already we have lost one man to a sickness. Soon we will have an oardeck full of lungfever. It is too cold for them if they are not working.'

'We have no blankets for them,' said the Captain, rather foolishly. Suleiman knew perfectly well that they had no blankets for the slaves. What would be the point? The blankets would get wet and filthy.

'Do we have braziers?' It was a rhetorical question, Suleiman knew perfectly well that the blacksmith had two.

'You want braziers in the oardeck? What about fire?'

Suleiman squinted up at the sky from which hung a steady soggy sheet of rain, that the wind folded over and slapped on wood or rope every so often like a washerwoman at a stream.

'I am more worried about lungfever, Señor,' he said. 'I've known an oardeck to lose half its men to fevers when they get cold. Señor.'

The Captain of the Oardeck havered for a while longer. Suleiman balanced in front of him, ignoring the rain on his face and rolling of the ship, staring the man out. He was a perfectly adequate Captain of the Oardeck, but he was weak.

And Suleiman knew that the galleases were important to the great Enterprise whose ships were sprinkled across the grey sea around them, fleeing from the storm that had broken their formation and scattered them. The galleases had been specially built for it, said the word in the wineshops, the great Santa Cruz had ordered them specially to carry out a great work for the glory of God, to provide him with a miracle. And if they were to be rowed, awkward ugly creatures that they were, they needed rowers. The *San Lorenzo* flagship, in particular, needed rowers or she would shame Don Hugo de Moncada.

The braziers were brought down in the late afternoon as the grey winds blew and the grey rain fell, and the sound of chattering teeth filled the oardeck. With a couple of hatches a little open to let the fumes out, the place started to warm up again.

Suleiman went up the companionway to talk to the Captain again. 'We should move the men or their bodies will seize up,' he said without preamble.

'What?'

'They will cramp and ache and be weak tomorrow. They must move. Have them grease the oarblades, then do rowing drill until they are warm. They won't like it, but it will be better for them.'

'How do you know?'

'Señor, have you ever rowed in a galley?'

'I have been Captain of the Oardeck, Simon—'

'Suleiman, Señor.'

'—Suleiman, for three years.'

'Yes, Señor. I myself have been rowing either at the oar or as a Padron for fifteen years, Señor, twelve of them as a voluntary.'

The Captain of the Oardeck blinked his eyes and Suleiman knew he had him. They brought out the lard they used for the oars and Suleiman made sure they had all the barrels open.

'We grease the oars to keep them supple,' he shouted as two hundred and fifty-two pairs of eyes stared dully at him, 'And we grease ourselves not for any impure reasons, but to keep ourselves warm. If I were you, I wouldn't eat it – it's heavily salted.'

Most of them had no idea what he was talking about, so he moved among them, grabbing handfuls of grease, rubbing it into arms, chests, giving a couple of pert buttocks a little slap. Careful not to enjoy yourself, couldn't have the Captain of the Oardeck getting worried about impurity again.

He came to the clerk who was looking dubiously at the handfuls of lard in his hand.

'Put it on,' he said. 'It's better to be unclean and a little warmer.'

'I don't believe I have ever been told not to wear pigfat,' whispered the clerk. 'Only it stinks.'

'Of course it does. The pig is an unclean animal and they're only going to send us the lard that's going off.'

'How did you know that the pig is unclean, Padron?' asked the clerk with interest. The black with the snake on his arm was already slapping the stuff on. He looked shiny, like an obsidian statue.

Suleiman bent close to the clerk. 'If you could look at me, *marrano*, you would know I am a Mussulman. We two are surrounded by the infidel heathen here.'

Surprisingly, the clerk smiled and began putting on the pigfat.

After another dank cold night of howling wind and rain, two more of the slaves were sick with fever, but at last *San Lorenzo* had turned and was sailing for shore again. Like many sailors, Suleiman could feel the loom of the land under his feet. This was not England, they were nowhere near far enough north, but the storm-battered fleet needed desperately to refit, repair broken spars and masts, take on more supplies.

They came to the harbour at Corunna, and Hugo de Moncada ordered the oars out again. So the galleas *San Lorenzo* led the other three into the harbour, at right angles to the wind, and the men rowed well, so well they only needed the warping ropes for the last few feet, and they ran up the oars as she came up against the quay, neat as a kiss. It was a pity that the pretty boy aristocrat with the tawny suit was suffering too badly from seasickness to enjoy it.

They had broken spars and oars and they needed provisions – more men, food and water, some of which had spoiled already in its raw green barrels. Suleiman forayed out to find more wineskins to fill with a mixture of cheap wine and water for his men. But the cold was more of a problem than thirst. This was summer, but you would hardly know it from the falling rain and the howling wind. Two more slaves caught the fever that had killed the black, and that made four, which worried Suleiman, who knew how sickness could sweep through an oardeck. All of the men were bluish and shivering and when the barber came to shave their heads again, some protested that they needed every scrap of warmth they could find.

Part of the trouble was that they were on half-rations and not doing any work, and because a large number of men getting bored in close confinement always led to that, there were fights, vicious ones. Mysteriously, one man lost an eye. Suleiman bandaged it and told him he could row even if he was completely blind. During winter in the Mediterranean the remaining slaves were often released from their benches, and kept in the bagnios where they could go out and work in the docks. But not here. While refitting went on and all the sailors slaved at recovering from the storm that had scattered them, the galley slaves idled away the hours.

Meanwhile more ships joined the great Enterprise. Suleiman could squint out of the oarport where it was open and see them, far away, coming into harbour under the guidance of the pilot boat.

One day Suleiman was returning to *San Lorenzo* after a night spent in boredom and drinking in the Corunna wineshops. He came on board to find a new group of men in grave discussions, grouped about a gun.

'Padron,' called one of the officers, and Suleiman came over, made obeisance. The officer who didn't know him, made an introduction to a tall, grey-haired, bitter-faced man with only one arm, who had standing at his side . . . A woman? A woman actually on board a galley? She was veiled, but even so . . .

Suleiman tried to hide his shock. Then the one-armed man spoke, in a guttural language that sounded as if it might be German, and the woman translated for him.

'My husband is a gunner,' she said in excellent Spanish to Suleiman. 'He wishes to examine the gun that broke loose and make sure it does not happen again.'

Suleiman bowed again, trying to control his scattered thoughts. 'Señora—'

'Mevrouw van den Berg,' said the woman. 'This is Mijnheer van den Berg.'

'Señora . . . your husband, of course. But . . . but not you, Señora. Under any circumstances.'

'How will you speak to him?' she said coldly. 'He speaks only Dutch.'

'I'll manage. I will have no woman on the oardeck, Señora, it would be . . . it would be unseemly.'

'As I am veiled, they will be unable to see me.'

'Yes . . . but . . .' Allah help him, how could he explain it quietly to the husband without the woman hearing?

He looked around the officers and saw that all of them, the Captain of the Oardeck included, had been unequal to the task of explaining why a woman could not possibly go down to the oardeck.

'It would be a very shocking thing,' he said feebly, 'against all—'

'Are you concerned that I might see the men's nakedness?' she asked him, and Suleiman saw all the group of officers wince at the question.

'Well . . . er . . .'

'I am a mother, and a wife. Why should I be shocked at what God gave all men?'

Typical woman, she wanted a look. How disgusting. She was quite small and slight, but clearly as overheated with lust as all women were. Suleiman looked desperately at the Captain of the Oardeck who shrugged.

The tall, one-armed gunner said something to his wife, and she nodded. 'I am quite heavily veiled, which makes it hard to see,' she said, 'and if you have the men squatting under the benches, there will be . . . less occasion for immodesty. I doubt you could shock me, in any case, as we have already inspected two of the other galleases where they had much worse injuries.'

'Ah,' said Suleiman, 'that was due to my little clerk. I might have lost as many as six men, but he had them jump up onto the bench in time.'

For all her coldness of manner, she shuddered. 'Shall we make the inspection?' she said.

De Moncada had given the order, the Captain of the Oardeck was too weak to stand against him and Suleiman had not the authority. He sighed, bowed again two-fisted, and led the way to the companionway.

As he came down into the half-light of the oardeck, where the men were muttering among each other, he roared out, 'Down!' and shook out his whip. They were learning, all of them went under the benches and only a few stuck their heads out when they saw the skirts of a woman following him. Suleiman took flicks off their noses for that. Lecherous bastards, lusting after a woman.

The oardeck became unnaturally still, every eye turned hungrily on the slight curves of Mevrouw van den Berg, as if by the mere force of staring they could shove aside her veil, rip off her gown and kirtle and petticoat and stays and smock, and make her as naked as they were, do to with her as they wanted.

Her husband followed and went straight to the gun that had broken loose, to examine it. He squinted in the dimness, but then there was a scrape and a clatter, and that useful clerk was standing by his oarport, one hand cupped around his privates, the other hooking up the hatch to let the grey light in.

Well, he had not been ordered to do it, but Suleiman would have ordered him, so the initiative could be allowed. The clerk turned to the gunner and his woman, quite slowly, bowed with ridiculous formality, then slipped back under the end of his bench. Suleiman thought the clerk was less bold than he seemed, for he was blushing red, all the way up his chest and face.

The woman, Mevrouw van den Berg was also less strong than she had thought she was. She bobbed, almost as if she was curtseying, which was impossible. Clearly the smell of the place and perhaps the starved gazing of the slaves was upsetting her, for she clung to her husband's good arm and translated in a low breathless voice as Suleiman explained how the gun had destroyed three lives when it broke loose. Mijnheer van den Berg pronounced that the gun was too heavy for its fastenings and ought really to be on the lowest deck, beneath the oardeck. Through his wife's stumbling words, he complimented Suleiman on being able to make it safe in a rolling ship. There would have to be changes made – such heavy guns ought to be bolted to the deck, not lashed ... and so on.

They looked at every gun while the air in the oardeck became a soup heavy with desire, and then climbed back up the companionway. A concerted sigh followed them, as if every mother's son there was letting out breath he had been holding the whole time the woman was before their eyes.

Suleiman supposed you couldn't blame them, most of them hadn't seen a woman for months and if women were what your fancy desired, that would be difficult. He thanked Allah that he was made as he was. Youths were better and a great deal easier to find, if only the Christian idiots were not so frightened of what they called impurity. Later in the voyage, when the Captain of the Oardeck and the Señor of the Benches stayed out of the stink as much as possible, then he would be able to find someone. And in due course he would have more offers than he knew what to do with, as the slaves got hungrier and realised they had only one thing left to sell. There was no reason to risk a beating. He could wait.

Except he was beginning to suspect he was falling in love. Not with the pretty boy and his round bum – already hollowing out and becoming sinewy. No, with the clerk who already looked sinewy, who had started scrawny, who looked carefully past him with cold pale eyes every time they spoke.

A part of Suleiman was amused and jeering. *It happens to you every voyage, Suleiman,* said that part to him, *you find someone you think is different, who stands out, and sometimes you get what you want, and sometimes not, but always it ends badly. You are worse than any mucky-minded woman.*

He couldn't help it, he thought, in response to his own jeering. It was lonely to be the Padron, and it was lonely to be the best.

*It will end badly,* said the jeering voice, *this will end very badly indeed.*

Mentally, Suleiman shrugged. So what? he thought cynically. He's only a slave and no doubt he will die. If necessary, I'll kill him.

The carpenters came the next day, under the supervision of the one-armed gunner, Mijnheer van den Berg, to bolt the heavy guns to the deck. With enormous care four new guns, two culverins and two smaller falconets were lowered into the oardeck and bolted into their solid wood cradles by the empty sternchaser gunports aft of the oars. Suleiman was vastly impressed by the complex moulding on them, the elaborate dragon. Perhaps these guns also came from England – he had heard that many of the guns in the Armada were English-cast.

Thanks be to Allah, the woman, Mevrouw van den Berg, stayed out of the oardeck this time. She had herself lowered on a sling to the gunners' gallery, and stood by the gun ports shouting the correct words through when Mijnheer van den Berg was at a loss. She brought with her a strange little creature, dressed as a child, who said nothing at all, but scampered busily up and down the gallery and the rigging. Once she peered in through the oarport when Suleiman was watching, and he saw that she was in fact a dwarf, afflicted by Allah with life-long childhood. He had seen such a creature when he was a boy and thrown stones at it too. His neck prickled superstitiously, but the creature was only there for the day, to attend its mistress.

A couple of times, Suleiman thought he saw Mevrouw van den Berg passing by the oarports, but he was busy making sure none of the slaves stole any carpenter's tool. When a file was missing at the end of the day, he went along the benches, looking in open mouths until he found the one that had it. Being fair-minded, since the man had not actually attempted to escape, only stolen a tool that would help him to do it, Suleiman offered him the choice of having his front teeth knocked out or a beating and wisely, the man chose a beating. The blacksmith came to put manacles on him since he had shown he could not be trusted. Once the carpenters and the gunner and his wife had gone, Suleiman hooked the manacles up to one of the oar-ropes and spent a happy half-hour thoroughly welting the man's back and chest.

When he finished, he came to rinse his whip in the gulley by the clerk's oarport. All the oardeck was quiet, even the other Padrons were staring at him with fear. What did they want? A mutiny? If you were soft on one, the others got cocky.

Spotting the clerk watching him round the end of the bench, Suleiman grinned and brushed his moustache. 'Well?' he said.

The clerk tilted his head at the other side of the ship where the would-be escaper sobbed quietly into his chained hands. 'How will he sleep, Padron?' he asked coolly. 'I understand why you did not beat his arse, since he must row, but surely he needs to rest as well?'

'Every time he turns over and can't get comfortable, he will remember not to try to escape.' Suleiman told him. 'And every time all of you hear him groan in the night, you will remember not to try and escape.'

'Will he not die of exhaustion, Padron?'

'Well, you know, clerk, all of you will probably die soon, but not immediately. You would not realise this because you have lived a sheltered life with your account books, but it is astonishing how tough men are. I myself have seen slaves no better than you row night and day on a bit of black bread and some olives, and hardly any of them died for many days. It always amazes me, clerk, how much work it takes to kill a man unless you stab him exactly right.'

The clerk nodded.

Suleiman went off the ship again to dull the tedium. They were still waiting for more supplies to reach them, to replace the ones that were already rotten. He passed an unsatisfactory evening in a wine shop in Corunna, gaming with dice. He won at first and even took a pair of spectacles off one of the gamesters, but then he lost. When at last he came back to the oardeck late, rocking with wine, angry at himself, he found the Padrons standing around his oarbench and yet another of his slaves dying. It was the soldier, hunched over, gargling himself to death.

Suleiman shoved past and turned the man over. Someone had broken the man's adam's apple in a fight, a particularly ugly way to die. There was nothing anyone could do. His knuckles were grazed, he had bruises on his ribs. Suleiman scowled around at the slaves nearby: the black called Snake had a swollen, bleeding nose, and the clerk . . .

Even in the dim light of the lantern, Suleiman could see that the clerk had a purpling swollen black eye and bruises around his ribs and his knuckles were bruised and broken as well. He was standing, looking unhappily down at the soldier while he choked.

Suleiman showed his teeth, rose up, grabbed the clerk's wrist, turned him over and wrapped an arm around his throat. The clerk made no attempt to fight, perhaps he was tired.

'You killed him, clerk?'

'By accident, Padron.'

'Why were you fighting?' There was no food around, not a scrap. They were on half-rations, nobody was going to save anything.

'He insulted m . . . me.'

Suleiman chuckled softly in the clerk's ear. 'And then you . . . ?'

'I hit him, Padron.'

'And then what?'

'He hit me back but missed and knocked Snake down, then he hit me and grappled me and I tried to break free and as I did, he slipped and hit the bench with his chin and so broke his throat and is dying.'

'Is that what happened?' Suleiman snapped at the other slaves on the bench. They all nodded at him, fearfully. 'So you admit you started the fight?'

'No, Padron, he did by making his insult.'

'Which was?'

'I prefer not to repeat it,' whispered the clerk.

Suleiman squeezed with his forearm and the clerk started to choke slightly. 'You can die now for destroying His Majesty's valuable property, or you can tell me what the insult was.'

'He said . . . ggghhh . . . he said that you, Padron, were staring at me the way I had been staring at the gunner's tight little cunt of a wife and that soon enough, I'd be making no noise when I fart.' The clerk spoke in a cold distant voice. 'I found that insulting and so I hit him.'

Suleiman let go. He scowled at the other slaves. 'Is that true? Did the soldier say that?'

Snake nodded, and the peasant furrowed his brow and said nervously, 'It was something like that, Padron. I think.'

It seemed everyone else had been asleep. Suleiman stood over the now quiet body of the soldier with his hands on his hips. Damn it. He had lost yet another man from his two benches, three so far. Never had he had such an unlucky voyage. But as for the clerk . . . Well, what could he do? He didn't want to lose another man. Especially not the clerk.

'You know that in the morning I must flog you, clerk,' he said and the little clerk licked his lips and nodded once. 'Strictly I should kill you for the murder, but on this occasion I shall be merciful.'

'Yes, Padron,' whispered the clerk sadly.

Suleiman paused, he couldn't help it, no matter what his jeering internal voice said, he was curious. 'Which was the insult that made you hit him, the one against me or the one against the woman?'

The clerk paused. 'Both, Padron,' he said at last. 'I see no reason why I should listen to any respectable woman being called a tight little cunt by any galley-slave and at least, you have not been unkind to me, Padron.'

They were cautious measured phrases, well-weighted not to be insulting. Clearly it had been the woman, not himself, Suleiman thought regretfully. Well, the clerk had much to learn yet. And it was quite admirable that he had been able to take on and beat that brawny soldier, given how little and scrawny he was.

Accordingly, in the morning, Suleiman was quite careful with the scourge, not to flay the man too badly. He couldn't help enjoying the sight of the clerk bent meekly over his bench, his arms cording as he braced himself against the blows, his head bent so no one could see his face. Suleiman indulged himself in fantasies of other reasons for bending the clerk over his bench. The Captain of the Oardeck brought the blacksmith and yet another replacement for the soldier and put the soldier out of the oarport and Suleiman didn't like the look of the replacement at all – skinny, hollow-eyed and coughing cavernously. Allah help them, they were down to the idiots and madmen already. And the consumptives.

At least extra food arrived from Don Hugo for the galley-slaves, to encourage them. Suleiman approved. If you wanted every last effort out of a man, you got it from him better with rewards than with beatings.

The next day the Armada set sail again from Corunna, newly replenished with supplies and water barrels that were supposedly sound and clean, and now the flagship was flying the banner of the Crusade, the one with images of Jesus and his Mother on it. Quite magnificent embroidery, you had to give them that. And the singing by the bald monks was wonderful, sonorous and deep-voiced, full of the sound of iron bells and righteous anger.

It was a slow business getting out of the port, but the galleases were in the van as the fighting ships they were. Also the wind was brisk and fair from the south-west, perfect to reach England while bottling the English up in their ports. They rowed hard to get out of the pool and to find enough searoom, hours of straining to heave the heavy unwilling mule of a ship through the waves of the Bay of Biscay. At last the sails plumped out and took the strain and they could haul the oars in again. Shortly after, all the faster ships hove to and waited in position for the slow clumsy transports to wallow after them into formation. They would stay in that formation until they landed in England; it was the only sure defence against the English ships. The Admiral of the Galleases, Hugo de Moncada made a speech in which he said that the Armada was like a herd of sheep and the galleases were the dogs, there to protect them all from the wolves.

That first night, the little clerk gave him cause for concern. In the evening, when they were greasing the oar, Suleiman spotted Snake rubbing some fat into the clerk's back to soften it up, which Suleiman let pass because it was a sensible idea. In fact he suggested it to the Padron of the man who had tried to escape, who was still moving very stiffly.

Seeing the clerk turning over and over to try and get comfortable, wincing away from Snake his benchmate, Suleiman went and squatted next to him. He felt like a chat before he lay down in his favoured place by the drums.

'How are you, clerk?'

In the lamplight, Suleiman saw the clerk's pale eyes glitter. 'I have been better, I have been worse.'

'How are your hands?'

For answer the clerk held up his hands so Suleiman could make out the broad weals on the palms, which had healed and formed satisfactory calluses, there were a few blisters on the fingers, but nothing too serious.

'Is your back bad?'

'Not as bad as the man you beat for stealing the file,' said the clerk and there was a touch of humour in his voice. 'Clearly what I did was not so terrible as that.'

Suleiman grinned. 'You destroyed valuable property of His Majesty's. Now he was trying to steal valuable property, namely himself, but if he had succeeded in it, both his benchmates would have had to die and so occasion His Majesty far more loss.'

'Why would his benchmates have to die?'

'Because they didn't stop him. You might be able to keep secrets from the Padron, but not from each other, as I'm sure you realise. And if the men on either side of him had let him file away his chain and said nothing about it, then they would have deserved to die for treachery.'

'Ah.'

The clerk tried to lie on his back, winced away from the hard deck, and turned on his side.

'By tomorrow night you will be able to sleep,' Suleiman promised.

'It's not so much my back that bothers me.'

'What then?' Perhaps Suleiman had been too careful with the scourge. He didn't want the clerk to think he could get away with killing people any time he felt like it.

'Well, Padron, I was thinking about my wife.'

Suleiman brushed his moustache with the back of his hand, balanced easily on the deck as it tilted and creaked. 'Clerk,' he said, 'I like you. I like you because you do your best and do not moan and complain and you can think when you are frightened and in danger, as when you got your benchmates up on the bench when the gun was loose. And you must be a better fighting man than you look. So I will speak to you as I would speak to my son, if I had any. You have no wife. All of that life died when you came into the galley and it can only give you pain now. You used to be a man with a trade of being a clerk, with a wife, perhaps children . . .'

'Three.'

'. . . perhaps a father, brothers, sisters. Now you have none of them. They are far away, they cannot come to you, you cannot come to them. All gone. All you have to think of is yourself and your bench. Your benchmates are your brothers. And I am your father. Think like this, and you might survive to go back to your family. Wear your heart out wishing for your wife, and you will certainly not last the year.'

Silence. The clerk was thinking. 'There's truth in what you say.' Suleiman put his hand on the man's bony shoulder, away from the welts and bruises, gripped. 'But I think it's more likely I'll die anyway. It's a race to see which will kill me first, the rowing, the bad food and water, your whip or plain boredom.'

The clerk's voice was cold and thoughtful. He was not complaining. Simply laying out the facts as he saw them.

It amused Suleiman greatly. 'Why clerk, I had no idea you were bored. Is this pleasure cruise not to your liking then?'

Again the clerk's eyes glittered, he smiled faintly. 'If I tell you the truth, will you start entertaining me with your whip, Padron?'

Suleiman shook his head, liking the clerk more and more, for his courage, for his irony. 'I had believed that galley-slaves prefer less excitement rather than more, but perhaps I am wrong,' he said, full of pleasure at the conversation. Perhaps the clerk could be weaned away from his wife.

'The truth is that I look at the same men's backs every day, I row the same oar in the same way, I look at the same piece of roof, of hull, all around me is the same. There is nothing to read and although I can talk to my benchmate a little, he has no great interest in the things that interest me – the stars, the Holy Names of the Almighty. The stink is the same except it gets worse every morning. And the food is the same and my belly gripes me the same way, at the same times, every day. Boredom is like pain for me.'

'Did you not find your fight with the soldier entertaining?'

The clerk blinked rapidly. 'Yes I did, Padron, and I was very surprised at myself. I was surprised I could kill him too, only I didn't think of it when I hit him because I was angry. I have killed before . . . But not that way. Not in a fight like that. And yesterday morning, I am afraid I was not at all amused despite your kind efforts.'

Suleiman chuckled. 'But you know, clerk, you have the best view of all your bench – you could look at the sea out of the oarport.'

'I told you, Padron, I can't see very well at a distance.'

Inspiration occurred to Suleiman then.

'Perhaps keeping a look-out would interest you if you had spectacles? Last night I won spectacles off a fool who could not play dice. Would you like them?' Suleiman knew the clerk's squinting eyes were resting on his face, cautious, not optimistic. Suleiman smiled down at him, enjoying the blankness and caution, relishing the fact of his power over the clerk. 'Of course, you must earn them from me.'

He squeezed the clerk's shoulder so there could be no mistake, saw the man's eyes shut, saw his adam's apple bob. Suleiman knew that that meant in the end, at last, he would get what he wanted from the clerk because in the end, he had something the clerk wanted more than his virginity. His sight.

At last they had reasonable winds still blowing from the south and west to fill the mainsail and give them some way to ride the swell. Suleiman decided he would have them rowing with the sails at least twice a day, even if de Moncada did not order it, to get them strengthened. He had the Captain of the Oardeck well under his thumb now.

Suleiman went to lie down next to his junior Padron. Thanks to the Christians' stupid fetish for purity, he dared do nothing with the clerk yet. It would have to wait until they were in a storm of some kind, perhaps even when the English were shooting at them with cannon and they were shooting back so the noise and smoke would be a distraction. If the clerk was already having a love affair with the black he had chosen to row next to him, well then Suleiman would kill the black and take the clerk anyway. Allah had clearly put the clerk on Suleiman's bench and kept him alive for Suleiman's benefit. It was intended, it was right, and one way or another, Suleiman knew he would prevail.

The anticipation put wine in his limbs. He spent his seed that night on a dream where the little whispering clerk came to him as his Padron, holding a whip in his hands, whispering of desire.

# Señor Josef Pasquale

Pasquale wrote two letters to his cousin and got no answer, then decided to go to the Ordnance office and try to find the man directly. At the office, clerks were busy at their desks, and in the courtyard workmen were loading barrels of ill-smelling powder onto a cart. Don Juan de Acuna Vela was at the docks, Señor, but Señor could wait and he might be back in the evening.

So Pasquale hurried down to the docks and enquired over and over and finally found Don Juan de Acuna Vela, a short peppery man, with a black scar on his cheek and bristling eyebrows. He was swearing at a sullen man who stood by the open door of a warehouse.

'So the Angel Gabriel and his seraphim came with a true docket from the King and took the guns away, eh?' he said to the sullen man, who shrugged.

'They were here last time I looked.'

Don Juan de Acuna Vela grabbed the man's beard and brought his head round so he could look into the warehouse. There were piles of round metal balls, cannon shot, Pasquale supposed, and some wooden trucks, but as for guns . . . None at all.

'So when did the Angel Gabriel come for the guns?'

'I was ill last week, Señor,' sniffed the man. 'I don't know what happened.'

'Did they at least go to one of His Majesty's ships? Please at least tell me that?'

'I don't know, I'm sure, sir,' said the man and de Acuna Vela spat and marched away from him towards a fat pony.

'Señor, Señor cousin,' said Pasquale urgently. 'Sir, may I speak with you?'

'If you can keep up.' De Acuna Vela jumped onto the fat pony's back and dug his heels in, so Pasquale had to trot alongside, his soutane flying behind him. It was undignified, but what would he not do to be there, helping, when the English were brought back to

Christ? Still trotting he stammered out something about his mother and his desire to be part of the great Enterprise.

'You're Josef at the Holy Office,' said de Acuna Vela. 'I know, you picked up a nice little pair of properties for my mother last year.'

The owner of them had died suddenly on the table and Josef had not wanted to keep the property since he was well provided for. Thank God that he had been inspired to be generous to his mother's aunt.

'Yes, cousin.'

'Holy Office ... hmm. So you can write. Can you speak Portuguese?'

'Both Spanish and Portuguese fluently, some Italian of course and a little French. And Latin. I can write both the new and the old hands and I can cast up accounts.'

'Priest?'

'No, sir, only minor orders.'

'Wonderful. My clerk died yesterday of some kind of jail fever. God must have sent you to help me find guns and powder for the King's Holy Enterprise. Come along.'

And for five bewildering hours, Pasquale trotted after de Acuna Vela, who seemed to him to be more a fleshly tornado than a man, as he rode about the docks and shouted at men who could not tell him how many barrels were coming and made lists and sent Pasquale to fetch languid young noblemen, who were supposed to be supervising the arrival of more guns by ship ...

The languid young men were clearly terrified of de Acuna Vela, who shouted at them in language well-larded with honorifics and polite terms and made it very clear how deeply he despised every single one of them. They scurried to do his bidding, as Pasquale did. De Acuna Vela told him brusquely that if he was hoping to be paid a wage or make anything from perks, he might as well go now. What de Acuna Vela did was for the honour of the King and the saving of England, that was all. Medina Sidonia would have every gun that could be scraped up, or bought from England itself. There was absolutely nothing spare for anyone who thought he could make money from ordnance contracts.

Pasquale stammered that he had never thought he would, that he had served the Holy Office for very little gain but still had enough that he did not want materially and the honour of the Holy Enterprise was good enough for him too.

Don Juan de Acuna Vela gripped his upper arm, stared into his eyes, nodded once and told him to be back an hour before dawn so they could supervise the lading of the *San Salvador*, one of the great store ships for munitions.

The days passed in a glorious, excited flurry. The ordained Dominican for whom Pasquale had done his work at the Holy Office was lugubrious to lose so fine an inquisitor, so objective and ungreedy a man, and wrote him a glowing letter of recommendation. Three days before the Enterprise left Lisbon harbour, Pasquale rode with his mother on her litter to the quiet, golden-stoned convent just north of Lisbon, where nuns who wore the sails of ships on their heads, received her gently and kindly and tucked her up in bed. The woman who had looked after his mother he let go in the teeth of wailing and recriminations, and most astonishing of all, a direct proposal of marriage, which he turned down coldly. He closed up the household, gave money to the other servants, and went to his cot in de Acuna Vela's cabin, with only a bag and the clothes he stood up in. Never in his whole life had he felt so happy.

The day before they sailed, he went to church with de Acuna Vela and the other clerks serving him, all gathered about the fiery, restless, little man to enter the Church of the Holy Virgin and hear Mass sung most beautifully by Dominicans, to kneel and bow his head as the Blessed Sacrament was raised above them, their Captain and their Lord, their leader into battle against the heretic English. All about him shone the light filtered by glass, the reds and golds of vestments, and the presence of Our Lord, right there, on the altar, raised before him, present as if he were sitting there at table with all of them. The glory of it brought him near to fainting.

He utterly pitied the cold and dank English for being deprived of Christ so cruelly by their Queen. No effort of his could be too great to bring them the happiness of hearing Mass and kneeling in the presence of God.

He looked covertly sideways as he knelt with his bent head and saw tears standing in the eyes of de Acuna Vela, and at that moment felt that in his cousin he had found a true elder brother.

Tears sprang into his eyes again as he watched the magnificent procession of the Holy Banner. The joy was something he could hold to himself as they sailed out into the Bay of Biscay, following the galleases into the choppy waves, which did not agree with him. By the time the storm struck, he was already in his cot, dry-heaving into a bucket and the new rolling from side to side just added a twist to his guts. But he kept in his mind's eye the Blessed Sacrament, raised into his sight like a battle standard, and once or twice, when he felt worst, he thought that Christ's mother, the Blessed Virgin herself was sitting next to him, stroking his sweat-stuck hair back from his face while his own belly tried to escape out of his mouth.

Since he had never sailed anywhere before, he had not realised just how weak his stomach was. But it didn't matter. De Acuna Vela came to visit him and reassured him with the smug jocularity of those immune to seasickness, that like all mortal pains, it would pass soon.

In fact, it was already gone by the time the ships struggled into harbour at Corunna to recover from the storm, straggling out across the grey restless seas and beating back and forth against the wind to get into the harbour's peace. He was as disorientated by the stillness once they were moored safely on the quay as he had been by the ship's rolling, which he told to de Acuna Vela who roared with laughter.

He spent a day sitting quietly on the quay watching as some barrels that were already rotten were heaved out of the ship by galley-slaves working the crane-wheels, drinking well-watered wine and eating soft manchet bread.

He rejoined de Acuna Vela's train, his belt a little loose but his mind sharp, and was immediately caught up in the inventorying and inspecting of a new load of munitions. It was on a ship they had been waiting for, which had finally joined them from England, with the last order of guns and shot and powder bought direct from the Witch-Queen's own Lord Treasurer. The little ship sailed cheekily into Corunna with her Flemish Hapsburg flag flying. De Acuna Vela said Pasquale had been lazing around for long enough and now he could go and see just how much the dishonest, scheming heretics had cheated them.

Among the munitions of war was a tall, thin Dutchman with only one arm and with him somebody else . . . Pasquale at first did not quite understand why the man was wearing skirts, and then his brain caught up with his eyes and he realised that the Dutchman had brought his wife. He had actually brought a woman on the Holy Enterprise, which had been dedicated to God and on which there were no other women at all, not sailors' drabs, not soldiers' whores, not courtiers' ladyloves and not officers' wives.

Stiff with anger, Pasquale went up to the gunner as he stood watching a gun being winched up out of the hold. 'Señor,' said

Pasquale, coldly, 'I am afraid it is not permitted for your wife to be present.'

The Dutchman answered him in Dutch. Pasquale tried Portuguese and the gunner answered him in Dutch. He tried French and Italian and got no further, even Latin, but no – this gunner was clearly not an educated man.

'Perhaps I can help, Señor?' said the woman, who had stood patiently by her husband throughout and whom Pasquale had studiously ignored.

Pasquale turned his face to her with great reluctance and then stopped. She was quite small, quite thin-boned and had a kind of fragility that you sometimes saw in the birds sold in cages at the market. The small wave of hair peeking out under her white cap was dark brown, her skin ivory, and her face was adorned with magnificent, brown eyes under winged brows, a small pink mouth and quite a pointed chin. There was a fleeting sense of familiarity and then Pasquale blinked and tried to stop staring because of the heat that began to rise in him at the sight of her. Of course. The woman at the Moorish Paradise, above her veil, had exactly such almond-shaped eyes. A very different body, of course, and Pasquale felt the sweat start on his skin as he suddenly remembered the veiled woman's gloriously ample hips turning and billowing, shining with sweat and oil as she slowly lowered herself onto his . . .

He coughed hard, desperately clutched at his rosary under his gown, gripped the beads so hard they hurt his knuckles and muttered an Ave Maria to himself against concupiscence.

The gunner's wife continued looking at him, quite candidly, and he looked at the deck, feeling his face prickling.

'Señora . . . it is not permitted . . . It is impossible for . . . I have to tell your husband that . . .' She waited for him to untangle his words. 'Señora, His Grace the Admiral has sworn a mighty oath that the Holy Enterprise shall be spotless and sinless to do God's work and so . . . So there can be no . . . no . . . um . . .' Why was his mouth dry and why could he not say the word 'women'? It was only a word for the weaker half of creation. What was wrong with him?

'No women?' she asked him, brazenly, her head tilted to one side. 'Do you speak Dutch, Señor?'

'No.' God above, why would he want to speak a barbaric tongue like that? It was almost as ugly as the obscure Dutch dialect spoken by the English themselves.

'Do you have anyone here who would be able to translate for my husband, Mijnheer van den Berg?' she asked.

'No.' Certainly there were Flemings and Dutchmen in the service of the King, but they were all in Flanders. 'Can he not do his work without translation?'

'Certainly, Señor, if you will explain how he can order the correct weights of powder for the shot and instruct the carpenters and riggers on how to mount the guns and inform the gunners that Señor de Acuna Vela has placed under his command how he wishes them to serve and lay the guns.'

Pasquale had listened to de Acuna Vela complain for an hour over supper the night before that it was all very well buying in guns from the English, but what he needed above all were the English gunners to shoot the damned things off, because none of his Spanish gunners had much notion of the matter and most of them were too afraid of the guns themselves to get near enough to fire them.

Still he turned on his heel and went immediately to de Acuna Vela to remonstrate. The man heard him out, then shook his head. 'Well, Pasquale, it's a good thing you're from the Holy Office with so much virtue in you. Find me an interpreter who knows Dutch and I'll have the man leave his wife here in a respectable nunnery until we return.'

Pasquale stayed silent. He had made some enquiries, drawn a blank. De Acuna Vela nodded. 'Of course, you're right, my dear cousin, but although this is a Holy Enterprise, it must be accomplished by practical means. Very unfortunately, Mijnheer van den Berg is an expert gunner, certainly compared to our own pathetic creatures. He has served in the Netherlands and he can even tell us something of the English ships' guns, since apparently he has traded into England. But he has no other language bar Dutch. If we want to speak to him, we need an interpreter. And as he explained to me, through his delightful wife, he has taken a vow of chastity out of respect for His Grace the Admiral and he and his wife will be as sister and brother for the duration of the Enterprise. They even have separate cots in different cabins.'

'Oh.' Pasquale felt embarrassed, 'Well, that's different. I had no idea they were ... um ...'

'Naturally,' said de Acuna Vela. 'And they volunteered to do it as well, they didn't need telling. I think they are both respectable people and God knows, we need that man's advice. They won't be here on the Duke's flagship like us, of course.'

Pasquale went back to the deck of the ship. 'My lord has explained the matter to me,' he said, trying to concentrate on speaking to the man. 'It seems that for the furtherance of the noble cause and since you have made your vow of chastity, this may be allowed.'

The woman curtseyed to him, her eyes lowered under lids so heavy with black lashes it seemed surprising they could be opened. 'I am honoured,' she said quite deep in her throat, 'to be allowed to be part of so great and wonderful an enterprise.'

Pasquale bowed back to her, thinking that he was still debilitated by the seasickness to be so breathless.

While the Holy Enterprise of England refitted at desperate speed so as not to miss any more of the summer than they had to, de Acuna Vela ordered Pasquale to accompany the Dutch gunner and his wife and make sure he had everything he needed. Perforce then, Pasquale found himself spending much of the day with the woman and speaking through her to her husband. They comported themselves very properly, indulging in no unseemly sensuality that he ever saw and they did indeed have separate cots in different cabins. The woman had brought a maidservant who was at first sight a child, but turned out to be a dwarf, such as the King's Majesty had at court, who was clever enough at climbing and did her mistress's bidding willingly enough but turned out to be a mute with no understanding more than a dog when Pasquale tried to speak with her. It was all perfectly respectable because of course, Mevrouw van den Berg must have a woman to be with her, but as her maidservant was not properly a woman there was no risk of any lewdness to her from the sailors.

The Dutch gunner, Mijnheer van den Berg, was full of excellent advice, which Pasquale passed on to de Acuna Vela. He recommen-ded that the guns be well bolted down to the decks so that they could not roll about in rough weather – and there had been some losses of galley slaves in the galleases when that happened during the storms after their first setting out. De Acuna Vela asked if the English had truly found a way of controlling the recoil of the guns so that they could be loaded from within the ship, rather than having to put the gunners out onto the gallery to reload. Mijnheer van den Berg agreed that the English had made some experiments that way, but they had decided that there was too much risk of a loose cannon during a battle and, of course, there was the added danger of fire.

Mijnheer van den Berg had also given invaluable advice to Pasquale, who found that he had to organise the transport of hundreds of barrels of gunpowder, hundreds of nets of shot. What should he do? Have them spread all about the ships of the Armada, or perhaps gather them into one or two ships where they could be carefully guarded?

Mijnheer van den Berg sucked on his long-stemmed pipe and narrowed his eyes. They had been eating a roasted chicken with some of the odd roots that had come from the New World, candied in syrup. Very strange tasting, almost dough-like, and quite hard to swallow. Pasquale noted that Van den Berg had eaten very little. His wife spoke to him unbidden, in a low urgent voice and he smiled at her. Then he spoke to her and when she turned to Pasquale at last, he was sweating with jealousy that the Dutchman should have the privilege of speaking at all to such a beautiful, delicate little person.

'Señor, my husband says that both ideas are good, but that of course, theft is easier and record-keeping much harder if the powder and shot is distributed amongst all the ships. He would recommend designating one or two large well-found ships as magazines and loading the powder and shot aboard them. As you will be keeping such a close formation, it will be easy for captains to send for more if they are so extravagant of their supplies as to need it. And in any case, surely you must be very careful to preserve plenty of powder and shot to use when the troops are ashore in England?'

Pasquale nodded at this good sense. He put the point to de Acuna Vela who frowned but agreed, and supplied him with the *San Salvador* as a transport ship. In the last few days at Corunna, while the Van den Bergs were inspecting the galleases and advising on the safe mounting of the new guns on their decks, barrel after barrel of powder went down into *San Salvador*'s hold, net after net of shot. This would be for the ordnance used to take English, here were the weapons of war that would do the holy work. Pasquale felt his neck thrill at the thought and at last he ticked off the items on the list with little Mevrouw van den Berg standing beside him. She had put back her heavy veil so she could breathe more freely, as she said. She looked drawn and weary, which was understandable if she had been forced to stand on a galleas oardeck amongst the terrible stink and lechery of the galley-slaves. Pasquale deeply disapproved of her husband for allowing it.

'There is such a lot of powder and shot,' she breathed to him. 'How is it possible to need so much?'

'An army eats powder and shot,' Pasquale told her wisely. 'And you would be shocked to hear how much an ordinary siege takes. This is gunpowder brought from all over the Holy Empire.'

She shook her head and then added hesitantly, 'I am only a woman, sir, perhaps you can tell me. Is the gunpowder valuable?'

Pasquale nodded.

'What happens if, perhaps, a man is disobedient and a spark makes one of the barrels explode? Will the others be safe or will they explode too?'

It was impossible not to smile at the earnestness and innocence of her questions, although Pasquale had asked questions that were very similar when he first began the unfamiliar work of clerk at the Ordnance.

'They will explode too from the heat and fire of the first explosion.'

'Oh.' Her voice was small and thoughtful. 'Then shouldn't they be spread about a bit? As I would put apples carefully separated on a shelf, so if one should be bad it wouldn't touch the others and make them bad too?'

Pasquale opened his mouth to explain how foolish it was to apply rules intended for apples to barrels of gunpowder, but then he thought for a moment. Of course, it was quite sensible. The barrels should be separated as much as possible. He had to store about ten in the magazine in the stern so that it was available to the gunners, but the rest could indeed be spread around the hold with shot and food to separate it. Delighted at her housewifely thinking, Pasquale caught the little bird-boned hand and bent over it to kiss it.

'Señora, you are a most wise and sagacious woman.'

She blushed and giggled a little, looking up at him sideways through the fur of her lashes, and then away. Thank God her husband was watching the cranes on the other side of the deck and had not noticed.

They left Corunna on 12 July with a God-given wind, pressing them north and east. The hulks and transports left first because they were the slowest sailors, and last of all was *San Martin*, towed by four longboats, banners flying, musicians playing on the aft deck. Every ship had been blessed with Holy Water, every man had heard Mass that morning and many had even received Communion because of the solemnity. It was a most glorious sight to see the great galleons with their sails spread, the vast number of ships assembling on the uncertain waves, swelling above each one the sacred red cross of the Crusade. Pasquale wept once more as he stood humbly in De Acuna Vela's train on the high deck of *San Martin*, watching the Duke of Medina Sidonia facing out to sea, his round anxious face almost smiling at the blessed sight.

It must be a great burden, even for so important a Duke, the right conduct of Santa Cruz's vast enterprise against heresy, the waging of a crusade against the evil Witch-Queen of England. While angels might come to fight on their side against the English devils, the responsibility for it was on Medina Sidonia's narrow shoulders.

The fleet had assembled and begun the long, slow voyage north with such bright skies and fair winds it was impossible not to realise that Jesus Christ Himself was their captain, the Virgin Mary their patroness.

The voyage north was surprisingly pleasant, with livestock to provide quite decent food in the early days. The Duke generally dined alone, not least because he was badly affected by seasickness. Pasquale found to his dismay that he spent a day and a half in squalid misery again, but he recovered a little more quickly.

Once he was recovered he went with de Acuna Vela to all the ships, one by one, dining with the gunners. *San Salvador*, the ordnance store ship, was last and they ate a suckling pig covered in biscuit crumbs somehow roasted in the galley, deep in the bilges. It had a slightly peculiar taste but nothing too bad. The Van den Bergs sat facing each other at the long table, Mevrouw van den Berg pale and slender, breaking up biscuits and nibbling them. She had no stomach for the meat, she explained, because she had been so sick.

'The answer is to well-water your wine,' Pasquale told her kindly. 'Here, let me serve you with some.' He poured water, added wine, and she sipped and drank, watched blankly by her servant, the little dwarf woman. De Acuna Vela grinned at Pasquale as if there was some sinful meaning to his perfectly simple act of courtesy and asked Mijnheer van den Berg, how was it that the English had so many gunners and such good ones?

Mijnheer van den Berg answered with his usual slow deliberation and the voice of his wife gave the Spanish for his words. 'The English gunners are well-paid and much respected. Every English pirate that preys on the Indies fleet needs gunners and so there is always plenty of demand for them and the English cast-guns rarely explode and so more of them survive. But I would not overrate them. Your Spanish gunners are full of faith and zeal for the cause.'

De Acuna Vela agreed that this was a good thing and proposed a school of gunnery where men could study the better laying and aiming of guns. There was something strange about guns: everyone knew that the balls flew in straight lines, and yet when you tried to shoot at something a long way away – a fortress wall, for instance – you often hit below the point you aimed at, as if the ball were like an arrow.

Mijnheer van den Berg sniffed when the words were relayed back to him. He had always understood that cannon balls flew in straight lines – perhaps the aiming was not quite as accurate as it should be.

Pasquale listened respectfully to this technical, almost alchemical talk, while Mevrouw van den Berg was the bridge between his master and the Dutch gunner. They seemed to like and respect each other. Pasquale could not quite like Mijnheer van den Berg, who seemed to stare at him coldly and made no attempt to be friendly or indeed to learn any Spanish. But his wife ... While she relayed meaning through the changing veil of words she could not help being animated and yet deferential. Her little fingers picked up bread and speared small morsels of pot herbs on her knife and dipped them in olive oil and were busy generally with the work of feeding her, and yet they were delicate, precise, like a bird's beak as it drank at a puddle. Never was she caught in mid-chew when she needed to translate. Never did she make any foolish womanish comment, nor did she seem to mind that the talk between her husband and De Acuna Vela was so military.

Pasquale gave up any intention of trying to make comments – in any case, he knew very little of the art of gunnery, having come to it so recently. He sat and ate and watched Mevrouw van den Berg at her work and wondered at the delicacy of her cheeks and the heavy fur of lashes on her eyes.

In the night he dreamed she came to him as a Moorish maiden, as one of the women at the house he visited, veiled across the lower half of her face, and he had struggled to undress her and take her clothes off, which seemed to be stuck to her. Appalled that sin was chasing him even here on the Holy Enterprise, although there had been no actual sinfulness in the dream, he had started up in his cot and prayed against the attentions of succubi.

Sometimes, when he was not careful, he found himself idly thinking of the rest of her body, wondering how her breasts would be and whether her hips were wide or narrow – impossible to tell when a woman was dressed in a farthingale. Of course he knew what female anatomy looked like from questioning suspected Jewesses, and from the women at that house of the Moorish paradise, but he was shocked at himself for speculating about a respectable married woman, who wore a crucifix and knelt reverently for Mass on the Sunday. Her husband had been taken ill with a stomach flux that day but the priest had visited him to offer the comfort of the Blessed Sacrament and Mijnheer van den Berg had explained through his wife that he was afraid that he would commit the sacrilege of vomiting it up again if he did.

At the time Pasquale approved the reverence.

After dinner the Van den Bergs went up to the poop deck, watching the sea slip by, occasionally staring north and east. Almost without intending it, Pasquale went to join them. Mijnheer van den Berg turned away angrily after a while, saying something incomprehensible in Dutch. He went below, muttering as he climbed down the companionway.

Pasquale found himself moving closer to Mevrouw van den Berg. She seemed not to notice him, blinking into the distance. And then he saw that there were tears hanging on her eyelashes, dropping down her face. She didn't touch them, didn't seem to notice them either.

'Mevrouw van den Berg . . .' he whispered, hesitantly. 'May I help you in your distress?'

She looked at him and smiled a little. 'No, I think not. This is a trouble I have made for myself.'

Pasquale bowed. 'I have no wish to pry—'

'I am afraid, Señor, that's all. I am afraid because here we are sailing nearer and nearer to England and soon that fierce El Draco will be coming out to fight the King's Armada and the guns will fire and . . . and men will be killed . . . Perhaps my husband, perhaps me. I'm sorry. I know it's very foolish. But I am afraid, so afraid, all the time.'

'You should never have come,' said Pasquale, 'Your husband is no better than a *marrano* to bring you with him. You should have stayed in a kindly nunnery like my mother until we had taken England and then come to join him.'

She smiled sadly at him. 'Alas, Señor, my husband needs me here. How else can Mijnheer van den Berg express himself except through me?'

'He could learn to speak Spanish.'

'Not in the time, Señor and besides, he has tried hard to learn the Spanish and the Italian tongue and never succeeded, he has no gifts that way. Whereas it is well-known that words come naturally to a woman.' She went to sit down upon a coil of rope and looked up at him, her small, pointed face as woebegone as a child's. 'Come, Señor, entertain me and take my mind off my fear. Tell me about yourself.'

Pasquale stammered and blushed. He was not used to talking to women. There had been a couple of strained and formal interviews with girls his mother thought might do for his wife, but none of the negotiations had succeeded. And of course he had never actually talked to any of the veiled women at the little house.

He talked about what might be understandable to little Mevrouw van den Berg, about his mother, about the terrible morning when she woke unable to move and he had run through the streets to find a doctor. There were very few doctors in Lisbon, or at least, very few respectable Old Christian doctors. It had taken him a long time. At last the man had come and at the cost of many gold pieces had pronounced that Señora Isabella Lopez Pasquale had been struck by a calenture and might never walk again. And nor had she.

Mevrouw van den Berg took his hand and clasped it. 'I am sorry for it. Where is she now?'

'Before we sailed, I took her myself to a beautiful and gentle nunnery where the nuns will care for her as a sister.'

'She must be proud of you.'

'She . . . I am not so good a son as I should be. She did not like my work at the Holy Office, although she said it was good that I serve the Catholic King. Alas, I have never married, Señora, which would have pleased her so greatly, for I am her only son, and born when she was quite old – in her late thirties, I believe.'

Mevrouw van den Berg nodded, her eyes wider than ever. 'The Holy Office,' she whispered. 'Is it hard to . . . to work there?'

'Very hard, Mevrouw van den Berg,' he told her sadly. 'It is very hard to question and interrogate sinners to find out their sins and not be marked by it, to hold oneself apart from ... from the unpleasantness of it.'

'And who do you question?' she asked. 'Traitors?'

'Of course, traitors to their Religion, traitors to the State.'

'Is there no difference?'

'Since the King is the Catholic King, no there is not. Most are New Christians that have backslid, returned to their vomit like dogs and worshipped as Jews or Moors again.'

'Mm. Do you question many Jews?'

'Certainly, of the New Christians. But not long ago I questioned one Jew who boasted of it, who said he had never been christened and already worshipped the true religion. Can you imagine it?'

Pasquale laughed at the pure shock and horror on her face. After a moment she swallowed and she laughed too.

'A Christ-Killer believing his religion is true! He was born in England where they permit such things, apparently. Nor would he listen to any priests or read any Holy Scripture, only saying that he had read them and was satisfied that his religion was better than ours. He was defiant.'

'It must be a terrible thing to meet such a person.'

'It was. Nor was he burned, unfortunately, despite his evil defiance and persistence in unreason. He was sentenced to the galleys.'

'So light a sentence?'

'Just what I said myself to the judge, Mevrouw van den Berg, but the judge told me that the burning of one Jew must wait for the success of His Majesty's Holy Enterprise. That is why I myself am here. Although I serve Don Juan de Acuna Vela in the matter of ordnance, when we have taken London, I will assist in setting up a branch of the Holy Office there, to help the poor lost English souls return to the safety of Mother Church.'

She smiled up at him, her eyes brilliant and velvet. 'A most wonderful thing, Señor.'

She understood him, the true centre of his life, his dedication to the Holy Virgin and the Catholic church. He tried to explain to her, how could he explain it? How the Mass filled his heart with light and happiness, how it gave him strength to do all the unpleasant sordid things he must do to wring confessions from obdurate sinners. How much he pitied the English that they were deprived of the Mass by their evil Queen.

And she listened to him, those marvellous eyes fixed on his face.

When he took her hand in his urgency to explain, she let him do it, and squeezed back.

He told her his plans for the Holy Office in London, for refounding monasteries and nunneries to provide places for the poor English who could not follow their vocations, for reforming schools so they could learn their Faith once more, for carefully extirpating heresy and all who would not gladly return to their true Mother Church.

'It will be a miracle,' said Mevrouw van den Berg, very fervent. 'A miracle of beauty.'

An odd phrase, very appropriate of course, but somehow sounding off key. If she had been a suspected heretic, he would have pounced on the words. But no doubt Mevrouw van den Berg was simply carried away by enthusiasm, and, of course, it summed up their Crusade most poetically. 'Of course,' he said, delighted, 'A miracle to return a whole nation back to the beautiful worship of God. Truly, a miracle of beauty.'

She smiled and kissed his cheek. 'You are so enthusiastic for the cause, so holy,' she said. 'I'm surprised your mother does not like it.'

'She wishes I had not taken minor orders for she fears I might go further to become a priest.'

'Surely she should be glad.'

'So I told her,' said Pasquale, not quite truthfully, because he had never dared to defy his mother in his life. 'But she begged me to wait until she had died and gone to Heaven and I swore to her I would.'

That wasn't quite true either, it was what he had quietly decided because he could not face her wrath.

The horizon faded into the dusk as they sat and talked. Mainly it was Pasquale who talked and Mevrouw van den Berg who listened gravely. Words bubbled out of him, into her graciously tilted ears. He was a little surprised at himself, talking so easily to a woman, when it had been so long . . . Not since he talked to the beautiful young cousin who became a nun because her father had no dowry for her, so many years ago, had he felt so relaxed and easy next to a woman . . . Even at the little house of women, he was never relaxed or comfortable: to begin with he was full of explosive tension and haste and afterwards he was as fluid in his bones as an alleycat. They were women for burying yourself in, for containing the explosion of your sin. Here was a woman who . . .

His mind balked at that train of thought. He talked about how

266

happy he was to be away from the Holy Office for a little, facing action as a true man should. He talked some more about his mother in his youth, how proud she was and her devotion to the Blessed Virgin.

'Did you ever know your grandparents?' asked Mevrouw van den Berg, still watching him with those marvellously, liquid, velvet eyes. They hypnotised him.

'Not really, mother didn't get on with them. I remember when I was a child they came to stay for a little while my father was away and it was ridiculous, really: neither of them would eat while they were there, except that grandmother would cook little messes for them on a chafing dish. Eggs and fish and so on. It was because of grandfather's stomach, it was bad. And then there was the fight . . .'

Pasquale had never told anyone about the fight because it was the only time he had ever seen his mother lose her poise and her pride and shout like a fishwife.

It was ridiculous. It was only his grandmother telling him a story about a Queen called Esther, one Friday evening and then lighting two candles. And his mother came sweeping in, knocked the candles over, shrieking at her own mother as if she were a dangerous enemy, and dragged him out by his arm so he never got the sweetmeats his grandmother had promised him. He had cried and been beaten for it, he remembered, and his grandparents had gone home the next day, without speaking to his mother.

Mevrouw van den Berg listened to this in silence, her own eyes growing bigger and bigger. 'How strange,' she said, in a very odd voice. 'And how sad that they went home.'

'It was sad,' agreed Pasquale, 'for I never saw them again. And my mother would never talk about them.'

'No.' Mevrouw van den Berg's voice was very thoughtful.

The next day the wind was still fair for them, the skies open and blue with herds of white clouds shepherded by the same winds. They made excellent progress and at last, at last, after so much struggle, at last, thanks be to God, at noon on Friday, 19 July, only a week after setting sail from Corunna, the King's mighty Armada sighted the Lizard, high black rocks weighting the horizon to the north-east. Their fleet had seen no English ships. Pasquale stared curiously at the English coast, deeply bitten by the sea, looking like the hem of a ragged green and black cloak laid on a restless mirror.

On *San Martin*, Medina Sidonia ordered the banner of the

Crucifixion unfurled from the mainmast, the superb embroidery showing the Passion of Our Lord with the Virgin Mary and Mary Magdalene kneeling at the foot of the cross, which had gone all the way to Rome to be blessed by the Holy Father himself. The priests said a Mass of thanksgiving at their safe passage and of special intention for the fighting to come. Kneeling behind de Acuna Vela on the hard deck, Pasquale thought his heart might burst with happiness, with the sense of Christ being near enough to touch, actually with them on the galleon, raised above his head by the priest while the bells rang. Even a great sinner like him might wipe out his sins by fighting on Crusade and if it pleased God that he should die in action, he would go straight to Heaven. Not, of course, the Moorish Paradise of fable, which was a false and evil mirage given out by the demon Mahomet. Pasquale squeezed his eyes shut and shifted his knees, worked to bring his mind back to the wonder of the Mass, the true Presence of the Saviour now being raised in the chalice of wine. Beautiful voices rang out, carrying holy words out across the waves, mixing them with the winds that had brought them. In his mind's eye, Pasquale saw the Latin chant drifting north on the air, falling like a sanctifying snow on the sad, bereft land of England.

They saw a barque in the distance, sails notching the horizon. As they watched, it seemed almost to skid to a halt, like a hunting dog scenting a bear, before tacking frantically to head back the way it had come. The priests lifted their voices again in the Te Deum.

The Duke of Medina Sidonia made a speech afterwards, his soft, rather dull voice straining to be heard, telling them that God was with them, that the Pope was with them, the King was, in his mind, with them and all Europe waited with bated breath for the return of England to the arms of Holy Mother Church. Mercifully it was a short speech as they sailed on up the Channel with the wind behind them. By that time, long white columns of smoke were rising all along the coast, from every high point.

So quickly did they move that the faster ships were outside Plymouth before the slow northern day had ended. Right there the *San Martin*'s sailors pulled on ropes so that the yards pointed at angles to each other and the great galleon slowed to a stop. Behind them a comet's trail of cross-sailed ships gradually caught up with them. The Duke's own trumpeter pealed brazen cries to join the seagulls, the flag for a council flew at the foremast. So the pinnaces began their busy flitting among the gracious chief ships.

De Acuna Vela paced up and down on the little patch of deck he had made his own, ducking a rope that hung down and chewing at his glove fingers. 'Go straight in, look at them, they're all in harbour, for God's sake, don't dither, go straight in!' he was muttering.

Straining his eyes Pasquale could see frenzied activity and white sails in the harbour. It was too far to make out much more than that. Soon the admirals of the other squadrons began arriving, De Leyva, the Lieutenant General of the Fleet running up the ladder from his pinnace, and vaulting the side before striding into the Great Cabin, blond hair flying under his hat, blond beard bristling like a northerner, his hot blue eyes flashing full of impatience and aggression. 'El Draco is trapped there, he must be or we would have seen him as we sailed up the channel and now we must . . .' Pasquale could hear the arrogant loud voice, the certainty. Other captains and admirals arrived, the sailors who helped them up the ladder muttering deferentially.

The council of war lasted for an hour and was punctuated by shouting, mostly by de Leyva. Medina Sidonia never raised his voice. Time passed, the meeting ended and the admirals departed, most of them angry and muttering.

The sailors shouted, ropes were hauled, the wind took the sails once more and swelled the crosses and the whole fleet sailed on, past the mouth to Plymouth harbour where the small English ships could be seen still struggling to get out in the teeth of the wind.

De Acuna Vela tutted angrily to himself. Pasquale watched with constant admiration as the crewmen of the *San Martin* trimmed he sails and the movement of the ship quickened. None of it made sense to him and yet it all worked – a good figure of religion, he thought. They were not very close to the shore, but you could still make out some of the little ports dotting the coast. Pasquale screwed up his eyes to look, imagined them deprived of the Mass, with nothing to sustain them or give them hope save the chilly Protestantism of words and intellect. Sometimes he could just make out a spire or church tower. Night fell slowly, as they sailed on, with the land blazing at its highest points as the beacons burned in the darkness, the land pockmarked with flame, the smell of burning drifting over to them from the land they had left astern.

He was dozing off in his uncomfortable swinging canvas cot, the haunch of one of the Duke's clerks knocking against his head, when the little door opened and a boy put his head in, holding up a lantern.

'Señor Pasquale, Señor, His Grace has need of you, please come, sir.'

Pasquale had scrambled out of his cot, his heart beating hard, fumbled his way into his doublet and hose, and was still shrugging his gown over his shoulders when the page showed him into the candle-shadowed great cabin where Medina Sidonia was pacing up and down, his thin shoulders hunched. His face with its baggy, anxious eyes frowned at the windows that pointed into a black night, golden-starred by the fallen constellation of the fleet's lanterns.

Pasquale stood, catching his breath, holding the doorpost against the heel of the ship while the page announced him between yawns and then on the Duke's nod, crawled under the table into a nest of blankets and curled up.

'Señor Pasquale,' said the Duke and Pasquale came forward, went to one knee and kissed his ring. 'Thank you for coming to see me so very late at night. I am afraid I have work for you to do.'

'I am at Your Grace's command.'

'Really, Señor, it's your experience at the Holy Office that I desire to use. It appears that there may be an English spy in the fleet ... Perhaps not. I hope not. Certainly, it is only suspicion at the moment. Well, at least he was recognised by one of the Catholic Englishmen who are serving with us. But I desire you to go and examine him, using all your abilities, and bring me a report by tomorrow night. We are likely to be in action against the English all of tomorrow – they are still clawing up to windward behind us – and I am sure that so honourable and gallant a soldier as El Draco will be anxious to join battle. At any rate, I will not be able to give this my attention until the evening ...'

A soldier had entered and was standing deferentially behind Pasquale, his morion helmet very polished in the candle glow. Two clerks came in behind him, carrying papers. The Duke's words trailed to a halt.

'Your Grace,' said Pasquale with a cough, 'am I permitted to use ... persuasion?'

'Use whatever you need, Señor Pasquale, only find out if the man is a spy and what he knows. But ... um ... try not to let him die.'

Pasquale bowed his head, rose to his feet and the soldier showed him out. However, instead of leading him to the hold of the *San Martin*, the soldier took him over to the rail and motioned that Pasquale should climb over and down the ladder to where he could just see that an eight-oared gig was waiting.

He gulped, gathered up his gown, put his hat in his teeth and very slowly climbed over and down the ladder into blackness, every limb trembling, his hands white-knuckled to hold onto the slippery rope.

Two of the sailors caught him as he dangled over the little boat, sat him down to catch his breath and stop shaking, then turned to help the soldier who was hampered by his sword. They rowed into the inky black night, the waves tossing their boat up and down and to and fro, the great shadowy hulls of ships suddenly looming out of the darkness and fading again.

Pasquale's treacherous stomach began playing him false again and he leaned helplessly over the side of the boat to empty out his supper. He could hardly see through the blur of tears when the boat nudged up against another steep wall of wood, and the sailors gave him a shove to get him moving up the ladder, the soldier came behind him and shouldered him over the rail when he paused there, paralysed by his own queasiness and trembling.

At least whatever ship he was on was reasonably stable. Pasquale paused, asked for a napkin and a drink of wine, fastidiously rinsed his mouth and spat over the side, then asked the Captain of the soldiers to bring him to see the captive.

There were two of them in the dank, cramped ship's brig, both of them in irons. The suspected spy had his right hand chained to a ringbolt on one of the ship's timbers, and his accomplice . . .

Mevrouw van den Berg sat in a pool of black damask kirtle on one of the beams that gave a little protection from the dirty planks. The manacles on her slight, slender wrists seemed enormous, a brutal mockery of jewellery. She was sitting staring at them and did not look up when Pasquale entered.

Mijnheer van den Berg stared at him as he came in, scowled, began shouting something in Dutch. Pasquale looked wildly from the gunner to his wife and back and then stepped quickly outside, shut the door and leaned against the wooden wall, shut his eyes. It was impossible . . . It could not be that . . .

The implications twisted out into the darkness. If the man truly was an English spy, then the implications for Pasquale's master, Don Juan de Acuna Vela, were very serious since Don Juan had employed the gunner. It was imperative that Pasquale find out what he was up to so there could be no question of complicity by either himself or his master. If Van den Berg was genuine and had been falsely accused, then there must be some kind of conspiracy, again aimed at de Acuna Vela.

'Señor?' The accent was hideous, heavy, somehow Germanic. Pasquale opened his eyes and saw another soldier there, a heavyset blond man with a dirty ruff. 'I am named William Probert, what said him for a spy – you be the inquisitor?'

Pasquale swallowed, got hold of himself. As coldly as he could, he said, 'And the reason for your accusation is?'

'That's never no Dutch gunner, sir, that's Anthony Fant, by God. I know him in Flushing many years back when I am young and so is he, four hundred of us who go to fight the Spaniard for the Dutch. Then I join Alva's army to fight the heretics.'

Pasquale nodded, fished in the pocket of his robe and brought out his breviary, held it out. 'Do you swear by Jesus Christ and your hope of heaven that what you say is true?'

'Certainly I do.' The square grubby hand banged on the cover. 'I swear by Jesus Christ, his Holy Virgin Mother, the Holy Ghost, the Holy Father and my soul that I know that man is Anthony Fant, an Englishman. Is there a reward for showing him to you?'

'His Grace the Duke of Medina Sidonia is known to be a generous prince and if I find that what you say is true, I am sure there will be some reward.'

Probert nodded. 'I could translate for you, Señor. I have before.'

'Thank you,' said Pasquale distantly. 'I would appreciate it. And the woman?'

'Never seen her, Señor. She is maybe his wife?'

'Hm.' Pasquale was still reeling with shock. He stood silently thinking for a while, trying to keep his head clear, between the shocking image of manacles on those delicate bird-boned wrists and the careful planning of his campaign. Interrogation was always in the nature of a war, a war between two intellects, that was what made it so fascinating. Given time, his jugs and gag and table, the strappado pulley, he could have guaranteed to crack the man, but he had only one day and no tools beyond what was available in a ship.

A thought struck him. He turned to the soldier who had accompanied him and asked him to fetch the ship's carpenter. Ingenuity must replace proper equipment.

'Now, William,' said Pasquale to the Englishman. 'I want you to go in there with me and translate but in addition, you must tell the prisoner in English that I intend to cut off his other hand.'

Probert nodded.

'Now I want you to do it only when I lift my hand, thus, in the blessing sign. Do you understand?'

'When you lift your hand, I tell him you cut his hand off.'

'Excellent.' To the soldier, Pasquale said, 'When the carpenter comes, knock once on the door. I shall open it to admit him if he is needed.'

'Ay, sir.'

'You will do this, cut his hand off?'

'Yes,' said Pasquale. 'Certainly.'

'Poor bastard – not even be able to piss for himself.'

Pasquale shrugged. It was irrelevant in any case, but he remembered that the English were famous for their unpredictable sentimentality.

When they entered, Van den Berg shouted at them both again, his wife remaining silent, still and quiet, with her heavy hands still in her lap. Pasquale dragged his eyes away. As far as he could tell, Van den Berg was still insisting he was the Dutch gunner, but it was almost impossible to tell Dutch and English apart in any case.

Pasquale stood and waited until Van den Berg stopped shouting. He said to Probert, 'Ask him his true name?'

'I told you, Señor, I told you it's—'

'Do as you're told.'

The Englishman sniffed, turned to Van den Berg and spat out some words in what Pasquale assumed was English. Van den Berg shouted more in Dutch.

'He tell you he a gunner from Haarlem, by name of Heinrich Van den Berg.'

'You speak Dutch as well?'

'Oh yes, and Portuguese.'

Pasquale wasn't sure whether to be angry or not. If only they had known . . . But if Probert had been the interpreter, he would never have met or spoken to Mevrouw van den Berg at all. He tried hard not to look at her but with no overt movement at all, she drew his gaze.

'I congratulate you. Ask him in English where he's from.'

Probert did as he was told and Van den Berg repeated himself in Dutch.

Pasquale hung his lantern on a hook let into a beam, gave the hook a little pull as he did so to see if it could be used for anything else, but it wasn't firm enough to support a man's weight. Possibly a woman's . . .

Pasquale swallowed hard against the ugly images rising unbidden from the place where original sin lurked in his heart. There came a single knock at the door and he nodded. Standing where he could see straight into Van den Berg's eyes, he raised his hand in the blessing.

'Ask him in English why he is here?'

Probert's eyes were on Pasquale's hand, he nodded, and spoke again in the ugly English sputter, a fair bit longer this time.

From where he stood, looking into Van den Berg's eyes, Pasquale could see the sudden pinpricking of the pupil, the blink, and Van den Berg's lips paled as well.

There was no question, the man knew English.

Pasquale sighed. He opened the door himself, found the carpenter there, a lanky man with sinewy arms and a completely bald head. There was barely space in the little brig for the carpenter and his toolbox, they had to ask Mevrouw van den Berg or whoever she was to move up.

'Translate for me exactly,' said Pasquale. 'Mr Fant, I approve your courage in coming to spy against my King . . . and I understand that you believe you are doing right . . . But I appeal to you to repent of your hard-heartedness . . . and confess all that you have done.'

Probert translated; Van den Berg shouted in Dutch again.

Sighing again, Pasquale motioned the carpenter to open the toolbox. If you were going to cut someone's arm off, you needed a saw. But if you were an inquisitor as experienced as he was, you understood that there was no point in doing it right away. So Pasquale ignored the saw for the moment. There were, of course, no thumbscrews, no pincers small enough for nails. But there was a mallet. He picked it up.

'Tell him in English to spread his fingers out on the beam.'

Confirmation, if confirmation was needed, for the spy clenched his only fist bone-tight in its manacle.

'Hold him,' Pasquale said to the carpenter, who shook his head firmly, and stepped out the door. Impatiently, Pasquale motioned in the soldier, who stolidly stepped behind Fant, and put a neck lock on him. Fant continued to shout in Dutch.

'Tell him again.'

The fist clenched tighter. Pasquale hit it with his mallet and Fant screamed. Pasquale caught the forefinger, held it against the beam and hit it a few times with the mallet while Fant roared and writhed. Longing for the civilised equipment of his office, of gags and restraints and so on, Pasquale caught the sweaty second finger and left the mashed first finger to hang.

'Tell him as long as he is willing to talk to me in English and not lie, I will leave his other fingers alone. As long as he remains silent, I will . . .'

Pasquale hit the middle finger with the mallet and Fant screamed again then, jabbered hoarsely at Probert.

'Is that English?' Pasquale asked.

Probert nodded, looking a little pale. He listened intently. 'Yes, Señor, he says he is English, he says his name's Anthony Fant what I told you, he says he come here to sell guns and thought of making money . . .'

Pasquale hit the second finger again. 'Tell him I expect no lying.'

Past Probert's blond bulk, Pasquale suddenly caught sight of Mevrouw van den Berg . . . the woman, bowed over and weeping into her small hands. He stopped. It would be better to separate them, in order to cross-check their stories.

He moved over, lifted the woman up by her armpit so she staggered to her feet and pushed her past her husband and the soldier. Fant began roaring in English again, and Pasquale ignored all the noise and undignified hysteria and pushed the woman out into the passageway.

'Look after her,' he ordered the carpenter who was leaning against the wall, staring up into space. 'Keep her here, don't let her escape.'

Shutting the door, Pasquale concentrated on Fant who was still jabbering away in English.

'He confessing, Señor,' said Probert excitedly. 'Say his wife knows nothing, she came because he order her . . . He say he come to learn the Duke's plans for invade England, something about a miracle of beauty, sir. That all he say, over and over, he come to find out the miracle of beauty, what is it.'

Fant was hunched over, tears streaking down his face, spittle bubbling in his mouth. It was hard to be sure. Pasquale gave the middle finger another whack with the mallet and Fant jumped as if he was a deer, screamed incoherently, bug-eyed, neck-corded.

'He say, what more do you want, Señor,' said Probert. 'Well, he say more but I leave it out.'

Pasquale frowned coldly at Probert. 'Never edit what he says. Tell me exactly.'

'Sorry, Señor. He say, what more do you want, oh illegitimate man who fornicates his mother, Señor. Sorry.'

The soldier sniggered until Pasquale had stared him into silence. 'Take his boots off,' he told Probert.

'Me, Señor?'

'You.'

It was a struggle and the soldier had to get a firmer grip against the flailing of Fant's stump, but in the end he was standing on his bare feet while the smell of sock added to the stink of fear filling the brig. Pasquale bent, took a grip on Fant's right foot, and beat the big toe with his mallet until it was a bag of purple jelly and Fant was howling like a dog.

'Tell him to keep a civil tongue in his head,' Pasquale told Probert who nodded, looking shocked and passed on the message. Fant didn't seem to be paying attention, lifting his wounded foot off the ground and crying.

Pasquale banged the mallet against the other toe, making Fant hop. 'Be quiet,' he said softly. 'Why are you making such a fuss? You have barely been touched.'

Whimpering, Fant stood still, staring at Pasquale in the way he had learnt to know was the beginning of truthfulness.

'Now, take us from the beginning.'

Fant had been ordered by the Queen to find out about a vital part of Santa Cruz's plan for the Armada. It was code-named the Miracle of Beauty and nobody in England knew what it meant, only they suspected it had to do with the galleases. That was all. He had brought the shipment of guns from Burghley and a woman to be his interpreter, and he had joined the Armada at Corunna as the Señor himself knew well . . .

They went through it again, in a different order and it was the same. Pasquale nodded, rubbed his eyes, used the man's doublet to wipe the end of the mallet clean. 'Let him go.'

The soldier unwrapped his arms from Fant's neck and the spy sagged against the beam. Pasquale nodded in approval – the chain was short so he would have to stand, which would tire him and the pain would keep him awake in case they needed any more from him. But Pasquale thought not. He had an instinct for these things and he thought that Fant genuinely knew very little more. Perhaps one more piece of information.

'One more thing,' he said. 'Who is your captain in this business?'

A slightly odd expression flitted across Fant's face, half-smile, half-sob. 'David Becket,' he said loudly and firmly. 'David Becket captain.'

'Hm.' Lifting the lantern high, Pasquale nodded to the soldier to pick up the toolbox and beckoned both him and Probert, leaving it dark behind him. He would report to Medina Sidonia before dawn, he thought, because this was clearly an important matter. First, of course, Pasquale had confirmed the existence of the spy and found out his mission, but if the code-name Miracle of Beauty was genuine, and was as secret as Fant had said, it meant that there had been a serious escape of information from Medina Sidonia's own court. The Duke needed to know as soon as possible . . .

Pasquale expected to find the carpenter holding onto the woman in the passageway, waiting for the return of his toolbox. But neither of them were there, only a splash of new blood on the wood.

For several heartbeats he stood and stared blankly at it, unable to understand what it meant. The carpenter . . . The man he had told to take care of Mevrouw van den Berg must have decided to take her with him somewhere, no doubt to commit the sin of fornication with her . . . Or perhaps she had tried to escape and there had been a struggle . . . No, surely not. She was only a little weak woman.

She must be found. Heart in mouth, Pasquale told Probert to tell the officer on watch that the woman had disappeared. He left the soldier on guard at the cell door. The brig was on the orlop deck, in the stern castle, just beneath the main magazine. Lantern held high he began searching frantically through the ship, checking every place he could think of that a woman might hide.

Dawn came and he was given ten soldiers to help in his search and they went through the ship methodically, from jib to afterdeck. Occasionally he would remember that he was on the *San Salvador* while the glorious Armada went into battle against the English. Except there didn't seem to be much battle going on. Certainly, the English admiral had sent a little ship close to *San Martin* to fire off a gun and then the other English ships who had somehow magically got themselves to the west of the fleet, sailed close to the fighting ships at each horn, north and south, of the half-moon formation. But *San Salvador* was a transport ship and so was protected in the middle of the moon shape, where the galleases scuttled up and down, eerily independent of the wind, pacing across the waves with their long caterpillar-like legs. Once Pasquale heard banging and thought someone was beating a drum, but the clouds of smoke from where the great Spanish and Portuguese warships sailed told him that this was cannon fire. It was even stranger to watch: there would be a flash and a puff of smoke, quite quiet, and then later would come the bang. What held back the noise of the gunpowder explosion? Pasquale wondered.

Then he remembered what he was about and returned to the search. At last, a soldier came to him and bowed, said that the door to the cartridge-filling room next to the magazine in the stern castle was locked on the inside and no answer when they knocked.

Pasquale strode over to the hatchway, and almost ran down the ladder in the quarterdeck, down into the deck where the main magazine was. A soldier was banging on the door of the cartridge-room. Pasquale motioned him back and tapped more gently on the door.

'Mevrouw van den Berg,' he said softly. 'Mevrouw van den Berg?'

There was a loud sniffle.

'Please don't be afraid, Señora, I don't intend to harm you.'

Another sniffle.

'If you would let me in . . .'

'You'll hurt me . . . You'll break my fingers . . .'

'No, no, Mevrouw van den Berg. I promise. I have learned all I need from your husband, nor would I put a good Christian woman like yourself to the question. If you would only trust me, I will see you are protected . . .'

'He never loved me, he only married me to translate . . .'

'Of course, Mevrouw van den Berg, of course, he is a wicked heretic Englishman and I know that you have been scandalously abused. Please let me in.'

There was another sniff, a scuffle and the door opened just enough to let him through.

He saw then that she was holding a pistol, a small wheel-lock dag, in both her small hands, the muzzle wobbling up and down because it was too heavy for her. Pasquale's heart nearly stopped. He knew that in a place where gunpowder was likely to be lying around, any spark at all was hideously dangerous, it would cause an explosion, a fire and then . . . They were right next to the magazine, there was even a chute for passing the gunpowder through the wall. The white canvas bags of cartridges were piled up on all sides. Just one spark was all it took . . .

'Mevrouw van den Berg,' he said, even more softly, heart thudding, not to startle her, 'don't shoot,' Not that she was likely to hit him the way she was waving the pistol around but the flash from the shot itself might ignite . . . 'Mevrouw van den Berg, I beseech you, give me the pistol. You are endangering yourself, if the spark lights the gunpowder . . .'

Even as he talked coaxingly to her a part of his mind was wondering how she came to have such a well-made small weapon. It was certainly the only firearm she had any chance at all of using but as far as he knew only officers carried them and she could not . . .

'Come in,' she said. 'Come in or I fire.'

'Then you will die in the explosion.'

'I know. I would rather die that way than have my fingers mashed.'

He came in, shut the door. 'Give me the pistol, mistress, I will take you under my protection. By God's Holy Mother, I swear I will take care of you.' She didn't give it to him. But she did put it down on a pile of cartridge bags. Somehow she had got rid of her manacles and he wondered how but then when her face crumpled into tears he forgot the question and only reached out for her, held her close against his chest so she could lean on him and weep. He swore to himself that after the execution of the evil English spy who had so used this gentle fragile creature, he himself would marry her, would take the advice of the priest who gave fasting for penance, and marry rather than burn. No more would he seek out the small house of women, no more beg to be tied and gagged so that they could unleash the swollen ecstasy of sin that he so weakly craved, he would be this delicate lady's most gentle and magnanimous husband and she would . . .

Something rustled behind him. He looked round. 'It's a rat,' whispered Mevrouw van den Berg. 'So many rats.'

'Come out of here with me, I will look after you . . . Mevrouw van den Berg . . . Tell me, what is your Christian name?'

She nestled her head in the hollow of his shoulder, her cap sideways from her escape, her black curling hair falling about her ivory face like a veil . . . Unable to help himself, he bent to her mouth, kissed her, marvelling at the delicacy of her bones and the softness of her lips, losing himself in the round tip-tilted scent of woman, of her body, in her . . .

Somebody punched him very hard on the back just under his ribcage and there seemed to be an enormous spike in it that impaled him on the most appalling pain he had ever felt, a vast, excruciating explosion of pain. It was so bad he could not even take breath to scream. He stared, staggered, let go of Mevrouw van den Berg and saw her face take on a feral, yes, devilish ferocity as she drew a carpenter's blade out of her sleeve and stabbed him in the gut with it.

His hands lifted reflexively as she slashed away at him, the awful shrieking pain in his kidney radiating down his bladder and up to his head, his knees wobbled, lost feeling, he dropped down, down . . . she kicked him, in the face with her pointed boot, smashing his teeth, again, smashing his nose, again and he started to lose hold on the world, his body had suddenly gone to a heap of pain, he simply didn't know what to do . . . Surely it couldn't be the delicate, the beautiful, the almond-eyed Mevrouw van den Berg who . . .

Her serving maid the dwarf stepped round from behind him with a bloody knife in her hand. A woman and a dwarf had murdered him . . . but why? He had only been trying to help? He loved her. He wanted to marry her. Why had she done this to him?

He was in a heap on some of the cartridge bags. The dwarf bent over him, put one manacle on one wrist, passed the chain behind the nearest beam and clicked it shut on his other wrist. He still couldn't scream or do more than gasp, but he was trying. Then Mevrouw van den Berg shoved a lump of tow in his mouth, making him retch, suffocating him, the blood from his nose was going down his throat with every breath, making him choke . . . It was terrible, agony, unendurable. Why? Why him?

'You want my Christian name?' hissed Mevrouw van den Berg in his ear. 'I am not a Christian, I am a Jewess, like your bitch of an apostate mother and her poor parents before her. *You have as much Jewish blood in you as I do*. And my name is Rebecca Anriques, wife of Simon Anriques whom you tortured and put in the galleys and now,' those magnificent almond eyes blazed, were beautiful still in their rage, 'now, you filthy Gentile bastard, now . . .'

She spat and slashed at his genitals, slashed again while he tried to wriggle away, protect himself, fighting the pain, the darkness. Her dwarf-woman put a hand on her arm and spoke to her in . . . in English? The woman, Rebecca Anriques, breathed deeply, stopped slashing and then answered, also in English.

Understanding suddenly flowered in Pasquale's head: it was she who was the spy, Fant was only her unfortunate helper. This was the true devil, this woman who had fooled him into desiring her, using his own sin as a weapon against him. The knowledge stood there, grinning at him, like a devil in itself.

She was standing now, moving to the door. She had laid slowmatch to the chute to the magazine where the main powder barrels were. Now, at hideous risk, she used the wheel-lock to make the sparks to light it and when it was glowing and smoking, she backed from the room, shut the door, locked it on him.

Pasquale watched it, unable to move, bleeding away inside, part-choked by the rope-fibres stuffing his mouth with its broken teeth, somehow watching from a great height as the bright glow travelled along the match, closer and closer to the spilled gunpowder from the magazine, the ship rocking and creaking along unconcernedly and then . . .

He felt the explosion, but never heard it. Blazing heat flayed off his skin, a giant hand made of air broke him, tossed him up as beams broke, though not the one he was chained to, and the end of the stern castle blew out into the fresh air. He looked down and found he no longer had his legs, only the mangled splintered wreckage of someone who had been given the Scottish boot.

The whole of the stern castle had been blown away, he was now looking out past splintered timbers, bits of body, white cartridge bags floating like flower blossoms down to the water . . . Somebody was screaming hoarsely . . . Was it him? No, he couldn't scream, but the screams he wanted to make seemed to be filling up his destroyed body, swelling it . . . Why wasn't he dead? Surely he could not have survived such an explosion, surely it couldn't be true that he was staring out across the water, part dangling by his flayed arms from the manacles that had chained Mevrouw van den Berg . . . Poor little Mevrouw van den Berg, the explosion would have frightened her . . .

There was something wrong with that thought, he didn't know what. He blinked blood from his eyes, waited for Death to come for him, the sunlight and the wind flaying him again . . . More screaming, shouting, flames and smoke – fire was taking hold on the ship, reaching to the upper rigging, the sails were flaming into brief beauty and clouds of foul-smelling smoke. Pasquale looked up and back, but it was hard, to move his head so much was too difficult, too tiring. So he looked out, aft of the ship, out of the vast window torn by the gunpowder, which had somehow avoided killing him completely.

Something was happening among the great galleons of the splendid Armada: one had somehow collided with another, he could see them clearly like model ships on a duck pond. Some of the rigging had come down in a cluttered tangle on the deck, sailors were crawling amongst it with axes flashing in the sunlight.

In the distance, Pasquale could just make out the small, low, despicable English ships, swooping towards them like jackals to take them now they were wounded. Then, thanks be to God, here came the Admiral on *San Martin* with his squadron, and two of the strange galleases tiptoeing over the waves towards them. The Admiral came between *San Salvador* and the hungry English, fired guns.

To watch from his ringside seat as the dogs and bears of the sea fought each other was really entertaining. Somehow the vast agony that was his body was fading into the distance, the brave sight of the ships under sail, the glistening waves, the clouds of grey gunpowder smoke making it all the more like a dream.

One of the galleases came near, moving precisely in close to the side of *San Salvador* that was not on fire. A rope twisted across the gap and was pulled taut. It was *San Lorenzo*, the flagship of the galleases. The ships were grappled together, as if boarding was planned ... And it was, for the soldiers on *San Lorenzo* leapt over the gap between the ships and began putting out the fires. How brave, how noble, to risk their lives to save a fellow ship.

A little voice was yammering at him, its source somewhere in the lower half of his body which was bleeding slowly away, its terrible wounds cauterised by the flash of the explosion. As I am going to die should I not perhaps say an act of contrition? Should I not turn to God in repentance for my sins? But why? thought the head-part of Pasquale. I was fooled by a woman but my intentions were noble. I am on crusade and I know I will go straight to heaven when I die. I have been Christ's most faithful servant, I have done nothing wrong since I made my confession for my last visit to the house of women, therefore why should I make an act of contrition? I would rather watch the ships.

The galleas was towing them along to keep up with the rest of the fleet, the wings of oars flashed in the sun and a sound came from the ship, as if the ship itself was singing. It was a strange rhythmic song, and the oars flashed in time with it. Pasquale could not hear very well because one of his eardrums had broken from the explosion, but he rather thought they were singing words, strange foreign words. '*Da meer a kuh is kallay, da meer a kuh is kallay.*' Probably some nonsense to help them keep the beat.

Rocking in a harsh bed with a wonderful view, Pasquale watched the galleas and its beautiful oars, listened to the singing of the galley-slaves, and gradually got colder. He shivered but was not present for the shivering, nor the pain it triggered off. The sun set and the night came down just as the towing cable to the galleas parted. *San Salvador* drifted on the tide, under the gleaming stars of the blackest night.

As Pasquale floated away he found a strange rocky passageway, heading towards light, which burnt his eyes, hurting him worse than the gunpowder explosion ever had, an agony of brightness and kindness. Someone was standing there, waiting for him. An angel, perhaps? To lead him away from what was obviously the Gate of Hell?

He looked at the person, found it was a shining man, naked, facing away from him. The man turned round and Pasquale looked into the face of Christ, pierced by its crown of thorns. But when Pasquale looked closer he saw that Christ was circumcised, was no different from that Jew he had tortured. Horror rooted him where he was, dread spread frosty fingers through all his heart.

'Josef,' said Christ to him sadly, '*Josef, why did you persecute Me?*'

# Simon Ames

## *Lisbon, Spring 1588*

It was a long time since Simon had been an inquisitor, and while he sat in the holding cell, he thought carefully about what he should do. Unfortunately, his memory was far too good, but at least most of his sensitive knowledge was five years old and he did not yet know what he had come to find out from his brother. In the summer of 1587, Francis Ames had sent the cargo to signal an emergency – myrtle leaves, sewn in a silk bag. Nunez and he had discussed deep into the night the best way to respond, in the state of war between England and Spain. Drake had just raided Cadiz and burned a lot of ships and also a vast many barrels, causing ruin to many of the Spanish industries. There was already a shortage of good sherry sack in London, although Nunez had bought up an entire cargo of it for the future. In the end they decided that Simon himself must voyage to Lisbon and make contact with Francis directly. It was possible that Francis wanted quiet extraction from his deep cover as the harbour master's clerk. Simon was the only available Ames brother with no vital work in Walsingham's service and he would be able to judge the situation.

There was no harm in trying to make some money and besides he needed good cover. Dr Nunez decided he would carry iron and guns and powder to the Slave Coast of Africa, there to load slaves and ship them over to the Caribbean, where the sugar plantations desperately needed manpower. Thence he would carry sugar to Lisbon and from Lisbon would bring the information and possibly his brother, together with Seville oranges, sherry sack, olive oil and spices for sale in England.

And so Simon had ventured out in a brig owned by Nunez through two intermediaries in Antwerp. His wife had forced him to take her with him, outrageously telling him that she would neither eat nor drink until he changed his mind and nor did she, for two and a half days until he broke. The last time she had let him out of her sight, as she said, he had ended by being chased by dogs through London and badly wounded in the shoulder. His children he knew would be safe with their grandfather, and perhaps it was no bad thing for her to be away from the Queen's England. Not that Elizabeth was the kind who took out her anger on men's wives, although her father had been such a man, only . . .

It was certainly comfortable to have a wife with him, until her maid had sickened and died with the flux and then Rebecca had taken the disease and been near enough to dying herself until Simon had brought the strange black woman to attend her and found he had somehow bought a witch. Had she really called the storm from the mast, or had that simply been insanity and madness followed by an accidental storm? It was what he had said to the interfering little drunk of a priest, who had almost certainly betrayed him.

Carrying sugar, he journeyed to Lisbon where he had never been before, where they could not possibly have known his face. Merula had been right, something had been scaring away the beggars. They must have been followed, very carefully, probably by relays of men, so they could take note of all his contacts. Who had betrayed him? Not Francis, he thought. Apart from it being utterly inconceivable, in plain fact they clearly did not yet know that Francis was his brother, nor that he was working as the harbour master's clerk. He thought it even possible that Francis might still be free. But he had been betrayed and it would be good to know who by, so he could curse them when he burned. He understood that curses made with the last breath of life were particularly effective.

He quite deliberately turned his mind away from the thought of burning. Now then, he thought. They never say what exactly they want because you never know what might come, and so they will . . . They will exert pressure without asking. I must be the outraged merchant, dealing only in sugar. When I must give them something, I will give them that I am English and I traded slaves without a licence. When I must give them something else, I will give them Walsingham's name. When I must give them a further thing, I will give them Phelippes' name. When the next thing must be given up, I will . . .

At the bottom of the pit of memory he was building was his brother.

He was very careful not to pray that his wife might escape. Almost certainly she would not. They would have soldiers at the ship, they might well have caught Francis by now, despite his coolness while the Holy Office arrested his brother in front of his eyes. Simon knew how much that must have cost Francis, to stand

and take notes, to watch his brother marched away, and do nothing . . .

What else could he give them? Unfortunately he knew nothing at all about Sir Francis Drake, never having even met the man, so he made up some interesting sounding tales about great ambushes in Cornwall, hellburner ships being created specially for El Draco.

He sat quietly, in the darkness of the cell they had put him in, which was quite civilised really: very, very dark, of course, with only a bench and a bucket for comfort, but not damp, not airless, big enough to stand up in and lie down. Much better than many of the cells at the Tower.

He found his fists had clenched up again and worked them to unknot the muscles in his shoulders. The Inquisition used the rack. They used thumbscrews. They used the strappado, which, in its lesser form of the manacles, had been worked to such devastating effect on David Becket in the Tower last year. They also used water torture of various kinds. They used darkness and silence, starvation and thirst if they had time, because these were the most effective, sapping the will without risking sudden death, leaving the mind unclouded by pain. If they had time to spend, but he thought they did not.

He stood up, climbed on his bench, waved his hand in the small current of air coming from the barred opening there. The opening wasn't a window because no light came from it. Carefully he tested the bars, moved all around checking for any weakness or crumbling in the stone. He might as well do it now, while he still could, so he would know it had been done.

When he had gone over the whole cell, inch by inch, searching for any possibility of escape, knowing many others had done so before and would after him, and found, as he expected, nothing, he pissed into the bucket and sat on the bench again.

He swallowed hard, blinked into the darkness, wondered again what it was Francis had been so urgent to tell him, prayed incoherently for mercy, then stopped. All the Holy Office knew of him was that he was a sugar merchant, that was all. It was entirely possible that they had picked him up on general principles, on simple suspicion of being English, since English merchants often made the triangle voyage illegally. It was possible he had been denounced in mistake for someone else. It was possible nothing bad . . . or nothing very bad would happen to him.

Of course, once they started work on him, if they stripped him naked, then, of course, they would see that he was circumcised. And then they would burn him.

After the interview with Pasquale, as he lay staring up into the darkness, Simon tried not to consider the future. His back and neck hurt, his stomach hurt terribly, his chest hurt, his throat hurt and his mouth hurt. Oh and his wrists and ankles were bruised. But all things considered, it could have been very much worse. He wondered if he had been close to dying the last time he drowned. All the pain and panic of struggling desperately to breathe against huge rocks of water and the pressure in his belly, it had all gone far away. He had felt as if he was floating. Unfortunately he had fallen back onto the table immediately. Was that what it felt like to die? It didn't seem so bad.

Certainly they would kill him, but how? Legally, he thought they could not burn him for heresy. He had forgotten earlier how punctilious was the Inquisition in its obedience to law. Spanish law, of course, was carefully designed to allow the Holy Office to do what it did, indeed to prescribe what it did, but nonetheless, legality itself was maintained. He remembered how he himself had been careful to get royal warrants for putting to the question in his days as an inquisitor. Now he looked back on the man he had been and hardly believed it had been him, Simon Ames, although he knew it had, knew they were the same person, though he was used now to people calling him Mr Anriques. At the time, of course, he had felt uneasily that he was serving a law he did not like but which was better than the death of the Queen, than anarchy.

From Pasquale's expression, Simon rather thought he fell outside their law and that this would upset the Holy Office deeply. Naturally they wanted to relax him to the secular arm and burn him immediately, and all things considered, he thought it would be better if they did. Another likelihood was that they would quietly forget about him and he would rot in his cell until he died. Another was that they would continue to question him, on general principles, until that killed him. But the legality of it hung over everything. Simon thought he understood Pasquale: as long as everything was tidily legal, Pasquale would have no mercy. Once a shadow fell on the purity of the law, Pasquale would be all at sea.

All at sea. A good metaphor. Simon liked the sea and relaxed comfortably into his memories of it. He had been astonished to find that he did not suffer from seasickness, even in the mighty storm that Merula had apparently summoned. He was not experienced in it at all, was no real seaman, but he had enjoyed watching the Master and Commander of his uncle's ship and asking what happened when this rope was pulled or that sail unfurled, watching the sailors at their work. The way it all fitted together was beautiful: angle upon angle, line upon line. It all made sense.

The Master had been complimentary of his understanding, had acceded to Simon's request to go aloft with one of the foremen of the tops. It had been one of the most exhilarating moments of his life, even if also terrifying. Halfway through his painful climb up the ratlines, he had felt them vibrating and stopped to wonder what was making that happen. Then he realised that it was the shaking of his knees, reverberating up and down the rope-web as if it were a plucked lute string. He took a deep breath, tried to settle himself. The futtock-shrouds had been the worst part: up went the foreman of the tops, hand over hand, hanging backwards like a monkey and Simon had followed in a terrified scramble and hung panting on the next set of ratlines while the crewman humiliated him by tying him on with a rope and patted his shoulder.

The platform of the fighting top seemed to be going round and round in circles as Simon clung on, but the sea all round . . . the wind . . . He had looked down at Rebecca, staring up at him white-faced, laughed and waved, somehow illogically cheered by her terror. Then he had clambered back down to the deck so she could scold him.

He had promised himself he would not think of Rebecca and yet he did, constantly. He assumed she had been arrested, the Almighty have mercy on her, probably tortured as he had been. It would be worse for her; she was only a woman, she knew so much less of the world, even though she was a mother and seemed to carry out a great deal of her father's business, she still appeared fragile to him. She had terrified him when she was so ill. He had been sure she would die like her tiring-maid and leave him completely bereft . . .

He had lived perfectly happily without women for many years, visited by the occasional succubus in his sleep, but never really missing them. Unlike Becket, he had never felt the need to risk his health and wits by visiting the whores in the South Bank stews. He had not been so very disappointed when Rebecca turned him down the first time, when he had still been serving the Queen and Walsingham as an inquisitor and pursuivant of Catholic priests. Later he had been very shocked when she had made it known to him through his aunt, Leonora Nunez that now he had left the Queen's service, she would consider his suit. As Aunt Leonora had pointed out, she was allowed to be imperious since she was the only child of a very rich merchant, and if the match could possibly be made it would be an excellent one.

Aunt Leonora had swung into action before he was fully recovered of the lungfever, a fact Simon occasionally thought suspicious. They had not known each other at all, apart from two very formal meetings, before they stood under the marriage tent. On their marriage night he had been too tense and too drunk to do more than carefully consummate his marriage with a delicate, fawn-like creature he could hardly believe really belonged to him. Only gradually had they come to know each other.

When had he first understood what was the matter with him, this strange sickness that attacked him with hollowness under his ribs and all the way up his back whenever he spent a day without her? She had seemed interested in the riddles of the stars which fascinated him and he had instructed her in the new ideas of Copernicus, through the Englishing of Thomas Digges. She had listened and questioned him and he had discovered that she could read, which impressed him. She had asked him resepectfully if he knew Cabbala, which was when he had first thought of studying it. But she was no bluestocking. She had quietly winnowed out of his wardrobe the clothes that made him feel uncomfortable and then restocked it with clothes that somehow magically made him seem taller and less spindly. She asked his advice when she dealt with the household accounts and never minded when he corrected her arithmetic, was even willing to learn the Arab notation from him, which Aunt Leonora felt was quite unsuitable for a woman.

Was it on the morning she brought him peaches in bed, and knelt in her smock, cutting up a peach and peeling it and eating it with such slow, teasing relish he had simply pushed her back so her head lay in the dark pool of her own hair and pleasured them both until they cried out. Or was it the night she screamed and worked as he gnawed his fingers downstairs in the kitchen, terrified that she would die as Agnes Fant had died, to give him a son? Or when she lost her temper with the wet-nurse for leaving the baby in wet swaddling clothes and punched the woman so hard she fell downstairs. That had been annoying but when Rebecca showed him the poor little creature's red buttocks he felt she had been quite gentle really.

Or did he truly fall in love with his wife by slow increments on every Sabbath when they lit the candles together and her skin took the candle glow and her hair became suddenly red like fire-embers . . . ?

Simon sighed, turned over on the bench, wished for a less hairy hairshirt and a warmer blanket, but then tutted at himself seeing they could have had him quite naked if they wanted, even though it seemed to upset them so.

Poor Rebecca. What would they . . . ?

Surely they would have shown her to him by now if they had her? Surely? Perhaps they didn't?

He was fooling himself. They must have her. Whoever had betrayed him would certainly have betrayed her as well. When he carefully chose a drunk for a chaplain, it hadn't occurred to him that even drunks were sometimes sober and it was hard to know when that happened.

He would think about his children who were safe with their doting grandfather; certainly they would miss him and their mother, but they loved the girl who had replaced the first wet-nurse, they loved their grandfather and the Queen would never vent her wrath on children. Of that he was completely certain.

The only pity of it was, what with casting up accounts and writing letters and studying Cabbala and so on, Simon had seen very little of his children.

There was the important moment when his son had first sat on a pony and . . .

For a moment the clattering came to him as the bridle and shoes of the nippy little beast he had bought for his son, but it was the door being unlocked and opened. Simon sat up a little, shaded his eyes from the torch.

They had a penitent's shirt for him, painted with lurid scenes of Calvary and martyrdom and hell, which frightened him. Would they burn him after all? They had him put it on over the hairshirt and then chained him and hustled him along black passageways, then into blinding sunlight that made his eyes run with tears after so long in the dark.

He had no idea where they were going because he couldn't see, but at last they came to a large, cool, marble building. He was ordered to sit on a marble bench and sat examining the complex Moorish patterns in the inlay on the walls, watching as black-robed priests and friars and lawyers and their serving men hustled to and fro. From the Hapsburg crest on the wall, he thought the Holy Office had referred him to the secular arm; this was a judicial building, at a quiet time. It was almost pleasant to sit and watch them, listening to his belly growling, watching his toes twiddle in the sandals they had given him. If he sat very still, the hairshirt didn't itch as much. At last there were orders and the clashing of halberds. He was hustled into a tall stately room where a weary-looking man in a judge's robes sat behind a high desk. Señor Pasquale stood behind another desk, his face drawn and pale.

Simon stood where he was placed, in front of the judge, his knees shaking just as they had on the ratlines, longing to scratch. It was unquestionably intimidating to be surrounded by men wearing so much in the way of doublets and hose and gowns and ruffs and tall velvet hats, while he was got up as a kind of religious clown. It occurred to him that Merula's dignity was remarkable when she had been wearing only her long leather skirt and an ill-fitting shirt. He tried to stand up a bit straighter, firmly squashed the urge to scratch. There was no point in looking like an ape when you were going to be sentenced to death.

Most of the indictment had already been heard while he waited outside. He still wasn't completely certain what they had accused and found him guilty of. They might not even ask him any questions and would certainly already have made up their minds.

There was no harm in a little courtesy. Simon bowed formally to the judge, who looked surprised and nodded his head in response.

'Señor Pasquale?' said the judge.

The inquisitor cleared his throat. 'Your Excellency, he admits it without any sign of penitence.'

The judge sighed and stared at Simon for a long time. Simon stared back.

'Anriques, you admit that you are a Jew?' said the examining judge.

'I have always been a Jew, yes,' whispered Simon, his voice still unhealed. He was relieved and a little surprised they were letting him speak.

'Will you at least convert to the True Religion?'

Simon's eyes narrowed. 'Since I already follow the true religion, it would be ridiculous to change,' he snapped.

There was sucked-in breath all round, a cold glare from the judge. Simon was amazed nobody had hit him. There was no point in trying to placate them, they had already decided sentence.

'He is, as you see, hard-hearted and unrepentant in his wicked error,' droned Señor Pasquale.

The judge put his long white hands on the desk and steepled them. 'Perhaps if we brought you a priest to dispute with you and lead you to a better understanding of—'

'Your Excellency,' said Simon, suddenly tired of the game, 'you have the power to bring any number of priests to dispute with me, but you do not have the power to make me believe what they say. Only the Almighty has that power. Why not leave it in His capable hands?'

The judge did not react in the way Simon had anticipated. He smiled. 'For entirely selfish reasons, I am afraid,' he said. 'For the safety of my own immortal soul, I must be entirely satisfied that every effort has been made to save you from damnation.'

'Then release me and let me go back home,' Simon reasoned. 'That will convince me you have my interests at heart. Legally you should banish me in accordance with the edict of Ferdinand and Isabella, and I am more than willing to be banished.'

'Legally, you should be executed for returning to this land as an obdurate Jew.'

'But I did not return, Your Excellency. I was visiting in my ship. I would have been long gone by now if I had not been arrested.'

'This is chopping logic,' said Señor Pasquale. 'The fact is, he is here and he is a Jew.'

'In any case, I would not send a soul in such danger back to lands cankered with the heresy of Protestantism,' said the judge. 'It would be like trying to wash off mud with pitch.' He paused, leafed through the pages in front of him. 'Anriques, are you married?'

What kind of trick was this? Didn't they know? Was it possible they did not in fact have Rebecca? The rush of hope in his heart made him feel faint.

'Why do you ask, Your Excellency?'

Señor Pasquale could not bear this insolence. 'The woman our informant told us you had with you. Where did she go?'

Hope was a heady wine when you had been steeling yourself against it. If Rebecca had escaped somehow, then anything was bearable. Simon had to pause for a moment because he was trembling, until he got control of himself, wishing his throat did not ache so much.

'What woman?' he asked.

The judge sighed again. 'Is she, was she a Jewess?'

'Naturally, I would not marry out of my religion. It is strictly forbidden us, according to the Book of Ezra, as you know,' said Simon piously. 'If I am married, it must be to a Jewess.'

'And these things are permitted in the heretic lands?'

'Yes, Your Excellency. The Queen's Gracious Majesty has permitted it.'

'We will need to establish a proper branch of the Holy Offce the minute we take London,' said the judge, making a note to himself. 'I will send His Grace a memorandum. In the meantime, I appeal to you again, Anriques: at least listen to the learned doctors of the church that I can send you. Hear what they say. I know that the Jews also wait for the Messiah. Can you not at least conceive the possibility that the Messiah was Christ Jesus?'

Simon was surprised to find himself responding honestly. 'It has been said, I forget by whom,' he said slowly, 'that both the Christians and the Jews await the arrival of the Messiah. If when He comes, He says, my fellow Jews, you were wrong and stiff-necked again when I was here last, then we will all repent. Since the Most High is merciful, He will forgive us. If when He comes, He says, my fellow Jews, thank you for waiting so long . . . Then, no doubt, the Christians will try to kill him.'

There was a pool of shocked silence, which Simon rather enjoyed. Perhaps he should not have been so flippant, but . . . Why not? What could he lose? He was so happy that Rebecca had escaped, he could have danced.

'You are indeed obdurate,' said the judge.

'Yes, Your Excellency. I am sorry for your immortal soul, but mine is safe. And since I am obdurate in my religion, you must sentence me and I make no doubt you have already decided what to say. Why waste more time? Sentence me and have an end to the farce.'

If he was going to be burned or hanged, let them get on with it. He wanted no more waiting in darkness.

'For the sake of your immortal soul, which I believe even Jews have,' said the judge sadly. 'To rescue you from hell and an eternity of suffering.'

Simon shut his eyes. Why did he have to come upon a conscientious judge? 'I think it is probably too late for me,' he said kindly, 'Why not get it over with?'

The judge looked down. 'May God have mercy on your soul. I hereby sentence you in the name of his most Catholic Majesty of

Spain, to hard labour in the galleys of this realm, the better to repent you of your evil. Perhaps honest work will help you to see the mercy of Jesus Christ Our Lord.'

Of all the horrors for which he had tried to prepare himself, this was the one he had never considered. Him? Simon Ames? In the galleys? *Him?*

The judge shook his head at the mad evil laughter of the Christ-Killer he was treating so gently.


At first, all that happened to Simon was that he was taken back to the prison and clapped in his cell again. The guards told him that they had been given orders to bring him a priest at any time of the day or night if he asked for one. Then they gave him a plate of bread and beans and a cup of well-watered vinegary wine, took his penitent's coloured shirt and sandals away and left him in the dark again.

He was glad, not just because it was the best food he had had in a long time, but also because he needed time to think.

First, he gave thanks to the Almighty that Rebecca had somehow eluded the Inquisition. They had made no mention of her black slave – perhaps Merula had truly managed to do something? He would never know. Otherwise, he could not imagine how it had happened, unless his brother Francis had somehow had a hand in it. Please let her get home to England, let the Queen's wrath be averted.

As for him, in the Spanish galleys. It was a terrifying thought. Was the judge blind? Simon had never been particularly strong and imprisonment had weakened him. You heard stories about the galleys . . .

Simon had been steeling himself for death and he thought this really made only a difference of time, perhaps a few months. But why him? Of all people you might set to an oar, he was the last. He said his evening prayers and tried not to scratch when he lay down on the bench to sleep. But he couldn't sleep. He was frightened and miserable.

In the morning, the guards came in early and marched him blinking out of the cell. In a brightly lit courtyard waited a hulking ugly man carrying a razor. Seriously wondering if he was hallucinating in some fever, Simon sat docile on the stool while the barber shaved both his scalp and chin. Having his head shaved made less difference than it had done the last time, when he was sick of lungfever, since Simon was going bald in the most unattractive way possible, with two long inlets of baldness climbing up his head, joining behind a tuft at the front and then spreading its hair-desert backwards leaving the tuft to grow in isolated splendour like a palm-tree at an oasis. His beard had never been very strong either. So although the wind around the back of his head felt very odd, all things considered, he thought perhaps he even looked better for being shaved. The man didn't give him a mirror though as a real barber would.

Next they made him walk through to a bigger yard, tripping on the leg chains as usual. There was a long line of hunched, battered men. They walked him up to the end of the line and locked manacles on his wrists with a chain that passed round the waist of the man in front. A few minutes later, a guard passed a chain round Simon's waist as another prisoner was attached. And so it went on. All of them were newly-bald, some licked their lips nervously, some waited stolidly and blank-faced, four of them were black. It occurred to Simon that he was by several inches the smallest of them and certainly the weakest and then he thought that the judge probably didn't care at all what kind of men he sent to row in the galleys, so long as he obeyed his royal instructions and sent enough.

Orders shouted out and they marched off through the town under guard. It must have been a common enough sight since none of the street-boys threw stones at the baldies passing by. Even at that time of the morning the sun was too bright for him and the cobbles hurt his bare feet as he hurried to keep up. He thought they were heading down to the docks. Yes, they passed the gate, even the quay where the ship had been moored and like a fool, he looked for it although it must have been long gone, impounded for use in the Enterprise. The docks were very interesting, after the boredom of his cell: the activity seemed frenetic, with ships being scoured and reballasted, work going on everywhere, all the huge wheels for the cranes manned with skilled walkers, who paced round like a dog in a spit-wheel. Some of them were bald like himself and Simon remembered that galley-slaves were used in the docks when there were no galleys to row. Perhaps they would use him that way . . .

They marched along the quay, down to one where four very strange-looking ships were tied up, being fitted out. What were they? Three masts, heavily built, wide oarports with benches visible through them . . . How fascinating. These must be the famous galleases from Naples, the very ships he had been trying to find out about when he was arrested. Was that the reason for it all? Was the Almighty using him for some great purpose?

Simon felt a thrill of irrational excitement and hope. Perhaps there really *was* a reason for what had happened to him. Perhaps the Almighty had not forgotten him. He looked more carefully at the strange ships, counting, observing.

There were other long chains of bald men standing about on the quay, some decorated with tattoos. Among them walked bald men who were not chained, many of them wearing magnificent moustaches. There was a gangplank to the nearest galleas and a row of six men were lined up next to it. The rigging was full of riggers, a crane on the quay lowered barrels and nets full of shot into the hold. All the time the guards watched them impassively, most with halberds, but some with calivers and cross-bows.

Another man with a moustache walked along the row of men, using a knife. Simon squinted his eyes, trying to make out what was happening: was he marking them? No, he was cutting their rags off so they were naked. Those who had shoes or clogs were told to take them off. Buckets of water were thrown at them, then handfuls of white powder. At last, the men were marched aboard, naked as the day the midwife saw them.

Almighty help me, Simon thought, and shivered. Some of the other men he was chained to were staring with just as much horror, others just watched impassively.

It took all morning to board the galley-slaves because the blacksmiths bolting them to their benches could only work so fast.

In fact, watching the blacksmith hammering the rivets on his leg chain was the last thing Simon consciously remembered for a long time. It seemed insane that he should sit quietly and watch while someone used a metal chain to turn him into part of a ship, and yet he did. He also paid attention to the men with calivers and crossbows and halberds standing around ready to kill anyone desperate enough to try an escape, as he sat, cupping his hands over his privates like all the other new slaves. He even felt pleased when his manacles finally came off and his arms felt wonderfully light. But really he was not present at all. He was hiding away, deep inside himself, like an animal in a burrow, as far as he could get from his body, which was now, it seemed, the property of His Most Catholic Majesty. When the Padron came and had them do things, he obeyed. The rest of the time he was curled with his naked back against the bench, staring around him and not seeing anything.

The black man next to him seemed in a similar state. There was scarring round his neck from the time when he had been captured and subdued with a forked treetrunk around his neck. Simon blinked at him, said nothing, the man he had once been who had traded in slaves, as distant from him as the inquisitor. He appreciated the irony, even considered that the Almighty must have a very sharp sense of humour, but all of this was simply a ruffle on the surface of a mind that was not truly there at all.

The Padron terrified him more than he could say. His heart pounded with fright like an animal's every time the Padron looked at him. A Turk of ordinary height, with a dark skin and a jutting nose over his flourishing moustache, he carried his whip like a sceptre, flicked it out lazily to take small bits of skin off whoever annoyed him.

Unwillingly, hating himself for his own slavishness, Simon tried to please him, to do as he was ordered promptly. He was terrified of the whip, terrified to white-minded sickness of being beaten. He tried to hide this, ashamed of it, strove to answer coolly and steadily when the Padron insisted on talking to him.

Early on the Padron had told him that he himself was a Mussulman, said something about their being surrounded by heathen. Apart from the blacks, the other men on the bench had seen he was a Jew and simply called him *marrano*. Padron called him 'clerk', which was marginally better. Nobody told names, or exchanged names, it was all nicknames or trades or what have you. So they had the soldier and the plowman and the tall willowy unfortunate who died so quickly that no one ever found out even his nickname.

They had been ignored, climbed over, shoved, kicked while the riggers brought in the oars. Occasionally one of them would be told to hold a rope or duck as something complex happened above. When the business was over and the work moved further up the ship, Simon had stared up at the oar hanging in its sling in the dimness, it seemed more enormous than he could believe. He was frightened of the oar as well, afraid every time they hauled on the ropes to bring it in and then let it out again, frightened he would accidentally clamp a thumb in the ring, afraid it would hit him on the head as it was pulled in and slipped out.

And then came the first time he fulfilled his function as muscular propulsion for the King of Spain's galleas. Padron had read them some kind of lecture about not letting go until they were told. The huge oar was in front of his nose, there was a kind of handrail clamped to it. Clearly no human hand could take hold on the oar, so they took hold on the rail and began to sit and stand in unison, to move it back and forth in the water.

It was very difficult. They had to move together, and there was no room for error. The first time Padron flicked him with the whip, Simon thought he had been stung by a wasp.

For the first hour or so until he began to feel the blisters on his hands and the bruises on his arse, he thought perhaps he would be able to do this, wrapped up inside himself as he was, hidden away from the Padron, from the oar, from this terrifying, impossible world.

As he sweated his way through the second hour, he began to realise why the King of Spain needed slaves for this work. Not only was it brutally hard, it was, beyond anything, dull. Over and over again, sit and stand, sit and stand, over and over again, always the same, push and pull, heave and pull . . .

It was mind-bending. For a while, Simon tried to keep his attention away from what was happening to his body, as his chest crowed for air and his bruised throat filled with phlegm and his arms and legs shook and burned and his hands . . .

His hands were the worst. They locked with cramp because he was frightened of being bitten by the Padron's insect whip – not because it hurt that badly but because it was negligent, immediate, humiliating. Because the Padron seemed to enjoy it? When the order came to let go, he couldn't manage it, his hands wouldn't obey him and the Padron came up behind him suddenly, making him quiver with fright, poured water, rubbed his forearms roughly with leathery palms, peeled back his fingers.

At the end of the hideous, unbelievable day, Simon lay on the boards and promised himself he would never move again. He was not hungry because his stomach was full of terror, he would tell his arms or legs to move and nothing would happen. In any case, his stomach still ached from what the inquisitor had done to him, and it was easy to refuse food. No doubt the black sitting next to him or the soldier whose nose the Padron had broken would have what he didn't eat. Then he might die quicker.

Padron seemed to take pleasure in men's pain. He insisted that Simon put his raw hands in aqua vitae for no better reason. Simon stayed stoical and quiet while his hands burnt in invisible flames in the spirits and his body went hot and cold with the pain. He would never have thought he could do it, except he was so frightened of more hurt from the Padron.

Then Padron brought him food, told him jovially in his accented Spanish, that if the clerk did not eat, he, the Padron, would tie Simon to the bench and stuff the food down his throat. The threat brought more terror. Since that day when the Inquisition had . . . questioned him, he could not bear to have anyone put anything in his mouth, or touch his mouth. It took him will-power to put the neck of a bottle between his chipped teeth.

So he ate. It didn't matter, he supposed, one more hour of rowing would kill him, for certain.

But it didn't. To his astonishment and anger, it didn't. There seemed no end to how much abuse his rickety frame could take. Every part of his body hurt, and his hands . . . He thought he knew how bad it had been for Becket, now, and sometimes he would remember with gut-churning pity and shame the times he had used thumbscrews to get a confession.

Exhausted as he was, he couldn't sleep that night, because the boards were too hard and his hands hurt too much and the night was too cold and the black lying next to him snorted through the hours. In the morning, when they brought black bread, olives and watered wine, he was so dizzy with weariness he ate without even noticing.

And then with all his grazes and bruises stiff and aching, with his hands so stiff with clots he could hardly bend them round the rail, with his arms shrieking as soon as he took hold, he had to row again.

He didn't know how long they rowed because he was only thinking about each individual movement, stand, sit, stand, sit. He heard somebody whimpering softly in the distance, wondered if it was the black and then realised the pathetic noises were coming from his own throat and he couldn't stop them.

Why am I not dead? he wondered at the end of that day. How come I'm still alive? He ate and drank, but he didn't know what, didn't know when. Perhaps I'll die in the night, he thought, and the blackness reached out so hungrily from the back of his skull that he fell unconscious, honestly convinced he was going to Sheol.

It was a terrible disappointment to him when he woke in the morning, to the groans and complaints of the other men on the bench, to the demands of his bladder and guts. Ashamed and disgusted he voided himself in the gulley and smelled his own stink all that day.

He wasn't sure, but he thought that was the day when one of the men on the other bench caused the boy who did the same duties on the hull-end of the bench as Simon to squeal in the early morning. There was a flurry and a beating. Later, a concerned knot of officers. The Padron was furious, his eyes flashing, brushing that moustache of his with his whip handle. The man who had caused the trouble was lash-scarred, sullen, unrepentent. Of course he had tried to have the boy. Who wouldn't? Such a pretty little arse.

The Padron called the blacksmith to free him, then winched him up by the feet and flogged him until the blood ran down and the man was a swollen, purple-faced lump of oozing flesh that moaned and wept and shuddered and finally was still, hanging limp and unbreathing, swaying with the ship's motion, a puddle of blood and urine staining the boards under it.

It's impossible, Simon thought, impossible. This is not happening to me, I did not see this. The smell of the butcher's shop filled the oardeck, adding to and warring with the already ever-present animal stench of men and ordure. The Padron passed by him to wash the scourge and Simon stayed absolutely still, breathing no more than he had to, terrified of those fierce eyes landing on him, taking some kind of offence, beating him . . .

They rowed most of the afternoon, he didn't know why or where or anything except the certain fact that every time he tried to let go and collapse, an insect bit him somewhere painful.

Cold blackness of the night, and in the morning the tall young man had died, was stiff and cold where he huddled by the walkway. Padron was not at all upset: he collected money and trinkets off the other Padrons who were ruefully admiring. The blacksmith came again, complaining at having to suffer the stink of the slaves, unbolted the ankle-rings, tipped the skinny corpse out through the nearest oarport. They rowed again.

Simon did his best not to be present. He couldn't understand why the tall young man had been lucky enough to die and he had not, he was envious of the young man, and he longed to find the way to unlock the ugly, burning, miserable body chained to the deck, that kept him from escaping. But he couldn't. He floated between the oar and the bench, he burned, he sweated, tried not to vomit when Padron forced water between his lips, and all the time he was waiting for his agonised carcass to break, to burst so he could fly free.

But he didn't. He came to, finding the Padron kicking him.

'Wait, I'm not dead yet,' he said in English, and then again in Spanish and then regretted it because if they put him out the oarport the salt water would give him much better mercy than the oardeck.

He had some kind of conversation with the Padron and he rather thought he had told the Padron he would not win bets on him so easily. Perhaps he was trying to goad the Padron into killing him. He thought there was something wrong with the black next to him. Surely it wasn't normal for a man to radiate so much heat, or squat to void his bowels in the stinking gulley so often. How often? He couldn't rightly remember, before sleep hit him on the head and he hoped that it was death disguised.

He woke stickily out of headlong sleep, lying in a pool of water, in darkness almost as black as his dreams, the howling of wind, the ship flinging itself from side to side so that the only thing keeping him from being thrown across the deck was some kind of iron entanglement around his ankles. The ship tilted sideways, he slid and crashed against the hull, water spewed in through some hole . . . The ship was sinking, the slaves would be lost. Where was Rebecca? Where was the Master of the ship?

He struggled to his feet, groping for the hatch to close the hole. Somebody was roaring orders over by the flickering watchlight, he couldn't work it out but he knew he had to shut the hatch where another great gout of water came in. As the ship heeled the other way, he braced his bare feet against the bench, fumbled for the hatch again, waited for the tilt, unhooked it and dropped it across, found the batten by touch and slotted it across, tried to go to the next hatch and nearly fell on his face when his ankle chains stopped him.

That was when he remembered where and what he was. Somebody got a lantern lit and the darkness was pushed back next to the Padron's hawklike face.

'Do as the clerk did,' roared the Padron, and Simon found himself shivering and panting in the stares of those men who were not busy clawing at their feet. Another moved to shut the hatch, and another. The Padron ran lightly down his bench, helped them shut the ports on that side, another Padron did the same on the other.

Above their heads swung the oars, groaning and creaking, thirty-six blunt swords of Damocles. Simon blinked up at them, wondering if one would fall on his head and finish it. But the Padron gave the order to go down under the bench, and Simon cowered there while he watched the Padrons climb up among the oars, hauling on ropes, making fast, with their own Padron always in the middle of it all, at the highest most dangerous points, clinging on with one enormous fist to a rope while he slipped another rope around the end of an oar that was about to drop down, then letting himself down the ropes like a monkey.

Then Simon had to sweep, get the water down the gulleys and out of the scuppers, pushing it uphill against the heel of the ship in the howling gale above, sweeping over and over until the planks were only an inch deep and they could rest. He stowed the sweeper, flopped down.

Simon wrapped his arms around his knees as the rest of the seawater emptied out of the scuppers slowly, shivering with the cold, every one of the many raw places on him shrieking at the salt and the cracked scabs on his hands bleeding again.

The black next to him was sitting likewise, with his head on his knees, teeth chattering, singing softly to himself. Was he insane? Well, why shouldn't he be? A spot of insanity would be a blessed relief, not to know yourself, to believe that perhaps you were a prince or some kind of animal.

Simon got the strange feeling that the black was encouraging the water, singing the storm onwards. Nonsense. Just because Merula claimed to be able to make storms, didn't mean that it was either true or common among the blacks. Simon had seen the black's blood and it was the same colour as his own. To be sure he smelled different, but he had five fingers on each hand and his privates were no different from any Christian's, even if they were bigger. The heat coming from the man was almost pleasant.

There was a whipping crack, more creaking, rumbling and a sudden screaming. Simon almost hit his head jumping up to see. A little way down the deck on the same side he saw a jumble of arms and legs and blood and in the middle of it, the fat shape of a gun. What was it doing there?

The ship tilted again and the gun rumbled again, rumbled over the deck on its heavy wooden field carriage – not a ship's gun either, but something taken from a fortress. It had broken free of its ropes, was loose on the oardeck. It was rolling inexorably over to the end man of the next bench who stood staring, tugging at his chains, wailing helplessly in its path as it bore down on him.

'Get on the bench!' shouted Simon, then realised he had shouted it in English.

The gun mowed the man down, rocked against the hull, started its rumbling journey back and its zigzag path would bring it right to their own bench.

'Listen,' said Simon in Spanish, 'Listen to me. It's coming this way. Get up on the bench. ON THE BENCH.' To show them what he meant he jumped up himself and found, as he had suspected, that the chains were just long enough to let him do it. He grabbed the black's shoulder and pulled him up likewise, said it again in Portuguese just in case.

Slowly, blinking, hearing Simon shouting over and over in the hoarse whisper that was all the inquisitor had left him, the other men got up on the bench and when the gun came rumbling towards them, none of them were in its path, they were all perched above it, clinging to each other for balance, the man next to the walkway grasping the netting to keep from pitching off.

The Padron was following the gun, face intent as he held a net in his hands. As the gun slammed into the hull he pounced, put the net over it, wrapped ropes around knightheads and others around posts to be held and so the gun was stopped. Other Padrons came and helped to lash it in place and then the Padron went and made sure of all the other guns.

Simon stayed perched on the bench until he was ordered down. The other men of his bench said things to him, he wasn't sure what, they seemed grateful to him. He tried to smile because what he really wanted was to laugh and cry. Whyever had he tried to escape the gun? As he watched the Padron kill the men who had been crushed, he thought that would be a good way to go. After all, there was really no such thing as a good death, all kinds of death involved pain and sickness and debility unless you were lucky enough to be executed or to die in battle. To be stabbed under the ear by the Padron seemed a much better thing than to stay alive to wrestle with enormous pieces of timber.

Padron came to talk to him just when he thought that and he shivered and tried to answer sensibly. He tried to hide his terror, which was surely foolish, for the Padron was not a coward, not perhaps even a bad man.

It was no good. The Padron roughly felt the black's forehead and scowled. 'He took sick yesterday,' Simon explained, feeling obscurely that it was his fault. The Padron told him to take care of the sick man and Simon was outraged, so angry he actually spoke back, risking the Almighty knew what vengeance.

But the Padron was not angry. 'Do what you can,' he said, quite gently, and then dared to praise Simon for his actions. He actually said that Simon had the heart of a Padron, Simon remembered it clearly, how it came as a compliment from the Padron's mouth and turned into an insult in the air midway between them. He tried not to show his fury and he thought the Padron hadn't noticed. Recklessly, he invited the Padron to kill the black, who seemed to want it, but the Padron spouted some kind of hypocritical nonsense about it being in the hands of Allah. He spoke quite gently to Simon while Simon blinked and clenched his teeth and tried to stop shivering.

As the ship scurried before the wind and the rain leaked in and the cold bit deeply into every part of Simon's frame, and the black lay shaking, panting and twitching next to him, the night passed and melted into day, which, was just as dark, just as miserable, just as cold. At first Simon was relieved not to be rowing, then realised that for all its brutality, at least rowing kept you warm. He had never shivered so much in his life, he thought his teeth would jump out of his head with it. After a while, the black stopped moaning and shivering. He gasped a couple of times. Guiltily, Simon watched, but did nothing. Could not even bring himself to unclamp his arms and reach out to hold the man's shoulder or hand so he would know he wasn't dying alone. He was too cold, too exhausted. At last the black lay still and the heat in him cooled and cooled as he stiffened.

The blacksmith had come and the black had splashed out of the briefly opened oarport, bitter grey rain spattering in and the wind making no headway at all against the stink of death around Simon.

There were four other slaves to take the places of the ones that had died. Two of them were black. Padron brought them along to where Simon sat and when Simon had climbed to his feet, wishing he could rest from the incessant shivering, he saw that one of them . . . one of the blacks . . . He had a snake climbing his arm, scarred there just like Merula's but with another kind of decorative pattern incised in it. The scar was magnificent and looked extremely painful to acquire.

No doubt it was another one of Merula's tribesmen, no doubt at all. Padron was giving him the choice of who should sit next to him and so he chose that young man, who looked the same to him as the black who had died, but who wore Merula's snake. It was something.

Idly he pointed at the snake when the blacksmith had gone away again. 'Is that the world-snake who climbed the tree and ate a bird and laid an egg?'

The black man stared at him, then nodded slowly. 'How you know?' he asked in stiff Spanish.

Simon stammered to tell him of Merula, the woman who had just such a snake on her left arm, who called herself upside-down, who summoned the storm, who was searching for her son, a prince who had been sold . . .

The black man gave a short cry and suddenly Simon found himself embraced, peering over the lash-scarred shoulders of an escaper, trying to blink back sudden inexplicable tears. It was ridiculous. Stupid. Though a prince who was the son of such as Merula would be more than likely to try to escape and find himself sentenced to the galleys as a nuisance . . . But still. Still.

Once Simon had believed quite firmly that he was held in the cupped hand of the Almighty. He had felt guarded and safe and confident that the Almighty would take care of him and his family. No longer. How could he believe such a thing, where he was? But here, this kind of thing . . . What could he make of it? The Almighty must have a hand in it, but with what bitter cruelty, what ugly practical jokery to give him Merula's son for his companion when he could do nothing whatever about it.

Eagerly, Merula's son told him his name, but try as he would, Simon could not say it. So they agreed that Snake would be perfectly adequate, and indeed an honour.

They huddled together for warmth, Simon wondering at himself that he felt no revulsion to do it, that for all its darkness, Snake's skin made goosepimples like his own. They fitted together well and with Snake there was at least one side of his body that wasn't freezing cold.

When at last they brought down braziers, that was almost worse, because Simon was furthest away from where they were set and felt the warmth coming from them far more feebly than the dank cold from the hull. He shivered and shook in rhythm with Snake's shaking and listened to the sound of coughing from some of his other fellow slaves. Surely lungfever would take hold.

A little while later some small, smelly barrels were lowered down to the walkway and the Padrons came and told them to lower the oarblades in the slings and grease the blades with pigfat. Padron told them to smear the fat on themselves – not for impurity, he said, laughing, to keep warm. Simon had to hold his breath at the smell, which had a flat sticky roundness of putrescence to it. He was not at all tempted to eat the stuff, even if the Padron had not advised against it. To his amazement, after he was as plastered in fat as a bird for spit-roasting, he did feel warmer and the water less chilling. Something about heathens from Padron – it was worrying. Padron seemed to like him.

Padron came along again and shouted at them until they got up, stiff and creaking and aching all over, exhausted from the effort of shivering. They were to lean on the benches and push themselves up by their arms. Over and over again. Padron would not listen to appeals for mercy, there had been no food and their guts were all rumbling, but for some ugliness inside him, the Padron wanted them to waste energy on pointless lifting themselves up and down.

Snake grinned sideways at him. 'This better,' he said haltingly, 'if . . . a woman, yes?'

Simon smiled back. 'A woman?' he said, puzzled.

'Here.' Snake held himself up on one arm, gestured in an expressively undulating line over the deck, and mimed mating with her until Simon had to choke down a laugh.

When they finished the push-ups, they were all breathless and a little warmed. The Padron had them jumping on and off the benches over and over.

At the end of it, the oardeck was no less dark and dank, but it was a little less cold. Padron stood on the walkway and said he had heard the Señors talking and they were making for Corunna now. Nobody cared, they just wanted their food. Simon and Snake sat back to back, chewing black bread, drinking the sour water. They were given permission to talk.

'You have woman?' asked Snake and Simon told him about Rebecca, had to admit that he only had the one wife so far, told of his children and found that Snake intended to marry at least five different women and keep them well-fed so they could be soft and fat and delightful to bury oneself in. When he was King. For Snake intended to be King, he would get free of this cold northland, he would go south until he found his tribelands and he would kill the King who had drugged him and sold him last summer and take his wives. With or without his upside-down mother's help, he would do this. And when he was a King, Simon could come and be his advisor and cunning-man. It was clearly either destiny and the world-snake's favour that had brought them together, or possibly Snake's strange and powerful mother had persuaded a couple of gods to do the work. But one way or another, Snake would be King. It was quite certain. The only question was how would he escape from the temporary hindrance of the galleas so he could begin his journey south.

Simon had not the heart to douse Snake's hopefulness in cold reality. He found it warming to be next to the young man, as if his soul could blink in Snake's light.

Snake had not the faintest idea where they were going or why and didn't care. When Simon tried haltingly to explain about Catholicism and Protestantism, Snake just laughed and shook his head at the barbarism of the northern ghost-peoples, to think that anyone knew all there was to know about any god. Surely there was a better reason for so much effort and war? Was England a fair country? Were the women there plump and beautiful? Were the men hard workers? Simon said that it was a fair country, even if the place was a bit cold and wet, the women were certainly sometimes beautiful and some of the men could work hard. Snake nodded wisely and said that it was a perfectly sensible war if you could take a rich farmland and some strong slaves, why not? He would do the same when he was King, if his adviser said he was strong enough and had enough guns and magic powder to make it easy. And he clapped Simon on the back and laughed.

In Corunna port, time passed slowly, the food was scanty, the water better because not from a half-rotten cask. There was work being done above by riggers, they could hear the shouts and hammering.

And then . . . And then it happened.

There had been the tramping up and down, the creaking, the shouts, that spoke of more people coming aboard from the quay. Padron's voice had been among them. Then the hatch was unbolted, and Padron came down the companionway, his whip curled snake-like around his great fist. Behind him were skirts first, moving uncertainly, then a tight bodice, then a veil draped around a woman's head.

Simon stared at her, not breathing. She was exactly Rebecca's size, exactly Rebecca's build. Her face . . . he couldn't see her face. Unaware of himself, he snuffed in air, actually sniffed for her like a dog. Yes. He thought it might be . . . Behind her came a tall, one-armed man who seemed familiar, couldn't quite place him . . .

He couldn't sit still, couldn't bear it. He stood up, caught the Padron's expression of complete disapproval, and reached for the hatch, to lift it up and bolt it out of the way, to get more air and light into the oardeck, perhaps penetrate that cursed veil. Just in time he remembered his nakedness, hid himself coyly with his hand.

She had one hand on the one-armed man's good arm. It was small, fine-boned, a little brown, the nails round, the rings on it . . . One was her mother's. One was his own ring, given to him from his mother's inheritance by his father when he got married. Given by him to Rebecca under the marriage-tent, when they were still strangers to each other.

Without even realising it, he bowed formally, as he would naturally do when seeing his wife after a long separation. She curtseyed to him.

It was ridiculous. It was outrageous. What in the name of Sheol was she doing here? How could she put herself in danger after her miraculous escape? He was hot with anger and shame. Almighty help him, his own wife was deliberately putting herself in the gaze of two hundred and fifty-two naked men to find him . . . Simon sat down again, shaking all over.

Snake gripped his shoulder and looked from Rebecca to him and back again. 'Is it . . . ?' he whispered.

'Shut up,' hissed Simon desperately. 'Shh.'

There was a grave conference about the gun that had escaped. The one-armed man spoke Dutch with an accent . . . He was . . . damn it, who was he? They had met years ago, back in the days when a quite different Simon had been Rackmaster Norton's most effective inquisitor. They had looked out from the Tower walls and spoken of the fall of Haarlem . . . Anthony Fant? But where was Becket? Surely, it was Becket who had brought Rebecca to find him . . . No, Becket would never be such a fool. And where was Merula?

'Your mother . . .' he whispered. 'Your mother serves m . . . her, that woman.'

Rebecca was translating fluently from Dutch to Spanish and back again, though he could see how she herself was trembling under the concealment of her veil and heavy gown. You could see it in the glitter of the jewel on her breast, in the way her hands gripped and let go of each other. Her voice was soft and a little textured, as if cobblestones were in it.

Simon couldn't look anymore, he couldn't bear to see Rebecca there, surrounded by the galley-slaves, some of them were so dead to shame they were showing their desire for her, they pointed at her with their ugly, naked members and leered . . .

Simon wanted to throttle each of them for disrespect, he was sick with rage, his hands clamped together and he put his face on his knees so he wouldn't see the disrespect, the ugly desire made manifest. Even he was feeling it, the shock of a woman's presence, Rebecca who could make him helpless with desire for her just by walking past him . . . He scrubbed his eyes with the heels of his palm and writhed with it all.

Snake's voice was in his ear. 'Look up,' said the man, face casual, eyes sharp and intent. 'Watch. You want Padron to know?'

Heart hammering with fear for Rebecca again, metal in the back of his mouth, Simon looked up, tried not to be there, tried to keep his face blank. They were there for hours, aeons, and Simon stared at her, looking away, felt sweat actually trickling down his back with the sheer effort of keeping still and acting like all the other men. The soldier was muttering lewdness about her to his benchmates who guffawed stupidly. I may not punch him, said Simon to himself, who had never been troubled by such rage in his life. I may not punch him. Thank the Almighty, not all of the men were as entranced by Rebecca as he was – Padron in particular was frowning with heavy disapproval.

At last the two of them went away and Simon sagged against Snake's solid back. Almighty help him, he had tears standing in his eyes. He stared at the deck, let them fall. If you didn't rub tears away, your eyes didn't get red and so no one would know. Snake's hand was on his shoulder, gripping hard enough to hurt.

'Good,' said Snake. 'Good.'

'Why is she here?' Simon whispered to him. 'Why take such a risk? Oh God . . .' His stomach started churning again. What if she was discovered? What if she was captured? His mind began restlessly bringing up horrible possibilities, more and more of them, each mutually exclusive of course, but still . . . It was like a fever in his blood, seeing Rebecca, actually seeing her with his eyes, not imagining her, as if the beams of light from his eyes that helped him to see took small particles of her flesh back into him and made him mad.

'She come find you,' said Snake simply. 'As my mother come find me. You come find her? No? If she taken by Arabs, you find her, no?'

Simon nodded, wondering if he would be able to do it, and then thinking that yes, damn it, he would. If Rebecca was in such a case, of course he would come after her.

'All the slaves we take,' he said to Snake, forgetting he hadn't explained about his slave-trading. 'Why don't their families come for them?'

Snake laughed. 'All dead, of course,' he said.

The next day brought great entertainment. From dawn the riggers and the carpenters were busy, and after the oardeck had been flushed out in the morning, the hatch at the amidships was raised as the slaves below were squinting and blinking at the sunlight coming through the square hole in the deck. Soldiers with calivers stood at the corners, ostentatiously coughing and gasping at the smell. Snake cheered at the sight of direct sunlight after so long, even Simon was entranced by the buttery yellow light lying on the stained deck, even though he was not directly under it. To see the blue sky and clouds above, even filtered through the busy tracery of rope and the extra rigging being built, to see gulls flying made his heart ache. It could have been heartburn, of course, there had been no food that morning.

The carpenters came to bolt down the guns and make them fast against recoil. Two more heavy guns were being added on both sides. Anthony Fant came down the companionway to supervise the matter and Simon craned his neck just like all the others to see if he had brought his wife with him. No, he hadn't. Thank the Almighty.

He heard a hiss and looked sideways to the oarport, and saw another face he knew: small, round, childlike but not childish . . . Thomasina!

He was so shocked to see her, he nearly gasped her name. She stared at him blankly, winked once and then stuck her tongue out, before pulling back. He forced himself to count to twenty before he moved casually to blink out of the oarport at the gunner's gallery. It was a little higher than the oarports because the gunners had to be able to move unobstructed along it, but if he craned his neck he could just see . . .

Only the edge of her skirts, only her feet in their small boots, a tiny peep of petticoat . . . Once she looked down at him, once, over the edge of the gallery and the shock of their eyes meeting was like a mallet on his chest-bone. She said nothing, only her face became ferocious and when he smiled from the sheer joy of seeing her, she simply nodded to him.

Other men's heads were sticking out of the oarports as far as they could: word had gone round that the woman was on the gunner's gallery. Simon saw Thomasina swinging from the gallery on a rope and throwing water onto the stubbled bald heads from a dripping swabber's rag. They tried to grab her but she shrieked with laughter and swung herself back up to the gallery, singing something nonsensical at the top of her voice.

All that day the carpenters hammered and sawed and drove bolts. One at a time the sakers were lowered into the oardeck by the heavy cranes, shifted across to their trucks at the gunports, hauled into place with a couple of benches of the slaves ordered to heave on lines to help, and carefully made fast there. Rebecca stayed on the gunners' gallery, calling out translations as needed, with Thomasina running up and down, climbing ratlines and generally making a nuisance of herself.

Simon was glad. The Padrons beat the slaves away from the oarports when they craned to look at her. Mostly his wife was hidden away from evil thoughts and worse bodies. He didn't think he could bear to look at her all day again and not touch her, not embrace her.

At the end of the day, they all had to stand by the bench, legs apart, hands held out and mouth wide open. The Padrons came along the lines of men looking in mouths, occasionally rummaging in crotches. Only one man had been stupid enough to think he could steal something – a file, found by their own Padron, who grinned wolfishly and gave the shaking slave the choice of no front teeth or a lashing.

They were ordered to watch while the blacksmith came to put manacles on the man's wrists, while Padron hooked the chain up high and beat the man all around his upper body, so it looked as if he was wearing a doublet of red and blue welts. Simon watched in sick fascination, every blow making his own skin twitch, and the Padron's careful aim and thoroughness as frightening as his clear enjoyment of it.

The Padron came to talk to him afterwards, and Simon was bold enough to ask him why he had taken such care to make it impossible for the man to sleep. He got a lecture on how hard it was to kill a man and how they would all listen to his groans and remember not to try to escape. It made perfect sense to Simon, who had himself used the groans of one man to gain a confession from another, but of course he could not say this nor commend the Padron for his attention to detail. He could only nod. Padron left him with a big smile and a knowing look, which anyone could see and which frightened Simon again. He felt sick again with relief when the Padron took himself off up the steps and away from the oardeck. Perhaps he had gone to spend his pay ashore.

It was when he shut and bolted the oarport that it happened. As he pushed the bolt across, something fell down, clattered into the gulley. At first he thought it was only a stone or a bit of wood from the carpentry earlier, but when he squinted at the thing, it was a tube, not very big, smooth-ended . . .

Simon kept his face blank, didn't even dare swallow. In any case his mouth was dry. It must have been there all day, since Thomasina peeked in . . . He squatted over the gulley, strained as if constipated, palmed the small metal thing. Not in his mouth, not after it had been in that gulley . . . He simply kept it palmed in his left hand, sick and sweaty with fright. Thank the Almighty that the Padron was not there, only his junior was keeping an eye on them. There had been some black bread and olives at noon and there would be nothing more until the next noon, so everyone was constipated. Nobody was bothering to look at him.

He curled up next to Snake, turned to the hull, where the planks of wood in all their dullness climbed up the side, every one more familiar to him than his own bed at home. He waited, vibrating with tension, until night had fallen, when the oardeck was dark and as full of noise as usual, whispers, farts, snoring, the dry sobbing of the man who had been beaten and his constant changes of position as he tried to find a comfortable way of sleeping, the coarse rumbling of the soldier having some kind of dirty argument with the peasant.

When his eyes had adjusted, Simon cupped the metal thing in his hands, brought it close to his face, found that it unscrewed. A bit of paper wrapped around the metal dropped out. The metal was a knife: sharp on one side, saw-edged on the other, it could screw deeply into the tube so it had a hilt. It was a gift . . . priceless, too high-priced. What would Padron do to him if he was found with it?

Fingers trembling, Simon unrolled the paper. He had to screw up his eyes to make out the tiny letters:

Beloved
    I am on *San Salvador*. The words Francis wanted to tell you

are: the third part of the Armada is the Miracle of Beauty. Becket had a message about it too. Nobody understands this. I will try to make sure *San Lorenzo* is taken by the English. Stay alive. I love you.

She had signed it only with their crest, a unicorn goring a book, in itself an ambiguous symbol, intended to give the Queen pause. As quickly as he could, Simon put the blade back inside its tube, screwed it together, chewed and swallowed the paper . . .

'What do you say, little clerk?' The soldier was laughing at him again. The soldier often did so, made no secret of his opinion that the Padron would soon have his way with Simon. There were in fact bets of individual olives being placed on how long it would take, by the soldier, the peasant and the black who had replaced the skinny young man.

Simon wedged the little knife in a gap between bench and deck, lifted himself up again. 'What?' he whispered irritably.

'We were wondering which would squeal louder, *marrano*? You or the gunner's tight little cunt of a wife.'

'What?' The word came out as a hiss because rage was constricting his throat. Snake heard the tone and sat up too. By her message, Rebecca had brought herself here, invisibly, into the oardeck again. Irrationally, it felt to him as if the soldier was calling his wife 'cunt' to her face.

'When Padron finally gets his prick up you, *marrano*, and gives you a new and silent fart. Which will squeal louder, you or the gunner's cunt?'

It was as if some invisible wall came down between him and the world, between his usual sensible self and a part of himself he had never met before. He launched himself at the soldier, fists flailing, the chain not quite short enough to stop him. He got one punch in with his left hand, before Snake was in the way, pushing him back, saying soothing things to him in broken Portuguese, which he couldn't understand because his brain was boiling with black anger that any stinking galley-slave should call his wife by that word.

The soldier had his fists up now, laughing at him, inviting him to try again.

Simon was in the grip of something totally new: his mind was cold, there were no longer any rules or fears. The soldier had to die. He found he could move very fast, the world around him was slow and unimportant. He brought his knee up and cracked Snake with his elbow, pushed past him. Something hit him in the eye, making sparks, somebody gripped him around the chest and quite calmly he cupped his hands, clapped them hard on the soldier's ears. When the grip loosened he dug with his elbow again and then turned, ignoring the flailing fists, reached up and grabbed the back of the man's bald head and his nose, shoved him down at the bench, shoved again, and finally got what he was aiming at the third time, he cracked the man's gullet on the edge of the bench and heard the satisfying crunch.

The soldier dropped to the deck. Snake pulled him back again and Simon found he was gasping, sweating, his face hurt. But now the Padrons were gathering, flailing with their whips, shouting at each other to bring water to throw. The end of a whip stung his flank, he hardly noticed it, shuddering in breath and staring as the soldier jack-knifed and clutched his throat and rattled and flopped like a fish and fought to die while he slowly drowned in his own blood. His benchmates were staring at him, muttering to each other, frightened of him now. They had liked and respected the soldier, the man who called him *marrano*, who laughed at him. Who was dead.

I killed him, Simon thought. Me, I killed him, myself. Intentionally. Because he insulted my wife. How did I do that? he wondered, bewildered, thinking of himself still as the skinny, scholarly code-breaker and student of Cabbala, not the sinewy, blank-faced clerk that the other slaves knew.

Still partly entranced, he stood and watched and when Padron came back and throttled him until he answered with his reasons, he answered steadily and quite forgot what he had hidden under the bench, the thing that would certainly cause Padron to kill him.

Padron seemed amused, grudging his admiration but giving it nonetheless, that he had been able to kill the soldier. You don't understand, Simon thought, something took me over, some devil, and I found it easy. Padron explained as if to an idiot that he would have to be flogged. Not me, Simon thought, it wasn't me, really, Padron, it was that devil that took me over.

When they had all gone, leaving the soldier's body to stink and stiffen among them and the other slaves to lie as far away from the mad little clerk as they could get, Snake whispered to him, 'You upside-down, eh?'

'No,' Simon told him. 'Not yet.' Snake shrugged, took his stiff, swelling hand and wrapped it round the little secret knife hilt.

'So hide it, not leave by the bench. Now.'

'Where? He moved to put it in his mouth, despite it having been in the gulley, and Snake laughed ... Pointed to Simon's arse and made an obscene gesture.

Everything is about arses tonight, thought a quite insane part of Simon as he clinked over to the gulley again, squatted and strained and covertly put the thing in the place it was obviously designed for. Obviously. A few months ago he would have been disgusted and ashamed even to think of putting something there, now he just did it. He was too naïve to live. Really, imagine thinking it belonged in his mouth.

He lay down again, uncomfortable, uneasy. His arse was the only piece of territory he still owned, that and the increasingly disordered country inside his skull. Will I go mad? he wondered. Or will it all turn me into a brute like the soldier was?

Yes, he thought, yes it will, one or the other. He squinted at his hands in the dimness, scarred by the oar rail, the knuckles and palms swelling from blows he could not rightly remember giving, hands, his own, he had killed with them now. Becket had said that killing your first man was like your first woman, the sort of inane thing an old soldier would say. It wasn't anything like that. Simon's first woman had not made him long to weep or curl up into a ball and hide away from the world; his first woman had been Rebecca and he had been her first man. It had been a perfectly ... well, adequate experience, on the whole. Aunt Leonora had seen to it that he was just drunk enough to be able to manage it but not so drunk he couldn't, which was a mercy. He had been as gentle as he could for as long as he could and then ... Rebecca had cried and bled, which proved her virginity. And he had stroked her hair, thanking her incoherently before he slept. Later they had learned each other, each Sabbath afternoon, they had studied each other's bodies, to glorify the Almighty with their love-making. Only a fool of a Christian could compare the two things. Killing a man was nothing like that. And in the morning the Padron would (quite justly) beat him.

To take his mind off that irredeemable fact, he sought for things that were not Rebecca to think about. He had considered all ten sephiroth, he had prayed, he had done manipulations in his mind of the numbers that surrounded him, the number of planks, the size of oars, the angles with the water, all kinds of things to keep his mind from scurrying about his skull like a spit dog. At least he had a new thing to mull over: he tried to imagine what the Miracle of Beauty might be.

Originally it must have been Santa Cruz's idea, the secret key that made the whole daft enterprise of the Armada feasible. The galleases were intended for it, of course, although they would be useful in any flat calm. Even so, they were terrible sailors and brutally hard to row; they were not good ships. He now knew far more about them than he had ever wanted to and although he had decided that the Almighty was playing with him to treat him so cruelly, still it gave his mind something to do.

Miracle of Beauty, Miracle of Beauty. What a foolish name. How could a warlike campaign, an invasion plan, be either miraculous or beautiful? It was stupid, ridiculous.

Simon slept, dreaming uneasily of statues that came to life, of the soldier shouting at him, of Rebecca, made tiny, but perfectly naked, peeking out of the little knife-hilt. Normally, now, he could sleep quite well on the deck, even when there had been no rowing to tire him out, but every time he turned over or rose out of a dream's muddy waters, he heard the sniffles and groans of the man who had been flogged the day before, prophesying the night he would have tomorrow. It made him feel sick each time he thought of it.

And in the morning, Padron came to him, with the knotted scourge in his hand and grinned under his moustache. Dry-mouthed, Simon looked past him, face blank.

'Now, clerk,' Padron said jovially. 'Must I tie you to the bench or will you stay still for me?'

'I'll stay still,' said Simon, skin prickling with the humiliation of it, determined not to show his fear to the other men on the bench, not even to the soldier who was still glaring sightlessly up at him because the blacksmith had not yet come to release him.

He tried to think of it as like a river to cross. Now he was on this side. Soon he would be on the other side. In between was unpleasantness. Obediently he gripped the other edge of the bench, hunched his shoulders over and ducked his head down as far as he could so nobody would see his face.

Padron stood on the bench and the scourge whistled, thumped. Once Simon caught a glimpse of the peasant grinning with satisfaction and rubbing himself. The newly discovered madman sitting gibbering quietly in the corner of Simon's mind made a note to kill the peasant just as soon as he had killed the Padron. Even the sensible part of him seemed to be flaking apart, like a flint. Becket had given him good advice, once, in his cups. 'Some of the whores say it's better to scream and wriggle,' he'd rumbled. 'That way, the man doing it doesn't lay on so hard because he thinks you're already suffering. Some of them say it's better not to say anything because then he doesn't get any fun out of it even if he lays on harder to try and get something out of you. As for me, I spent my time cursing the bastard, which was some help.'

At the time Simon had thought he could not be so stoical, but now he found that a solid mass of rage born of shame kept him silent by blocking up his throat. It hurt more with each blow, a peculiar, unbearable, spreading itch under his ribs each time, getting worse each time as the blows started crossing and re-crossing previous welts, until the pain itself was breath-stopping. He gripped the bench tighter and tighter, tried to remember not to bite his tongue or his lip and tried not to move, not to give Padron any fun. He wasn't sure whether he had succeeded because he kept his eyes tight shut, terrified he might cry.

At the end of it, Padron sluiced him down with seawater and jumped up from the bench to the walkway to talk to the blacksmith, who had also been watching with a lascivious grin on his face. The two of them moved the soldier's corpse so the chain could be taken off, then out the oarport went the soldier and all his experience of Lepanto and the great three days looting of Antwerp and wherever else he had been, which changed each time he told stories.

Sick and shaking and cold from the water, which stung his back like fire, Simon sat under the bench, curled his back and tried to get his breath. He was panting as if he had been rowing. Snake inspected the damage for him.

'He got worse than you,' Snake pronounced eventually, nodding across at the one who had stolen the file who still moved like an old man. 'It not bad.'

'Not bad,' Simon repeated dully, easing his shoulders and wishing he could swap bodies with someone else. I am now a member of the company of whores and peasants and soldiers, he thought, and also priests who must scourge themselves for the better worship of God. Those who have been flogged. Well, why not?

He thought of Rebecca and what she might say when she saw him. Almost certainly she would be furious with him for taking the risk of fighting the soldier only for words, only because he had called her a name, not even knowing what she was to him. Of course she would never get the chance because he would probably never tell her. Would he ever feel her next to him in bed again? Would he ever be able to lay his head on her shoulder and hold the small, pointed mound of her breast? No. Almost certainly not. He had seen her, that should be enough, but it wasn't. Like the food they got at noon, half rations because of still being in port, it was enough only to whet hunger, not satisfy it.

He thought of her and then forced himself to stop thinking of her. He was not like the soldier or the peasant, to relieve his carnal desires right there, in the oardeck. It didn't happen often anyway, he was too hungry and tired most of the time. By running through possible codes for the Miracle of Beauty, changing the letters to others by sequences of combinations and getting nothing but gibberish, he even managed to forget the fire in his back enough to doze off. The other men on the bench looked at him sidelong.

Every movement hurt, that morning, not only his back but as if his whole body had been beaten, he ached the way he had in the first few days of rowing. He said this to Snake who said that of course it wasn't his back alone, what did he think? Which reminded Simon that Snake was an escaper and also a member of the fellowship of those who had been flogged. Snake said the same as Becket, which was that you had to move about, stretch your back muscles and so he conscientiously touched his toes every hour or so no matter what it felt like or how badly the scabs cracked and burned.

At noon they got more food than they bargained for. Not only black bread and olives and cheese and sausage, but also, each of them, an orange. A whole orange, each one a warm sun of scent and sweetness in the dim oardeck, like a promise from another world. Everyone on the oardeck was muttering and suspicious at such largesse, which was right because Padron stood on the walkway with his whip and told them that the oranges were a gift from Don Hugo de Moncada, a great and generous gift, because soon they would be leaving Corunna and heading north to fight the English.

Simon held his orange in his cupped hand, nearly laughing at the brightness, the outrageous vividness of the colour, admiring it as if it were a jewel. The peasant looked greedily at him. The last time they had something special to eat, a piece of chicken each, the soldier had reached over and stolen his, and Simon had done nothing. This time Simon met the peasant's eyes and grinned. The man looked away. Shall I take his orange from him? Simon thought with a festive flare, and then was ashamed of himself.

He ate the orange slowly, every bit of it except the pips – skin and pith and meat and all, dribbling at the powerful tastes, the sourness, the bitterness. It was a Seville orange. He had heard from Dr Nunez of rare oranges from China that needed no sugar, but this was fine, this was good, as if taking a small sun into his body warmed him up.

And then, in the afternoon, they rowed again, out of Corunna harbour, out into the Atlantic, where the sailors could set the sails and catch the perfect south-westerly wind that would take them north-east to England. In the distance, he could hear sacred music, he supposed there was flag-flying and religious pageantry for the occasion. The Spaniards loved a procession almost as much as the English.

It was hard to row again, but not so hard as the first days. Simon suspected that nothing in his life would ever be as hard as that and found a kind of wonder in himself that he had in fact lived through it. He looked at the other men on the bench and wondered if they thought the same, or if they thought at all. He didn't feel any fellowship with them, really, except when they were all heaving on the huge oar and they had to move together. Then the peasant would often give a rhythm for them, a worksong from when peasants were breaking rocks on the road. Snake listened with interest to it and then set up a song of his own, one with a strange beat to it that somehow caught them up and swung them along, and nonsensical foreign words that meant nothing to them, which they sang by rote. Some Padrons did not allow singing but their Padron was neutral about it. he allowed them to sing so long as they never missed the beat with the other oars and when he realised that the other benches caught the rhythm of Snake's song as well, he even joined in with obscene Spanish.

Even so, after the long rest in Corunna, they were all more easily tired. When at last they could stop heaving, and catch their breath, and feel the heel and lift of the ship as the wind took her, Padron came along with the barrels of grease for the oars as they drew them up. Snake put grease on Simon's back to make it more supple; that had burned him when they worked, his sweat had stung and all the bruises ached.

While he was trying to sleep that night, Padron came and talked to him, quite friendly, really, advising him to forget his wife. Simon answered cautiously and neutrally, only telling Padron about the terrible ache of boredom in his gut, which Padron seemed to find witty.

All Simon wanted was for the Padron was to go away, so he could try to sleep a little, but the man seemed to enjoy talking to him. He spoke of spectacles, of Simon keeping a look out through the oarport for him, of Simon earning the gift of sight.

The friendly squeeze of Simon's shoulder by the Padron's wide horny hand told him exactly how he could earn the spectacles, exactly how he could negotiate one of the last territories he owned, where he kept the little knife Rebecca had sent him, and it made him feel sick and sweaty. The Padron grinned down at him, completely sure of his power, of his right to get what he wanted from His Majesty's property.

Simon stared into the night, at the seaming on Snake's back, trying to think about it. Trying not to think about it. Yes, he thought, perhaps he could resist, for a time anyway. But Padron could make sure that his life was hell, could stop his food, beat him, even stop his water. He lived with only a thin border of resource between him and death, he knew that. At the moment the Padron seemed to like him and the soldier had been right, the Padron wanted him. And he had no power at all to say no and make it stick. One day, sooner or later, when he was nearer to death perhaps, but one day, Padron would . . . The thought of the sin sickened him, tightened up his gut like a tangled string. His back burned, his muscles ached and Snake snored softly and he couldn't sleep because he wanted to weep. Once he dozed off and found himself sitting up, tearing at the rings round his ankles, where they had made bruises and sore places. What could he do? Nothing. He couldn't escape, he couldn't die quick enough unless he used Rebecca's little knife to slit his own throat. Of course, he could do that, said the quiet little madman sitting in the corner of his skull, the devil who had taken him over when he killed the soldier. It would mean never seeing Rebecca again, of making Sheol for himself. It might be worth doing though, rather than lose sovereignty over his last bit of territory. If he stabbed himself hard under the ear, where Padron had killed the men who were crushed, it wouldn't take long to die or hurt that badly. Of course, he could stab the Padron when he came to take him, and then they would beat him to death.

It was a tempting thought.

He couldn't sleep in the dimness of the oardeck, the heel and lift of the swell under the ship, all the great Holy Enterprise, which he couldn't see, which he probably would never see, hove to with their lanterns burning, so they could keep contact in the wastes of the ocean, sacrificing speed for cohesion as they had been ordered by the King. Everybody else was asleep, snoring, grunting. One man moaning. Oh him.

Simon sat cross-legged to examine the chain that made him a part of the ship. There were ankle chains that could be locked and unlocked, but these were the kind that had a rivet hammered into place. To get them off you had to hammer the rivet out again. Which could be done if you wanted the slaves to work in the docks while the galleys were laid up for the winter, but not without a hammer and anvil. The chain between his ankles was made of good steel links about an inch across, and it passed through the ringbolt in the deck. Out of sheer animal frustration, he pissed on the ringbolt, and watched as the piss drained out through the hole in the deck that the ring was bolted into. Blinking, not quite sure if he was seeing right, or if what he was seeing actually meant anything good, Simon jiggled the bolt. There was movement, give. Something had damaged the timbers . . . Perhaps the iron wheels of the gun truck as it went past, something like that. Or perhaps the timbers were a bit young, unseasoned and were already starting to rot.

Simon looked round, particularly for Padron. He was curled up against the junior Padron, cuddling the young man as if they were husband and wife, a disgusting sight. Everybody was asleep. Very quietly, Simon reached behind and retrieved the little knife, screwed it together, tried the saw blade.

The timbers splintered and gave to his tenative sawing, he rubbed away sawdust with his finger. He could enlarge the hole the ringbolt was in and when it was big enough he would be able to pull it out. He would still have chains on his ankles but he would not be bolted to the deck. It was something.

He thought of Snake. What had Padron said? If one escaped, his benchmates died too because they must have known, you couldn't keep secrets. Very well. He would make sure Snake was freed too: he could reach Snake's bolt. Not the peasant's nor anyone else's, because they were further up the bench and too high. He was the last man, on the end, right by the hull. Quite lucky.

Simon worked away carefully on the wood around the ringbolt, then formed the sawdust into a kind of cement with more piss to hide what he'd done, put his little knife away. He was terrified it might break or wear down, but so far so good.

He slept badly, afraid of so many things, jumped when the Padron spoke to him in the morning, asking how his back was. He eased his shoulders to hide his instant cringe as his skin remembered pain. He said it was recovering, Padron. They sang as they rowed north that day, so that Hugo de Moncada came to listen at the hatch and commend the Captain of the Oardeck on the high morale of his slaves. Perhaps the slaves could sing some sacred hymns, Salve Regina, perhaps? No, the Captain thought they were too ignorant for that. Never mind, said Don Hugo, it was good to listen to and they were making excellent progress. Simon squinted up at the man standing like a giant by the hatch, catching the grave bony face, the immense dignity and the ease with which he stood on the deck, and thought, after the Padron, after the peasant, you, Don Hugo. Or not him, the devil. The little devil that had entered his skull with his killing of the soldier, or just before perhaps. He was quite grateful to it because it had revealed to him how easy it was to kill someone. Not easy physically, true, he had been lucky he had been able to crack the soldier's gullet on the bench, but easy mentally. He saw that now. Killing was only what you did when someone was in your way or disrespected you or threatened you. The soldier and the devil together had taught him that.

At least they got more rations now they were working. Not enough, of course, never enough. Simon had folds of skin on his belly where he had lost the little pot that Rebecca's care had given him. Inside his stomach seemed permanently in a knot of craving. When he had grinned at the peasant, it had been a feral showing of teeth: take my orange and I'll kill you, he'd thought, and the peasant had understood.

Instead of being fed at noon, they were fed in the morning and evening. As they sailed north, they rowed, they drank the water, which started tasting strange after only a few days, they ate bread, then bread and worms, then biscuit. The worms had horrified Simon when he first found them in his bread but Snake showed him they were edible and even satisfying. Cold, slimy, but edible. So he ate them. It was almost disappointing when the food changed from bread with worms to hardtack biscuit without worms. He often thought of his orange and he thought of entire meals from the past, some invented, some remembered. His body swung and heaved at the oar, his mouth sang reedily along with Snake's deep gong of a voice and in his mind he was in the land of Cockayne, where the wells ran with wine and the tables groaned with chicken and game birds and rabbit and bread and sauces sharpened with verjuice, and apple pasties of French bisket bread, and marchpane subtleties, and beer and ale ... At night he slept fitfully, woke in the middle watches. Sometimes there were things happening: Padron playing dice with the other Padrons, or a fight or somebody crying out in their sleep. Sometimes it was all quiet and then he would lie curled around the ringbolt, gently sawing away at the wood like a very large ship's worm. If he got the chance, he sawed away at Snake's ringbolt as well, which didn't start off loose as his had been. He was quite artistic in his care to hide the work: not only urine and sawdust, but carefully saved up turds to match the pale scraped wood to the stained old wood.

Padron gave him a heart attack every time he came for a chat. Padron treated him as a favourite, gave him tips on rowing, brought him better food, fish, cooked salt beef, dried fruit. Padron wanted Simon to like him, how ridiculous. Simon would look carefully past Padron or at the deck, just occasionally focusing at the place on Padron's thick neck where Rebecca's knife would one day make a hole. He tried not to twitch when Padron put his hands on some part of him; once on his shoulders, supposedly checking to see if he was better from the flogging, another time a rough, calloused caress on his bum. Every time it happened, his skin itched and prickled at the place for hours afterwards.

Snake was sympathetic, the peasant made coarse jokes and further up the bench there was envy at his favourable treatment, occasional snide comments. They had forgotten that he had saved their worthless lives when the cannon broke loose and he hated all of them.

One morning, very early, Padron brought their rations and while they gobbled the food and squatted to shit, he stood on the bench and announced to all the oardeck that the Armada was now in sight of the Lizard, which apparently was some southern part of England.

Simon immediately turned to look out of the oarport but there was nothing but blurred sea. His heart momentarily lifted and then sank deeper than ever. The only good thing was that there would be less time for Padron to come and smile at him from under his moustache, less opportunity for his arse to get squeezed. Only the fact that Simon was starving all the time allowed him to eat the biscuit and olives. The low boiling rage in the pit of his gut would have killed any ordinary appetite. And he was near England. Round and round his heart twisted, tighter and tighter. He was close but not close enough, the tentacles of the Inquisition still held him, the chains were still on his sore ankles, he would likely die in this galleas and the Almighty had brought him so far, so close only to mock him. Miracle of Beauty, Miracle of Beauty. What the hell use was that to anyone? How could anybody riddle it out? Even if he did, what use would it be?

The motion of the ship changed to the rolling that told Simon it was stationary somewhere. Trumpets sounded and there was the clatter and thud of a small boat coming alongside, presumably to take Don Hugo de Moncada for his council of war.

Again there were extra rations. More sausage, pickled onions as well as olives and . . . another orange. Simon held it in his hands like a grenado, or an orangeado. Memory attacked him: outside the bearpit in London was a woman with wonderful breasts who sold Seville oranges stuffed with broken sugar-loaf and you could suck on the juices and then throw the orange peel on a midden for the rats of London to fight over. He himself had done so quite often, in fact he had not even finished his orangeado when he went with Becket to visit Harry Hunks . . . The memory of the orangeado laughed at him from its mouth of sugar, sitting on a midden benefiting rats when now he would crunch it all up in one go. Even without sugar, the orange was bitter, sour, but delightful. He peeled it with trembling fingers, dribbling slightly, and ate it all in a few gulps, then chewed the skin he had kept carefully in his lap and then picked up the little flecks of peel and flesh that had dropped and ate them.

Snake smiled at him round his own mouthful of orange.

'I never saw such fruit,' he said and Simon told him that they had been unknown in his grandfather's time but had come out of the furthest east with the silks, little trees that grew and flourished in the heat of Spain.

'Battle tomorrow,' said Snake wisely.

Padron said the same thing from the bench. He told them they were in the English Channel, that they would likely be in action the next day when the English infidel would surely attack and with Allah's help they would ram and board El Draco's own ship and the soldiers cluttering up the galleas would finally do some of the work for a change. That got a laugh. Simon shook his head. Under no circumstances would Drake permit the Spanish to board.

Luckily Padron either didn't see or didn't notice his head shake, continuing with his speech. Now they, the oarsmen, were slaves of His Majesty and as rowers in the galleas, they were the soul of the galleas. Some of them might perhaps be thinking that when the fleets were fighting would be a good opportunity for an escape attempt. Any such thinkers should think again. In action the hatch would be battened down from outside. There would not be the slightest point in trying to overpower him or the other Padrons in the heat of battle because the slaves would still not be able to escape. In any case it was in their interests to row their hearts out to keep the ships afloat and moving because it was harder to hit a moving target and in any case, if the galleas sank, they all died. But if they succeeded and were victorious, there was an excellent chance that all of the slaves who had served His Majesty so well would be released. It had happened after Lepanto. So they could choose foolishness and death or sensible obedience and perhaps, Inshallah, freedom.

It was a good speech, Simon thought, and perfectly reasonable. And probably quite true. Nonetheless that night, in the darkness and quiet, he sawed away at the wood around his ringbolt and Snake's ringbolt and then hid the damage. He thought one more night's work would make the bolts come straight out of the wood and after that it was a case of waiting his chance.

He woke to find Padron's hand caressing his arse, Padron squatting right next to him, right next to the ringbolt that was still a little dusty from being worked on. He lurched up, nearly hitting his head on the bench, heart thudding.

'Well, clerk,' said the Padron, 'today we will fight the English. Who knows: perhaps they'll board and take us and then you will be freed and I will be the slave?'

'Perhaps,' said Simon.

'What will you do then, clerk?'

Simon smiled. 'I will eat spit-roasted beef, venison pasties, comfits and bread and butter, and drink wine until my guts ache. And then I will seek out my wife and take her to bed.'

Padron put his head on one side and sighed. 'What would you do if I kissed you?'

'I would fight,' said Simon, trying to hide the fact that his mouth had gone dry. 'I know I would probably lose, but I would have to fight.'

Padron's eyes narrowed. Simon found himself sweating. He forced himself to stare steadily back.

'Unfortunately the noise of our fighting would get us both found out and because they are so hot for purity in this Holy Enterprise, we will both be hanged. Which will suit me but might not suit you.' Simon was careful to keep his voice light, cold, unafraid, despite the sick terror inside. A thought occurred to him. 'And . . . and . . . since the Inquisition examined me I have been liable to bite anything that goes in my mouth.'

Simon was measuring up the Padron, who balanced easily against the heel of the deck as he squatted. Snake was awake by now, Simon knew it, waiting quietly.

'I could free you,' offered Padron.

Simon shook his head, knowing this was a lie, wondering if hitting him first would be worthwhile. 'You are a man of honour, Padron,' he said, voice wobbling. He stopped, breathed deeply, so close, to be so close to England and then to die in a sordid scramble, 'is there no one in all this deck who would desire to be your catamite?'

Padron smiled. 'Many.' He dropped his heavy hand on Simon's shoulder and gripped hard. Then he straightened from his squat and went to fetch the food so that the routine of an oardeck could begin.

After eating too little biscuit and olives for his clenched-up stomach, because Padron only brought him half-rations, alone of all the bench, Simon dutifully swept out the filth as best he could, the stink of his own and other men's wastes all about him like smoke. Above, in the sunshine and the clean air, the soldiers were singing a Kyrie Eleison, and it sounded like martial angels if you were light-headed from want of food and heart-sick fear. Death didn't frighten him at all; pain, another worse flogging, starvation, being raped did. All he had left was himself. His body was the city where his soul lived, and as with any city, the gates were the weak places. The inquisitor of the Holy Office had forced one of Simon's gates, with his cloth funnel and metal gag and jugs of water, and by so doing had let in the devil that had killed the soldier. Under siege by the Padron, the metaphor extended itself. The army was camped outside, ready to take the city by starvation. If his other gate fell by storm, at least he would have done himself the honour of resistance although he felt that to be raped would reduce him to nothing . . . But to surrender his city without a fight would make him less than nothing . . . Almighty, please have mercy on me, give me strength. Simon had no doubt at all that Padron would be back, prayed incoherently to the God of Israel whom he no longer believed to be on his side. May the Almighty have mercy on Simon His servant, whom He has tormented and destroyed and exiled into the galleys for no reason unless it was for being an inquisitor and a slaver . . . A ridiculous idea.

Above the soldiers' singing echoed his thoughts: Kyrie Eleison, Lord have mercy; Christe Eleison, Christ have mercy. It was in Greek, which had been the language of the gospels. Like all his family he had been brought up as a linguist: he spoke English, Portuguese, Spanish. He knew Latin and thence could puzzle out Italian. He could read and write some Hebrew, thanks to his father-in-law's Dutch rabbi. He knew a few words of Greek . . .

It came to him like a flower opening, like an evening primrose unfolding itself yellow in the dusk. The word for 'beauty' in Greek was 'kalos/kalle'.

He said it to himself under his breath, over and over. *Kalos*. Could it be that simple? Could it really be so incredibly simple? Could Santa Cruz have hidden the key to his plan for the Enterprise of England behind a simple Greek pun? The Miracle of Beauty, the Miracle of Kalle, the Miracle of *Calais* . . .

They were ordered abruptly to put the oars out. Simon fumbled to hang up the sweeper, open the oarport, stood ready to clip on the ring as the oar thundered out on its restraining line.

He stepped up to the great oar and when Padron shouted, 'Take hold' he took hold next to Snake, locked his hands and tried to forget about them while he begin the rhythm of sitting and standing, sweeping the huge oar to and fro. They were quite good at it now, they could vary the rhythm and back water and lift the blade out of the waves – the hardest thing because there was no momentum, just the strain of holding the vast double tree balanced on the ring while the ship manoeuvred, muscles burning and quivering, back breaking and then at last to dip it down again on the order.

He swung into the rhythm with one of Snake's worksongs and his lips were muttering, 'Calais, Calais.'

It made sense. It was the only thing that made sense. When Medina Sidonia finally got the Armada to the narrow seas off Dover, with the best will in the world, Parma would have to spend at least a week, possibly two, embarking his troops from Sluys. He couldn't do it before because there was no point until Medina Sidonia was in place in the Channel and when he would get there depended on imponderables like wind, water and the activities of the English fleet.

But Medina Sidonia could not possibly anchor in a place like the Calais Roads where the cross-currents were famously fiendish and the weather as unguessable and explosive as the Queen's temper. It would be dangerous to do it for a day, let alone for the week that Parma must take. You couldn't embark that many troops on barges in less time, much less get them down to the Scheldt. And so . . .

Somewhere in the distance, in the world outside the oardeck there were deep thunderous booms. Then more booms. Shouting. Trumpet calls. More banging. Giants playing the drums very badly.

Padron shouted, the rhythm doubled, they rowed harder and the sweat began to pop, the heat began to build, you had to remember to breathe deeply and not gasp or you would faint. Whistling the ugly-smelling air in and out of his lungs, Simon thought about his discovery.

It was the obvious answer to the impossible temporal conundrum of the Armada. Simply take the town of Calais.

Put four heavily armed galleases full of soldiers into Calais harbour where the lack of wind would do them no harm. Bring them up close to the quay and batter the citadel into submission in a devastating surprise attack. Let the soldiers on board storm the town. Then the Armada could take shelter in the deep-water harbour, could refit, resupply and wait for wind and water and constant patrolling to exhaust the English and Dutch fleets while Parma embarked. And then . . . hop across the channel when the English fleet was forced to refit and resupply. It only took a couple of days of good weather, once you had the troops loaded, as Duke William of Normandy had proved six centuries ago.

Of course, Calais was supposed to be neutral and the Governor, Gourdan would not go quietly, but France was in thrall to civil war. For such a prize as England, Philip of Spain could plead necessity and pay off the French crown with the spoils of London if need be.

Simon stared ahead at the lash-scarred backs in front of him, heaving and pulling on the oar in front of him while his own scars itched and pulled, his guts gurgled with hunger, his lungs and arms and back burned and his head spun in excitement. How could he tell anybody? Here he was, he had the answer. The riddle his brother Francis had summoned him to Lisbon to pass on, the riddle that had brought him into the jaws of the Inquisition, that had brought him to this oar. But how could he pass it to the English commanders in their fleet? They were so close. On land he could hope to run that far before he was caught. Here, in the galleas . . . Every time he sat or stood, the bruising ache in his ankles reminded him why escape was impossible.

Perhaps he could wrench out his weakened bolt when the oar was drawn up that night, jump out of the oarport . . . No, the chain on his ankles would sink him. That was why they made them thick and heavy. He could swim but not that well. Shout? Don't be ridiculous, the best he could do since the Inquisition was a breathy croak. Write a message. On what? With what? When exactly?

He could have swept with frustration. He growled English curses under his breath and Snake sweating and grunting with effort next to him, looked sideways at him.

'What?' asked Snake.

Simon shook his head, talking was strictly forbidden when they were rowing and in any case, he couldn't possibly spare the breath to explain. Padron had spotted them, though. He reached with his whip and caught Simon over and over across the shoulders and neck and face, never pausing as he handled the end of the oar, never missing the beat, burying Simon in a deft flurry of cracking leather. You had to admire his skill.

Simon ducked his head between his arms like a turtle and carried on heaving and pulling, waiting for the storm to stop. Padron was angry with him: any excuse would do for a beating until Simon gave up his honour and there was nothing whatever he could do about it. Except let Padron bugger him, of course.

After a while the whip stopped cracking around him and he could put his head up again, catch glimpses of the red weals and bruises all over his shoulders and arms. His face was stiff and sore as well. He kept on, swinging with the oar, singing along with Snake.

The order came to stop, to back water. Their side of the galleas shipped oars for a moment. And that was when the guns boomed on the deck above them, a vast bellowing roar and then another and another, the sound like a blow in the face, making the ears ring. Smoke drifted down. There were two gunners on the oardeck as well, now. They passed down between the benches, a cloth across their faces against the stench, and one after another the enormous fifty-pounder guns roared and belched smoke stinking of eggs.

Whips cracked again, Padron shouting orders. Simon's body heard before his battered brain caught up, he was still coughing helplessly at the smoke, like all the others, but they backed water, turned the galleas around in nearly its own length and the other broadside roared, the gunners again fired the fifty-pounders on the oardeck and yet more bellows of thunder, more pain in his ears, more grey smoke filling the place like a pall and the sense that it was a hot grey flannel across your mouth and nose, stopping half your breath every time you wanted air. Snake crowed and puked beside him, Simon croaked helplessly and they heaved the oar forwards and back, forwards and back, blind, deaf, muscles on fire, keeping the ship moving, registering the flick of Padron's whip but not noticing the pain in comparison with the awful hunger for air in his lungs.

The smoke didn't disperse: where was it going to go? The hatches were shut, the two gratings blocked by soldiers' feet. There was a little space in the oarport as the oars moved to and fro. Whips cracked again and again, as some men on the benches collapsed, but the Padrons were as blind in the smoke as the rowers. There was a booming, someone was hammering on the hatch. At last, it opened and some of the smoke started to escape, the gunners rushed choking up the ladder. Through drifts of grey, Simon saw Padron's legs as he stood on the ladder, shouting angrily. He went all the way up and the noise of an argument, but not what it was about, floated down to them.

They rowed on, coughing, gasping, eyes streaming. At last there came the order to stop. Feet on the ladder, you saw everyone's feet first, became adept at recognising boots. These belonged to the Admiral, Hugo de Moncada. Leaning on his oar, crowing for breath, Simon watched the black damask back of a true Spanish grandee as he stood on the walkway and inspected the damage wrought by no more than smoke. No cannon balls had hit the ship yet.

Don Hugo did not have a napkin clasped to his mouth, he breathed deeply, coughed and nodded at Padron who was standing with his legs wide, brawny arms folded.

The hatch wasn't shut again, but a boarding net was laid across it. Padron came among the rowers with his water skin and Simon expected to be missed out when it was his turn. No, he got to gulp his fill of wine-soured water, at least Padron was fair in that.

They waited for the gunners to get out on the gunners' gallery and reload the heavy oardeck guns, the shot lowered on nets by pulleys, the swabbing and charging, a long complex operation and all carried out exposed on a balcony hanging over the water. The other guns were being reloaded as well.

There was more banging from far off. Simon snatched a peek past the oar through the oarport and saw English ships worrying the great galleons of the flag squadron like dogs. Their guns fired over and over and Simon grinned. He knew nothing of gunnery, but he could tell a fast rate of fire when he heard it.

Then all was ready and they rowed again, double speed, backed water and spun, rowed once more. The guns fired again. This time there was a booming from nearby, the crash and crunch of shot hitting the galleas. All high above, no serious damage, one sailor shrieking, no doubt from splinters. More rowing, push, pull, push pull, the fifty-pounders fired on the oardeck, the oardeck full of smoke.

Streaming eyes shut, mouth hanging open, breath sobbing in and out and his ribs on fire, Simon knew that someone was behind him in the smoke. Then, there was suddenly an enormous explosion not far away, echoing and cracking across the sea.

They kept rowing, shouts above, the sound of crackling. Each rower was in his own smoke-filled little world, the walkway swam in bleary mistiness. A different smell added to the gunpowder stink.

'Clerk, look and see what's happening?' shouted the peasant anxiously.

Simon squinted carefully. Smoke drifted, black now. They were near something that was on fire. A ship on fire – how had that happened? Surely none of the cannon could do that much damage? They passed the prow and he could see the name through the drifts, almost close enough to touch, so that even he could make it out: *San Salvador*.

*San Salvador* was the ship Rebecca was on. It had somehow been caused to explode. What had happened? Was she alive? Almighty Lord, please let her be alive.

They were getting a line aboard, more shouting, the sound of long poles being used to keep the flaming ship far enough away. The order came to row again and they rowed, twice the weight now, twice as hard to get moving, and every muscle in Simon's body was exhausted, protesting, burning, towing the crippled munitions ship *San Salvador* so she could be protected by the rest of the Armada.

He bent his back. Again and again. They rowed and rowed, harder than they had ever rowed before, the oardeck silent now apart from the drum, and the hoarse hiss and gasp of two hundred and fifty men labouring their hearts out, the creak of the oars, the hissing of the flames as *San Lorenzo*'s sailors put out the flames. Sometimes they could hear a far off wailing from the casualties on *San Salvador*. And still they rowed on. Snake had his eyes shut, foam on his lips. Simon elbowed him, filled with a sudden certainty and understanding. Surely the Almighty had bent down in his unfathomable way with the red hot coal of inspiration.

'Sing,' croaked Simon, 'Sing these words. The Miracle is Calais. The Miracle is Calais. They're an English spell.'

Snake blinked, wiped his eyes with his shoulder, frowned, repeated Simon's phrase. Simon sang with him, the simple rhythmic tune Snake had first taught them. The rhythm eased the work, the words nobody really cared about so long as they helped to carry the tune. Other rowers picked it up, sang what were nonsense words to them, but their voices swelled out the sound, built it up, all of them singing and swinging together to pull not one but two ships through the resistant waters.

After a moment Simon's voice closed on him, he wanted to weep. He could hear it clearly now, all the rowers on the galleas singing, 'The Miracle is Calais.' If Rebecca were still alive, if she could hear it, if she could make it out, if she could guess who had told them what to sing . . . if if if . . .

The sound was travelling, he knew that. He picked it up again because the music helped with the pain, made you forget how tired you were, how your hands were hurting and your shoulders sore and how impossible was what you were doing and all the rest of it. 'The Miracle is Calais,' he croaked, 'the Miracle is Calais.'

Long into the night they rowed, still towing the crippled ship, lamps lit and swinging from the beams so that the Padrons could see them, their new song still passing from one bench to the other. Rows of shoulders and arms and heads as mechanical as a waterwheel, working away in a daze of exhaustion.

Boots on the ladder again, Don Hugo's. A conference with the Captain of the Oardeck, Padron standing with his arms folded fiercely scowling behind the Captain. Shouted orders up above, the order to ship oars and then row again, and the weight was lessened, half what it had been.

Simon had to puzzle for several strokes before he understood that they had dropped the tow rope, they were no longer hauling *San Salvador* through the water. *San Salvador* was slipping to aft, a few lamps alight, a hulk with a wailing cargo of burned flesh already starting to stink ... Mentally Simon bade his wife goodbye, wondering if what he had done was enough, if he had performed what the Almighty in His sarcastic and bitter humour had clearly desired of him.

Another order. Simon's body obeyed while his battered mind caught up, they were drawing up the oar so he must open the ring and close the hatch, they were making fast, so he must coil the rope.

'Down,' said Padron gently. It wasn't the universal collapse of the first few days' rowing. The men sought their usual sleeping positions slowly, like old men in the throes of arthritis, not speaking. Padron came along the bench with more water, not so much this time, carefully doled out in a horn cup. Then he came again with bags of dried figs, raisins, biscuit, oily little fish. 'Well done,' he said to each man. 'Well done, my son.'

Simon was sitting with his legs drawn up and his arms wrapped round his knees, sharpening chin on his shoulder. The Turk squatted beside him.

'Well,' said the Padron, quite cheerfully, 'How are you, clerk?'

Simon shrugged, his belly a ravening wolf inside him, but not expecting to get fed.

Padron grinned. 'Are you hungry, clerk?'

Simon stared at him, fury making his breath come short. 'In the name of Allah,' he said, 'do you think I am a fool? I have played this game myself, many times.' He mimicked the Padron's Turkish accent. 'Are you hungry, clerk? Would you like to eat? All you have to do is give me what I want and this unpleasantness will end. So simple, why do you make yourself suffer, you silly slave?'

For the first time in his memory of the man, Padron looked puzzled.

'I have been an inquisitor in my time,' Simon hissed, leaning forward. 'I understand you very well. When I am ready to sell my arse to you for food, I will say to you, Padron, I am tired of resisting you, do what you like only let me eat. Until then, find someone else to play with.'

He ostentatiously turned his back on the Padron, rested his head on his tightly wrapped arms, biting his lip to stop the stupid childish tears of self-pity and hunger. He had never realised before, in the days when he had played just such games with food as the Padron to get information from suspected traitors, he had never understood how sickeningly it hurt, how it gnawed away at your mind and made

333

your thoughts tedious with memories of food and thoughts of food. Perhaps this was part of the Almighty's joke.

The heavy paw of the Padron landed on his shoulder, gripped hard, then there was a swift movement and the Padron was gone.

'You want eat?' came Snake's soft rumble. Simon looked over his shoulder to see a little pile of biscuits and a couple of figs on the deck. Another half ration. Was it worth stirring up his stomach to eat it?

He couldn't help it, his hands shook as he grabbed the biscuits and the dried fruit, gulped down the first ones quickly. He forced himself to slow down, suck each raisin individually, gutting it inside his mouth for its sweet innards and then chewing up the skin and swallowing the pips whole. He thought about saving a fig for the morning, but knew he would never be able to sleep for fear of someone stealing it. Some of his teeth were getting loose and sore, which was hardly a surprise.

Snake shook his head, took Simon's hard, scarred palm and put some things in it, curled the fingers over. There was half a salted anchovy, some olives, another fig. Simon blinked at it stupidly. 'Eat,' said Snake. 'Is good. My belly full.' He patted his hollow stomach and grinned, enjoying the polite lie.

Simon blinked, hunger was blurring his eyes, his eyes were watering . . . No, damn it, he was weeping. Why? He should be happy. Well, he was, he crunched up the anchovy, bones and all, spat olive stones, chewed the fig carefully to save his painful teeth. He shook his head because he had come so low that a handful of food could lift him out of despair.

An awful thought struck him. Was Snake perhaps made the same way as Padron? Did Snake desire him? He didn't know, couldn't think how to ask. And was suspicion a courteous answer to generosity like this? He shook his head and wished his head would stay still instead of wobbling.

The answer came to him that if Snake had wanted to do more than simply huddle up to him for warmth, then Snake had been perfectly placed to do it. Snake was not tall but he was far more strongly built than Simon and even in the total lack of privacy of the oardeck, he could have found a moment or two, just as Simon had for his sawing activities. There were puritans who were frightened of all kinds of love because they feared impurity in all of them. Their minds were too small to understand that bodily desire was only one variety of a great wide sweep of love. Was it dog-like of

Simon to love Snake because he had shared his food? Perhaps. But it was natural for men to love each other because they were naturally similar, just as it was natural for men to love women because they were so different. And no doubt women loved women as well. It was *agape* not *eros* between two who were the same, and *eros* between two that were different. Difference was important. Look how different he and Rebecca were and how well they fitted together. Oh please God, let her be alive still, not hurt by the explosion on *San Salvador*. Perhaps Merula had caused it, or Thomasina. Let Rebecca be all right ... Had she heard their singing? Had she understood? Please, God, let her be all right.

Simon knew that his mind was spinning out of control, knew that he was lying curled up against Snake's back for warmth but also for human contact, found parts of him wondering about killing the Padron and parts of him wondering about how he would get the knife out when the time came and parts of him revolving restlessly around the food he would eat when he was free, when he got to heaven. His guts cramped again, rumbled and cramped. One remaining shard of clarity continued to think about the Miracle of Calais and that was the part that made the central spine of all his spinning thoughts as he dozed. What else could he do to get the message to the English fleet? No inspiration came, nothing. He dozed into torturing dreams of banquets laid on the walkway, just out of reach of where he was chained.

The next day they did no rowing and the last replacements were brought out of the hold to fill the spaces made by two men who had collapsed and died when they were rowing in the smoke. They could hear Mass being said for the soldiers and sailors above and many of the slaves crossed themselves reverently as the bell rang for the Consecration. Afterwards there was some food, and Simon got a half ration again with Padron watching him intently. Simon kept his face stony until Padron went away. With Snake's help the two of them were getting three quarters the ration, which was bad, but not impossible.

'Clerk, why is Padron punishing you?' asked the peasant anxiously. 'What have you done?'

'Padron wants my arse,' said Simon coldly. 'I want to keep it mine.'

The peasant stared in silence. He looked over his shoulder at the other three men further up the bench who were playing some kind of game with their fingers. Then he looked at Simon again, and slowly held out his smallest fig.

Snake grinned as Simon slowly took the offering.

'It isn't so bad,' said the peasant seriously. 'Padron is gentle and he gives you fruit afterwards, and you can confess to the padre later, if you want.'

Simon blinked, wondering how he had managed to miss so much of what had been going on. Snake laughed. Simon only shook his head at the peasant as he split the fig between him and Snake.

The peasant shook his head as well and tutted. 'Goats get used to it too, you know,' he added so seriously that Simon swallowed down his urge to giggle.

'Oh.'

Given the choice between Padron and a goat, Simon had no idea which he would choose. In the end, he didn't care. He felt too exhausted to do more than sit and stare ahead, peering occasionally out of the oarport, while the light airs pushed the whole Armada at the pace of a snail, across a wide bay he supposed might be Lyme Bay, and the two fleets glared at each other. The English ships kept their distance but did not come in close. Why not?

In the evening neither he nor Snake got any rations. Simon was furious. He scowled at Padron who played chequers with the junior Padron in the long soft light of a summer's evening, and pretended to ignore him.

Padron sauntered over when the game finished, squatted by Simon. 'Well?'

'I had always thought you were at least a man of honour, Padron,' said Simon as disdainfully as he could, his heart pounding as always with fear. 'Clearly I was wrong.'

The Padron shrugged. 'Why are you making such a problem?'

'Why do you insist on . . . on this?' Simon made a fierce gesture with his fist because the words were tangling themselves in his head. 'Why aren't the others and your junior Padron enough for you? Why me?'

Padron looked at him sideways. 'What did you mean about being an inquisitor?'

Simon hesitated, then decided to tell the truth, because after all, what could they do to him? Kill him? Good. Send him to the galleys? Hah! 'Many years ago I was an inquisitor in England. There they do not have the Holy Office but they are very afraid of priests and hunt them down for spies and infidel.'

Such a long time ago, he had been another man entirely. For a start there had been no devil inside him, poking its head between the whirling curtains of dizziness and sticking its tongue out at the Padron.

'I was an inquisitor for Don Francisco Walsingham.' Padron, who had never heard of Walsingham, showed no interest in this. 'I had to break men open for him and I was good at it. Starvation is a very efficient way to go about it, if you have the time. I often used it because I felt it was a lesser evil than torture. And it was effective. What you are doing, starving me and my friend, will get you what you want in the end, if we are alive, if the ship isn't sunk.'

Padron was squatting, watching, his face still. Simon smiled a little, only with his mouth, not realising how cold it made his face. He hesitated, not sure how to say the thing that was in his heart, against the weariness and cold and the encroaching sense of hopelessness.

'I am not a very carnal man,' he said, spreading his hands open between himself and the Padron. 'I have never lusted after women particularly. I have known one who did, who was a soldier, but who said that to take any woman unwilling was to dishonour yourself as well as her, that what you stole from her for your pleasure was less than what you destroyed in yourself. A man who would force a woman is only half a man, with no more than strength on his side. To win a woman, to persuade her . . . that's a true prize.' Padron was at least listening to this convoluted speech, his face unreadable. Hollow in the pit of his protesting belly, Simon was sure he would get at least a beating. He swallowed, tried to lick his lips without spit, croaked clumsily on. 'I am not a woman, but you want to treat me as one and in truth I can fight but I can't stop you. When you . . . when you win, in the end, what have you shown? That you can treat me as your woman when you wish. That the Padron is stronger than this slave?'

Padron held his gaze for a few moments, then looked down at the deck. Brushed his moustache. Looked up again. 'You have forgotten love,' he said, quite lightly and rose, passed back along the bench to the walkway.

Simon put his face in his hands and tried very hard not to sob. He knew his shoulders were shaking. One part of him said, what does it matter, it's only my arse he wants, not my soul. I need food. Another part, the devil, said, kill him next time he comes near, he won't expect it and it will be easy, and another part wrung its hands like a child and wanted to know, why me? Almighty, why me?

Snake patted his shoulder, said nothing reproachful about losing his own ration.

In the night Simon lay unsleeping, wrapped around the knot of his belly, alternating between dreaming of food and trying not to think at all. There was a stir and clinking further along the bench, all along it, stealthy covert movement. A moment later, Snake sat up on his elbow, then turned over to face Simon. His face was lit up by his smile.

'Look,' he said, and gave Simon a handful of figs and raisins.

Simon crammed them into his mouth quickly, his mouth aching with the flood of spit. 'Where . . . ?' he asked. Snake pointed his thumb over his shoulder where the peasant and the other black, the cavernous cougher and the replacement for the willowy boy peered back at him. Simon wanted to thank them, but could think of no way of doing it except by knuckling his forehead and lying down to chew and swallow. It was not enough, it was never enough, but it was better than nothing at all.

He still couldn't sleep though. He had to revise his plans for escape. He couldn't leave all of them when him and Snake broke free, they would be killed for it.

His mind chewed away on the problem, dipping in and out of sleep like a swallow snatching flies from the surface of a pond. Calais, the Miracle was Calais.

The next day they did a little rowing, just enough to stop them stiffening up as Padron explained. There was only biscuit to eat and only at midday. Simon thought that he and Snake would go without again, but Padron came up to them and told Snake to put his hands out. Snake got the same double handful of biscuit that the others on the bench had got. Simon stared stonily past Padron's left ear as Padron stood in front of him with his bag of biscuit.

'Do you want to eat, clerk?' asked Padron.

'Yes, of course I do,' said Simon haughtily.

'Kneel down.'

Simon stared into his eyes, incredulous. Padron took the whip he had under his arm as always and shook it out. 'Kneel.'

Simon knelt, slowly, clearing the chain out of the way, legs on either side of the bolt he had been working on.

'Open your mouth.'

Simon stared up at Padron, rippling muscles at a strange angle, moustache like an animal hanging on Padron's hooked nose.

'Don't be afraid, clerk.' It was impossible not to be afraid at that contemptuous tone.

Simon opened his mouth, ready to bite hard if need be.

Padron put a piece of biscuit in, popping it in like a priest giving communion. Simon chewed, swallowed, a very small part of him demanding that he proudly spit it out and a much larger, more practical part of him insisting that this was food and why waste it? Padron gave him all the ration like that, occasionally teasing by holding the biscuit just a little out of reach, as you might tease a dog. Like a dog, Simon drooled because he couldn't help it. The silence, broken by nervous giggles from the peasant, made the ceremony worse. At last it was finished.

'Did you enjoy your meal, clerk?' asked the Padron.

'The biscuit was good,' said Simon after a moment, with a lawyerly care. The Padron snorted, stepped back and brought the whip slashing across Simon's face, whiting out the oardeck.

He found himself already on his feet, his fists bunched, Snake's shoulder blocking him from going after the Padron.

'No,' said Snake, quite quietly, in a voice that broke through Simon's rage. 'Later.'

'You are too stiff-necked to live, clerk,' said Padron.

'Quiet,' hissed Snake still blocking him, until Padron had turned on his heel and walked back up the bench, past the other slaves who were silent.

Simon's rage faded, leaving him sweating and shaking and wrung out, with a long burning pain in his chest. The biscuit lay on his stomach, making him feel sick for hours. As the slow warm day passed and the Armada wallowed its way past the English coast at the pace of the slowest hulk in this lightest of airs, he sat on the bench, or curled up under it, silent. Snake examined the long whip cut that marked his face on the diagonal and tutted.

'Now is not good time for become a warrior,' he said.

The next day, it was still half light when Simon woke again, knowing from the brighter heel and lift of the deck under him that there was wind. Only a little time later, he heard the banging and crashing of fighting, lifted the oarport hatch a little way and peered out at the toy ships blowing smoke puffs at each other. He couldn't see well enough to know who they were. Only the speed of the banging told him that the English were fighting.

339

There was a scurry on deck: the heavy hatches were being lifted, gunners came down the ladders, cloths over their faces, and boarding nets laid over the openings, the sailors were manning the yards to set the sails to catch the easterly breeze.

Simon looked out of the oarport again. More smoke blew in from the battle over the southern horn of the Armada crescent.

A trumpet blew. Simon turned to find Padron already bringing biscuit and a water skin to his rowers, waited his turn. He expected no water either this morning, but Padron put a double handful of biscuit into his hands, let him gulp his fill of the flat slightly sour water. It was as if the past few days had not happened. Simon kept his expression cold. Padron said, 'We will be in battle soon, Don Hugo announced it. Here, take these, look out the port for me and tell me what you see.'

A pair of pince-nez spectacles were pressed into Simon's hands and, with his hands trembling, he put them on. They weren't as good as his own, but they were better than nothing at all. He looked again at the battle to the south and saw the individual sails, the low race-built galleons frisking about the rearguard Spaniards.

'I see the English fighting the Spaniards,' he said. 'The English are better sailors and faster with their guns.'

Padron brushed his moustache. 'We will be attacking some English ships that have got stuck near the headland over there.'

Simon barely had time to gulp down his biscuit before the order came to put out the oars, and take hold. He took hold, already light-headed, his chest already tight in anticipation of the gunsmoke.

Using sails and oars, the four galleases of Hugo de Moncada's squadron bore down on the five English ships that had dropped anchor to avoid going aground on Portland Bill in the light easterly breeze of the morning. For the first time, the Armada had the weather gauge on the English. *San Lorenzo* was in the van, the other three in line abreast.

Simon stared at the oar, the pattern of the wood and knotholes that he knew as intimately as his wife's skin, that he suspected he would be able to remember on his deathbed – assuming this oar was not to be where he died.

Snake was singing again beside him, very softly, a slow chant that lifted the stubbly hairs on Simon's neck. The snake on his right arm pulsed with his muscles and Simon settled into the rhythm of it, let his body become a thing with a will of its own. Which it had. It wasn't different from himself, no matter how separated his thoughts felt.

Simon was too intent on rowing to realise that the larboard row of oars had been ordered to back water, they were swinging round. As they did the fore guns roared, and then one after another the upperdeck guns fired, and the fifty-pounders between the banks of oars fired. Once again the oardeck was full of smoke, once again he was rowing with all his might in a fog of grey stink and air starvation, his muscles cramping into knots and sweat dripping from his face. They rowed forwards, backed. The galleas was being twirled around the English ships like a dancer. So far, no answering fire.

They rowed again, one stroke, two strokes.

'Clerk, what do you see? Can we board?'

Simon looked past the flank of the oar through the oarport and saw the English ship, near enough to see the guns pointing through the gun ports, the men on the rigging.

'No, too far . . .'

His hoarse voice was lost in the roar of the English guns, one after another. There was a crash, another crash, shrieking towards the aft of the ship. Simon looked over his shoulder and saw that an oarport had been broken by a cannon ball, splinters sticking out of the nearest rowers making them look like bloody hedgehogs. Another roar, more crashing, more shrieking. Simon stared open-mouthed at one of the rowers behind him, who had a splinter sticking out of his eye and was still rowing.

'Stroke!' shouted Padron. 'Back water.' They couldn't fire in return yet because the gunners had to go out on the gallery to reload the guns. First they had to get out of range of caliver and arquebus shot. Above them there was a peppery clatter of handgun-fire. Simon was looking directly into the mouth of a gun, almost on a level. Smoke was coming from it, thank the Almighty it had fired without harming him . . . He bent to back water with the others, looking again. Some kind of flurry was going on behind the English oarport. There was a name written on the ship . . . *Triumph*. Suddenly there was another sequence of bangs, and the same row of guns spouted smoke again, there were crashes. More screams behind him, another cannon ball had splintered the oar two banks behind and one man was staring stupidly at his arm, which had been somehow ripped off.

Simon turned away, metal in his mouth, bent to gag and puke, then felt the sting of Padron's lash.

'Stroke.' Padron was handling the oar almost alone, one-handed, he broke the rowers around him out of their horror-struck trances, the ship backed water, twirled, more of its guns fired, the fifty-pounders on the other side fired and then they rowed for their lives out of small arms range while the gunners ran for the steps to get out on the gallery and reload.

Simon was standing, still holding the rail, still sick at the stink of butchery around him. Padron was suddenly beside him and his heart lurched again.

'How many guns have the English ships? How can they fit them all in?'

'The English ships fire three times for our once,' Simon told him.

'How? Is it witchcraft?'

'No ... Yes, it's witchcraft. By their magic they can reload the guns without need for a gunner's gallery. Look for yourself.'

Padron pushed past him, peered out. He chewed the moustache that Simon was beginning to think of giving a separate name. 'Hmph. We must row quicker.'

Padron disappeared, they listened to the shouting and booming as the other galleases went into action against the English who did not seem to be in any particular hurry to up their anchors. Behind him the Padrons were sorting amongst the rowers, the one without an arm was already dead, but the one with the splinter in his eye had it pulled out while he screamed, roughly bandaged. Simon heard the Padron tell him he could row with both his eyes out, if necessary, and not to make such a fuss.

Then the guns were ready and they went into action again, rowing double speed, heavier going now there were fewer whole rowers to do it and smoke still swirling amongst the benches, air soup made of bad eggs.

It became a terrible fever dream, full of crashing and sour spit at the back of the throat and aching arms and legs and movements that went on and on and on, unrelenting, and more crashing and more smoke and more screaming and Simon gazing stupidly at a long gouge in the top of the oar, inches from his hands, made by a bit of flying metal, and he had no memory of it happening and he counted his fingers, looked for bloody stumps, but they were still there. The order came to stop and the whole oardeck hung, sobbing for breath, then the blessed order to draw up the oars, which they did, some having to unpeel their hands finger by finger, and Simon unlocked the ring and made the rope fast and coiled it and then dropped under the bench still in a trance. His head was ringing so badly from the noise of the guns that Snake had to shout at him.

There was food, the same double handfuls of biscuit that everyone else got, there was water, poured stone-faced by Padron into Simon's gasping, foam-rimmed mouth so he could eat the salty hardtack, not enough, never ever enough.

That was a while after they stopped rowing though, for the wind had changed in the morning, from easterly to south south-westerly, which had somehow changed the battle, for more quick-firing English ships had sailed across Simon's limited view, before disappearing behind the smoke again. That was after the galleases had been ordered to disengage by Hugo de Moncada himself, apparently, seeing the terrible execution done by the English cannon on the rowers and the easy targets of the oars. They were having to replace some of the oars with new ones from the hold and mend others with long staves bolted on. And shortly after, the five English ships, supposedly trapped behind the headland of Portland Bill, had upped their anchors, filled their sails with the new south-westerly breeze and impudently sailed away. Simon had laughed.

He finished his biscuit, barely noticed that Padron again took the waterskin away before he had finished drinking, and plunged headfirst into exhausted sleep. Morning came with the knowledge that the ship was sluggish again but that there was some kind of way on her from the breeze. He felt hungover, as if he had spent the night drinking aqua vitae with David Becket, which was unjust. His stomach was queasy, his head sore, his eyes and mouth felt sandy.

After morning biscuit, this time again a half ration for both him and Snake, Padron gave him one gulp of water to drink but stopped him before he had drunk any more. Simon said nothing, suddenly understanding what was going on. He looked stonily past Padron's neck again.

Padron grinned. 'You're a fool, clerk,' he said.

They rowed again, more smoke, more noise. At one time they were towing another ship, singing in short gasps, hotter and hotter. Sweat poured down Simon's face as he fought the oar in a daze until the order came to draw in the oars and rest.

Simon sat on the bench for a while, shaking, his mouth utterly dry and his head pounding. It was cruel to give him salt biscuit without water, he thought, cruel to ask him to row without water or food, cruel. His head hurt so badly he could hardly see. Padron came along the bench with the waterskin, gave some to Snake, missed him out completely, leaving him staring. Padron was going to break him by drought, since famine took too long. Drought would work, his mouth was already a desert and he couldn't think straight.

Ironically, he had to make water. He watched the stream playing on the ring bolt, and wondered if it tasted as bad as it smelled. But his piss looked less like water than sherry sack, dark coloured and stinking of fish. He couldn't do it. The salt sea clopping and splashing on the wood, on the other side of the ship's hull so near was laughing at him.

At least when I am this thirsty, I don't feel hungry, he thought to himself as he huddled up under the bench and tried not to shiver any more, I feel sick. His head was the worst thing. He looked around for Padron, wondering if he agreed to Padron's will, if he gave in now, would he at least get a drink? Padron was nowhere to be seen, but the junior Padron saw him and suddenly jumped up, brought the waterskin and very carefully poured water into Simon's mouth. He gulped and swallowed and gulped and the water made a glorious track, slimy, sour and bad-tasting as it was, it cleared the dried spittle and cleared his head until his belly was full with it.

Junior Padron said nothing to him, only took the waterskin away again. Not being thirsty was wonderful and Simon could look out at the soft cloudy sunlight through the oarport and realise that there was only the very lightest of wind, that the sea was calm again, and that they were moving with utter slowness past the English coast, while the English ships stayed dourly behind them. And for that moment, he was happy. He would eat nothing more so the salt wouldn't make him so thirsty, and he would be able to hold Padron off for another day at least . . .

He was peacefully taking on Snake in a game of draughts played with light and dark stones on a board scratched on the deck, when there was a flurry and tension among the other men of the bench. He looked up, at the Padron with his whip and his striped breeches, and next to him the tall, high-nosed, white-ruffed dignity of the black-damask-clad Admiral of the Galleases.

Quite slowly, as he realised Padron might have thought of a way to take a most complex revenge, his blood froze inside him. He blinked up stupidly for a while, and then when Padron twitched the end of his whip, scrambled to his feet.

'I told my lord Hugo what you said to me the other day,' said Padron, 'that you have been an inquisitor for the English. He wishes to know if you were taken as a spy?'

To be ambushed by it now, here, and as a result of his own carelessness. Simon swallowed hard.

'No, my lord,' he said, gesturing at himself. 'As a Jew.'

Don Hugo was surrounded by bad smells but now looked as if something even worse was under his nose.

'My lord wishes to know what you can tell us about the English navy and about El Draco in particular.'

'Nothing, my lord. I know very little of Her Majesty's navy and have never even met Sir Francis Drake although I have heard—'

The whip had to be lifted up to come down across his face and this time, Simon had time to duck, put his arms up. It wrapped round his arm, leaving a burning weal. Here it came. He was done for and it was his own stupid fault, boasting about his knowledge to Padron.

Don Hugo stopped Padron as he lifted his arm again, spoke quietly into his ear. Padron grinned and turned, cracked the whip across Snake's head and shoulders.

Don Hugo took out a stiletto knife, handed it to Padron, spoke softly again. He was not an ugly or an evil man, Simon thought, as he stared, imagining his heart leaning to its oar inside his chest. He just needs information desperately.

'You can row if you're blind,' said Padron. 'In fact it's better if you're blind for you obey orders better. Don Hugo wants information. If you answer well, he might let you keep your eyes. And your black catamite too will keep his eyes.'

Don Hugo looked down at them both from a great height of pure blood, and rock-solid unimpeachable nobility. He had dark brown eyes, very fine, very intelligent. He would have his answers.

Almighty, you brought me here. Was it to betray the English?

The answer came to him, clear as a bell, wrapped in the kind of ineffable smile a faceless God might smile. *Yes, entertain them.*

Simon put his face in his hands, his shoulders shook. But he hid his face because he was laughing hysterically. Because it had come to him what he could do loyally to serve the land wherein he dwelled as all good Jews were enjoined to do. Hysterical was right, there were tears as well. He was so twisted up in trapped fear and disgust, he could hardly speak.

He sat down on the bench and let himself weep, moaned, cried. Padron and Don Hugo stared at him, lips curling. Snake stared as well, sweating with fear. To be blind and at the oar, nothing could possibly be worse and death would be much better. If Snake lost even one eye, he could never be king in his country.

Padron's hand was heavy on his shoulder again. 'Tell Don Hugo about the English guns.'

'The English have an enchantment for their guns, called a flail. It is an arrangement of ropes,' said Simon breathlessly, who had seen the recoil-control for the stern-chaser on his own ship, 'it controls the way the gun rolls back. So you fire the gun, it jerks back by itself on its carriage—'

'The English guns are not bolted to the deck?' demanded Don Hugo, speaking directly to him for the first time.

'No, my lord, they are on wheeled carriages. When they fire, they jerk back a way, but the ropes stop them. Then the gunners reload and haul on the ropes to bring the guns back up to the gun ports. It is very quick – the sailors who sail with El Draco can fire many shots in an hour, I believe.'

Don Hugo stroked his pointed beard and nodded. 'Tell me about how the English can sail so close to the wind.'

'I am not a sailor, my lord,' said Simon. 'I believe they can make their yards move further round but I don't know how.'

Padron had the stiletto in his fist. He jabbed it at Snake's eye, where he squatted, still bent over the draughts board, too afraid to move.

'It . . . it's true, my lord, I don't know. Perhaps their yards are kept loose, not lashed tight to the masts. I truly do not know any more about it. I am a merchant not a sailor and—'

Don Hugo nodded again, gestured at the Padron to wait. 'Will the English use fireships?'

'Yes, most certainly,' gabbled Simon, at last in an area of questioning where he could use his imagination. 'As soon as they can, or as soon as you are outside Calais, they will use their special fireships, which have been prepared. They are bigger than usual, they are filled with guns and gunpowder and if you thought what happened on *San Salvador* was ugly, wait until you see the English hellburners go off. My father-in-law lost a cousin at Antwerp when the hellburners were used there. You will lose many more ships and men. The English are crazy and El Draco craziest of all, they have men who will sail them right into the middle of your line and then set them off and take their chances by jumping in the sea . . .'

'They have hellburners?' said Don Hugo.

Inspiration seemed to be picking Simon up and cuffing him along like a kitten. 'Oh yes, my lord, it is their secret weapon to stop you entering Calais.'

Don Hugo stood perfectly still, face of cold ivory.

Now Simon was well aware that Hugo de Moncada and Medina Sidonia must be the only two men in the fleet who knew about the Miracle of Calais. In fact, since Don Hugo had been in Santa Cruz's confidence, had been instrumental in ordering the galleases, he might even be the only other man in the fleet who knew about Calais, apart from Simon, if Medina Sidonia had sealed orders and had not yet opened them. The Spanish understood security: to keep a thing secret, you must not tell anyone.

'Calais?' repeated Don Hugo, as if he was having trouble getting the words out. 'What about Calais?'

'I was sent to find out about it,' said Simon recklessly. 'All about your plans to enter Calais harbour with the galleases and force the citadel.'

Hugo de Moncada's pursed lips and intent face was all the confirmation he needed that his guess was right.

'Who sent you?'

They would hang him as a spy, but so what?

'The Queen of England, Walsingham, Sir Francis Drake.'

'They speak about Calais?'

'Of course they do, my lord,' lied Simon with as much servile eagerness as he could muster. 'There are many traitors at the Spanish court and Parma has a few as well. They are like worms in a ship, they get everywhere. It is common knowledge at the English court that the Spanish are sailing in the expectation of the Miracle of Calais.'

Don Hugo sucked breath through his teeth, turned away briefly to stare out the oarport, as if he was afraid an English spy might be listening there.

Internally Simon could almost laugh at the expressions warring away on Don Hugo's face, at his own madness, at the daft simplicity of it. Only inside himself. The outside of his face he kept twisted up with fear and obsequiousness.

'The English know that we plan to take Calais?' It was not in fact a question, it was Hugo de Moncada repeating to himself the thing that, had it been true, would have made all his efforts, all the security of the password, all the careful control of who had the knowledge, a waste of time. It was heartwarming to hear him.

'Yes, my lord.' It seemed to Simon that Don Hugo was inexperienced as an interrogator. Simon himself would never have given such easy confirmation to anybody.

'What have they done about it?'

'They sent me to find out more about it, but I was unable to do so before the Holy Office captured me. They have the hellburners, of course. What else they might have done I do not know because I have been a prisoner of the Inquisition for so long.'

Don Hugo was twiddling a ring on his gloved hand. 'What does El Draco plan?'

'I'm sorry, my lord. I am not a wizard or a warlock. How could I know what El Draco plans?' Padron jabbed at him with the stiletto and Simon made himself stare coldly at Padron. 'Blind, I will still know nothing more. You would do better to ask yourself what El Draco plans because experienced sailors are more like each other than they are like other men and so more apt to know each other's minds.' It was a compliment, smoothly done, Simon thought to himself, comparing the great El Draco with Don Hugo.

Don Hugo stared down at Simon for a long time. Aware that he was sitting in front of the Admiral, Simon slipped down to his knees. His chest was burning again with his trapped anger, watching Padron with his stiletto, the casual threat to Snake who had done nothing but be his friend.

'My lord,' he said timidly, 'I told you everything you asked.'

Don Hugo blinked his eyes. Lost in thought, he had been staring at Simon but not seeing him.

'Whatever else you ask me about the English, if I know the answer, I will tell you, but—'

'Yes?' said Don Hugo.

Simon took a deep breath, and dived forwards, clasped Don Hugo's polished boots. 'Please, please, my lord, do not leave me here, don't abandon me here to the Padron's hatred.'

Don Hugo tried to step back but was trapped by Simon's grip round his ankles.

'The Padron hates me, he starves me, he beats me and my friend, he only brought you here because he thought I would be punished ... Don't leave me here where the Padron can kill me.'

There were blows, a whole hornet's nest biting at Simon's back. They stopped. He peeked up from where he had been protecting his head under his arms, saw Padron standing back, bewildered, Don Hugo's arm put up to stop the beating.

'Why does the Padron hate you?' asked Don Hugo.

Simon looked up, surprised to find quite genuine tears in his eyes. He must be even more frightened and weary than he thought, and was surprised again by the prickling all up his face and the way his throat locked. He had wanted to tell Don Hugo that the Padron was laying siege to his arse and found he was as blushful and tongue-tied as a maid about it.

'Padron want lie with him,' came Snake's rumbling voice. 'Padron lie with all the white men on his benches, here is clerk, he say, no, it a sin. Padron not like that.'

Snake looked suddenly stricken and dropped to his knees as well. 'Padron kill me for say that.'

Oh, that was artful of Snake, thought Simon, and one look at Padron's face will convince Don Hugo that what we accuse him of is true. Besides, he's an experienced captain of galleys, he must know what goes on. What will he say?

Simon started to pray again. If I can get off the oardeck, if I can be on the upper deck, please Almighty, if I have done your will here, please let me get away from the oar, please let me have some freedom of movement . . . Let me get away from Padron, let me be a man again and not part of the ship . . . I will serve you, I will . . . I don't know what I'll do. Almighty, help me anyway, please.

'He's lying,' said Padron, his face still telling the truth, 'he is a very disobedient slave, for this I punish him . . .'

Don Hugo looked down the bench at the other rowers. The other slaves on the bench who had been watching the drama with de Moncada like an audience at a theatre, began a chorus of agreement, even the peasant spoke up, 'Yes, your lordship, he does this, he is worse than my cousin . . .'

Don Hugo was looking less than shocked, but very angry. 'There can be no place for such impurity on the Holy Enterprise of England,' he said sternly to Padron, beckoning the Captain of the Oardeck.

Simon and Snake stayed hunkered on their knees while Don Hugo issued cold orders, and Padron seemed to wilt where he stood. The blacksmith came hurrying down the steps with his hammer and little anvil and Simon watched nervously as his ankle chain was taken off one anklet, unthreaded from the now-loose ringbolt. The blacksmith had brought a bag with him, handed over a pair of canvas breeches, tied with rope at the waist and Simon made himself decent. It felt most peculiar and quite constricting and uncomfortable. Then the chain was riveted back in place on the anklet. The same happened to Snake. Don Hugo jerked his head and Simon and Snake jumped to their feet and for the first time in weeks took more than a couple of steps away from the oarbench.

The blacksmith had brought an extra set of chains. Padron had to give up his whip and his striped breeches and, his face utterly blank with shock found himself back at the oar where he had started, fifteen years ago, in Simon's place. They left one space between him and the next man in case anyone should want to take revenge. The peasant was grinning and rubbing himself again, which showed that the peasant was not thinking too clearly at all.

Privately Simon thought it was a foolish decision because the obvious place to put a man of Padron's strength and experience was at the other end of the oar, but never mind. It was balm to his heart to watch. The whole oardeck was watching the fall of their Padron, his demotion to the bench, and some of the other Padrons cheered and clapped.

And then he and Snake passed along between the rowers, most of them watching him enviously, but some smiling and patting his back. He felt very lightheaded at the change, the sudden parting from the bench. Besides, he thought they would now go down into the hold for safekeeping and he was afraid of it, of the helplessness and darkness and certain death if the ship sank. Except that had always been true, the only difference between being in the hold and at the oar was that in the hold he was protected from English fire and did not have to sweat his guts out wrestling with an oar in a fog of gunpowder smoke.

It was difficult to climb the ladder behind Don Hugo because his chains were heavy and, as he was not used to different kinds of movement than rowing, sitting and standing, his knees were stiff. They came out on the deck Simon had last seen in the brilliant light of Lisbon harbour, then clean and newscraped, but now distinctly stained by the boots of the sailors and by blood. It made him gasp to see the sun with its courtly attendance of clouds, to see the sky, to feel wind on his face, to be away from the stink of the oardeck. The air smelled extraordinary, as if newly made. He passed the cannon, sakers and falconets mostly, all bolted securely to the deck, saw the way the soldiers and sailors drew back from him and Snake. They had last been shaved by the barber a few days before and were bristly enough to look as ugly as they smelled.

They passed the rail and Simon looked down on the sparkling waters, peered out at the vast curve of Spanish ships and into the haze where the English lay in wait.

He was giddy, lightheaded with happiness, he even had Rebecca's knife securely hidden in the lower gate of his body, and he did not at all care about the way the soldiers and sailors stared at him. De Moncada called over a young soldier, spoke to him and the young soldier looked resentful, beckoned Simon and Snake towards a pump that served to flush out the oardeck. They stood over the grating and while sailors pumped, Simon and Snake washed for the first time in months and months, in fact Simon had forgotten how long. The cold salt stung and burned in his various cuts and weals and rashes and sores but when it was over Simon felt he had been born anew, become a fresh creature. Snake laughed in pure delight at it, shook his head like a dog so the droplets spun.

When they had dried off on bits of tarpaulin, they were both led aft to the Great Cabin where another soldier put manacles on their wrists and told them curtly to wait.

'You are not yet pardoned,' said Don Hugo as he stalked into the cabin and stood by the desk. 'But this might be achieved for both of you if you cooperate now. You, black, if your friend does not do as he is bid, you go back to the oar, to your old place. If you annoy me in any way, you go back to the oar.'

Right next to Padron, who would no doubt be very vengeful. Snake nodded and salaamed like an Arab.

'As for you, Jew, if you do as you're told and help me as I require, it might be possible for you to be pardoned or at least given leave to depart for Constantinople, since England will no longer be sloppy and heretical enough to offer your kind a safe haven. If you give me any reason to doubt you or annoy me in any way, I will hang you from the yard by your hands and bring your ex-Padron up to do as he will with you.'

Simon nodded and bowed.

'So we understand each other?'

'Yes, my lord,' whispered Simon.

Don Hugo narrowed his eyes. 'You may speak up.'

Simon gave back a cold stare. 'My lord, since the Inquisition used the jugs on me, I cannot do more than whisper.' He was still full of the recklessness that had taken hold of him when he pretended to break down in front of de Moncada.

Moncada put his hand flat on paper and a pen and ink. 'The Padron called you the clerk. Can you write?'

Simon blinked and lifted up his right hand. It had swollen and stiffened over the weeks and was so hardened with calluses and the deep scar across the palm that it was hard for him to make a fist. 'I used to be able to, my lord. Secretary or Italic, whichever you please.'

'Write down what you told me.'

Still floating in a dream of release, Simon moved to where Moncada had pointed to a stool, sat himself down with the little automatic tuck of his elbows that had kept the long hanging sleeves of his robe from being sat upon when he went to work in his study. He drew up the paper, picked up the pen between fingers that could hardly feel it, and checked the nib, which was adequate enough. He dipped it in the ink and began to write but then stopped.

'How shall I begin?'

'With the date?'

'I don't know the date.'

Moncada told him, which was according to the Spanish system not the English. But Simon didn't care. He watched his clumsy fingers and the nib as the pen travelled its dancing path on the white floor of paper and out came a month and a number, quite well penned in fact. Wednesday, 24 July in the English system, he thought. To be writing again. It was almost as wonderful as the smell of fresh air and the sight of the sky had been. He couldn't help it, he smiled.

He wrote the appropriate salutation to the Grand Admiral of the Fleet, the Duke of Medina Sidonia, then paused to think.

'My lord, I would not want to write anything that might be offensive,' he said humbly. 'Can you advise me?'

Two officers were beside de Moncada, making reports, receiving orders. They stared at the two half-naked galley-slaves. In his own good time, de Moncada turned his attention to Simon.

'Write about the hellburners and whatever the Queen's court knows or believes about Calais,' said Don Hugo.

Simon nodded and began with some flowery sentiments full of humility and requests for favour, mentioned that he knew that a Monsignor Giambelli had been engaged by the Queen as an advisor and that hellburners full of gunpowder were in preparation to send against the Armada. This would be done if they looked likely to proceed against Calais, or to take any safe harbour where the Spanish fleet could resupply and wait for Parma to embark his troops. Or at any time they were anchored in the right place, in fact. He finished with some more flowery phrases, signed himself Simon the Clerk and after sanding and shaking, handed the sheet to de Moncada. Snake was watching him with fascination.

Don Hugo read and nodded. 'One alteration,' he said. 'You must sign in your own name.'

Obediently Simon put Simon Anriques under his first signature.

'And you swear that you have written only what you know to be true.

'I swear it by Jesus Christ and every saint in heaven,' said Simon with great piety.

It seemed that Don Hugo had not the imagination to ask Simon to swear by Torah and Talmud. Instead he went to the corner of the Great Cabin where there was a glorious silver-gilt altar, painted with St. Lawrence being burnt to death on a gridiron and lit with two wax candles. Don Hugo genuflected and brought out a little chased silver box. He put it on the desk very reverently.

'It is a sacred relic, a toe of San Lorenzo, the patron saint of this ship,' said Don Hugo. 'Put your hand on it and swear that what you have written is the truth.'

Fighting a very ill-bred urge to laugh, Simon put his hand on what was no doubt a lightly toasted pig-joint inside a very fancy box, and intoned, 'By this sacred relic of San Lorenzo I swear that what I have written is the truth.'

Don Hugo looked a little relieved. He wrote his own short note to go with Simon's and sent the sealed package off with a junior officer who presented himself at the door. A soldier presented himself a moment later, backed by five men, saluted.

'Hang both of them,' said Don Hugo, gesturing negligently at Simon and Snake, 'for impurity.'

'My lord,' shouted Simon, furiously. 'I trusted you.'

Don Hugo's face was shut. 'The Padron said that the black is your catamite.'

'He lied,' said Simon through his teeth, knees banging to the deck again. 'He lied because that is the only way he can imagine friendship. I have had impure thoughts about women, certainly, I make no claim to special virtue. But I have never committed that sin, never! Or do you think I would have taken the risk of reporting him to you?'

'Then hang them for treason to the Queen of England,' said Don Hugo with a certain lift to his lip. 'At least that is a fair accusation.'

And it was, in a way. Simon looked down, thought faster than he had ever thought in his life. This was a trap. It would test whether he believed what he said to be true: if it was a lie, Don Hugo was calculating that he would say so to try to save his life. 'At least let my friend Snake go free, my lord. He has done nothing wrong, he is a prince in his own land, he was tricked and drugged and taken by his enemies and sold into slavery, and in all this time of rowing, he has suffered for being my friend. You are right that I deserve to hang for betraying my Queen, but he does not and you will be doing a great injustice.'

Don Hugo looked genuinely shocked. 'You are pleading for the life of a black?' he said.

'Yes, my lord,' whispered Simon. 'I am.'

'But he isn't . . . He bears the mark of Cain. He is a heathen. He has no soul. Why?'

Pointless to argue about souls with a Spanish grandee. 'For friendship's sake, my lord. When I was hungry, he gave me food, when Padron beat me he looked after me. Even if he is a heathen, he has acted as a true Christian would act.' Which in Simon's own opinion, traduced Snake appallingly, but never mind. 'And only the Almighty, blessed be He, knows who has souls and who has not.'

Don Hugo was watching Simon carefully. 'You are saying that you will not argue for your own life, but you want the black saved.'

'Yes, my lord.' What did it matter? When de Moncada found out that the English did not in fact have hellburners and that Giambelli had in fact been employed to fortify London, when he realised that neither the Queen nor any of her advisors had the least idea what the Miracle of Beauty meant, then he would hang Simon anyway.

'Very well. Take the black to the hold, he can be a replacement when we lose more men. Take the Jew out to the mainmast and hang him from the yardarm.'

Snake knew enough Spanish to follow this. He shouted and lunged at de Moncada and it took all five of the soldiers to hold him and drag him still shouting in his own language down to the hold. Simon stayed kneeling where he was, looking down at the deck, suddenly very taken by the arrangement of the woodgrain and the knotholes in it, the wax polish on it. Despite the wash under the pump, his knees were still filthy. He wished he could have a proper bath with soap before he died, eat good food again, sleep with his wife again . . .

All the things he had done without realising they were the last time he would do them, things he had done without even noticing them, thinking of other matters, finding fault. He was going to lose his life on the end of the rope and he had barely lived it, being so busy in his head for so much of it. The last intense memory of food he had before the Seville orange at the oar had been of eating goat's cheese with marmelada quince paste at a wineshop in Lisbon and being briefly fascinated by the way the salty and sharp and scented and sweet married together like man and wife. And then he had gone to his worries about Rebecca, his brothers and the galleases and so could not say what else he had eaten or what the wine had tasted like.

Two more soldiers came, picked him up under the armpits and marched him out of the great cabin and out onto the maindeck. They had him kneeling there by the mainmast while one of them pointed a caliver at his head, which was a very poor weapon for the purpose and he turned over in his mind the possibility of taking his chances with the soldier's aim and making a run for the side of the ship, jumping over the side . . . sinking like a stone to the bottom of the sea from the weight of his chains. Anyway, his knees felt soft, his belly heavy as if he had eaten raw dough, he was suddenly utterly weary. At least the Padron would be pleased.

The sun was setting on what was nearly a flat calm, the water ruffled by the lightest of breezes, turned to molten bronze with a blackwork of English ships, all their sails set to catch the teasing little cats' paws of wind, waiting behind them in the eye of the sun. After the close quarters of the oardeck, after the boredom and misery and drudgery of the oardeck, here was the Almighty, negligently spreading His cloak to show its beauty. For Simon alone? It was a sort of kindness, from an ineffable, cruel and unknowable god.

Tears prickled his eyes to see the light on the water. He disdained to pray for rescue. The Almighty knew he wanted to live and embrace his wife, kiss his children and eat spiced lamb pasties with proper attention, instead of reading a scholarly book at the same time. The Almighty knew this and the Almighty knew what would happen to him and it was up to the Almighty to save his servant, Simon. Frankly, Simon felt it was well past time for the

355

Almighty to make amends with him, rather than the other way about. But the sea gone to molten metal and the ships in the sunset, that was a kind of gift, and Simon would graciously accept it and allow his heart to be lifted by it.

They had the noose rigged, a soldier was coming towards him with a hood. Simon's throat closed up. Don't take the sky from me again.

'Sir, I do not fear to die, you don't need to—'

'It's for us,' said the soldier, quite kindly, 'so we don't have to see your face go blue and your tongue and eyes stick out.'

'You are afraid of seeing something nasty?'

The soldier, who was too young to have more than a fluffy sprinkling of beard, looked down.

'Be careful,' Simon advised. 'What if His Excellency the Grand Admiral Medina Sidonia wants to question me and he finds you have hanged me?'

Now the boy was looking from side to side and twisting his precious hood between his hands.

'Why don't you ask Don Hugo about it?'

Simon considered it quite possible that Don Hugo was bluffing in any case. But the soldier didn't understand that, he wanted to do the job he had been given.

Simon looked up at the noose from where he knelt. Unpleasantness. Like a river. Now he was on this side of it. Soon he would be on the other side. He would be able to make his case directly to the Almighty.

The soldier did what panicking boys often do, he decided on action. He grabbed Simon, shoved the hood over his head and pinned his manacled arms to his side with a few turns of rope.

Suffocating inside the canvas, deprived of the sky once more, trying not to cry or fall or do anything except stand patiently, Simon eventually heard the yammering of a priest nearby, smelled incense. He began to sing in defiance, something they had probably never heard, something he had only learned quite recently from a Dutch rabbi. 'Shema Yisrael . . .' Hear O Israel, the Lord is your God, the Lord is one . . . They moved him forward, put the noose round his neck. He was standing on the deck, so they were going to hoist him up. Oh this was going to be bad, it would take him half an hour to die. Almighty spare me this . . . He stopped singing because his throat had locked and he couldn't breathe properly.

There was a pause. A long pause. Sweat tickled his nose, his eyes, he was breathing hard from suffocation, yes, from fear. There was talking nearby, he couldn't make it out because of the hood. Damn it. Get this over with.

# Rebecca Anriques

## San Salvador, *near Plymouth*, 20 *July 1588*

Thomasina hung in the rigging like a monkey, her kirtle pulled up between her sturdy white legs and through her belt. The light was fading, the sound of crackling and burning from the back end of the ship too, counterpointed by a chorus of groans and moans from the poor creatures who had been exploded and burned in it.

*San Lorenzo* still strained away at the towing cables but was losing ground. She thought of Mr Anriques as she had seen him when she peeked through the oarport, shockingly naked, bony and scabby, with his bald head uglier than any beggar she had ever seen. She tried not to think of him sweating to haul a crippled ship through the water. Ahead the great crescent of the Spanish fleet was pulling away from them, even in the feeble wind. And what would happen to them all now?

Thomasina swore, her voice straight from the gutters of London. Never again would she venture on the ocean, nor cross the sea nor venture into any foreign parts, never again.

Rebecca Anriques, the main cause of the trouble, sat quietly by the rail, watching *San Lorenzo*, her head tilted as if she was listening. Thomasina listened too, the sound of the men at the oars, singing a rhythmic worksong ... The words were hard to make out but sounded familiar, as if they might be English.

Thomasina climbed hand over hand to the foremast ratlines near where Rebecca sat, her feet curled under her, and every part of her neat like a cat, as if she had never been taken prisoner by the terrifying skinny man with the burning eyes. There were some smuts of gunpowder and soot on the hem of her dark red woollen dress and her white cap, which hid her dark brown hair, was certainly not as white as it should have been, but otherwise she looked calm and respectable. Thomasina hung on the ratlines and called down to her, 'Are you well, mistress?'

It was a real relief to be able to talk English normally, without fear. She had learned enough Dutch from the men of the Steelyard in her days as a tumbler in Paris Garden to obey Rebecca's orders in

Dutch, but that was all. It was a pity she knew no Spanish. But she had been only a clever pet to most of the men Rebecca had dealt with, including the bloody inquisitor, whom she hoped was dead or dying.

'Shh,' said Rebecca. 'Listen. What are they singing?'

Thomasina cupped her ear with one hand, held on tight. 'Da meer a kul is kall lay,' she said finally.

Rebecca nodded. 'I thought so.' She smiled, her pale pointed face lit up by it. 'I thought so.' She stood up, kissed Thomasina most unexpectedly on her nose, and blew a kiss at the galleas.

The singing went on, repetitive, swinging. At last, it ceased and the oars lifted, all at once together, how did they manage it? The rope fell slack and was cut. Poor crippled *San Salvador* seemed to stand still as the wings of the galleas dipped again and the ship moved away towards the now distant fleet.

Thomasina grunted, and started climbing, up to the foremast fighting top, up and backwards to get up the futtock shrouds, then scramble over amongst the heavily tarred ropes and blocks that steadied the topmast. It was high enough. Across the smooth darkening waters, she could see the sleek English ships, like a pack of wolves watching a wounded deer. *San Salvador* was a wreck, drifting, most of her mainmast in a heap where the aftdeck had been, completely at the mercy of wind and tide.

To be fair to them, Spaniards had come to take off the living as well as the big chest of bullion. The survivors were mostly sailors as nearly all the officers were dead. They spoke gently to Mevrouw van den Berg. They had found a bloody piece of her husband's doublet, he was certainly dead. She should come with them to the safety of the fleet.

Rebecca had replied in Spanish, at length. The officer who had asked her bowed most lavishly to her, spoken urgently and then shrugged at her answer, bowed again and climbed down the ladder to the waiting skiff.

Abstractedly Rebecca had explained what he said: he had been reminding Mevrouw van den Berg of the frightful savagery of the English heretics, who were uncontrollable when hopeful of loot. But she had said she would stay and try to find her husband.

Thomasina grinned again, and stared out at the waiting English heretics, waved. 'Come and get us, boys.'

Rebecca stood looking out at the English as well, balancing as the

359

ship wallowed with the soft waves. If there had been the smallest amount of swell, *San Salvador* would have been sinking, but the weather was on their side with a miraculous flat calm.

Silently Rebecca walked amongst the slippery stinking carnage she had made, the men she had condemned to an agonising death. She had intended to blow up the inquisitor, had been full of glee at the thought of such revenge, but she had been forced to blow up poor Anthony Fant as well because the brig was directly below the powder magazine. She was less regretful than she should have been about it because she thought the man stupid and, when it came down to it, cowardly as well. So what if the inquisitor broke his remaining hand? Did he think he was going to be allowed to live once they knew he was English?

When the stocky blond soldier had stared at Fant so strangely and then spoken to him in English, she had told Anthony that it was time to make their move. But Anthony Fant had been determined to wait until battle was properly joined. He was sure he had fooled the man, whoever it was. The cartridge filling room was all prepared, he only needed to enter it to fill cartridges and charges he had set could be lit . . . But they should wait for the right moment, when it would do the Spanish the most damage.

She had wept and raged, and he had reassured her, clasped her hand in his and told her that he was a man experienced in the ways of foreigners and there was no danger yet, not to worry her pretty little head, he would make sure she was safe.

Finally he had shouted her down, ordered her to be silent, told her she was nothing but a foolish woman who knew nothing and must do as she was told by the wiser, stronger sex who were not made hysterical by their wandering wombs. Then he had stalked out, leaving her trembling with fury.

Knowing the ways of foreigners much better than he did, she had told Thomasina to be sure she was well up the rigging when the soldiers came to take them. She had gambled that no one would be interested in the midget maid servant who scampered about the rigging like a child but never spoke. But never had she imagined such terrible hours, for the soldiers had clamped heavy metal chains on her wrists so she could hardly lift her hands, and they had been shut in the dark, stinking brig with Anthony Fant praying rather audibly for strength. She had said nothing to him, no reproaches, nothing. He was the wiser, stronger one, let him rescue them.

And Señor Pasquale had come, no longer a hesitant clerkly

figure, but a man full of black certainty and cold efficiency, who had wasted no time in doing the worst that Anthony Fant feared and more, so she couldn't bear it, she had hidden her eyes and wept with fear and horror. He had grabbed her and pushed her out the door where the ship's carpenter was holding his fingers in his ears and praying busily, but blocking her path when she tried to go past him to escape.

And then he had suddenly gasped. Somebody was behind him, had hamstrung him with a sharp knife, so he went down and before Rebecca could say anything, Thomasina was on him with her knife. He flailed her off, crawled desperately backwards along the passage and fell down an open companionway where he was immediately silent.

Thomasina had pulled Rebecca's skirts, took her to the ladder that led up, and then up again and as they rounded a narrow corner, she had recognised the door to the cartridge room next to the magazine.

There should have been a soldier guarding it, it should have been locked. But Rebecca remembered Anthony's preparations and decided he must have bribed someone. Anyway, it was open. She whisked in, sank down behind a pile of white canvas cartridge bags and watched from far away while Thomasina used a couple of little tools to open the manacles bruising her wrists. Anthony's screams and prayers for mercy could be heard, echoing through the wood, straight up from the brig.

This is not what I am used to, she suddenly thought to herself. I am really not the kind of person who can do this. I am an excellent housewife and a good woman for business, all my husband's enterprises have prospered under my direction, I have always chosen the best nurses to take care of my children and spent much ill-afforded time to be with them myself . . . this is simply not what I can do.

*You escaped from Lisbon,* came the internal voice that had bullied her into coming to find Simon, *you gave the Inquisition the slip.*

That was Merula's doing, not mine, said Rebecca to herself, and I left Merula in Flanders.

*You have Thomasina,* said herself. *Look how small she is, yet she tackled the carpenter for you.*

They will find us, Rebecca thought, shaking at the sobs coming from below, they will most certainly find us and then Pasquale will come and then . . .

Thomasina put the manacles behind a beam and plumped down on her knees, staring at her. 'Mr Fant showed me where the fuses are, in case I should need to do this,' she said in her high, firm London voice. 'Now the cramp-rings are off, you can do it.'

There was slowmatch cunningly laid to travel sideways into the magazine and down into the barrels of powder below.

But they had no fire, nor any means of making one in a cartridge room, where the men must wear soft list-slippers in case the nails in their boots caused a spark.

In her seachest was hidden her small pistol, the wheel-lock dag of German make she had pointed at Becket. It was still there, left behind in her cabin, never used. Thomasina nodded when she mentioned it.

'Pasquale will search the ship soon enough, when he sees you're gone. I'll run and fetch it, but I may not be able to bring it to you soon. Can you stay here and wait?'

The smell of gunpowder caught in her throat and the sounds of Anthony's pain were still coming up to her. Why had she listened to him? Why had she let him . . . Well, Becket had been determined to leave her behind in Flanders, that was clear. As Fant had warned her. Once a coat-changer, always a coat-changer, he had said. And Anthony was the perfect answer to the problem of a man to give her countenance, since he was not only willing but insistent on coming with her. But Anthony Fant had been . . . still was a fool.

Because of his foolishness, they would probably both die, leaving Simon still chained to his oar where she could not get to him. She had tried everything she could at Corunna to free him, offered three times his worth to the Captain of the Oardeck of *San Lorenzo*, and nearly got herself arrested for it. They were so short of men to row, they certainly would not free him, certainly not.

It had shocked her to see him naked, amongst so many naked men. Although heavily veiled, she had still been able to see . . . too much. It had sickened her in fact, more than she could say, the animal stench of the oardeck, the hungry staring of the men, the hostility of the officers, the tension and ugliness of the whole place. But then Simon had lifted up the hatch so light could come in and turned and bowed to her courteously. They could strip him of all the things that men valued, chain him like a dog, and yet he could not help his instinctive civility. She had risked both their lives in curtseying back, then made it look like a faint of horror. She had been mute with the … the awful pain in her chest from her longing, from being so close to Simon and still not able to help him.

She had to haul her mind back to the present. There was the sound of boots. She pulled in her skirts, left the cartridge room door closed, burrowed under the piles of cartridges, making herself as small as possible.

A man wearing a morion opened the door, leaned in, blinked about. He was holding a candle, which made her guts freeze in fright. Getting blown up with the gunpowder … Somebody roared at him and he pulled back, shut the door immediately, said that there was nobody there.

She huddled up in the cartridges, shifted position so her hand wouldn't go to sleep, and dozed off, watching the door and the grill above, which would give light during the day for the filling of cartridges.

Light dawned and with it a hollow booming in the distance. Was it thunder? Ships crashing into each other to board? Perhaps cannon fire? She didn't know and *San Salvador* sailed slowly on, well away from any fighting in the centre of the defensive formation with ships close about her.

And then Thomasina was back with the dag in its case, whispering breathlessly of Pasquale's searching of the ship for her. Rebecca took it, the heavy thing that had bruised her every time she fired it in the past, and worked carefully and conscientiously to follow the recipe that would load it, first the powder, then the wad, then the ball, then another wad and tamp it down, then the priming powder in the pan and to be sure there was a clear path and then to wind it and lock it. She held it in her lap and then told Thomasina that she must get away.

Thomasina spat on the deck. 'Do you want that long streak of misery that hurt Mr Fant?' she asked. 'For he's leading the search and frantic to find you. If you can give him a cuddle, I'll get behind him.'

'A what?'

'Didn't you know? He wants your cunny, not your confession.'

It was extremely strange to hear such obscenity from so small a face and Rebecca had to suppress the impulse to scold her for it. Thomasina was neither a child nor a servant and must be treated carefully, she had learned that.

The men had banged on the door then and Thomasina had

363

whisked herself into the gunpowder chute, just the tip of her head poking out to watch.

Rebecca winced at the memory of what happened next. Pasquale had indeed wanted her cunny, as Thomasina had said, seemed to have convinced himself that he was in love with her after the shy conversation with him when she had discovered who he was and had to hold her hands together as tight as she could to stop herself from attacking him.

It had sickened her but also obscurely pleased her to feel her power over him, his desperate urgency to believe her innocent and frightened, his desire for her. She had acted the part, yes, of course, but it had been easy for her. And then when Thomasina had stuck her knife in Pasquale's kidneys . . .

The words Rebecca had hissed then had come scalding out of her soul, unpremeditated, designed to hurt, to bewilder. Never had she kicked or hit anyone with intent to destroy, not a servant, not even an animal. But she had enjoyed the crunch of her boot in his mouth, gasped with laughter at the wonderful irony of the manacles to chain him there, and lit the fuse with the sparks from her dag by moving the powderpan out of the way.

Once the slowmatch was hissing on its journey, she had left him there, and with Thomasina to guide her, threaded her way between decks, bent almost double in places, sweating with the expectation of the explosion, before climbing a ladder and finding herself forward, near the prow of the ship, where the ordinary crewmen lived, to be greeted with ironic cheers and half a dozen pairs of arms out to catch hold of her. They were ignorant sea-peasants, they knew nothing but rumours about her.

And that was when the ship had blown up. Not all of it, just the after part, with the captain and most of the officers, setting light to the main mast and the mizzen, breaking the deck, a great roaring boom that had made both Thomasina and herself deaf for an hour and showered them with splinters that wounded and shredded the men around them and yet Thomasina had pulled them both under a tarpaulin and they had been safe.

She had killed Pasquale, killed whatever was left of Anthony Fant, killed about fifty sailors who had done her no harm at all, and in fact treated her with rough courtesy when she need have dealings with them.

She had killed for Simon, for the Queen, for herself to revenge herself on Pasquale, for policy. She had killed like a soldier, although she was no such thing. The thought sickened her, she had sat shaking by the rail while the remaining sailors tried to put out the fires and do something about the shattered steerage, while the *San Lorenzo* had put a line aboard and the muscles of Simon and the slaves strained to tow the destroyed hulk. She had sat there, cold and sick and staring while the singing came to her across the water, and with it her husband's answer to the riddle that had taken him to Lisbon and into the jaws of the Inquisition in the first place. With Thomasina's help she had taken it to him, and now he was sending it back to her with the voices of his fellow slaves.

She could understand it. Once she knew that 'meer a kul' was miracle, she knew that the second half meant 'is Calais'.

Even she knew enough geography to understand it, her last gift from her husband. She explained it to Thomasina who was horrified at the perfidy of the plan, at how easily it might succeed. She knew she should be shocked as well but was not. She was inside a glass case, she decided, safely sealed away like one of the Spaniards' superstitious reliquaries. Yes, she thought, I am like a saint's bone, looking out of my glass box at the wild activities of men.

The Spanish were clearing the ship of everyone who could still walk, of everything they could carry. Four men heaved the great paychest of bullion over the side into a gig. The officer came and appealed to her, she had no idea what she said to him. Evening came and Thomasina tucked her up where she was in a cloak and a tarpaulin.

It was only a matter of waiting until the greedy English snapped up the prize of *San Salvador*. But they were frightened to do it, she realised as the long night passed, as the fire at the aft end gradually burnt itself out. They had seen the explosion and were afraid of another one. They didn't know she had made sure all the barrels of powder were stored between other things so the fire couldn't reach them. Nothing catches fire less willingly than a barrel of wet-cured salt beef or pickled herrings, despite the saltpetre in it. She couldn't tell them, only sit immobile by the rail, staring at the English ships as *San Salvador* wallowed. She was mercifully locked behind her glass walls, while Thomasina brought her cups of watered wine and chafed her hands and talked to her gently in her rough voice and called her ma'am and in general seemed most concerned about her, of which there was no need.

It's the screaming, poor Anthony Fant's screaming, I have to keep it out of my head, she wanted to say, but didn't. And also Pasquale's

365

screaming, which mixed with it. And the weak moaning and wailing of the men she had killed. Her fault. All of them children of mothers like her, all of them dying because of her.

All she wanted was Simon to hold her, but she couldn't have him for he was rowing busily away from her in the galleas, had rowed, was long gone. Dead, probably. Only she and Thomasina were still alive.

The gulls were swooping and shrieking at the stern now, where it was all broken and blackened and stinking. What were they squabbling over, she wondered, guts? Broken store-barrels? Anthony Fant's eyes? Who knows?

At last there was the scraping of a boathook, the creak as men came up the side of the ship. They popped their heads over the side, looking nervous, behind a loaded and lit caliver.

She sat still with Thomasina, watching them climb over. They spread out through the ship, searching for loot of course, and found none for there had been plenty of time for the Spaniards to take off even the table plate and candlesticks. Nor would they know about the treasure of powder and shot below. She watched them, still locked behind the glass. Perhaps someone should tell them about it. One of them, the leader looked slightly familiar. She wasn't sure.

'Scuttle her,' said the older man. 'She'm barely worth the work of taking her in.'

Thomasina nudged her and as she sat, still locked behind glass, Thomasina marched forwards, curtseyed as the men stared and blinked at her, and lifted her voice.

What was she saying? Rebecca shook her head. She was not still deaf but something was wrong with her hearing. She could barely move, for stiffness, she could not make out perfectly plain English words.

The men came forward, staring. Thomasina held up a ring she had carried around her neck on a chain, a very fine emerald ring carved with an elaborate E.

'Be gentle with her, sirs,' came Thomasina's piping voice, 'she is a most brave lady but it has been hard for her, so hard. Sirs, please, you must take me to my Lord Admiral, I have intelligence for him that this lady has paid dear to get and her husband too. I am Thomasina de Paris, the Queen's most private servant in these matters.'

What was that, now? wondered Rebecca. Anything interesting? She picked at a seam on her kirtle where it was coming unpicked, poor sewing by someone, she thought, not double-stitched at all but single.

The gentlemen wanted her to come with them but she was very disinclined to move, very unhappy. There was something she needed to tell them, something very important about the *San Salvador*. What was it? Oh yes.

'Be sure to salvage the ship, sirs,' she murmured. 'Her hold is full of gunpowder and shot.'

They stopped again as they eased her towards the rail, exchanged glances.

'It's true,' said Thomasina, 'she came for to get it, you know, amongst other things. Here, I'll show you.'

She took the younger of the two leaders by the hand, led him towards a hatchway and they disappeared from sight, while Rebecca stared at her boot toes and wondered how they had become so scuffed and stained with brown.

The younger man came up the ladder again at the run, 'It's true, Mr Hawkins,' he shouted, his face alight. 'Barrels and barrels of the best Venetian powder.'

They waited while John Hawkins investigated and when he came back the thing was all changed. He left three men to help with the prize, and clambered back down the side to his skiff, laughing like a boy.

Rebecca looked down and could not bring herself to do it. She had climbed up and down ladders to get to different decks, but was no monkey like Thomasina to run about the rigging. She had been brought aboard the *San Salvador* in a sling, which had been uncomfortable and undignified but better than climbing a slippery wooden ladder.

Thomasina had already shinned down to the skiff, was staring up at her. She couldn't find the words to say anything more, only shook her head and clutched tight at the rail, shuddering.

'Your pardon, Mrs Anriques,' said the younger man, caught her sore wrist, put his shoulder against her stomach and lifted her up. She yelped and went rigid with terror. 'Please be still, lady, and you'll get down safe.'

And the insane boy climbed over the rail and went down the creaking steps and into the skiff where there were hands outstretched to catch her as he slid her off his shoulder and sat down looking pleased with himself.

It had all been done so quickly, she was dizzy and gasping with it.

'How ... how dare you ...' she stuttered and Thomasina elbowed her and grinned. She shut her lips and scowled at the waves while the sailors rowed them over the sea and the younger man introduced himself as Captain Thomas Howard and the older man as Mr John Hawkins, Secretary of the Navy.

But as the great black flank of the English flagship, *Ark Royal*, rose above her, she gulped hard and caught the ladder and with the young men pushing her up from behind and other men ready to pull her from above, she managed to climb aboard the English flagship, followed in an impudent scamper by Thomasina.

At which point, of course, very inconveniently, she fainted.

Thomasina was trapped in a nightmare while still wide awake. She and Rebecca had been all the way to Lisbon (never again, she swore to herself) and back, had suffered days and days of stuffy tedium in the wallowing hulk that was *San Salvador*, nights of agonising seasickness in the tiny odd-shaped cabin that was entirely filled by a cot they had to share, the tension of the fear of discovery, the increasingly stinking food and worse water, the dangerous stupidity of Anthony Fant, all in order to get the precious nugget of information that the Spanish planned to take Calais.

And now they could get no one to listen to them. They were on *Ark Royal*, certainly, in one of the better cabins in fact, where Rebecca had been solicitously laid in a cot, attended by the ship's barber surgeon, who had bled her, in Thomasina's opinion, far too much. They were in the same ship as the Lord Admiral of Elizabeth's fleet, and yet they could not come to him.

He sent a young officer to attend on them and find out who they were. Thomasina told him and found herself being stared at and laughed at by a boy who simply reported that one was a German woman, sick with jail fever, and the other a mad midget. Nobody would carry a message for her.

Thomasina tried to use Elizabeth's ring to get herself past the officers who surrounded the Lord Admiral and had it stolen by an impudent man who had claimed to be a clerk. She had even tried the expedient of climbing the ratlines and using the rigging to reach the poopdeck where the Admiral was watching the Spanish crescent with a Dutch spyglass. Only to be scooped off a rope by one of the soldiers and carried squawking back to Rebecca in her cabin, Rebecca who lay white and silent and half-conscious thanks to the bleeding.

The only good thing about it was that the Armada was travelling so slowly east across the glassy sea they were still not past the Isle of Wight. *San Salvador* had been towed into Weymouth and the next day, pinnaces and fishing smacks came with barrels of Venetian powder and shot to resupply all the English ships that were short. By herself, Rebecca had given the English the means to fight for an extra day.

Now there was fighting again. Over in the distance the ships gathered slowly, fired guns, parted slowly, leaving great feathers of smoke that faded slowly in the still airs. The Admiral called a council of war and the captains came climbing aboard from their skiffs, Drake himself at the head of them, his round face full of good humour and frustration mixed. There was a guard on the door of their cabin now, so Thomasina only saw him from the porthole.

She busied herself with caring for Rebecca and writing furious letters to the Queen as her report, though with no expectation of being able to find anyone to carry them for her. When she slept, she found Rebecca still and cold, breathing very slowly, and was terrified she might die. She dared not call the idiot of a ship's surgeon again in case he bled her again. All that had been wrong with her was exhaustion and her nerves being overwrought by the terrible result of the explosion. Even so, Thomasina thought that without that fool Anthony Fant to be with them and give them a man's voice to carry weight, none of the overgrown boys delighting in their stern adventure would pay any attention to either of them.

She kicked the door of the cabin and hurt her toes, then contented herself with another furious letter and staring from the little porthole.

A two-master was bearing up as close to the *Ark Royal* as it could get, every sail spread, before it hove to. The ship's boat was launched. As it rowed into sight Thomasina could see a brightly clothed group of men sitting in it, and muttered sourly to herself of yet more idiotic court gallants coming aboard to be treated with all courtesy when she and her mistress were slighted . . . And then she heard a voice she thought she recognised, leaned out as far as she could to see none other than Mr Robert Carey, handsome courtier, unofficial cousin to the Queen and rackety youngest son of the Lord Chamberlain, hopping across the gap between the boat and the side of the *Ark Royal*, laughing when he nearly fell in.

'Mr Carey!' she shrieked. 'Mr Carey, here!'

Carey carried on up the ladder, then paused. Had he seen her?

Yes, he had, he lifted his hat to her, a very dangerous thing to do in view of the slippery rope he was holding and his sword threatening to tangle itself between his legs. There was a reason why experienced seamen used short-swords.

'Come and see me!' she shouted. 'Quickly!'

And then she had nothing to do but pace up and down gnawing her fingernails, hoping that he would do it, but he didn't. Nothing happened. He must have forgotten who she was, he wouldn't come, damn him. If they ever got back to court, by God she would make his life a misery for him. Misery? She'd see to it he never so much as came near the Queen, the half-witted, salf-satisfied, glory-hunting, money-grubbing . . .

There was a knock at the cabin door. She called 'Come,' expecting the young soldier who would not let her out bringing the usual cheese and biscuits.

Carey, bent almost double, came in looking cautiously amused. He was also clearly near to dying of curiosity to know how the Queen's Fool came to be aboard *Ark Royal*. He saw her scowl and instinctively began by trying to smooth her mood, courtier-wise, telling how he had almost decided that he was mistaken in who she was, until he heard one of the other courtiers infesting the flagship laughing over a tale of a muliercula who tried sliding down a rope to reach the Admiral and had been locked up with her mistress since she was clearly insane. It had been the work of a few minutes and two shillings to find her.

To Carey, it seemed Thomasina was as grim-faced and furious as she had been at the time of their first proper meeting, although considerably less battered. The hem of her little kirtle was stained with smoke and seawater. He kissed her hand as he would any other lady of the court, and found himself hearing a tale of such outrageous unlikelihood that he was not at all surprised the officers had kept her away from the Admiral. Why should they believe a couple of women, one of whom was clearly very sick, and the other a dwarf?

Carey looked at Mrs Anriques, who lay limp and white in her cot and only opened her eyes to drink some of the watered wine Thomasina brought. He had accompanied the Queen to the Mews for their meeting, but that was all. He knew no more of her, though he could at least tell that she was who she said she was. But Thomasina he knew well.

'Mistress de Paris,' he said, putting up his hand to stem the flow.

He was sitting on a seachest by that time, appalled at what he was hearing. 'Mistress, if I can persuade my lord Admiral to hear you, will that be enough?'

'It's all I want,' said Thomasina. 'I know he still may not listen because I am small and Mrs Anriques is only a woman, I know this. But at least if I have told him the tale, then my conscience is clear.'

Carey nodded. 'I make no promises,' he said. 'I am only one of half a hundred courtiers pestering up this ship and none of us know a farthing's worth about the sea...'

'Why did you come then?' demanded Thomasina.

'To kill me some Spaniards and make a lot of money,' said Carey with a grin, 'Why do you think? Oh yes, and fight for the Queen against the Papists, of course.'

'I'd put the whole pack of you in the hold and use you as ballast,' sniffed Thomasina. 'At least that way you might do some good.'

Carey clasped his chest as if wounded. 'Cruel mistress, how can I appeal to my lord on your behalf if my eyes are red from your sharp words.'

Thomasina only growled at him and so he bowed and left them. She got a note under the door much later that evening. It read:

To Mrs Thomasina de Paris, Queen's Fool

I have done what I can for you, although I fear it is little enough. Cumberland and I are off to his ship, the *Elizabeth Bonaventure* since this ship has a surfeit of volunteers. God speed.

Rbt Carey, gent

At which Thomasina began to pace again and chew her fingernails and swear under her breath. She wrote another letter, which would ruin Carey, and then burnt it because she was sure he would have done what he could, only like all of them, he could not take any woman seriously, much less one under four foot high.

In the dim early morning, they were woken by the clattering of the longboat being launched, and then the rhythmic shouting and creak as it and other longboats took the *Ark Royal* under tow. They had been still in the night, rolling from side to side a little. When Thomasina stuck her head out of the porthole as far as she could go, she saw every yard on the ship white with sails, which hung wrinkled like washing on a line. The sea sparkled with the sunlight and there were some kind of sea creatures with pointed fins swimming around and about the ship. It was a beautiful day and far too hot to be cooped up in a wooden cabin.

The soldier was adamant that Mrs Anriques could not possibly leave her cabin, since the longboats were rowing them into battle to stop the Spaniards landing on the Isle of Wight.

They could hear booming, and saw other ships, Hawkins' *Victory* and another beyond that, with two Spanish ships wallowing in difficulties. Beyond them was the bulk of the Isle of Wight, dotted with white houses.

The galleases were coming from the Spanish fleet, the only ships able to move easily. It was all immensely slow. When the first guns spoke from the ship, both Rebecca and Thomasina leapt and shuddered and then Thomasina laughed.

All through the long day, as *Ark Royal* struggled to the battle Hawkins had started with the two lagging Spanish galleons and the guns roared in their slow sequence, Thomasina hung as far as she could get out of the porthole, cheering them on. The galleases were trying to tow the ships Hawkins had attacked, and as *Ark Royal* came nearer, gun after gun barked at them. She could see between the drifts of smoke that blood was coming from the gallery of the *San Lorenzo* where rowers had been killed, some of the oars were broken. Rebecca pulled her away to look and then sat down in despair, full of terror that Simon must have been killed by the terrible cannon-fire from the *Ark Royal*. Next thing there were more Spanish ships coming, with light breezes at last springing up to favour the Spanish. One was the Spanish fleet's flagship, *San Martin* and the two great flagships sailed past each other while the Spanish guns fired once and the English guns, by some miracle, managed to fire twice each. Once a lump of metal lodged in the brightly painted wood just above the cabin and another time a flying splinter of wood nearly took Thomasina's ear off as she turned at that moment to speak to Rebecca.

Then something else happened, there was a kind of popping from far off, and a little while later, *San Martin* and its companions turned to sail away from the entrance to the Solent.

As evening came down the sailors in the rigging cheered, for the Spanish ships were well past their chance to take the Isle of Wight. Thomasina shouted up at them that they were fools, that it wasn't the Isle of Wight the Spaniards wanted but Calais, and Rebecca told her to hush.

Rebecca looked like a little brown sparrow, so slender was she.

She nibbled at the biscuit and sipped the wine, and Thomasina wondered how she had ever had the strength to convince the Queen to back her crazy mission, how she could have spent all that time surrounded by enemies, patronised by Anthony Fant, and kept to her purpose as she did.

In the evening, she told Rebecca what she had tried with Carey and Rebecca only nodded, silent, looking quite old as she sat neatly, staring at the porthole where a most outrageous sunset was blazing down into the west, foretelling more heat for the morrow. At last she demanded a candle from the boy outside, paper and pen and ink, and sat down to write a letter telling of what she had seen and heard and done.

Thomasina had the distinct sense of the quiet before the storm. In the morning it was a day so calm that they could hear the peculiar singing of the mermaids through the hull of the ship, while the little ripples clopped on the side of the ship, like tongues. Their tiny cabin was worse than a steam bath at the stews.

When Thomasina craned out of the porthole, the slack hanging sails told her that nothing would happen that day, even if there had been powder and shot to do it with. The men who had rowed the longboats to tow *Ark Royal* and its fellows into shot to protect the Isle of Wight needed to rest since they were not galley slaves who could be worked to death, but free men.

In any case there was no need, since the currents would stop Medina Sidonia if he had any mind to turn back and try for the Solent again.

And in the morning, the fluffy-chinned boy who had first refused to listen to them, came and sullenly told them that they could wait upon my lord High Admiral in half an hour.

'I am too sick and weak from my labours amongst the Spaniards to go to him,' said Rebecca primly. 'Would you beg him to be so good as to come here to us? Also, that we should not be the cause of any distraction to his sailors.'

This had been another reason given for their confinement in the cabin. The boy winced and went away, looking haunted.

There was a pause, during which Rebecca disposed herself on the bed and had Thomasina lay a damp cloth on her brow.

At last there was a knock, the boy opened the door and Lord Charles Howard of Effingham ducked his head to enter the cabin, which he seemed to fill completely. Thomasina was standing by the bed, still scowling furiously, for she had last seen my Lord Admiral when Her Majesty gave him audience in the Presence Chamber. Evidently, he had not noticed her.

'Mrs . . . Mrs Anriques?' said the Admiral nervously, a tall, white-bearded man in his vigorous fifties, a consummate diplomat and leader of men, who had succeeded in working with the volcanic Drake, well-known to take subordination very hard indeed.

'Please forgive me, my lord Admiral,' said Rebecca in a faint voice, 'I am too exhausted from my labours to rise to greet you.'

'I heard a very strange tale from Mr Carey,' said the Admiral, towering over the cot. 'Can it be true that you have travelled from Lisbon with the Spanish fleet?'

'Yes, my lord.' In a low soft voice, that the Admiral must visibly strain to hear, Rebecca told exactly what she had done and what she had seen. She gave numbers as well: a businesslike count of the guns on each ship that she had seen, which she had made as Anthony Fant's translator, an estimate of the amount of powder and shot available, how the guns were mounted, how loaded, how served for reloading, how long it might take.

At first the Admiral's eyes bugged at a woman telling him these things, but after a while he sat down on the seachest and began asking sharp questions.

'You are the one who blew up *San Salvador*?'

'At risk of her life, my lord,' scolded Thomasina, who wanted some glory herself. 'After I knifed the man that was guarding her and another that tried to dishonour her.'

The Admiral looked at the planks of the floor and shook his head. 'And you have been kept in this cabin since Mr Hawkins brought you aboard *Ark Royal*?'

'Yes, my lord, although Mr Hawkins and your brother treated us with all civility and gentleness, we have been dealt with as if we were mad and unaccountable ever since. I have been ill only with strain and fatigue, not, as has been said, with jail fever. Nor hysteria.'

The Admiral made a noise in his throat midway between a cough and a laugh. 'And the matter of Calais? It seems . . . tenuous. How sure are you?'

'I am sure that any one of the galleases have the firepower to take Calais by themselves. I am sure that my husband was taken by the Inquisition when he went to enquire about it, that my brother-in-law gained the knowledge at risk of his life. I am only a woman, my lord, and know little of such warlike matters, but it seems to me a

374

most wise thing, to take a port such as Calais where the Spaniards will be safe from storms and the English—'

'Yes, indeed. A disaster. Mistress, my heartiest apologies. Would you choose to go ashore now, since we could put you aboard a pinnace I am sending for resupplies of powder and shot and water.'

'Thank you, my lord, but no. I came upon this venture for to find my husband who I have seen rowing on *San Lorenzo*. I stay until I free him or know he is dead.'

The Lord Admiral took her hand and kissed it, did the same for Thomasina. 'Two most valiant ladies. I should be honoured if you will stay aboard and perhaps speak at a council if it should be necessary.'

Things changed. They were brought to a much better cabin, near the Great Cabin where the Admiral slept, passing court gallants bunking down uncomfortably in nooks and crannies. Thomasina heard one of them moaning that it was worse even than being on progress, where you had to share beds, because here there were no beds . . .

The day passed with the ships almost still in the grip of the hot sun. It was as if the Spaniards had brought the weather with them from Lisbon. She and Rebecca reclined on cushions on the poop deck with the boy who had first spoken to them and misreported what they said, now given the job of waving a fan for them to keep them cool. The Council of War took place in the Great Cabin with the Lord High Admiral, greatly daring, knighting some of his captains. John Hawkins walked in a Mr and came pacing out as Sir John, glowing with pride. All his painstaking service at the Navy Board, his Herculean labours to convince the obstinate shipbuilders of Southampton and London that the more a ship looked like a fish the better it sailed, all well-rewarded in his shining eyes, by the mere addition of a Sir to his name. Men are very strange creatures, Thomasina reflected, very, very strange.

With the next day came some clouds and cooling showers of rain, with fitful gusts of wind pushing cats' paws over the waters. The land began to move as the sails bellied out a little and there was motion, up and down, side to side, but forwards now. The Spanish sailed on, as slowly as the slowest of them, the English stalked their trail, and Kent passed to the left of them until they could see white cliffs at the cape of Margate, where the Spaniards dropped anchor still in formation in Calais Roads only a couple of miles from Calais itself.

After another Council of War they beat the drum for Divine Service. Thomasina found to her surprise that she had tears in her eyes to hear the stately English words, the English gospel, the fine sermon given by the chaplain, and none of your foreign Latinising, no incense, no bells, no shaven-head men in fancy silk frocks. Some of the ships' boys piped up a psalm for them, which they had been reedily practising since the day before and an extra ration of beer was ordered on the grounds that it was a hot day for singing.

The Admiral spoke to the men, mincing no words. Medina Sidonia on the *San Martin* and Parma at the mouth of the Rhine were only 25 miles apart, two armies large enough separately, but perhaps unbeatable if they joined. No matter. With the Englishmen between them, they would not join. And if any man thought the odds in numbers and size of ships unjust, well, that man was Medina Sidonia for any one English sailor outnumbered ten Spaniards by ten to one, and the same for their guns.

The sailors cheered and waved their statute caps before the next shower came down and wetted them all to the skin.

They could see the French boats going out to the Spanish ships, laden with provisions, causing much muttering among men who were already on biscuit and cheese with salt beef every other day. Only the fear of being taken for ransome or perhaps missing some notable prize-taking kept the court gallants crowding the waist from stealing a skiff and going off to seek wine and venison pasties in Calais.

The Lord Admiral had paused by the little corner Rebecca and Thomasina had made their own and said, 'I've sent for the fireships, Mrs Anriques, they should be here by tomorrow.'

Rebecca's narrow face tightened at that. 'Tomorrow? But we are here, Calais is only a few miles away. Look!'

'Do you know more, Mrs Anriques? Something else has come to mind?'

Rebecca stared into the white-streaked blue sky. 'I have met Don Hugo de Moncada, Admiral of the Galleases. He is a bold active man, very like Sir Francis Drake. But they will not leave it all to the galleases, be sure of it.'

The Admiral nodded and passed on.

A squadron of forty ships, led by Lord Henry Seymour joined them in the afternoon. And then a small ship came tacking up from the French coast, sliding past the outliers of the Spanish fleet and sending its boat out before it had slowed. The young man in it climbed aboard and hurried straight to the Admiral.

As evening fell another Council was called and the boy who had first discounted them was sent to bring Mrs Anriques and Mrs de Paris to speak at it.

At first Rebecca refused point-blank to go. She had told the Admiral her story, he could tell it to his captains, she could not possibly speak to such a gathering of men, she had never done such a thing, it was not her place . . . And Thomasina stood on the cot to hiss at her, to tell her that if the Admiral wanted her to talk to his captains, he had a good reason and what kind of coward was she, not to do what the Queen did every day.

The Great Cabin was lit by candles as well as the orange streaks of sunset, maps of the seaways outside Calais laid out on the table. Around it stood the captains of the English fleet, muttering and arguing with each other in broad Devon, Cornish or Norfolk tones.

Silence fell as Thomasina and Rebecca entered. Thomasina was delighted with Rebecca: she stepped inside the cabin and stood there like a Queen, before the Admiral brought them both to the table.

'Mrs Anriques, ma'am, tell these gentlemen what you discovered and how you discovered it,' said the Admiral.

Thomasina narrowed her eyes. She was familiar with the uses of drama and recognised that the Admiral was after something.

Speaking softly and shyly, Rebecca told of the coded phrase Miracle of Beauty, which she had been trying to understand, and how it meant that Calais was now in desperate danger.

There was silence when she finished, as the men about the table digested the thought of having to try and keep the Spanish fleet bottled up in Calais harbour while they struggled with the weather in Calais Roads themselves.

The Admiral cleared his voice and opened a letter. 'This was brought to me by fast ship from Mr Robert Cecil, who was with the peace commissioners in Dunkirk for the purpose of watching the Spaniards:

My lord Admiral

I write in haste to let you know that a renegade Englishman and a force of mercenaries and rebels of about 200 strong, have taken the road to Calais in the expectation of holding the citadel to prevent the cannons from defending the harbour.

377

They will be there tonight. I have gone in pursuit but can only take twenty men.

Your respectful servant.

Rbt Cecil, gent

The noise of Howard refolding the letter was like quiet cannon-fire against the blue wash of the sea beneath them.

Hawkins broke the silence. 'When will the fireships of Walsingham's be ready?'

'I expect them tomorrow, midday on Monday.'

More silence. Thomasina was watching Sir Francis Drake, who was staring at the map with a scowl on his face. So was everyone else. He spoke slowly, to himself so it seemed. 'I think that God has sent us word of the Spaniard's evil by the most marvellous means of a woman and a muliercula, to show his might that even the weakest vessels can be His prophets. Are we to be like the elders of Jerusalem when they would not listen to Ezekiel?'

He looked up, blue eyes very bright, and a grin spread all across his round, weathered face.

'My lord Admiral, we dare not wait. I'll give you my ship, the *Thomas*, two hundred tons burden, and my Captain John Yonge for to set her afire and sail her at the Spaniards with the tide tonight.'

'I can give you no compensation for her, Sir Francis,' said the Admiral gravely.

'Nor will I ask none. She's a gift to Her Majesty, only so you singe the Spaniard's lower beard and his arse with it. Begging your pardon, ma'am.'

There was a rumble of laughter, some clearing of throats. Hawkins was scowling as well, rather put out.

'I'll give Her Majesty my ship, the *Bark Bond*,' he growled. 'One hundred and fifty tons burden, and Captain Prouse to be Yonge's second-in-command.'

The Admiral nodded and looked quizzically at the other captains. Within ten minutes, they had eight large ships and a quantity of tar and gunpowder and paint to make fireships with.

The Admiral smiled at Rebecca, who smiled back for the first time with perfect understanding of what his game had been, curtseyed and left the cabin.

By evening the eight ships were at the centre of the gathered English fleet with small boats plying furiously back and forth with anything and everything that would burn. There was even a box of fireworks.

As night fell, they worked on by lamplight, the men tarring the rigging and the oldest sails in the fleet being hoisted into place. For all that half the court gallants on the *Ark Royal* volunteered to sail the fireships, they were mostly crewed with wide-shouldered pigtailed Cornishmen in their fifties, who would have the nerve to get as close to the Spaniards as they could before taking to their boats.

Thomasina and Rebecca stayed at the rail in the warm night, feeling the freshening wind on their faces, as the frantic work continued. At last, just as the ships at anchor began to turn around with the tide, there were shouts and a scurry of boats carrying workers away from the fireships. Men manned the rigging of the ships that had been screening them from the Spaniards and began taking their craft out of their path.

The ships began to sail, silent and black in the blackness, with lanterns hanging from the yards. They could smell smoke but see no flame because the fires had been started below decks.

Slowly at first, then speeding with the wind pressing their sails the eight ships began to flower with flame as they drew near the Spanish fleet, the fire licking up the rigging and crowning the masts. Dark figures still worked them, daring each other to stay aboard longer, working the steerages to aim the beautiful, short-lived vessels of gold and red and orange straight at the Spanish fleet.

There was someone behind them. Thomasina turned to find the long legs of the Lord Admiral standing there, watching as they were.

'Beautiful,' she said fiercely. 'May they kill many Spaniards.'

'Just so long as they break the formation, Mrs de Paris,' said the Admiral. 'Mrs Anriques, I am much indebted to you for speaking to my council to such good effect. If there is any service I may—'

Rebecca turned on him, the side of her face lit by the now distant fireships. 'Oh yes, my lord Admiral, you may do me a service. If there is any opportunity, any chance no matter how slim, to board and take the galleas *San Lorenzo*, will you give me your word that you will do it?'

'I can't promise that any—'

'This is the only service that I would ask of you. That you help me save my husband from the galley-bench. Promise me that if you can, you will.'

379

The Admiral tilted his head. 'Your husband is a man most fortunate in his wife and her loyalty.'

'Will you take *San Lorenzo*?'

'Yes,' rumbled the Lord High Admiral, 'I give you my word. If I can take that galleas, I will.'

# Edward Dormer

*Flanders, 1588*

When he came back from killing the mapmaker, Parma saw him personally, clapped him personally on the back, shook his hand. Edward glowed with the honour, pleased with the purse of gold, but far more delighted with the praise given out, lavishly by Parma's standards and by his own. In fact nobody had ever praised him so much before, never had he done anything so wholeheartedly approved of. His struggles with the priesthood, his exhausting efforts to subdue his body to the service of God, they all fell into the background because here at last was something he understood and could do.

He escorted ten barges down a canal and drove off some ragged-arsed beggars who tried to take them back. He took a couple of small forts and rounded up several herds of Butter-eaters' cows to supply the troops. He spent much of his time patrolling up and down the length of the new canal that Parma had built to bring his army to the North Sea when the Armada was in the Channel.

He had a wonderful time. Piers Lammett came to join him, as leathery and enigmatic as before and they went drinking together in dark little alehouses that supplied wonderful dark sticky beer made from cherries.

'Did you ever find out why His Grace wanted Van Groenig killed?' asked Lammett, as the potboy opened another barrel of cherry-ale.

Edward scowled with the effort of memory, not helped by several quarts of beer. 'Who?'

'The man you were sent to kill in England. God, I pitied you then, Ned, I thought you were certain sure to be arrested and Walsingham would have you dangling from a pillar being flogged to improve your memory.'

'When I went to England, I didn't know anything at all about Parma or the Holy Enterprise,' said Edward, substantially slowed by the beer.

'Exactly. Nobody expected to see you again. When you bounced back on the *Fortune*, we thought for a bit that perhaps you'd been turned, but obviously you hadn't. Very impressed, His Grace was, and I told him that you were clearly naturally talented.'

Edward accepted the praise as his due. He looked back on the raw untested boy he had been six months before and felt a kindly patronage for him. 'Did you know I killed Becket?'

'Did you now?' Lammett smiled and lifted his tankard. 'How?'

'Same way you taught me, come up behind him, grab his hair and stab him in the eye. Worked a treat on both of them.'

'Oh, yes. And he gave you no trouble?'

'Not much. He tried to fight but couldn't draw his sword in time—'

Lammett's eyebrows went up. 'I'm surprised he'd bother. He'd know a sword's no good for close work.'

It came to Edward that Lammett was quietly doubting that he had in fact killed Becket at all – not exactly saying it, just not looking entirely convinced. Edward grunted, lifted his feet off the table, and scrabbled out the canvas wallet he kept in his pouch, which one of his men had made for him to keep the trophies of the men he had personally killed. He felt it was good for his soul to keep track of it, how many he had actually sent to Hell in God's service. There was something important about the numbers, not that he was childish enough to think he would get another room to his mansion in Heaven for each heretic he had destroyed, but still . . . You had to stop them blurring into each other, for each was in fact a man, had been a child full of hope, had been corrupted and led astray by the evils of heresy and had ended choking out his life on Edward's blade. God's justice was a terrible thing.

Lammett watched with grave interest as he opened up the little wallet and pointed to the second lock of hair, the wiry sandy one, not very long.

'There. That's Becket's hair.'

'Ah,' said Lammett, taking another pull of his beer. 'And there was I thinking he was dark-haired.'

'No, for he introduced himself as Mr Becket when he asked the sailors about me,' said Edward, his jaw sticking out a little at this continued doubt.

'Well, then,' said Lammett, lifting his tankard to Edward. 'No doubt about it. Many congratulations, sir, I cannot think of a greater blow struck for His Majesty's Holy Enterprise than the killing of David Becket.'

Edward tilted his head in courtesy, wondering why he was being so touchy at the moment. It seemed an awfully slow business, waiting for the great Armada to be in the Channel so they could begin to board the barges and take ship across the sea. Everything he was doing was working to that end, but it all seemed piddling and unreal in comparison to his longing to go home, to retake England for the True Faith.

'As for Van Groenig ...' Edward felt a little stirring of guilt there, foolishly because after all the man had been about to betray Parma for money. 'Van Groenig was no trouble either,' he said smiling, and drank more cherry beer.

As it happened, the next time he saw Lammett, they were both in Parma's antechamber, waiting for an interview with him. The attendant showed them both in and as they knelt beside each other, Parma waved his hand for them to rise, called for wine.

'I have a special mission for both of you,' he said, 'in which you shall be partners, and which shall be for the God-favoured liberation of England from the toils of heresy.'

Alexander Farnese, Duke of Parma rarely spoke in such a flowery manner and Edward blinked at him in puzzlement. Lammett caught his eye and looked deliberately at one of the tapestries where there was a slight bulge.

Parma smiled faintly. 'This mission, as ordered by His Most Catholic Majesty King Philip of Spain and the Low Countries, is contained in these sealed orders. You shall together recruit a troop of about four hundred men, all experienced soldiers, with the proviso that none shall be Frenchmen or Spaniards, and then you shall attend upon the peace commissioners at Dunkirk. At the moment when the King's invincible Armada is sighted in the channel you shall open the orders and follow them to the letter.'

Raw excitement made Edward's ears hammer.

'As a precaution against accidents, the orders are in two halves and each of you holds one half, written in code, for which each of you holds half of the key. Thus, if one of you should unfortunately fall prey to one of Sir Francis Walsingham's men, at least the secret shall still be safe.'

'What do we do if that happens?'

'When the Armada arrives, you must row out to them and explain your problem to the Duke of Medina Sidonia, who will also have opened his sealed orders. He will tell you what you must do and with God's grace you shall do it and achieve the miracle by which the Armada shall be able to hold the narrow seas against the English until I and my troops can board our barges and sail across. Otherwise the thing is impossible, as I am sure you realise.'

Lammett's head had come snapping up as Parma spoke. His eyes seemed to be burning holes in his head to Edward, so fierce was his intent to serve the cause of right.

'Does it all depend upon us, Your Grace?'

'Not entirely. But you have a most important part to play and so it is imperative that you hold yourselves ready in Dunkirk. You will be attached to my commissioners as guardians, but I expect your troop to be ready for action the minute the Holy Cross is seen in the channel. Do you understand?'

'Yes, Your Grace,' said Lammett. 'Thank you.'

'Any questions, Mr Dormer?'

'Do we have money and weapons for the troops or must we find them ourselves?'

Parma smiled kindly at Edward. 'Of course they will be provided. The last thing I want is any independent campaign to gain funds or munitions. In matters of policy, Mr Dormer shall lead. In matters of war, Mr Lammett shall advise. And you will be given everything you need.'

And they were. They were also given Imperial warrants and twenty men to guard the two wagons full of bullion and guns. They headed south at once in the hopes of finding soldiers in the campaign bedevilled borderland between Flanders and France.

Two weeks later, having recruited a bare three hundred in the teeth of the furious opposition of the various Captains in the area, most of whom had contracts to supply Parma with troops for the invasion of England, and having immediately lost a third of them to desertion, Dormer and Lammett came to Dunkirk. It was a muddy, miserable little fishing village blinking out onto the English Channel, and they found it overpressed with people, since Her Majesty Queen Elizabeth's peace commissioners were in lodgings there and so were His Majesty King Philip's peace commissioners, their respective trains of servants and their guards. There was no space to be had anywhere, not even in the stables of the meanest inn, and so, much against their will and all best practice, they sprinkled their troops in billets around the surrounding muddy farming hamlets. Most of the farmers protesting at the evil intrusion were well-used to having soldiers billeted on them and eyed up Dormer's ugly-looking Germans and Italians and renegade Englishmen very much as they might have assessed pigs they were buying at market. Their daughters did much the same. As for the price of food . . .

'A barrel of salt fish for a gold piece?' Dormer groaned. 'They catch them out there, they salt them here, how can they possibly be—'

'Where else will we go?' pointed out Lammett philosophically. 'The country's eaten bare and the peace commissioners offer top prices.'

'Bastards,' snorted Dormer. 'What do we want peace for?'

Lammett laughed. 'Mostly it's in the nature of seeing who blinks first.'

They settled down like everyone else, arguing over prices, trying to buy beer on credit from alewives who always bit coins first, waiting like everyone else with bated breath for the ships to appear in the channel.

Dormer flogged the first three deserters he caught and hanged the fourth and fifth. After that, their rate of attrition slowed a little. The peace commissioners were making good progress on the question of the size and shape of the table where they would discuss peace and also on the issue of who would sit where. The hunchbacked son of Elizabeth's Lord Treasurer, Robert Cecil could be seen sometimes, taking the air along the little fishing quay, attended by large surly Englishmen. Everyone was miserable.

Dormer himself was needing more aqua vitae every night to get to sleep. The sealed waxed package that held his orders was never out of his doublet-front, and seemed to burn him when it crackled. Sometimes, when he was drunk, he would take it out and look at it, but he knew that it had been kept so dark a secret for a good reason and tried his best to trust in the lords and King who knew what they were doing. He repelled the many whores who tried to tempt him to mortal sin, but found himself also suffering from nightly attacks by succubi, which made him conclude that Dunkirk must be full of witches. He went to confession regularly to rid himself of the venial sins of looking at the whores with lust or thinking of them with lust, but the only alternatives were sturdy fishwives and their daughters, who were only marginally less sturdy and stank of fish. It occurred to him to wonder, heretically, just how badly St Peter and the other apostles who were fishermen had stunk. He confessed that fault as well, to the downtrodden curate of the Dunkirk church, and was told to say yet another rosary.

They lost a few more men to raging fluxes and wearily set themselves to recruit more. Around that time Lammett turned up with the sorriest pair of probable deserters that Dormer had ever seen.

One was a wide, black-haired, black-bearded, scowling bully with a face that seemed teasingly familiar. The other, at first sight, was his slave boy, but then when she stood up, it became clear she was his slave woman.

Dormer gulped in shock at the sight of a woman dressed as a man, when she was so very obviously a woman and forgot to wonder where he had seen her master before.

'New recruits,' said Lammett triumphantly.

'Them?'

They were ragged and looked hungry. Both had short swords but no other armament and no armour or horses. They exchanged glances when he spoke and the woman grinned.

'I'll take the man, the woman can go and ... do laundry, I suppose.'

The man looked highly amused at this and the woman scowled. 'I'll fight,' she said. 'I'll fight you to prove I can.'

In the end she crossed swords perfectly effectively with Lammett and showed she knew the use of a caliver as well. Lammett shrugged and said that what they needed were warm bodies who could fight, never mind what they were, and against his better judgement Dormer gave way.

The man claimed to be called Smith and said he had so much experience it would be foolish to go into it all, but that he had been at the siege of Haarlem and also the battle of Zutphen where the English commander Sir Philip Sidney took his death-wound, which he claimed to have given him. He was clumsy with a sword owing to an old injury to his shoulder and wrists, but he would undertake to turn any troop of deserters and cripples into soldiers.

Lammett seemed to like him and so they were signed on, one as David Smith and the other, making only her mark, as Merula.

The waiting went on, enlivened by the occasional rain storm and slate-skied days. It was a bad summer and, as Lammett said grimly when they tripped over a sickening corpse in the town ditch once, you knew the people were expecting famine when the women started killing their new babies.

Then the wind changed and blew from the south-west, the sun came out, most of the rain departed and the muddy streets of Dunkirk began converting to dust. At last the peace commissioners established the shape of the table as round, to their mutual satisfaction, and settled down to deciding where everyone should sit and in what order they should enter the chamber.

It was on a day with a few bright showers that Dormer went into a small dank inn that charged marginally less for its aqua vitae on account of watering it drastically. He asked the potman if he knew where David Smith was and the man shrugged, drew breath to speak.

'He will be here in an hour,' said an indeterminate voice, deep, soft, clear, hard to tell whether it was male or female. Dormer blinked into the shadows at the back of the common room and after he squinted hard, he made out the figure of David Smith's slave woman, Merula, her cloak lapped around her despite sitting next to the fire, staring gloomily at a leather jack of truly abysmal mild ale. Dormer had learned better than to order mild ale at that establishment.

'Do you know where he's gone?' he asked and the woman shrugged, then sighed, put down her drink and gestured at the bench opposite her.

'You wait for him with me?' she said, her voice a little singsong. Dormer had never met an African before, much less sat down opposite one, although he had known some who had black slaves working for them and highly recommended them for their strength and toughness.

Dormer had no idea how to treat her, what sort of person she was. She was not a girl but a woman, yet she had a sword on her belt. She was so dark that her eyes and teeth seemed to glare out of the firelight by themselves. Some of her teeth were pointed like a dog's, and yet she spoke quite gently. Was she . . . did she sleep in the same bed as David Smith?

Even the thought made his skin prickle and his breath come short, he was in such a state of tension about the whores. If she did it with David Smith . . . For several seconds he just blinked down at her stupidly, not even answering her perfectly civil invitation because he was so hypnotised by the alien look of her and his own twining speculations.

387

Suddenly she looked straight at him and smiled. 'I have my manumission, a thing you find important. I am not in the trade yet of selling my woman's cave to men I do not know. So please do not waste my time with offering me of money or beads or food or marriage.'

What was she talking about? Woman's cave? She made a soldier's gesture so crude that Dormer found himself blushing. Oh. How had she read his mind?

And she smiled again, secretly, drank, gestured at the bench. Almost against his will he sat down and ordered aqua vitae, even found himself offering her a drink as if she was a man.

She smiled and shook her head. 'I am trying not to drink booze too much,' she said.

'Why?' asked Dormer, who had heard of heretic Protestants who were against drink as it led to licentiousness and sin – vide, they would say, the tale of Lot and his daughters.

She shook her head. 'It cuts me from my gods.'

Dormer blinked stupidly at her again as the boy brought a cupful of spirits. Heretics he was used to, he had heard of the Moors and the Jews who refused Christ's message, but never before had he met a real pagan.

'Gods?' he asked.

'Oh . . . I should call them angels.'

'Who are you?'

'I am sister to a great King in my country where there is a proper sun, and more importantly I am the finest upside-down woman there has ever been. Or I was. Now I am right-side up, alas, and I think it is the booze has done it.' She looked at her tankard and tutted. 'I would drink water, but it makes me too sick. You have a great many flux demons here.' She looked shrewdly at him.

He was fascinated. 'Tell me about your gods?' he said.

'Why? They are not your gods. You serve some kind of northern god.'

He couldn't let this pass as a true son of the Church, even though he was not a priest and would never be ordered overseas to bring the benighted savages of the New World to the Truth. On the other hand, here was a benighted savage opposite him and God must have some purpose in bringing them together. He shook his head at the woman's simplicity.

'I serve only one god, the only true God, who made everything.'

She blinked owlishly at him. 'Truly?'

'Yes.' He couldn't help smiling at the wonderful opportunity. 'It may seem strange to you that there is only one God over all, beyond all, infinite and all-powerful—'

'No, not at all,' she interrupted him, 'Only I am surprised that a . . .' She used strange words he didn't understand, '. . . should know this.'

'Know what?'

'That there is only One who made all.'

'What did you call me . . . those words you used?'

'Oh,' she coughed. 'Do not be offended, please, but to me you northerners are all so strange and ugly-coloured, I call you . . . um . . . hairy . . . ghosts . . . also, I called you one-who-follows-after-demons-mistaking-them-for-gods, which was unfair of me since you know of the One.'

Somehow the aqua vitae he was drinking as she said this went down the wrong way and he coughed and choked. She frowned and looked worried, put out a long, hard, black hand to touch his arm as he crowed.

'I am sorry if I offend,' she said, 'but also Mr . . . Mr Smith tells me I should have a care of the priests here, if they should hear me to say that I follow one True God, and so should you, for if they find you do not serve their Suffering Jesus god in this land, then they will burn you for it.'

Another gulp of aqua vitae did not help at all, in fact it made his coughing fit worse. He managed to gasp, 'Of course I serve Our Lord Jesus Christ.'

'Good,' said the woman, 'that's more healthy for you. Now, I have said, I will be baptised and serve the Jesus god as well, if it will satisfy the priests here, I will learn his songs and make sacrifice, for I do not wish to burn. But when I am upside-down I serve the One Who Made All as my Lady Leopard because I must. When I am right-side up, I will serve whichever god is best for me, of course.'

He had never heard such outrageous nonsense in his life, but something in him stopped him getting angry with the savage. It was hardly her fault she was innocent and unwise, after all.

'You don't understand,' he whispered, wiping the tears of coughing from his eyes, 'there is only one god and Our Lord Jesus is His Son.'

'Ah,' she nodded wisely. 'A half-god, then. I am descended from one, for a woman climbed a tree when the Lady Leopard chased her

389

and found the King Snake and mated with him and so bore children that were half-gods.'

'No, no, no . . . Only One, but three persons . . . You see, it is a matter of the Holy Trinity.' He racked his brain to find a way of explaining such a theological subtlety to a heathen, and wished that he had a shamrock nearby like St Patrick. 'Think of a stalk with three leaves on it, and yet only one stalk, all one same plant. That is like the Holy Trinity. One God, three persons, the Father, the Son and the Holy Spirit, all of one substance . . .'

She looked unimpressed. 'Only three? Surely God is a great tree with many branches, many trunks, but only one tree. And each of us a tiny leaf.'

'Eh?'

'In my country we have wonderful trees – that kind of tree that Snake woman climbed. It starts from a seed, like any plant, and grows like any tree and sends out branches. And then the branches send down roots to the ground and if the earth is good, they root there and make another trunk to send out more branches. There are so many branches to some of them, they are like a forest in themselves. Each trunk is a god. This is a song we have about the gods and where to go hunting them – I could sing it for you, if you like?'

Dormer stared at her. Surely what she was saying was heresy, theological nonsense . . . Yet it seemed to make sense, if there were indeed such trees? No, surely not. 'Um. Let me tell you about Our Lord Jesus Christ?'

She looked pleased. 'That would be very fine. Nobody tells me about him, but they say I should serve him.'

He did his best to make the story understandable by a simple savage, and yet still she asked questions that worried him. She seemed to find the idea that mankind needed saving in the first place very hard to grasp, and yet she didn't balk at all at the Resurrection and Ascension into Heaven. At the end she nodded approvingly.

'Now that is a fine god-tale,' she said. 'I'm sure it must take many days to sing it properly. Would you like to hear any of my god-tales now? I know many good ones from many tribes, many about the Great Mother of All.'

Dormer had no time for the childish tales of heathens. He had to go and see if there was any message from Parma, he had to go and search the horizon for signs of the Armada, which must surely be making its way up the Channel by now. Two days before he had thought he heard a kind of rumbling that might have been distant cannon.

'No, thank you,' he said, trying to be polite. After all, she too was a child of God, despite her strange skin and stranger ideas, only she didn't know it yet. 'But you must remember that your gods are all demons.'

She stared at him. 'Is that how you think?'

'It's true. All gods are false, except the Almighty in His three persons.'

And she opened her onyx eyes very wide and started to laugh heartily, slapped her thigh like a man. At last she said, 'How can the Almighty be a man? You say He – does God have privates?'

It was evidently heresy, and yet it was difficult to argue against. And embarrassing.

Edward fled, to find that a pacquet boat was struggling along the coast, every sail set and wrinkling in the weak air, heading for Dunkirk. When it finally came in on the rising tide, he found the dock buzzing with excitement, all the commissioners there and their bodyguards as well.

Yes, the Armada was in the channel. Yes, the King's ships had been fighting the Queen's ships. There had been great battles by Portland Bill, Medina Sidonia would be somewhere near the Isle of Wight now.

It was time. Beckoning Lammett, Dormer went back to his lodgings and they both slit open their sealed packages putting the halves of the two documents together. Dormer decoded laboriously while Lammett watched the door and when he had the whole of it, he laughed at the perfect sense of the plan.

In the name of His Most Catholic Majesty, greetings.

When the Holy Enterprise is at the Cape of Margate or Calais Roads, take all your men, ride westwards along the coast to the easternmost gate of Calais. On the night after the first day that the Enterprise is anchored in Calais Roads, it shall be opened to you by a friend who will greet you in the name of St Augustine. Enter the city, ride for the Citadel and take it by the Grace of God and the strength of your arms. Raise this my banner there as a sign for the ships that the place is ours. At all costs, prevent the guns of the Citadel from firing on the four galleases, which will take the city for His Most Catholic

Majesty at first light. Render them any other assistance you can and when they have the port, join with His Grace the Duke of Medina Sidonia when he brings his ships into the harbour. Burn this letter.

Enclosed was a tightly folded silk banner and the map Dormer himself had taken from the body of the mapmaker, now adorned with the labels and key that established it as the French city of Calais.

The whole was sealed with the seal of the Duke of Parma and his own proper signature.

They would be attacking a neutral city. That was why the order had been for there to be no Spaniards, only English, Allemaynes, Scots, Dutch – any ragtag and bobtail but no subjects of the King. That way he could deny them if he had to.

'Where are we going then?' said Lammett.

Dormer smiled, rolled up the paper. 'It's best not to know until the last minute.' He kept the paper, just in case, put it in his doublet front.

Lammett nodded, and left the little tavern. Dormer called for beer and a good meal, not sure if he could eat it or not. He had an enormous responsibility. The immense weight of it made him feel shaky and elated at the same time. Perhaps they had overestimated his abilities, perhaps he would fail.

No. He would not fail. He would see what he had dreamed of all that time ago at the Seminary in Rheims; he would see the soldiers of God leaping ashore to retake poor, enslaved England for the True Faith. Soon. Very soon now. He would return to his native land as a hero, a rescuer, not some poor starveling priest hunted from door to door by Walsingham's pursuivants. This was why God had spoken to him in the chapel that day, in the fumes of cabbage soup, why God had directed all his movements since. When he went to the little room that had been his lodgings for so many weary weeks, he packed, oiled his sword, cleaned his pistols. Then he knelt at his prie-dieu under the figure of the Blessed Virgin and Christchild in the corner of his room and prayed happily, bubbling over with gratitude that at last he could do God's work.

As he crossed himself and rose, a little stiffly, his knees being less used to bearing his weight than they had been, he saw the shadowy shape waiting in the doorway. It clearly was not Lammett, and he drew his dagger and advanced, only to find that it was the black woman, Merula.

She didn't look at all alarmed by his knife, even before he put it away, only smiled and lifted her hands, palms upwards to show she had no weapon.

'What is it?' he asked, suspicions starting to crowd him.

'I only came to say sorry that I upset you with my talk of gods. Mr Smith, who is not my master, but my friend, he said I had most certainly offended you with my nonsense, since you were once working to be a priest. And I, as an upside-down woman, was also something like a priest. I should be more careful . . . Not to burn, eh?'

There was something odd in the way she looked at him, something unfocused and not quite human. The darkness made her seem more demonic, all eyes and teeth. Was she . . . ? Perhaps. Perhaps she had been possessed by the demons she worshipped.

Well, there was an easy way to tell, and he thought he should do so before he rode through the night to Calais with her behind him. He would need to allow her to come, alas, since men had been deserting again, despite Mr Smith's taking of them in hand.

And so he drew her into the room he shared with Lammett. He sat her down at the little table where he did his paperwork and checked his musters against the paychest.

'Merula, I am very concerned at the state of your soul. I am concerned in case you have been possessed by a demon, which might make you say the things you have.'

Merula smiled. 'Of course my Lady Leopard rides me, but she does not own me. She takes me where it is right for me to go, if only I have the courage. But I am not upside-down now, so my Lady Leopard is not here.'

'You know you must abjure all demons such as your Lady Leopard. But first, let me test you. Say these words after me . . . Pater noster, qui es in caelis . . .'

'But I do not know what they mean. Are they a spell?'

'No, of course not. They are a prayer made by Jesus Christ himself when he was amongst us and it doesn't matter that you don't understand it, the demons will know who it came from and be afraid.'

'So if my Lady Leopard is a demon and evil, as you say, she will be chased away by these words.'

'Yes.'

'I would call that a very powerful spell, to be able to cast out demons so easily. But yes, certainly, Mr Dormer, I will say your spell with you since I know my Lady Leopard is no demon.'

'Then do so.' Poor woman, she was so caught in the toils of deviltry, she had no idea how near her soul was to hell. At least he should rescue her from that, in case she were to die. The limbo of the unbaptised was better than hell at any rate.

'Pater noster . . .'

'Pater noster . . .'

They went through the whole of the Lord's Prayer and when they came to the significant words, 'Et libera nos a malo, Amen,' Edward could not help his voice rising and shaking a little. She said the words carefully and he waited. Nothing.

'Should I see anything?' she asked.

'Say it again.'

'Libera nos a malo, Amen. Will you tell me the meaning of the words, or is it secret?'

'No, only . . . It means, Our Father, who art in Heaven . . .' She listened as carefully and docilely as he could have hoped to the words given by Christ. No smoke came from her ears or nostrils, no screams or groans from her belly, nothing. It was very puzzling.

'That is a very fine and beautiful prayer. I am surprised that the Suffering Jesus should have made such a good prayer.'

Now she looked into the corner and smiled at something she saw there. Dormer shook himself out of his musing and asked her why.

'Only you call her a demon, but I see you worship my Lady Leopard as well.' She gestured and when Dormer looked the way of her pointing finger he saw the figure of the Blessed Virgin that he had been praying to.

'Eh?'

'I have seen her like this, my Lady Leopard showed herself so when I was in one of your empty temples.'

Dormer blinked owlishly at the Negress for several minutes while he tried to make sense of this. He felt that somehow it was very important, almost as important as the orders regarding the taking of Calais.

Was it possible that what she had said was true?

'You have seen a vision of Our Lady?'

'Yes, standing on the moon, the serpent at her feet, crowned with stars,' said Merula, leaning forward with eagerness. 'This is what it means to be upside-down, to see things like this. It was my Lady Leopard in another shape, as all the gods are the great tree of God

394

in other shapes, you cannot divide the infinite Light, only turn towards it or away. You see? I have no demons because I pray to Our Lady as you do. Only for me, she wears a beautiful golden yellow coat with the fingerprints of God on it.'

Just for a moment, he felt as if something inside him was splitting and breaking, as if a steady even pressure from inside had finally broken a hard shell and was bursting out, like a leaf bursting out of a seed. Perhaps there was something in what she said . . .

No. It was impossible. It was impossible that a black savage could be reverencing the Virgin Mary as he did, it was impossible that she could tell him anything about God, he who had been studying for the priesthood for as long as he could remember, and had only turned to soldiering because God had told him to. How dare she try and instruct him. The impertinence of it, of her filthy ignorance and savage pagan lies . . .

'How dare you!' he hissed at her. 'How dare you call the Virgin Mary by the name of your demoness. You know nothing of the True Religion. Get out.'

She rose, looking at him steadily. 'Be careful. I am upside-down now, again, at last, after so long,' she said, quiet and thoughtful, 'I see in your godspace that you reverence the Suffering Jesus, but are also a seeker for the true God beyond him. I see you reverence Our Lady, but do not understand her nature. I see following you the men you have killed, the Dutch mapmaker and . . . and . . . another man, a man I saw once only, who is winking at me and putting his finger to his lips and smiling . . .'

She stood utterly still and he felt a chill down his neck as the candles moved in the breeze from the door. Only the breeze from the door, nothing else.

'We are all followed by those we killed, which is why we must be careful how and why we do it, and to do it with respect. You should be wary of the first two you killed.'

His mouth had gone dry, to be faced with the devil in this woman he had tried to help, before his great enterprise, his lynchpin effort . . . He began to repeat the Pater Noster.

'Yes, this is a great prayer,' she said, her voice becoming singsong as her demons took her captive again. 'I would like to warn you, since you have been kind to me and taken care for my soul, which is more than any other hairy ghost has done . . . I would like to warn you not to go to Calais and not to take the Citadel for the sake of the Spanish. I would like to tell you not to betray your people, but I see you will do it anyway . . .'

Dormer croaked, held fascinated by those onyx eyes under the wide brown brows. Her demon must have told her his secrets. The devil was opposing his holy work, a devil no doubt conjured by the Witch-Queen of England, who had sent this poor heathen woman against him . . . His cold fingers reached convulsively for his dagger.

She shook her head, then suddenly stopped and turned as if someone had called her. Over in the corner she looked, the opposite corner from the prie-dieu which was empty except for the shadows thrown by the firelight, and her face lit up, her eyes and mouth opened wide and she held out her hands to her demon . . .

Now, strike now! Edward told himself, snatched out his dagger and lunged for her chest, she staggered back with a cry, pulled out her own weapon, tried to defend herself . . . She was no worse than any other man would have been, except she had a slash in her chest, and when she ducked under his dagger strike, he punched her in the face with his fist, punched her again, got her on the ground and raised his dagger to strike . . .

Something dark grabbed at him, he heard a whistling, smelled a terrible animal stink, heard a creaking of wooden beams as if in a ship, he felt sick as he always did in a ship. He was being held by something. He struck out, struck again . . . There was a shout, again he tangled with darkness, that was less than solid, but harder than air, as it were an unmoving wind in the shape of a stocky powerful man fighting him and the woman was shouting, shrieking angrily . . . Suddenly he felt an arm about his throat, heard a voice in his ear . . .

'Dormer, stop it! What the hell are you doing! Stop it, Ned.'

It was Lammett, holding him, stopping him from killing the woman whose chest he was sitting on, whose face he had made bloody with his fists, whose wound in her chest was welling with blood.

'Get off.' There was a snarl in Lammett's voice, he was genuinely shocked. 'What happened?'

'She . . . she attacked me, with demons . . . There was a demon here, she called a devil to her, she's a witch . . .'

He could feel every part of himself shaking, spittle from his mouth, he could hardly speak from fear and fury.

The black woman lay where she was, then looked up at Lammett with one purpling eye. 'He wished to kill me and I fought,' she said, her voice slurred. 'He tried to stab me with his dagger, but my son . . . My son came and fought him. Calais will be his grave.'

The eye shut, the woman passed out.

Lammett hoisted Edward up, dusted him down, took his dagger, cleaned it. 'I'll fetch a surgeon and say we found her in the alley, no doubt it was footpads that attacked her,' he said coldly.

Dormer sat for a moment, the woman's voice still in his ears. Her son? Calais his grave? The son's grave or Dormer's grave? How had she known?

He followed after Lammett, still shaking.

The surgeon clucked his tongue and said he thought the slash would either kill her that night if it was deep enough, or better itself without his help. He bound up the wound well enough, though the blood kept welling, soaking the lint and bandages.

The soldier, David Smith came hurrying to find her, smelling, as he always did, strongly of booze, tried to rouse her and failed. Lammett repeated over and over, quite steadily to Smith's sharp questions, that they had found her in an alley. And it was clear that Smith did not believe them.

Dormer went along with all of this, silent, still shaking, still horrified at his near escape from a witch and her familiar demons. He insisted on calling in at the nearest church, only to find that it was a church of Our Lady and that the figure Merula had described to him looked down at him from the altar, crowned in stars, standing on the moon, dancing with the serpent . . . No. Crushing the serpent. Destroying it with her heel.

He lit a candle in any case, knelt, tried to say the Ave Maria, found it would not come to him because he was so upset and crossed himself again. His candle went out, blown by a sudden draught.

Still they had to wait. The next day, the feast of St Anne, dawned hot and breathless, not the slightest catspaw of wind ruffling the surface of the sea, where the waves slid themselves like oil up the beach and back again and urchins from Dunkirk went and risked their health to swim in it. It was clear no sailing ship could make any progress and particularly not the large store ships that the whole of the Armada would have to nanny all the way up the channel.

Dormer did not visit the Negress, who lay still in Smith's lodgings, grey under the ebony of her skin, the skin stretched tight on her face and fever raging from the wound in her chest. Smith had offered a reward to find the man who stabbed her.

And the Saturday came, as slow as the waves, Saturday, 28 July, the feast of Saints Nazarius and Celsus, Martyrs. There were a few showers of rain while Dormer paced through the town. He laid a bet with one of Robert Cecil's servants that the Armada would not be seen near Calais on the Monday, and another bet that it would not arrive on Sunday with one of the Spanish commissioner's doorkeepers.

On Sunday morning a rider came hammering into the Spanish commissioner's lodgings. By noon Dormer knew that the Armada was at anchor outside Calais with M. Gourdain the governor allowing all non-martial supplies to be sent aboard. Three miles further down the coast were the English.

It was time.

Quietly Dormer sent Lammett and Smith among the various billets they had put the men in, counting them, taking names, being sure they had swords and were, if not sober, at least capable of riding a horse that evening. Dormer went to Mass in a fog of excitement and fear; he had made his confession the day before, was careful to receive Holy Communion, and yet he could not say what the Gospel had been, only thought it might have been Christ cleansing the Temple. Which was a good omen he thought.

He felt hollow with fright, with the knowledge that the Holy Enterprise of England rested on him alone. It made him unnaturally sensitive. He knew that Smith and Lammett were watching him carefully, that they spoke together often. Once he thought he saw Lammett talking to one of the English commissioner's servants, but wasn't sure. Perhaps he was only passing the time of day.

They had to wait until the evening. In the last half hour before the gates shut, he had all his men filter out of the city by all the gates, meeting in an orchard under the walls. Some of the men had sold their horses to buy drink, one had a lame horse, another had no caliver. Dormer went among them rectifying the things they had not, relieving them of things they did not need, such as bedrolls and sacks to carry plunder.

'We will head south-west along the coast road,' he said in English first, then French before he had Lammett translate it to Dutch. 'We are going to take the Calais Citadel, spike the guns if we can. They must not be able to fire at ships coming into the harbour.'

There was the sound of someone sucking air in through his teeth, some muttering among the Frenchmen they had had no choice but to recruit.

One spoke up. 'There is no war between the King of Spain and the King of France,' he protested. 'Why is the King of Spain attacking Calais?'

Many of the others started to explain, but Dormer held up his hand for silence. 'The King of Spain is not attacking the King of France. This is an assistance that the Governor of Calais is rendering the King of Spain, but the King of France does not want the English to realise what he is doing or blame him for it. So it must seem as if it is by force.'

The man scowled and subsided. It was an explanation sufficiently labyrinthine to appeal to their cynicism – Lord, it might even be near enough true. Dormer waited for questions, perhaps protests from Smith and Lammett, but got none, a little to his surprise.

Instead, Smith came to him and said that Lammett had found someone he suspected was an English spy and wanted Dormer to come and question him. They were outside the orchard, behind a hedge so the men would not be upset by it. Dormer went where Smith pointed, wondering a little, hearing something not quite right in Smith's voice, not quite sure of himself.

And found that Lammett was waiting for him in the dip formed by the road that led to Dunkirk, his back turned. Dormer's feet crunched on the gravel of the road, Lammett turned and Dormer saw that he had a dag in his hand, the match lit.

Dormer stared, glimpsed the light travelling like a falling star down to the pan and threw himself down and forwards, heard the bellow of the gun, cannoned into Lammett with his dagger already drawn, and his hand stabbing before his mind had even caught up with the treachery, slicing Lammett's neck at the vein so the blood gouted. Lammett bucked, kicked and choked, then his eyes turned up and Dormer could not ask what had caused the treachery, why now of all times ... But there was no time. If Lammett was an English spy, then by God they had better ride as fast as they could.

Dormer climbed off Lammett's body, dusted himself down, waited for a moment until his heart had steadied down to a slower rhythm and then ran back to where the men waited.

'We had a traitor amongst us,' Dormer said, staring hard at Smith who had been so thick with Lammett, whose woman had been a heathen witch, 'but Jesus Christ gave me his protection and help and now Mr Lammett is answering for his evil at the throne of God.'

Smith bowed his head a moment. The whole troop mounted up, and Dormer set his jaw, rode over to Smith.

'Did you know what he planned?'

'Of course not,' Smith answered evenly, 'but I would hardly admit it even if I did, now would I, sir?' And he smiled gap-toothed.

Dormer smiled back, the whole of his face tight with cold fury. 'Forgive my injustice, but I must have your pistol,' he said.

Smith looked down for a moment, as the rest of the men jostled around them. 'Are you relieving me of my command?'

'No, Mr Smith,' Dormer said. 'I only want your pistol.'

Another hesitation, Smith seemed to be studying his horse's hooves. Then he looked up, grey eyes looking peculiarly transparent as the last light of the slow summer sun caught them. He smiled again, very charming. 'Of course, Captain. Here you are.'

He unbuckled the case from the front of his saddle and handed it over. Dormer buckled it in place next to his own pistol, astonished that his hands weren't trembling at all with his rage.

Should they take the road or go by a different route? No, by God. Speed was now of the essence, since he must assume that Lammett had warned Cecil and he wanted no troop of heretics hammering after him. In any case, they had twenty miles to ride and a Citadel to take before dawn.

He was experienced enough a soldier to know better than to gallop. He kept them all at a canter for the better parts of the road nearer to Dunkirk, went down to a trot where the animals must pick their way amongst the pot holes and back to a canter. Riding post, the twenty miles might have taken him an hour. For a man running, it might be three hours. Dormer estimated the time to be near midnight when the walls of Calais loomed up before them out of the darkness, scattered houses and market gardens around it and the road leading fine and clear to the gate.

He turned off it and went to the side, to one of the many places where the wall had been pierced for the convenience of the people. Was it the right one? Would the traitor be there? Behind him Smith was supervising the padding of the horses' hooves and their bridles.

Dormer went up to it on his own, in case of treachery, the map carefully drawn by the man he had killed clutched in his hand. It was the correct postern gate. He knocked twice.

'Who's there?' asked a voice.

'St Augustine.'

There was the sound of a bolt, the door opened. Dormer couldn't help himself, he punched the air in silent triumph. Then he turned to his men, waved them on. They dismounted, led their horses through the small gate, the man who had opened it huddled up in his cloak in the shadows. One by one they passed through, Smith last of all.

Dormer, who had been counting, hissed at him, 'We're ten short.'

'I told them to wait on the road and kill any messengers coming from Dunkirk.'

Maybe he hadn't known what Lammett was up to. Dormer nodded, gripped Smith's shoulder. He passed through, waited while the door was bolted shut again and locked. The one who had opened it didn't wait for thanks but slipped away down an alley. Dormer consulted his map again.

'Follow me, stay together.'

Calais was the usual maze of little tiny streets, with a few lanterns and lights making the shadows worse. Now his nightsight was in, the stars were bright enough to give plenty of light, the sea was a gentle cat snoring on the other side of the town. Dormer took it slowly: the map was good, but it was only a map. Every time he saw a church he checked it against the labelling on the map, every time he saw a large inn, he checked it too. He took his time, despite the thudding of his heart in his throat where it seemed to have taken up residence, despite the sweat dripping down under his breastplate as one bridle jingled, another man sneezed, a third one swore when his horse pecked.

They were going up, they were on the street that led up to the Citadel ... There would be guards of course at the gate, but probably sleepy in the warm night, probably not expecting trouble despite the entire might of the Spanish fleet anchored just outside the harbour. Just a little further and ...

One of the horses whinnied and shrieked, reared up on its hind legs, pawing the air, kicked its back legs up and shook its rider off into the drain with a clatter of armour and fallen helmet. Two more horses whinnied and sidled while their riders swore at them loudly and a third bolted suddenly down the street.

'Quiet!' That was Smith, cuffing the spooking horses and somehow managing to roar in a whisper.

Shutters opened above them. There were cries, then someone worked out what was happening. The shouting started, a woman emptied a metal chamber pot on the end man and began banging it with a candle stick. '*Alarme! Au secours!*'

Well, the guards were awake now.

'Follow me!' shouted Dormer, kicked his horse to a gallop, pulled out Smith's pistol and shot the guard who was levelling a crossbow at him, pulled out his own pistol and missed the other one, reversed the pistol and cracked the man across the face with it as he rode through, so the guard collapsed. He heard the thudding as some of the other horses followed him, not all of them, but what could you expect, they were only mercenaries . . . Somebody was trying to shut the gate, he turned his horse's hindquarters to thrust against it, heard a gasp, there were men behind him now. Where was Smith? There, right behind him, shortsword strapped in his hand.

They rode across the small courtyard, choked with huts and chicken coops and slippery straw, then Dormer vaulted from his horse onto one of the garrison who was swinging a halberd and the fight began in earnest.

It was wonderful, he had never felt happier in his life. He felt invulnerable, almost like an angel, as he exchanged cuts and slashes with some poor man who was slow and sleepy and cut his head off, ducked a crossbow aimed at him and heard the grunt of the man behind him who took the bolt, shoulder charged the archer, took his crossbow, threw it to one of the stronger of his German soldiers who shouted, '*Danke*' and stolidly began winding the weapon up again in the middle of the wild whirling chaos. Smith was near him, but in all the confusion, Dormer kept an eye on him, never let him get too close, made sure he was ahead at all times. It added to his exhilaration, not knowing whether Smith might attack him, but knowing that if he did, Dormer himself would win. Perhaps Smith realised it too.

They had to cut their way to the main gate of the tower . . . Dormer picked up one of the benches in the courtyard, threw it into the gap as the soldiers behind tried to shut the great doors, and jumped after it roaring something, he wasn't sure what, perhaps it was even 'St George and England!'

There was another flurry of blades and sweating bodies, both of them fell away, black blood in the darkness, somebody else was running up the stairs, more men behind him following, Smith was there too, breathing hard, he had lost his helmet.

Dormer ran for the stairs, slowed, pleased to have the German behind him. Somebody peeked out and the German said, '*Ja.*' Dormer began reloading his pistol as quickly as he could. They waited until the man peeked again over a crossbow and the German shot him in the face.

Dormer ran up the steps, took the garrison soldier's crossbow and passed it to the German who nodded.

He went on up the spiral stairs more cautiously, heart thudding, crashing through each door. He found a dormitory on the second storey, waited for a few more of them to follow him and then took the grenado he had carefully carried on his baldric all this way, lit the short fuse, lobbed it into the room and shut the door.

There was a firm hollow boom, the whole building shook, the door rattled and the shrieking started.

Dormer ran on up the stairs, to the top of the Citadel, leaving the German to hold the stairs for him.

There he found himself on a broad gun platform with a perfect view of the harbour entrance. Something was happening out there on the dark waters under the stars, something he couldn't quite make out, red stars sliding across the water.

He felt for the bag of spikes he had brought to drive into the touch-holes of the great cannon all around him and make them impossible to fire. He only had to hold the gun platform for a couple of hours, for at first light the galleases would do the work they had been designed for by the great Admiral Santa Cruz, they would row into the harbour no matter what the wind was doing and with their heavy ordnance they would beat Calais into submission and take the harbour for God and the King.

He went to the stairs, called down it, 'Up, up here.'

Only a few of them answered him, perhaps ten of them, with Smith among them, his face dark and brooding.

'Smith,' hissed Dormer. 'Tell the men to finish off the wounded in the dormitory and then close the gates of the Citadel and be ready to hold it against the Governor's men. Make a fighting retreat from there up to this platform and we'll hold it until the town belongs to us.'

Smith nodded, clattered down the stairs, calling orders. He reappeared and shut the door that led onto the gun platform ahead of him, leaving the German and his crossbow to guard it on the other side.

It was a beautiful night. Dormer looked out to sea, over the

403

harbour wall, far out where the white cliffs of his country could just be made out, glimmering. They took the light of the sun early, he supposed. Soon, he told himself, soon I'll be there. This is the key. All I have to do is prevent the guns from firing until the galleases are in the harbour. Whatever is going on out there, the galleases will be rowing for the harbour mouth as soon as they can see which way to go . . . Once they have the harbour and the quayside, my part is done because M. Gourdain will make terms or be replaced by whoever sanctioned the opening of the postern gate.

He knew why he and Lammett had been chosen for the mission: Englishmen loyal to the True Church taking Calais to help in the rescue of their country was an easier thing for the King of France to swallow politically than the same venture led by Spaniards or Flemings. It was all in the look of the thing.

Edward looked across at where Smith was staring thoughtfully across harbour to the confusion of ships in Calais Roads. They could hear faint cries and the formation seemed to be breaking up, if the stern lights gave any guides. Two fireships were beaching on the sandbank, burning away to give some kind of light.

He was sure no mere launching of fireships could have harmed the austere discipline of the Spanish fleet. Surely it was a ruse to fool the heretics.

Smith took out his pipe and tobacco, made and lit it. He offered it, friendlywise, but Dormer refused, never having liked the American weed.

'Now?' asked Smith.

'We wait until the galleases are in and the harbour is taken.'

Smith nodded as if this confirmed his impressions. 'We spike the guns?'

Dormer shook his head. 'I will.' Casually he took out his pistol, checked that it was loaded and primed. Then he pointed it at Smith.

Smith stared, blinking slowly.

'Give me your sword, Mr Smith.'

'Why?'

'For the sufficient reason that I believe you were plotting with Lammett to sabotage this venture. *Now*, Mr Smith.' Smith licked his lips, unbuckled his belt and slid the sword over. 'And your poniard.'

'How can I fight when the French come to retake the Citadel?'

'Surely it's better for you if you don't fight, considering your injured hands.'

Smith's face was quite blank, hard to read, doubtless he was a good primero player, but there was a muscle twitching under his beard. Perhaps once he would have tried something, but now ... Now he had the air of a man who has already been defeated. He took out the poniard by the quillions and threw it gently in Dormer's direction. Then he crossed his arms, sucked smoke from his pipe and blew a smoke ring. 'Well?'

'I won't ask why you turned your coat,' Dormer said. 'I'm sure your reasons seemed good to you. I'll even say nothing of it if we make it to the Spanish fleet, because by then it will be irrelevant.'

'Kind of you.'

'How did you know Lammett?'

Smith smiled again, a tired, wary smile and shook his head. 'We need to start this conversation again, my friend,' he said. 'Firstly, as I expect you're planning to kill me, you should know whom you are killing. No? My name is David Becket. I am the Queen's man now and always have been, though many think me a turncoat as you do. Lammett was the real turncoat, for he could not stomach a Spaniard ruling England. He told me that you believed you had killed me very easily. It was my brother you killed, Mr Dormer, my brother Philip Becket, who was a man of peace, had lived all his life in the place he was born and never fought in anger once he grew to manhood. I have been looking very carefully for you.'

Dormer stared. This was the great David Becket? Who had prevented the likeliest assassination attempt against the Witch-Queen, who had been somehow involved in the failure of Fr Tom Hart's mission? This broad, dark, weary looking, grubby man with the clumsy, weak hands?

Becket saw his astonishment. 'Did you think I'd be killed by Lammett's favourite stab in the eye, boy? It's a perfectly good method, but you'd have to get behind me first.'

'I'm sorry I killed your brother in mistake for you,' said Dormer. 'I had no wish to kill anybody but you.'

Becket tilted his head in acknowledgement. 'As for why you stabbed my woman ...'

'She attacked me with witchcraft. At your orders, no doubt.'

'No, not my orders. Perhaps you offended her. She most certainly is a witch and can look after herself. As for the other ... No apology can make up for my brother's death and his widow's sorrow, which is very heavy. She blamed me for it and in a way she was right.' Becket sighed. 'It seems all I can do is harm those around me. So here we are and soon Calais will be Spanish and then . . . Then, Mr Dormer? The tercios landing in Gravesend. Marching up the road to London, burning as they go. London Bridge blown up, the city a broken, burning hulk and the streets littered with corpses, the Oxford Road sounding to the stamp of the tercios and the rumble of their guns. Battle joined outside Oxford.'

Dormer stared at him, mouth open.

Becket sneered. 'Had you not thought of that? Did you think the English would roll over with their paws in the air like dogs for the Spanish to lord it over them?' He shook his head and chuckled without any humour at all. 'Such an innocent you are, Mr Dormer, really. Do you think we're living in a knightly romance? I have seen it all, in my dreams. Since early spring I have been plagued by them. It started with a dream of my father's house – no very great mansion but a fair and good house – burnt and broken, my brother hanged from the rafters by the troops, my sister-in-law raped and my nephews and nieces killed.'

'The soldiers of God would never—'

'You have evidently not seen as much war as I have, Mr Dormer. Do you think any soldiers hold themselves back when they see a woman they can rape easily and without consequence? Do you think they hold their hands when the woman's little son tries to protect her? Do you think war is a gentle and gracious sport, where the righteous win and the evil die and cannon balls only hit the sinful? Do you think that?'

'God disposes—'

'Certainly He does. But I have seen the soldiers of Spain starving out a city until all the children died of their swollen bellies, I have seen them burn and break poor folks' houses for the pleasure of seeing the flames leap and hearing glass tinkle . . . Christ, I've done it myself . . . soldiers are only men, an army is only a mob, somewhat held in by discipline. Do you think the Spanish soldiers are angels because they cross themselves and pray to Our Lady?'

'I'm sure they're no worse than the Protestants—'

'Of course they aren't. When men are as bestial as they can be, there's very little to choose between them. You were in England recently, you saw how fertile it is, how none of the towns are fortified, how peaceful it is. And now you plan to take bloody war into England, have the Spanish destroy it, put Philip of Spain into Whitehall and the Holy Office in Westminster. Lammett wanted to stop you – he was no less a Catholic than you – but he was no

God-*damned Spaniard!*' Becket was shouting now. 'He was no traitor like you.'

In all his phantasies and all his plans, it had not in fact occurred to Dormer that the rulers of England would be foreign as well as Catholics.

Becket was talking again, quite softly, his eyes holding Dormer's as if by a spell, brilliant and intense with urgency. 'Walsingham fears the Catholics. My liege, the Queen, does not. Do you know why? She knows they will not fight for Spain because they are true Englishmen who would never see England crushed by the Spaniards. Unlike you . . . you filth.' Becket spat, quite accurately, between Dormer's feet.

For a moment Dormer's fists bunched, he nearly stepped up close. But then he stopped, understanding what Becket was about. He sat again, levelled his pistol. 'You can goad me, Mr Becket, but with God's help I shall resist. Now will you spike that gun.'

'No,' said Becket, full of contempt. 'Do it yourself, boy.'

He should have shot Becket as soon as they were on the gun-platform. But the last traces of priesthood in him prevented it: since he had the chance, he must teach Becket to see that the Catholic church was his only hope of Heaven, that Dormer was right to try and save England from Hell. Then he could shoot the man with a clear conscience.

So Dormer walked over to the largest gun, still pointing his pistol at Becket, put the iron spike in the touch-hole and using the mallet awkwardly left-handed, hammered it in. Then he went to the next gun and the next, working in concentrated silence, never letting the muzzle of his pistol waver from Becket's chest. It would take a few hours to bore out new touch-holes so the guns could be fired again. All he needed to do was hold out until the galleases were in harbour.

'Mr Becket,' said Dormer as he worked. 'I have let you live to hear this. The Catholic Church is the only true church, the word of God carried down the centuries in the arms of our Holy Mother. Only turn away from heresy, turn back to God and you will understand why . . .'

'Keep your sermons for someone that is in fact a heretic, Dormer,' said Becket wearily. 'I see no God up there, no God in Churches, no God anywhere. Just a great emptiness full of puppets men make for themselves to fight over.'

Dormer paused in his hammering. 'No God at all?'

'Never seen sign of one. Or if there is, he's an ugly bastard, full of bile and rage and not an ounce of pity.'

It was pitiful to hear the abandonment in his voice. Dormer suddenly felt his eyes prickling with sadness for a man who felt so alone. 'I'll pray for you, Mr Becket, pray that you can come back to the Truth.'

Becket shrugged, sucked his pipe, looked out over the battlements. The sun was coming up and two more fireships had grounded on the beach. Dormer looked out. His breath stopped.

An oared ship was struggling for the harbour mouth, she had taken some kind of damage, she seemed clumsy in the water. The other ships . . . There was now no crescent formation visible. The sea was scattered with ships and puffs of smoke. A thunder of guns came rolling slowly across the water.

Becket stood, looked, saw the galleas and his face lit with understanding. 'Weren't there four galleases?'

'One galleas can do it.'

The oars gleamed in the rising sun, a ship seeming to walk on the sea.

'We could sink it with cannon fire from here,' said Becket, 'just the two of us. There's a couple of guns left that can fire.'

Dormer gripped his pistol, his hand had suddenly become sweaty. Becket's voice was coaxing, not angry.

'I know how to lay and serve a gun, there's powder and ball here. Come on, Dormer, help me save England from war.'

Something was wrong. Surely, there should be more galleases . . . No matter. Once the officers of the Armada realised that Calais was held for them, others would come into the harbour. Perhaps that was why they had lost formation, perhaps they were coming in for shelter.

'Dormer.' Becket's voice was rough-edged, he was nearer.

'Stand still,' snapped Dormer. 'Put your hands on your head.'

Becket stood still, put his hands on his head.

Dormer had the holy banner, packaged in his breast. As fast as he could he hammered in the spikes for the last couple of guns, then went to the flagpole that was empty, for the garrison had not had a chance to raise the fleur-de-lis of France. He clipped the banner to the cord, pulled it up and it spread out slackly on the soft breeze, the badge of the Duke of Parma, the signal that Calais was ripe for the taking.

There were voices on the stairs, thundering, a crossbow being fired, somebody shrieked, the sound of a woman's voice and a sudden hammering on the door onto the gun platform.

'I warned Cecil and told the others they could go,' Becket said casually. 'No point asking them to stay and get killed when the French wanted their guns back.'

Of course he had. Of course. The talking had been playing for time.

There was a steady solid banging, then the crunch of an axe in the wood of the door.

Becket was moving again, his hands hanging loose and relaxed. 'Edward Dormer,' he said softly, 'you can put down your pistol, give me your surrender and I will perhaps let you live.'

Dormer backed, full of black panic, his world suddenly empty of God's guidance. The door splintered to the axe.

# Merula

## Dunkirk

*Never assume you know what a god is thinking.*

It was Lady Leopard. At last, at last, she had climbed on my shoulder, finally she had opened up the gates of my mind and allowed my godsight in its fullest flood to crash into the busy town of my hairy ghost thinking and utterly wreck it. Except for speaking the blue-green hairy ghost tongue of English, I was as I had been in the flower of my power, when I walked the forests of the lands ruled by the great Lion Sun and hunted gods in the dreamtime.

Never could there have been a worse time for it.

We had come to Dunkirk utterly without money, our horses stolen, with our bellies empty for two days. Becket had seen a paper with marks on it, among them a little picture of a horse with a horn on it, and laughed delightedly. So we took service with Piers Lammett and Edward Dormer, and received our ten guilders pourboire money. Becket called himself David Smith and he and Lammett laughed knowingly about that too.

Why did we not take ship and travel back to England with the pourboire money when we first took service and I made my mark on their great book of names? Partly for the reason that there was no ship to be had, all the craft hiding from the Dutch who were out waiting for the Spanish fleet, and notorious pirates every one of them. Partly for the reason that Becket drank the pourboire money and I helped him. And partly for the reason that he wished to stay near Dormer. At first he would not say why, but then when he was drunk one night, he showed me a tattered piece of paper he kept in his jerkin, partly covered with their writing, but with a most fairly done picture of a young man that certainly did have the look of Edward Dormer.

'This is the man that killed my brother,' said Becket. 'This is also the man who killed the mapmaker who would have sold us Parma's plan to take England.'

He explained it to me, about the three parts to the Spanish plan, then smiled cynically. 'If you ever get the chance, Merula,' he said, 'try to see if he has a map on him anywhere?'

And I sat next to him as he swallowed down the aqua vitae that stunned him enough so he could sleep and watched my Lady Leopard blinking complacently in her guise as the tabby cat. What is this about, I wondered as Becket became more and more surly as the drink took him down into his own pit, why is this?

The gods too have rivalries and enmities, perhaps my Lady Leopard had taken against the Spaniards' Suffering Jesus and was friends with Thundering Jehovah of the English. Or perhaps it was only her whim.

*Never think you understand a god*, said my Lady Leopard, tickling my ear.

A man came to fetch us once, when Dormer was out of Dunkirk to recruit more men. Becket scowled and went, loosening his sword because of a name mentioned to him. We were taken to the back room of an alehouse where the tables had been covered with Turkey rugs to hide their stains and there was bad wine served in silver goblets for the benefit of the hunchbacked man in black damask that sat waiting for us. Becket bowed to him and so I salaamed.

'It *is* Mr Becket, then,' said Mr Robert Cecil, narrowing his eyes, 'that was Clerk of the Ordnance.'

'Ay, sir,' said Becket in a flat tone that answered none of the questions hanging in Cecil's voice.

Cecil gestured that Becket should sit, should drink, should be less on his dignity and Becket sat, drank and remained on his dignity. I stood by the wall as was expected of me, with my hands behind my back. Then I was hoping there would be no upside-downness just yet, since this was an important man among the hairy ghosts and I had no wish to offend him. So far was I fallen then, so separated from my Lady.

'I had heard . . .' said Cecil, smiling judiciously, 'I had heard that you were taking a shipload of ordnance to the Hague for the Queen.'

'Ay, sir,' said Becket, still a blank wall.

'It went not as well as you had hoped?'

'No, sir.'

'Have you heard anything of Mr Fant recently?'

And Becket stopped and looked at Cecil, who was smiling blandly, and Becket's eyes fluttered like a maid's just for a second. There was a fleeting smile from him.

'Ah.'

'Ah, indeed, Mr Becket,' said Cecil. 'My father warned me you might be seeking employment with me here.'

'Hm.' Becket was thinking now, I could see that. 'So Fant was working for my lord Burghley?'

'Not necessarily,' scolded Cecil. 'Only my father thought he should be kept informed of your doings, that was all. I have no doubt he contacted Mrs Anriques himself.'

Becket nodded. 'Did my lord Treasurer Burghley, your esteemed father, not like my informing the Queen of his dealings in guns with the Spanish?'

Cecil looked away, coughed. 'It was less sinister than it may have seemed,' he said. 'My father may have dealt in guns and indeed he may have made money at it, but all the guns and shot he sold was the smaller weights, the sakers and falconets, never the culverins or demi-culverins. The Spanish are well outgunned by us still and always shall be.'

Becket inclined his head.

'Further it was no small help to him, as a way of gathering intelligence.'

'Indeed.'

'Although he has never been thoroughly convinced that the Spanish intend war.'

'I am.'

Cecil leaned back in his chair, shifted his hunchback a little, nodded. 'So am I, Mr Becket, but my father will not have it so. As for me, whenever I desire to understand what the Spanish might do, I imagine Mr Secretary Walsingham as the King of Spain and then I know. It has never failed.'

Becket smiled back at him.

'What do you want from me?'

'Why did you take service with Edward Dormer?'

I waited for Becket to explain about his brother, but he did not. He shrugged. 'I need money, he offered it. Why should I not?'

'He is one of Parma's men. I have it on good authority that he was sent into England last autumn with a mission to kill a mapmaker for Parma and that he did his work well and further killed your own brother.'

Becket was very still. 'How do you know this?'

'I have ... sources.'

'Ah.'

'I have been wondering why an independent captain with Parma's money to spend, is sitting about in Dunkirk with two hundred men idle and half a dozen likely little forts to take within a day's ride.' Cecil put his fingers together and made points of them, 'Only wondering, you understand, I do not know for a fact that he is planning anything. Yet here he is, here is Parma's gold and I would like to know why.'

'And?'

'I should take it as a great favour from you, Mr Becket, if you could stay your hand for long enough to find out what he is up to. Hmm?'

Becket nodded. 'And if I find it out?'

For the first time Mr Cecil looked at me. 'Send me your black with a message. I shall do whatever is necessary.'

Becket smiled, his first true smile for a long time, quite a charming gentle smile for so big and ugly a man. 'Mr Cecil, it shall be a pleasure.'

And Cecil stood, Becket stood, Cecil held out his well-ringed hand for to shake right hands and show there were no hidden weapons, and then we left him there.

Becket got in a fight that night with an ugly bruiser that stared at me and then made offers to buy me off him. The man laughed when Becket said I was freed and had my manumission with me, saying that no one frees a slave until they are too old to work and by God she was juicy enough to have plenty of work in her. And Becket struck him with his fist, struck again and again, until Lammett and I pulled him off the man.

Lammett saw no offence in what the man had said, while Becket growled, 'I've never done the work of a pimp and nor will I start now.'

And then he looked at me sidelong and considering. Next morning he roused me early, said he would make an honest woman of me. Which offended me, for I told him I am always honest. But he brought me to one of their smaller plain temples that was for the English to worship in, and spoke to the priest who would not do what he desired since I am not a Christian.

Becket was angry and protested, and the priest fluttered his hands as if Becket were upside-down instead of me and told him many times that until I was a Christian he could not do it. Nor would he baptise me on the spot at Becket's orders, no matter how Becket might shout.

'What was it you asked of him?' I said, as he stamped away from the place.

'I desired him to marry us.'

And I smiled. Men are so strange. He had never asked me, after all. Nor had he asked my family, nor paid a bride-price. It warmed my heart even so, and I put my arms around him and kissed him.

'You know I killed my last husband for beating me?' I told him. 'Are you not afraid?'

'Of you, Merula?' he said, then looked up through his eyelashes with the boy's grin that always melted me. 'No, never.'

That night we held hands and jumped over the candleflames three times, which a friend of his said was as good as a priest and better for the thing being sealed in drink and no damned prosing.

We drank ourselves dizzy on bad aqua vitae, dancing around the tables to their whistles and drums. Even their music was strange to my ears, though beautiful, but without any bones to it, music like the cows and sheep of their country, no music with leopards or elephants in it at all. Nor did they dance in ways I understood and when I sang for them they found it strange also, although they liked it when I took their big drum and beat it in ways they hadn't heard before, to make a song out of drumbeats as we do at home.

So there I sat, the next night, thinking of the forest, thinking of the wide plains, thinking of the round houses and carved compound of my King, thinking of the horses we herd and thinking of the Lion Sun that hunts clouds to eat them.

And this was how I spoke of gods to the young man, whose Spanish money we had taken, Edward Dormer. At first there had only been the hungry writhing of his desires in his godspace. Here was another hairy ghost hopeful of exploring my woman's cave, I thought, to find out if a black cave was darker than a pink cave perhaps. Would he offer money or trinkets, food or marriage, I wondered, since I had shown him I could fight. Although Becket had said grudgingly that he was a fine swordsman, far better than Becket himself now his hands were bad.

It would be better not to waste time. I told him I was free and I told him I was not a whore, which shocked him. But he ordered aqua vitae and even offered me some, which was more courteous than many of them.

He was, in his own northern way, upside-down and had studied for to be a priest of the Suffering Jesus before deciding to serve him with a sword instead. It was interesting and he told me the god-tale of his Suffering Jesus, which I was glad to hear, but in the end I said something that upset him and he ran away.

That was the day that word came: the Spanish were in the English Channel, they were fighting the English ships. Becket was angry with me that I had talked about gods with the man, which was ungrateful since I had kept Dormer with me so he would not know of Becket having another meeting with Cecil. But Becket said that the followers of the Suffering Jesus burned anyone who worshipped other gods, or even the same one differently, and so I must go and apologise and be sure Dormer wouldn't arrest me or hang me, which Becket said he could do nothing to prevent if it was for heresy.

When I found Dormer in his lodging he was in a strange state, full of excitement with his Suffering Jesus god vast and bright in his godspace. I was afraid to speak to him. And then he desired to make a spell to drive out what he thought was a demon, which was my Lady Leopard. I let him do it, said the words he asked me to, and of course Lady Leopard, who is only one trunk of the great Tree of God, smiled with her whiskers and lay down to stretch and purr and was not in the least driven off by it.

That was when my godsight began to rise and I made my mistake. I saw the gracefully carved thing he worshipped, the idol in the shape of the Queen Moon, the Lady of All, and I told him of seeing her in the Jesus temple, and I told him how no one can divide the infinite Light, although our eyes make smaller patterns of it to save our sanity. All we can do is turn towards or away. And for a moment I thought I had helped him, but then all in his godspace turned black and he became full of rage and hatred and fear.

But I could not leave him with such black and hungry hatred in his godspace. Why am I upside-down if not to be a speaker of gods to men and of men to gods? So I spoke to Dormer, tried to explain to him and all that happened was he became more and more frightened and angry until he was clutching for his dagger and I, inconveniently upside-down, stupidly upside-down, with Lady Leopard dancing about me, I spoke on, telling him what I knew of his most secret plans and thoughts, confirming all his terror.

Then he was there. My son. His fetch had come to find me. The little boy I had left behind such a long while ago, little fat-fisted chubby boy, who smiled and laughed and shouted for me and I turned to embrace him and then . . . Then . . .

The flash of a knife in the corner of my eye, the white stiffening and focusing of Dormer's, like a snake striking, the blow in my chest . . .

Fire in my chest, fingers round my neck, so sudden and when I was full of sorrow and love for my son's fetch, I went down . . . My little boy shouted, and suddenly his fetch turned and swelled and became a handsome man, very like his father, with his now-living snake wrapped round his arm. He became a shadow-warrior, he took power from the fever that was killing him and fought Dormer for me, wrestled him out of the dreamtime, held Dormer off for long enough that Lammett could come and see and save my life.

Only I was half-dead. Not afraid. The pain was on the floor in my bleeding body. I was standing up, naked but for my leather skirt, smiling at my handsome son, who told me his name was Snake for the moment. This was wonderful and right. But my heart was breaking, for if he come here to me, he must be close to death, very close. Those who are not upside-down hardly ever go spirit-walking in the dreamtime, and I had never found my son in the dreamtime before, which I would have if he were upside-down as well. So he was dying and I knew nothing of where he was.

And yet it was not important to me then. I spoke to him and embraced him and I showed him my Lady Leopard, and he showed me his god, the clever Trickster, and we spoke as we had never done before. We walked together in the wide plains of the dreamtime, where the zebra and the leopard are reflections of each other. He said if I had such a place to hunt in, he understood now why I had left him for it. And I wept then for his strength and kindness, such a fine man my sister had made of him. We climbed mountains together, my son and I, and travelled across lakes; we hunted words as they scuttled over the sky, herded songs that shook their manes and dipped their horns and pawed the stars, and bowed kindly to let us ride them.

Perhaps you hairy ghosts who are so like gods in what you can do, perhaps you would say we did no such thing and it was all a fever dream. Both of these things can be true, you know. You wish the world to be tidy with a thing either one thing or the other, each answer yes or no. And I say the world is luxuriantly curled upon itself like a fern, and a thing can be one thing and the other, both yes and no, and each speck of dust may choose where it lands. And we are both right.

But at last I said farewell to my darling son who was grown so fine and strong and said he had something more to do before he could return to the dreamtime. Perhaps the kindly sun of that place had given him strength to fight his fever. So I jumped down into myself again and found I was sick and burning and my chest like fire. Becket had gone, had left me to ride with Dormer and Lammett.

A hairy ghost boy that was not my son was sitting next to the bed, staring at me. I rubbed my eyes and sat up with the sweat rolling down my back under my ugly shirt and reached with a shaking hand for the horn cup of watered wine that Becket had put there.

The boy flinched away and said to me, 'You do it.'

'What?' I had learned a little Dutch, only because it is like English in its way.

'You ... something, something ... tell Englishmen.'

He held up a packet of paper with black marks and wax on it. I took it from him and the boy ran out the door and clattered down the stairs.

It was enough. My fever was low enough so I could think and function in the world, my chest hurt with the wound and the bandages griped and burned and every move made my head rock and hurt. I swallowed down all the watered wine, poured myself more and slopped half of it out on the rushes, drank it down and shivered. Then I pulled on my doublet and a leather jerkin that I could not fasten for the cause it was not made for anyone with breasts and pulled on my breeches also, and my cloak and boots and went to the door.

The place was almost empty for many of those who had stayed there were in Dormer's service. I staggered to the stables, needing to pause and take a breath every ten steps, and found one boy feeding horses. First I asked, then I shouted and frightened him into letting me take one, and then I mounted and rode out the gate, still light-headed, wobbling in the saddle as if I had never ridden before.

I asked in the streets of Dunkirk, and found that the councillors were mainly at supper or had gone to bed and that yes, many horsemen had taken the road westwards and southwards along the coast, which led after only a few miles to the great port and Citadel of Calais.

In the end it was easy because the Englishman at the door who asked my business heard what I said of David Becket and immediately led me to where Robert Cecil was drinking tobacco smoke by the very fine fire in his lodgings. I longed to get near to it, since I was shivering and sick and my head felt it would burst like a rotten melon. I bent one knee to him, since he was important among the English, and gave him the packet, then waited, rocking and basking in the warmth, while he read it.

Then he smiled at me as he drew paper towards him and began writing very fast.

'So Her Majesty was right all along. It *is* Calais. Where is Becket?'

'He went with Dormer. The boy he told to bring you this, wouldn't do it and gave it to me.'

Cecil nodded and rang a bell. A slender young man came and bowed. Cecil gave him the packet with his letter. 'Take this to my lord Admiral Howard on *Ark Royal* immediately, and if the Prince of Nassau's ships stop you, he may read the letter also. Waste no time.' The young man touched his cap and strode out, leaving Cecil to look at me and lift his brows. 'Will you take some wine?'

'Thank you, sir,' I said, enjoying his expedient courtesy, and he poured with his own hands and I drank, wishing for water in it, but no matter. It was warming.

'Are you recovered from Dormer's attack now?'

I knew what he was about. He had only his train of servants, perhaps twenty at best. He would take anyone else who could wield a weapon, even a mad black savage. And I was desperate to find Becket who had left me to ride with his friend Lammett the spy, and Dormer, the killer of his brother. So I smiled and said, 'A little weak, a little lightheaded, but good enough.'

'Will you come with me?' His smile was rueful. 'Becket told me of your ... ah ... abilities and I have very few men.'

Which was how it came about that half an hour later, with the little hunchbacked councillor and all the men he could gather up in the time, about twenty of them, we too were riding down the road to Calais. That was on the Sunday night when the Armada was anchored in Calais Roads.

And we were there in good time, before dawn, but the man on the gate would not open to Cecil, for all he spoke good French and gave many details of the urgency of the matter. No, M. Gourdain must first be consulted, and in fact, M. Gourdain the Governor must first be wakened and have time to eat his morning bread and beer and sit on the stool and then be dressed by his valet before any of his underlings would undertake to mention Englishmen hammering at the gate to him. There had been some kind of disorder in the town during the night as well, this too must be reported to him.

It all took time and meanwhile the English councillor's son must unfortunately cool his heels outside the gate of the town.

Cecil showed his teeth and eased his bent shoulders and muttered under his breath about how much he hated the French. But there was nothing to do except wait. No doubt Dormer had had a helper to let him in.

At last there was shouting within and much explanation, the doors swung open and there was M. Gourdain himself on foot, with soldiers about him, coming to speak to Her Majesty's Commissioner. Cecil dismounted as quickly as he could and came forwards with much bowing and courtesy and then explained the matter. What he heard made him very angry.

'They have taken the Citadel and there is at least one galleas making for the harbour entrance,' he said to me and his men. 'I have said that as they are led by a renegade Englishman, we shall be in the van when they retake, especially as M. Gourdain will need to place most of his men on the quayside to deal with the galleases.'

And so it was that Cecil remounted and we swept in an escorted group through the little streets of Calais where many hairy ghosts of another tribe stared and pointed at me until we came to the gate of the Citadel shut against us.

Gourdain and his men hid well back with crossbows and calivers to give us cover and Cecil's men ran forward with a battering ram to break the gate.

It took a number of tries but no one shot at us and in the end the gate broke and there was none behind it but corpses. And so up the stairs and a man dying by a smoke-blackened and shattered door with groans coming from the darkness and up more stairs and a man sitting with a crossbow at the top of the steps, smoking a pipe.

He stood as we came up, lifted his crossbow, and I stopped gratefully, to lean against the wall and hold my ribs and breathe hard, with the Lady Leopard swirling around me and the chattering about me of those I had killed, for there was a thing coming that might mean my death, and they were naturally full of interest and excitement.

*Not now*, I said to my godsight as it threatened to break through the walls of the world and overwhelm me thanks to the pain in my chest and the fever in my blood. Cecil went and spoke in halting Dutch to the man with the crossbow who smiled and lowered his weapon. One named Becket had given him gold to wait for Mr Cecil and let him through.

The door to the gun platform was locked. Cecil tried it, waved forward the man with the axe and I shoved past the others, past Cecil, to be first onto the platform. I heard speech, I heard the rumble of Becket's voice.

Did I love him? Well, the hairy ghosts call the game of the two-backed beast by many strange names but one of them is 'making love' and there's a truth in it rare to the hairy ghosts. To lie with someone, to welcome his mansnake into my woman's cave, certainly there can be no more than pleasure and the warmth of another body in it. But there can be more and in itself it can be made by the game. Becket had bedded me because he was curious to try a black woman and, like many men, unwilling to let a willing cave escape his mansnake. And I had bedded him because I was lonely and curious to try a white man. And from such simplicity, a more complicated thing had grown.

And so as soon as the door looked shattered enough, I pushed the man with the axe aside, kicked it in, felt the lift and beat as my Lady Leopard leaped on my shoulder, and charged through with my shortsword in my hand, ready to fight Dormer and kill him . . .

And so it was that he turned his pistol from Becket to me. And so it was that Becket put himself between the pistol and me. I saw it in the slowness of my Lady's rage, I saw him step sideways deliberately when he saw Dormer's knuckle whiten on the trigger, and his left arm was blown off by the pistol-ball at such short range. He charged upon Dormer and head-butted him, bore him down by sheer rage and weight, struck him one-handed, blood-spattered white face snarling and Dormer was strong enough and fast enough to slash him with a knife in the gut.

Becket gasped, hunched, rolled bonelessly off Dormer, who staggered up again, kicked him. But I was there. I came close, I turned his shoulder gently, for I wished him to see me, to see the black demon of his fearful godspace and know that I would send him to the place he called Hell.

He turned, his knife ready, but he was battered, and he had some godsight, and so he saw me with my Lady Leopard, saw the truth of me. He hesitated, only for a heartbeat, and in that time of filling and swelling and the great heart-muscle clenching, like a fist, I raised my shortsword and struck sideways, severing his neckbone with the heavy blade, crunch through the gristle and nerve, and so he crumpled and fell.

I picked up his head, happy to have taken it. 'You are mine now,'

I told him as his eyes blinked and blinked. 'Your spirit will serve me until I let you go.' And the fluttering was quicker, quicker, moths escaping from a dead tree, before they stilled and his eyes were only meat. Lady Leopard greeted his spirit with a playful pat from her paw.

Then I turned to my candle-husband. He had seen me kill Dormer but was dying, bleeding from his destroyed arm, bleeding from his ripped belly. Oh now, I thought, now you can come to me, godsight. The Lady Leopard made her shapeshift to the Lady of All, filled me with the knowledge I got all alone in the forests, the wisdom for which I gave up my child.

I reached out to David's face, pushed away the sweaty curls, as he fought the demon of pain, fought not to cry out or groan. There are few wounds more agonising and bloody than a ripped liver. I put gentleness on his forehead, stole pain from him. He calmed.

'Which will you have, my lover?' I asked him softly in English. 'The death which will come soon, perhaps tonight or tomorrow, or the death I give you with my knife?'

It was hard for him to take enough breath to speak. 'Your . . . knife.'

He lifted his hand again, and held mine tight. He knew what had happened. His arm he might recover from, but a knife in his guts and liver as well . . . No. And it would be hard to die unhelped since his lungs were not pierced. But I hesitated, my own heart invisibly torn, and he gripped harder with the pain. So I showed the knife to him, to be sure I understood, and then when he nodded, I drove the blade up between his ribs and into his heart. So I killed my friend.

Up, up I went, borne up by the wind of his passing into the dreamtime, borne up by rage and sorrow and revenge, by fever and the madness of my Lady. And in that time I saw my son's warrior spirit too, broken free, carried by his favourite god. He knew where he was and smiled to see me there again.

It was time to put a stop to the Spaniards and their Suffering Jesus and their greedy plan to take England. There is nothing to choose between one tribe of hairy ghosts and the other, but David Becket had been blue-green English and his spirit had no trouble choosing.

So I looked to the north and east and saw Thundering Jehovah dancing and bellowing among the rocks of the north. Such a crazy, charming, little boy of a god. Here, I called, come and play. He caught my scent, grown large with my pain, saw the frail wooden cockleshells of his enemy and brother god Suffering Jesus, and boomed his challenge, swooping down upon them, his cloud-chariots scudding before him, scooping up the waves with his fists made of air.

It was the work of less than a moment, stepping sideways out of time and back again. Then I was back in myself, unwelcome there, the knife still in my hand.

However, when I lifted my knife again to go with my dear, strange lover, the Lady stopped me. And I knelt weeping and dirty with blood, shaking with fever and sorrow and the hard ending of dream-walking, while Cecil allowed the Frenchmen back onto the gun platform and they began the labour of boring out new touch-holes in the spiked guns. None dared come near me for they saw the bloody knife, the head I had taken, and feared me.

David was there again, a tall, strong young man, playing a laughing veney with his spirit-sword. No longer were his black curls sprinkled with silver, no gut hanging over his swordbelt, no longer were his hands clumsy and unreliable, here he was again as he had been in his prime. I had killed him and might have asked him to stay with me for company, but to love someone is to let them go.

In my dreamsight he came close and kissed me, then blinked at my lower belly, looked again and laughed. What had he seen hiding in my woman's place? I smiled back at him, suddenly understanding. If she should live to be born, if she should live to receive her woman's snake, then I would tell her the tale of her strange father.

He saluted with his sword as the hairy ghosts do, then turned. I saw him tramping up the sunshine to make report to his Captain, the one he had stopped believing in but had never deserted. Who stood, as David expected, with a red banner of lions and the open gate of Paradise behind Him.

When we look at the Lady of All, we see what our hearts truly expect. Do you think She is only one thing or another? Do you think She is too small to hold all of us?

But then, I have never seen any spirit fly anywhere else, even if they go a roundabout way or spend time locked in confusion in the world. This might be a shock to the strange, heathen hairy ghosts who have made such a fuss and a botheration over where their spirits will end up.

In the end, naturally, we all fly home.

# Simon Ames

## San Lorenzo

It was taking them a stupidly long time to hang him, giving him every chance to shout out that he had lied. The thing was enraging. What kind of fool did they think he was? He had told them he had been an inquisitor . . .

May they rot before and after they get to hell, Simon thought, a pulse of fear still beating in his jaw, for all his knowledge and all his wisdom, he still had to concentrate hard to keep the gates of his body shut tight, sweat was trickling in maddening rivulets down his face.

At last they shoved him in another direction, unbound his arms, pulled the hood off and he gasped and blinked at the sun. Don Hugo was standing there, face impassive.

'You are correct that His Excellency may want to question you. For this reason, I will not hang you yet.'

Simon just stared and panted. You liar, he thought, you were testing me.

He was shoved the same way they had taken Snake, down two ladders, through the ill-smelling crew's quarters and down another ladder into the hold, where they unlocked a cage and shoved him in. Snake was there and a dead body and a great deal of filth. But Snake came to him and embraced him with tears of joy in his eyes, speaking in his own language, then haltingly in Spanish.

'You not hang! So fine a scribe, upside-down scribe. Good, I am happy.'

Simon smiled wanly and had to sit down, the weakness in his legs still there. He could breathe, he was not hanging by his neck slowly kicking his way to heaven, but to lose the sky, the air . . . He tried to feel gratitude. No, he would be honest with the Almighty. Hear, Oh Lord God of Israel, your servant is *not* satisfied.

There was a waterskin that Snake brought to him, the water in it smelled bad but not actually poisoned and Simon drank, still thirsty. It felt strangely defiant to drink when he wanted, rather than having to wait for Padron to come with the water. Once the cage had been

423

locked and the soldiers had climbed the ladder out of the hold and shut the trapdoor the dim light became an utterly thick blanket of blackness.

Is this better than being hanged? Simon asked himself and decided that it was, just. He was going to be hanged anyway, or shot or possibly tortured if Medina Sidonia liked to use that to establish truth. Poor Snake, who was no better off, was feeling his way around the cage, kicking all the turds into the furthest corner, rolling the corpse in the same direction. It will only take a few days for the foul airs to kill us both, Simon thought. If he wants to talk to me, Medina Sidonia had better hurry up.

Time passed. Simon decided that if he was going to be Snake's advisor when Snake became King of his country, he had better learn the language. Snake found this very funny but began with enthusiasm.

Two soldiers with lamps brought waterskins and biscuit in the evening. Simon demanded that they take out the corpse before it started to rot really badly – its belly was already swollen.

Night passed in a strengthening stink, with the ship rocking in the calm and the lips of waves making obscene kissing noises against the hull. Rats came pattering and whispering in the blackness, nibbling on the corpse.

In the morning Simon shouted at the two young soldiers who brought a little more biscuit and they fetched ropes, trussed the gnawed corpse Simon and Snake had rolled to the gate of the cage and dragged it away, farting foulness as it went.

Darkness again. And then they heard something they had never heard before, a kind of rhythmic *swish-unk*, *swish-unk*, and the motion of the ship changed. Simon thought hard and then Snake's voice smiled in the darkness.

'Padron rowing for us now.'

Simon laughed. Of course, they had never heard it because they had always been too busy rowing. The sound went on for a very long time, and then the booming and crashing of guns was all around. They heard a screeling, crashing, crumpling sound, and the ship rocked; again, more thunder of English guns. There was an echoing crash and the whole ship juddered, again and again.

Next there was a pause and the *swish-unk*, *swish-unk* started again, slower, harder, a rolling chant transmitting through the wood. Snake was by the bars of the cage and he hammered with his hands in a complicated beat.

'We are towing something.'

Another crash of guns. Once a splintering crunch followed by screaming. Snake and Simon sat still in the filth of the cage, protected womb-like in the bowels of the ship, their ears straining to see past the wooden walls to the benches. You knew little enough of what was happening when you were at the oar – but in the cage, nothing. In frustration, Simon began banging his head gently against the bars until Snake's hand on his shoulder stopped him.

'Not to start,' rumbled Snake's voice, 'or it become pleasant.'

We will only know we are about to die when we smell the smoke or see the water gushing in, thought Simon, and to know that he could do nothing and was trapped made fear become something like a rat in his chest, running around its own cage, biting to be let out.

Still the smell of gunpowder got to them, clouds of it. So much. More banging, more crashing, more screaming. There was a pattering and squeaking all around and Simon suddenly realised that the rats had come to join them after all, because where they were was the least frightening place. Perhaps not for you, he thought as the pattering and swishing went on on the blackness, but for me this is far worse than the oar. He would never have thought he could say such a thing.

The rowers were still towing, the cannon were still firing, but not their own any more, the noises weren't near enough and didn't make the ship vibrate enough. English cannon. It must be an enormous battle, thought Simon, wishing his spirit could be light enough to fly through a knothole and away.

After a while the crashing faded. They were rowing out of the battle area. From the lift to the ship's keel, Simon thought that there was at last some wind and renewed cannon fire in another direction told him that the great sailing ships were now at last able to come into the battle. But *San Lorenzo* seemed not to be taking any further part, which was hardly surprising, considering how long the men had been rowing. Simon could see it, almost taste the metal in his mouth, feel his lips crack as he bent with the others over the oar, trying to catch his breath.

'Poor bastards.'

'Not Padron.'

'No, apart from Padron. Let him row the ship by himself.'

'He like that.'

Nobody came, so there was no food and the waterskin was down to one third, which they decided to save for the morning. They

425

slept at last, not curled against each other since there was enough room in the cage to stretch out, it had been designed to pack in ten men after all. But they were close enough that the sound of the other man's breathing could reassure each of them that he was not lost alone in a black pit that moved mysteriously.

Not until midday the next black day was the trapdoor raised again, and by that time Simon was frantic with worry about Snake.

'How long did you have the headache?' he was demanding, trying to feel Snake's forehead in pitch black, while Snake fended him off. His skin felt burning hot and slick with sweat.

'Long time, since we get near England.'

'Why didn't you say?'

'Why? If I sick, two ways to go: out the oarport, in the cage. Both bad. Why say?'

Simon put his face in his hands. He heard Snake lift himself up on an elbow.

'You know what it is?'

'Not yet. My uncle is a physician, I've learned some things from him ... Headache, fever ...'

'My nose bleeding again.'

Simon sighed shakily. 'Most likely it's jail fever, there are two kinds, very like each other. Have you ever had jail fever?'

'I had fevers ...' He said some words in his own tongue, which Simon assumed were the names. Snake coughed and lay down again. 'Not jail fever.'

Have I had jail fever? Simon wondered and honestly could not say, except that if he had so much as sniffed its miasma when he was a boy he would most certainly have caught it, since he seemed to catch every other fever it was possible to have. Or yes, perhaps he had, when he first started acting for Walsingham and had gone to the Clink, to interrogate someone in a cell so full of rats, it had seemed like a furry sea. That had put him in bed for three months with a raging headache and a fever that convinced him at one point that he was a bird and must fly out the window. Perhaps he'd had this kind of jail fever. Well, if he hadn't caught it yet, he almost certainly would now.

He was furious with the Almighty. In fact, all his frustration and fright of yesterday and all his fears for Snake today and the blackness and the cramping hunger of his belly and the hopelessness of everything, all boiled together into a great black ball of fury. I am no Job, to worship you defiantly in spite of everything, he said to the nothingness above and around him, I am not some Christian godling either. How dare you treat me like this, in all your power and might, to crush me like a worm and then crush me again. How dare you!

The trapdoor opened, sullen looking soldiers put down a ladder, came with biscuit and a new waterskin, which they pushed through the hatch in the gate, and left again.

Simon called after them, 'The battle yesterday. Who won?'

The soldiers, fluff-faced both of them, looked at each other and shrugged. 'Many galley-slaves hurt and many of us too,' said one, 'We were towing *Rata Encoranada* to fire her guns at the English. She did some damage, but I heard we were meant to take the White Island and we did not.'

The Isle of Wight, Simon thought. It was the last possible place for a refuge before the Straits of Dover. And we are past – no wonder the cannon fire was fierce. The English know as well as the Spanish how vital it is.

There was no *swish-unk*, *swish-unk*, but they were moving, *San Lorenzo* was sailing. Dimly he could hear the sounds of hammering and carpentry through the hull. It seemed there was enough wind to keep them moving without the oars. No doubt the oarsmen are exhausted, some of them hurt or dead. Why haven't they brought us out as replacements?

His skin crawled. What if they did? What if he was chained to a bench again – not Padron's of course, but any bench would do. Well, no doubt the Almighty would find it amusing, which made it almost a certainty.

Snake's fever rose higher and higher through the day, and he smelled bad, although he had no flux. By the evening, he was muttering incomprehensibly in his own tongue, speaking to someone, shouting. Once he swept his arm out and almost knocked Simon over. All Simon could do was pour water into him and sponge him gently with a rag ripped from the striped breeches he had been given, and water from the nearly empty waterskin.

The night was hideous, the next day worse. Simon only dozed, trying to get water into Snake as he cried and raved and fought demons in his delirium, trying not to be caught and strangled by Snake, who seemed to regard him as a mortal enemy.

By the morning after, Snake's skin burned a little less – temperate enough for a custard, rather than hot enough to fry a lamb chop,

Simon thought to himself who tended by now to divide his thinking solely between worrying and food.

The trapdoor opened, the ladder came down. First they handed up some sacks and a barrel. Next four soldiers came to the cage and looked in.

'What's wrong with the black?'

'I think he has a jail fever.'

'What about you?'

Simon grinned. 'I'm well,' he said and hoped sincerely that it wasn't true. 'I've had jail fever.'

The soldiers looked at each other, one staggered as the ship heeled in the waves. We are at anchor somewhere, Simon realised, his attention not focused on Snake for a moment. I wonder where.

'Come with us now.'

Snake was lying still, dozing, eyes half-shut, his skin running with sweat. Remembering the corpse and the rats, Simon moved him so that the rats couldn't come at any part of him – the bars were too close together to let them in, which was a mercy, although the mice and cockroaches were a constant nuisance. He gave Snake more water, splashed a little on his forehead, left the waterskin where Snake could reach it, then stood and waited for the soldiers to unlock the gate.

When he came out, he saw them gingerly step near him and grinned like a wolf. If only he had no chains on his hands and feet, a quick dodge and run and he would be in the sea paddling with all his might for the English.

But it wasn't sensible and in any case, how could he abandon Snake? He went with them meekly, their spears poised to stab if he wasn't, and up the ladder, through the crew deck, up again aft of the oardeck and not interconnecting, up once more and out onto the quarterdeck. Wondering if he was going to be hanged, Simon blinked out at the dazzling sea, remembered his spectacles, which he had kept hooked on his breeches, put them on and blinked around him. White cliffs. So they were in Calais Roads. Twenty-five miles from Dover, the place where time and tide disagreed so radically, that Calais was the only answer. Westwards, still clinging to the weather gauge, were the English ships, more of them than there had ever been.

'Why aren't we fighting?' he asked the soldiers who were waiting for the pump to be rigged again.

One soldier crossed himself. 'Who wants to start a fight on a Sunday?'

Simon nodded and squinted at the carnival of little boats plying out from Calais across the shining water to the great crescent of ships. All of the gigs and skiffs were weighed down with food, bread, cheese, eggs, hams, barrels, fruit, many being rowed by determined-looking women with their smocks pulled low and their stays unlaced at the top. Simon found them sticky to his eyes: he had looked on male bodies for so long, to see such ripeness and softness had him swallowing hard.

The boys too were staring sadly over the rail at the women. One tore his eyes away and sighed, then saw Simon looking too and cuffed him. The other one beckoned up the blacksmith who hammered out the rivets on Simon's ankle-chains, so his feet were free for the first time in months. It felt very peculiar, quite unnatural. He had crusty sores where the ankle-rings had been. Soldiers ringed him round so he could not leap into the sea.

'Strip,' said the boy.

Simon frowned. 'Why?'

'So you can wash and have more decent clothes.'

Simon nodded, took his cloth breeches off. The coldness of the water of the pump made him jump, but he was abstracted from it all. They wouldn't give him decent clothes to hang him because they would be soiled, therefore he would not be hanged immediately. That was something.

When he was still sticky from the seawater they gave him a sailor's canvas shirt and woollen hose and a jerkin which hung crazily loose from his bones. They even gave him a pair of turnshoes to put on his feet.

Feeling very odd and much chafed in sensitive places, Simon followed after the four soldiers and climbed carefully over the side of the ship, down the ladder, barking his knuckles painfully, into the waiting gig. A young soldier took hold of his arm, twisted it up behind him and growled threats in his ear. Simon relaxed, ignoring the strain in his shoulder. Oarsmen not chained there, sailors, bent to their work and Simon watched critically. You had to admit that handling individual oars together was probably more skilled than wrestling a tree trunk on an oardeck. It was fun to watch the work for a change.

They were threading through all the little rowing boats and skiffs buzzing about the Armada, very much like flies around a horse.

429

Except that these were beneficent flies, bringing sustenance. One passed so close they nearly collided. Volcanic French cursing from the blonde woman in the stern made Simon's ears burn.

Later he thought how clever it would have been to pretend to curse back but tell the woman that the Spanish intended to take her town, but there again, Spanish wasn't so different from French that the soldiers might not be able to guess, and one of them might actually speak French as well. Besides, who would believe a woman?

Yes, as he thought. They were coming to *San Martin*, the flagship. It towered enormous over the waves, showing damage from shot in the carvings and the sails being frantically mended. It took several tries for Simon to get hold of the ladder, and he had to pause several times as he scrambled upwards. He climbed over the side and collapsed on the deck, panting with exhaustion until the youngest soldier toed him in the ribs and he struggled to his feet again.

He was brought to the stern gallery off the Great Cabin. They passed through while Simon feasted his eyes on the Turkey rug on the map table, just like the one he had had once, aeons ago, in another life, the cushions on the curtained bed, a fine painted altar complete with a tabernacle in the corner, and paintings of St Martin splitting his red soldier's cloak in half for the beggar.

On the gallery stood many tall and handsome men, their hands elegantly tilting their swords out of the way, their heads strained high by their perfect ruffs, many wearing polished and chased breastplates over their marvellous dark damask doublets. Among them was Don Hugo de Moncada. Now, if only I were stuffed with gunpowder like a hellburner, Simon thought to himself, what a wondrous execution I might do amongst all the Armada's high command. He had to content himself with the thought that he might have taken the jail fever that Snake had and they might breathe in its miasma from him. He hoped so.

The soldiers crashed a salute, and he was pushed forwards amongst the admirals and great captains to a slight, round-faced man sitting in a chair, his knees covered by a rug, leaning back green-faced, a politely covered bowl beside him and some very watered wine at his elbow on a little table.

The captains and admirals stopped their arguing and turned to look down on him. Simon felt like a child in the presence of hostile adults and went to one knee when he saw the elaborate ruby ring on the hand of the man in the chair.

'Do you know me?' asked that man faintly, in the purest Castilian, his green cheeks taking a sheen of sweat as the bulk of the *San Martin* rolled briskly in the swell.

'Are you His Excellency the Duke of Medina Sidonia?'

The man nodded, swallowed again and turned aside to retch into the bowl. Simon stared at the polished planks and thought very hard, his heart thumping loud and slow inside him. What will they ask me? Will they use torture?

'You are Simon Anriques, the clerk?'

'Yes, Your Excellency.'

'You wrote this confession?'

'Yes, Your Excellency.'

'Was any persuasion used?'

'Only fear of going back to the oarbenches, Your Excellency.'

There was a chorus of protest at that.

'Not tortured? How in the name of God can we know it's true then?'

'A galley-slave? What does he know?'

Medina Sidonia waved them down, swallowing once more. 'What has happened since then?'

'First Don Hugo nearly hanged me, and then I was locked up in the cage in the hold, Your Excellency.'

'Mm. What can you tell me about hellburners?'

So that's what had worried them. Not Calais. Well, maybe Calais *was* worrying Medina Sidonia, but he couldn't say so because it was supposed to be so secret.

'They are ships filled with gunpowder, which were used against the pontoon bridge at Antwerp and they were invented by Signor Giambelli who—'

'The hellburners as planned by your English Queen?' snapped Don Hugo, leaning over him.

'Ah. All I know, Your Excellency, because I have been a prisoner of the Holy Office for so long and had left England months before that, all I know is that when I took my leave of her, the Queen was mightily pleased with herself because she had hired the best siege engineer in Italy, Signor Giambelli, and that he made hellburners.'

The captains and admirals stirred and murmured amongst themselves. Simon blinked humbly down at the deck. No need to mention the fact that there was not, at that time, enough gunpowder in all England to fill even one genuine hellburner.

'What do you understand by hellburners?' Poor Medina Sidonia

431

was having to retch and spit again, and this question was peremptorily asked by one of the other admirals.

'They are larger ships than usually used for fireships, filled with gunpowder and ironware, with the guns double-shotted, set alight and sailed into the middle of a fleet or, indeed, as at Antwerp, a pontoon bridge, for to blow it up.'

'Why are you telling us this?' That was another voice, less harsh, more confiding. 'Is it not treason to your Queen to give us her plans.'

'Perhaps it is, Señor,' said Simon consideringly. 'But as I do not think there is much you can do if the English use hellburners, and as Don Hugo threatened me and my oarmate with blinding if I did not tell him what I knew, and as you will surely hang me afterwards, why not tell you?'

'Perhaps this story of hellburners is all a lie. Perhaps you are simply trying to frighten us?' suggested the soft-voiced one.

Simon looked up at the man and thought for a moment. 'Certainly, Señor, you do not have to believe me. But in any case, how could a poor miserable galley-slave like myself frighten so many great captains?'

This got a very cold stare in response, but the other captains muttered and jostled. Medina Sidonia sipped some wine and leaned back exhausted. From the black rings around his eyes, he had not slept for many days. Good, thought Simon, I hope your seasickness gets worse.

'Leave us,' he said to the captains who filed out with very ill grace. Medina Sidonia then spent some minutes with his head back on the cushions behind him, blinking at Simon whose knee was getting sore.

'The other matter,' the Admiral whispered at last, 'the matter of the Miracle.'

'Your Excellency?'

'It is a lie.'

Simon dared to look up at the Admiral's sad brown eyes. 'Your Excellency?'

'I am a man of honour. To attack unannounced and without declaration of war, with no justification except expediency, the city of a friendly nation, neutral in our fight . . . No. This I will never permit. Calais belongs to the King of France, and they are even sending us food and drink. Monsieur Gourdan, the governor has

432

offered all help short of the military. To make a sneak attack on our friends . . . No.'

'Your Excellency, have you opened all your sealed orders?'

'Yes, I have. All of them.' The bloodshot brown eyes were like pebbles. 'His Most Catholic Majesty of Spain, my leige Philip the second of that name, would never order such an outrage. If there had been such an order, it would of course have been a forgery and I would have burned it. In any case, His Grace the Duke of Parma will be joining us tomorrow. Your Queen must have been fed false information by some double agent.'

Simon bowed his head, thinking that if Parma could move his troops onto his barges and out of the Rhine estuary in a day, then that truly would be worthy of the name of miracle. 'Alas that I cannot tell her in person she is mistaken, Your Excellency.'

'I shall have Don Hugo keep you alive until we land in England and then I shall hand you over to the English to do with as they wish.'

'Your Excellency is a fair and honourable prince,' said Simon. 'I ask no better mercy.'

Another cold stare, and then the Admiral rang the little bell at his hand and the captains and admirals filed back in again, all arguing about the best means of responding to hellburners.

Since it would be very unsuitable for a mere galley-slave to travel in the same boat as the Admiral of the Galleases, Simon waited at the rail with his two young guards and looked happily out across the waters. The sky was no longer a calm blue, but full of puffs of cloud under a thin striation of higher cloud. The Armada rocked at anchor in possibly the most exposed and dangerous searoad of Europe, with the English anchored a few miles to the west where they still had the weather-gauge. All along the cliffs on both sides, dimly visible as a dark fringe on the English side, audible as a festival on the French side, were the people who had come out to see the ships and hope for a good battle to watch.

The little boat that carried him was full of bread and big, wax-covered roundels of cheese and the smells rose up around Simon, making him drool helplessly like a dog. He had to keep swallowing and his belly growled and grumbled as if it was full of demons. No hope of stealing anything, the young soldier had twisted his arm behind him again. Climbing the rope ladder up the side of the ship made him dizzy again and he had to pause to catch his breath.

He went back into darkness meekly enough, down the ladders, deeper and deeper into the ship. For the first time he noticed the smell, an animal stench of dung and old piss. In the cage with the gate locked, Simon picked up the sack of biscuit that the young soldier had carelessly dropped, and the waterskin, only half full and distinctly slimy. Snake was lying quietly, coughing occasionally. He was so quiet that Simon felt him anxiously, found his fever low enough to give him a rest from delirium.

Snake said something in his own tongue, which Simon didn't understand. He bent closer to hear. Snake lifted his head weakly, grabbed Simon's arm. He was hot but not delirious.

'Get me out of here,' whispered Snake. 'Take your knife, get me out.'

Simon nodded. If Snake wanted to die under the sky, well, Simon would arrange it for him. In some way.

'How?' he asked.

'Kill someone,' whispered Snake and coughed with laughter.

Making sure he was armed couldn't hurt, Simon thought. He knew that if the English were going to attack, or do anything, they would do it soon. Of course, they would not in fact know about Calais, that part of what he had said had been a lie, but even so, Calais Roads was too good an opportunity to ignore.

So Simon strained and pushed, too empty gutted to find it easy, until he had retrieved Rebecca's gift to him, he washed it in urine and then dried it on his breeches. Once assembled, he held it lightly in his hand. The bag that the biscuits had been in, that was useful. He waited, wondering if the manacles would hamper him too much. What did it matter. If the Almighty chose to help, he would succeed, if the Almighty was still aloof and enjoying his predicament, then he would not. So he waited quite patiently for the thing to happen.

And waited.

Suddenly, there was a confused shouting, the sound of a single gun, more guns firing at random. A thunder of feet above him. More shouting. Simon's empty stomach tightened into a wizened knot. He felt sick, dizzy with tension. What was happening?

The long rolling rattle as the oars went out, the command 'Take hold'. Reflexively, Simon's fists closed. And then *swish-unk, swish-unk*. They were rowing frantically away from something.

The trapdoor clattered. A soldier came sliding down the ladder, holding a lantern. 'You!' he gasped. 'Out, help with the oars.'

Meekly Simon stood up, backed into the shadows. 'I think the black is dead.'

The soldier unlocked the gate, came to bend over Snake who was obligingly staying very still. A booted toe prodded Snake's ribs and then suddenly Snake made a lunge and wrapped his arms around the boy's legs.

'Quick!' yelled Snake.

Simon stepped forward, shaking, could he do this? He was no David Becket . . .

The biscuit bag slipped over the boy's head, Rebecca's knife went into the boy's neck, the boy fell choking in blood to the floor.

He'd done it. Simon felt the boy all over; a dag, shotted and wound, which Simon put in his belt, a very elegant sword, which Simon had no hope of wielding with his hands still manacled, a nice poniard dagger, which he took.

Panting for breath, Simon helped Snake get up, doddering like an old man, and got him out of the cage, then slammed the gate shut on the still-bleeding soldier. Snake went up the ladder, coughing, slipping, but he went up. In the crew quarters, there was no one except a couple of moaning bodies in piles of blankets in the corner. Snake had not been the only one to get jail fever.

Up another ladder, and another, Simon shoving Snake up from behind, frantic to get into the open. Just as they neared the quarterdeck, the galleas suddenly swung sideways, nearly knocking them off the ladder, there was a hideous crunch and screaming from the stern. Simon popped his head out of the trapdoor – there was a mêlée on deck, the sailors were shouting, wielding poles, trying to fend off another smaller ship that had somehow collided in the darkness with them, and seemed to be impaled on the rudder. The oars swept again, the whole ship shuddered. Out in the darkness, there was fire, a ship ablaze from the hull to the mast sailed past them, majestic in her fury.

Simon suddenly had the most ridiculous urge to laugh. He finished climbing the ladder, hauled Snake up by his shoulders from where he had collapsed with the collision, dragged him to the rail. 'Look!' Simon cheered. 'Look at them! Drake's hellburners.'

He had shouted in English, so he said it again in Spanish in case anybody could hear him. Snake smiled wanly, clutched the rail gasping and shivering and Simon danced for sheer joy to see the fireships, hear the screaming and shouting, the vast ponderous galleons cutting their anchor ropes and swinging out into the south-westerly wind on a lee shore . . . There was another rending crunch in the darkness, more shouting. Wonderful! The whole Armada was panicking, cutting and running before the wind from the terror of the fireships, its magnificent defensive formation broken, every ship for itself and crashing into each other in the packed choppy waters.

'Ha ha!' he yelled, dancing a jig on a box and nearly falling. 'You're scared, you're scared, shit your fancy hose why don't you, sons of whores . . .'

A sailor loomed out of the darkness, swung a cudgel. Simon dodged and buried the poniard in the man's guts, let the rush take the man over the rail and nearly lost the poniard in the process.

The sweeps swung again and again, first one side, then the other, and the galleas wiggled from side to side like an eel until the other ship caught in her rudder was freed and dropped behind. They needed to hide. Simon and Snake climbed over the railing and onto the metal beakhead itself, just under the bowsprit, where they clung on, hidden by the curve of the ship's prow. Simon used a rope-end to tie Snake more securely because he was panting and sweating and looked ready to pass out. Together they squinted into the darkness. Another ship of fire floated past and it was true, they were very large. For a moment Simon started to believe his own lie, but then he remembered that there was simply not enough gunpowder in England to pack so many big ships with the stuff. The Queen had indeed been charmed with the idea and had hired Signor Giambelli for the purpose, until Signor Giambelli gave her the estimates of the amount of gunpowder needed and the Queen had exploded like a hellburner herself at the very notion of spending so much on a gamble.

Simon enjoyed himself immensely that night, although the early chaos subsided as the eight English fireships floated past and grounded on Calais beach to burn harmlessly down to the waterline. The Armada was well and truly scattered, while *San Lorenzo* could not steer properly without her rudder. She could do something with the oars but not much.

By the time dawn came in a magnificent tapestry of bloody clouds, *San Lorenzo* was firmly underway again. Dimly, Simon could make out Don Hugo on the poopdeck, roaring orders through a speaking trumpet. He was doing his best to get the galleas turned, to head for the shore . . . why? They weren't so badly damaged?

With the larboard oars backing water and the starboard oars rowing double-time, the galleas turned ponderously round. Simon and Snake were the first to see that there was another ship there, low in the water, one of the pinnaces . . . They could have shouted warning, but instead clung on tighter as the galleas prow ground sideways into and over the other ship, with more screaming, more crunching of broken wood . . .

Don Hugo looked over the side at the damage, continued to shout orders. What the devil was he playing at, rowing like a maniac for the shore?

Revelation came to Simon. Don Hugo de Moncada as Admiral of the Galleases and Santa Cruz's particular favourite, was the only other man in the Armada who knew that Calais was the lynchpin of the whole enterprise. His ship was damaged, he could be expected to make for a beach so he could ground her . . . But in fact he was making for Calais harbour, with his ordnance. If one ship could take the town unsuspecting, Don Hugo would make the attempt.

You had to admire the obstinacy of the man. Whether it was true or not that Medina Sidonia had burned His Majesty's orders that had instructed him to do something against his honour as a Spanish nobleman or whether his mind was simply clouded by seasickness and exhaustion, Don Hugo would try to save the Armada single-handed.

There was nothing Simon could do. He had to cling to the beakhead and watch as the opening to Calais harbour came closer and closer . . . There was a chain across it, but the beakhead was sharp and serrated and if that failed, then men with axes could usually break through. Once in the harbour, Don Hugo could use his two hundred and thirty-odd soldiers to take the harbour, perhaps even get into the Citadel. Maybe there was some kind of land-bound attack as well, to back up the galleases and cause a diversion. And Medina Sidonia would be forced to support Don Hugo if he gained possession of Calais, or see all his captains mutiny.

It was a brilliant act in the face of defeat, worthy of El Draco himself. The oars went *swish-unk*, *swish-unk*, and among the sounds of the oars came the concerted gasp and thud of the men. Then someone started up Snake's song, with an independent life now, singing of the Miracle of Calais, which they were, unwittingly, about to effect.

They were over the shoal waters, near the bar, negotiating one of the channels that led into the port, the oars dipping precisely . . .

The idea came to Simon like a musket shot through the head. Before he could think too much about it, he swung himself down

437

onto the gunner's gallery above the oar decks. There were the heavy fifty-pounder shot waiting to be swung down in their nets for reloading the cannon on the oardeck. Simon ran all the way along the gallery to the stern, swung the shot-net out and while it moved to and fro, he sawed frantically at the ropes with his poniard until the shot dropped out, crunched onto the gallery, rolled off and onto the oars, making them bounce, cracking one. He was already at the next shot-net, sawing through it; the shot dropped, he went to the next.

The fifty-pound lumps of metal were heavy enough to make the oars bounce as they rolled off the gallery and through to the sea, and that was enough to disrupt the careful rhythm of the rowers. The oars on that side suddenly pointed in all directions, two collided with each other and broke. With no oars countering the unbroken rhythm on the other side, and no rudder to provide a correction, the galleas suddenly swerved to the disrupted side, swerved again with the next stroke. Simon panted as he released another shot from its net, nearly lost his toes as it crashed down, taking the edge off the gallery and bounced among the oars. There was screaming and shouting from the oardeck. Someone looked out – Simon knew that face and he jeered and waved at the Padron. Perhaps it wasn't wise, two soldiers had hopped over onto the gallery and were coming after him. A musket shot from the rigging cracked past him.

Simon swung another net out, positioned it just above the gallery, sawed through the net and the shot dropped straight through between him and his pursuers. The two young soldiers stared at him across the gap, easy to jump across – if you weren't afraid of falling in the water, through the meat-pounding oars.

Another stroke from the other side, the rowers settled into their rhythm, they were hard to stop . . .

And the grinding heaving crash, the juddering of the ship, the slow heeling over made Simon clutch for the nearest handhold, the ratline chains. Another soldier was coming after him. The ship was going over and over . . . screaming and crying from the oardeck, crashing as some of the cannon got loose again, the whole galleas tilting at a crazy angle with the oars gradually pointing at the sky, the gunner's gallery going lower and lower to the water.

Simon kicked with his legs, clung like a monkey, got a toe into a bit of carving, hoisted himself up and over the rail. Somebody struck at him, he fought back yelling, 'You fool, I'm Spanish,' and the soldier let him pass. All the sailors were climbing the rigging, trying to get off the deck. There was a crash of a gun, then a rattle of musket-fire.

In the chaos on the sharply angled deck, still juddering as the hull ground on the shoal, Simon ran forwards, saw English ships gathering a hundred yards away unable to come closer because of the shoals. One was the *Ark Royal*, the English Admiral's ship and it was lowering a longboat full of shouting Englishmen. Other ships lowered their boats.

Simon ducked his head, vaulted the rail to where Snake was still clinging to the beakhead, gasping helplessly as he dangled over the water, until Simon untied the rope and got him upright again. Peeping over the rail, Simon saw that Don Hugo was still on the poopdeck at the stern, surrounded by soldiers and seamen with muskets and swords. They waited until the boats came close enough and the sailors on it started throwing grappling hooks and trying to board. Then the Spanish soldiers, many of them from the tercios, the finest troops in Europe, began to fire their guns, calm and collected on Don Hugo's orders.

One man and then another exploded in blood in the boats. The longboats backed off a little way, and the English returned fire, the caliver and arquebus bullets snapping and whining through the air, lodging in carvings, causing explosions of deadly splinters where they hit.

As the water came in, the wailing from the oardeck grew stronger and more hysterical. Simon fought not to see the picture, the men wrenching their ankles bloody to try to get away from the water.

On impulse he leaned in through the gunport and shouted in Spanish, 'We've run aground, the ship won't sink, we're stuck on a sandbank.' He repeated it in Portuguese.

Suddenly there was a crash, a shocked silence, more shouting. Simon recognised Padron's bellow in amongst it all. The wailing changed to a cheer.

Snake was shaking his arm, the fingers burning. Simon looked around. It was a stand-off between the English in the boats and the Spanish gathered on the highest part of the galleas. More boats were coming in, but they could not get nearer as long as the Spanish went on firing their muskets, careful to kill with each shot if they could, Don Hugo at the centre of them, still shouting orders.

Snake was pointing at the boats surrounding them. 'English?'

'Yes, my . . . my friends.'

Snake pointed in the direction of Don Hugo. 'Kill the king, stop the fight.'

Once again, Simon had the sensation of a hand sweeping down from the sky and lifting him. He took the dag out from his breeches waistband, checked it was still shotted and wound – it was and he'd been lucky not to blow his own balls off, only it was one of the new-fangled kind with a safety catch. He put it back, grabbed Snake's arm. 'Stay here. I'll kill the captain.'

Snake laughed. 'I too,' he said and when Simon hesitated because he was still sick, Snake just laughed louder. 'Stop me?' he asked and shook his head.

They climbed from the beakhead, cautiously over the reddening waters, onto the other gunner's gallery, now at a forty-five degree angle so they had to walk partly on the hull of the ship as the cannon pointed fruitlessly at the sky. Simon still had manacles on his wrists, Snake had both wrist and leg chains still, but the noise from the musketry and shouting on the poop was so loud he thought no one would hear them picking their way along. He focused on climbing up with the sweep of the gallery, towards the built-up poop, clinging to the ship, dizzy now with the lack of motion as the galleas stayed grounded on the sandbank. They were in range of the guns in the Citadel, why didn't they fire at the galleas? What was going on in the town of Calais?

Snake hissed air through his teeth behind him. Simon glanced over his shoulder, and saw Padron heaving himself through one of the oarports where the oar had broken . . . How had Padron got free?

Suddenly Simon remembered spending so many nights whittling away at the wood round the bolt that kept him where he was, how he had disguised the work, how close he had been when Padron decided to bring him down with drought . . . Padron had been put in his place on the bench and in the terror of the grounding and partial sinking must have pulled the bolt right out.

Padron climbed onto the gunner's gallery, intent and ferocious, spattered with someone else's blood. Simon took out the dag to shoot the bastard, his mouth watering at the thought of putting a bullet through Padron's muscular chest, getting revenge . . .

Snake held him. 'No,' he insisted. 'Kill him,' he said, pointing to where Don Hugo was still directing the fire. Nobody was looking at them yet, apart from the Padron climbing up towards them. But somebody would see them soon. And then that somebody would shoot them with a musket. 'I get Padron,' Snake added as he reached over, drew the poniard that Simon had taken from the young soldier and turned.

For a split second Simon wanted to argue, Padron was the man he wanted to kill, not Don Hugo, who had only used perfectly normal interrogation techniques on him, had not even tortured him . . .

Snake looked over his shoulder, saw Simon hesitating. He lifted his arm, pointing at Don Hugo, shouted imperiously. It was in his own language, but Simon understood the meaning. As Padron reached for Snake with a wolfish snarl on his face, Simon climbed closer to the poop, knowing how inaccurate a dag was, wanting to be as close to Don Hugo as he could get. He crept the last few feet, peered over the rail, there was Don Hugo and only a few feet away. Everyone was looking the other way, at an English longboat edging closer. A boy in a glittering, gold-brocade encrusted, tawny doublet, stained with seawater and vomit, suddenly popped his head up, swung his leg over the rail ready to run away. He was so intent on escaping, he never noticed Simon until Simon hit him and knocked him back, sprawling on the deck.

Simon took aim, heard Becket's rumble in his ear as if the man was standing there, 'Take your time, aim for the body, hold your breath and squeeze.'

Nothing. What was wrong, it wasn't a misfire? The boy in the tawny doublet staggered to his feet, tried climbing over again. Simon reversed the dag and cracked the pretty face across with the heavy ball on the butt-end intended for just that purpose. Why didn't it fire? Ah, the safety catch was on. Simon unhooked it, took aim again. Just in that moment, Don Hugo turned and looked at him, stared at the dag transfixed. The man's lips moved, he was saying, 'Holy Jesus.' Simon held his breath, squeezed, the dag shouted, his hand was hit by something like a rock so he nearly dropped the weapon. He turned.

He was just in time to see Padron and Snake wrestling behind him. Padron was on top, beating Snake's head against the wood.

Simon stepped up, whispered, 'Padron.'

Padron looked round and Simon hit him across the face with the ball-stock of the dag, hit him again, holding the dag like a club by the barrel, not caring that it was hot, struck again and now Padron's face was a mask of blood, his nose gone to pulp, his jaw hanging . . . Padron let go of Snake, launched himself on Simon, Simon was overborne, Padron's hands around his scrawny neck, he beat feebly with the dag, his eyes were going black, he couldn't breathe . . .

Another crunch, the fingers relaxed, he gulped breath, sat up punching wildly, his fist connected. Snake had his hands around Padron's neck, Padron choked, eyes bulging, then he threw himself backwards, taking Snake off balance. Simon watched, transfixed, as they teetered, fell, rolling over the wood of the hull, past the crazy forest of abandoned oars, still fighting until there was a double splash. Simon ran down the hull, squeezing between the oars, careful now of the other slaves who were starting to climb out of the oarports, most of them bloody, trailing their broken bolts and chains behind them. The water boiled, too shallow for a galleas but still deep enough to drown a man, Padron and Snake fighting in a maelstrom of blood and muscle, he couldn't see which to grab until at last he caught a black wrist still wrapped with the tail of a carved snake, and hauled.

It was a deadweight. Snake's head hung sideways. Padron had broken his neck for him.

Padron's body was bobbing in the shallow waters, perhaps only eight foot deep, but he was weighted down by his ankle-chains and the bolt he had pulled out of the deck. Blood flowered round him like purple lawn curtains in the sea. He glared up at them as he fought for the surface, trying to climb the water and the bubbles coming from his nose as his body fought to breathe. Simon stared at him coldly, at those calloused hands clutching for the silvery surface like sea anemones. Of course he could have reached down and pulled Padron up, and he could see the desperate appeal in Padron's eyes. I don't think so, Simon thought, although he knew the pain of drowning. Simon pulled Snake's body up as far as he could and squatted there until the last mighty bubble and heave. Padron fought death for a long time, it seemed, but then at last his eyes were sightless.

Simon tried to pull Snake's body with him, further up the side of the ship, but he was shaking and his hand hurt. He laid Snake down, put his head in his hands. The bubble in his own chest expanded until it burst. Snake would never be a King now, would never lead his people well-equipped with guns and gunpowder that Simon would advise on manufacturing, against the slave-traders, the Arabs and the Portuguese. He would never be the richest king in his lands, he would never rule an empire, never take fifty fat wives and plant fine sons and daughters in all of them. Simon wished he could weep to ease the pain in his chest, but found his eyes dry although he was shaking all over, not caring about the mayhem around him, the boats rowing closer, the occasional musket shot.

After a while, Simon lifted his head, crept up the side of the ship again. On the poopdeck the soldiers were gathered around Hugo de Moncada. When Simon could look, he saw that the Admiral of the Galleases had a perfect hole in the middle of his forehead. A white handkerchief had already been attached to a pike and was waving frantically at the surrounding English longboats.

Next moment the English had thrown grappling hooks and climbed aboard in a determined swarm. Thuggish thickset sailors and gentlemen in breastplates glanced at Simon as they climbed past, dismissed him as ragged and therefore unprofitable and headed for the officers and men still on the poop. Moments later the Spanish were being stripped of their shirts. Shouts and yells of delight echoed as the English found the Great Cabin and the officers' belongings. A Spanish officer who dared to protest was clubbed to the ground.

A flurry saw another longboat being lowered from the English flagship. More sailors shoved past Simon. At last he caught one and said, in English, 'I must see an English officer immediately.'

The sailor blinked at him stupidly. 'You a Spaniard?'

'No, sir,' said Simon patiently. 'I'm as English as you are, I was taken as a galley-slave and I—'

The sailor embraced him, said, 'Welcome home, mate,' and rushed on to join in the looting.

Simon caught hold of another one, a skinny lad. 'Bring me to my lord Howard of Effingham or to Sir Francis Drake, goodman, I must see him immediately.'

'Hang on, I've got to get something out of this.' And the sailor was off into the galleas cabins with his friends, crazed by the legendary English lust for gold.

And so Simon sat peacefully on the side of the galleas while the English behaved like a column of ants that had found a sugar loaf. A little later, when the frenzy of theft was at its height, a boat that had been rowing laboriously out from the port of Calais came near. The rowers backed water and a gentleman stood up in it and shouted in French, 'We claim salvage of this ship for the King of France.'

The English sailors shouted and jeered, some of them pulled their breeches down and bared their arses. The gentleman patiently repeated himself in Spanish, Italian and Latin. At last an aristocratic looking man leaned over and said, in accented French, 'No, sir, our prize, I think.'

'Ours,' insisted the Frenchman, stood up in his boat and fired a caliver straight up in the air, which nearly knocked him over, causing more jeering and hilarity among the English.

The next moment the great guns in the Calais Citadel began to speak, enormous shot, crashing into the water and drenching everyone, first one side of the sandbank, then the other, and at last the shot began hitting the galleas, while the shot that missed nearly swamped the longboats still gathered round.

There was a stampede. All the English swarmed off the galleas and into their boats. Simon stood, hesitated. What about Snake's body? But then sense prevailed and he simply went with the throng as they scrambled for any boat and rowed as fast as they could away from the cannon in the fortress, waving muskets and swords at the Frenchmen and shouting elaborate obscenities about the French and their sexual diseases.

Simon found himself thinking that it was quite funny, but the capacity to laugh seemed as frozen in him as his tears. Nor did he care about the guns of the ferocious sea battle going on out in the Channel rumbling like thunder.

Somebody elbowed him in the ribs. 'Who're you?'

'I'm English, I was a galley-slave—'

'Well if you know how to row, why ain't you rowing?' The sailor had a wounded hand, roughly wrapped with a bit of torn sheet.

Simon blinked, took the toothpick of an oar that the sailor gave him, dropped it in the rollock and bent with the stroke. So strange, it was so small, he was facing the wrong way. In his mind Simon heard Snake singing, an eerie ferocious song, and found himself humming along with it. Then he shook his head to clear it. Snake was dead, gone to Sheol, he couldn't sing any more.

Simon blinked over his shoulder at the gaily painted blur of wooden hull and flying sails they were approaching, his spectacles gone in the fight with Padron.

'Which ship are we going to?'

'*Ark Royal*. Look what I got.'

It was the reliquary box, the holy relic of San Lorenzo on which Simon had sworn. The sailor shook it in his ear, opened it with his teeth. 'Urgh, what's that?'

Simon stared owlishly at the carbonised bone. 'I believe the Spaniards say it's a toe of St Lawrence.' It was many months since he had spoken English, it came quite slowly and strangely to his tongue.

'Ugh. Stinks.' The sailor tipped the toe of St Lawrence in the sea, shook out the box, then examined it again. 'This is good though, look, pearls. And rubies. Did you get anything, mate, any gold pieces or jewelled crosses?'

'No, but my friend killed the Padron and I . . . shot the Spanish captain, Don Hugo de Moncada.'

It was obvious the sailor didn't believe him, only nodded noncommittally. Rowing such a tiny ship, such small oars . . . It should be funny, really it should. When they came up alongside the *Ark Royal*, the sailor next to Simon caught his hand as he drew in the oar, looked at the palm.

'Well, you ain't lying at least.'

'Now take me to my lord the Admiral, I must see him at once.'

The sailor shook his head. 'Not yet, mate, if you take my advice. His lordship's very upset, he didn't want to come in after just one galleas, it was the madwoman made him do it . . . Hoy, you can't go up there!'

In the waist of the *Ark Royal*, Simon looked about, saw sailors, soldiers, cannon, gunners . . . Crowds of people, all busy. He made his way to the stern, to the poopdeck where the Admiral would be, saying only to all the crowds of blurred people who tried to stop him that he must speak with the Admiral. The ship was trimming her sails, turned away from the lee shore and tacking towards the peppering of ships out to sea, all of them clotted into furiously fighting groups. More cannon bellowed, the clouds of smoke drifting like bog-cotton over the waves.

Somebody stopped him again as he climbed up to the quarter-deck, just as he came to the top of the stepladder. He could hear a person speaking higher than a man, not a boy's voice either, he squinted, looked again. The hairs on neck and arms prickled.

A small woman was standing facing the Admiral, her fists on her hips, defiance in every inch of her. Lord Howard of Effingham was leaning over her, roaring; she was arguing with him fiercely.

Once again something lifted him. He sidestepped and shoved his shoulder into the man trying to stop him, passed between another two soldiers who tried to lay hands on him as if they weren't there, climbed another ladder, and got to the small woman, reached her, stopped, suddenly terrified it might not be her.

'Rebecca?' he said and she spun to face him.

It was ridiculous but now he was suddenly, breath-stoppingly afraid she might not know him. She stared, her mouth opened as if to scream, and then she ran to him.

She did. She knew him. Bony, stubble-headed, filthy with blood and smoke, stinking, in rags, eyes squinting without spectacles, she knew him. *She knew him.*

Lord Howard was shouting something at him now, but he really couldn't be bothered to understand it. What did it matter what anyone said or did now he had found Rebecca again? He was making strange noises, seesaw noises, there was water flooding his face.

His arms were wrapped so tight around her he was lifting her off the deck, her arms went round him, she gripped so he could not breathe and all his heart was a fireship floating out of night, into dawn and exploding with happiness.

# The Last of Gloriana

For the first and only time, the Queen of England gives a private and most secret audience to an African princess, who stands before her in her ill-fitting men's clothes, her belly swelling more than could be explained by beer.

'What can I give you, Merula, to thank you for your service to me?' says the Queen carefully.

Merula smiles at her, something about her face wild and not quite human, or so the Queen thinks who has never really looked at a black woman before.

'Give me a ship, O Queen of England, a ship with guns and powder and shot, and I shall take my son's ashes home. There I shall raise an army of men and gods and spirits, and bring to battle and kill the man who sold him.'

She says it without much emphasis, but the Queen feels that all this might well come to pass. She would never admit it but is not at all happy to have such a creature in her realm as could call any kind of angel. It is bad enough that Dr Dee traffics with them, although he is in Bohemia. And so the Queen takes paper and herself drafts an order that names the black woman a princess of Africa and gives her a small ship and men to sail it and money to pay them. Perhaps they will pounce on the woman while she sleeps and make a slave of her or perhaps they will bear her to the Slave Coast and let her go. But at least she will not be in England.

The black witch takes the paper and salaams the Queen before being conducted from her Presence.

Thomasina herself had come back to London, but not yet to court. She was resting at the house of Dr Nunez, since Simon came down with a jail fever after his exertions and those who had been near him were waiting to see if they had taken the infection before coming near the Queen herself. But Thomasina had dictated a most complete report, which made the Queen laugh till she cried at its tactless descriptions of half-witted court gallants and withering

447

contempt for useless men that thought themselves too clever for the Spaniards to detect.

... It remains only for me to confirm what Mrs Anriques has said, that she it was persuaded my lord Admiral Howard of Effingham to spend three hours to take the galleas *San Lorenzo* while it lay beached since she knew her husband was upon it, and that by so doing his lordship prevented any other attempt at the harbour until it was too late. Many have spoken ill of him in this matter, saying he is as bad as Sir Francis Drake in his greed for a prize, and other worse things, but he knew he could not come off with the galleas for a prize once the French had the Calais Citadel under their control again and so indeed, he did not. But Mr Anriques escaped and he brought him home, which will be a great benefit to Your Majesty.

We have performed your mission, Your Majesty. We have used a sprat to catch a mackerel, or a little ship to catch a great fleet. There may be other Armadas, but never one so dangerous, I hope.

The Queen lifted her head to stare into space, imagining she saw the storm angel that Merula claimed to have called as he hunted the ships of Spain northwards. It had been close to a disaster, near enough, without what was written in the report from her muliercula.

She already knew how she would commemorate the great victory. It would give the credit to the storms of God, visible and invisible, that had blown both men and ships into their best places for the defeat of Spain.

It could very easily have been utterly otherwise, and the fingers of the dreams that had plagued her all summer, wherein she was a black-browed, broad-beamed general by the name of David Becket, trailed their last icy nails down her back as she thought of her last dream of him, riding across the sky with the Wild Hunt.

She would see to it that Becket's family and Fant's family also were looked after by honest gentlemen that would not try to make their fortunes from their lands.

She put Thomasina's report in her chased silver cabinet and went, after suitable ceremony by her women, ignored in her abstraction, to her samite-curtained bed, sleeping alone in the warmth of summer. As she slept she found herself dreaming for the last time of what might have been, of her new husband Ralegh, Earl of Sherborne, Duke of Cornwall, now recovered of his amputated leg, bringing her most gently to a belated nuptial bed in the best chamber of Merton college. And there, in her dream, he taught her that not all men were rough bears with musk-scented boots and that pleasure as well as pain could come from the dry empty place between her legs. She woke in the grey of morning with tears on her face.

And we gods shall leave her to her mortal dreaming, pulling back from her bedchamber and through the window over the Privy Garden, flying low with one of the carrion kites over Westminster and London, to Paul's churchyard. It lies in the shadow of the great Gothic cathedral with its twenty-year-old temporary roof: the old spire was struck with lightning at the beginning of the Queen's reign, and all men shook their heads at the ill luck of a mere woman being supreme Governor of the Church of England. They have forgotten it now, forgotten that St Paul's even had a spire.

There in the courtyard are the stalls of the stationers, the book-sellers, each with his sign by his stall, as of a fountain, a black swan, a Greek temple, a little lapdog, the starry huntsman. Some print and sell small pamphlets about the terrible levels of street crime in London, others the latest phantastical romances of knights and swords and damsels in distress and ferocious giants. One, with the Archbishop's permission, has a most lucrative trade and sells a fine range of Bibles, in Tyndale's version.

A balding young man that came up from the country with the muster of pikemen from Stratford-upon-Avon is wandering like a child in a king's pastry kitchen, fingering all the books: here poetry, Englished from Greek; there plays, the very latest of all disgraceful entertainments, inveighed against by preachers and legislated against by councils. He has already gone to see one performance, at the Bel Sauvage Inn, Ludgate. He was left open-mouthed and staggered by it, as entranced and bedazzled as he was as a boy by the entertainments for Her Majesty at Kenilworth. The poetry and magic is still whirling around his head even now, making him feverish and vague. Nor will they ever leave him in peace.

He picks up in his hands one of the Bibles, weighs it, considers buying it, puts it down again, incidentally leaving a dirty thumb-print on its facing page. Eventually he is seduced by a new edition of English histories.

Had the Spanish landed he would have died in a muddy field, his head blown off by a musket ball and no one would have heard of him nor said that a rose by any other name would smell as sweet.

And so, it's time to go. You need not stare at the stars, which are hidden by sunlight in any case, only take that holy book rejected by Shakespeare. Its leather cover is beautifully tooled in gold, its pages crackle creamy white as we turn them with a breath; we read the verse in Isaiah wherein God says, most clearly, that His ways are not our ways, His thoughts not our thoughts.

The pages brown at the edges, subtly burned by sunlight and air and the passing of time. And now the sound of cars and the chirrup of telephones tell us we are home.

# Historical Note

Anyone who is anxious to make sense of Merula's section of the book should read *Surfing Through Hyperspace* by Clifford A. Pickover, but it would probably be better if you just went along for the ride. I tried to base her on what research I could manage into the area at the time, but I decided to use invention rather than fact, because it seemed to me that a lifetime would be too short to study the great empires and peoples of 16th century Western Africa and I would have to learn Arabic to do it properly.

I have often had to guess or make up the physical detail of my heroes' lives aboard ship. The ships of the 18th century were very different from those of 1588. In fact the pace of technological development in ship-building was so fast during the 16th and 17th centuries that the ships of 1588 were quite different from the famous *Mary Rose* of 1547 and ships of the mid-17th century almost unrecognisable. Imagine basing your knowledge of a Sopwith Camel of WWI on a modern fighter jet and you will get some idea of the difficulties I have had researching the subject. It has often seemed to me that the historians of the period are as much at sea as I was. It was immensely helpful to be able to pick the brains of the craftsmen and women at Square-Sail Experience, Square-Sail Shipyard in Charlestown, Cornwall who have the experience of actually building and sailing reproduction square-rigged ships for the film industry. It was the sailmaker there, Alfred Readman, who came up with the suggestion that the English yards were not lashed to the mast but suspended, so they could be hauled round further and sail closer to the wind. But with all this, I have still had to make things up or arbitrarily decide whether one or another hotly contested detail was more likely. As a primer, I have relied heavily on the splendid illustrations of Mark Bergin in Richard Humble & Mark Bergin's *A 16th Century Galleon* published by Simon & Schuster Young Books [1993] and was inspired by the relevant chapters in *The Safeguard of the Sea* by N. A. M. Rodger [1997]. I used *State Papers Relating to the Defeat of the Spanish Armada* ed. John

Knox Laughton [Navy Records Society 1987] and *The Spanish Armadas* by Winston Graham [1987] as my main sources for the movements of the Armada and the English fleet, except where I decided that history had to make way for the sake of a good tale.

This applies doubly to the galleases and galley-slaves. Again, perhaps I was looking in the wrong places or books or, most likely, in the wrong language but I have found it very difficult to get information about them. Accordingly, I read what I could on Greek triremes, normal Mediterranean galleys and ships, and made the rest up.

The central theme of this book is inspired by my deep irritation with the various theories I have read about the Armada and what Philip II thought he was doing. I do not think that the Enterprise of England was an outrageously expensive exercise in sabre-rattling. Nor do I think that Philip, Santa Cruz, Medina-Sidonia or Parma were stupid men.

Accordingly, I asked myself how could the Armada, exactly as it set sail, have been made to work – and developed my novel from the obvious answer to that question. The fact that it *didn't* work should not be taken as proof that it could *never* have worked. Much less likely enterprises have succeeded perfectly well: the seaborne invasion of a powerful, cultured and martial country by an obscure, struggling, bastard Duke of Normandy in 1066 comes to mind, as does the defiance of a few ill-armed, scrawny Colonists against the foremost sea-power of the time in 1776.

As for the problems over dating caused by the English affection for an obsolete calendar, I have taken the coward's way out and ignored them completely. All dates are English.

Lastly, please remember that the religious opinions of my characters are not necessarily my opinions and nor are their various prejudices.